New York Times bestselling author Anne Perry lives
Portmahomack, Scotland. She writes the Victorian mystery
series featuring Thomas and Charlotte Pitt, which
was adapted for television. THE CATER STREET
HANGMAN was watched by millions of viewers when
it was broadcast by ITV. She is also the author of the
critically acclaimed William and Hester Monk series. Her
most recent novel, the next in a series of novels set at the
dawn of World War I, is SHOULDER THE SKY. All her
titles are available from Headline.

Praise for Anne Perry:

'Her finely drawn characters couldn't be more
comfortable within the customs and sensibility of their
historical period, for which Ms Perry once again
demonstrates her true and lively passion' *New York Times
Book Review*

'A surpassingly excellent historical and psychologically
intricate mystery' *Publishers Weekly*

'A complex plot supported by superb storytelling'
Scotland on Sunday

'Master storyteller Anne Perry moves closer to Dickens
as she lifts the lace curtain from Victorian society to
reveal its shocking secrets' Sharyn McCrumb

Also by Anne Perry and available from Headline

Tathea
Come Armaggedon
The One Thing More
A Christmas Journey
The Christmas Visitors

World War I series
No Graves as Yet
Shoulder the Sky

The William Monk series
A Dangerous Mourning
Defend and Betray
A Sudden, Fearful Death
The Sins of the Wolf
Cain His Brother
Weighed in the Balance
The Silent Cry
The Whited Sepulchres
The Twisted Root
Slaves and Obsession
A Funeral in Blue
Death of a Stranger
The Shifting Tide

The Inspector Pitt series
Bedford Square
The Whitechapel Conspiracy
Southampton Row
Seven Dials

The Face
of a Stranger

and

Half Moon Street

Anne Perry

Copyright © 1990, 2000 Anne Perry

The right of Anne Perry to be identified as the Author of
the Work has been asserted by her in accordance with
the Copyright, Designs and Patents Act 1988.

THE FACE OF A STRANGER first published in Great Britain in 1998
by HEADLINE BOOK PUBLISHING

HALF MOON STREET first published in Great Britain in 2000
by HEADLINE BOOK PUBLISHING

First published in this omnibus edition in 2005
by HEADLINE BOOK PUBLISHING

A HEADLINE paperback

10 9 8 7 6 5 4 3 2 1

Apart from any use permitted under UK copyright law,
this publication may only be reproduced, stored, or transmitted,
in any form, or by any means, with prior permission in writing
of the publishers or, in the case of reprographic production,
in accordance with the terms of licences issued by the
Copyright Licensing Agency.

All characters in this publication are fictitious and any resemblance
to real persons, living or dead, is purely coincidental.

ISBN 0 7553 2664 4

Typeset in Times

Printed and bound in Great Britain by
Clays Ltd, St Ives plc

Headline's policy is to use papers that are natural, renewable and
recyclable products and made from wood grown in sustainable
forests. The logging and manufacturing processes are expected to
conform to the environmental regulations of the country of origin.

HEADLINE BOOK PUBLISHING
A division of Hodder Headline
338 Euston Road
London NW1 3BH

www.headline.co.uk
www.hodderheadline.com

The Face
of a Stranger

To Christine M J Lynch,
in gratitude for old friendship renewed

Chapter One

He opened his eyes and saw nothing but a pale greyness above him, uniform, like a winter sky, threatening and heavy. He blinked and looked again. He was lying flat on his back; the greyness was a ceiling, dirty with the grime and trapped fumes of years.

He moved slightly. The bed he was lying on was hard and short. He made an effort to sit up and found it acutely painful. Inside his chest a fierce pain stabbed him, and his left arm was heavily bandaged and aching. As soon as he was half up his head thumped as if his pulse were a hammer behind his eyes.

There was another wooden cot just like his own a few feet away, and a pasty-faced man lay on it, moving restlessly, grey blanket mangled and sweat staining his shirt. Beyond him was another, blood-soaked bandages swathing the legs; and beyond that another, and so on down the great room to the black-bellied stove at the far end and the smoke-scored ceiling above it.

Panic exploded inside him, hot prickling through his skin. He was in a workhouse! God in heaven, how had he come to this?

But it was broad daylight! Awkwardly, shifting his

position, he stared around the room. There were people in all the cots; they lined the walls, and every last one was occupied. No workhouse in the country allowed that! They should be up and labouring, for the good of their souls, if not for the workhouse purse. Not even children were granted the sin of idleness.

Of course; it was a hospital. It must be! Very carefully he lay down again, relief overwhelming him as his head touched the bran pillow. He had no recollection of how he had come to be in such a place, no memory of having hurt himself – and yet he was undoubtedly injured, his arm was stiff and clumsy, he was aware now of a deep ache in the bone. And his chest hurt him sharply every time he breathed in. There was a thunderstorm raging inside his head. What had happened to him? It must have been a major accident: a collapsing wall, a violent throw from a horse, a fall from a height? But no impression came back, not even a memory of fear.

He was still struggling to recall something when a grinning face appeared above him and a voice spoke cheerfully.

'Now then, you awake again, are you?'

He stared upwards, focusing on the moon face. It was broad and blunt with a chapped skin and a smile that stretched wide over broken teeth.

He tried to clear his head.

'Again?' he said confusedly. The past lay behind him in dreamless sleep like a white corridor without a beginning.

'You're the right one, you are.' The voice sighed good-humouredly. 'You dunno nuffin' from one day ter the next, do yer? It wouldn't surprise me none if yer didn't remember yer own name! 'Ow are yer then? 'Ow's yer arm?'

'My name?' There was nothing there, nothing at all.

'Yeah.' The voice was cheerful and patient. 'Wot's yer name, then?'

He must know his name. Of course he must! It was . . . Blank seconds ticked by.

'Well then?' the voice pressed.

He struggled. Nothing came except a white panic, like a snowstorm in the brain, whirling and dangerous, and without focus.

'Yer've forgot!' The voice was stoic and resigned. 'I thought so. Well, the Peelers was 'ere, day afore yesterday; an' they said as you was "Monk" – "William Monk". Now wot 'a you gorn an' done that the Peelers is after yer?' He pushed helpfully at the pillow with enormous hands and then straightened the blanket. 'You like a nice 'ot drink then, or summink? Proper parky it is, even in 'ere. July – an' it feels like ruddy November! I'll get yer a nice 'ot drink o' gruel, 'ow's that then? Raining a flood outside, it is. Ye're best off in 'ere.'

'William Monk?' he repeated the name.

'That's right, leastways that's wot the Peelers says. Feller called Runcorn, 'e was; Mr Runcorn, a hinspector, no less!' He raised scruffy eyebrows. 'Wot yer done, then? You one o' them Swell Mob wot goes around pinchin' gennelmens' wallets and gold watches?' There was no criticism in his round, benign eyes. 'That's wot yer looked like when they brought yer in 'ere, proper natty dressed yer was, hunderneath

3

the mud and torn-up stuff, like, and all that blood.'

Monk said nothing. His head reeled, pounding in an effort to perceive anything in the mists, even one clear, tangible memory. But even the name had no real significance. 'William' had a vague familiarity but it was a common enough name. Everyone must know dozens of Williams.

'So yer don't remember,' the man went on, his face friendly and faintly amused. He had seen all manner of human frailty and there was nothing so fearful or so eccentric it disturbed his composure. He had seen men die of the pox and the plague, or climb the wall in terror of things that were not there. A grown man who could not remember yesterday was a curiosity, but nothing to marvel at. 'Or else yer ain't saying,' he went on. 'Don't blame yer.' He shrugged. 'Don't do ter give the Peelers nothin' as yer don't 'ave ter. Now d'yer feel like a spot of 'ot gruel? Nice and thick, it is, bin sitting on that there stove a fair while. Put a bit of 'eart inter yer.'

Monk was hungry, and even under the blanket he realized he was cold.

'Yes please,' he accepted.

'Right-oh-then, gruel it is. I suppose I'll be a'tellin' yer yer name termorrer jus' the same, an' yer'll look at me all gormless again.' He shook his head. 'Either yer 'it yer 'ead summink 'orrible, or ye're scared o' yer wits o' them. Peelers. Wot yer done? You pinched the crown jools?' And he went off chuckling with laughter to himself, up to the black-bellied stove at the far end of the ward.

Police! Was he a thief? The thought was repellent, not

only because of the fear attached to it but for itself, what it made of him. And yet he had no idea if it might be true.

Who was he? What manner of man? Had he been hurt doing something brave, rash? Or chased down like an animal for some crime? Or was he merely unfortunate, a victim, in the wrong place at the wrong time?

He racked his mind and found nothing, not a shred of thought or sensation. He must live somewhere, know people with faces, voices, emotions. And there was nothing! For all that his memory held, he could have sprung into existence here in the hard cot in this bleak hospital ward.

But he was known to someone! The police.

The man returned with the gruel and carefully fed it to Monk, a spoonful at a time. It was thin and tasteless, but he was grateful for it. Afterwards he lay back again, and struggle as he might, even fear could not keep him from deep, apparently dreamless sleep.

When he woke the following morning at least two things were perfectly clear this time: his name, and where he was. He could remember the meagre happenings of the previous day quite sharply: the nurse, the hot gruel, the man in the next cot turning and groaning, the grey-white ceiling, the feel of the blankets, and the pain in his chest.

He had little idea of time, but he judged it to be somewhere in the mid-afternoon when the policeman came. He was a big man, or he appeared so in the caped coat and top hat of Peel's Metropolitan Police Force. He had a bony face, long nose and wide mouth, a good brow, but deep-set eyes too small to tell the colour of easily; a pleasant enough countenance, and intelligent, but showing small signs of temper between the brows and about the lips. He stopped at Monk's cot.

'Well, do you know me this time, then?' he asked cheerfully.

Monk did not shake his head; it hurt too much.

'No,' he said simply.

The man mastered his irritation and something that might even have been disappointment. He looked Monk up and down closely, narrowing one eye in a nervous gesture as if it would concentrate his vision.

'You look better today,' he pronounced.

Was that the truth; did he look better? Or did Runcorn merely want to encourage him? For that matter, what did he look like? He had no idea. Was he dark or fair, ugly or pleasing? Was he well built, or ungainly? He could not even see his hands, let alone his body beneath the blankets. He would not look now – he must wait till Runcorn was gone.

'Don't remember anything, I suppose?' Runcorn continued. 'Don't remember what happened to you?'

'No.' Monk was fighting with a cloud totally without shape. Did this man know him, or merely of him? Was he a public figure Monk ought to recognize? Or did he pursue him for some dutiful and anonymous purpose? Might he only be looking for information, or could he tell Monk something about himself more than a bare name, put flesh and memory to the bleak fact of his presence?

Monk was lying on the cot clothed up to his chin, and yet

he felt mentally naked, vulnerable as the exposed and ridiculous are. His instinct was to hide, to conceal his weakness. And yet he must know. There must be dozens, perhaps scores of people in the world who knew him, and he knew nothing. It was a total and paralyzing disadvantage. He did not even know who loved or hated him, whom he had wronged, or helped. His need was like that of a man who starves for food, and yet is terrified that in any mouthful may lurk poison.

He looked back at the policeman. Runcorn, the nurse had said his name was. He must commit himself to something.

'Did I have an accident?' he asked.

'Looked like it,' Runcorn replied matter-of-factly. 'Hansom was turned over, right mess. You must have hit something at a hell of a lick. Horse frightened out of its wits.' He shook his head and pulled the corners of his mouth down. 'Cabby killed outright, poor devil. Hit his head on the kerb. You were inside, so I suppose you were partly protected. Had a swine of a job to get you out. Dead weight. Never realized you were such a solid feller. Don't remember it, I suppose? Not even the fright?' Again his left eye narrowed a little.

'No.' No images came to Monk's mind, no memory of speed, or impact, not even pain.

'Don't remember what you were doing?' Runcorn went on, without any real hope in his voice. 'What case you were on?'

Monk seized on a brilliant hope, a thing with shape; he was almost too afraid to ask, in case it crumbled at his touch.

He stared at Runcorn. He must know this man, personally, perhaps even daily. And yet nothing in him woke the slightest recall.

'Well, man?' Runcorn demanded. 'Do you remember? You weren't anywhere we sent you! What the devil were you doing? You must have discovered something yourself. Can you remember what it was?'

The blank was impenetrable.

Monk moved his head fractionally in negation, but the bright bubble inside him stayed. He was a Peeler himself, that was why they knew him! He was not a thief – not a fugitive.

Runcorn leaned forward a little, watching him keenly, seeing the light in his face.

'You do remember something!' he said triumphantly. 'Come on, man – what is it?'

Monk could not explain that it was not memory that changed him, but a dissolving of fear in one of the sharpest forms it had taken. The entire, suffocating blanket was still there, but characterless now, without specific menace.

Runcorn was still waiting, staring at him intently.

'No,' Monk said slowly. 'Not yet.'

Runcorn straightened up. He sighed, trying to control himself. 'It'll come.'

'How long have I been here?' Monk asked. 'I've lost count of time.' It sounded reasonable enough; anyone ill might do that.

'Over three weeks – it's the thirty-first of July – 1856,' he added with a touch of sarcasm.

Dear God! Over three weeks, and all he could remember was yesterday. He shut his eyes; it was infinitely worse than that – a whole lifetime of how many years? And all he could remember was yesterday! How old was he? How many years were lost? Panic boiled up inside him again and for a moment he could have screamed. Help me, somebody, who am I? Give me back my life, my self!

But men did not scream in public, even in private they did not cry out. The sweat stood cold on his skin and he lay rigid, hands clenched by his sides. Runcorn would take it for pain, ordinary physical pain. He must keep up the appearance. He must not let Runcorn think he had forgotten how to do his job. Without a job the workhouse would be a reality – grinding, hopeless, day after day of obedient, servile, pointless labour.

He forced himself back to the present.

'Over three weeks?'

'Yes,' Runcorn replied. Then he coughed and cleared his throat. Perhaps he was embarrassed. What does one say to a man who cannot remember you, who cannot even remember himself? Monk felt for him.

'It'll come back,' Runcorn repeated. 'When you're up again; when you get back on the job. You want a break to get well, that's what you need, a break till you get your strength. Take a week or two. Bound to. Come back to the station when you're fit to work. It'll all come clear then, I dare say.'

'Yes,' Monk agreed, more for Runcorn's sake than his own. He did not believe it.

* * *

Monk left the hospital three days later. He was strong enough to walk, and no one stayed in such places longer than they had to. It was not only financial consideration, but the sheer danger. More people died of cross-infection than of any illness or injury that brought them there in the first place. This much was imparted to him in a cheerfully resigned matter by the nurse who had originally told him his name.

It was easy to believe. In the short days he could remember he had seen doctors move from one bloody or festering wound to another, from fever patient to vomiting and flux, then to open sores, and back again. Soiled bandages lay on the floor; there was little laundry done, although no doubt they did the best they could on the pittance they had.

And to be fair, they did their utmost never knowingly to admit patients suffering from typhoid, cholera or smallpox; and if they did discover these illnesses afterwards, they rectified their error. Those poor souls had to be quarantined in their own houses and left to die, or recover if God were willing. There they would be of least peril to the community. Everyone was familiar with the black flag hanging limply at the ends of a street.

Runcorn had left for him his Peeler's coat and tall hat, carefully dusted off and mended after the accident. At least they fitted him, apart from being a trifle loose because of the weight he had lost lying on his back since the injury. But that would return. He was a strong man, tall and lean muscled, but the nurse had shaved him so he had not yet seen his face. He had felt it, touching with his fingertips when no one was watching him. It was strong boned, and his mouth seemed wide, that was all he knew; and his hands were smooth and uncallused by labour, with a scattering of dark hairs on the backs.

Apparently he had had a few coins in his pocket when they brought him in, and these were handed to him as he left. Someone else must have paid for his treatment – presumably his police salary had been sufficient? Now he stood on the steps with eight shillings and elevenpence, a cotton handkerchief and an envelope with his name and '27 Grafton Street' written on it. It contained a receipt from his tailor.

He looked around him and recognized nothing. It was a bright day with fast-scudding clouds and a warm wind. Fifty yards away there was an intersection, and a small boy was wielding a broom, keeping the crossing clear of horse manure and other rubbish. A carriage swirled past, drawn by two high-stepping bays.

Monk stepped down, still feeling weak, and made his way to the main road. It took him five minutes to see a vacant hansom, hail it and give the cabby the address. He sat back inside and watched as streets and squares flickered by, other vehicles, carriages, some with liveried footmen, more hansoms, brewers' drays, costermongers' carts. He saw pedlars and vendors, a man selling fresh eels, another with hot pies, plum duff – it sounded good, he was hungry, but he had no idea how much the fare would be, so he did not dare stop.

A newspaper boy was shouting something, but they passed him too quickly to hear above the horse's hooves.

A one-legged man sold matches.

There was a familiarity about the streets, but it was at the back of his mind. He could not have named a single one, simply that they did not seem alien.

Tottenham Court Road. It was very busy: carriages, drays, carts, women in wide skirts stepping over refuse in the gutter, two soldiers laughing and a little drunk, red coats a splash of colour, a flower seller and two washerwomen.

The cab swung left into Grafton Street and stopped.

''Ere y'are, sir, Number Twenty-seven.'

'Thank you.' Monk climbed out awkwardly; he was still stiff and unpleasantly weak. Even that small exertion had tired him. He had no idea how much money to offer. He held out a florin, two sixpences, a penny and a halfpenny in his hand.

The cabby hesitated, then took one of the sixpences and the halfpenny, tipped his hat and slapped the reins across his horse's rump, leaving Monk standing on the pavement. He hesitated, now that the moment was come, overtaken with fear. He had not even the slightest idea what he should find – or whom.

Two men passed, looking at him curiously. They must suppose him lost. He felt foolish, embarrassed. Who would answer his knock? Should he know them? If he lived here, they must know him. How well? Were they friends, or merely landlords? It was preposterous, but he did not even know if he had a family!

But if he had, surely they would have visited him. Runcorn had come, so they would have been told where he was. Or had he been the kind of man who inspires no love, only professional courtesy? Was that why Runcorn had called, because it was his job?

Had he been a good policeman, efficient at his work? Was he liked? It was ridiculous – pathetic.

He shook himself. This was childish. If he had a family, a wife or brother or sister, Runcorn would have told him. He must discover each thing as he could; if he was fit to be employed by the Peelers, then he was a detective. He would learn each piece till he had enough to cobble together a whole, the pattern of his life. The first step was to knock on this door, dark brown and closed in front of him.

He lifted his hand and rapped sharply. It was long, desperate minutes with the questions roaring in his mind before it was opened by a broad, middle-aged woman in an apron. Her hair was scraped back untidily, but it was thick and clean and her scrubbed face was generous.

'Well I never!' she said impulsively. 'Save my soul, if it in't Mr Monk back again! I was only saying to Mr Worley this very morning, as 'ow if you didn't come back again soon I'd 'ave ter let yer rooms; much as it'd go against me ter do it. But a body 'as ter live. Mind that Mr Runcorn did come around an' say as yer'd 'ad a haccident and bin terrible 'urt and was in one 'o them 'orstipitals.' She put her hand to her head in despair. 'Gawd save us from such places. Ye're the first man I've seen as 'as come out o' there on 'is own two feet. To tell you the truth, I was expectin' every day to 'ave some messenger boy come and say as you was dead.' She screwed up her face and looked at him carefully. 'Mind yer does still look proper poorly. Come in and I'll make yer a good meal. Yer must be starved, I'll dare swear yer 'aven't 'ad a decent dish since yer left 'ere! It were as cold as a workhouse master's 'eart the day yer went!' And she whisked her enormous skirts around and led him inside.

He followed her through the panelled hallway hung with sentimental pictures and up the stairs to a large landing. She produced a bunch of keys from her girdle and opened one of the doors.

'I suppose you gorn and lost your own key, or you wouldn't 'ave knocked; that stands ter reason, don't it?'

'I had my own key?' he asked before realizing how it betrayed him.

'Gawd save us, o' course yer did!' she said in surprise. 'Yer don't think I'm goin' ter get up and down at all hours o' the night ter let yer in and out, do yer? A Christian body needs 'er sleep. 'Eathen hours yer keeps, an' no mistake. Comes o' chasin' after 'eathen folk, I expec'.' She turned to look at him. ''Ere, yer does look ill. Yer must 'ave bin 'it summink terrible. You go in there an' sit down, an' I'll bring yer a good 'ot meal an' a drink. Do you the world o' good, that will.' She snorted and straightened her apron fiercely. 'I always thought them 'orstipitals din't look after yer proper. I'll wager as 'alf o' them wot dies in there dies o' starvation.' And with indignation at the thought twitching in every muscle under her black taffeta, she swept out of the room, leaving the door open behind her.

Monk walked over and closed it, then turned to face the room. It was large, dark brown panelling and green wallpaper.

The furniture was well used. A heavy oak table with four matching chairs stood in the centre, Jacobean with carved legs and decorated claw feet. The sideboard against the far wall was similar, although what purpose it served he did not know; there was no china on it, and when he opened the drawers, no cutlery. However the lower drawers did contain table linen and napkins, freshly laundered and in good repair. There was also an oak desk with two small, flat drawers. Against the near wall, by the door, there was a handsome bookcase full of volumes. Part of the furniture? Or his own? Later he would look at the titles.

The windows were draped rather than hung with fringed plush curtains of a mid shade of green. The gas brackets on the walls were ornate, with pieces missing. The leather easy chair had faded patches on the arms, and the pile on the cushions was flat. The carpet's colours had long since dimmed to muted plums, navies and forest greens – a pleasant background. There were several pictures of a self-indulgent tone, and a motto over the mantelpiece with the dire warning GOD SEES ALL.

Were they his? Surely not; the emotions jarred on him and he found himself pulling a face at the mawkishness of the subjects, even feeling a touch of contempt.

It was a comfortable room, well lived in, but peculiarly impersonal, without photographs or mementoes, no mark of his own taste. His eyes went around it again and again, but nothing was familiar, nothing brought even a pinprick of memory.

He tried the bedroom beyond. It was the same:

comfortable, old, shabby. A large bed stood in the centre, made up ready with clean sheets, crisp white bolster, and wine-coloured eiderdown, flounced at the edges. On the heavy dresser there was a rather pleasant china washbowl and a jug for water. A handsome silver-backed hairbrush lay on the tallboy.

He touched the surfaces. His hands came away clean. Mrs Worley was at least a good housekeeper.

He was about to open the drawers and look further when there was a sharp rap on the outer door and Mrs Worley returned, carrying a tray with a steaming plate piled with steak and kidney pudding, boiled cabbage, carrots and beans, and another dish with pie and custard.

'There yer are,' she said with satisfaction, setting it down on the table. He was relieved to see knife, fork and spoon with it, and a glass of cider. 'You eat that, and yer'll feel better!'

'Thank you, Mrs Worley.' His gratitude was genuine; he had not had a good meal since . . .?

'It's my duty, Mr Monk, as a Christian woman,' she replied with a little shake of her head. 'And yer always paid me prompt, I'll say that for yer – never argued ner was a day late, fer ought else! Now you eat that up, then go ter bed. Yer look proper done in. I don't know what yer bin doin', an' I don't want ter. Prob'ly in't fit fer a body to know anyway.'

'What shall I do with the . . .' He looked at the tray.

'Put it outside the door like yer always does!' she said with raised eyebrows. Then she looked at him more closely and sighed. 'An' if yer gets took poorly in the night, yer'd best shout out, an I'll come an' see to yer.'

'It won't be necessary – I shall be perfectly well.'

She sniffed and let out a little gasp, heavy with disbelief, then bustled out, closing the door behind her with a loud click. He realized immediately how ungracious he had been. She had offered to get up in the night to help him if he needed it, and all he had done was assure her she was not needed. And she had not looked surprised, or hurt. Was he always this discourteous? He paid – she said he paid promptly and without quibble. Was that all there was between them, no kindness, no feeling, just a lodger who was financially reliable, and a landlady who did her Christian duty by him, because that was her nature?

It was not an attractive picture.

He turned his attention to the food. It was plain, but of excellent flavour, and she was certainly not ungenerous with her portions. It flickered through his mind with some anxiety to wonder how much he paid for these amenities, and if he could much longer afford them while he was unable to work. The sooner he recovered his strength, and enough of his wits to resume his duties for the police, the better. He could hardly ask her for credit, particularly after her remarks, and his manners. Please heaven he did not owe her already for the time he was in the hospital!

When he had finished the meal he placed the tray outside on the landing table where she could collect it. He went back into the room, closed the door and sat in one of the armchairs, intending to look through the desk in the window corner, but in weariness, and the comfort of the cushions, he fell asleep.

When he woke, cold now and stiff, his side aching, it was dark, and he fumbled to light the gas. He was still tired, and would willingly have gone to bed, but he knew that the temptation of the desk, and the fear of it, would trouble even the most exhausted sleep.

He lit the lamp above it and pulled open the top. There was a flat surface with an inkstand, a leather writing block and a dozen small closed drawers.

He started at the top left-hand side, and worked through them all. He must be a methodical man. There were receipted bills; a few newspaper clippings, entirely of crimes, usually violent, and describing brilliant police work in solving them; three railway timetables; business letters; and a note from a tailor.

A tailor. So that was where his money went – vain beggar. He must take a look through his wardrobe and see what his taste was. Expensive, according to the bill in his hand. A policeman who wanted to look like a gentleman! He laughed sharply: a ratcatcher with pretensions – was that what he was? A somewhat ridiculous figure. The thought hurt and he pushed it away with a black humour.

In other drawers there were envelopes, notepaper, good quality – vanity again! Whom did he write to? There was also sealing wax, string, a paper knife and scissors, a number of minor items of convenience. It was not until the tenth drawer that he found the personal correspondence. They were all in the same hand, to judge from the formation of the letters a young person, or someone of slight education. Only one person wrote to him – or only one whose letters he had considered worth keeping. He opened the first, angry with himself that his hands were shaking.

It was very simple, beginning 'Dear William', full of homely news, and ending 'your loving sister, Beth'.

He put it down, the round characters burning in front of him, dizzy and overwhelmed with excitement and relief, and perhaps a shadow of disappointment he forced away. He had a sister, there was someone who knew him, had always known him; more than that, who cared. He picked up the letter again quickly, almost tearing it in his clumsiness to reread it. It was gentle, frank, and yes, it was affectionate; it must be, one did not speak so openly to someone one did not trust, and care for.

And yet there was nothing in it that was any kind of reply, no reference to anything he had written to her. Surely he did write? He could not have treated such a woman with cavalier disregard.

What kind of a man was he? If he had ignored her, not written, then there must be a reason. How could he explain himself, justify anything, when he could not remember? It was like being accused, standing in the dock with no defence.

It was long, painful moments before he thought to look for the address. When he did it came as a sharp, bewildering surprise – it was in Northumberland. He repeated it over and over to himself, aloud. It sounded familiar, but he could not place it. He had to go to the bookcase and search for an atlas to look it up. Even so he could not see it for several minutes. It was very small, a name in fine letters on the coast, a fishing village.

A fishing village? What was his sister doing there? Had she married and gone there? The surname on the envelope was Bannerman. Or had he been born there, and then come south to London? He laughed sharply. Was that the key to his pretension? He was a provincial fisherman's son, with eyes on passing himself off as something better?

When? When had he come?

He realized with a shock he did not know how old he was. He still had not looked at himself in the glass. Why not? Was he afraid of it? What did it matter how a man looked? And yet he was trembling.

He swallowed hard and picked up the oil lamp from the desk. He walked slowly into the bedroom and put the lamp on the dresser. There must be a glass there, at least big enough to shave himself.

It was on a swivel; that was why he had not noticed it before, his eye had been on the silver brush. He set the lamp down and slowly tipped the glass.

The face he saw was dark and very strong, broad, slightly aquiline nose, wide mouth, rather thin upper lip, lower lip fuller, with an old scar just below it, eyes intense luminous grey in the flickering light. It was a powerful face, but not an easy one. If there was humour it would be harsh, of wit rather than laughter. He could have been anything between thirty-five and forty-five.

He picked up the lamp and walked back to the main room, finding the way blindly, his inner eye still seeing the face that had stared back at him from the dim glass. It was not that it displeased him especially, but it was the face of a stranger, and not one easy to know.

The following day he made his decision. He would travel north to see his sister. She would at least be able to tell him his childhood, his family. And to judge from her letters, and the recent date of the last, she still held him in affection, whether he deserved it or not. He wrote in the morning telling her simply that he had had an accident but was considerably recovered now, and intended to visit her when he was well enough to make the journey, which he expected to be no more than another day or two at the outside.

Among the other things in the desk drawer he found a modest sum of money. Apparently he was not extravagant except at the tailor, the clothes in his wardrobe were impeccably cut and of first-quality fabric, and possibly the bookshop – if the contents of the case were his. Other than that he had saved regularly, but if for any particular purpose there was no note of it, and it hardly mattered now. He gave Mrs Worley what she asked for, a further month's rent on account – minus the food he would not consume while he was away – and informed her he was going to visit his sister in Northumberland.

'Very good idea.' She nodded her head sagaciously. 'More'n time you paid her a visit, if yer ask me. Not that yer did, o' course! I'm not one to interfere' – she drew in her breath – 'but yer in't bin orf ter see 'er since I known yer – an' that's some years now. An' the poor soul writes to yer regular – although w'en yer writes back I'm blessed if I know!'

She put the money in her pocket and looked at him closely.

'Well, you look after yerself – eat proper and don't go doin' any daft caperin's around chasin' folk. Let ruffians alone an' mind for yerself for a space.' And with that parting advice she smoothed her apron again and turned away, her boot heels clicking down the corridor towards the kitchen.

It was 4 August when he boarded the train in London and settled himself for the long journey.

Northumberland was vast and bleak, wind roaring over treeless, heather-darkened moors, but there was a simplicity about its tumultuous skies and clean earth that pleased him enormously. Was it familiar to him, memories stirring from childhood, or only beauty that would have woken the same emotion in him had it been as unknown as the plains of the moon? He stood a long time at the station, bag in his hand, staring out at the hills before he finally made move to begin. He would have to find a conveyance of some kind: he was eleven miles from the sea and the hamlet he wanted. In normal health he might well have walked it, but he was still weak. His rib ached when he breathed deeply, and he had not yet the full use of his broken arm.

It was not more than a pony cart, and he had paid handsomely for it, he thought. But he was glad enough to have the driver take him to his sister's house, which he asked for by name, and deposit him and his bag on the narrow street in front of the door. As the wheels rattled away over the cobbles he conquered his thoughts, the apprehension and the sense of an irretrievable step, and knocked loudly.

He was about to knock again when the door swung open and a pretty, fresh-faced woman stood on the step. She was bordering on the plump and had strong dark hair and features reminiscent of his own only in the broad brow and some echo of cheekbones. Her eyes were blue and her nose had the strength without the arrogance, and her mouth was far softer. All this flashed into his mind, with the realization that she must be Beth, his sister. She would find him inexplicable, and probably be hurt, if he did not know her.

'Beth.' He held out his hands.

Her face broke into a broad smile of delight.

'William! I hardly knew you, you've changed so much! We got your letter – you said an accident – are you hurt badly? We didn't expect you so soon—' She blushed. 'Not that you aren't very welcome, of course.' Her accent was broad Northumberland, and he found it surprisingly pleasing to the ear. Was that familiarity again, or only the music of it after London?

'William?' She was staring at him. 'Come inside – you must be tired out, and hungry.' She made as if to pull him physically into the house.

He followed her, smiling in a sudden relief. She knew him; apparently she held no grudge for his long absence or the letters he had not written. There was a naturalness about her that made long explanations unnecessary. And he realized he was indeed hungry.

The kitchen was small but scrubbed clean; in fact the table was almost white. It woke no chord of memory in him at all. There were warm smells of bread and baked fish and salt wind from the sea. For the first time since waking in the hospital, he found himself beginning to relax, to ease the knots out.

Gradually, over bread and soup, he told her the facts he knew of the accident, inventing details where the story was so bare as to seem evasive. She listened while she continued to stir her cooking on the stove, warm the flatiron and then begin on a series of small children's clothes and a man's Sunday white shirt. If it was strange to her, or less than credible, she gave no outward sign. Perhaps the whole world of London was beyond her knowledge anyway, and inhabited by people who lived incomprehensible lives which could not be hoped to make sense to ordinary people.

It was the late summer dusk when her husband came in, a broad, fair man with wind-scoured face and mild features. His grey eyes still seemed tuned to the sea. He greeted Monk with friendly surprise, but no sense of dismay or of having been disturbed in his feelings, or the peace of his home.

No one asked Monk for explanations, even the three shy children returned from chores and play, and since he had none to give, the matter was passed over. It was a strange mark of the distance between them, which he observed with a wry pain, that apparently he had never shared enough of himself with his only family that they noticed the omission.

Day succeeded day, sometimes golden bright, sun hot when the wind was offshore and the sand soft under his feet. Other times it swung east off the North Sea and blew with sharp chill and the breath of storm. Monk walked along the beach, feeling it rip at him, beating his face, tearing at his hair, and the very size of it was at once frightening and comforting. It had nothing to do with people; it was impersonal, indiscriminate.

He had been there a week, and was feeling the strength of life come back to him, when the alarm was called. It was nearly midnight and the wind screaming around the stone corners of the houses when the shouts came and the hammering on the door.

Rob Bannerman was up within minutes, oilskins and seaboots on still almost in his sleep. Monk stood on the landing in bewilderment, confused; at first no explanation came to his mind as to the emergency. It was not until he saw Beth's face when she ran to the window, and he followed her and saw below them the dancing lanterns and the gleam of light on moving figures, oilskins shining in the rain, that he realized what it was. Instinctively he put his arm around Beth, and she moved fractionally closer to him, but her body was stiff. Under her breath she was praying, and there were tears in her voice.

Rob was already out of the house. He had spoken to neither of them, not even hesitated beyond touching Beth's hand as he passed her.

It was a wreck, some ship driven by the screaming winds onto the outstretched fingers of rock, with God knew how many souls clinging to the sundering planks, water already swirling around their waists.

After the first moment of shock, Beth ran upstairs again to dress, calling to Monk to do the same, then everything

25

was a matter of finding blankets, heating soup, rebuilding fires ready to help the survivors – if, please God, there were any.

The work went on all night, the lifeboats going backwards and forwards, men roped together. Thirty-five people were pulled out of the sea, ten were lost. Survivors were all brought back to the few homes in the village. Beth's kitchen was full of white-faced shivering people and she and Monk plied them with hot soup and what comforting words they could think of.

Nothing was stinted. Beth emptied out every last morsel of food without a thought as to what her own family might eat tomorrow. Every stitch of dry clothing was brought out and offered.

One woman sat in the corner too numb with grief for her lost husband even to weep. Beth looked at her with a compassion that made her beautiful. In a moment between tasks Monk saw her bend and take the woman's hands, holding them between her own to press some warmth into them, speaking to her gently as if she had been a child.

Monk felt a sudden ache of loneliness, of being an outsider whose involvement in this passion of suffering and pity was only chance. He contributed nothing but physical help; he could not even remember whether he had ever done it before, whether these were his people or not. Had he ever risked his life without grudge or question as Rob Bannerman did? He hungered with a terrible need for some part in the beauty of it. Had he ever had courage, generosity? Was there anything in his past to be proud of, to cling to?

There was no one he could ask—

The moment passed and the urgency of the present need overtook him again. He bent to pick up a child shaking with terror and cold, and wrapped it in a warm blanket, holding it close to his own body, stroking it with soft, repetitive words as he might a frightened animal.

By dawn it was over. The seas were still running high and hard, but Rob was back, too tired to speak and too weary with loss of those the sea had taken. He simply took off his wet clothes in the kitchen and climbed up to bed.

A week later Monk was fully recovered physically; only dreams troubled him, vague nightmares of fear, sharp pain and a sense of being violently struck and losing his balance, then a suffocation. He woke gasping, his heart racing and sweat on his skin, his breath rasping, but nothing was left except the fear, no thread to unravel towards recollection. The need to return to London became more pressing. He had found his distant past, his beginnings, but memory was virgin blank and Beth could tell him nothing whatsoever of his life since leaving, when she was still little more than a child. Apparently he had not written of it, only trivialities, items of ordinary news such as one might read in the journals or newspapers, and small matters of his welfare and concern for hers. This was the first time he had visited her in eight years, something he was not proud to learn. He seemed a cold man, obsessed with his own ambition. Had that compelled him to work so hard, or had he been so poor? He would like to think there was some excuse, but to judge from the money in his desk at Grafton Street, it had not lately been finance.

He racked his brains to recall any emotion, any flash of memory as to what sort of man he was, what he had valued, what sought. Nothing came, no explanations for his self-absorption.

He said good-bye to her and Rob, thanking them rather awkwardly for their kindness, surprising and embarrassing them, and because of it, himself too; but he meant it so deeply. Because they were strangers to him, he felt as if they had taken him in, a stranger, and offered him acceptance, even trust. They looked confused, Beth colouring shyly. But he did not try to explain; he did not have words, nor did he wish them to know.

London seemed enormous, dirty and indifferent when he got off the train and walked out of the ornate, smoke-grimed station. He took a hansom to Grafton Street, announced his return to Mrs Worley, then went upstairs and changed his clothes from those worn and crumpled by his journey. He took himself to the police station Runcorn had named when speaking to the nurse. With the experience of Beth and Northumberland behind him he began to feel a little confidence. It was still another essay into the unknown, but with each step accomplished without unpleasant surprise, his apprehension lessened.

When he climbed out of the cab and paid the driver he stood on the pavement. The police station was as unfamiliar as everything else – not strange, simply without any spark of familiarity at all. He opened the doors and went inside, saw the sergeant at the duty desk and wondered how many hundreds of times before he had done exactly this.

'Arternoon, Mr Monk.' The man looked up with slight surprise, and no pleasure. 'Nasty haccident. Better now, are yer, sir?'

There was a chill in his voice, a wariness. Monk looked at him. He was perhaps forty, round-faced, mild and perhaps a trifle indecisive, a man who could be easily befriended, and easily crushed. Monk felt a stirring of shame, and knew no reason for it whatever, except the caution in the man's eyes. He was expecting Monk to say something to which he would not be able to reply with assurance. He was a subordinate, and slower with words, and he knew it.

'Yes I am, thank you.' Monk could not remember the man's name to use it. He felt contempt for himself – what kind of a man embarrasses someone who cannot retaliate? Why? Was there some long history of incompetence or deceit that would explain such a thing?

'You'll be wantin' Mr Runcorn, sir.' The sergeant seemed to notice no change in Monk, and to be keen to speed him on his way.

'Yes, if he's in – please?'

The sergeant stepped aside a little and allowed Monk through the counter.

Monk stopped, feeling ridiculous. He had no idea which way to go, and he would raise suspicion if he went the wrong way. He had a hot, prickly sensation that there would be little allowance made for him – he was not liked.

'You o'right, sir?' the sergeant said anxiously.

'Yes – yes I am. Is Mr Runcorn still' – he took a glance around and made a guess – 'at the top of the stairs?'

'Yes, sir, right w'ere 'e always was!'

'Thank you.' And he set off up the steps rapidly, feeling a fool.

Runcorn was in the first room on the corridor. Monk knocked and went in. It was dark and littered with papers and cabinets and baskets for filing, but comfortable, in spite of a certain institutional bareness. Gas lamps hissed gently on the walls. Runcorn himself was sitting behind a large desk, chewing a pencil.

'Ah!' he said with satisfaction when Monk came in. 'Fit for work, are you? About time. Best thing, work. Good for a man to work. Well, sit down then, sit down. Think better sitting down.'

Monk obeyed, his muscles tight with tension. He imagined his breathing was so loud it must be audible above the gas.

'Good. Good,' Runcorn went on. 'Lot of cases, as always; I'll wager there's more stolen in some quarters of this city than is ever bought or sold honestly.' He pushed away a pile of papers and set his pen in its stand. 'And the Swell Mob's been getting worse. All these enormous crinolines. Crinolines were made to steal from, so many petticoats on no one can feel a dip. But that's not what I had in mind for you. Give you a good one to get your teeth into.' He smiled mirthlessly.

Monk waited.

'Nasty murder.' He leaned back in his chair and looked

30

directly at Monk. 'Haven't managed to do anything about it, though heaven knows we've tried. Had Lamb in charge. Poor fellow's sick and taken to his bed. Put you on the case; see what you can do. Make a good job of it. We've got to turn up some kind of result.'

'Who was killed?' Monk asked. 'And when?'

'Feller called Joscelin Grey, younger brother of Lord Shelburne, so you can see it's rather important we tidy it up.' His eyes never left Monk's face. 'When? Well, that's the worst part of it – rather a while ago, and we haven't turned up a damned thing. Nearly six weeks now – about when you had your accident; in fact, come to think of it, exactly then. Nasty night, thunderstorm and pouring with rain. Probably some ruffian followed him home, but made a very nasty job of it, bashed the poor feller about to an awful state. Newspapers in an outrage, naturally, crying for justice, and what's the world coming to, where are the police, and so on. We'll give you everything poor Lamb had, of course, and a good man to work with, name of Evan, John Evan; worked with Lamb till he took ill. See what you can do, anyway. Give them something!'

'Yes, sir.' Monk stood up. 'Where is Mr Evan?'

'Out somewhere; trail's pretty cold. Start tomorrow morning, bright and early. Too late now. Go home and get some rest. Last night of freedom, eh! Make the best of it; tomorrow I'll have you working like one of those railway diggers!'

'Yes, sir.' Monk excused himself and walked out. It was already darkening in the street and the wind was laden with the smell of coming rain. But he knew where he was going, and he knew what he would do tomorrow, and it would be with identity – and purpose.

Chapter Two

Monk arrived early to meet John Evan and find out what Lamb had so far learned of the murder of Lord Shelburne's brother, Joscelin Grey.

He still had some sense of apprehension; his discoveries about himself had been commonplace, such small things as one might learn of anyone, likes and dislikes, vanities – his wardrobe had plainly shown him those – discourtesies, such as had made the desk sergeant nervous of him. But the remembered warmth of Northumberland was still with him and it was enough to buoy up his spirits. And he must work! The money would not last much longer.

John Evan was a tall young man, and lean almost to the point of appearing frail, but Monk judged from the way he stood that it was a deception; he might well be wiry under that rather elegant jacket, and the air with which he wore his clothes was a natural grace rather than effeminacy. His face was sensitive, all eyes and nose, and his hair waved back from his brow thick and honey brown. Above all he appeared intelligent, which was both necessary to Monk and frightening. He was not yet ready for a companion of such quick sight, or subtlety of perception.

But he had no choice in the matter. Runcorn introduced

Evan, banged a pile of papers on the wide, scratched wooden table in Monk's office, a good-sized room crammed with filing drawers and bookcases and with one sash window overlooking an alley. The carpet was a domestic castoff, but better than the bare wood, and there were two leather-seated chairs. Runcorn went out, leaving them alone.

Evan hesitated for a moment, apparently not wishing to usurp authority, then as Monk did not move, he put out a long finger and touched the top of the pile of papers.

'Those are all the statements from the witnesses, sir. Not very helpful, I'm afraid.'

Monk said the first thing that came to him.

'Were you with Mr Lamb when they were taken?'

'Yes, sir, all except the street sweeper; Mr Lamb saw him while I went after the cabby.'

'Cabby?' For a moment Monk had a wild hope that the assailant had been seen, was known, that it was merely his whereabouts that were needed. Then the thought died immediately. It would hardly have taken them six weeks if it were so simple. And more than that, there had been in Runcorn's face a challenge, even a kind of perverse satisfaction.

'The cabby that brought Major Grey home, sir,' Evan said, demolishing the hope apologetically.

'Oh.' Monk was about to ask him if there was anything useful in the man's statement, then realized how inefficient he would appear. He had all the papers in front of him. He picked up the first and Evan waited silently by the window while he read.

It was in neat, very legible writing, and headed at the top was the statement of Mary Ann Brown, seller of ribbons and laces in the street. Monk imagined the grammar to have been altered somewhat from the original, and a few aspirates put in, but the flavour was clear enough.

'I was standing in my usual place in Doughty Street near Mecklenburgh Square, like as I always do, on the corner, knowing as how there is ladies living in many of them buildings, especially ladies as has their own maids what does sewing for them, and the like.'

Question from Mr Lamb: 'So you were there at six o'clock in the evening?'

'I suppose I must have been, though I carsen't tell the time, and I don't have no watch. But I see'd the gentleman arrive what was killed. Something terrible, that is, when even the gentry's not safe.'

'You saw Major Grey arrive?'

'Yes, sir. What a gentleman he looked, all happy and jaunty, like.'

'Was he alone?'

'Yes, sir, he was.'

'Did he go straight in? After paying the cabby, of course.'

'Yes, sir, he did.'

'What time did you leave Mecklenburgh Square?'

'Don't rightly know, not for sure. But I heard the church clock at St Mark's strike the quarter just afore I got there.'

'Home?'

'Yes, sir.'

'And how far is your home from Mecklenburgh Square?'

'About a mile, I reckon.'

'Where do you live?'

'Off the Pentonville Road, sir.'

'Half an hour's walk?'

'Bless you, no, sir, more like a quarter. A sight too wet to be hanging around, it was. Besides, girls as hang around that time of an evening gets themselves misunderstood, or worse.'

'Quite. So you left Mecklenburgh Square about seven o'clock.'

'Reckon so.'

'Did you see anyone else go into Number Six, after Major Grey?'

'Yes, sir, one other gentleman in a black coat with a big fur collar.'

There was a note in brackets after the last statement to say it had been established that this person was a resident of the apartments, and no suspicion attached to him.

The name of Mary Ann Brown was written in the same hand at the bottom, and a rough cross placed beside it.

Monk put it down. It was a statement of only negative value; it made it highly unlikely that Joscelin Grey had been followed home by his murderer. But then the crime had happened in July, when it was light till nine in the evening. A man with murder, or even robbery, on his mind would not wish to be seen so close to his victim.

By the window Evan stood still, watching him, ignoring the clatter in the street beyond, a drayman shouting as he backed his horse, a coster calling his wares and the hiss and rattle of carriage wheels.

Monk picked up the next statement, in the name of Alfred Cressent, a boy of eleven who swept a crossing at the corner of Mecklenburgh Square and Doughty Street, keeping it clear of horse droppings principally, and any other litter that might be let fall.

His contribution was much the same, except that he had not left Doughty Street until roughly half an hour after the ribbon girl.

The cabby claimed to have picked Grey up at a regimental club a little before six o'clock, and driven him straight to Mecklenburgh Square. His fare had done no more than pass the time of day with him, some trivial comment about the weather, which had been extraordinarily unpleasant, and wished him a good night upon leaving. He could recall nothing more, and to the best of his knowledge they had not been followed or especially remarked by anyone. He had seen no unusual or suspicious characters in the neighbourhood of Guilford Street or Mecklenburgh Square, either on the way there or on his departure, only the men of unobtrusive appearance who might have been clerks returning home after a long day's work, or pickpockets awaiting a victim, or any of a hundred other things. This statement also was of no real help.

Monk put it on top of the other two, then looked up and found Evan's gaze still on him, shyness tinged with a faint, self-deprecating humour. Instinctively he liked Evan – or could it be just loneliness, because he had no friend, no human companionship deeper than the courtesies of office or the impersonal kindness of Mrs Worley fulfilling her 'Christian duty'. Had he had friends before, or wanted them? If so, where were they? Why had no one welcomed him back? Not even a letter. The answer was unpleasant, and obvious: he had not earned such a thing. He was clever, ambitious – a rather superior ratcatcher. Not appealing. But he must not let Evan see his weakness. He must appear professional, in command.

'Are they all like this?' he asked.

'Pretty much,' Evan replied, standing more upright now that he was spoken to. 'Nobody saw or heard anything that has led us even to a time or a description. For that matter, not even a definitive motive.'

Monk was surprised; it brought his mind back to the business. He must not let it wander. It would be hard enough to appear efficient without woolgathering.

'Not robbery?' he asked.

Evan shook his head and shrugged very slightly. Without effort he had the elegance Monk strove for, and Runcorn missed absolutely.

'Not unless he was frightened off,' he answered. 'There was money in Grey's wallet, and several small, easily portable ornaments of value around the room. One fact that might be worth something, though: he had no watch on. Gentlemen of his sort usually have rather good watches, engraved, that sort of thing. And he did have a watch chain.'

Monk sat on the edge of the table.

'Could he have pawned it?' he asked. 'Did anyone see

him with a watch?' It was an intelligent question, and it came to him instinctively. Even well-to-do men sometimes ran short of ready money, or dressed and dined beyond their means and were temporarily embarrassed. How had he known to ask that? Perhaps his skill was so deep it was not dependent on memory?

Evan flushed faintly and his hazel eyes looked suddenly awkward.

'I'm afraid we didn't find out, sir. I mean, the people we asked didn't seem to recall clearly; some said they remembered something about a watch, others that they didn't. We couldn't get a description of one. We wondered if he might have pawned it too; but we didn't find a ticket, and we tried the local pawnshops.'

'Nothing?'

Evan shook his head. 'Nothing at all, sir.'

'So we wouldn't know it, even if it turned up?' Monk said disappointedly, jerking his hand at the door. 'Some miserable devil could walk in here sporting it, and we should be none the wiser. Still, I daresay if the killer took it, he will have thrown it into the river when the hue and cry went up anyway. If he didn't he's too daft to be out on his own.' He twisted around to look at the pile of papers again and riffled through them untidily. 'What else is there?'

The next was the account of the neighbour opposite, one Albert Scarsdale, very bare and prickly. Obviously he had resented the inconsideration, the appalling bad taste of Grey in getting himself murdered in Mecklenburgh Square, and felt the less he said about it himself the sooner it would be forgotten, and the sooner he might dissociate himself from the whole sordid affair.

He admitted he thought he had heard someone in the hallway between his apartment and that of Grey at about eight o'clock, and possibly again at about quarter to ten. He could not possibly say whether it was two separate visitors or one arriving and then later leaving; in fact he was not sure beyond doubt that it had not been a stray animal, a cat, or the porter making a round – from his choice of words he regarded the two as roughly equal. It might even have been an errand boy who had lost his way, or any of a dozen other things. He had been occupied with his own interests, and had seen and heard nothing of remark. The statement was signed and affirmed as being true with an ornate and ill-natured signature.

Monk looked across at Evan, still waiting by the window.

'Mr Scarsdale sounds like an officious and unhelpful little beggar,' he observed dryly.

'Very, sir,' Evan agreed, his eyes shining but no smile touching his lips. 'I imagine it's the scandal in the buildings; attracts notice from the wrong kind of people, and very bad for the social reputation.'

'Something less than a gentleman.' Monk made an immediate and cruel judgment.

Evan pretended not to understand him, although it was a patent lie.

'Less than a gentleman, sir?' His face puckered.

Monk spoke before he had time to think, or wonder why he was so sure.

'Certainly. Someone secure in his social status would not be affected by a scandal whose proximity was only a geographical accident, and nothing to do with him personally. Unless, of course, he knew Grey well?'

'No, sir,' Evan said, but his eyes showed his total comprehension. Obviously Scarsdale still smarted under Grey's contempt, and Monk could imagine it vividly. 'No, he disclaimed all personal acquaintance with him. And either that's a lie or else it's very odd. If he were the gentleman he pretends to be, he would surely know Grey, at least to speak to. They were immediate neighbours, after all.'

Monk did not want to court disappointment.

'It may be no more than social pretension, but worth inquiring into.' He looked at the papers again. 'What else is there?' He glanced up at Evan. 'Who found him, by the way?'

Evan came over and sorted out two more reports from the bottom of the pile. He handed them to Monk.

'Cleaning woman and the porter, sir. Their accounts agree, except that the porter says a bit more, because naturally we asked him about the evening as well.'

Monk was temporarily lost. 'As well?'

Evan flushed faintly with irritation at his own lack of clarity.

'He wasn't found until the following morning, when the woman who cleans and cooks for him arrived and couldn't get in. He wouldn't give her a key, apparently didn't trust her; he let her in himself, and if he wasn't there then she just

41

went away and came another time. Usually he leaves some message with the porter.'

'I see. Did he go away often? I assume we know where to?' There was an instinctive edge of authority to his voice now, and impatience.

'Occasional weekend, so far as the porter knows; sometimes longer, a week or two at a country house, in the season,' Evan answered.

'So what happened when Mrs—what's her name? – arrived?'

Evan stood almost to attention. 'Huggins. She knocked as usual, and when she got no answer after the third attempt, she went down to see the porter, Grimwade, to find out if there was a message. Grimwade told her he'd seen Grey arrive home the evening before, and he hadn't gone out yet, and to go back and try again. Perhaps Grey had been in the bathroom, or unusually soundly asleep, and no doubt he'd be standing at the top of the stairs by now, wanting his breakfast.'

'But of course he wasn't,' Monk said unnecessarily.

'No. Mrs Huggins came back a few minutes later all fussed and excited – these woman love a little drama – and demanded that Grimwade do something about it. To her endless satisfaction' – Evan smiled bleakly – 'she said that he'd be lying there murdered in his own blood, and they should do something immediately, and call the police. She must have told me that a dozen times.' He pulled a small face. 'She's now convinced she has the second sight, and I spent a quarter of an hour persuading her that she should stick to cleaning and not give it up in favour of fortune-telling – although she's already a heroine, of sorts, in the local newspaper – and no doubt the local pub!'

Monk found himself smiling too.

'One more saved from a career in the fairground stalls – and still in the service of the gentry,' he said. 'Heroine for a day – and free gin every time she retells it for the next six months. Did Grimwade go back with her?'

'Yes, with a master key, of course.'

'And what did they find, exactly?' This was perhaps the most important single thing: the precise facts of the discovery of the body.

Evan concentrated till Monk was not sure if he was remembering the witness's words or his own sight of the rooms.

'The small outer hall was perfectly orderly,' Evan began. 'Usual things you might expect to see, stand for coats and things, and hats, rather a nice stand for sticks, umbrellas and so forth, box for boots, a small table for calling cards, nothing else. Everything was neat and tidy. The door from that led directly into the sitting room; and the bedroom and utilities were off that.' A shadow passed over his extraordinary face. He relaxed a little and half unconsciously leaned against the window frame.

'That next room was a different matter altogether. The curtains were drawn and the gas still burning, even though it was daylight outside. Grey himself was lying half on the floor and half on the big chair, head downward. There was a lot of blood, and he was in a pretty dreadful state.' His eyes

43

did not waver, but it was with an effort, and Monk could see it. 'I must admit,' he continued, 'I've seen a few deaths, but this was the most brutal, by a long way. The man had been beaten to death with something quite thin – I mean not a bludgeon – hit a great many times. There had pretty obviously been a fight. A small table had been knocked over and one leg broken off, several ornaments were on the floor and one of the heavy stuffed chairs was on its back, the one he was half on.' Evan was frowning at the memory, and his skin was pale. 'The other rooms hadn't been touched.' He moved his hands in a gesture of negation. 'It was quite a while before we could get Mrs Huggins into a sane state of mind, and then persuade her to look at the kitchen and bedroom; but eventually she did, and said they were just as she had left them the previous day.'

Monk breathed in deeply, thinking. He must say something intelligent, not some fatuous comment on the obvious. Evan was watching him, waiting. He found himself self-conscious.

'So it would appear he had a visitor some time in the evening,' he said more tentatively than he had wished. 'Who quarrelled with him, or else simply attacked him. There was a violent fight, and Grey lost.'

'More or less,' Evan agreed, straightening up again. 'At least we don't have anything else to go on. We don't even know if it was a stranger, or someone he knew.'

'No sign of a forced entry?'

'No, sir. Anyway, no burglar is likely to force an entry into a house when all the lights are still on.'

'No.' Monk cursed himself for an idiotic question. Was he always such a fool? There was no surprise in Evan's face. Good manners? Or fear of angering a superior not noted for tolerance? 'No, of course not,' he said aloud. 'I suppose he wouldn't have been surprised by Grey, and then lit the lights to fool us?'

'Unlikely, sir. If he were that coolheaded, he surely would have taken some of the valuables? At least the money in Grey's wallet, which would be untraceable.'

Monk had no answer for that. He sighed and sat down behind the desk. He did not bother to invite Evan to sit also. He read the rest of the porter's statement.

Lamb had asked exhaustively about all visitors the previous evening, if there had been any errand boys, messengers, even a stray animal. Grimwade was affronted at the very suggestion. Certainly not: errand boys were always escorted to the appropriate place, or if possible their errands taken over by Grimwade himself. No stray animals had ever tainted the buildings with their presence – dirty things, stray animals, and apt to soil the place. What did the police think he was – were they trying to insult him?

Monk wondered what Lamb had replied. He would certainly have had a pointed answer to the man on the relative merits of stray animals and stray humans! A couple of acid retorts rose to his mind even now.

Grimwade swore there had been two visitors and only two. He was perfectly sure no others had passed his window. The first was a lady, at about eight o'clock, and he would sooner not say upon whom she called; a question of private affairs must be treated with discretion, but she had not visited Major Grey, of that he was perfectly certain. Anyway, she was a very slight creature, and could not possibly have inflicted the injuries suffered by the dead man. The second visitor was a man who called upon a Mr Yeats, a longtime resident, and Grimwade had escorted him as far as the appropriate landing himself and seen him received.

Whoever had murdered Grey had obviously either used one of the other visitors as a decoy or else had already been in the building in some guise in which he had so far been overlooked. So much was logic.

Monk put the paper down. They would have to question Grimwade more closely, explore even the minutest possibilities; there might be something.

Evan sat down on the window ledge.

Mrs Huggins's statement was exactly as Evan had said, if a good deal more verbose. Monk read it only because he wanted time to think.

Afterwards he picked up the last one, the medical report. It was the one he found most unpleasant, but maybe also the most necessary. It was written in a small, precise hand, very round. It made him imagine a small doctor with round spectacles and very clean fingers. It did not occur to him until afterwards to wonder if he had ever known such a person, and if it was the first wisp of memory returning.

The account was clinical in the extreme, discussing the corpse as if Joscelin Grey were a species rather than an individual, a human being full of passions and cares, hopes and humours who had been suddenly and violently cut off from life, and who must have experienced terror and extreme pain in the few minutes that were being examined so unemotionally.

The body had been looked at a little after nine thirty a.m. It was that of a man in his early thirties, of slender build but well nourished, and not apparently suffering from any illness or disability apart from a fairly recent wound in the upper part of the right leg, which might have caused him to limp. The doctor judged it to be a shallow wound, such as he had seen in many ex-soldiers, and to be five or six months old. The body had been dead between eight and twelve hours; he could not be more precise than that.

The cause of death was obvious for anyone to see: a succession of violent and powerful blows about the head and shoulders with some long, thin instrument. A heavy cane or stick seemed the most likely.

Monk put down the report, sobered by the details of death. The bare language, shorn of all emotion, perversely brought the very feeling of it closer. His imagination saw it sharply, even smelled it, conjuring up the sour odour and the buzz of flies. Had he dealt with many murders? He could hardly ask.

'Very unpleasant,' he said without looking up at Evan.

'Very,' Evan agreed, nodding. 'Newspapers made rather a lot of it at the time. Been going on at us for not having found the murderer. Apart from the fact that it's made a lot of people nervous, Mecklenburgh Square is a pretty good area, and if one isn't safe there, where is one safe? Added to that, Joscelin Grey was a well-liked, pretty harmless young ex-officer, and of extremely good family. He served in the Crimea and was invalided out. He had rather a good record, saw the Charge of the Light Brigade, badly wounded at Sebastopol.' Evan's face pinched a little with a mixture of embarrassment and perhaps pity. 'A lot of people feel his country has let him down, so to speak, first by allowing this to happen to him, and then by not even catching the man who did it.' He looked across at Monk, apologizing for the injustice, and because he understood it. 'I know that's unfair, but a spot of crusading sells newspapers; always helps to have a cause, you know! And of course the running patterers have composed a lot of songs about it – returning hero and all that!'

Monk's mouth turned down at the corners.

'Have they been hitting hard?'

'Rather,' Evan admitted with a little shrug. 'And we haven't a blind thing to go on. We've been over and over every bit of evidence there is, and there's simply nothing to connect him to anyone. Any ruffian could have come in from the street if he dodged the porter. Nobody saw or heard anything useful, and we are right where we started.' He got up gloomily and came over to the table.

'I suppose you'd better see the physical evidence, not that there is much. And then I daresay you'd like to see the flat, at least get a feeling for the scene?'

Monk stood up also.

'Yes, I would. You never know, something might suggest itself.' Although he could imagine nothing. If Lamb had not succeeded, and this keen, delicate young junior, what was he going to find? He felt failure begin to circle around him, dark and enclosing. Had Runcorn given him this knowing he would fail? Was it a discreet and efficient way of getting rid of him without being seen to be callous? How did he even know for sure that Runcorn was not an old enemy? Had he done him some wrong long ago? The possibility was cold and real. The shadowy outline of himself that had appeared so far was devoid of any quick acts of compassion, any sudden gentlenesses or warmth to seize hold of and to like. He was discovering himself as a stranger might, and what he saw so far did not excite his admiration. He liked Evan far more than he liked himself.

He had imagined he had hidden his complete loss of memory, but perhaps it was obvious, perhaps Runcorn had seen it and taken this chance to even some old score? God, how he wished he knew what kind of man he was, had been. Who loved him, who hated him – and who had what cause? Had he ever loved a woman, or any woman loved him? He did not even know that!

Evan was walking quickly ahead of him, his long legs carrying him at a surprisingly fast pace. Everything in Monk wanted to trust him, and yet he was almost paralyzed by his ignorance. Every foothold he trod on dissolved into quicksand under his weight. He knew nothing. Everything was surmise, constantly shifting guesses.

He behaved automatically, having nothing but instinct and ingrained habit to rely on.

The physical evidence was astonishingly bare, set out like luggage in a lost-and-found office, ownerless; pathetic and rather embarrassing remnants of someone else's life, robbed now of their purpose and meaning – a little like his own belongings in Grafton Street, objects whose history and emotion were obliterated.

He stopped beside Evan and picked up a pile of clothes. The trousers were dark, well cut from expensive material, now spotted with blood. The boots were highly polished and only slightly worn on the soles. Personal linen was obviously changed very recently; shirt was expensive; cravat silk, the neck and front heavily stained. The jacket was tailored to high fashion, but ruined with blood, and a ragged tear in the sleeve. They told him nothing except a hazard at the size and build of Joscelin Grey, and an admiration for his pocket and his taste. There was nothing to be deduced from the bloodstains, since they already knew what the injuries had been.

He put them down and turned to Evan, who was watching him.

'Not very helpful, is it, sir?' Evan looked at them with a mixture of unhappiness and distaste. There was something in his face that might have been real pity. Perhaps he was too sensitive to be a police officer.

'No, not very,' Monk agreed dryly. 'What else was there?'

'The weapon, sir.' Evan reached out and picked up a heavy ebony stick with a silver head. It too was encrusted with blood and hair.

Monk winced. If he had seen such grisly things before, his immunity to them had gone with his memory.

'Nasty.' Evan's mouth turned down, his hazel eyes on Monk's face.

Monk was conscious of him, and abashed. Was the distaste, the pity, for him? Was Evan wondering why a senior officer should be so squeamish? He conquered his revulsion with an effort and took the stick. It was unusually heavy.

'War wound,' Evan observed, still watching him. 'From what witnesses say, he actually walked with it: I mean it wasn't an ornament.'

'Right leg.' Monk recalled the medical report. 'Accounts for the weight.' He put the stick down. 'Nothing else?'

'Couple of broken glasses, sir, and a decanter broken too. Must have been on the table that was knocked over, from the way it was lying; and a couple of ornaments. There's a drawing of the way the room was, in Mr Lamb's file, sir. Not that I know of anything it can tell us. But Mr Lamb spent hours poring over it.'

Monk felt a quick stab of compassion for Lamb, then for himself. He wished for a moment that he could change places with Evan, leave the decisions, the judgments to someone else, and disclaim the failure. He hated failure! He realized now what a driving, burning desire he had to solve this crime – to win – to wipe that smile off Runcorn's face.

'Oh – money, sir.' Evan pulled out a cardboard box and opened it. He picked up a fine pigskin wallet and, separately, several gold sovereigns, a couple of cards from a club and an exclusive dining room. There were about a dozen cards of his own, engraved 'Major the Honourable Joscelin Grey,

Six, Mecklenburgh Square, London'.

'Is that all?' Monk asked.

'Yes, sir, the money is twelve pounds, seven shillings and sixpence altogether. If he were a thief, it's odd he didn't take that.'

'Perhaps he was frightened – he may have been hurt himself.' It was the only thing he could think of. He motioned Evan to put the box away. 'I suppose we'd better go and have a look at Mecklenburgh Square.'

'Yes, sir.' Evan straightened up to obey. 'It's about half an hour's walk. Are you well enough for it yet?'

'A couple of miles? For heaven's sake, man, it was my arm I broke, not both my legs!' He reached sharply for his jacket and hat.

Evan had been a little optimistic. Against the wind and stepping carefully to avoid pedlars and groups of fellow travellers on the footpath, and traffic and horse dung in the streets, it was a good forty minutes before they reached Mecklenburgh Square, walked around the gardens and stopped outside Number Six. The boy sweeping the crossing was busy on the corner of Doughty Street, and Monk wondered if it was the same one who had been there on that evening in July. He felt a rush of pity for the child, out in all weather, often with sleet or snow driving down the funnel of the high buildings, dodging in among the carriages and drays, shovelling droppings. What an abysmal way to earn your keep. Then he was angry with himself – that was stupid and sentimental nonsense. He must deal with reality. He squared his chest and marched into the foyer. The porter was standing by a small office doorway, no more than a cubbyhole.

'Yes, sir?' He moved forward courteously, but at the same time blocking their further progress.

'Grimwade?' Monk asked him.

'Yes, sir?' The man was obviously surprised and embarrassed. 'I'm sorry, sir, I can't say as I remember you. I'm not usually bad about faces—' He let it hang, hoping Monk would help him. He glanced across at Evan, and a flicker of memory lit his face.

'Police,' Monk said simply. 'We'd like to take another look at Major Grey's flat. You have the key?'

The man's relief was very mixed.

'Oh yes, sir, and we ain't let nobody in. Lock's still as Mr Lamb left it.'

'Good, thank you.' Monk had been preparing to show some proof of his identity, but the porter was apparently quite satisfied with his recognition of Evan, and turned back to his cubbyhole to fetch the key.

He came with it a moment later and led them upstairs with the solemnity due the presence of the dead, especially those who had died violently. Monk had the momentarily unpleasant impression that they would find Joscelin Grey's corpse still lying there, untouched and waiting for them.

It was ridiculous, and he shook it off fiercely. It was beginning to assume the repetitive quality of a nightmare, as if events could happen more than once.

'Here we are, sir.' Evan was standing at the door, the porter's key in his hand. 'There's a back door as well, of course, from the kitchen, but it opens onto the same landing, about twelve yards along, for services, errands, and the like.'

Monk recalled his attention.

'But one would still have to pass the porter at the gate?'

'Oh yes, sir. I suppose there's not much point in having a porter if there's a way in without passing him. Then any beggar or pedlar could bother you.' He pulled an extraordinary face as he pondered the habits of his betters. 'Or creditors!' he added lugubriously.

'Quite.' Monk was sardonic.

Evan turned and put the key in the lock. He seemed reluctant, as if a memory of the violence he had seen there still clung to the place, repelling him. Or was Monk projecting his own fancies onto someone else?

The hallway inside was exactly as Evan had described it: neat, blue Georgian with white paint and trims, very clean and elegant. He saw the hat stand with its place for sticks and umbrellas, the table for calling cards and so forth. Evan was ahead of him, his back stiff, opening the door to the main room.

Monk walked in behind him. He was not sure what he was expecting to see; his body was tight also, as if waiting for an attack, for something startling and ugly on the senses.

The decoration was elegant, and had originally been expensive, but in the flat light, without gas or fire, it looked bleak and commonplace enough. The Wedgwood-blue walls seemed at a glance immaculate, the white trims without scar, but there was a fine rime of dust over the polished wood of the chiffonier and the desk and a film dulling the colours of the carpet. His eye travelled automatically to the window first, then around the other furniture – ornate side table with piecrust edges, a jardinière with a Japanese bowl on it, a mahogany bookcase – till he came to the overturned heavy chair, the broken table, companion to the other, the pale inner wood a sharp scar against its mellowed satin skin. It looked like an animal with legs in the air.

Then he saw the bloodstain on the floor. There was not a lot of it, not widespread at all, but very dark, almost black. Grey must have bled a lot in that one place. He looked away from it, and noticed then that much of what seemed pattern on the carpet was probably lighter, spattered blood. On the far wall there was a picture crooked, and when he walked over to it and looked more carefully, he saw a bruise in the plaster, and the paint was faintly scarred. It was a bad watercolour of the Bay of Naples, all harsh blues with a conical Mount Vesuvius in the background.

'It must have been a considerable fight,' he said quietly.

'Yes, sir,' Evan agreed. He was standing in the middle of the floor, not sure what to do. 'There were several bruises on the body, arms and shoulders, and one knuckle was skinned. I should say he put up a good fight.'

Monk looked at him, frowning.

'I don't remember that in the medical report.'

'I think it just said "evidences of a struggle", sir. But that's pretty obvious from the room here, anyway.' His eyes glanced around at it as he spoke. 'There's blood on that chair as well.' He pointed to the heavy stuffed one lying on its back. 'That's where he was, with his head on the floor. We're looking for a violent man, sir.' He shivered slightly.

'Yes.' Monk stared around, trying to visualize what must have happened in this room nearly six weeks ago, the fear and the impact of flesh on flesh, shadows moving, shadows because he did not know them, furniture crashing over, glass splintering. Then suddenly it became real, a flash sharper and more savage than anything his imagination had called up, red moments of rage and terror, the thrashing stick; then it was gone again, leaving him trembling and his stomach sick. What in God's name had happened in this room that the echo of it still hung here, like an agonized ghost, or a beast of prey?

He turned and walked out, oblivious of Evan behind him, fumbling for the door. He had to get out of here, into the commonplace and grubby street, the sound of voices, the demanding present. He was not even sure if Evan followed him.

Chapter Three

As soon as Monk was out in the street he felt better, but he could not completely shake the impression that had come to him so violently. For an instant it had been real enough to bring his body out in hot, drenching sweat, and then leave him shivering and nauseous at the sheer bestiality of it.

He put up his hand shakily and felt his cheek wet. There was a hard, angular rain driving on the wind.

He turned to see Evan behind him. But if Evan had felt that savage presence, there was no sign of it in his face. He was puzzled, a little concerned, but Monk could read no more in him than that.

'A violent man,' Monk repeated Evan's words through stiff lips.

'Yes, sir,' Evan said solemnly, catching up to him. He started to say something, then changed his mind. 'Where are you going to begin, sir?' he asked instead.

It was a moment before Monk could collect his thoughts to reply. They were walking along Doughty Street to Guilford Street.

'Recheck the statements,' he answered, stopping on the corner kerb as a hansom sped past them, its wheels spraying filth. 'That's the only place I know to begin. I'll do the least promising first. The street sweeper is there.' He indicated the child a few yards from them, busy shovelling dung and at the same time seizing a penny that had been thrown him. 'Is he the same one?'

'I think so, sir; I can't see his face from here.' That was something of a euphemism: the child's features were hidden by dirt and the hazards of his occupation, and the top half of his head was covered by an enormous cloth cap, to protect him from the rain.

Monk and Evan stepped out onto the street towards him.

'Well?' Monk asked when they reached the boy.

Evan nodded.

Monk fished for a coin; he felt obliged to recompense the child for the earnings he might lose in the time forfeited. He came up with twopence and offered it.

'Alfred, I am a policeman. I want to talk to you about the gentleman who was killed in Number Six in the square.'

The boy took the twopence.

'Yeah, guv. I dunno anyfink what I din't tell the ovver rozzer as asked me.' He sniffed and looked up hopefully. A man with twopence to spend was worth pleasing.

'Maybe not,' Monk conceded, 'but I'd like to talk to you anyway.' A tradesman's cart clattered by them towards Gray's Inn Road, splashing them with mud and leaving a couple of cabbage leaves almost at their feet. 'Can we go to the footpath?' Monk inquired, hiding his distaste. His good boots were getting soiled and his trouser legs were wet.

The boy nodded, then acknowledging their lack of skill in dodging wheels and hooves with the professional's condescension for the amateur, he steered them to the kerb again.

'Yers, guv?' he asked hopefully, pocketing the twopence somewhere inside the folds of his several jackets and sniffing hard. He refrained from wiping his hand across his face in deference to their superior status.

'You saw Major Grey come home the day he was killed?' Monk asked with appropriate gravity.

'Yers, guv, and there weren't nob'dy followin' 'im, as fer as I could see.'

'Was the street busy?'

'No, wicked night, it were, for July, raining summink 'orrible. Nob'dy much abaht, an' everyone goin' as fast as their legs'd carry 'em.'

'How long have you been at this crossing?'

'Couple o' years.' His faint fair eyebrows rose with surprise; obviously it was a question he had not expected.

'So you must know most of the people who live around here?' Monk pursued.

'Yers, I reckon as I do.' His eyes sparked with sudden sharp comprehension. 'Yer means did I see anyone as don't belong?'

Monk nodded in appreciation of his sagacity. 'Precisely.'

''E were bashed ter deaf, weren't 'e?'

'Yes.' Monk winced inwardly at the appropriateness of the phrase.

'Then yer in't lookin' fer a woman?'

'No,' Monk agreed. Then it flashed through his mind that a man might dress as a woman, if perhaps it were not some

59

stranger who murdered Grey, but a person known to him, someone who had built up over the years the kind of hatred that had seemed to linger in that room. 'Unless it were a large woman,' he added, 'and very strong, perhaps.'

The boy hid a smirk. 'Woman as I saw was on the little side. Most women as makes their way that fashion gotta look fetchin' like, or leastways summink as a woman oughter. Don't see no great big scrubbers 'round 'ere, an' no dolly-mops.' He sniffed again and pulled his mouth down fiercely to express his disapproval. 'Only the class for gentlemen as 'as money like wot they got 'ere.' He gestured towards the elaborate house fronts behind him towards the square.

'I see.' Monk hid a brief amusement. 'And you saw some woman of that type going into Number Six that evening?' It was probably not worth anything, but every clue must be followed at this stage.

'No one as don't go there reg'lar, guv.'

'What time?'

'Jus' as I were goin' 'ome.'

'About half past seven?'

'S' right.'

'How about earlier?'

'Only wot goes inter Number Six, like?'

'Yes.'

He shut his eyes in deep concentration, trying to be obliging; there might be another twopence. 'One of the gennelmen wot lives in Number Six come 'ome wiv another gent, little feller wiv one o' them collars wot looks like fur, but all curly.'

'Astrakhan?' Monk offered.

'I dunno wot yer calls it. Anyway, 'e went in abaht six, an' I never sawed 'im come aht. That any 'elp to yer, guv?'

'It might be. Thank you very much.' Monk spoke to him with all seriousness, gave him another penny, to Evan's surprise, and watched him step blithely off into the thoroughfare, dodging in between traffic, and take up his duties again.

Evan's face was brooding, thoughtful, but whether on the boy's answers or his means of livelihood, Monk did not ask.

'The ribbon seller's not here today.' Evan looked up and down the Guilford Street footpath. 'Who do you want to try next?'

Monk thought for a moment. 'How do we find the cabby? I presume we have an address for him?'

'Yes, sir, but I doubt he'd be there now.'

Monk turned to face the drizzling east wind. 'Not unless he's ill,' he agreed. 'Good evening for trade. No one will walk in this weather if they can ride.' He was pleased with that – it sounded intelligent, and it was the merest common sense. 'We'll send a message and have him call at the police station. I don't suppose he can add anything to what he's already said anyway.' He smiled sarcastically. 'Unless, of course, he killed Grey himself!'

Evan stared at him, his eyes wide, unsure for an instant whether he was joking or not. Then Monk suddenly found he was not sure himself. There was no reason to believe the cabby. Perhaps there had been heated words between them, some stupid quarrel, possibly over nothing more important than the fare. Maybe the man had followed Grey upstairs, carrying a case or a parcel for him, seen the flat, the warmth, the space, the ornaments, and in a fit of envy become abusive. He may even have been drunk; he would not be the first cabby to bolster himself against cold, rain and long hours a little too generously. God help them, enough of them died of bronchitis or consumption anyway.

Evan was still looking at him, not entirely sure.

Monk spoke his last thoughts aloud.

'We must check with the porter that Grey actually entered alone. He might easily have overlooked a cabby carrying baggage, invisible, like a postman; we become so used to them, the eye sees but the mind doesn't register.'

'It's possible.' Belief was strengthening in Evan's voice. 'He could have set up the mark for someone else, noted addresses or wealthy fares, likely-looking victims for someone. Could be a well-paying sideline?'

'Could indeed.' Monk was getting chilled standing on the kerb. 'Not as good as a sweep's boy for scouting the inside of a house, but better for knowing when the victim is out. If that was his idea, he certainly mistook Grey.' He shivered. 'Perhaps we'd better call on him rather than send a message; it might make him nervous. It's late; we'll have a bit of lunch at the local public house, and see what the gossip is. Then you can go back to the station this afternoon and find out if anything is known about this cabby, what sort of reputation he has – if we know him, for example, and who his associates are. I'll try the porter again, and if possible some of the neighbours.'

The local tavern turned out to be a pleasant, noisy place which served them ale and a sandwich with civility, but something of a wary eye, knowing them to be strangers and perhaps guessing from their clothes that they were police. One or two ribald comments were offered, but apparently Grey had not patronized the place and there was no particular sympathy for him, only the communal interest in the macabre that murder always wakens.

Afterwards Evan went back to the police station, and Monk returned to Mecklenburgh Square, and Grimwade. He began at the beginning.

'Yes, sir,' Grimwade said patiently. 'Major Grey came in about quarter after six, or a bit before, and 'e looked 'is usual self to me.'

'He came by cab?' Monk wanted to be sure he had not led the man, suggested the answer he wanted.

'Yes, sir.'

'How do you know? Did you see the cab?'

'Yes, sir, I did.' Grimwade wavered between nervousness and affront. 'Stopped right by the door 'ere; not a night to walk a step as you didn't 'ave to.'

'Did you see the cabby?'

''Ere, I don't understand what you're getting after.' Now the affront was definitely warning.

'Did you see him?' Monk repeated.

Grimwade screwed up his face. 'Don't recall as I did,' he conceded.

'Did he get down off the box, help Major Grey with a parcel, or a case or anything?'

'Not as I remember; no, 'e didn't.'

'Are you sure?'

'Yes I am sure. 'E never got through that door.'

That theory at least was gone. He should have been too old at this to be disappointed, but he had no experience to call on. It seemed to come to him easily enough, but possibly most of it was common sense.

'He went upstairs alone?' He tried a last time, to remove every vestige of doubt.

'Yes, sir, 'e did.'

'Did he speak to you?'

'Nothing special, as I can think of. I don't remember nothin', so I reckon it can't 'ave bin. 'E never said nothin' about bein' afraid, or as 'e was expecting anyone.'

'But there were visitors to the buildings that afternoon and evening?'

'Nobody as would be a-murderin' anyone.'

'Indeed?' Monk raised his eyebrows. 'You're not suggesting Major Grey did that to himself in some kind of bizarre accident, are you? Or of course there is the other alternative – that the murderer was someone already here?'

Grimwade's face changed rapidly from resignation through extreme offence to blank horror. He stared at Monk, but no words came to his brain.

'You have another idea? I thought not – neither have I.' Monk sighed. 'So let us think again. You said there were two visitors after Major Grey came in: one woman at about seven o'clock, and a man later on at about quarter to ten.

64

Now, who did the woman come to see, Mr Grimwade, and what did she look like? And please, no cosmetic alterations for the sake of discretion!'

'No wot?'

'Tell me the truth, man!' Monk snapped. 'It could become very embarrassing for your tenants if we have to investigate it for ourselves.'

Grimwade glared at him, but he took the point perfectly.

'A local lady of pleasure, sir; called Mollie Ruggles,' he said between his teeth. ''Andsome piece, with red 'air. I know where she lives, but I expec' you understand it would come real gratifyin' if you could see your way clear to bein' discreet about 'oo told yer she was 'ere?' His expression was comical in its effort to expunge his dislike and look appealing.

Monk hid a sour amusement – it would only alienate the man.

'I will,' he agreed. It would be in his own interest also. Prostitutes could be useful informants, if well treated. 'Who did she come to see?'

'Mr Taylor, sir; 'e lives in flat Number Five. She comes to see 'im quite reg'lar.'

'And it was definitely her?'

'Yes, sir.'

'Did you take her to Mr Taylor's door?'

'Oh no, sir. Reckon as she knows 'er way by now. And Mr Taylor – well . . .' He hunched his shoulders. 'It wouldn't be tactful, now would it, sir? Not as I suppose you 'as ter be tactful, in your callin'!' he added meaningfully.

'No.' Monk smiled slightly. 'So you didn't leave your position when she came?'

'No, sir.'

'Any other women come, Mr Grimwade?' He looked at him very directly.

Grimwade avoided his eyes.

'Do I have to make my own inquiries?' Monk threatened. 'And leave detectives here to follow people?'

Grimwade was shocked. His head came up sharply.

'You wouldn't do that, sir! They're gentlemen as lives 'ere! They'd leave. They won't put up with that kind o' thing!'

'Then don't make it necessary.'

'You're an 'ard man, Mr Monk.' But there was a grudging respect behind the grievance in his voice. That was small victory in itself.

'I want to find the man who killed Major Grey,' Monk answered him. 'Someone came into these buildings, found his way upstairs into that flat and beat Major Grey with a stick, over and over until he was dead, and then went on beating him afterwards.' He saw Grimwade wincing, and felt the revulsion himself. He remembered the horror he had felt when actually standing in the room. Did walls retain memory? Could violence or hatred remain in the air after a deed was finished, and touch the sensitive, the imaginative with a shadow of the horror?

No, that was ridiculous. It was not the imaginative, but the nightmare-ridden who felt such things. He was letting his own fear, the horror of his still occasionally recurring dreams and the hollowness of his past extend into the present and warp his judgment. Let a little more time pass, a little more identity build, learn to know himself, and he would grow firmer memories in reality. His sanity would come back; he would have a past to root himself in, other emotions, and people.

Or could it be – could it possibly be that it was some sort of mixed, dreamlike, distorted recollection coming back to him? Could he be recalling snatches of the pain and fear he must have felt when the coach turned over on him, throwing him down, imprisoning him, the scream of terror as the horse fell, the cab driver flung headlong, crushed to death on the stones of the street? He must have known violent fear and, in the instant before unconsciousness, have felt sharp, even blinding pain as his bones broke. Was that what he had sensed? Had it been nothing to do with Grey at all, but his own memory returning, just a flash, a sensation, the fierceness of the feeling long before the clarity of actual perception came back?

He must learn more of himself, what he had been doing that night, where he was going, or had come from. What manner of man had he been, whom had he cared for, whom wronged, or whom owed? What had mattered to him? Every man had relationships, every man had feelings, even hungers; every man who was alive at all stirred some sort of passions in others. There must be people somewhere who had feelings about him – more than professional rivalry and resentment – surely? He could not have been so negative, of so little purpose that his whole life had left no mark on another soul.

As soon as he was off duty, he must leave Grey, stop building the pattern piece by piece of his life, and take up the few clues to his own, place them together with whatever skill he possessed.

Grimwade was still waiting for him, watching curiously, knowing that he had temporarily lost his attention.

Monk looked back at him.

'Well, Mr Grimwade?' he said with sudden softness. 'What other women?'

Grimwade mistook the lowering tone for a further threat.

'One to see Mr Scarsdale, sir; although 'e paid me 'andsome not to say so.'

'What time was it?'

'About eight o'clock.'

Scarsdale had said he had heard someone at eight. Was it his own visitor he was talking about, trying to play safe, in case someone else had seen her too?

'Did you go up with her?' He looked at Grimwade.

'No, sir, on account o' she bin 'ere before, an' knew 'er way, like. An' I knew she was expected.' He gave a slight leer, knowingly, as man to man.

Monk acknowledged it. 'And the one at quarter to ten?' he asked. 'The visitor for Mr Yeats, I think you said? Had he been here before too?'

'No, sir. I went up with 'im, 'cos 'e didn't know Mr Yeats very well an' 'adn't called 'ere before. I said that to Mr Lamb.'

'Indeed.' Monk forbore from criticizing him over the omission of Scarsdale's woman. He would defeat his own purpose if he antagonized him any further. 'So you went up with this man?'

'Yes, sir.' Grimwade was firm. 'Saw Mr Yeats open the door to 'im.'

'What did he look like, this man?'

Grimwade screwed up his eyes. 'Oh, big man, 'e was, solid and—'ere!' His face dropped. 'You don't think it was 'im wot done it, do yer?' He breathed out slowly, his eyes wide. 'Gor'—it must 'a' bin. When I thinks of it now!'

'It might have,' Monk agreed cautiously. 'It's possible. Would you know him if you saw him again?'

Grimwade's face fell. 'Ah, there you 'ave me, sir; I don't think as I would. Yer see, I didn't see 'im close, like, when 'e was down 'ere. An' on the stairs I only looked where I was goin', it bein' dark. 'E 'ad one o' them 'eavy coats on, as it was a rotten night an' rainin' somethin' wicked. A natural night for anyone to 'ave 'is coat turned up an' 'is 'at drawn down. I reckon 'e were dark, that's about all I could say fer sure, an' if 'e 'ad a beard, it weren't much of a one.'

'He was probably clean-shaven, and probably dark.' Monk tried to keep the disappointment out of his voice. He must not let irritation push the man into saying something to please him, something less than true.

''E were big, sir,' Grimwade said hopefully. 'An' 'e were tall, must 'ave bin six feet. That lets out a lot o' people, don't it?'

'Yes, yes it does,' Monk agreed. 'When did he leave?'

'I saw 'im out o' the corner o' me eye, sir. 'E went past me window at about 'alf past ten, or a little afore.'

'Out of the corner of your eye? You're sure it was him?'

''Ad ter be; 'e didn't leave before, ner after, an' 'e looked the same. Same coat, and 'at, same size, same 'eight. Weren't no one else like that lives 'ere.'

'Did you speak to him?'

'No, 'e looked like 'e was in a bit of an 'urry. Maybe 'e wanted ter get 'ome. It were a beastly rotten night, like I said, sir; not fit fer man ner beast.'

'Yes I know. Thank you, Mr Grimwade. If you remember anything more, tell me, or leave a message for me at the police station. Good day.'

'Good day, sir,' Grimwade said with intense relief.

Monk decided to wait for Scarsdale, first to tax him with his lie about the woman, then to try and learn something more about Joscelin Grey. He realized with faint surprise that he knew almost nothing about him, except the manner of his death. Grey's life was as blank an outline as his own, a shadow man, circumscribed by a few physical facts, without colour or substance that could have induced love or hate. And surely there had been hate in whoever had beaten Grey to death, and then gone on hitting and hitting him long after there was any purpose? Was there something in Grey, innocently or knowingly, that had generated such a passion, or was he merely the catalyst of something he knew nothing of – and its victim?

He went back outside into the square and found a seat from which he could see the entrance of Number Six.

It was more than an hour before Scarsdale arrived, and already beginning to get darker and colder, but Monk was compelled by the importance it had for him to wait.

He saw him arrive on foot, and followed a few paces after him, inquiring from Grimwade in the hall if it was indeed Scarsdale.

'Yes, sir,' Grimwade said reluctantly, but Monk was not interested in the porter's misfortunes.

'D'yer need me ter take yer up?'

'No thank you; I'll find it.' And he took the stairs two at a time and arrived on the landing just as the door was closing. He strode across from the stair head and knocked briskly. There was a second's hesitation, then the door opened. He explained his identity and his errand tersely.

Scarsdale was not pleased to see him. He was a small, wiry man whose handsomest feature was his fair moustache, not matched by slightly receding hair and undistinguished features. He was smartly, rather fussily dressed.

'I'm sorry, I can't see you this evening,' he said brusquely. 'I have to change to go out for dinner. Call again tomorrow, or the next day.'

Monk was the bigger man, and in no mood to be summarily dismissed.

'I have other people to call on tomorrow,' he said, placing himself half in Scarsdale's way. 'I need certain information from you now.'

'Well, I haven't any—' Scarsdale began, retreating as if to close the door.

Monk stepped forward. 'For example, the name of the young woman who visited you the evening Major Grey was killed, and why you lied to us about her.'

It had the result Monk had wished. Scarsdale stopped dead. He fumbled for words, trying to decide whether to bluff it out or attempt a little late conciliation. Monk watched him with contempt.

'I – er,' Scarsdale began. 'I – think you have misunderstood – er . . .' He still had not made the decision.

Monk's face tightened. 'Perhaps you would prefer to discuss it somewhere more discreet than the hallway?' He looked towards the stairs, and the landing where other doorways led off – including Grey's.

'Yes – yes I suppose so.' Scarsdale was now acutely uncomfortable, a fine beading of sweat on his brow. 'Although I really cannot tell you anything germane to the issue, you know.' He backed into his own entranceway and Monk followed. 'The young lady who visited me had no connection with poor Grey, and she neither saw nor heard anyone else!'

Monk closed the main door, then followed him into the sitting room.

'Then you asked her, sir?' He allowed his face to register interest.

'Yes, of course I did!' Scarsdale was beginning to regain his composure, now that he was among his own possessions. The gas was lit and turned up; it glowed gently on polished leather, old Turkey carpet and silver-framed photographs. He was a gentleman, facing a mere member of Peel's police. 'Naturally, if there had been anything that could have assisted you in your work, I should have told you.' He used the word *work* with a vague condescension, a mark of the gulf between them. He did not invite Monk to sit, and remained standing himself, rather awkwardly between the sideboard and the sofa.

'And this young lady, of course, is well known to you?' Monk did not try to keep his own sarcastic contempt out of his voice.

Scarsdale was confused, not sure whether to affect insult or to prevaricate because he could think of nothing suitably crushing. He chose the latter.

'I beg your pardon?' he said stiffly.

'You can vouch for her truthfulness,' Monk elaborated, his eyes meeting Scarsdale's with a bitter smile. 'Apart from her . . . *work*' – he deliberately chose the same word – 'she is a person of perfect probity?'

Scarsdale coloured heavily and Monk realized he had lost any chance of cooperation from him.

'You exceed your authority!' Scarsdale snapped. 'And you are impertinent. My private affairs are no concern of yours. Watch your tongue, or I shall be obliged to complain to your superiors.' He looked at Monk and decided this was not a good idea. 'The woman in question has no reason to lie,' he said stiffly. 'She came up alone and left alone, and saw no one at either time, except Grimwade, the porter; and you can ascertain that from him. No one enters these buildings without his permission, you know.' He sniffed very slightly. 'This is not a common rooming house!' His eyes glanced for a second at the handsome furnishings, then back at Monk.

'Then it follows that Grimwade must have seen the murderer,' Monk replied, keeping his eyes on Scarsdale's face.

Scarsdale saw the imputation, and paled; he was arrogant,

73

and perhaps bigoted, but he was not stupid.

Monk took what he believed might well be his best chance.

'You are a gentleman of similar social standing' – he winced inwardly at his own hypocrisy – 'and an immediate neighbour of Major Grey's; you must be able to tell me something about him personally. I know nothing.'

Scarsdale was happy enough to change the subject, and in spite of his irritation, flattered.

'Yes, of course,' he agreed quickly. 'Nothing at all?'

'Nothing at all,' Monk conceded.

'He was a younger brother of Lord Shelburne, you know?' Scarsdale's eyes widened, and at last he walked to the centre of the room and sat down on a hard-backed, carved chair. He waved his arm vaguely, giving Monk permission to do so too.

'Indeed?' Monk chose another hard-backed chair so as not to be below Scarsdale.

'Oh yes, a very old family,' Scarsdale said with relish. 'The Dowager Lady Shelburne, his mother, of course, was the eldest daughter of the Duke of Ruthven, at least I think it was he; certainly the duke of somewhere.'

'Joscelin Grey,' Monk reminded him.

'Oh. Very pleasant fellow; officer in the Crimea, forgotten which regiment, but a very distinguished record.' He nodded vigorously. 'Wounded at Sebastopol, I think he said, then invalided out. Walked with a limp, poor devil. Not that it was disfiguring. Very good-looking fellow, great charm, very well liked, you know.'

'A wealthy family?'

'Shelburne?' Scarsdale was faintly amused by Monk's ignorance and his confidence was beginning to return. 'Of course. But I suppose you know, or perhaps you don't.' He looked Monk up and down disparagingly. 'But naturally all the money went to the eldest son, the present Lord Shelburne. Always happens that way, everything to the eldest, along with the title. Keeps the estates whole, otherwise everything would be in bits and pieces, d'you understand? All the power of the land gone!'

Monk controlled his sense of being patronized; he was perfectly aware of the laws of primogeniture.

'Yes, thank you. Where did Joscelin Grey's money come from?'

Scarsdale waved his hands, which were small, with wide knuckles and very short nails. 'Oh, business interests, I presume. I don't believe he had a great deal, but he didn't appear in any want. Always dressed well. Tell a lot from a fellow's clothes, you know.' Again he looked at Monk with a faint curl of his lip, then saw the quality of Monk's jacket and the portion of his shirt that was visible, and changed his mind, his eyes registering confusion.

'And as far as you know he was neither married nor betrothed?' Monk kept a stiff face and hid at least most of his satisfaction.

Scarsdale was surprised at his inefficiency.

'Surely you know that?'

'Yes, we know there was no official arrangement,' Monk said, hastening to cover his mistake. 'But you are in a position to know if there was any other relationship, anyone in whom he – had an interest?'

Scarsdale's rather full mouth turned down at the corners.

'If you mean an arrangement of convenience, not that I am aware of. But then a man of breeding does not inquire into the personal tastes – or accommodations – of another gentleman.'

'No, I didn't mean a financial matter,' Monk answered with the shadow of a sneer. 'I meant some lady he might have — admired – or even been courting.'

Scarsdale coloured angrily. 'Not as far as I know.'

'Was he a gambler?'

'I have no idea. I don't gamble myself, except with friends, of course, and Grey was not among them. I haven't heard anything, if that's what you mean.'

Monk realized he would get no more this evening, and he was tired. His own mystery was heavy at the back of his mind. Odd, how emptiness could be so intrusive. He rose to his feet.

'Thank you, Mr Scarsdale. If you should hear anything to throw light on Major Grey's last few days, or who might have wished him harm, I am sure you will let us know. The sooner we apprehend this man, the safer it will be for everyone.'

Scarsdale rose also, his face tightening at the subtle and unpleasant reminder that it had happened just across the hall from his own flat, threatening his security even as he stood there.

'Yes, naturally,' he said a little sharply. 'Now if you will be good enough to permit me to change – I have a dinner engagement, you know.'

Monk arrived at the police station to find Evan waiting for him. He was surprised at the sharpness of his pleasure at seeing him. Had he always been a lonely person, or was this just the isolation from memory, from all that might have been love or warmth in himself? Surely there was a friend somewhere – someone with whom he had shared pleasure and pain, at least common experience? Had there been no woman – in the past, if not now – some stored-up memory of tenderness, of laughter or tears? If not he must have been a cold fish. Was there perhaps some tragedy? Or some wrong?

The nothingness was crowding in on him, threatening to engulf the precarious present. He had not even the comfort of habit.

Evan's acute face, all eyes and nose, was infinitely welcome.

'Find out anything, sir?' He stood up from the wooden chair in which he had been sitting.

'Not a lot,' Monk answered with a voice that was suddenly louder, firmer than the words warranted. 'I don't see much chance of anyone having got in unseen, except the man who visited Yeats at about quarter to ten. Grimwade says he was a biggish man, muffled up, which is reasonable on a night like that. He says he saw him leave at roughly half past ten. Took him upstairs, but didn't see him closely, and wouldn't recognize him again.'

Evan's face was a mixture of excitement and frustration.

'Damn!' he exploded. 'Could be almost anyone then!' He looked at Monk quickly. 'But at least we have a fair idea how he got in. That's a great step forward; congratulations, sir!'

Monk felt a quick renewal of his spirits. He knew it was not justified; the step was actually very small. He sat down in the chair behind the desk.

'About six feet,' he reiterated. 'Dark and probably clean-shaven. I suppose that does narrow it a little.'

'Oh, it narrows it quite a lot, sir,' Evan said eagerly, resuming his own seat. 'At least we know that it wasn't a chance thief. If he called on Yeats, or said he did, he had planned it, and taken the trouble to scout the building. He knew who else lived there. And of course there's Yeats himself. Did you see him?'

'No, he wasn't in, and anyway I'd rather find out a little about him before I face him with it.'

'Yes, yes of course. If he knew anything, he's bound to deny it, I suppose.' But the anticipation was building in Evan's face, his voice; even his body was tightening under the elegant coat as if he expected some sudden action here in the police station. 'The cabby was no good, by the way. Perfectly respectable fellow, worked this area for twenty years, got a wife and seven or eight children. Never been any complaints against him.'

'Yes,' Monk agreed. 'Grimwade said he hadn't gone into the building, in fact doesn't think he even got off the box.'

'What do you want me to do about this Yeats?' Evan asked, a very slight smile curling his lips. 'Sunday tomorrow, a bit hard to turn up much then.'

Monk had forgotten.

'You're right. Leave it till Monday. He's been there for nearly seven weeks; it's hardly a hot trail.'

Evan's smile broadened rapidly.

'Thank you, sir. I did have other ideas for Sunday.' He stood up. 'Have a good weekend, sir. Good night.'

Monk watched him go with a sense of loss. It was foolish. Of course Evan would have friends, even family, and interests, perhaps a woman. He had never thought of that before. Somehow it added to his own sense of isolation. What did he normally do with his own time? Had he friends outside duty, some pursuit or pastime he enjoyed? There had to be more than this single-minded, ambitious man he had found so far.

He was still searching his imagination uselessly when there was a knock on the door, hasty, but not assertive, as though the person would have been pleased enough had there been no answer and he could have left again.

'Come in!' Monk said loudly.

The door opened and a stout young man came in. He wore a constable's uniform. His eyes were anxious, his rather homely face pink.

'Yes?' Monk inquired.

The young man cleared his throat. 'Mr Monk, sir?'

'Yes?' Monk said again. Should he know this man? From his wary expression there was some history in their past that had been important at least to him. He stood in the middle of the floor, fidgeting his weight from one foot to the other. Monk's wordless stare was making him worse.

'Can I do something for you?' Monk tried to sound reassuring. 'Have you something to report?' He wished he could remember the man's name.

'No, sir—I mean yes, sir, I 'ave something to ask you.' He took a deep breath. 'There's a report of a watch turned up at a pawnbroker's wot I done this arternoon, sir, an' – an' I thought as it might be summink ter do with your gennelman as was murdered – seein' as 'e didn't 'ave no watch, just a chain, like? Sir.' He held a piece of paper with copperplate handwriting on it as if it might explode.

Monk took it and glanced at it. It was the description of a gentleman's gold pocket watch with the initials J.G. inscribed ornately on the cover. There was nothing written inside.

He looked up at the constable.

'Thank you,' he said with a smile. 'It might well be – right initials. What do you know about it?'

The constable blushed scarlet. 'Nuffink much, Mr Monk. 'E swears blind as it was one of 'is reg'lars as brought it in. But you can't believe anyfink 'e says 'cause 'e would say that, wouldn't 'e? He don't want ter be mixed up in no murder.'

Monk glanced at the paper again. The pawnbroker's name and address were there and he could follow up on it any time he chose.

'No, he'd doubtless lie,' he agreed. 'But we might learn something all the same, if we can prove this was Grey's watch. Thank you – very observant of you. May I keep it?'

'Yes, sir. We don't need it; we 'as lots more agin 'im.'

Now his furious pink colour was obviously pleasure, and considerable surprise. He still stood rooted to the spot.

'Was there anything else?' Monk raised his eyebrows.

'No, sir! No there in't. Thank you, sir.' And the constable turned on his heel and marched out, tripping on the doorsill as he went and rocketing out into the passage.

Almost immediately the door was opened again by a wiry sergeant with a black moustache.

'You o'right, sir?' he asked, seeing Monk's frown.

'Yes. What's the matter with – er?' He waved his hand towards the departing figure of the constable, wishing desperately that he knew the man's name.

''Arrison?'

'Yes.'

'Nothin' – just afeared of you, that's all. Which in't 'ardly surprisin', seein' as 'ow you tore 'im off such a strip in front o' the 'ole station, w'en that macer slipped through 'is fingers – which weren't 'ardly 'is fault, seein' as the feller were a downright contortionist. 'Arder to 'old than a greased pig, 'e were. An' if we'd broke 'is neck wo'd be the ones for the 'igh jump before breakfast!'

Monk was confused. He did not know what to say. Had he been unjust to the man, or was there cause for whatever he had said? On the face of it, it sounded as if he had been gratuitously cruel, but he was hearing only one side of the story – there was no one to defend him, to explain, to give his reasons and say what he knew and perhaps they did not.

And rack and tear as he might, there was nothing in his

81

mind, not even Harrison's face – let alone some shred about the incident.

He felt a fool sitting staring up at the critical eyes of the sergeant, who plainly disliked him, for what he felt was fair cause.

Monk ached to explain himself! Even more he wanted to know for his own understanding. How many incidents would come up like this, things he had done that seemed ugly from the outside, to someone who did not know his side of the story?

'Mr Monk, sir?'

Monk recalled his attention quickly. 'Yes, Sergeant?'

'Thought you might like to know as we got the magsman wot snuffed ol' Billy Marlowe. They'll swing 'im for sure. Right villain.'

'Oh – thank you. Well done.' He had no idea what the sergeant was talking about, but obviously he was expected to. 'Very well done,' he added.

'Thank you, sir.' The sergeant straightened up, then turned and left, closing the door behind him with a sharp snick.

Monk bent to his work again.

An hour later he left the police station and walked slowly along the dark, wet pavements and found the way back to Grafton Street.

Mrs Worley's rooms were at least becoming familiar. He knew where to find things and, better than that, they offered privacy; no one would disturb him, intrude on his time to think, to try again to find some thread.

After his meal of mutton stew and dumplings, which were hot and filling, if a little heavy, he thanked Mrs Worley when she collected the tray, saw her down the stairs, and then began once more to go through the desk. The bills were of little use; he could hardly go to his tailor and say, 'What kind of man am I? What do I care about? Do you like, or dislike me, and why?' One small comfort he could draw from his accounts was that he appeared to have been prompt in paying them; there were no demand notices, and the receipts were all dated within a few days of presentation. He was learning something, a crumb: he was methodical.

The personal letters from Beth told him much of her: a simplicity, an unforced affection, a life of small detail. She said nothing of hardships or of bitter winters, nothing even of wrecks or the lifeboatmen. Her concern for him was based on her feelings, and she seemed to be without knowledge; she simply translated her own affections and interests to his life, and assumed his feelings were the same. He knew without needing deeper evidence that it was because he had told her nothing; perhaps he had not even written regularly. It was an unpleasant thought, and he was harshly ashamed of it. He must write to her soon, compose a letter that would seem rational, and yet perhaps elicit some answer from her which would tell him more.

The following morning he woke late to find Mrs Worley knocking on the door. He let her in and she put his breakfast on the table with a sigh and a shake of her head. He was obliged to eat it before dressing or it would have gone cold.

Afterwards he resumed the search, and again it was fruitless for any sharpening of identity, anything of the man behind the immaculate, rather expensive possessions. They told him nothing except that he had good taste, if a little predictable – perhaps that he liked to be admired? But what was admiration worth if it was for the cost and discretion of one's belongings? A shallow man? Vain? Or a man seeking security he did not feel, making his place in a world that he did not believe accepted him?

The flat itself was impersonal, with traditional furniture, sentimental pictures. Surely Mrs Worley's taste rather than his own?

After luncheon he was reduced to the last places to seek: the pockets of his other clothes, jackets hanging in the cupboard. In the best of them, a well-cut, rather formal coat, he found a piece of paper and, on unfolding it carefully, saw that it was a printed sheet for a service of Evensong at a church he did not know.

Perhaps it was close by. He felt a quickening of hope. Maybe he was a member of the congregation. The minister would know him. He might have friends there, a belief, even an office or a calling of some sort. He folded up the paper again carefully and put it in the desk, then went into the bedroom to wash and shave again, and change into his best clothes, and the coat from which the sheet had come. By five o'clock he was ready, and he went downstairs to ask Mrs Worley where St Marylebone Church might be.

His disappointment was shattering when she showed complete ignorance. Temper boiled inside him at the frustration. She must know. But her placid, blunt face was expressionless.

He was about to argue, to shout at her that she must know, when he realized how foolish it would be. He would only anger her, drive from himself a friend he sorely needed.

She was staring at him, her face puckered.

'My, you are in a state. Let me ask Mr Worley for yer; he's a rare fine understanding o' the city. O' course, I expect it's on the Marylebone Road, but ezac'ly where I'm sure I wouldn't know. It's a long street, that is.'

'Thank you,' he said carefully, feeling foolish. 'It's rather important.'

'Going to a wedding, are yer?' She looked at his carefully brushed dark coat. 'What you want is a good cabby, what knows 'is way, and'll get you there nice and prompt, like.'

It was an obvious answer, and he wondered why he had not thought of it himself. He thanked her, and when Mr Worley had been asked, and given his opinion that it might be opposite York Gate, he went out to look for a cab.

Evensong had already begun when he hurried up the steps and into the vestry. He could hear the voices lifted rather thinly in the first hymn. It sounded dutiful rather than joyous. Was he a religious man; or, it would be truer to ask, had he been? He felt no sense of comfort or reverence now, except for the simple beauty of the stonework.

He went in as quickly as he could, walking almost on the sides of his polished boots to make no noise. One or two heads turned, sharp with criticism. He ignored them and slid into a back pew, fumbling for a hymnbook.

Nothing sounded familiar; he followed the hymn because the tune was trite, full of musical clichés. He knelt when everyone else knelt, and rose as they rose. He missed the responses.

When the minister stepped into the pulpit to speak, Monk stared at him, searching his face for some flicker of memory. Could he go to this man and confide in him the truth, ask him to tell him everything he knew? The voice droned on in one platitude after another; his intention was benign, but so tied in words as to be almost incomprehensible. Monk sank deeper and deeper into a feeling of helplessness. The man did not seem able to remember his own train of thought from one sentence to the next, let alone the nature and passions of his flock.

When the last amen had been sung, Monk watched the people file out, hoping someone would touch his memory, or, better still, actually speak to him.

He was about to give up even that when he saw a young woman in black, slender and of medium height, dark hair drawn softly back from a face almost luminous, dark eyes and fragile skin, mouth too generous and too big for it. It was not a weak face, and yet it was one that could have moved easily to laughter, or tragedy. There was a grace in the way she walked that compelled him to watch her.

As she drew level she became aware of him and turned. Her eyes widened and she hesitated. She drew in her breath as if to speak.

He waited, hope surging up inside him, and a ridiculous

excitement, as if some exquisite realization were about to come.

Then the moment vanished; she seemed to regain a mastery of herself, her chin lifted a little, and she picked up her skirt unnecessarily and continued on her way.

He went after her, but she was lost in a group of people, two of whom, also dressed in black, were obviously accompanying her. One was a tall, fair man in his mid-thirties with smooth hair and a long-nosed, serious face; the other was a woman of unusual uprightness of carriage and features of remarkable character. The three of them walked towards the street and waiting vehicles and none of them turned their heads again.

Monk rode home in a rage of confusion, fear, and wild, disturbing hope.

Chapter Four

But when Monk arrived on Monday morning, breathless and a little late, he was unable to begin investigation on Yeats and his visitor. Runcorn was in his room, pacing the floor and waving a piece of blue notepaper in his hand. He stopped and spun around the moment he heard Monk's feet.

'Ah!' He brandished the paper with a look of bright, shimmering anger, his left eye narrowed almost shut.

The good-morning greeting died on Monk's tongue.

'Letter from upstairs.' Runcorn held up the blue paper. 'The powers that be are after us again. The Dowager Lady Shelburne has written to Sir Willoughby Gentry, and confided to the said member of Parliament' – he gave every vowel its full value in his volume of scorn for that body – 'that she is not happy with the utter lack of success the Metropolitan Police Force is having in apprehending the vile maniac who so foully murdered her son in his own house. No excuses are acceptable for our dilatory and lackadaisical attitude, our total lack of culprits to hand.' His face purpled in his offence at the injustice of it, but there was no misery in him, only a feeding rage. 'What the hell are you doing, Monk? You're supposed to be such a damn good detective, you've got your eyes on a superintendency – the commissionership, for all I know! So what do we tell this – this ladyship?'

Monk took a deep breath. He was more stunned by Runcorn's reference to himself, to his ambition, than anything in the letter. Was he an overweeningly ambitious man? There was no time for self-defence now; Runcorn was standing in front of him commanding an answer.

'Lamb's done all the groundwork, sir.' He gave Lamb the praise that was due him. 'He's investigated all he could, questioned all the other residents, street pedlars, locals, anyone who might have seen or known anything.' He could see from Runcorn's face that he was achieving nothing, but he persisted. 'Unfortunately it was a particularly foul night and everyone was in a hurry, heads down and collars up against the rain. Because it was so wet no one hung around, and with the overcast it was dark earlier than usual.'

Runcorn was fidgeting with impatience.

'Lamb spent a lot of time checking out the villains we know,' Monk continued. 'He's written up in his report that he's spoken to every snout and informer in the area. Not a peep. No one knows anything; or if they do, they're not saying. Lamb was of the opinion they were telling the truth. I don't know what else he could have done.' His experience offered nothing, but neither could his intelligence suggest any omission. All his sympathy was with Lamb.

'Constable Harrison found a watch with the initials J.G. on it in a pawnbroker's – but we don't know it was Grey's.'

'No,' Runcorn agreed fiercely, running his finger with distaste along the deckle edge of the notepaper. It was a luxury he could not afford. 'Indeed you don't! So what are you doing, then? Take it to Shelburne Hall – get it identified.'

'Harrison's on his way.'

'Can't you at least find out how the bloody man got in?'

'I think so,' Monk said levelly. 'There was a visitor for one of the other residents, a Mr Yeats. He came in at nine forty-five and left at roughly ten thirty. He was a biggish man, dark, well muffled. He's the only person unaccounted for; the others were women. I don't want to leap to conclusions too soon, but it looks as if he could be the murderer. Otherwise I don't know any way a stranger could have got in. Grimwade locks up at midnight, or earlier if all the residents are in, and after that even they have to ring the bell and get him up.'

Runcorn put the letter carefully on Monk's desk.

'And what time did he lock up that night?' he asked.

'Eleven,' Monk replied. 'No one was out.'

'What did Lamb say about this man who visited Yeats?' Runcorn screwed up his face.

'Not much. Apparently he only spoke to Yeats once, and then he spent most of the time trying to find out something about Grey. Maybe he didn't realize the importance of the visitor at that time. Grimwade said he took him up to Yeats's door and Yeats met him. Lamb was still looking for a thief off the street then—'

'Then!' Runcorn leapt on the word, sharp, eager. 'So what are you looking for now?'

Monk realized what he had said, and that he meant it. He frowned, and answered as carefully as he could.

'I think I'm looking for someone who knew him, and

hated him; someone who intended to kill him.'

'Well, for God's sake don't say so to Dowager Lady Shelburne!' Runcorn said dangerously.

'I'm hardly likely to be speaking to her,' Monk answered with more than a trace of sarcasm.

'Oh yes you are!' There was a ring of triumph in Runcorn's voice and his big face was glowing with colour. 'You are going down to Shelburne today to assure Her Ladyship that we are doing everything humanly possible to apprehend the murderer, and that after intensive effort and brilliant work, we at last have a lead to discovering this monster.' His lip curled very faintly. 'You're generally so blunt, damn near rude, in spite of your fancy airs, she won't take you for a liar.' Suddenly his tone altered again and became soft. 'Anyway, why do you think it was someone who knew him? Maniacs can kill with a hell of a mess; madmen strike over and over again, hate for no reason.'

'Possibly.' Monk stared back at him, matching dislike for dislike. 'But they don't scout out the names of other residents, call upon them, and then go and kill someone else. If he was merely a homicidal lunatic, why didn't he kill Yeats? Why go and look for Grey?'

Runcorn's eyes were wide; he resented it, but he took the point.

'Find out everything you can about this Yeats,' he ordered. 'Discreetly, mind! I don't want him scared away!'

'What about Lady Shelburne?' Monk affected innocence.

'Go and see her. Try to be civil, Monk – make an effort! Evan can chase after Yeats, and tell you whatever he finds when you get back. Take the train. You'll be in Shelburne a day or two. Her Ladyship won't be surprised to see you, after the rumpus she's raised. She demanded a report on progress, in person. You can put up at the inn. Well, off you go then. Don't stand there like an ornament, man!'

Monk took the train on the Great Northern line from King's Cross Station. He ran across the platform and jumped in, slamming the carriage door just as the engine belched forth a cloud of steam, gave a piercing shriek and jolted forward. It was an exciting sensation, a surge of power, immense, controlled noise, and then gathering speed as they emerged from the cavern of the station buildings out into the sharp late afternoon sunlight.

Monk settled himself into a vacant seat opposite a large woman in black bombazine with a fur tippet around her neck (in spite of the season) and a black hat on at a fierce angle. She had a packet of sandwiches, which she opened immediately and began to eat. A little man with large spectacles eyed them hopefully, but said nothing. Another man in striped trousers studiously read his *Times*.

They roared and hissed their way past tenements, houses and factories, hospitals, churches, public halls and offices, gradually thinning, more interspersed with stretches of green, until at last the city fell away and Monk stared with genuine pleasure at the beauty of soft countryside spread wide in the lushness of full summer. Huge boughs clouded green over fields heavy with ripening crops and thick hedgerows starred with late wild roses. Coppices of trees huddled in folds of

93

the slow hills, and villages were easily marked by the tapering spires of churches, or the occasional squarer Norman tower.

Shelburne came too quickly, while he was still drinking in the loveliness of it. He grabbed his valise off the rack and opened the door hastily, excusing himself past the fat woman in the bombazine and incurring her silent displeasure. On the platform he inquired of the lone attendant where Shelburne Hall lay, and was told it was less than a mile. The man waved his arm to indicate the direction, then sniffed and added, 'But the village be two mile in t'opposite way, and doubtless that be w'ere you're a-goin'.'

'No thank you,' Monk replied. 'I have business at the Hall.'

The man shrugged. 'If'n you say so, sir. Then you'd best take the road left an' keep walking.'

Monk thanked him again and set out.

It took him only fifteen minutes to walk from the station entrance to the drive gates. It was a truly magnificent estate, an early Georgian mansion three storeys high, with a handsome frontage, now covered in places by vines and creepers, and approached by a sweeping carriageway under beech trees and cedars that dotted a parkland which seemed to stretch towards distant fields, and presumably the home farm.

Monk stood in the gateway and looked for several minutes. The grace of proportion, the way it ornamented rather than intruded upon the landscape, were all not only extremely pleasant but also perhaps indicative of something in the nature of the people who had been born here and grown up in such a place.

Finally he began walking up the considerable distance to the house itself, a further third of a mile, and went around past the outhouses and stables to the servants' entrance. He was received by a rather impatient footman.

'We don't buy at the door,' he said coldly, looking at Monk's case.

'I don't sell,' Monk replied with more tartness than he had intended. 'I am from the Metropolitan Police. Lady Shelburne wished a report on the progress we have made in investigating the death of Major Grey. I have come to give that report.'

The footman's eyebrows went up.

'Indeed? That would be the Dowager Lady Shelburne. Is she expecting you?'

'Not that I know of. Perhaps you would tell her I am here.'

'I suppose you'd better come in.' He opened the door somewhat reluctantly. Monk stepped in, then without further explanation the man disappeared, leaving Monk in the back hallway. It was a smaller, barer and more utilitarian version of a front hall, only without pictures, having only the functional furniture necessary for servants' use. Presumably he had gone to consult some higher authority, perhaps even that autocrat of below-stairs – and sometimes above – the butler. It was several minutes before he returned, and motioned Monk to go with him.

'Lady Shelburne will see you in half an hour.' He left

Monk in a small parlour adjacent to the housekeeper's room, a suitable place for such persons as policemen; not precisely servants or tradesmen, and most certainly not to be considered as of quality.

Monk walked slowly around the room after the footman had gone, looking at the worn furniture, brown upholstered chairs with bow legs and an oak sideboard and table. The walls were papered and fading, the pictures anonymous and rather puritan reminders of rank and the virtues of duty. He preferred the wet grass and heavy trees sloping down to ornamental water beyond the window.

He wondered what manner of woman she was who could control her curiosity for thirty long minutes rather than let her dignity falter in front of a social inferior. Lamb had said nothing about her. Was it likely he had not even seen her? The more he considered it, the more certain he became. Lady Shelburne would not direct her inquiries through a mere employee, and there had been no cause to question her in anything.

But Monk wanted to question her; if Grey had been killed by a man who hated him, not a maniac in the sense of someone without reason, only insofar as he had allowed a passion to outgrow control until it had finally exploded in murder, then it was imperative Monk learn to know Grey better. Intentionally or not, Grey's mother would surely betray something of him, some honesty through the memories and the grief, that would give colour to the outline.

He had had time to think a lot about Grey and formulate questions in his mind by the time the footman returned and conducted him through the green baize door and across the corridor to Lady Fabia's sitting room. It was decorated discreetly with deep pink velvet and rosewood furniture. Lady Fabia herself was seated on a Louis Quinze sofa and when Monk saw her all his preconceptions fled his tongue. She was not very big, but as hard and fragile as porcelain, her colouring perfect, not a blemish on her skin, not a soft, fair hair out of place. Her features were regular, her blue eyes wide, only a slight jutting chin spoiled the delicacy of her face. And she was perhaps too thin; slenderness had given way to angularity. She was dressed in violet and black, as became someone in mourning, although on her it looked more like something to be observed for one's own dignity than any sign of distress. There was nothing frail in her manner.

'Good morning,' she said briskly, dismissing the footman with a wave of her hand. She did not regard Monk with any particular interest and her eyes barely glanced at his face. 'You may sit if you wish. I am told you have come to report to me the progress you have made in discovering and apprehending the murderer of my son. Pray proceed.'

Opposite him Lady Fabia sat, her back ramrod-straight from years of obedience to governesses, walking as a child with a book on her head for deportment, and riding upright in a sidesaddle in the park or to hounds. There was little Monk could do but obey, sitting reluctantly on one of the ornate chairs and feeling self-conscious.

'Well?' she demanded when he remained silent. 'The watch your constable brought was not my son's.'

Monk was stung by her tone, by her almost unthinking assumption of superiority. In the past he must have been used to this, but he could not remember; and now it stung with the shallow sharpness of gravel rash, not a wound but a blistering abrasion. A memory of Beth's gentleness came to his mind. She would not have resented this. Why was the difference between them? Why did he not have her soft Northumbrian accent? Had he eradicated it intentionally, washing out his origins in an attempt to appear some kind of gentleman? The thought made him blush for its stupidity.

Lady Shelburne was staring at him.

'We have established the only time a man could have gained entry to the buildings,' he replied, still stiff with his own sense of pride. 'And we have a description of the only man who did so.' He looked straight into her chilly and rather surprised blue eyes. 'He was roughly six feet tall, of solid build, as far as can be judged under a greatcoat. He was dark-complexioned and clean-shaven. He went ostensibly to visit a Mr Yeats, who also lives in the building. We have not yet spoken to Mr Yeats—'

'Why not?'

'Because you required that I come and report our progress to you, ma'am.'

Her eyebrows rose in incredulity, touched with contempt. The sarcasm passed her by entirely.

'Surely you cannot be the only man directed to conduct such an important case? My son was a brave and distinguished soldier who risked his life for his country. Is this the best with which you can repay him?'

'London is full of crimes, ma'am; and every man or woman murdered is a loss to someone.'

'You can hardly equate the death of a marquis's son with that of some thief or indigent in the street!' she snapped back.

'Nobody has more than one life to lose, ma'am; and all are equal before the law, or they should be.'

'Nonsense! Some men are leaders, and contribute to society; most do not. My son was one of those who did.'

'Some have nothing to—' he began.

'Then that is their own fault!' she interrupted. 'But I do not wish to hear your philosophies. I am sorry for those in the gutter, for whatever reason, but they really do not interest me. What are you doing about apprehending this madman who killed my son? Who is he?'

'We don't know—'

'Then what are you doing to find out?' If she had any feelings under her exquisite exterior, like generations of her kind she had been bred to conceal them, never to indulge herself in weakness or vulgarity. Courage and good taste were her household gods and no sacrifice to them was questioned, nor too great, made daily and without fuss.

Monk ignored Runcorn's admonition, and wondered in passing how often he had done so in the past. There had been a certain asperity in Runcorn's tone this morning which surpassed simply frustration with the case, or Lady Shelburne's letter.

'We believe it was someone who knew Major Grey,' he answered her. 'And planned to kill him.'

'Nonsense!' Her response was immediate. 'Why should anyone who knew my son have wished to kill him? He was a man of the greatest charm; everyone liked him, even those who barely knew him.' She stood up and walked over towards the window, her back half to him. 'Perhaps that is difficult for you to understand; but you never met him. Lovel, my eldest son, has the sobriety, the sense of responsibility, and something of a gift to manage men; Menard is excellent with facts and figures. He can make anything profitable; but it was Joscelin who had the charm, Joscelin who could make one laugh.' There was a catch in her voice now, the sound of real grief. 'Menard cannot sing as Joscelin could; and Lovel has no imagination. He will make an excellent master of Shelburne. He will govern it well and be just to everyone, as just as it is wise to be – but my God' – there was sudden heat in her voice, almost passion – 'compared with Joscelin, he is such a bore!'

Suddenly Monk was touched by the sense of loss that came through her words, the loneliness, the feeling that something irrecoverably pleasing had gone from her life and part of her could only look backwards from now on.

'I'm sorry,' he said, and he meant it deeply. 'I know it cannot bring him back, but we will find the man, and he will be punished.'

'Hanged,' she said tonelessly. 'Taken out one morning and his neck broken on the rope.'

'Yes.'

'That is of little use to me.' She turned back to him. 'But it is better than nothing. See to it that it is done.'

It was dismissal, but he was not yet ready to go. There were things he needed to know. He stood up.

'I mean to, ma'am; but I still need your help—'

'Mine?' Her voice expressed surprise, and disapproval.

'Yes, ma'am. If I am to learn who hated Major Grey enough to kill him' – he caught her expression – 'for whatever reason. The finest people, ma'am, can inspire envy, or greed, jealousy over a woman, a debt of honour that cannot be paid—'

'Yes, you make your point.' She blinked and the muscles in her thin neck tightened. 'What is your name?'

'William Monk.'

'Indeed. And what is it you wish to know about my son, Mr Monk?'

'To start with, I would like to meet the rest of the family.'

Her eyebrows rose in faint, dry amusement.

'You think I am biased, Mr Monk, that I have told you something less than the truth?'

'We frequently show only our most flattering sides to those we care for most, and who care for us,' he replied quietly.

'How perceptive of you.' Her voice was stinging. He tried to guess what well-covered pain was behind those words.

'When may I speak to Lord Shelburne?' he asked. 'And anyone else who knew Major Grey well?'

'If you consider it necessary, I suppose you had better.' She went back to the door. 'Wait here, and I shall ask him to see you, when it is convenient.' She pulled the door open and walked through without looking back at him.

He sat down, half facing the window. Outside a woman in a plain stuff dress walked past, a basket on her arm. For a wild moment memory surged back to him. He saw in his mind a child as well, a girl with dark hair, and he knew the cobbled street beyond the trees, going down to the water. There was something missing; he struggled for it, and then knew it was wind, and the scream of gulls. It was a memory of happiness, of complete safety. Childhood – perhaps his mother, and Beth?

Then it was gone. He fought to add to it, focus it more sharply and see the details again, but nothing else came. He was an adult back in Shelburne, with the murder of Joscelin Grey.

He waited for another quarter of an hour before the door opened again and Lord Shelburne came in. He was about thirty-eight or forty, heavier of build than Joscelin Grey, to judge by the description and the clothes; but Monk wondered if Joscelin had also had that air of confidence and slight, even unintentional superiority. He was darker than his mother and the balance of his face was different, sensible, without a jot of humour in the mouth.

Monk rose to his feet as a matter of courtesy – and hated himself for doing it.

'You're the police fellow?' Shelburne said with a slight frown. He remained standing, so Monk was obliged to also. 'Well, what is it you want? I really can't imagine how anything I can tell you about my brother could help you find the lunatic who broke in and killed him, poor devil.'

'No one broke in, sir,' Monk corrected him. 'Whoever it was, Major Grey gave entrance to him himself.'

'Really?' The level brows rose a fraction. 'I find that very unlikely.'

'Then you are not acquainted with the facts, sir.' Monk was irked by the condescension and the arrogance of a man who presumed to know Monk's job better than he did, simply because he was a gentleman. Had he always found it so hard to bear? Had he been quick-tempered? Runcorn had said something about lack of diplomacy, but he could not remember what it was now. His mind flew back to the church the day before, to the woman who had hesitated as she passed him down the aisle. He could see her face as sharply here at Shelburne as he had then; the rustle of taffeta, the faint, almost imaginary perfume, the widening of her eyes. It was a memory that made his heart beat faster and excitement catch in his throat.

'I know my brother was beaten to death by a lunatic.' Shelburne's voice cut across him, scattering his thoughts. 'And you haven't caught him yet. Those are facts!'

Monk forced his attention to the present.

'With respect, sir.' He tried to choose his words with tact. 'We know that he was beaten to death. We do not know by whom, or why; but there were no marks of forced entry, and the only person unaccounted for who could possibly have entered the building appears to have visited someone else. Whoever attacked Major Grey took great care about the way he did it, and, so far as we know, did not steal anything.'

'And you deduce from that that it was someone he knew?' Shelburne was sceptical.

'That, and the violence of the crime,' Monk agreed, standing across the room from him so he could see Shelburne's face in the light. 'A simple burglar does not go on hitting his victim long after he is quite obviously dead.'

Shelburne winced. 'Unless he is a madman! Which was rather my point. You are dealing with a madman, Mr – er.' He could not recall Monk's name and did not wait for it to be offered. It was unimportant. 'I think there's scant chance of your catching him now. You would probably be better employed stopping muggings, or pickpockets, or whatever it is you usually do.'

Monk swallowed his temper with difficulty. 'Lady Shelburne seems to disagree with you.'

Lovel Grey was unaware of having been rude; one could not be rude to a policeman.

'Mama?' His face flickered for an instant with unaccustomed emotion, which quickly vanished and left his features smooth again. 'Oh, well; women feel these things. I am afraid she has taken Joscelin's death very hard, worse than if he'd been killed in the Crimea.' It appeared to surprise him slightly.

'It's natural,' Monk persisted, trying a different approach. 'I believe he was a very charming person – and well liked?'

Shelburne was leaning against the mantelpiece and his boots shone in the sun falling wide through the French window. Irritably he kicked them against the brass fender.

'Joscelin? Yes, I suppose he was. Cheerful sort of fellow,

always smiling. Gifted with music, and telling stories, that kind of thing. I know my wife was very fond of him. Great pity, and so pointless, just some bloody madman!' He shook his head. 'Hard on Mother.'

'Did he come down here often?' Monk sensed a vein more promising.

'Oh, every couple of months or so. Why?' He looked up. 'Surely you don't think someone followed him from here?'

'Every possibility is worth looking into, sir.' Monk leaned his weight a little against the sideboard. 'Was he here shortly before he was killed?'

'Yes, as a matter of fact he was; couple of weeks, or less. But I think you are mistaken. Everyone here had known him for years, and they all liked him.' A shadow crossed his face. 'Matter of fact, I think he was pretty well the servants' favourite. Always had a pleasant word, you know; remembered people's names, even though he hadn't lived here for years.'

Monk imagined it: the solid, plodding older brother, worthy but boring; the middle brother still an outline only; and the youngest, trying hard and finding that charm could bring him what birth did not, making people laugh, unbending the formality, affecting an interest in the servants' lives and families, winning small treats for himself that his brothers did not – and his mother's love.

'People can hide hatred, sir,' Monk said aloud. 'And they usually do, if they have murder in mind.'

'I suppose they must,' Lovel conceded, straightening up and standing with his back to the empty fireplace. 'Still, I think you're on the wrong path. Look for some lunatic in London, some violent burglar; there must be loads of them. Don't you have contacts, people who inform to the police? Why don't you try them?'

'We have, sir – exhaustively. Mr Lamb, my predecessor, spent weeks combing every possibility in that direction. It was the first place to look.' He changed the subject suddenly, hoping to catch him less guarded. 'How did Major Grey finance himself, sir? We haven't uncovered any business interest yet.'

'What on earth do you want to know that for?' Lovel was startled. 'You cannot imagine he had the sort of business rivals who would beat him to death with a stick? That's ludicrous!'

'Someone did.'

He wrinkled his face with distaste. 'I had not forgotten that! I really don't know what his business interests were. He had a small allowance from the estate, naturally.'

'How much, sir?'

'I hardly think that needs to concern you.' Now the irritation was back; his affairs had been trespassed upon by a policeman. Again his boot kicked absently at the fender behind him.

'Of course it concerns me, sir.' Monk had command of his temper now. He was in control of the conversation, and he had a direction to pursue. 'Your brother was murdered, probably by someone who knew him. Money may well come into it; it is one of the commonest motives for murder.'

Lovel looked at him without replying.

Monk waited.

'Yes, I suppose it is,' Lovel said at last. 'Four hundred pounds a year – and of course there was his army pension.'

To Monk it sounded a generous amount; one could run a very good establishment and keep a wife and family, with two maids, for less than a thousand pounds. But possibly Joscelin Grey's tastes had been a good deal more extravagant: clothes, clubs, horses, gambling, perhaps women, or at least presents for women. They had not so far explored his social circle, still believing it to have been an intruder from the streets, and Grey a victim of ill fortune rather than someone of his own acquaintance.

'Thank you,' he replied to Lord Shelburne. 'You know of no other?'

'My brother did not discuss his financial affairs with me.'

'You say your wife was fond of him? Would it be possible for me to speak to Lady Shelburne, please? He may have said something to her the last time he was here that could help us.'

'Hardly, or she would have told me; and naturally I should have told you, or whoever is in authority.'

'Something that meant nothing to Lady Shelburne might have meaning for me,' Monk pointed out. 'Anyway, it is worth trying.'

Lovel moved to the centre of the room as if somehow he would crowd Monk to the door. 'I don't think so. And she has already suffered a severe shock; I don't see any purpose in distressing her any further with sordid details.'

'I was going to ask her about Major Grey's personality,

sir,' Monk said with the shadow of irony in his voice. 'His friends and his interests, nothing further. Or was she so attached to him that would distress her too much?'

'I don't care for your impertinence!' Lovel said sharply. 'Of course she wasn't. I just don't want to rake the thing over any further. It is not very pleasant to have a member of one's family beaten to death!'

Monk faced him squarely. There was not more than a yard between them.

'Of course not, but that surely is all the more reason why we must find the man.'

'If you insist.' With ill humour he ordered Monk to follow him, and led him out of the very feminine sitting room along a short corridor into the main hall. Monk glanced around as much as was possible in the brief time as Shelburne paced ahead of him towards one of the several fine doorways. The walls were panelled to shoulder height in wood, the floor parqueted and scattered with Chinese carpets of cut pile and beautiful pastel shades, and the whole was dominated by a magnificent staircase dividing halfway up and sweeping to left and right at either end of a railed landing. There were pictures in ornate gold frames on all sides, but he had no time to look at them.

Shelburne opened the withdrawing room door and waited impatiently while Monk followed him in, then closed it. The room was long and faced south, with French windows looking onto a lawn bordered with herbaceous flowers in brilliant bloom. Rosamond Shelburne was sitting on a brocade chaise longue, embroidery hoop in her hand. She looked up when they came in. She was at first glance not unlike her mother-in-law: she had the same fair hair and good brow, the same shape of eye, although hers were dark brown, and there was a different balance to her features, the resolution was not yet hard, there was humour, a width of imagination waiting to be given flight. She was dressed soberly, as befitted one who had recently lost a brother-in-law, but the wide skirt was the colour of wine in shadow, and only her beads were black.

'I am sorry, my dear.' Shelburne glanced pointedly at Monk. 'But this man is from the police, and he thinks you may be able to tell him something about Joscelin that will help.' He strode past her and stopped by the first window, glancing at the sun across the grass.

Rosamond's fair skin coloured very slightly and she avoided Monk's eyes.

'Indeed?' she said politely. 'I know very little of Joscelin's London life, Mr—?'

'Monk, ma'am,' he answered. 'But I understand Major Grey had an affection for you, and perhaps he may have spoken of some friend, or an acquaintance who might lead us to another, and so on?'

'Oh.' She put her needle and frame down; it was a tracery of roses around a text. 'I see. I am afraid I cannot think of anything. But please be seated, and I will do my best to help.'

Monk accepted and questioned her gently, not because he expected to learn a great deal from her directly, but because indirectly he watched her, listening to the intonations of her voice, and the fingers turning in her lap.

Slowly he discovered a picture of Joscelin Grey.

'He seemed very young when I came here after my marriage,' Rosamond said with a smile, looking beyond Monk and out of the window. 'Of course that was before he went to the Crimea. He was an officer then; he had just bought his commission and he was so' – she searched for just the right word – 'so jaunty! I remember that day he came in in his uniform, scarlet tunic and gold braid, boots gleaming. One could not help feeling happy for him.' Her voice dropped. 'It all seemed like an adventure then.'

'And after?' Monk prompted, watching the delicate shadows in her face, the search for something glimpsed but not understood except by a leap of instinct.

'He was wounded, you know?' She looked at him, frowning.

'Yes,' he said.

'Twice – and ill, too.' She searched his eyes to see if he knew more than she, and there was nothing in his memory to draw on. 'He suffered very much,' she continued. 'He was thrown from his horse in the charge at Balaclava and sustained a sword wound in his leg at Sebastopol. He refused to speak much to us about being in hospital at Scutari; he said it was too terrible to relate and would distress us beyond bearing.' The embroidery slipped on the smooth nap of her skirt and rolled away on the floor. She made no effort to pick it up.

'He was changed?' Monk prompted.

She smiled slowly. She had a lovely mouth, sweeter and

more sensitive than her mother-in-law's. 'Yes – but he did not lose his humour, he could still laugh and enjoy beautiful things. He gave me a musical box for my birthday.' Her smile widened at the thought of it. 'It had an enamel top with a rose painted on it. It played "Für Elise" – Beethoven, you know—'

'Really, my dear!' Lovel's voice cut across her as he turned from where he had been standing by the window. 'The man is here on police business. He doesn't know or care about Beethoven and Joscelin's music box. Please try to concentrate on something relevant – in the remote likelihood there is anything. He wants to know if Joscelin offended someone – owed them money – God knows what!'

Her face altered so slightly it could have been a change in the light, had not the sky beyond the windows been a steady cloudless blue. Suddenly she looked tired.

'I know Joscelin found finances a little difficult from time to time,' she answered quietly. 'But I do not know of any particulars, or whom he owed.'

'He would hardly have discussed such a thing with my wife.' Lovel swung around sharply. 'If he wanted to borrow he would come to me – but he had more sense than to try. He had a very generous allowance as it was.'

Monk glanced frantically at the splendid room, the swagged velvet curtains, and the garden and parkland beyond, and forbore from making any remark as to generosity. He looked back at Rosamond.

'You never assisted him, ma'am?'

Rosamond hesitated.

'With what?' Lovel asked, raising his eyebrows.

'A gift?' Monk suggested, struggling to be tactful. 'Perhaps a small loan to meet a sudden embarrassment?'

'I can only assume you are trying to cause mischief,' Lovel said acidly. 'Which is despicable, and if you persist I shall have you removed from the case.'

Monk was taken aback; he had not deliberately intended offence, simply to uncover a truth. Such sensibilities were peripheral, and he thought a rather silly indulgence now.

Lovel saw his irritation and mistook it for a failure to understand. 'Mr Monk, a married woman does not own anything to dispose of – to a brother-in-law or anyone else.'

Monk blushed for making a fool of himself, and for the patronage in Lovel's manner. When reminded, of course he knew the law. Even Rosamond's personal jewellery was not hers in law. If Lovel said she was not to give it away, then she could not. Not that he had any doubt, from the catch in her speech and the flicker of her eyes, that she had done so.

He had no desire to betray her; the knowledge was all he wanted. He bit back the reply he wished to make.

'I did not intend to suggest anything done without your permission, my lord, simply a gesture of kindness on Lady Shelburne's part.'

Lovel opened his mouth to retort, then changed his mind and looked out of the window again, his face tight, his shoulders broad and stiff.

'Did the war affect Major Grey deeply?' Monk turned back to Rosamond.

'Oh yes!' For a moment there was intense feeling in her,

then she recalled the circumstances and struggled to control herself. Had she not been as schooled in the privileges and the duties of a lady she would have wept. 'Yes,' she said again. 'Yes, although he mastered it with great courage. It was not many months before he began to be his old self – most of the time. He would play the piano, and sing for us sometimes.' Her eyes looked beyond Monk to some past place in her own mind. 'And he still told us funny stories and made us laugh. But there were occasions when he would think of the men who died, and I suppose his own suffering as well.'

Monk was gathering an increasingly sharp picture of Joscelin Grey: a dashing young officer, easy mannered, perhaps a trifle callow; then through experience of war with its blood and pain, and for him an entirely new kind of responsibility, returning home determined to resume as much of the old life as possible; a youngest son with little money but great charm, and a degree of courage.

He had not seemed like a man to make enemies through wronging anyone – but it did not need a leap of imagination to conceive that he might have earned a jealousy powerful enough to have ended in murder. All that was needed for that might lie within this lovely room with its tapestries and its view of the parkland.

'Thank you, Lady Shelburne,' he said formally. 'You have given me a much clearer picture of him than I had. I am most grateful.' He turned to Lovel. 'Thank you, my lord, if I might speak with Mr Menard Grey—'

'He is out,' Lovel replied flatly. 'He went to see one of

the tenant farmers, and I don't know which so there is no point in your traipsing around looking. Anyway, you are looking for who murdered Joscelin, not writing an obituary!'

'I don't think the obituary is finished until it contains the answer,' Monk replied, meeting his eyes with a straight, challenging stare.

'Then get on with it!' Lovel snapped. 'Don't stand here in the sun – get out and do something useful.'

Monk left without speaking and closed the withdrawing room door behind him. In the hall a footman was awaiting discreetly to show him out – or perhaps to make sure that he left without pocketing the silver card tray on the hall table, or the ivory-handled letter opener.

The weather had changed dramatically; from nowhere a swift overcast had brought a squall, the first heavy drops beginning even as he left.

He was outside, walking towards the main drive through the clearing rain, when quite by chance he met the last member of the family. He saw her coming towards him briskly, whisking her skirts out of the way of a stray bramble trailing onto the narrower path. She was reminiscent of Fabia Shelburne in age and dress, but without the brittle glamour. This woman's nose was longer, her hair wilder, and she could never have been a beauty, even forty years ago.

'Good afternoon.' He lifted his hat in a small gesture of politeness.

She stopped in her stride and looked at him curiously.

'Good afternoon. You are a stranger. What are you doing here? Are you lost?'

'No, thank you, ma'am. I am from the Metropolitan Police. I came to report our progress on the murder of Major Grey.'

Her eyes narrowed and he was not sure whether it was amusement or something else.

'You look a well-set-up young man to be carrying messages. I suppose you came to see Fabia?'

He had no idea who she was, and for a moment he was at a loss for a civil reply.

She understood instantly.

'I'm Callandra Daviot; the late Lord Shelburne was my brother.'

'Then Major Grey was your nephew, Lady Callandra?' He spoke her correct title without thinking, and only realized it afterwards, and wondered what experience or interest had taught him. Now he was only concerned for another opinion of Joscelin Grey.

'Naturally,' she agreed. 'How can that help you?'

'You must have known him.'

Her rather wild eyebrows rose slightly.

'Of course. Possibly a little better than Fabia. Why?'

'You were very close to him?' he said quickly.

'On the contrary, I was some distance removed.' Now he was quite certain there was a dry humour in her eyes.

'And saw the clearer for it?' He finished her implication.

'I believe so. Do you require to stand here under the trees, young man? I am being steadily dripped on.'

He shook his head, and turned to accompany her back along the way he had come.

'It is unfortunate that Joscelin was murdered,' she continued. 'It would have been much better if he could have died at Sebastopol – better for Fabia anyway. What do you want of me? I was not especially fond of Joscelin, nor he of me. I knew none of his business, and have no useful ideas as to who might have wished him such intense harm.'

'You were not fond of him yourself?' Monk said curiously. 'Everyone says he was charming.'

'So he was,' she agreed, walking with large strides not towards the main entrance of the house but along a gravelled path in the direction of the stables, and he had no choice but to go also or be left behind. 'I do not care a great deal for charm.' She looked directly at him, and he found himself warming to her dry honesty. 'Perhaps because I never possessed it,' she continued. 'But it always seems chameleon to me, and I cannot be sure what colour the animal underneath might be really. Now will you please either return to the house, or go wherever it is you are going. I have no inclination to get any wetter than I already am, and it is going to rain again. I do not intend to stand in the stable yard talking polite nonsense that cannot possibly assist you.'

He smiled broadly and bowed his head in a small salute. Lady Callandra was the only person in Shelburne he liked instinctively.

'Of course, ma'am; thank you for your . . .' He hesitated, not wanting to be so obvious as to say 'honesty'. '. . . time. I wish you a good day.'

116

She looked at him wryly and with a little nod, strode past into the harness room calling loudly for the head groom.

Monk walked back along the driveway again – as she had surmised, through a considerable shower – and out past the gates. He followed the road for the three miles to the village. Newly washed by rain, in the brilliant bursts of sun it was so lovely it caught a longing in him as if once it was out of sight he would never recall it clearly enough. Here and there a coppice showed dark green, billowing over the sweep of grass and mounded against the sky, and beyond the distant stone walls wheat fields shone dark gold with the wind rippling like waves through their heavy heads.

It took him a little short of an hour and he found the peace of it turning his mind from the temporary matter of who murdered Joscelin Grey to the deeper question as to what manner of man he himself was. Here no one knew him; at least for tonight he would be able to start anew, no previous act could mar it, or help. Perhaps he would learn something of the inner man, unfiltered by expectations. What did he believe, what did he truly value? What drove him from day to day – except ambition, and personal vanity?

He stayed overnight in the village public hostelry, and asked some discreet questions of certain locals in the morning, without significantly adding to his picture of Joscelin Grey, but he found a very considerable respect for both Grey's brothers, in their different ways. They were not liked – that was too close a relationship with men whose lives and stations were so different – but they were trusted. They fitted into expectations of their kind, small courtesies were observed, a mutual code was kept.

Of Joscelin it was different. Affection was possible. Everyone had found him more than civil, remembering as many of the generosities as were consistent with his position as a son of the house. If some had thought or felt otherwise they were not saying so to an outsider like Monk. And he had been a soldier; a certain honour was due the dead.

Monk enjoyed being polite, even gracious. No one was afraid of him – guarded certainly, he was still a Peeler – but there was no personal awe, and they were as keen as he to find who had murdered their hero.

He took luncheon in the taproom with several local worthies and contrived to fall into conversation. By the door with the sunlight streaming in, with cider, apple pie and cheese, opinions began to flow fast and free. Monk became involved, and before long his tongue got the better of him, clear, sarcastic and funny. It was only afterwards as he was walking away that he realized that it was also at times unkind.

He left in the early afternoon for the small, silent station, and took a clattering, steam-belching journey back to London.

He arrived a little after four, and went by hansom straight to the police station.

'Well?' Runcorn inquired with lifted eyebrows. 'Did you manage to mollify Her Ladyship? I'm sure you conducted yourself like a gentleman?'

Monk heard that slight edge to Runcorn's voice again, and the flavour of resentment. What for? He struggled desperately to recall any wisp of memory, even a guess as to what he might have done to occasion it. Surely not mere abrasiveness of manner? He had not been so stupid as to be positively rude to a superior? But nothing came. It mattered – it mattered acutely: Runcorn held the key to his employment, the only sure thing in his life now, in fact the very means of it. Without work he was not only comparatively anonymous, but within a few weeks he would be a pauper. Then there would be only the same bitter choice for him as for every other pauper: beggary, with its threat of starvation or imprisonment as a vagrant; or the workhouse. And God knew, there were those who thought the workhouse the greater evil.

'I believe Her Ladyship understood that we are doing all we can,' he answered. 'And that we had to exhaust the more likely-seeming possibilities first, like a thief off the streets. She understands that now we must consider that it may have been someone who knew him.'

Runcorn grunted. 'Asked her about him, did you? What sort of feller he was?'

'Yes, sir. Naturally she was biased—'

'Naturally,' Runcorn agreed tartly, shooting his eyebrows up. 'But you ought to be bright enough to see past that.'

Monk ignored the implication. 'He seems to have been her favourite son,' he replied. 'Considerably the most likable. Everyone else gave the same opinion, even in the village. Discount some of that as speaking no ill of the dead.' He smiled twistedly. 'Or of the son of the big house. Even so, you're still left with a man of unusual charm, a good war record, and no especial vices or weaknesses, except that he found it hard to manage on his allowance, bit of a temper now and then, and a mocking wit when he chose; but generous, remembered birthdays and servants' names – knew how to amuse. It begins to look as if jealousy could have been a motive.'

Runcorn sighed.

'Messy,' he said decidedly, his left eye narrowing again. 'Never like having to dig into family relationships, and the higher you go the nastier you get.' He pulled his coat a little straighter without thinking, but it still did not sit elegantly. 'That's your society for you; cover their tracks better than any of your average criminals, when they really try. Don't often make a mistake, that lot, but oh my grandfather, when they do!' He poked his finger in the air towards Monk. 'Take my word for it, if there's something nasty there, it'll get a lot worse before it gets any better. You may fancy the higher classes, my boy, but they play very dirty when they protect their own; you believe it!'

Monk could think of no answer. He wished he could remember the things he had said and done to prompt Runcorn to these flavours, nuances of disapproval. Was he a brazen social climber? The thought was repugnant, even pathetic in a way, trying to appear something you are not, in order to impress people who don't care for you in the slightest, and can most certainly detect your origins even before you open your mouth!

But did not most men seek to improve themselves, given

opportunity? But had he been over ambitious, and foolish enough to show it?

The thing lying at the back of his mind, troubling him all the time, was why he had not been back to see Beth in eight years. She seemed the only family he had, and yet he had virtually ignored her. Why?

Runcorn was staring at him.

'Well?' he demanded.

'Yes, sir.' He snapped to attention. 'I agree, sir. I think there may be something very unpleasant indeed. One has to hate very much to beat a man to death as Grey was beaten. I imagine if it is something to do with the family, they will do everything they can to hush it up. In fact the eldest son, the present Lord Shelburne, didn't seem very eager for me to probe it. He tried to guide me back to the idea that it was a casual thief, or a lunatic.'

'And Her Ladyship?'

'She wants us to continue.'

'Then she's fortunate, isn't she?' Runcorn nodded his head with his lips twisted. 'Because that is precisely what you are going to do!'

Monk recognized a dismissal.

'Yes, sir; I'll start with Yeats.' He excused himself and went to his own room.

Evan was sitting at the table, busy writing. He looked up with a quick smile when Monk came in. Monk found himself overwhelmingly glad to see him. He realized he had already begun to think of Evan as a friend as much as a colleague.

'How was Shelburne?' Evan asked.

'Very splendid,' he replied. 'And very formal. What about Mr Yeats?'

'Very respectable.' Evan's mouth twitched in a brief and suppressed amusement. 'And very ordinary. No one is saying anything to his discredit. In fact no one is saying anything much at all; they have trouble in recalling precisely who he is.'

Monk dismissed Yeats from his mind, and spoke of the thing which was more pressing to him.

'Runcorn seems to think it will become unpleasant, and he's expecting rather a lot from us—'

'Naturally.' Evan looked at him, his eyes perfectly clear. 'That's why he rushed you into it, even though you're hardly back from being ill. It's always sticky when we have to deal with the aristocracy; and let's face it, a policeman is usually treated pretty much as the social equal of a parlour maid and about as desirable to be close to as the drains; necessary in an imperfect society, but not fit to have in the withdrawing room.'

At another time Monk would have laughed, but now it was too painful, and too urgent.

'Why me?' he pressed.

Evan was frankly puzzled. He hid what looked like embarrassment with formality.

'Sir?'

'Why me?' Monk repeated a little more harshly. He could hear the rising pitch in his own voice, and could not govern it.

Evan lowered his eyes awkwardly.

122

'Do you want an honest answer to that, sir; although you must know it as well as I do?'

'Yes I do! Please?'

Evan faced him, his eyes hot and troubled. 'Because you are the best detective in the station, and the most ambitious. Because you know how to dress and to speak; you'll be equal to the Shelburnes, if anyone is.' He hesitated, biting his lip, then plunged on. 'And – and if you come unstuck either by making a mess of it and failing to find the murderer, or rubbing up against Her Ladyship and she complains about you, there are a good few who won't mind if you're demoted. And of course worse still, if it turns out to be one of the family – and you have to arrest him—'

Monk stared at him, but Evan did not look away. Monk felt the heat of shock ripple through him.

'Including Runcorn?' he said very quietly.

'I think so.'

'And you?'

Evan was transparently surprised. 'No, not me,' he said simply. He made no protestations, and Monk believed him.

'Good.' He drew a deep breath. 'Well, we'll go and see Mr Yeats tomorrow.'

'Yes, sir.' Evan was smiling, the shadow gone. 'I'll be here at eight.'

Monk winced inwardly at the time, but he had to agree. He said good-night and turned to go home.

But out in the street he started walking the other way, not consciously thinking until he realized he was moving in the general direction of St Marylebone Church. It was over two miles away, and he was tired. He had already walked a long way in Shelburne, and his legs were aching, his feet sore. He hailed a cab and when the driver asked him, he gave the address of the church.

It was very quiet inside with only the dimmest of light through the fast-greying windows. Candelabra shed little yellow arcs.

Why the church? He had all the peace and silence he needed in his own rooms, and he certainly had no conscious thought of God. He sat down in one of the pews.

Why had he come here? No matter how much he had dedicated himself to his job, his ambition, he must know someone, have a friend, or even an enemy. His life must have impinged on someone else's – besides Runcorn's.

He had been sitting in the dark without count of time, struggling to remember anything at all – a face, a name, even a feeling, something of childhood, like the momentary glimpse at Shelburne – when he saw the girl in black again, standing a few feet away.

He was startled. She seemed so vivid, familiar. Or was it only that she seemed to him to be lovely, evocative of something he wanted to feel, wanted to remember?

But she was not beautiful, not really. Her mouth was too big, her eyes too deep. She was looking at him.

Suddenly he was frightened. Ought he to know her? Was he being unbearably rude in not speaking? But he could know any number of people, of any walk of life! She could be a bishop's daughter, or a prostitute!

No, never with that face.

Don't be ridiculous, harlots could have faces with just that warmth, those luminous eyes; at least they could while they were still young, and nature had not yet written itself on the outside.

Without realizing it, he was still looking at her.

'Good evening, Mr Monk,' she said slowly, a faint embarrassment making her blink.

He rose to his feet. 'Good evening, ma'am.' He had no idea of her name, and now he was terrified, wishing he had never come. What should he say? How well did she know him? He could feel the sweat prickly on his body, his tongue dry, his thoughts in a stultified, wordless mass.

'You have not spoken for such a long time,' she went on. 'I had begun to fear you had discovered something you did not dare to tell me.'

Discovered! Was she connected with some case? It must be old; he had been working on Joscelin Grey since he came back, and before that the accident. He fished for something that would not commit him and yet still make sense.

'No, I'm afraid I haven't discovered anything else.' His voice was dry, artificial to his own ears. Please God he did not sound so foolish to her!

'Oh.' She looked down. It seemed for a moment as if she could not think of anything else to say, then she lifted her head again and met his eyes very squarely. He could only think how dark they were − not brown, but a multitude of shadows. 'You may tell me the truth, Mr Monk, whatever it is. Even if he killed himself, and for whatever reason, I would rather know.'

'It is the truth,' he said simply. 'I had an accident about seven weeks ago. I was in a cab that overturned and I broke my arm and ribs and cracked my head. I can't even remember it. I was in hospital for nearly a month, and then went north to my sister's to regain my strength. I'm afraid I haven't done anything about it since then.'

'Oh dear.' Her face was tight with concern. 'I am sorry. Are you all right now? Are you sure you are better?'

She sounded as if it mattered to her. He found himself warmed ridiculously by it. He forced from his mind the idea that she was merely compassionate, or well mannered.

'Yes, yes thank you; although there are blanks in my memory.' Why had he told her that? To explain his behaviour – in case it hurt her? He was taking too much upon himself. Why should she care, more than courtesy required? He remembered Sunday now; she had worn black then too, but expensive black, silk and fashionable. The man accompanying her had been dressed as Monk could not afford to be. Her husband? The thought was acutely depressing, even painful. He did not even think of the other woman.

'Oh.' Again she was lost for words.

He was fumbling, trying to find a clue, sharply conscious of her presence; even faintly, although she was several feet away, of her perfume. Or was it imagination?

'What was the last thing I told you?' he asked. 'I mean—' He did not know what he meant.

But she answered with only the merest hesitation.

'Not a great deal. You said Papa had certainly discovered

that the business was fraudulent but you did not know yet whether he had faced the other partners with it or not. You had seen someone, although you did not name him, but a certain Mr Robinson disappeared every time you went after him.' Her face tightened. 'You did not know whether Papa could have been murdered by them, to keep his silence, or if he took his own life, for shame. Perhaps I was wrong to ask you to discover. It just seemed so dreadful that he should choose that way rather than fight them, show them for what they are. It's no crime to be deceived!' There was a spark of anger in her now, as though she were fighting to keep control of herself. 'I wanted to believe he would have stayed alive, and fought them, faced his friends, even those who lost money, rather than—' She stopped, otherwise she would have wept. She stood quite still, swallowing hard.

'I'm sorry,' he said very quietly. He wanted to touch her, but he was hurtfully aware of the difference between them. It would be a familiarity and would break the moment's trust, the illusion of closeness.

She waited a moment longer, as if for something which did not come; then she abandoned it.

'Thank you. I am sure you have done everything you could. Perhaps I saw what I wished to see.'

There was a movement up the aisle, towards the door of the church, and the vicar came down, looking vague, and behind him the same woman with the highly individual face whom Monk had seen on the first occasion in the church. She also was dressed in dark, plain clothes, and her thick hair with a very slight wave was pulled back in a manner that owed more to expediency than fashion.

'Mrs Latterly, is that you?' the vicar asked uncertainly, peering forward. 'Why, my dear, what are you doing here all by yourself? You mustn't brood, you know. Oh!' He saw Monk. 'I beg your pardon. I did not realize you had company.'

'This is Mr Monk,' she said, explaining him. 'From the police. He was kind enough to help us when Papa . . . died.'

The vicar looked at Monk with disapproval.

'Indeed. I do think, my dear child, that it would be wiser for all of us if you were to let the matter rest. Observe mourning, of course, but let your poor father-in-law rest in peace.' He crossed the air absently. 'Yes – in peace.'

Monk stood up. Mrs Latterly; so she was married – or a widow? He was being absurd.

'If I learn anything more, Mrs Latterly' – his voice was tight, almost choking – 'do you wish me to inform you?' He did not want to lose her, to have her disappear into the past with everything else. He might not discover anything, but he must know where she was, have a reason to see her.

She looked at him for a long moment, undecided, fighting with herself. Then she spoke carefully.

'Yes please, if you will be so kind, but please remember your promise! Good night.' She swivelled around, her skirts brushing Monk's feet. 'Good night, Vicar. Come, Hester, it is time we returned home; Charles will be expecting us for dinner.' And she walked slowly up towards the door. Monk watched her go arm in arm with the other woman as if she had taken the light away with her.

*　*　*

Outside in the sharper evening air Hester Latterly turned to her sister-in-law.

'I think it is past time you explained yourself, Imogen,' she said quietly, but with an edge of urgency in her voice. 'Just who is that man?'

'He is with the police,' Imogen replied, walking briskly towards their carriage, which was waiting at the kerbside. The coachman climbed down, opened the door and handed them in, Imogen first, then Hester. Both took his courtesy for granted and Hester arranged her skirts merely sufficiently to be comfortable, Imogen to avoid crushing the fabric.

'What do you mean, "with"?' Hester demanded as the carriage moved forward. 'One does not accompany the police; you make it sound like a social event! "Miss Smith is with Mr Jones this evening".'

'Don't be pedantic,' Imogen criticized. 'Actually you can say it of a maid as well – "Tilly is with the Robinsons at present"!'

Hester's eyebrows shot up. 'Indeed! And is that man presently playing footman to the police?'

Imogen remained silent.

'I'm sorry,' Hester said at length. 'But I know there is something distressing you, and I feel so helpless because I don't know what it is.'

Imogen put out her hand and held Hester's tightly.

'Nothing,' she said in a voice so low it could only just be heard above the rattle of the carriage and the dull thud of hooves and the noises of the street. 'It is only Papa's death, and all that followed. None of us are over the shock of it yet, and I do appreciate your leaving everything and coming home as you did.'

'I never thought of doing less,' Hester said honestly, although her work in the Crimean hospitals had changed her beyond anything Imogen or Charles could begin to understand. It had been a hard duty to leave the nursing service and the white-hot spirit to improve, reform and heal that had moved not only Miss Nightingale but so many other women as well. But the death of first her father, then within a few short weeks her mother also, had made it an undeniable duty that she should return home and be there to mourn, and to assist her brother and his wife in all the affairs that there were to be attended to. Naturally Charles had seen to all the business and the finances, but there had been the house to close up, servants to dismiss, endless letters to write, clothes to dispose of to the poor, bequests of a personal nature to be remembered, and the endless social façade to be kept up. It would have been desperately unfair to expect Imogen to bear the burden and that responsibility alone. Hester had given no second thought as to whether she should come, simply excused herself, packed her few belongings and embarked.

It had been an extraordinary contrast after the desperate years in the Crimea with the unspeakable suffering she had seen, the agony of wounds, bodies torn by shot and sword; and to her even more harrowing, those wasted by disease, the racking pain and nausea of cholera, typhus and dysentery, the cold and the starvation; and, driving her almost beyond herself with fury, the staggering incompetence.

She, like the other handful of women, had worked herself

close to exhaustion, cleaning up human waste where there were no sanitary facilities, excrement from the helpless running on the floor and dripping through to the packed and wretched huddled in the cellars below. She had nursed men delirious with fever, gangrenous from amputations of limbs lost to everything from musket shot, cannon shot, sword thrust, even frostbite on the exposed and fearful bivouacs of the winter encampments where men and horses had perished by the thousands. She had delivered babies of the hungry and neglected army wives, buried many of them, then comforted the bereaved.

And when she could bear the pity no longer she had expended her last energy in fury, fighting the endless, idiotic inadequacy of the command, who seemed to her not to have the faintest grasp of ordinary sense, let alone management ability.

She had lost a brother, and many friends, chief among them Alan Russell, a brilliant war correspondent who had written home to the newspapers some of the unpalatable truths about one of the bravest and foolhardiest campaigns ever fought. He had shared many of them with her, allowing her to read them before they were posted.

Indeed in the weakness of fever he had dictated his last letter to her and she had sent it. When he died in the hospital at Scutari she had in a rash moment of deep emotion written a dispatch herself, and signed his name to it as if he were still alive.

It had been accepted and printed. From knowledge gleaned from other injured and feverish men she had learned their accounts of battle, siege and trench warfare, crazy charges and long weeks of boredom, and other dispatches had followed, all with Alan's name on them. In the general confusion no one realized.

Now she was home in the orderly, dignified, very sober grief of her brother's household mourning both her parents, wearing black as if this were the only loss and there were nothing else to do but conduct a gentle life of embroidery, letter writing and discreet good works with local charities. And of course obey Charles's continuous and rather pompous orders as to what must be done, and how, and when. It was almost beyond bearing. It was as if she were in suspended animation. She had grown used to having authority, making decisions and being in the heart of emotion, even if overtired, bitterly frustrated, full of anger and pity, desperately needed.

Now Charles was driven frantic because he could not understand her or comprehend the change in her from the brooding, intellectual girl he knew before, nor could he foresee any respectable man offering for her in marriage. He found the thought of having her living under his roof for the rest of her life well nigh insufferable.

The prospect did not please Hester either, but then she had no intention of allowing it to come to pass. As long as Imogen needed her she would remain, then she would consider her future and its possibilities.

However, as she sat in the carriage beside Imogen while they rattled through the dusk streets she had a powerful conviction that there was much troubling her sister-in-law and it was something that, for whatever reasons, Imogen was keeping secret, telling neither Charles nor Hester, and bearing the weight of it alone. It was more than grief, it was something that lay not only in the past but in the future also.

Chapter Five

Monk and Evan saw Grimwade only briefly, then went straight up to visit Yeats. It was a little after eight in the morning and they hoped to catch him at breakfast, or possibly even before.

Yeats opened the door himself; he was a small man of about forty, a trifle plump, with a mild face and thinning hair which fell forward over his brow. He was startled and there was still a piece of toast and marmalade in his hand. He stared at Monk with some alarm.

'Good morning, Mr Yeats,' Monk said firmly. 'We are from the police; we would like to speak to you about the murder of Major Joscelin Grey. May we come in please?' He did not step forward, but his height seemed to press over Yeats and vaguely threaten him, and he used it deliberately.

'Y-yes, y-yes of course,' Yeats stuttered, backing away, still clutching the toast. 'But I assure you I d-don't know anything I haven't already t-told you. Not you – at least – a Mr Lamb who was – a—'

'Yes I know.' Monk followed him in. He knew he was being oppressive, but he could not afford to be gentle. Yeats must have seen the murderer face-to-face, possibly even been in collusion with him, willingly or unwillingly. 'But we have learned quite a few new facts,' he went on, 'since Mr Lamb was taken ill and I have been put on the case.'

'Oh?' Yeats dropped the toast and bent to pick it up, ignoring the preserve on the carpet. It was a smaller room than Joscelin Grey's and overpoweringly furnished in heavy oak covered in photographs and embroidered linen. There were antimacassars on both the chairs.

'Have you—' Yeats said nervously. 'Have you? I still don't think I can – er – could—'

'Perhaps if you were to allow a few questions, Mr Yeats.' Monk did not want him so frightened as to be incapable of thought or memory.

'Well – if you think so. Yes – yes, if . . .' He backed away and sat down sharply on the chair closest to the table.

Monk sat also and was conscious of Evan behind him doing the same on a ladder-back chair by the wall. He wondered fleetingly what Evan was thinking, if he found him harsh, overconscious of his own ambition, his need to succeed. Yeats could so easily be no more than he seemed, a frightened little man whom mischance had placed at the pivot of a murder.

Monk began quietly, thinking with an instant's self-mockery that he might be moderating his tone not to reassure Yeats but to earn Evan's approval. What had led him to such isolation that Evan's opinion mattered so much to him? Had he been too absorbed in learning, climbing, polishing himself, to afford friendship, much less love? Indeed, had anything at all engaged his higher emotions?

Yeats was watching him like a rabbit seeing a stoat, and too horrified to move.

'You yourself had a visitor that night,' Monk told him quite gently. 'Who was he?'

'I don't know!' Yeats's voice was high, almost a squeak. 'I don't know who he was! I told Mr Lamb that! He came here by mistake; he didn't even really want me!'

Monk found himself holding up his hand, trying to calm him as one would with an overexcited child, or an animal.

'But you saw him, Mr Yeats.' He kept his voice low. 'No doubt you have some memory of his appearance, perhaps his voice? He must have spoken to you?' Whether Yeats was lying or not, he would achieve nothing by attacking his statement now; Yeats would only entrench himself more and more deeply into his ignorance.

Yeats blinked.

'I – I really can hardly say, Mr— Mr—'

'Monk – I'm sorry,' he said, apologizing for not having introduced himself. 'And my colleague is Mr Evan. Was he a large man, or small?'

'Oh, large, very large,' Yeats said instantly. 'Big as you are, and looked heavy; of course he had a thick coat on, it was a very bad night – wet – terribly.'

'Yes, yes I remember. Was he taller than I am, do you think?' Monk stood up helpfully.

Yeats stared up at him. 'No, no, I don't think so. About the same, as well as I can recall. But it was some time ago now.' He shook his head unhappily.

Monk seated himself again, aware of Evan discreetly taking notes.

'He really was here only a moment or two,' Yeats protested, still holding the toast, now beginning to break and drop crumbs on his trousers. 'He just saw me, asked a question as to my business, then realized I was not the person he sought, and left again. That is really all there was.' He brushed ineffectively at his trousers. 'You must believe me, if I could help, I would. Poor Major Grey, such an appalling death.' He shivered. 'Such a charming young man. Life plays some dreadful tricks, does it not?'

Monk felt a quick flicker of excitement inside himself.

'You knew Major Grey?' He kept his voice almost casual.

'Oh, not very well, no, no!' Yeats protested, shunning any thought of social arrogance – or involvement. 'Only to pass the time of day, you understand? But he was very civil, always had a pleasant word, not like some of these young men of fashion. And he didn't affect to have forgotten one's name.'

'And what is your business, Mr Yeats? I don't think you said.'

'Oh, perhaps not.' The toast shed more pieces in his hand, but now he was oblivious to it. 'I deal in rare stamps and coins.'

'And this visitor, was he also a dealer?'

Yeats looked surprised.

'He did not say, but I should imagine not. It is a small business, you know; one gets to meet most of those who are interested, at one time or another.'

138

'He was English then?'

'I beg your pardon?'

'He was not a foreigner, whom you would not expect to have known, even had he been in the business?'

'Oh, I see.' Yeats's brow cleared. 'Yes, yes he was English.'

'And who was he looking for, if not for you, Mr Yeats?'

'I – I – really cannot say.' He waved his hand in the air. 'He asked if I were a collector of maps; I told him I was not. He said he had been misinformed, and he left immediately.'

'I think not, Mr Yeats. I think he then went on to call on Major Grey, and within the next three quarters of an hour, beat him to death.'

'Oh my dear God!' Yeats's bones buckled inside him and he slid backwards and down into his chair. Behind Monk, Evan moved as if to help, then changed his mind and sat down again.

'That surprises you?' Monk inquired.

Yeats was gasping, beyond speech.

'Are you sure this man was not known to you?' Monk persisted, giving him no time to regather his thoughts. This was the time to press.

'Yes, yes I am. Quite unknown.' He covered his face with his hands. 'Oh my dear heaven!'

Monk stared at Yeats. The man was useless now, either reduced to abject horror, or else very skilfully affecting to be. He turned and looked at Evan. Evan's face was stiff with embarrassment, possibly for their presence and their part in

the man's wretchedness, possibly merely at being witness to
it.

Monk stood up and heard his own voice far away. He
knew he was risking a mistake, and that he was doing it
because of Evan.

'Thank you, Mr Yeats. I'm sorry for distressing you. Just
one more thing: was this man carrying a stick?'

Yeats looked up, his face sickly pale; his voice was no
more than a whisper.

'Yes, quite a handsome one; I noticed it.'

'Heavy or light?'

'Oh, heavy, quite heavy. Oh no!' He shut his eyes,
screwing them up to hide even his imagination.

'There is no need for you to be frightened, Mr Yeats,'
Evan said from behind. 'We believe he was someone who
knew Major Grey personally, not a chance lunatic. There is
no reason to suppose he would have harmed you. I daresay
he was looking for Major Grey in the first place and found
the wrong door.'

It was not until they were outside that Monk realized
Evan must have said it purely to comfort the little man. It
could not have been true. The visitor had asked for Yeats by
name. He looked sideways at Evan, now walking silently
beside him in the drizzling rain. He made no remark on it.

Grimwade had proved no further help. He had not seen
the man come down after leaving Yeats's door, nor seen him
go to Joscelin Grey's. He had taken the opportunity to attend
the call of nature, and then had seen the man leave at a
quarter past ten, three quarters of an hour later.

'There's only one conclusion,' Evan said unhappily, striding along with his head down. 'He must have left Yeats's door and gone straight along the hallway to Grey, spent half an hour or so with him, then killed him, and left when Grimwade saw him go.'

'Which doesn't tell us who he was,' Monk said, stepping across a puddle and passing a cripple selling bootlaces. A rag and bone cart trundled by, its driver calling out almost unintelligibly in a singsong voice. 'I keep coming back to the one thing,' Monk resumed. 'Why did anyone hate Joscelin Grey so much? There was a passion of hate in that room. Someone hated him so uncontrollably he couldn't stop beating him even after he was dead.'

Evan shivered and the rain ran off his nose and chin. He pulled his collar up closer around his ears and his face was pale.

'Mr Runcorn was right,' he said miserably. 'It's going to be extremely nasty. You have to know someone very well to hate them as much as that.'

'Or have been mortally wronged,' Monk added. 'But you're probably right; it'll be in the family, these things usually are. Either that, or a lover somewhere.'

Evan looked shocked. 'You mean Grey was —'

'No.' Monk smiled with a sharp downward twist. 'That wasn't what I meant, although I suppose it's possible; in fact it's distinctly possible. But I was thinking of a woman, with a husband perhaps.'

Evan's face relaxed a fraction.

'I suppose it's too violent for a simple debt, gambling or

141

something?' he said without much hope.

Monk thought for a moment.

'Could be blackmail,' he suggested with genuine belief. The idea had only just occurred to him seriously, but he liked it.

Evan frowned. They were walking south along Gray's Inn Road.

'Do you think so?' He looked sideways at Monk. 'Doesn't ring right to me. And we haven't found any unaccounted income yet. Of course, we haven't really looked. And blackmail victims can be driven to a very deep hatred indeed, for which I cannot entirely blame them. When a man has been tormented, stripped of all he has, and then is still threatened with ruin, there comes a point when reason breaks.'

'We'll have to check on the social company he kept,' Monk replied. 'Who might have made mistakes damaging enough to be blackmailed over, to the degree that ended in murder.'

'Perhaps if he was homosexual?' Evan suggested it with returning distaste, and Monk knew he did not believe his own word. 'He might have had a lover who would pay to keep him quiet – and if pushed too far, kill him?'

'Very nasty.' Monk stared at the wet pavement. 'Runcorn was right.' And thought of Runcorn set his mind on a different track.

He sent Evan to question all the local tradesmen, people at the club Grey had been at the evening he was killed, anything to learn about his associates.

* * *

Evan began at the wine merchant's whose name they had
found on a bill head in Grey's flat. He was a fat man with a
drooping moustache and an unctuous manner. He expressed
desolation over the loss of Major Grey. What a terrible misfortune. What an ironic stroke of fate that such a fine officer
should survive the war, only to be struck down by a madman
in his own home. What a tragedy. He did not know what to
say – and he said it at considerable length while Evan
struggled to get a word in and ask some useful questions.

When at last he did, the answer was what he had guessed
it would be. Major Grey – the Honourable Joscelin Grey –
was a most valued customer. He had excellent taste – but
what else would you expect from such a gentleman? He
knew French wine, and he knew German wine. He liked the
best. He was provided with it from this establishment. His
accounts? No, not always up to date – but paid in due
course. The nobility were that way with money – one had to
learn to accommodate it. He could add nothing – but
nothing at all. Was Mr Evan interested in wine? He could
recommend an excellent Bordeaux.

No, Mr Evan, reluctantly, was not interested in wine; he
was a country parson's son, well educated in the gentilities
of life, but with a pocket too short to indulge in more than
the necessities, and a few good clothes, which would stand
him in better stead than even the best of wines. None of
which he explained to the merchant.

Next he tried the local eating establishments, beginning
with the chophouse and working down to the public alehouse,

which also served an excellent stew with spotted dick pudding, full of currants, as Evan could attest.

'Major Grey?' the landlord said ruminatively. 'You mean 'im as was murdered? 'Course I knowed 'im. Come in 'ere reg'lar, 'e did.'

Evan did not know whether to believe him or not. It could well be true; the food was cheap and filling and the atmosphere not unpleasant to a man who had served in the army, two years of it in the battlefields of the Crimea. On the other hand it could be a boost to his business – already healthy – to say that a famous victim of murder had dined there. There was a grisly curiosity in many people that would give the place an added interest to them.

'What did he look like?' Evan asked.

''Ere!' The landlord looked at him suspiciously. 'You on the case – or not, then? Doncher know?'

'I never met him alive,' Evan replied reasonably. 'It makes a lot of difference, you know.'

The landlord sucked his teeth. ''Course it do – sorry, guv, a daft question. 'E were tall, an' not far from your build, kind o' slight – but 'e were real natty wiv it! Looked like a gennelman, even afore 'e opened 'is mouf. Yer can tell. Fair 'air, 'e 'ad; an' a smile as was summat lov'ly.'

'Charming,' Evan said, more as an observation than a question.

'Not 'alf,' the landlord agreed.

'Popular?' Evan pursued.

'Yeah. Used ter tell a lot o' stories. People like that – passes the time.'

'Generous?' Evan asked.

'Gen'rous?' The landlord's eyebrows rose. 'No – not gen'rous. More like 'e took more'n 'e gave. Reckon as 'e din't 'ave that much. An' folk liked ter treat 'im – like I said, 'e were right entertainin'. Flash sometimes. Come in 'ere of an occasion an' treat everyone 'andsome – but not often, like – mebbe once a monf.'

'Regularly?'

'Wotcher mean?'

'At a set time in the month?'

'Oh no – could be any time, twice a monf, or not fer two monfs.'

Gambler, Evan thought to himself. 'Thank you,' he said aloud. 'Thank you very much.' And he finished the cider and placed sixpence on the table and left, going out reluctantly into the fading drizzle.

He spent the rest of the afternoon going to bootmakers, hatters, shirtmakers and tailors, from whom he learned precisely what he expected – nothing that his common sense had not already told him.

He bought a fresh eel pie from a vendor on Guilford Street outside the Foundling Hospital, then took a hansom all the way to St James's, and got out at Boodles, where Joscelin Grey had been a member.

Here his questions had to be a lot more discreet. It was one of the foremost gentlemen's clubs in London, and servants did not gossip about members if they wished to retain their very agreeable and lucrative positions. All he acquired in an hour and a half of roundabout questions was confirmation that Major Grey was indeed a member, that he came quite regularly when he was in town, that of course, like other gentlemen, he gambled, and it was possible his debts were settled over a period of time, but most assuredly they were settled. No gentleman welshed on his debts of honour – tradesmen possibly, but never other gentlemen. Such a question did not arise.

Might Mr Evan speak with any of Major Grey's associates?

Unless Mr Evan had a warrant such a thing was out of the question. Did Mr Evan have such a warrant?

No Mr Evan did not.

He returned a little wiser, but with several thoughts running through his head.

When Evan had gone, Monk walked briskly back to the police station and went to his own room. He pulled out the records of all his old cases, and read. It gave him little cause for comfort.

If his fears for this case proved to be real – a society scandal, sexual perversion, blackmail and murder – then his own path as detective in charge lay between the perils of a very conspicuous and well-publicized failure and the even more dangerous task of probing to uncover the tragedies that had precipitated the final explosion. And a man who would beat to death a lover, turned blackmailer, to keep his secret, would hardly hesitate to ruin a mere policeman. 'Nasty' was an understatement.

Had Runcorn done this on purpose? As he looked through

the record of his own career, one success after another, he wondered what the price had been; who else had paid it, apart from himself? He had obviously devoted everything to work, to improving his skill, his knowledge, his manners, his dress and his speech. Looking at it as a stranger might, his ambition was painfully obvious: the long hours, the meticulous attention to detail, the flashes of sheer intuitive brilliance, the judgement of other men and their abilities – and weaknesses, always using the right man for any task, then when it was completed, choosing another. His only loyalty seemed to be the pursuit of justice. Could he have imagined it had all gone unnoticed by Runcorn, who lay in its path?

His rise from country boy from a Northumbrian fishing village to inspector in the Metropolitan Police had been little short of meteoric. In twelve years he had achieved more than most men in twenty. He was treading hard on Runcorn's heels; at this present rate of progress he could shortly hope for another promotion, to Runcorn's place – or better.

Perhaps it all depended on the Grey case?

He could not have risen so far, and so fast, without treading on a good many people as he passed. There was a growing fear in him that he might not even have cared. He had read through the cases, very briefly. He had made a god of truth, and – where the law was equivocal, or silent – of what he had believed to be justice. But if there was anything of compassion and genuine feeling for the victims, he had so far failed to find it. His anger was impersonal: against the forces of society that produced poverty and bred helplessness and crime; against the monstrosity of the rookery slums, the sweatshops, extortion, violence, prostitution and infant mortality.

He admired the man he saw reflected in the records, admired his skill and his brain, his energy and tenacity, even his courage; but he could not like him. There was no warmth, no vulnerability, nothing of human hopes or fears, none of the idiosyncrasies that betray the dreams of the heart. The nearest he saw to passion was the ruthlessness with which he pursued injustice; but from the bare written words, it seemed to him that it was the wrong itself he hated, and the wronged were not people but the by-products of the crime.

Why was Evan so keen to work with him? To learn? He felt a quick stab of shame at the thought of what he might teach him; and he did not want Evan turned into a copy of himself. People change, all the time; every day one is a little different from yesterday, a little added, a little forgotten. Could he learn something of Evan's feeling instead and teach him excellence without his accompanying ambition?

It was easy to believe Runcorn's feelings for him were ambivalent, at best. What had he done to him, over the years of climbing; what comparisons presented to superiors? What small slights made without sensitivity – had he ever even thought of Runcorn as a man rather than an obstacle between him and the next step up the ladder?

He could hardly blame Runcorn if now he took this perfect opportunity to present him with a case he had to lose; either in failure to solve, or in too much solving, and the uncovering of scandals for which society, and therefore the commissioner of police, would never excuse him.

Monk stared at the paper files. The man in them was a stranger to him, as one-dimensional as Joscelin Grey; in fact more so, because he had spoken to people who cared for Grey, had found charm in him, with whom he had shared laughter and common memories, who missed him with a hollowness of pain.

His own memories were gone, even of Beth, except for the one brief snatch of childhood that had flickered for a moment at Shelburne. But surely more would return, if he did not try to force them and simply let them come?

And the woman in the church, Mrs Latterly; why had he not remembered her? He had only seen her twice since the accident, and yet her face seemed always at the back of his mind with a sweetness that never quite let him go. Had he spent much time on the case, perhaps questioned her often? It would be ridiculous to have imagined anything personal – the gulf between them was impassable, and if he had entertained ideas, then his ambition was indeed overweening, and indefensible. He blushed hot at the imagination of what he might have betrayed to her in his speech, or his manner. And the vicar had addressed her as 'Mrs' – was she wearing black for her father-in-law, or was she a widow? When he saw her again he must correct it, make it plain he dreamed no such effrontery.

But before then he had to discover what on earth the case was about, beyond that her father-in-law had died recently.

He searched all his papers, all the files and everything in his desk, and found nothing with the name Latterly on it. A wretched thought occurred to him, and now an obvious one – the case had been handed on to someone else. Of course it would be, when he had been ill. Runcorn would hardly abandon it, especially if there really was a question of suspicious death involved.

Then why had the new person in charge not spoken to Mrs Latterly – or more likely her husband, if he were alive? Perhaps he was not. Maybe that was the reason it was she who had asked? He put the files away and went to Runcorn's office. He was startled in passing an outside window to notice that it was now nearly dusk.

Runcorn was still in his office, but on the point of leaving. He did not seem in the least surprise to see Monk.

'Back to your usual hours again?' he said dryly. 'No wonder you never married; you've taken a job to wife. Well, cold comfort it'll get you on a winter night,' he added with satisfaction. 'What is it?'

'Latterly.' Monk was irritated by the reminder of what he could now see of himself. Before the accident it must have been there, all his characteristics, habits, but then he was too close to see them. Now he observed them dispassionately, as if they belonged to someone else.

'What?' Runcorn was staring at him, his brow furrowed into lines of incomprehension, his nervous gesture of the left eye more pronounced.

'Latterly,' Monk repeated. 'I presume you gave the case to someone else when I was ill?'

'Never heard of it,' Runcorn said sharply.

'I was working on the case of a man called Latterly. He

either committed suicide, or was murdered—'

Runcorn stood up and went to the coat stand and took his serviceable, unimaginative coat off the hook.

'Oh, that case. You said it was suicide and closed it, weeks before the accident. What's the matter with you? Are you losing your memory?'

'No I am not losing my memory!' Monk snapped, feeling a tide of heat rising up inside him. Please heaven it did not show in his face. 'But the papers are gone from my files. I presumed something must have occurred to reopen the case and you had given it to someone.'

'Oh.' Runcorn scowled, proceeding to put on his coat and gloves. 'Well, nothing has occurred, and the file is closed. I haven't given it to anyone else. Perhaps you didn't write up anything more? Now will you forget about Latterly, who presumably killed himself, poor devil, and get back to Grey, who most assuredly did not. Have you got anything further? Come on, Monk – you're usually better than this! Anything from this fellow Yeats?'

'No, sir, nothing helpful.' Monk was stung and his voice betrayed it.

Runcorn turned from the hat stand and smiled fully at him, his eyes bright.

'Then you'd better abandon that and step up your inquiries into Grey's family and friends, hadn't you?' he said with ill-concealed satisfaction. 'Especially women friends. There may be a jealous husband somewhere. Looks like that kind of hatred to me. Take my word, there's something very nasty at the bottom of this.' He tilted his hat slightly on his head, but it simply looked askew rather than rakish. 'And you, Monk, are just the man to uncover it. You'd better go and try Shelburne again!' And with that parting shot, ringing with jubilation, he swung his scarf around his neck and went out.

Monk did not go to Shelburne the next day, or even that week. He knew he would have to, but he intended when he went to be as well armed as possible, both for the best chance of success in discovering the murderer of Joscelin Grey, whom he wanted with an intense and driving sense of justice, and – fast becoming almost as important – to avoid all he could of offence in probing the very private lives of the Shelburnes, or whoever else might have been aroused to such a rage, over whatever jealousies, passions or perversions. Monk knew that the powerful were no less frail than the rest of men, but they were usually far fiercer in covering those frailties from the mockery and the delight of the vulgar. It was not a matter of memory so much as instinct, the same way he knew how to shave, or to tie his cravat.

Instead he set out with Evan the following morning to go back to Mecklenburgh Square, this time not to find traces of an intruder but to learn anything he could about Grey himself. Although they walked with scant conversation, each deep in his own thought, he was glad not to be alone. Grey's flat oppressed him and he could never free his mind from the violence that had happened there. It was not the blood, or even the death that clung to him, but the hate. He must have seen death before, dozens, if not scores of times, and he could not possibly have been troubled by it like this each time. It must usually have been casual death, pathetic or brainless murder, the utter selfishness of the mugger who wants and takes, or murder by the thief who finds his escape blocked. But in the death of Grey there was a quite different passion, something intimate, a bond of hatred between the killer and the killed.

He was cold in the room, even though the rest of the building was warm. The light through the high windows was colourless as if it would drain rather than illuminate. The furniture seemed oppressive and shabby, too big for the place, although in truth it was exactly like any other. He looked at Evan to see if he felt it also, but Evan's sensitive face was puckered over with the distaste of searching another man's letters, as he opened the desk and began to go through the drawers.

Monk walked past him into the bedroom, a little stale smelling from closed windows. There was a faint film of dust, as last time. He searched cupboards and clothes drawers, dressers, the tallboy. Grey had an excellent wardrobe; not very extensive, but a beautiful cut and quality. He had certainly possessed good taste, if not the purse to indulge it to the full. There were several sets of cuff links, all gold backed, one with his family crest engraved, two with his own initials. There were three stickpins, one with a fair-sized pearl, and a set of silver-backed brushes, a pigskin toilet kit. Certainly no burglar had come this far. There were many fine pocket handkerchiefs, monogrammed, silk and linen shirts, cravats, socks, clean underwear. He was surprised and somewhat disconcerted to find he knew to within a few shillings the price one would pay for each article, and wondered what aspirations had led him to such knowledge.

He had hoped to find letters in the top drawers, perhaps those too personal to mix with bills and casual correspondence in the desk, but there was nothing, and eventually he went back to the main room. Evan was still at the desk, standing motionless. The place was totally silent, as though both of them were aware that it was a dead man's room, and felt intrusive.

Far down in the street there was a rumble of wheels, the sharper sound of hooves, and a street seller's cry which sounded like 'Ole clo' – ole clo'!'

'Well?' He found his voice sunk to a near whisper.

Evan looked up, startled. His face was tight.

'Rather a lot of letters here, sir. I'm not sure really what to make of them. There are several from his sister-in-law, Rosamond Shelburne; a rather sharp one from his brother Lovel – that's Lord Shelburne, isn't it? A very recent note from his mother, but only one, so it looks as if he didn't keep hers. There are several from a Dawlish family, just prior to his death; among them an invitation to stay at their home for a week. They seem to have been friendly.' He puckered his mouth slightly. 'One is from Miss Amanda Dawlish, sounds quite eager. In fact there are a number of invitations, all for dates after his death. Apparently he didn't keep old ones. And I'm afraid there's no diary. Funny.' He looked up at Monk. 'You'd think a man like that would have a social diary, wouldn't you?'

'Yes you would!' Monk moved forward. 'Perhaps the murderer took it. You're quite sure?'

'Not in the desk.' Evan shook his head. 'And I've checked for hidden drawers. But why would anyone hide a social diary anyway?'

'No idea,' Monk said honestly, taking a step nearer to the desk and peering at it. 'Unless it was the murderer who took it. Perhaps his name figures heavily. We'll have to try these Dawlishes. Is there an address on the letters?'

'Oh yes, I've made a note of it.'

'Good. What else?'

'Several bills. He wasn't very prompt in paying up, but I knew that already from talking to the tradesmen. Three from his tailor, four or five from a shirtmaker, the one I visited, two from the wine merchant, rather terse letter from the family solicitor in reply to a request for an increased allowance.'

'In the negative, I take it?'

'Very much so.'

'Anything from clubs, gambling and so on?'

'No, but then one doesn't usually commit gambling debts to paper, even at Boodles, unless you are the one who is collecting, of course.' Then he smiled suddenly. 'Not that I can afford to know – except by hearsay!'

Monk relaxed a little. 'Quite,' he agreed. 'Any other letters?'

'One pretty cool one from a Charles Latterly, doesn't say much—'

'Latterly?' Monk froze.

'Yes. You know him?' Evan was watching him.

Monk took a deep breath and controlled himself with an effort. Mrs Latterly at St Marylebone had said 'Charles', and he had feared it might have been her husband.

'I was working on a Latterly case some time ago,' he said, struggling to keep his voice level. 'It's probably coincidence. I was looking for the file on Latterly yesterday and I couldn't find it.'

'Was he someone who could have been connected with Grey, some scandal to hush up, or—'

'No!' He spoke more harshly than he had intended to, betraying his feelings. He moderated his tone. 'No, not at all. Poor man is dead anyway. Died before Grey did.'

'Oh.' Evan turned back to the desk. 'That's about all, I'm afraid. Still, we should be able to find a lot of people who knew him from these, and they'll lead us to more.'

'Yes, yes quite. I'll take Latterly's address, all the same.'

'Oh, right.' Evan fished among the letters and passed him one.

Monk read it. It was very cool, as Evan had said, but not impolite, and there was nothing in it to suggest positive dislike, only a relationship which was not now to be continued. Monk read it three times, but could see nothing further in it. He copied down the address, and returned the letter to Evan.

They finished searching the apartment, and then with careful notes went outside again, passing Grimwade in the hall.

'Lunch,' Monk said briskly, wanting to be among people,

hear laughter and speech and see men who knew nothing about murder and violent, obscene secrets, men engrossed in the trivial pleasures and irritations of daily life.

'Right.' Evan fell in step beside him. 'There's a good public house about half a mile from here where they serve the most excellent dumplings. That is—' he stopped suddenly. 'It's very ordinary – don't know if you—'

'Fine,' Monk agreed. 'Sounds just what we need. I'm frozen after being in that place. I don't know why, but it seems cold, even inside.'

Evan hunched his shoulders and smiled a little sheepishly. 'It might be imagination, but it always chills me. I'm not used to murder yet. I suppose you're above that kind of emotionalism, but I haven't got that far—'

'Don't!' Monk spoke more violently than he had meant to. 'Don't get used to it!' He was betraying his own rawness, his sudden sensitivity, but he did not care. 'I mean,' he said more softly, aware that he had startled Evan by his vehemence, 'keep your brain clear, by all means, but don't let it cease to shock you. Don't be a detective before you're a man.' Now that he had said it it sounded sententious and extremely trite. He was embarrassed.

Evan did not seem to notice.

'I've a long way to go before I'm efficient enough to do that, sir. I confess, even that room up there makes me feel a little sick. This is the first murder like this I've been on.' He sounded self-conscious and very young. 'Of course I've seen bodies before, but usually accidents, or paupers who died in the street. There are quite a few of them in the winter. That's why I'm so pleased to be on this case with you. I couldn't learn from anyone better.'

Monk felt himself colour with pleasure – and shame, because he did not deserve it. He could not think of anything at all to say, and he strode ahead through the thickening rain searching for words, and not finding them. Evan walked beside him, apparently not needing an answer.

The following Monday Monk and Evan got off the train at Shelburne and set out towards Shelburne Hall. It was one of the summer days when the wind is fresh from the east, sharp as a slap in the face, and the sky is clear and cloudless. The trees were huge green billows resting on the bosom of the earth, gently, increasingly moving, whispering. There had been rain overnight, and under the shadows the smell of damp earth was sweet where their feet disturbed it.

They walked in silence, each enjoying it in his own way. Monk was not aware of any particular thoughts, except perhaps a sense of pleasure in the sheer distance of the sky, the width across the fields. Suddenly memory flooded back vividly, and he saw Northumberland again: broad, bleak hills, north wind shivering in the grass. The milky sky was mackerel shredded out to sea, and white gulls floated on the currents, screaming.

He could remember his mother, dark like Beth, standing in the kitchen, and the smell of yeast and flour. She had been very young then. He remembered a room with sun in it, the vicar's wife teaching him letters, Beth in a smock staring at him in awe. She could not read. He could almost feel himself teaching her, years after, slowly, outline by outline. Her writing still carried echoes of those hours, careful, conscious of the skill and its long learning. She had loved him so much, admired him without question. Then the memory disappeared and it was as if someone had drenched him in cold water, leaving him startled and shivering. It was the most acute and powerful memory he had recaptured and its sharpness left him stunned. He did not notice Evan's eyes on him, or the quick glance away as he strove to avoid what he realized would be intrusion.

Shelburne Hall was in sight across the smooth earth, less than a thousand yards away, framed in trees.

'Do you want me to say anything, or just listen?' Evan asked. 'It might be better if I listened.'

Monk realized with a start that Evan was nervous. Perhaps he had never spoken to a woman of title before, much less questioned her on personal and painful matters. He might not even have seen such a place, except from the distance. He wondered where his own assurance came from, and why he had not ever thought of it before. Runcorn was right, he was ambitious, even arrogant – and insensitive.

'Perhaps if you try the servants,' he replied. 'Servants notice a lot of things. Sometimes they see a side of their masters that their lordships manage to hide from their equals.'

'I'll try the valet,' Evan suggested. 'I should imagine you are peculiarly vulnerable in the bath, or in your underwear.' He grinned suddenly at the thought, and perhaps in some amusement at the physical helplessness of his social superiors to need assistance in such common matters. It offset his own fear of proving inadequate to the situation.

Lady Fabia Shelburne was somewhat surprised to see Monk again, and kept him waiting nearly half an hour, this time in the butler's pantry with the silver polish, a locked desk for the wine book and the cellar keys, and a comfortable armchair by a small grate. Apparently the housekeeper's sitting room was already in use. He was annoyed at the casual insolence of it, and yet part of him was obliged to admire her self-control. She had no idea why he had come. He might even have been able to tell her who had murdered her son, and why.

When he was sent for and conducted to the rosewood sitting room, which seemed to be peculiarly hers, she was cool and gracious, as if he had only just arrived and she had no more than a courteous interest in what he might say.

At her invitation he sat down opposite her on the same deep rose-pink chair as before.

'Well, Mr Monk?' she inquired with slightly raised eyebrows. 'Is there something further you want to say to me?'

'Yes, ma'am, if you please. We are even more of the opinion that whoever killed Major Grey did so for some personal reason, and that he was not a chance victim. Therefore we need to know everything further we can about him, his social connections—'

Her eyes widened. 'If you imagine his social connections are of a type to indulge in murder, Mr Monk, then you are extraordinarily ignorant of society.'

'I am afraid, ma'am, that most people are capable of murder, if they are hard-pressed enough, and threatened in what they most value—'

'I think not.' Her voice indicated the close of the subject and she turned her head a little away from him.

'Let us hope they are rare, ma'am.' He controlled his impulse to anger with difficulty. 'But it would appear there is at least one, and I am sure you wish to find him, possibly even more than I do.'

'You are very slick with words, young man.' It was grudgingly given, even something of a criticism. 'What is it you imagine I can tell you?'

'A list of his closest friends,' he answered. 'Family friends, any invitations you may know of that he accepted in the last few months, especially for weeks or weekends away. Perhaps any lady in whom he may have been interested.' He saw a slight twitch of distaste cross her immaculate features. 'I believe he was extremely charming.' He added the flattery in which he felt was her only weakness.

'He was.' There was a small movement in her lips, a change in her eyes as for a moment grief overtook her. It was several seconds till she smoothed it out again and was as perfect as before.

Monk waited in silence, for the first time aware of the force of her pain.

'Then possibly some lady was more attracted to him than was acceptable to her other admirers, or even her husband?' he suggested at last, and in a considerably softer tone, although his resolve to find the murderer of Joscelin Grey

161

was if anything hardened even further, and it allowed of no exceptions, no omissions for hurt.

She considered this thought for a moment before deciding to accept it. He imagined she was seeing her son again as he had been in life, elegant, laughing, direct of gaze.

'It might have been,' she conceded. 'It could be that some young person was indiscreet, and provoked jealousy.'

'Perhaps someone who had a little too much to drink?' He pursued it with a tact that did not come to him naturally. 'And saw in it more than there was?'

'A gentleman knows how to conduct himself.' She looked at Monk with a slight turn downwards at the corners of her mouth. The word *gentleman* was not lost on him. 'Even when he has had too much to drink. But unfortunately some people are not as discriminating in their choice of guests as they should be.'

'If you would give me some names and addresses, ma'am; I shall conduct my inquiries as cautiously as I can, and naturally shall not mention your name. I imagine all persons of good conscience will be as keen to discover who murdered Major Grey as you are yourself.'

It was a well-placed argument, and she acknowledged it with a momentary glance directly into his eyes.

'Quite,' she agreed. 'If you have a notebook I shall oblige you.' She reached across to the rosewood table almost at her side and opened a drawer. She took out a leather-bound and gold-tooled address book.

He made ready and was well started when Lovel Grey came in, again dressed in casual clothes – this time breeches and a Norfolk jacket of well-worn tweed. His face darkened when he saw Monk.

'I really think, Mr Monk, that if you have something to report, you may do so to me!' he said with extreme irritation. 'If you have not, then your presence here serves no purpose, and you are distressing my mother. I am surprised you should come again.'

Monk stood up instinctively, annoyed with himself for the necessity.

'I came, my lord, because I needed some further information, which Lady Shelburne has been kind enough to give me.' He could feel the colour hot in his face.

'There is nothing we can tell you that could be of the least relevance,' Lovel snapped. 'For heaven's sake, man, can't you do your job without rushing out here every few days?' He moved restlessly, fidgeting with the crop in his hand. 'We cannot help you! If you are beaten, admit it! Some crimes are never solved, especially where madmen are concerned.'

Monk was trying to compose a civil reply when Lady Shelburne herself intervened in a small, tight voice.

'That may be so, Lovel, but not in this case. Joscelin was killed by someone who knew him, however distasteful that may be to us. Naturally it is also possible it was someone known here. It is far more discreet of Mr Monk to ask us than to go around inquiring of the whole neighbourhood.'

'Good God!' Lovel's face fell. 'You cannot be serious. To allow him to do that would be monstrous. We'd be ruined.'

'Nonsense!' She closed her address book with a snap and replaced it in the drawer. 'We do not ruin so easily. There have been Shelburnes on the land for five hundred years, and will continue to be. However I have no intention of allowing Mr Monk to do any such thing.' She looked at Monk coldly. 'That is why I am providing him with a list myself, and suitable questions to ask – and to avoid.'

'There is no need to do either.' Lovel turned furiously from his mother to Monk and back again, his colour high. 'Whoever killed Joscelin must have been one of his London acquaintances – if indeed it really was someone he knew at all, which I still doubt. In spite of what you say, I believe it was purely chance he was the victim, and not someone else. I daresay he was seen at a club, or some such place, by someone who saw he had money and hoped to rob him.'

'It was not robbery, sir,' Monk said firmly. 'There were all sorts of valuable items quite visible and untouched in his rooms, even the money in his wallet was still there.'

'And how do you know how much he had in his wallet?' Lovel demanded. 'He may have had hundreds!'

'Thieves do not usually count out change and return it to you,' Monk replied, moderating the natural sarcasm in his voice only slightly.

Lovel was too angry to stop. 'And have you some reason to suppose this was a "usual" thief? I did not know you had proceeded so far. In fact I did not know you had proceeded at all.'

'Most unusual, thank heaven.' Monk ignored the jibe. 'Thieves seldom kill. Did Major Grey often walk about with hundreds of pounds in his pocket?'

Lovel's face was scarlet. He threw the crop across the room, intending it to land on the sofa, but it fell beyond and rattled to the floor. He ignored it. 'No of course not!' he shouted. 'But then this was a unique occasion. He was not simply robbed and left lying, he was beaten to death, if you remember.'

Lady Fabia's face pinched with misery and disgust.

'Really, Lovel, the man is doing his best, for whatever that is worth. There is no need to be offensive.'

Suddenly his tone changed. 'You are upset, Mama; and it's quite natural that you should be. Please leave this to me. If I think there is anything to tell Mr Monk, I shall do so. Why don't you go into the withdrawing room and have tea with Rosamond?'

'Don't patronize me, Lovel!' she snapped, rising to her feet: 'I am not too upset to conduct myself properly, and to help the police find the man who murdered my son.'

'There is nothing whatsoever we can do, Mama!' He was fast losing his temper again. 'Least of all assist them to pester half the country for personal information about poor Joscelin's life and friends.'

'It was one of poor Joscelin's "friends" who beat him to death!' Her cheeks were ashen white and a lesser woman might well have fainted before now, but she stood ramrod stiff, her white hands clenched.

'Rubbish!' Lovel dismissed it instantly. 'It was probably someone he played at cards and who simply couldn't take losing. Joscelin gambled a damned sight more than he led you to believe. Some people play for stakes they can't afford, and then when they're beaten, they lose control of themselves and go temporarily off their heads.' He breathed in and out hard. 'Gaming clubs are not always as discriminating as they should be as to whom they allow in. That is quite probably what happened to Joscelin. Do you seriously imagine anyone at Shelburne would know anything about it?'

'It is also possible it was someone who was jealous over a woman,' she answered icily. 'Joscelin was very charming, you know.'

Lovel flushed and the whole skin of his face appeared to tighten.

'So I have frequently been reminded,' he said in a soft, dangerous little voice. 'But not everyone was as susceptible to it as you, Mama. It is a very superficial quality.'

She stared at him with something that bordered on contempt.

'You never understood charm, Lovel, which is your great misfortune. Perhaps you would be good enough to order extra tea in the withdrawing room.' Deliberately she ignored her son and contravened propriety, as if to annoy him. 'Will you join us, Mr Monk? Perhaps my daughter-in-law may be able to suggest something. She was accustomed to attend many of the same functions as Joscelin, and women are frequently more observant of other women, especially where' – she hesitated – 'affairs of the emotions are concerned.'

Without waiting for his reply she assumed his compliance and, still ignoring Lovel, turned to the door and stopped.

Lovel wavered for only the barest second, then he came forward obediently and opened the door for her. She swept through without looking again at either of them.

In the withdrawing room the atmosphere was stiff. Rosamond had difficulty hiding her amazement at being expected to take tea with a policeman as if he were a gentleman; and even the maid with the extra cups and muffins seemed uncomfortable. Apparently the below-stairs gossip had already told her who Monk was. Monk silently thought of Evan, and wondered if he had made any progress.

When the maid had handed everyone their cups and plates and was gone Lady Fabia began in a level, quiet voice, avoiding Lovel's eyes.

'Rosamond, my dear, the police require to know everything they can about Joscelin's social activities in the last few months before he died. You attended most of the same functions, and are thus more aware of any relationships than I. For example, who might have shown more interest in him than was prudent?'

'I?'. Rosamond was either profoundly surprised or a better actress than Monk had judged her to be on their earlier meeting.

'Yes you, my dear.' Lady Fabia passed her the muffins, which she ignored. 'I am talking to you. I shall, of course, also ask Ursula.'

'Who is Ursula?' Monk interrupted.

'Miss Ursula Wadham; she is betrothed to my second son, Menard. You may safely leave it to me to glean from her any information that would be of use.' She dismissed Monk and turned back to Rosamond. 'Well?'

'I don't recall Joscelin having any . . . relationship in – in particular.' Rosamond sounded rather awkward, as if the subject disturbed her. Watching her, Monk wondered for a moment if she had been in love with Joscelin herself, if perhaps that was why Lovel was so reluctant to have the matter pursued.

Could it even have gone further than a mere attraction?

'That is not what I asked,' Lady Fabia said with thin patience. 'I asked you if anyone else had shown any interest in Joscelin, albeit a one-sided one?'

Rosamond's head came up. For a moment Monk thought she was about to resist her mother-in-law, then the moment died.

'Norah Partridge was very fond of him,' she replied slowly, measuring her words. 'But that is hardly news; and I cannot see Sir John taking it badly enough to go all the way up to London and commit murder. I do believe he is fond of Norah, but not enough for that.'

'Then you are more observant than I thought,' Lady Fabia said with acid surprise. 'But without much understanding of men, my dear. It is not necessary to want something yourself in order profoundly to resent someone else's having the ability to take it away from you; especially if they have the tactlessness to do it publicly?' She swivelled to Monk. He was not offered the muffins. 'There is somewhere for you to begin. I doubt John Partridge would be moved to murder – or that he would use a stick if he were.' Her face flickered with pain again. 'But Norah had other admirers. She is a somewhat extravagant creature, and not possessed of much judgment.'

'Thank you, ma'am. If you think of anything further?'

For another hour they raked over past romances, affairs and supposed affairs, and Monk half listened. He was not interested in the facts so much as the nuances behind their expression. Joscelin had obviously been his mother's favourite, and if the absent Menard was like his elder brother, it was easy to understand why. But whatever her feelings, the laws of primogeniture ruled that not only the title and the lands, but also the money to support them and the way of life that went with them, must pass to Lovel, the firstborn.

Lovel himself contributed nothing, and Rosamond only enough to satisfy her mother-in-law, of whom she seemed in awe far more than of her husband.

Monk did not see Lady Callandra Daviot, rather to his disappointment. He would have liked her candour on the subject, although he was not sure she would have expressed herself as freely in front of the grieving family as she had in the garden in the rain.

He thanked them and excused himself in time to find Evan and walk down to the village for a pint of cider before the train back to London.

'Well?' Monk asked as soon as they were out of sight of the house.

'Ah.' Evan could scarcely suppress his enthusiasm; his stride was surprisingly long, his lean body taut with energy, and he splashed through puddles on the road with complete disregard for his soaking boots. 'It's fascinating. I've never been inside a really big house before, I mean inside to know it. My father was a clergyman, you know, and I went along to the manor house sometimes when I was a child – but it was nothing like this. Good Lord, those servants see things that would paralyze me with shame – I mean the family treat them as if they were deaf and blind.'

'They don't think of them as people,' Monk replied. 'At least not people in the same sense as themselves. They are two different worlds, and they don't impinge, except physically. Therefore their opinions don't matter. Did you learn anything else?' He smiled slightly at Evan's innocence.

Evan grinned. 'I'll say, although of course they wouldn't intentionally tell a policeman, or anyone else, anything they thought confidential about the family. It would be more than their livelihood was worth. Very closemouthed, they thought they were.'

'So how did you learn?' Monk asked curiously, looking at Evan's innocent, imaginative features.

Evan blushed very slightly. 'Threw myself on Cook's mercy.' He looked down at the ground, but did not decrease his pace in the slightest. 'Slandered my landlady appallingly, I'm afraid. Spoke very unkindly about her cooking – oh, and I stood outside for some time before going in, so my hands were cold—' He glanced up at Monk, then away again. 'Very motherly sort, Lady Shelburne's cook.' He smiled rather smugly. 'Daresay I did a lot better than you did.'

'I didn't eat at all,' Monk said tartly.

'I'm sorry.' Evan did not sound it.

'And what did your dramatic debut earn you, apart from luncheon?' Monk asked. 'I presume you overheard a good deal – while you were busy being pathetic and eating them out of house and home?'

'Oh yes – did you know that Rosamond comes from a well-to-do family, but a bit come-lately? And she fell for Joscelin first, but her mother insisted she marry the eldest brother, who also offered for her. And she was a good, obedient girl and did as she was told. At least that is what I read between the lines of what the tweeny was saying to the laundry maid – before the parlour maid came in and stopped them gossiping and they were packed off to their duties.'

Monk whistled through his teeth.

'And,' Evan went on before he could speak, 'they had no children for the first few years, then one son, heir to the title, about a year and a half ago. Someone particularly spiteful is said to have observed that he has the typical Shelburne looks, but more like Joscelin than Lovel – so the second footman heard said in the public house. Blue eyes – you see, Lord Shelburne is dark – so is she – at least her eyes are—'

Monk stopped in the road, staring at him.

'Are you sure?'

'I'm sure that's what they say, and Lord Shelburne must have heard it – at last—' He looked appalled. 'Oh God! That's what Runcorn meant, isn't it? Very nasty, very nasty indeed.' He was comical in his dismay, suddenly the enthusiasm gone out of him. 'What on earth are we going to do? I can imagine how Lady Fabia will react if you try opening that one up!'

'So can I,' Monk said grimly. 'And I don't know what we are going to do.'

Chapter Six

Hester Latterly stood in the small withdrawing room of her brother's house in Thanet Street, a little off the Euston Road, and stared out of the window at the carriages passing. It was a smaller house, far less attractive than the family home on Regent Square. But after her father's death that house had had to be sold. She had always imagined that Charles and Imogen would move out of this house and back to Regent Square in such an event, but apparently the funds were needed to settle affairs, and there was nothing above that for any inheritance for any of them. Hence she was now residing with Charles and Imogen, and would be obliged to do so until she should make some arrangements of her own. What they might be now occupied her thoughts.

Her choice was narrow. Disposal of her parents' possessions had been completed, all the necessary letters written and servants given excellent references. Most had fortunately found new positions. It remained for Hester herself to make a decision. Of course Charles had said she was more than welcome to remain as long as she wished – indefinitely, if she chose. The thought was appalling. A permanent guest, neither use nor ornament, intruding on what should be a private house for husband and wife, and in time their children. Aunts were all very well, but not for breakfast, luncheon and dinner every day of the week.

Life had to offer more than that.

Naturally Charles had spoken of marriage, but to be frank, as the situation surely warranted, Hester was very few people's idea of a good match. She was pleasing enough in feature, if a little tall – she looked over the heads of rather too many men for her own comfort, or theirs. But she had no dowry and no expectations at all. Her family was well bred, but of no connection to any of the great houses; in fact genteel enough to have aspirations, and to have taught its daughters no useful arts, but not privileged enough for birth alone to be sufficient attraction.

All of which might have been overcome if her personality were as charming as Imogen's – but it was not. Where Imogen was gentle, gracious, full of tact and discretion, Hester was abrasive, contemptuous of hypocrisy and impatient of dithering or incompetence and disinclined to suffer foolishness with any grace at all. She was also fonder of reading and study than was attractive in a woman, and not free of the intellectual arrogance of one to whom thought comes easily.

It was not entirely her fault, which mitigated blame but did not improve her chances of gaining or keeping an admirer. She had been among the first to leave England and sail, in appalling conditions, to the Crimea and offer her help to Florence Nightingale in the troop hospital in Scutari.

She could remember quite clearly her first sight of the city, which she had expected to be ravaged by war, and how her breath had caught in her throat with delight at the vividness of the white walls and the copper domes green against the blue sky.

Of course afterwards it had been totally different. She had witnessed such wretchedness and waste there, exacerbated by incompetence that beggared the imagination, and her courage had sustained her, her selflessness never looked for reward, her patience for the truly afflicted never flagged. And at the same time the sight of such terrible suffering had made her rougher to lesser pain than was just. Each person's pain is severe to him at the time, and the thought that there might be vastly worse occurs to very few. Hester did not stop to consider this, except when it was forced upon her, and such was most people's abhorrence of candour on unpleasant subjects that very few did.

She was highly intelligent, with a gift for logical thought which many people found disturbing – especially men, who did not expect it or like it in a woman. That gift had enabled her to be invaluable in the administration of hospitals for the critically injured or desperately ill – but there was no place for it in the domestic homes of gentlemen in England. She could have run an entire castle and marshalled the forces to defend it, and had time to spare. Unfortunately no one desired a castle run – and no one attacked them any more.

And she was approaching thirty.

The realistic choices lay between nursing at a practical level, at which she was now skilled, although more with injury than the diseases that occur most commonly in a temperate climate like that of England, and, on the other hand, a post in the administration of hospitals, junior as that was likely to be; women were not doctors, and not generally considered for more senior posts. But much had changed in the war, and the work to be done, the reforms that might be achieved, excited her more than she cared to admit, since the possibilities of participating were so slight.

And there was also the call of journalism, although it would hardly bring her the income necessary to provide a living. But it need not be entirely abandoned—?

She really wished for advice. Charles would disapprove of the whole idea, as he had of her going to the Crimea in the first place. He would be concerned for her safety, her reputation, her honour – and anything else general and unspecified that might cause her harm. Poor Charles, he was a very conventional soul. How they could ever be siblings she had no idea.

And there was little use asking Imogen. She had no knowledge from which to speak; and lately she seemed to have half her mind on some turmoil of her own. Hester had tried to discover without prying offensively, and succeeded in learning nothing at all, except close to a certainty that whatever it was Charles knew even less of it than she.

As she stared out through the window into the street her thoughts turned to her mentor and friend of pre-Crimean days, Lady Callandra Daviot. She would give sound advice both as to knowledge of what might be achieved and how to go about it, and what might be dared and, if reached, would make her happy. Callandra had never given a fig for doing what she was told was suitable, and she did not assume a person wanted what society said they ought to want.

She had always said that Hester was welcome to visit her either in her London house or at Shelburne Hall at any time she wished. She had her own rooms there and was free to entertain as pleased her. Hester had already written to both addresses and asked if she might come. Today she had received a reply most decidedly in the affirmative.

The door opened behind her and she heard Charles's step. She turned, the letter still in her hand.

'Charles, I have decided to go and spend a few days, perhaps a week or so, with Lady Callandra Daviot.'

'Do I know her?' he said immediately, his eyes widening a fraction.

'I should think it unlikely,' she replied. 'She is in her late fifties, and does not mix a great deal socially.'

'Are you considering becoming her companion?' His eye was to the practical. 'I don't think you are suited to the position, Hester. With all the kindness in the world, I have to say you are not a congenial person for an elderly lady of a retiring nature. You are extremely bossy – and you have very little sympathy with the ordinary pains of day-to-day life. And you have never yet succeeded in keeping even your silliest opinions to yourself.'

'I have never tried!' she said tartly, a little stung by his wording, even though she knew he meant it for her well-being.

He smiled with a slightly twisted humour. 'I am aware of that, my dear. Had you tried, even you must have done better!'

'I have no intention of becoming a companion to anyone,' she pointed out. It was on the tip of her tongue to add that, had she such a thing in mind, Lady Callandra would be her first choice; but perhaps if she did that, Charles would question Callandra's suitability as a person to visit. 'She is the widow of Colonel Daviot, who was a surgeon in the army. I thought I should seek her advice as to what position I might be best suited for.'

He was surprised. 'Do you really think she would have any useful idea? It seems to me unlikely. However do go, by all means, if you wish. You have certainly been a most marvellous help to us here, and we are deeply grateful. You came at a moment's notice, leaving all your friends behind, and gave your time and your affections to us when we were sorely in need.'

'It was a family tragedy.' For once her candour was also gracious. 'I should not have wished to be anywhere else. But yes, Lady Callandra has considerable experience and I should value her opinion. If it is agreeable to you, I shall leave tomorrow early.'

'Certainly—' He hesitated, looking a trifle uncomfortable. 'Er—'

'What is it?'

'Do you – er – have sufficient means?'

She smiled. 'Yes, thank you – for the time being.'

He looked relieved. She knew he was not naturally generous, but neither was he grudging with his own family. His reluctance was another reinforcement of the observations she had made that there had been a considerable tightening of circumstances in the last four or five months. There had been other small things: the household had not the complement of servants she remembered prior to her leaving for the Crimea; now there were only the cook, one kitchen maid, one scullery maid, one housemaid and a parlour maid who doubled as lady's maid for Imogen. The butler was the only male indoor servant; no footman, not even a bootboy. The scullery maid did the shoes.

Imogen had not refurbished her summer wardrobe with the usual generosity, and at least one pair of Charles's boots had been repaired. The silver tray in the hall for receiving calling cards was no longer there.

It was most assuredly time she considered her own position, and the necessity of earning her own way. Some academic pursuit had been a suggestion; she found study absorbing, but the tutorial positions open to women were few, and the restrictions of the life did not appeal to her. She read for pleasure.

When Charles had gone she went upstairs and found Imogen in the linen room inspecting pillow covers and sheets. Caring for them was a large task, even for so modest a household, especially without the services of a laundry maid.

'Excuse me.' She began immediately to assist, looking at embroidered edges for tears or where the stitching was coming away. 'I have decided to go and visit Lady Callandra Daviot, in the country, for a short while. I think she can advise me on what I should do next—' She saw Imogen's look of surprise, and clarified her statement. 'At least she

179

will know the possibilities open to me better than I.'

'Oh.' Imogen's face showed a mixture of pleasure and disappointment and it was not necessary for her to explain. She understood that Hester must come to a decision, but also she would miss her company. Since their first meeting they had become close friends and their differences in nature had been complementary rather than irritating. 'Then you had better take Gwen. You can't stay with the aristocracy without a lady's maid.'

'Certainly I can,' Hester contradicted decisively. 'I don't have one, so I shall be obliged to. It will do me no harm whatsoever, and Lady Callandra will be the last one to mind.'

Imogen looked dubious. 'And how will you dress for dinner?'

'For goodness sake! I can dress myself!'

Imogen's face twitched very slightly. 'Yes, my dear, I have seen! And I am sure it is admirable for nursing the sick, and fighting stubborn authorities in the army—'

'Imogen!'

'And what about your hair?' Imogen pressed. 'You are likely to arrive at table looking as if you had come sideways through a high wind to get there!'

'Imogen!' Hester threw a bundle of towels at her, one knocking a front lock of her hair askew and the rest scattering on the floor.

Imogen threw a sheet back, achieving the same result. They looked at each other's wild appearance and began to laugh. Within moments both were gasping for breath and sitting on the floor in mounds of skirts with previously crisp laundry lying around them in heaps.

The door opened and Charles stood on the threshold looking bemused and a trifle alarmed.

'What on earth is wrong?' he demanded, at first taking their sobs for distress. 'Are you ill? What has happened?' Then he saw it was amusement and looked even more confounded, and as neither of them stopped or took any sensible notice of him, he became annoyed.

'Imogen! Control yourself!' he said sharply. 'What is the matter with you?'

Imogen still laughed helplessly.

'Hester!' Charles was growing pink in the face. 'Hester, stop it! Stop it at once!'

Hester looked at him and found it funnier still.

Charles sniffed, dismissed it as women's weakness and therefore inexplicable, and left, shutting the door hard so none of the servants should witness such a ridiculous scene.

Hester was perfectly accustomed to travel, and the journey from London to Shelburne was barely worth comment compared with the fearful passage by sea across the Bay of Biscay and through the Mediterranean to the Bosporus and up the Black Sea to Sebastopol. Troopships replete with terrified horses, overcrowded, and with the merest of accommodations, were things beyond the imagination of most Englishmen, let alone women. A simple train journey through the summer countryside was a positive pleasure, and the warm, quiet and sweet-scented mile in the dog cart at the far end before she reached the hall was a glory to the senses.

She arrived at the magnificent front entrance with its Doric columns and portico. The driver had no time to hand her down because she had grown unaccustomed to such courtesies and scrambled to the ground herself while he was still tying the reins. With a frown he unloaded her box and at the same moment a footman opened the door and held it for her to pass through. Another footman carried in the box and disappeared somewhere upstairs with it.

Fabia Shelburne was in the withdrawing room where Hester was shown. It was a room of considerable beauty, and at this height of the year, with the French windows open onto the garden and the scent of roses drifting on a warm breeze, the soft green of the rolling parkland beyond, the marble-surrounded fireplace seemed unnecessary, and the paintings keyholes to another and unnecessary world.

Lady Fabia did not rise, but smiled as Hester was shown in.

'Welcome to Shelburne Hall, Miss Latterly. I hope your journey was not too fatiguing. Why, my dear, you seem very blown about! I am afraid it is very windy beyond the garden. I trust it has not distressed you. When you have composed yourself and taken off your travelling clothes, perhaps you would care to join us for afternoon tea? Cook is particularly adept at making crumpets.' She smiled, a cool, well-practised gesture. 'I expect you are hungry, and it will be an excellent opportunity for us to become acquainted with each other. Lady Callandra will be down, no doubt, and my daughter-in-law, Lady Shelburne. I do not believe you have met?'

'No, Lady Fabia, but it is a pleasure I look forward to.'
She had observed Fabia's deep violet gown, less sombre
than black but still frequently associated with mourning.
Apart from that Callandra had told her of Joscelin Grey's
death, although not in detail. 'May I express my deepest
sympathy for the loss of your son. I have a little understanding
of how you feel.'

Fabia's eyebrows rose. 'Have you!' she said with disbelief.

Hester was stung. Did this woman imagine she was the
only person who had been bereaved? How self-absorbed
grief could be.

'Yes,' she replied perfectly levelly. 'I lost my elder brother
in the Crimea, and a few months ago my father and mother
within three weeks of each other.'

'Oh——' For once Fabia was at a loss for words. She had
supposed Hester's sober dress merely a travelling
convenience. Her own mourning consumed her to the
exclusion of anyone else's. 'I am sorry.'

Hester smiled; when she truly meant it it had great
warmth.

'Thank you,' she accepted. 'Now if you permit I will
accept your excellent idea and change into something suitable
before joining you for tea. You are quite right; the very
thought of crumpets makes me realize I am very hungry.'

The bedroom they had given her was in the west wing,
where Callandra had had a bedroom and sitting room of her
own since she had moved out of the nursery. She and her
elder brothers had grown up at Shelburne Hall. She had left

it to marry thirty years ago, but still visited frequently, and in her widowhood had been extended the courtesy of retaining the accommodation and the hospitality that went with it.

Hester's room was large and a little sombre, being hung with muted tapestries on one entire wall and papered in a shade that was undecided between green and grey. The only relief was a delightful painting of two dogs, framed in gold leaf which caught the light. The windows faced westward, and on so fine a day the evening sky was a glory between the great beech trees close to the house, and beyond was a view of an immaculately set-out walled herb garden with fruit trees carefully lined against it. On the far side the heavy boughs of the orchard hid the parkland beyond.

There was hot water ready in a large blue-and-white china jug, and a matching basin beside it, with fresh towels, and she wasted no time in taking off her heavy, dusty skirts, washing her face and neck, and then putting the basin on the floor and easing her hot, aching feet into it.

She was thus employed, indulging in the pure physical pleasure of it, when there was a knock on the door.

'Who is it?' she said in alarm. She was wearing only a camisole and pantaloons and was at a considerable disadvantage. And since she already had water and towels she was not expecting a maid.

'Callandra,' came the reply.

'Oh—' Perhaps it was foolish to try to impress Callandra Daviot with something she could not maintain. 'Come in!'

Callandra opened the door and stood with a smile of delight on her face.

184

'My dear Hester! How truly pleased I am to see you. You look as if you have not changed in the slightest – at the core at least.' She closed the door behind her and came in, sitting down on one of the upholstered bedroom chairs. She was not and never had been a beautiful woman; she was too broad in the hip, too long in the nose, and her eyes were not exactly the same colour. But there was humour and intelligence in her face, and a remarkable strength of will. Hester had never known anyone she had liked better, and the mere sight of her was enough to lift the spirits and fill the heart with confidence.

'Perhaps not.' She wriggled her toes in the now cool water. The sensation was delicious. 'But a great deal has happened: my circumstances have altered.'

'So you wrote to me. I am extremely sorry about your parents – please know that I feel for you deeply.'

Hester did not want to talk of it; the pain was still very sharp. Imogen had written and told her of her father's death, although not a great deal of the circumstances, except that he had been shot in what might have been an accident with a pair of duelling pistols he kept, or that he might have surprised an intruder, although since it had happened in the late afternoon it was unlikely, and the police had implied but not insisted that suicide was probable. In consideration to the family, the verdict had been left open. Suicide was not only a crime against the law but a sin against the Church that would exclude him from being buried in hallowed ground and be a burden of shame the family would carry indefinitely.

Nothing appeared to have been taken, and no robber was

ever apprehended. The police did not pursue the case.

Within a week another letter had arrived, actually posted two weeks later, to say that her mother had died also. No one had said that it was of heartbreak, but such words were not needed.

'Thank you,' Hester acknowledged with a small smile.

Callandra looked at her for a moment, then was sensitive enough to see the hurt in her and understood that probing would only injure further, discussion was no longer any part of the healing. Instead she changed the subject to the practical.

'What are you considering doing now? For heaven's sake don't rush into a marriage!'

Hester was a trifle surprised at such unorthodox advice, but she replied with self-deprecatory frankness.

'I have no opportunity to do such a thing. I am nearly thirty, of an uncompromising disposition, too tall, and have no money and no connections. Any man wishing to marry me would be highly suspect as to his motives or his judgment.'

'The world is not short of men with either shortcoming,' Callandra replied with an answering smile. 'As you yourself have frequently written to me. The army at least abounds with men whose motives you suspect and whose judgment you abhor.'

Hester pulled a face. 'Touché,' she conceded. 'But all the same they have enough wits where their personal interest is concerned.' Her memory flickered briefly to an army surgeon in the hospital. She saw again his weary face, his sudden smile, and the beauty of his hands as he worked. One dreadful morning during the siege she had accompanied him to the redan. She could smell the gunpowder and the corpses and feel the bitter cold again as if it were only a moment ago. The closeness had been so intense it had made up for everything else – and then the sick feeling in her stomach when he had spoken for the first time of his wife. She should have known – she should have thought of it – but she had not.

'I should have to be either beautiful or unusually helpless, or preferably both, in order to have them flocking to my door. And as you know, I am neither.'

Callandra looked at her closely. 'Do I detect a note of self-pity, Hester?'

Hester felt the colour hot up her cheeks, betraying her so no answer was necessary.

'You will have to learn to conquer that,' Callandra observed, settling herself a little deeper in the chair. Her voice was quite gentle; there was no criticism in it, simply a statement of fact. 'Too many women waste their lives grieving because they do not have something other people tell them they should want. Nearly all married women will tell you it is a blessed state, and you are to be pitied for not being in it. That is arrant nonsense. Whether you are happy or not depends to some degree upon outward circumstances, but mostly it depends how you choose to look at things yourself, whether you measure what you have or what you have not.'

Hester frowned, uncertain as to how much she understood, or believed, what Callandra was saying.

Callandra was a trifle impatient. She jerked forward, frowning. 'My dear girl, do you really imagine every woman with a smile on her face is really happy? No person of a healthy mentality desires to be pitied, and the simplest way to avoid it is to keep your troubles to yourself and wear a complacent expression. Most of the world will then assume that you are as self-satisfied as you seem. Before you pity yourself, take a great deal closer look at others, and then decide with whom you would, or could, change places, and what sacrifice of your nature you would be prepared to make in order to do so. Knowing you as I do, I think precious little.'

Hester absorbed this thought in silence, turning it over in her mind. Absently she pulled her feet out of the basin at last and began to dry them on the towel.

Callandra stood up. 'You will join us in the withdrawing room for tea? It is usually very good as I remember; there is nothing wrong with your appetite. Then later we shall discuss what possibilities there are for you to exercise your talents. There is so much to be done; great reforms are long overdue in all manner of things, and your experience and your emotion should not go to waste.'

'Thank you.' Hester suddenly felt much better. Her feet were refreshed and clean, she was extremely hungry, and although the future was a mist with no form to it as yet, it had in half an hour grown from grey to a new brightness. 'I most certainly shall.'

Callandra looked at Hester's hair. 'I shall send you my maid. Her name is Effie, and she is better than my appearance would lead you to believe.' And with that she went cheerfully out of the door, humming to herself in a rich contralto voice, and Hester could hear her rather firm tread along the landing.

Afternoon tea was taken by the ladies alone. Rosamond appeared from the boudoir, a sitting room especially for female members of the household, where she had been writing letters. Fabia presided, although of course there was the parlour maid to pass the cups and the sandwiches of cucumber, hothouse grown, and later the crumpets and cakes.

The conversation was extremely civilized to the point of being almost meaningless for any exchange of opinion or emotion. They spoke of fashion, what colour and what line flattered whom, what might be the season's special feature, would it be a lower waist, or perhaps a greater use of lace, or indeed more or different buttons? Would hats be larger or smaller? Was it good taste to wear green, and did it really become anyone; was it not inclined to make one sallow? A good complexion was so important!

What soap was best for retaining the blush of youth? Were Dr So-and-so's pills really helpful for female complaints? Mrs Wellings had it that they were little less than miraculous! But then Mrs Wellings was much given to exaggeration. She would do anything short of standing on her head in order to attract attention.

Frequently Hester caught Callandra's eyes, and had to look away in case she should giggle and betray an unseemly and very discourteous levity. She might be taken for mocking her hostess, which would be unforgivable – and true.

Dinner was a quite different affair. Effie turned out to be a very agreeable country girl with a cloud of naturally wavy auburn hair many a mistress would have swapped her dowry for and a quick and garrulous tongue. She had hardly been in the room five minutes, whisking through clothes, pinning here, flouncing there, rearranging everything with a skill that left Hester breathless, before she had recounted the amazing news that the police had been at the Hall, about the poor Major's death up in London, twice now. They had sent two men, one a very grim creature, with a dark visage and manner grand enough to frighten the children, who had spoken with the mistress and taken tea in the withdrawing room as if he thought himself quite the gentleman.

The other, however, was as charming as you could wish, and so terribly elegant – although what a clergyman's son was doing in such an occupation no one could imagine! Such a personable young man should have done something decent, like taking the cloth himself, or tutoring boys of good family, or any other respectable calling.

'But there you are!' she said, seizing the hairbrush and beginning on Hester's hair with determination. 'Some of the nicest people do the oddest things, I always say. But Cook took a proper fancy to him. Oh dear!' She looked at the back of Hester's head critically. 'You really shouldn't wear your hair like that, ma'am; if you don't mind me saying.' She brushed swiftly, piled, stuck pins and looked again. 'There now – very fine hair you have, when it's done right. You should have a word with your maid at home, miss – she's not doing right by you – if you'll excuse me saying so. I hope that gives satisfaction?'

'Oh indeed!' Hester assured her with amazement. 'You are quite excellent.'

Effie coloured with pleasure. 'Lady Callandra says I talk too much,' she essayed modestly.

Hester smiled. 'Definitely,' she agreed. 'So do I. Thank you for your help – please tell Lady Callandra I am very grateful.'

'Yes, ma'am.' And with a half-curtsy Effie grabbed her pin-cushion and flew out of the door, forgetting to close it behind her, and Hester heard her feet along the passage.

She really looked very striking; the rather severe style she had worn for convenience since embarking on her nursing career had been dramatically softened and filled out. Her gown had been masterfully adapted to be less modest and considerably fuller over a borrowed petticoat, unknown to its owner, and thus height was turned from a disadvantage into a considerable asset. Now that it was time she swept down the main staircase feeling very pleased with herself indeed.

Both Lovel and Menard Grey were at home for the evening, and she was introduced to them in the withdrawing room before going in to the dining room and being seated at the long, highly polished table, which was set for six but could easily have accommodated twelve. There were two joins in it where additional leaves could be inserted so it might have sat twenty-four.

Hester's eye swept over it quickly and noticed the crisp linen napkins, all embroidered with the family crest, the gleaming silver similarly adorned, the cruet sets, the crystal goblets reflecting the myriad lights of the chandelier, a tower of glass like a miniature iceberg alight. There were flowers from the conservatory and from the garden, skilfully arranged in three flat vases up the centre of the table, and the whole glittered and gleamed like a display of art.

This time the conversation was centred on the estate, and matters of more political interest. Apparently Lovel had been in the nearest market town all day discussing some matter of land, and Menard had been to one of the tenant farms regarding the sale of a breeding ram, and of course the beginning of harvest.

The meal was served efficiently by the footmen and parlour maid and no one paid them the slightest attention.

They were halfway through the remove, a roast saddle of mutton, when Menard, a handsome man in his early thirties, finally addressed Hester directly. He had similar dark brown hair to his elder brother, and a ruddy complexion from much time spent in the open. He rode to hounds with great pleasure, and considerable daring, and shot pheasant in season. He smiled from enjoyment, but seldom from perception of wit.

'How agreeable of you to come and visit Aunt Callandra, Miss Latterly. I hope you will be able to stay with us for a while?'

'Thank you, Mr Grey,' she said graciously. 'That is very kind of you. It is a quite beautiful place, and I am sure I shall enjoy myself.'

'Have you known Aunt Callandra long?' He was making polite conversation and she knew precisely the pattern it would take.

'Some five or six years. She has given me excellent advice from time to time.'

Lady Fabia frowned. The pairing of Callandra and good advice was obviously foreign to her. 'Indeed?' she murmured disbelievingly. 'With regard to what, pray?'

'What I should do with my time and abilities,' Hester replied.

Rosamond looked puzzled. 'Do?' she said quietly. 'I don't think I understand.' She looked at Lovel, then at her mother-in-law. Her fair face and remarkable brown eyes were full of interest and confusion.

'It is necessary that I provide for myself, Lady Shelburne,' Hester explained with a smile. Suddenly Callandra's words about happiness came back to her with a force of meaning.

'I'm sorry,' Rosamond murmured, and looked down at her plate, obviously feeling she had said something indelicate.

'Not at all,' Hester assured her quickly. 'I have already had some truly inspiring experiences, and hope to have more.' She was about to add that it is a marvellous feeling to be of use, then realized how cruel it would be, and swallowed the words somewhat awkwardly over a mouthful of mutton and sauce.

'Inspiring?' Lovel frowned. 'Are you a religious, Miss Latterly?'

Callandra coughed profusely into her napkin; apparently she had swallowed something awry. Fabia passed her a glass of water. Hester averted her eyes.

'No, Lord Shelburne,' she said with as much composure as she could. 'I have been nursing in the Crimea.'

There was a stunned silence all around, not even the clink of silver on porcelain.

'My brother-in-law, Major Joscelin Grey, served in the Crimea,' Rosamond said into the void. Her voice was soft and sad. 'He died shortly after he returned home.'

'That is something of a euphemism,' Lovel added, his face hardening. 'He was murdered in his flat in London, as no doubt you will hear. The police have been inquiring into it, even out here! But they have not arrested anyone yet.'

'I am terribly sorry!' Hester meant it with genuine shock. She had nursed a Joscelin Grey in the hospital in Scutari, only briefly; his injury was serious enough, but not compared with the worst, and those who also suffered from disease. She recalled him: he had been young and fair-haired with a wide, easy smile and a natural grace. 'I remember him—' Now Effie's words came back to her with clarity.

Rosamond dropped her fork, the colour rushing to her cheeks, then ebbing away again leaving her ash-white. Fabia closed her eyes and took in a very long, deep breath and let it go soundlessly.

Lovel stared at his plate. Only Menard was looking at her, and rather than surprise or grief there was an expression in his face which appeared to be wariness, and a kind of closed, careful pain.

'How remarkable,' he said slowly. 'Still, I suppose you

194

saw hundreds of soldiers, if not thousands. Our losses were staggering, so I am told.'

'They were,' she agreed grimly. 'Far more than is generally understood, over eighteen thousand, and many of them needlessly – eight-ninths died not in battle but of wounds or disease afterwards.'

'Do you remember Joscelin?' Rosamond said eagerly, totally ignoring the horrific figures. 'He was injured in the leg. Even afterwards he was compelled to walk with a limp – indeed he often used a stick to support himself.'

'He only used it when he was tired!' Fabia said sharply.

'He used it when he wanted sympathy,' Menard said half under his breath.

'That is unworthy!' Fabia's voice was dangerously soft, laden with warning, and her blue eyes rested on her second son with chill disfavour. 'I shall consider that you did not say it.'

'We observe the convention that we speak no ill of the dead,' Menard said with irony unusual in him. 'Which limits conversation considerably.'

Rosamond stared at her plate. 'I never understand your humour, Menard,' she complained.

'That is because he is very seldom intentionally funny,' Fabia snapped.

'Whereas Joscelin was always amusing.' Menard was angry and no longer made any pretence at hiding it. 'It is marvellous what a little laughter can do – entertain you enough and you will turn a blind eye on anything!'

'I loved Joscelin,' Fabia met his eyes with a stony glare. 'I enjoyed his company. So did a great many others. I love you also, but you bore me to tears.'

'You are happy enough to enjoy the profits of my work!' His face was burning and his eyes bright with fury. 'I preserve the estate's finances and see that it is properly managed, while Lovel keeps up the family name, sits in the House of Lords or does whatever else peers of the realm do – and Joscelin never did a damn thing but lounge around in clubs and drawing rooms gambling it away!'

The blood drained from Fabia's skin leaving her grasping her knife and fork as if they were lifelines.

'And you still resent that?' Her voice was little more than a whisper. 'He fought in the war, risked his life serving his Queen and country in terrible conditions, saw blood and slaughter. And when he came home wounded, you grudged him a little entertainment with his friends?'

Menard drew in his breath to retort, then saw the pain in his mother's face, deeper than her anger and underlying everything else, and held his tongue.

'I was embarrassed by some of his losses,' he said softly. 'That is all.'

Hester glanced at Callandra, and saw a mixture of anger, pity and respect in her highly expressive features, although which emotion was for whom she did not know. She thought perhaps the respect was for Menard.

Lovel smiled very bleakly. 'I am afraid you may find the police are still around here, Miss Latterly. They have sent a very ill-mannered fellow, something of an upstart, although

I daresay he is better bred than most policemen. But he does not seem to have much idea of what he is doing, and asks some very impertinent questions. If he should return during your stay and give you the slightest trouble, tell him to be off, and let me know.'

'By all means,' Hester agreed. To the best of her knowledge she had never conversed with a policeman, and she had no interest in doing so now. 'It must all be most distressing for you.'

'Indeed,' Fabia agreed. 'But an unpleasantness we have no alternative but to endure. It appears more than possible poor Joscelin was murdered by someone he knew.'

Hester could think of no appropriate reply, nothing that was not either wounding or completely senseless.

'Thank you for your counsel,' she said to Menard, then lowered her eyes and continued with her meal.

After the fruit had been passed the women withdrew and Lovel and Menard drank port for half an hour or so, then Lovel put on his smoking jacket and retired to the smoking room to indulge, and Menard went to the library. No one remained up beyond ten o'clock, each making some excuse why they had found the day tiring and wished to sleep.

Breakfast was the usual generous meal: porridge, bacon, eggs, devilled kidneys, chops, kedgeree, smoked haddock, toast, butter, sweet preserves, apricot compôte, marmalade, honey, tea and coffee. Hester ate lightly; the very thought of partaking of all of it made her feel bloated. Both Rosamond and Fabia ate in their rooms, Menard had already dined and

197

left and Callandra had not arisen. Lovel was her only companion.

'Good morning, Miss Latterly. I hope you slept well?'

'Excellently, thank you, Lord Shelburne.' She helped herself from the heated dishes on the sideboard and sat down. 'I hope you are well also?'

'What? Oh – yes thank you. Always well.' He proceeded with his heaped meal and it was several minutes before he looked up at her again. 'By the way, I hope you will be generous enough to disregard a great deal of what Menard said at dinner yesterday? We all take grief in different ways. Menard lost his closest friend also – fellow he was at school and Cambridge with. Took it terribly hard. But he was really very fond of Joscelin, you know, just that as immediately elder brother he had— er— He searched for the right words to explain his thoughts, and failed to find them. 'He – er— had—'

'Responsibilities to care for him?' she suggested.

Gratitude shone in his face. 'Exactly. Sometimes I daresay Joscelin gambled more than he should, and it was Menard who— er . . .'

'I understand,' she said, more to put him out of his embarrassment and end the painful conversation than because she believed him.

Later in a fine, blustery morning, walking under the trees with Callandra, she learned a good deal more.

'Stuff and nonsense,' Callandra said sharply. 'Joscelin was a cheat. Always was, even in the nursery. I shouldn't be at all surprised if he never grew out of it, and Menard had to pick up after him to avoid a scandal. Very sensitive to the family name, Menard.'

'Is Lord Shelburne not also?' Hester was surprised.

'I don't think Lovel has the imagination to realize that a Grey could cheat,' Callandra answered frankly. 'I think the whole thing would be beyond him to conceive. Gentlemen do not cheat; Joscelin was his brother – and so of course a gentleman – therefore he could not cheat. All very simple.'

'You were not especially fond of Joscelin?' Hester searched her face.

Callandra smiled. 'Not especially, although I admit he was very witty at times, and we can forgive a great deal of one who makes us laugh. And he played beautifully, and we can also overlook a lot in one who creates glorious sound – or perhaps I should say re-creates it. He did not compose, so far as I know.'

They walked a hundred yards in silence except for the roar and rustle of the wind in giant oaks. It sounded like the torrent of a stream falling, or an incessant sea breaking on rocks. It was one of the pleasantest sounds Hester had ever heard, and the bright, sweet air was a sort of cleansing of her whole spirit.

'Well?' Callandra said at last. 'What are your choices, Hester? I am quite sure you can find an excellent position if you wish to continue nursing, either in the army hospital or in one of the London hospitals that may be persuaded to accept women.' There was no lift in her voice, no enthusiasm.

'But?' Hester said for her.

Callandra's wide mouth twitched in the ghost of a smile. 'But I think you would be wasted in it. You have a gift for administration, and a fighting spirit. You should find some cause and battle to win it. You have learned a great deal about better standards of nursing in the Crimea. Teach them here in England, force people to listen – get rid of cross-infection, insanitary conditions, ignorant nurses, incompetent treatments that any good housekeeper would abhor. You will save more lives, and be a happier woman.'

Hester did not mention the dispatches she had sent in Alan Russell's name, but a truth in Callandra's words rested with an unusual warmth in her, a kind of resolution as if discord had been melted into harmony.

'How do I do it?' The writing of articles could wait, find its own avenue. The more she knew, the more she would be able to speak with power and intelligence. Of course she already knew that Miss Nightingale would continue to campaign with every ounce of the passion which all but consumed her nervous strength and physical health for a reformation of the entire Army Medical Corps, but she could not do it alone, or even with all the adulation the country offered her or the friends she had in the seats of power. Vested interests were spread through the corridors of authority like the roots of a tree through the earth. The bonds of habit and security of position were steel-like in endurance. Too many people would have to change, and in doing so admit they had been ill advised, unwise, even incompetent.

'How can I obtain a position?'

'I have friends,' Callandra said with quiet confidence. 'I

shall begin to write letters, very discreetly, either to beg favours, prompt a sense of duty, prick consciences, or else threaten disfavour both public and private, if someone does not help!' There was a light of humour in her eyes, but also a complete intention to do exactly what she had said.

'Thank you,' Hester accepted. 'I shall endeavour to use my opportunities so as to justify your effort.'

'Certainly,' Callandra agreed. 'If I did not believe so, I should not exert them.' And she matched her stride to Hester's and together they walked in the wood under the branches and out across the park.

Two days later General Wadham came to dinner with his daughter Ursula, who had been betrothed for several months to Menard Grey. They arrived early enough to join the family in the withdrawing room for conversation before the meal was announced, and Hester found herself immediately tested in her tact. Ursula was a handsome girl whose mane of hair had a touch of red in its fairness and whose skin had the glow of someone who spends a certain amount of time in the open. Indeed, conversation had not proceeded far before her interest in riding to hounds became apparent. This evening she was dressed in a rich blue which in Hester's opinion was too powerful for her; something more subdued would have flattered her and permitted her natural vitality to show through. As it was she appeared a trifle conspicuous between Fabia's lavender silk and her light hair faded to grey at the front, Rosamond in a blue so dull and dark it made her flawless cheeks like alabaster, and Hester herself

201

in a sombre grape colour rich and yet not out of keeping with her own recent state of mourning. Actually she thought privately she had never worn a colour which flattered her more!

Callandra wore black with touches of white, a striking dress, but somehow not quite the right note of fashion. But then whatever Callandra wore was not going to have panache, only distinction; it was not in her nature to be glamorous.

General Wadham was tall and stout with bristling side whiskers and very pale blue eyes which were either farsighted or nearsighted, Hester was unsure which, but they certainly did not seem to focus upon her when he addressed her.

'Visiting, Miss— er— Miss—'

'Latterly,' she supplied.

'Ah yes – of course – Latterly.' He reminded her almost ludicrously of a dozen or so middle-aged soldiers she had seen whom she and Fanny Bolsover had lampooned when they were tired and frightened and had sat up all night with the wounded, then afterwards lain together on a single straw pallet, huddled close for warmth and telling each other silly stories, laughing because it was better than weeping, and making fun of the officers because loyalty and pity and hate were too big to deal with, and they had not the energy or spirit left.

'Friend of Lady Shelburne's, are you?' General Wadham said automatically. 'Charming – charming.'

'No,' she contradicted. 'I am a friend of Lady Callandra Daviot's. I was fortunate enough to know her some time ago.'

'Indeed.' He obviously could think of nothing to add to that, and moved on to Rosamond, who was more prepared to make light conversation and fall in with whatever mood he wished.

When dinner was announced there was no gentleman to escort her into the dining room, so she was obliged to go in with Callandra, and at table found herself seated opposite the general.

The first course was served and everyone began to eat, the ladies delicately, the men with appetite. At first conversation was slight, then when the initial hunger had been assuaged and the soup and fish eaten, Ursula began to speak about the hunt, and the relative merits of one horse over another.

Hester did not join in. The only riding she had done had been in the Crimea, and the sight of the horses there injured, diseased and starving had so distressed her she put it from her mind. Indeed so much did she close her attention from their speech that Fabia had addressed her three times before she was startled into realizing it.

'I beg your pardon!' she apologized in some embarrassment.

'I believe you said, Miss Latterly, that you were briefly acquainted with my late son, Major Joscelin Grey?'

'Yes. I regret it was very slight – there were so many wounded.' She said it politely, as if she were discussing some ordinary commodity, but her mind went back to the reality of the hospitals when the wounded, the frostbitten and those wasted with cholera, dysentery and starvation were lying so close there was barely room for more, and the rats scuttled, huddled and clung everywhere.

And worse than that she remembered the earthworks in the siege of Sebastopol, the bitter cold, the light of lamps in the mud, her body shaking as she held one high for the surgeon to work, its gleam on the saw blade, the dim shapes of men crowding together for a fraction of body's warmth. She remembered the first time she saw the great figure of Rebecca Box striding forward over the battlefield beyond the trenches to ground lately occupied by Russian troops, and lifting the bodies of the fallen and hoisting them over her shoulder to carry them back. Her strength was surpassed only by her sublime courage. No man fell injured so far forward she would not go out for him and carry him back to hospital hut or tent.

They were staring at her, waiting for her to say something more, some word of praise for him. After all, he had been a soldier – a major in the cavalry.

'I remember he was charming.' She refused to lie, even for his family. 'He had the most delightful smile.'

Fabia relaxed and sat back. 'That was Joscelin,' she agreed with a misty look in her blue eyes. 'Courage and a kind of gaiety, even in the most dreadful circumstances. I can still hardly believe he is gone – I half think he will throw the door open and stride in, apologizing for being late and telling us how hungry he is.'

Hester looked at the table piled high with food that would have done half a regiment at the height of the siege. They used the word *hunger* so easily.

General Wadham sat back and wiped his napkin over his lips.

'A fine man,' he said quietly. 'You must have been very proud of him, my dear. A soldier's life is all too often short, but he carries honour with him, and he will not be forgotten.'

The table was silent but for the clink of silver on porcelain. No one could think of any immediate reply. Fabia's face was full of a bleak and terrible grief, an almost devastating loneliness. Rosamond stared into space, and Lovel looked quietly wretched, whether for their pain or his own was impossible to know. Was it memory or the present which robbed him?

Menard chewed his food over and over, as if his throat were too tight and his mouth too dry to swallow it.

'Glorious campaign,' the general went on presently. 'Live in the annals of history. Never be surpassed for courage. Thin Red Line, and all that.'

Hester found herself suddenly choked with tears, anger and grief boiling up inside her, and intolerable frustration. She could see the hills beyond the Alma River more sharply than the figures around the table and the winking crystal. She could see the breastwork on the forward ridges as it had been that morning, bristling with enemy guns, the Greater and Lesser Redoubts, the wicker barricades filled with stones. Behind them were Prince Menshikoff's fifty thousand men. She remembered the smell of the breeze off the sea. She had stood with the women who had followed the army and watched Lord Raglan sitting in frock coat and white shirt, his back ramrod stiff in the saddle.

At one o'clock the bugle had sounded and the infantry advanced shoulder to shoulder into the mouths of the Russian guns and were cut down like corn. For ninety minutes they were massacred, then at last the order was given and the Hussars, Lancers and Fusiliers joined in, each in perfect order.

'Look well at that,' a major had said to one of the wives, 'for the Queen of England would give her eyes to see it.'

Everywhere men were falling. The colours carried high were ragged with shot. As one bearer fell another took his place, and in his turn fell and was succeeded. Orders were conflicting, men advanced and retreated over each other. The Grenadiers advanced, a moving wall of bearskins, then the Black Watch of the Highland Brigade.

The Dragoons were held back, never used. Why? When asked, Lord Raglan had replied that he had been thinking of Agnes!

Hester remembered going over the battlefield afterwards, the ground soaked with blood, seeing mangled bodies, some so terrible the limbs lay yards away. She had done all she could to relieve the suffering, working till exhaustion numbed her beyond feeling and she was dizzy with the sights and sounds of pain. Wounded were piled on carts and trundled to field hospital tents. She had worked all night and all day, exhausted, dry-mouthed with thirst, aching and drenched with horror. Orderlies had tried to stop the bleeding; there was little to do for shock but a few precious drops of brandy. What she would have given then for the contents of Shelburne's cellars.

The dinner table conversation buzzed on around her, cheerful, courteous, and ignorant. The flowers swam in her vision, summer blooms grown by careful gardeners, orchids tended in the glass conservatory. She thought of herself walking in the grass one hot afternoon with letters from home in her pocket, amid the dwarf roses and the blue larkspur that grew again in the field of Balaclava the year after the Charge of the Light Brigade, that idiotic piece of insane bungling and suicidal heroism. She had gone back to the hospital and tried to write and tell them what it was really like, what she was doing and how it felt, the sharing and the good things, the friendships, Fanny Bolsover, laughter, courage. The dry resignation of the men when they were issued green coffee beans, and no means to roast or grind them, had evoked her admiration so deeply it made her throat ache with sudden pride. She could hear the scratching of the quill over the paper now – and the sound as she tore it up.

'Fine man,' General Wadham was saying, staring into his claret glass. 'One of England's heroes. Lucan and Cardigan are related – I suppose you know? Lucan married one of Lord Cardigan's sisters – what a family.' He shook his head in wonder. 'What duty!'

'Inspires us all,' Ursula agreed with shining eyes.

'They hated each other on sight,' Hester said before she had time for discretion to guard her tongue.

'I beg your pardon!' The general stared at her coldly, his rather wispy eyebrows raised. His look centred all his incredulity at her impertinence and disapproval of women who spoke when it was not required of them.

Hester was stung by it. He was exactly the sort of blind, arrogant fool who had caused such immeasurable loss on the battlefield through refusal to be informed, rigidity of thought, panic when they found they were wrong, and personal emotion which overrode truth.

'I said that Lord Lucan and Lord Cardigan hated each other from the moment they met,' she repeated clearly in the total silence.

'I think you are hardly in a position to judge such a thing, madame.' He regarded her with total contempt. She was less than a subaltern, less than a private, for heaven's sake – she was a woman! And she had contradicted him, at least by implication, and at the dinner table.

'I was on the battlefield at the Alma, at Inkermann and at Balaclava, and at the siege of Sebastopol, sir,' she answered without dropping her gaze. 'Where were you?'

His face flushed scarlet. 'Good manners, and regard for our hosts, forbid me from giving you the answer you deserve, madame,' he said very stiffly. 'Since the meal is finished, perhaps it is time the ladies wished to retire to the withdrawing room?'

Rosamond made as if to rise in obedience, and Ursula laid her napkin beside her plate, although there was still half a pear unfinished on it.

Fabia sat where she was, two spots of colour in her cheeks, and very carefully and deliberately Callandra reached for a peach and began to peel it with her fruit knife and fork, a small smile on her face.

No one moved. The silence deepened.

'I believe it is going to be a hard winter,' Lovel said at last. 'Old Beckinsale was saying he expects to lose half his crop.'

'He says that every year,' Menard grunted and finished the remnant of his wine, throwing it back without savour, merely as if he would not waste it.

'A lot of people say things every year.' Callandra cut away a squashy piece of fruit carefully and pushed it to the side of her plate. 'It is forty years since we beat Napoleon at Waterloo, and most of us still think we have the same invincible army and we expect to win with the same tactics and the same discipline and courage that defeated half Europe and ended an empire.'

'And by God, we shall, madame!' The general slammed down his palm, making the cutlery jump. 'The British soldier is the superior of any man alive!'

'I don't doubt it,' Callandra agreed. 'It is the British general in the field who is a hidebound and incompetent ass.'

'Callandra! For God's sake!' Fabia was appalled.

Menard put his hands over his face.

'Perhaps we should have done better had you been there, General Wadham,' Callandra continued unabashed, looking at him frankly. 'You at least have a very considerable imagination!'

Rosamond shut her eyes and slid down in her seat. Lovel groaned.

Hester choked with laughter, a trifle hysterically, and

stuffed her napkin over her mouth to stifle it.

General Wadham made a surprisingly graceful strategic retreat. He decided to accept the remark as a compliment.

'Thank you, madame,' he said stiffly. 'Perhaps I might have prevented the slaughter of the Light Brigade.'

And with that it was left. Fabia, with a little help from Lovel, rose from her seat and excused the ladies, leading them to the withdrawing room, where they discussed such matters as music, fashion, society, forthcoming weddings, both planned and speculated, and were excessively polite to one another.

When the visitors finally took their leave, Fabia turned upon her sister-in-law with a look that should have shrivelled her.

'Callandra – I shall never forgive you!'

'Since you have never forgiven me for wearing the exact shade of gown as you when we first met forty years ago,' Callandra replied, 'I shall just have to bear it with the same fortitude I have shown over all the other episodes since.'

'You are impossible. Dear heaven, how I miss Joscelin.' She stood up slowly and Hester rose as a matter of courtesy. Fabia walked towards the double doors. 'I am going to bed. I shall see you tomorrow.' And she went out, leaving them also.

'You are impossible, Aunt Callandra,' Rosamond agreed, standing in the middle of the floor and looking confused and unhappy. 'I don't know why you say such things.'

'I know you don't,' Callandra said gently. 'That is because

you have never been anywhere but Middleton, Shelburne Hall or London society. Hester would say the same, if she were not a guest here – indeed perhaps more. Our military imagination has ossified since Waterloo.' She stood up and straightened her skirts. 'Victory – albeit one of the greatest in history and turning the tide of nations – has still gone to our heads and we think all we have to do to win is to turn up in our scarlet coats and obey the rules. And only God can measure the suffering and the death that pigheadedness has caused. And we women and politicians sit here safely at home and cheer them on without the slightest idea what the reality of it is.'

'Joscelin is dead,' Rosamond said bleakly, staring at the closed curtains.

'I know that, my dear,' Callandra said from close behind her. 'But he did not die in the Crimea.'

'He may have died because of it!'

'Indeed he may,' Callandra conceded, her face suddenly touched with gentleness. 'And I know you were extremely fond of him. He had a capacity for pleasure, both to give and to receive, which unfortunately neither Lovel nor Menard seem to share. I think we have exhausted both ourselves and the subject. Good night, my dear. Weep if you wish; tears too long held in do us no good. Composure is all very well, but there is a time to acknowledge pain also.' She slipped her arm around the slender shoulders and hugged her briefly, then knowing the gesture would release the hurt as well as comfort, she took Hester by the elbow and conducted her out to leave Rosamond alone.

* * *

The following morning Hester overslept and rose with a headache. She did not feel like early breakfast, and still less like facing any of the family across the table. She felt passionately about the vanity and the incompetence she had seen in the army, and the horror at the suffering would never leave her; probably the anger would not either. But she had not behaved very well at dinner; and the memory of it churned around in her mind, trying to fall into a happier picture with less fault attached to herself, and did not improve either her headache or her temper.

She decided to take a brisk walk in the park for as long as her energy lasted. She wrapped up appropriately, and by nine o'clock was striding rapidly over the grass getting her boots wet.

She first saw the figure of the man with considerable irritation, simply because she wished to be alone. He was probably inoffensive, and presumably had as much right to be here as herself – perhaps more? He no doubt served some function. However she felt he intruded, he was another human being in a world of wind and great trees and vast, cloud-racked skies and shivering, singing grass.

When he drew level he stopped and spoke to her. He was dark, with an arrogant face, all lean, smooth bones and clear eyes.

'Good morning, ma'am. I see you are from Shelburne Hall—'

'How observant,' she said tartly, gazing around at the totally empty parkland. There was no other place she could

212

conceivably have come from, unless she had emerged from a hole in the ground.

His face tightened, aware of her sarcasm. 'Are you a member of the family?' He was staring at her with some intensity and she found it disconcerting, and bordering on the offensive.

'How is that your concern?' she asked coldly.

The concentration deepened in his eyes, and then suddenly there was a flash of recognition, although for the life of her she could not think of any occasion on which she had seen him before. Curiously he did not refer to it.

'I am inquiring into the murder of Joscelin Grey. I wonder if you had known him.'

'Good heavens!' she said involuntarily. Then she collected herself. 'I have been accused of tactlessness in my time, but you are certainly in a class of your own.' A total lie – Callandra would have left him standing! 'It would be quite in your deserving if I told you I had been his fiancée – and fainted on the spot!'

'Then it was a secret engagement,' he retorted. 'And if you go in for clandestine romance you must expect to have your feelings bruised a few times.'

'Which you are obviously well equipped to do!' She stood still with the wind whipping her skirts, still wondering why he had seemed to recognize her.

'Did you know him?' he repeated irritably.

'Yes!'

'For how long?'

'As well as I remember it, about three weeks.'

'That's an odd time to know anyone!'

'What would you consider a usual time to know someone?' she demanded.

'It was very brief,' he explained with careful condescension. 'You can hardly have been a friend of the family. Did you meet him just before he died?'

'No. I met him in Scutari.'

'You what?'

'Are you hard of hearing? I met him in Scutari!' She remembered the general's patronizing manner and all her memories of condescension flooded back, the army officers who considered women out of place, ornaments to be used for recreation or comfort but not creatures of any sense. Gentlewomen were for cossetting, dominating and protecting from everything, including adventure or decision or freedom of any kind. Common women were whores or drudges and to be used like any other livestock.

'Oh yes,' he agreed with a frown. 'He was injured. Were you out there with your husband?'

'No I was not!' Why should that question be faintly hurtful? 'I went to nurse the injured, to assist Miss Nightingale, and those like her.'

His face did not show the admiration and profound sense of respect close to awe that the name usually brought. She was thrown off balance by it. He seemed to be single-minded in his interest in Joscelin Grey.

'You nursed Major Grey?'

'Among others. Do you mind if we proceed to walk? I am getting cold standing here.'

'Of course.' He turned and fell into step with her and they began along the faint track in the grass towards a copse of oaks. 'What were your impressions of him?'

She tried hard to distinguish her memory from the picture she had gathered from his family's words, Rosamond's weeping, Fabia's pride and love, the void he had left in her happiness, perhaps Rosamond's also, his brothers' mixture of exasperation and – what – envy?

'I can recall his leg rather better than his face,' she said frankly.

He stared at her with temper rising sharply in his face.

'I am not interested in your female fantasies, madame, or your peculiar sense of humour! This is an investigation into an unusually brutal murder!'

She lost her temper completely.

'You incompetent idiot!' she shouted into the wind. 'You grubby-minded, fatuous nincompoop. I was nursing him. I dressed and cleaned his wound – which, in case you have forgotten, was in his leg. His face was uninjured, therefore I did not regard it any more than the faces of the other ten thousand injured and dead I saw. I would not know him again if he came up and spoke to me.'

His face was bleak and furious. 'It would be a memorable occasion, madame. He is eight weeks dead – and beaten to a pulp.'

If he had hoped to shock her he failed.

She swallowed hard and held his eyes. 'Sounds like the battlefield after Inkermann,' she said levelly. 'Only there at least we knew what had happened to them – even if no one had any idea why.'

'We know what happened to Joscelin Grey – we do not know who did it. Fortunately I am not responsible for explaining the Crimean War – only Joscelin Grey's death.'

'Which seems to be beyond you,' she said unkindly. 'And I can be of no assistance. All I can remember is that he was unusually agreeable, that he bore his injury with as much fortitude as most, and that when he was recovering he spent quite a lot of his time moving from bed to bed encouraging and cheering other men, particularly those closest to death. In fact when I think of it, he was a most admirable man. I had forgotten that until now. He comforted many who were dying, and wrote letters home for them, told their families of their deaths and probably gave them much ease in their distress. It is very hard that he should survive that, and come home to be murdered here.'

'He was killed very violently – there was a passion of hatred in the way he was beaten.' He was looking at her closely and she was startled by the intelligence in his face; it was uncomfortably intense, and unexpected. 'I believe it was someone who knew him. One does not hate a stranger as he was hated.'

She shivered. Horrific as was the battlefield, there was still a world of difference between its mindless carnage and the acutely personal malevolence of Joscelin Grey's death.

'I am sorry,' she said more gently, but still with the stiffness he engendered in her. 'I know nothing of him that would help you find such a relationship. If I did I should tell you. The hospital kept records; you would be able to find out who else was there at the same time, but no doubt you have already done that—' She saw instantly from the shadow in his face that he had not. Her patience broke. 'Then for heaven's sake, what have you been doing for eight weeks?'

'For five of them I was lying injured myself,' he snapped back. 'Or recovering. You make far too many assumptions, madame. You are arrogant, domineering, ill tempered and condescending. And you leap to conclusions for which you have no foundation. God! I hate clever women!'

She froze for an instant before the reply was on her lips.

'I love clever men!' Her eyes raked him up and down. 'It seems we are both to be disappointed.' And with that she picked up her skirts and strode past him and along the path towards the copse, tripping over a bramble across her way. 'Drat,' she swore furiously. 'Hellfire.'

Chapter Seven

'Good morning, Miss Latterly,' Fabia said coolly when she came into the sitting room at about quarter past ten the following day. She looked smart and fragile and was already dressed as if to go out. She eyed Hester very briefly, noting her extremely plain muslin gown, and then turned to Rosamond, who was sitting poking apologetically at an embroidery frame. 'Good morning, Rosamond. I hope you are well? It is a most pleasant day, and I believe we should take the opportunity to visit some of the less fortunate in the village. We have not been lately, and it is your duty, my dear, even more than it is mine.'

The colour deepened a trifle in Rosamond's cheeks as she accepted the rebuke. From the quick lift in her chin Hester thought there might be far more behind the motion than was apparent. The family was in mourning, and Fabia had quite obviously felt the loss most keenly, at least to the outward eye. Had Rosamond tried to resume life too quickly for her, and this was Fabia's way of choosing the time?

'Of course, Mama-in-law,' Rosamond said without looking up.

'And no doubt Miss Latterly will come with us,' Fabia added without consulting her. 'We shall leave at eleven.

That will allow you time to dress appropriately. The day is most warm – do not be tempted to forget your position.' And with that admonition, delivered with a frozen smile, she turned and left them, stopping by the door for a moment to add, 'And we might take luncheon with General Wadham, and Ursula.' And then she went out.

Rosamond threw the hoop at her workbasket and it went beyond and skittered across the floor. 'Drat,' she said quietly under her breath. Then she met Hester's eyes and apologized.

Hester smiled at her. 'Please don't,' she said candidly. 'Playing Lady Bountiful 'round the estates is enough to make anyone resort to language better for the stable, or even the barracks, than the drawing room. A simple "drat" is very mild.'

'Do you miss the Crimea, now you are home?' Rosamond said suddenly, her eyes intent and almost frightened of the answer. 'I mean—' She looked away, embarrassed and now finding it hard to speak the words which only a moment before had been so ready.

Hester saw a vision of endless days being polite to Fabia, attending to the trivial household management that she was allowed, never feeling it was her house until Fabia was dead; and perhaps even afterwards Fabia's spirit would haunt the house, her belongings, her choices of furniture, of design, marking it indelibly. There would be morning calls, luncheon with suitable people of like breeding and position, visits to the poor – and in season there would be balls, the races at Ascot, the regatta at Henley, and of course in winter the hunt. None of it would be more than pleasant at best, tedious at worst – but without meaning.

But Rosamond did not deserve a lie, even in her loneliness – nor did she deserve the pain of Hester's view of the truth. It was only her view; for Rosamond it might be different.

'Oh yes, sometimes I do,' she said with a small smile. 'But we cannot fight wars like that for long. It is very dreadful as well as vivid and real. It is not fun being cold and dirty and so tired you feel as if you've been beaten – nor is it pleasant to eat army rations. It is one of the finest things in life to be truly useful – but there are less distressing places to do it, and I am sure I shall find many here in England.'

'You are very kind,' Rosamond said gently, meeting her eyes again. 'I admit I had not imagined you would be so thoughtful.' She rose to her feet. 'Now I suppose we had better change into suitable clothes for calling – have you something modest and dowdy, but very dignified?' She stifled a giggle and turned it into a sneeze. 'I'm sorry – what a fearful thing to ask!'

'Yes – most of my wardrobe is like that,' Hester replied with an amused smile. 'All dark greens and very tired-looking blues – like faded ink. Will they do?'

'Perfectly – come!'

Menard drove the three of them in the open trap, bowling along the carriageway through the park towards the edge of the home estate and across heavy cornfields towards the village and the church spire beyond the slow swell of the hill. He obviously enjoyed managing the horse and did it with the skill of one who is long practised. He did not even try to make conversation, supposing the loveliness of the land, the sky and the trees would be enough for them, as it was for him.

Hester sat watching him, leaving Rosamond and Fabia to converse. She looked at his powerful hands holding the reins lightly, at the ease of his balance and the obvious reticence in his expression. The daily round of duties in the estate was no imprisonment to him; she had seen a brooding in his face occasionally in the time she had been at Shelburne, sometimes anger, sometimes a stiffness and a jumpiness of the muscles which made her think of officers she had seen the night before battle, but it was when they were all at table, with Fabia's conversation betraying the ache of loneliness underneath as if Joscelin had been the only person she had totally and completely loved.

The first house they called at was that of a farm labourer on the edge of the village, a tiny cottage, one room downstairs crowded with a sunburned, shabby woman and seven children all sharing a loaf of bread spread with pork drippings. Their thin, dusty legs, barefooted, splayed out beneath simple smocks and they were obviously in from working in the garden or fields. Even the youngest, who looked no more than three or four, had fruit stains on her fingers where she had been harvesting.

Fabia asked questions and passed out practical advice on financial management and how to treat croup which the woman received in polite silence. Hester blushed for the condescension of it, and then realized it had been a way of life with little substantial variation for over a thousand years, and both parties were comfortable with its familiarity; and she had nothing more certain to put in its place.

Rosamond spoke with the eldest girl, and took the wide pink ribbon off her own hat and gave it to her, tying it around the child's hair to her shy delight.

Menard stood patiently by the horse, talking to it in a low voice for a few moments, then falling into a comfortable silence. The sunlight on his face showed the fine lines of anxiety around his eyes and mouth, and the deeper marks of pain. Here in the rich land with its great trees, the wind and the fertile earth he was relaxed, and Hester saw a glimpse of a quite different man from the stolid, resentful second son he appeared at Shelburne Hall. She wondered if Fabia had ever allowed herself to see it. Or was the laughing charm of Joscelin always in its light?

The second call was similar in essence, although the family was composed of an elderly woman with no teeth and an old man who was either drunk or had suffered some seizure which impaired both his speech and his movement.

Fabia spoke to him briskly with words of impersonal encouragement, which he ignored, making a face at her when her back was turned, and the old woman bobbed a curtsy, accepted two jars of lemon curd, and once again they climbed into the trap and were on their way.

Menard left them to go out into the fields, high with ripe corn, the reapers already digging the sickles deep, the sun hot on their backs, arms burned, sweat running freely. There was much talk of weather, time, the quarter of the wind, and when the rain would break. The smell of the grain and the broken straw in the heat was one of the sweetest things Hester had ever known. She stood in the brilliant light with her face lifted to the sky, the heat tingling on her skin, and gazed across the dark gold of the land – and thought of those who had been willing to die for it – and prayed that the heirs to so much treasured it deeply enough, to see it with the body and with the heart as well.

Luncheon was another matter altogether. They were received courteously enough until General Wadham saw Hester, then his florid face stiffened and his manner became exaggeratedly formal.

'Good morning, Miss Latterly. How good of you to call. Ursula will be delighted that you are able to join us for luncheon.'

'Thank you, sir,' she replied equally gravely. 'You are very generous.'

Ursula did not look particularly delighted to see them at all, and was unable to hide her chagrin that Menard had seen fit to be out with the harvesters instead of here at the dining room table.

Luncheon was a light meal: poached river fish with caper sauce, cold game pie and vegetables, then a sorbet and a selection of fruit, followed by an excellent Stilton cheese.

General Wadham had obviously neither forgotten nor forgiven his rout by Hester on their previous meeting. His chill. rather glassy eye met hers over the cruet sets a number of times before he actually joined battle in a lull between Fabia's comments on the roses and Ursula's speculations as to whether Mr Danbury would marry Miss Fothergill or Miss Ames.

'Miss Ames is a fine young woman,' the general remarked, looking at Hester. 'Most accomplished horsewoman, rides to hounds like a man. Courage. And handsome too, dashed handsome.' He looked at Hester's dark green dress sourly. 'Grandfather died in the Peninsular War – at Corunna – 1810. Don't suppose you were there too, were you, Miss Latterly? Bit before your time, eh?' He smiled, as if he had intended it to be good-natured.

'1809,' Hester corrected him. 'It was before Talavera and after Vimiero and the Convention of Cintra. Otherwise you are perfectly correct – I was not there.'

The general's face was scarlet. He swallowed a fish bone and choked into his napkin.

Fabia, white with fury, passed him a glass of water.

Hester, knowing better, removed it instantly and replaced it with bread.

The general took the bread and the bone was satisfactorily coated with it and passed down his throat.

'Thank you,' he said freezingly, and then took the water also.

'I am happy to be of assistance,' Hester replied sweetly. 'It is most unpleasant to swallow a bone, and so easily done, even in the best of fish – and this is delicious.'

Fabia muttered something blasphemous and inaudible under her breath and Rosamond launched into a sudden and over enthusiastic recollection of the Vicar's midsummer garden party.

Afterwards, when Fabia had elected to remain with Ursula and the general, and Rosamond hurried Hester out to the trap to resume their visiting of the poor, she whispered to her rapidly and with a little self-consciousness.

'That was awful. Sometimes you remind me of Joscelin. He used to make me laugh like that.'

'I didn't notice you laughing,' Hester said honestly, climbing up into the trap after her and forgetting to arrange her skirts.

'Of course not.' Rosamond took the reins and slapped the horse forward. 'It would never do to be seen. You will come again some time, won't you?'

'I am not at all sure I shall be asked,' Hester said ruefully.

'Yes you will – Aunt Callandra will ask you. She likes you very much – and I think sometimes she gets bored with us here. Did you know Colonel Daviot?'

'No.' For the first time Hester regretted that she had not. She had seen his portrait, but that was all; he had been a stocky, upright man with a strong-featured face, full of wit and temper. 'No, I didn't.'

Rosamond urged the horse faster and they careered along the track, the wheels bouncing over the ridges.

'He was very charming,' she said, watching ahead. 'Sometimes. He had a great laugh when he was happy – he also had a filthy temper and was terribly bossy – even with Aunt Callandra. He was always interfering, telling her how she ought to do everything – when he got the whim for it. Then he would forget about whatever it was, and leave her to clear up the mess.'

226

She reined in the horse a little, getting it under better control.

'But he was very generous,' she added. 'He never betrayed a friend's confidence. And the best horseman I ever saw – far better than either Menard or Lovel – and far better than General Wadham.' Her hair was coming undone in the wind, and she ignored it. She giggled happily. 'They couldn't bear each other.'

It opened up an understanding of Callandra that Hester had never imagined before – a loneliness, and a freedom which explained why she had never entertained the idea of remarriage. Who could follow such a highly individual man? And perhaps also her independence had become more precious as she became more used to its pleasures. And perhaps also there had been more unhappiness there than Hester had imagined in her swift and rather shallow judgments?

She smiled and made some acknowledgment of having heard Rosamond's remarks, then changed the subject. They arrived at the small hamlet where their further visiting was to be conducted, and it was late in the afternoon, hot and vividly blue and gold as they returned through the heavy fields past the reapers, whose backs were still bent, arms bare. Hester was glad of the breeze of their movement and passing beneath the huge shade trees that leaned over the narrow road was a pleasure. There was no sound but the thud of the horse's hooves, the hiss of the wheels and the occasional bird song. The light gleamed pale on the straw stalks where the labourers had already passed, and darker on the ungathered heads. A few faint clouds, frail as spun floss, drifted across the horizon.

Hester looked at Rosamond's hands on the reins and her quiet, tense face, and wondered if she saw the timeless beauty of it, or only the unceasing sameness, but it was a question she could not ask.

Hester spent the evening with Callandra in her rooms and did not dine with the family, but she took breakfast in the main dining room the following morning and Rosamond greeted her with evident pleasure.

'Would you like to see my son?' she invited with a faint blush for her assumption, and her vulnerability.

'Of course I would,' Hester answered immediately; it was the only possible thing to say. 'I cannot think of anything nicer.' Indeed that was probably true. She was not looking forward to her next encounter with Fabia and she certainly did not wish to do any more visiting with General Wadham, any more 'good works' among those whom Fabia considered 'the deserving poor', nor to walk in the park again where she might meet that peculiarly offensive policeman. His remarks had been impertinent, and really very unjust. 'It will make a beautiful beginning to the day,' she added.

The nursery was a bright south-facing room full of sunlight and chintz, with a low nursing chair by the window, a rocking chair next to the large, well-railed and guarded fireplace, and at present, since the child was so young, a day crib. The nursery maid, a young girl with a handsome face and skin like cream, was busy feeding the baby, about a year and a half old, with fingers of bread and butter dipped in a chopped and buttered boiled egg. Hester and Rosamond did not interrupt but stood watching.

The baby, a quiff of blond hair along the crown of his head like a little bird's comb, was obviously enjoying himself immensely. He accepted every mouthful with perfect obedience and his cheeks grew fatter and fatter. Then with shining eyes he took a deep breath and blew it all out, to the nursery maid's utter consternation. He laughed so hard his face was bright pink and he fell over sideways in his chair, helpless with delight.

Rosamond was filled with embarrassment, but all Hester could do was laugh with the baby, while the maid dabbed at her once spotless apron with a damp cloth.

'Master Harry, you shouldn't do that!' the maid said as fiercely as she dared, but there was no real anger in her voice, more simple exasperation at having been caught yet again.

'Oh, you dreadful child.' Rosamond went and picked him up, holding him close to her and laying the pale head with its wave of hair close to her cheek. He was still crowing with joy, and looked over his mother's shoulder at Hester with total confidence that she would love him.

They spent a happy hour in gentle conversation, then left the maid to continue with her duties, and Rosamond showed Hester the main nursery where Lovel, Menard and Joscelin had played as children: the rocking horse, the toy soldiers, the wooden swords, the musical boxes, and the kaleidoscope; and the dolls' houses left by an earlier generation of girls – perhaps Callandra herself?

Next they looked at the schoolroom with its tables and shelves of books. Hester found her hands picking at first idly over old exercises of copperplate writing, a child's early, careful attempts. Then as she progressed to adolescent years and essays she found herself absorbed in reading the maturing hand. It was an essay in light, fluent style, surprisingly sharp for one so young and with a penetrating, often unkind wit. The subject was a family picnic, and she found herself smiling as she read, but there was pain in it, an awareness under the humour of cruelty. She did not need to look at the spine of the book to know it was Joscelin's.

She found one of Lovel's and turned the pages till she discovered an essay of similar length. Rosamond was searching a small desk for a copy of some verses, and there was time to read it carefully. It was utterly unlike, diffident, romantic, seeing beyond the simple woodland of Shelburne a forest where great deeds could be done, an ideal woman wooed and loved with a clean and untroubled emotion so far from the realities of human need and difficulty. Hester found her eyes prickling for the disillusion that must come to such a youth.

She closed the pages with their faded ink and looked across at Rosamond, the sunlight on her bent head as she fingered through duty books looking for some special poem that caught her own high dream. Did either she or Lovel see beyond the princesses and the knights in armour, the fallible, sometimes weak, sometimes frightened, often foolish people beneath – who needed immeasurably more courage, generosity and power to forgive than the creatures of youth's dreams – and were so much more precious?

She wanted to find the third essay, Menard's – and it took her several minutes to locate a book of his and read it. It was stiff, far less comfortable with words, and all through it there was a passionate love of honour, a loyalty to friendship and a sense of history as an unending cavalcade of the proud and the good, with sudden images borrowed from the tales of King Arthur. It was derivative and stilted, but the sincerity still shone through, and she doubted the man had lost the values of the boy who had written so intensely – and awkwardly.

Rosamond had found her poem at last, and was so absorbed in it that she was unaware of Hester's movement towards her, or that Hester glanced over her shoulder and saw that it was an anonymous love poem, very small and very tender.

Hester looked away and walked to the door. It was not something upon which to intrude.

Rosamond closed the book and followed a moment after, recapturing her previous gaiety with an effort which Hester pretended not to notice.

'Thank you for coming up,' she said as they came back into the main landing with its huge jardinières of flowers. 'It was kind of you to be so interested.'

'It is not kindness at all,' Hester denied quickly. 'I think it is a privilege to see into the past as one does in nurseries and old schoolrooms. I thank you for allowing me to come.

And of course Harry is delightful! Who could fail to be happy in his presence?'

Rosamond laughed and made a small gesture of denial with her hand, but she was obviously pleased. They made their way downstairs together and into the dining room, where luncheon was already served and Lovel was waiting for them. He stood up as they came in, and took a step towards Rosamond. For a moment he seemed about to speak, then the impulse died.

She waited a moment, her eyes full of hope. Hester hated herself for being there, but to leave now would be absurd; the meal was set and the footman waiting to serve it. She knew Callandra had gone to visit an old acquaintance, because it was on Hester's behalf that she had made the journey, but Fabia was also absent and her place was not set.

Lovel saw her glance.

'Mama is not well,' he said with a faint chill. 'She has remained in her room.'

'I am sorry,' Hester said automatically. 'I hope it is nothing serious?'

'I hope not,' he agreed, and as soon as they were seated, resumed his own seat and indicated that the footman might begin to serve them.

Rosamond nudged Hester under the table with her foot, and Hester gathered that the situation was delicate, and wisely did not pursue it.

The meal was conducted with stilted and trivial conversation, layered with meanings, and Hester thought of the boy's essay, the old poem, and all the levels of dreams and realities where so much fell through between one set of meanings and another, and was lost.

Afterwards she excused herself and went to do what she realized was her duty. She must call on Fabia and apologize for having been rude to General Wadham. He had deserved it, but she was Fabia's guest, and she should not have embarrassed her, regardless of the provocation.

It was best done immediately; the longer she thought about it the harder it would be. She had little patience with minor ailments; she had seen too much desperate disease, and her own health was good enough she did not know from experience how debilitating even a minor pain can be when stretched over time.

She knocked on Fabia's door and waited until she heard the command to enter, then she turned the handle and went in.

It was a less feminine room than she had expected. It was plain light Wedgwood blue and sparsely furnished compared with the usual cluttered style. A single silver vase held summer roses in full bloom on the table by the window; the bed was canopied in white muslin, like the inner curtains. On the farthest wall, where the sun was diffused, hung a fine portrait of a young man in the uniform of a cavalry officer. He was slender and straight, his fair hair falling over a broad brow, pale, intelligent eyes and a mobile mouth, humorous, articulate, and, she thought in that fleeting instant, a little weak.

Fabia was sitting up in her bed, a blue satin bedjacket

covering her shoulders and her hair brushed and knotted loosely so it fell in a faded coil over her breast. She looked thin and much older than Hester was prepared for. Suddenly the apology was not difficult. She could see all the loneliness of years in the pale face, the loss which would never be repaired.

'Yes?' Fabia said with distinct chill.

'I came to apologize, Lady Fabia,' Hester replied quietly. 'I was very rude to General Wadham yesterday, and as your guest it was inexcusable. I am truly sorry.'

Fabia's eyebrows rose in surprise, then she smiled very slightly.

'I accept your apology. I am surprised you had the grace to come – I had not expected it of you. It is not often I misjudge a young woman.' Her smile lifted the corners of her mouth fractionally, giving her face a sudden life, echoing the girl she must once have been. 'It was most embarrassing for me that General Wadham should be so – so deflated. But it was not entirely without its satisfactions. He is a condescending old fool – and I sometimes get very weary of being patronized.'

Hester was too surprised to say anything at all. For the first time since arriving at Shelburne Hall she actually liked Fabia.

'You may sit down,' Fabia offered with a gleam of humour in her eyes.

'Thank you.' Hester sat on the dressing chair covered with blue velvet, and looked around the room at the other, lesser paintings and the few photographs, stiff and very posed for the long time that the camera required to set the image. There was a picture of Rosamond and Lovel, probably at their wedding. She looked fragile and very happy; he was facing the lens squarely, full of hope.

On the other chest there was an early daguerreotype of a middle-aged man with handsome side-whiskers, black hair and a vain, whimsical face. From the resemblance to Joscelin, Hester assumed it to be the late Lord Shelburne. There was also a pencil sketch of all three brothers as boys, sentimental, features a little idealized, the way one remembers summers of the past.

'I'm sorry you are feeling unwell,' Hester said quietly. 'Is there anything I can do for you?'

'I should think it highly unlikely; I am not a casualty of war – at least not in the sense that you are accustomed to,' Fabia replied.

Hester did not argue. It rose to the tip of her tongue to say she was accustomed to all sorts of hurt, but then she knew it would be trite – she had not lost a son, and that was the only grief Fabia was concerned with.

'My elder brother was killed in the Crimea.' Hester still found the words hard to say. She could see George in her mind's eye, the way he walked, hear his laughter, then it dissolved and a sharper memory returned of herself and Charles and George as children, and the tears ached in her throat beyond bearing. 'And both my parents died shortly after,' she said quickly. 'Shall we speak of something else?'

For a moment Fabia looked startled. She had forgotten, and now she was faced with a loss as huge as her own.

'My dear – I'm so very sorry. Of course – you did say so. Forgive me. What have you done this morning? Would you care to take the trap out later? It would be no difficulty to arrange it.'

'I went to the nursery and met Harry.' Hester smiled and blinked. 'He's beautiful—' And she proceeded to tell the story.

She remained at Shelburne Hall for several more days, sometimes taking long walks alone in the wind and brilliant air. The parkland had a beauty which pleased her immensely and she felt at peace with it as she had in few other places. She was able to consider the future much more clearly, and Callandra's advice, repeated several times more in their many conversations, seemed increasingly wise the more she thought of it. The tension among the members of the household changed after the dinner with General Wadham. Surface anger was covered with the customary good manners, but she became aware through a multitude of small observations that the unhappiness was a deep and abiding part of the fabric of their lives.

Fabia had a personal courage which might have been at least half the habitual discipline of her upbringing and the pride that would not allow others to see her vulnerability. She was autocratic, to some extent selfish, although she would have been the last to think it of herself. But Hester saw the loneliness in her face in moments when she believed herself unobserved, and at times beneath the old woman so immaculately dressed, a bewilderment which laid bare the child she had once been. Undoubtedly she loved her two surviving sons, but she did not especially like them, and no one could charm her or make her laugh as Joscelin had. They were courteous, but they did not flatter her, they did not bring back with small attentions the great days of her beauty when dozens had courted her and she had been the centre of so much. With Joscelin's death her own hunger for living had gone.

Hester spent many hours with Rosamond and became fond of her in a distant, non-confiding sort of way. Callandra's words about a brave, protective smile came to her sharply on several occasions, most particularly one late afternoon as they sat by the fire and made light, trivial conversation. Ursula Wadham was visiting, full of excitement and plans for the time when she would be married to Menard. She babbled on, facing Rosamond but apparently not seeing anything deeper than the perfect complexion, the carefully dressed hair and the rich afternoon gown. To her Rosamond had everything a woman could desire, a wealthy and titled husband, a strong child, beauty, good health and sufficient talent in the arts of pleasing. What else was there to desire?

Hester listened to Rosamond agreeing to all the plans, how exciting it would be and how happy the future looked, and she saw behind the dark eyes no gleam of confidence and hope, only a sense of loss, a loneliness and a kind of desperate courage that keeps going because it knows no way to stop. She smiled because it brought her peace, it prevented question and it preserved a shred of pride.

Lovel was busy. At least he had purpose and as long as

237

he was fulfilling it any darker emotion was held at bay. Only at the dinner table when they were all together did the occasional remark betray the underlying knowledge that something had eluded him, some precious element that seemed to be his was not really. He could not have called it fear – he would have hated the word and rejected it with horror – but staring at him across the snow-white linen and the glittering crystal, Hester thought that was what it was. She had seen it so often before, in totally different guises, when the danger was physical, violent and immediate. At first because the threat was so different she thought only of anger, then as it nagged persistently at the back of her mind, unclassified, suddenly she saw its other face, domestic, personal, emotional pain, and she knew it was a jar of familiarity.

With Menard it was also anger, but a sharp awareness too of something he saw as injustice; past now in act, but the residue still affecting him. Had he tidied up too often after Joscelin, his mother's favourite, protecting her from the truth that he was a cheat? Or was it himself he protected, and the family name?

Only with Callandra did she feel relaxed, but it did on one occasion cross her mind to wonder whether Callandra's comfort with herself was the result of many years' happiness or the resolution within her nature of its warring elements, not a gift but an art. It was one evening when they had taken a light supper in Callandra's sitting room instead of dinner in the main wing, and Callandra had made some remark about her husband, now long dead. Hester had always assumed the marriage to have been happy, not from anything she knew of it, or of Callandra Daviot, but from the peace within Callandra.

Now she realized how blindly she had leaped to such a shortsighted conclusion.

Callandra must have seen the idea waken in her eyes. She smiled with a touch of wryness, and a gentle humour in her face.

'You have a great deal of courage, Hester, and a hunger for life which is a far richer blessing than you think now – but, my dear, you are sometimes very naive. There are many kinds of misery, and many kinds of fortitude, and you should not allow your awareness of one to build to the value of another. You have an intense desire, a passion, to make people's lives better. Be aware that you can truly help people only by aiding them to become what they are, not what you are. I have heard you say "If I were you, I would do this – or that." "I" am never "you" – and my solutions may not be yours.'

Hester remembered the wretched policeman who had told her she was domineering, overbearing and several other unpleasant things.

Callandra smiled. 'Remember, my dear, you are dealing with the world as it is, not as you believe, maybe rightly, that it ought to be. There will be a great many things you can achieve not by attacking them but with a little patience and a modicum of flattery. Stop to consider what it is you really want, rather than pursuing your anger or your vanity to charge in. So often we leap to passionate judgments – when if we but knew the one thing more, they would be so different.'

Hester was tempted to laugh, in spite of having heard very clearly what Callandra had said, and perceiving the truth of it.

'I know,' Callandra agreed quickly. 'I preach much better than I practise. But believe me, when I want something enough, I have the patience to bide my time and think how I can bring it about.'

'I'll try,' Hester promised, and she did mean it. 'That miserable policeman will not be right – I shall not allow him to be right.'

'I beg your pardon?'

'I met him when I was out walking,' Hester explained. 'He said I was overbearing and opinionated, or something like that.'

Callandra's eyebrows shot up and she did not even attempt to keep a straight face.

'Did he really? What temerity! And what perception, on such a short acquaintance. And what did you think of him, may I ask?'

'An incompetent and insufferable nincompoop!'

'Which of course you told him?'

Hester glared back at her. 'Certainly!'

'Quite so. I think he had more of the right of it than you did. I don't think he is incompetent. He had been given an extremely difficult task. There were a great many people who might have hated Joscelin, and it will be exceedingly difficult for a policeman, with all his disadvantages, to discover which one it was – and even harder, I imagine, to prove it.'

'You mean, you think—' Hester left it unsaid, hanging in the air.

'I do,' Callandra replied. 'Now come, we must settle what you are to do with yourself. I shall write to certain friends I have, and I have little doubt, if you hold a civil tongue in your head, refrain from expressing your opinion of men in general and of Her Majesty's Army's generals in particular, we may obtain for you a position in hospital administration that will not only be satisfying to you but also to those who are unfortunate enough to be ill.'

'Thank you.' Hester smiled. 'I am very grateful.' She looked down in her lap for a moment, then up at Callandra and her eyes sparkled. 'I really do not mind walking two paces behind a man, you know – if only I can find one who can walk two paces faster than I! It is being tied at the knees by convention I hate – and having to pretend I am lame to suit someone else's vanity.'

Callandra shook her head very slowly, amusement and sadness sharp in her face. 'I know. Perhaps you will have to fall a few times, and have someone else pick you up, before you will learn a more equable pace. But do not walk slowly simply for company – ever. Not even God would wish you to be unequally yoked and result in destroying both of you – in fact God least of all.'

Hester sat back and smiled, lifting up her knees and hugging them in a most unladylike fashion. 'I daresay I shall fall many times – and look excessively foolish – and give

rise to a good deal of hilarity among those who dislike me –
but that is still better than not trying.'

'Indeed it is,' Callandra agreed. 'But you would do it
anyway.'

Chapter Eight

The most productive of Joscelin Grey's acquaintances was one of the last that Monk and Evan visited, and not from Lady Fabia's list, but from the letters in the flat. They had spent over a week in the area near Shelburne, discreetly questioning on the pretence of tracing a jewel thief who specialized in country houses. They had learned something of Joscelin Grey, of the kind of life he led, at least while home from London. And Monk had had the unnerving and extremely irritating experience one day while walking across the Shelburne parkland of coming upon the woman who had been with Mrs Latterly in St Marylebone Church. Perhaps he should not have been startled – after all, society was very small – but it had taken him aback completely. The whole episode in the church with its powerful emotion had returned in the windy, rain-spattered land with its huge trees, and Shelburne House in the distance.

There was no reason why she should not have visited the family, precisely as he later discovered. She was a Miss Hester Latterly, who had nursed in the Crimea, and was a friend of Lady Callandra Daviot. As she had told him, she had known Joscelin Grey briefly at the time of his injury. It was most natural that once she was home she should give her condolences in person. And also certainly within her nature that she should be outstandingly rude to a policeman.

And give the devil her due, he had been rude back – and gained considerable satisfaction from it. It would all have been of no possible consequence were she not obviously related to the woman in the church whose face so haunted him.

What had they learned? Joscelin Grey was liked, even envied for his ease of manner, his quick smile and a gift for making people laugh; and perhaps even more rather than less, because the amusement had frequently an underlying caustic quality. What had surprised Monk was that he was also, if not pitied, then sympathized with because he was a younger son. The usual careers open to younger sons such as the church and the army were either totally unsuitable to him or else denied him now because of his injury, gained in the service of his country. The heiress he had courted had married his elder brother, and he had not yet found another to replace her, at least not one whose family considered him a suitable match. He was, after all, invalided out of the army, without a merchandisable skill and without financial expectations.

Evan had acquired a rapid education in the manners and morals of his financial betters, and now was feeling both bemused and disillusioned. He sat in the train staring out of the window, and Monk regarded him with a compassion not unmixed with humour. He knew the feeling, although he could not recall experiencing it himself. Was it possible he had never been so young? It was an unpleasant thought that he might always have been cynical, without that particular kind of innocence, even as a child.

Discovering himself step by step, as one might a stranger, was stretching his nerves further than he had been aware of until now. Sometimes he woke in the night, afraid of knowledge, feeling himself full of unknown shames and disappointments. The shapelessness of his doubt was worse than certainty would have been; even certainty of arrogance, indifference, or of having overridden justice for the sake of ambition.

But the more he pulled and struggled with it, the more stubbornly it resisted; it would come only thread by thread, without cohesion, a fragment at a time. Where had he learned his careful, precise diction? Who had taught him to move and to dress like a gentleman, to be so easy in his manners? Had he merely aped his betters over the years? Something very vague stirred in his mind, a feeling rather than a thought, that there had been someone he admired, someone who had taken time and trouble, a mentor – but no voice, nothing but an impression of working, practising – and an ideal.

The people from whom they learned more about Joscelin Grey were the Dawlishes. Their house was in Primrose Hill, not far from the Zoological Gardens, and Monk and Evan went to visit them the day after returning from Shelburne. They were admitted by a butler too well trained to show surprise, even at the sight of policemen on the front door-step. Mrs Dawlish received them in the morning room. She was a small, mild-featured woman with faded hazel eyes and brown hair, which escaped its pins.

'Mr Monk?' She queried his name because it obviously meant nothing to her.

Monk bowed very slightly.

'Yes, ma'am; and Mr Evan. If Mr Evan might have your permission to speak to the servants and see if they can be of assistance?'

'I think it unlikely, Mr Monk.' The idea was obviously futile in her estimation. 'But as long as he does not distract them from their duties, of course he may.'

'Thank you, ma'am.' Evan departed with alacrity, leaving Monk still standing.

'About poor Joscelin Grey?' Mrs Dawlish was puzzled and a little nervous, but apparently not unwilling to help. 'What can we tell you? It was a most terrible tragedy. We had not known him very long, you know.'

'How long, Mrs Dawlish?'

'About five weeks before he . . . died.' She sat down and he was glad to follow suit. 'I believe it cannot have been more.'

'But you invited him to stay with you? Do you often do that, on such short acquaintance?'

She shook her head, another strand of hair came undone and she ignored it.

'No, no hardly ever. But of course he was Menard Grey's brother—' Her face was suddenly hurt, as if something had betrayed her inexplicably and without warning, wounding where she had believed herself safe. 'And Joscelin was so charming, so very natural,' she went on. 'And of course he also knew Edward, my eldest son, who was killed at Inkermann.'

'I'm sorry.'

Her face was very stiff, and for a moment he was afraid she would not be able to control herself. He spoke to cover the silence and her embarrassment.

'You said "also". Did Menard Grey know your son?'

'Oh, yes,' she said quietly. 'They were close friends – for years.' Her eyes filled with tears. 'Since school.'

'So you invited Joscelin Grey to stay with you?' He did not wait for her to reply; she was beyond speech. 'That's very natural.' Then quite a new idea occurred to him with sudden, violent hope. Perhaps the murder was nothing to do with any current scandal, but a legacy from the war, something that had happened on the battlefield? It was possible. He should have thought of it before – they all should.

'Yes,' she said very quietly, mastering herself again. 'If he knew Edward in the war, we wanted to talk with him, listen to him. You see – here at home, we know so little of what really happened.' She took a deep breath. 'I am not sure if it helps, indeed in some ways it is harder, but we feel . . . less cut off. I know Edward is dead and it cannot matter to him any more; it isn't reasonable, but I feel closer to him, however it hurts.'

She looked at him with a curious need to be understood. Perhaps she had explained precisely this to other people, and they had tried to dissuade her, not realizing that for her, being excluded from her son's suffering was not a kindness but an added loss.

'Of course,' he agreed quietly. His own situation was utterly different, yet any knowledge would surely be better than this uncertainty. 'The imagination conjures so many things, and one feels the pain of them all, until one knows.'

Her eyes widened in surprise. 'You understand? So many friends have tried to persuade me into acceptance, but it gnaws away at the back of my mind, a sort of dreadful doubt. I read the newspapers sometimes' – she blushed – 'when my husband is out of the house. But I don't know what to believe of them. Their accounts are—' She sighed, crumpling her handkerchief in her lap, her fingers clinging around it. 'Well, they are sometimes a little softened so as not to distress us, or make us feel critical of those in command. And they are sometimes at variance with each other.'

'I don't doubt it.' He felt an unreasonable anger for the confusion of this woman, and all the silent multitude like her, grieving for their dead and being told that the truth was too harsh for them. Perhaps it was, perhaps many could not have borne it, but they had not been consulted, simply told; as their sons had been told to fight. For what? He had no idea. He had looked at many newspapers in the last few weeks, trying to learn, and he still had only the dimmest notion – something to do with the Turkish Empire and the balance of power.

'Joscelin used to speak to us so – so carefully,' she went on softly, watching his face. 'He told us a great deal about how he felt, and Edward must have felt the same. I had had no idea it was so very dreadful. One just doesn't know, sitting here in England—' She stared at him anxiously. 'It wasn't very glorious, you know – not really. So many men dead, not because the enemy killed them, but from the cold and the disease. He told us about the hospital at Scutari. He was there, you know; with a wound in his leg. He suffered quite appallingly. He told us about seeing men freezing to death in the winter. I had not known the Crimea was cold like that. I suppose it was because it was east from here, and I always think of the East as being hot. He said it was hot in the summer, and dry. Then with winter there was endless rain and snow, and winds that all but cut the flesh. And the disease.' Her face pinched. 'I thanked God that if Edward had to die, at least it was quickly, of a bullet, or a sword, not cholera. Yes, Joscelin was a great comfort to me, even though I wept as I hadn't done before; not only for Edward, but for all the others, and for the women like me, who lost sons and husbands. Do you understand, Mr Monk?'

'Yes,' he said quickly. 'Yes I do. I'm very sorry I have to distress you now by speaking of Major Grey's death. But we must find whoever killed him.'

She shuddered.

'How could anyone be so vile? What evil gets into a man that he could beat another to death like that? A fight I deplore, but I can understand it; but to go on, to mutilate a man after he is dead! The newspapers say it was dreadful. Of course my husband does not know I read them – having known the poor man, I felt I had to. Do you understand it, Mr Monk?'

'No, I don't. In all the crimes I have investigated, I have not seen one like this.' He did not know if it was true, but he felt it. 'He must have been hated with a passion hard to conceive.'

'I cannot imagine it, such a violence of feeling.' She closed her eyes and shook her head fractionally. 'Such a wish to destroy a – a creature. It would frighten me even to think someone could feel such an intensity of hatred for me, even if I were quite sure they could not touch me, and I were innocent of its cause. I wonder if poor Joscelin knew?'

It was a thought that had not occurred to Monk before – had Joscelin Grey had any idea that his killer hated him? Had he known, but merely thought him impotent to act?

'He cannot have feared him,' he said aloud. 'Or he would hardly have allowed him into his rooms while he was alone.'

'Poor man.' She hunched her shoulders involuntarily, as if chilled. 'It is very frightening to think that someone with that madness in their hearts could walk around, looking like you or me. I wonder if anyone dislikes me intensely and I have no idea of it. I had never entertained such a thought before, but now I cannot help it. I shall be unable to look at people as I used to. Are people often killed by those they know quite well?'

'Yes, ma'am, I am afraid so; most often of all by relatives.'

'How appalling.' Her voice was very soft, her eyes staring at some spot beyond him. 'And how very tragic.'

'Yes it is.' He did not want to seem crass, nor indifferent to her horror, but he had to pursue the business of it. 'Did Major Grey ever say anything about threats, or anyone who might be afraid of him—'

She lifted her eyes to look at him; her brow was puckered

and another strand of hair escaped the inadequate pins. 'Afraid of him? But it was he who was killed!'

'People are like other animals,' he replied. 'They most often kill when they are afraid themselves.'

'I suppose so. I had not thought of that.' She shook her head a little, still puzzled. 'But Joscelin was the most harmless of people! I never heard him speak as if he bore real ill will towards anyone. Of course he had a sharp wit, but one does not kill over a joke, even if it is a trifle barbed, and possibly even not in the kindest of taste.'

'Even so,' he pressed, 'against whom were these remarks directed?'

She hesitated, not only in an effort to remember, but it seemed the memory was disturbing her.

He waited.

'Mostly against his own family,' she said slowly. 'At least that was how it sounded to me – and I think to others. His comments on Menard were not always kind, although my husband knows more of that than I – I always liked Menard – but then that was no doubt because he and Edward were so close. Edward loved him dearly. They shared so much—' She blinked and screwed up her mild face even more. 'But then Joscelin often spoke harshly of himself also – it is hard to understand.'

'Of himself?' Monk was surprised. 'I've been to his family, naturally, and I can understand a certain resentment. But in what way of himself?'

'Oh, because he had no property, being a third son; and after his being wounded he limped, you know. So of course there was no career for him in the army. He appeared to feel he was of little – little standing – that no one accounted him much. Which was quite untrue, of course. He was a hero – and much liked by all manner of people!'

'I see.' Monk was thinking of Rosamond Shelburne, obliged by her mother to marry the son with the title and the prospects. Had Joscelin loved her, or was it more an insult than a wound, a reminder that he was third best? Had he cared, it could only have hurt him that she had not the courage to follow her heart and marry as she wished. Or was the status more important to her, and she had used Joscelin to reach Lovel? That would perhaps have hurt differently, with a bitterness that would remain.

Perhaps they would never know the answer to that.

He changed the subject. 'Did he at any time mention what his business interests were? He must have had some income beyond the allowance from his family.'

'Oh yes,' she agreed. 'He did discuss it with my husband, and he mentioned it to me, although not in any great detail.'

'And what was it, Mrs Dawlish?'

'I believe it was some investment, quite a sizable one, in a company to trade with Egypt.' The memory of it was bright in her face for a moment, the enthusiasm and expectation of that time coming back.

'Was Mr Dawlish involved in this investment?'

'He was considering it; he spoke highly of its possibilities.'

'I see. May I call again later when Mr Dawlish is at home, and learn more details of this company from him?'

'Oh dear.' The lightness vanished. 'I am afraid I have

expressed myself badly. The company is not yet formed. I gathered it was merely a prospect that Joscelin intended to pursue.'

Monk considered for a moment. If Grey were only forming a company, and perhaps persuading Dawlish to invest, then what had been his source of income up to that time?

'Thank you.' He stood up slowly. 'I understand. All the same, I should like to speak to Mr Dawlish. He may well know something about Major Grey's finances. If he were contemplating entering business with him, it would be natural he should inquire.'

'Yes, yes of course.' She poked ineffectually at her hair. 'Perhaps about six o'clock.'

Evan's questioning of the half-dozen or so domestic servants yielded nothing except the picture of a very ordinary household, well run by a quiet, sad woman stricken with a grief she bore as bravely as she could, but of which they were all only too aware and each in their own way shared. The butler had a nephew who served as a foot soldier and had returned a cripple. Evan was suddenly sobered by the remembrance of so many other losses, so many people who had to struggle on without the notoriety, or the sympathy, of Joscelin Grey's family.

The sixteen-year-old between-stairs maid had lost an elder brother at Inkermann. They all recalled Major Grey, how charming he was, and that Miss Amanda was very taken with him. They had hoped he would return, and were horrified that he could be so terribly murdered right here in his home. They had an obvious duality of thought that confounded Evan – it shocked them that a gentleman should be so killed, and yet they viewed their own losses as things merely to be borne with quiet dignity.

He came away with an admiration for their stoicism, and an anger that they should accept the difference so easily. Then as he came through the green baize door back into the main hallway, the thought occurred to him that perhaps that was the only way of bearing it – anything else would be too destructive, and in the end only futile.

And he had learned little of Joscelin Grey that he had not already deduced from the other calls.

Dawlish was a stout, expensively dressed man with a high forehead and dark, clever eyes, but at present he was displeased at the prospect of speaking with the police, and appeared distinctly ill at ease. There was no reason to assume it was an unquiet conscience; to have the police at one's house, for any reason, was socially highly undesirable, and judging from the newness of the furniture and the rather formal photographs of the family – Mrs Dawlish seated in imitation of the Queen – Mr Dawlish was an ambitious man.

It transpired that he knew remarkably little about the business he had half committed himself to support. His involvement was with Joscelin Grey personally, and it was this which had caused him to promise funds, and the use of his good name. 'Charming fellow,' he said, half facing Monk as he stood by the parlour fire. 'Hard when you're brought up in a family, part of it and all that, then the eldest brother marries and suddenly you're nobody.' He shook his head grimly. 'Dashed hard to make your way if you're not suited to the church, and invalided out of the army. Only thing really is to marry decently.' He looked at Monk to see if he understood. 'Don't know why young Joscelin didn't, certainly a handsome enough chap, and pleasing with women. Had all the charm, right words to say, and so on. Amanda thought the world of him.' He coughed. 'My daughter, you know. Poor girl was very distressed over his death. Dreadful thing! Quite appalling.' He stared down at the embers and a sharp sadness filled his eyes and softened the lines around his mouth. 'Such a decent man. Expect it in the Crimea, die for your country, and so on; but not this. Lost her first suitor at Sebastopol, poor girl; and of course her brother at Balaclava. That's where he met young Grey.' He swallowed hard and looked up at Monk, as if to defy his emotions. 'Damned good to him.' He took a deep breath and fought to control a conflict of emotions that were obviously acutely painful. 'Actually spoke to each other night before the battle. Like to think of that, someone we've met, with Edward the night before he was killed. Been a great source of—' He coughed again and was forced to look away, his eyes brimming. 'Comfort to us, my wife and me. Taken it hard, poor woman; only son, you know. Five daughters. And now this.'

'I understand Menard Grey was also a close friend of your son's,' Monk said, as much to fill the silence as that it might have mattered.

Dawlish stared at the coals. 'Prefer not to speak of it,' he replied with difficulty, his voice husky. 'Thought a lot of him – but he led Edward into bad ways – no doubt about it. It was Joscelin who paid his debts – so he did not die with dishonour.'

He swallowed convulsively. 'We became fond of Joscelin, even on the few weekends he stayed with us.' He lifted the poker out of its rest and jabbed at the fire fiercely. 'I hope to heaven you catch the madman who did it.'

'We'll do everything we can, sir.' Monk wanted to say all sorts of other things to express the pity he felt for so much loss. Thousands of men and horses had died, frozen, starved, or been massacred or wasted by disease on the bitter hillsides of a country they neither knew nor loved. If he had ever known the purpose of the war in the Crimea he had forgotten it now. It could hardly have been a war of defence. Crimea was a thousand miles from England. Presumably from the newspapers it was something to do with the political ramifications of Turkey and its disintegrating empire. It hardly seemed a reason for the wretched, pitiful deaths of so many, and the grief they left behind.

Dawlish was staring at him, waiting for him to say something, expecting a platitude.

'I am sorry your son had to die in such a way.' Monk held out his hand automatically. 'And so young. But at least Joscelin Grey was able to assure you it was with courage and dignity, and that his suffering was brief.'

Dawlish took his hand before he had time to think.

'Thank you.' There was a faint flush on his skin and he was obviously moved. He did not even realize until after

Monk had gone that he had shaken hands with a policeman as frankly as if he had been a gentleman.

That evening Monk found himself for the first time caring about Grey personally. He sat in his own quiet room with nothing but the faint noises from the street in the distance below. In the small kindnesses to the Dawlishes, in paying a dead man's debts, Grey had developed a solidity far more than in the grief of his mother or the pleasant but rather insubstantial memories of his neighbours. He had become a man with a past of something more than a resentment that his talent was wasted while the lesser gifts of his elder brother were over-rewarded, more than the rejected suitor of a weak young woman who preferred the ease of doing as she was told and the comfort of status to the relative struggle of following her own desires. Or perhaps she had not really wanted anything enough to fight for it?

Shelburne was comfortable, physically everything was provided; one did not have to work, morally there were no decisions – if something was unpleasant one did not have to look at it. If there were beggars in the street, mutilated or diseased, one could pass to the other side. There was the government to make the social decisions, and the church to make the moral ones.

Of course society demanded a certain, very rigid code of conduct, of taste, and a very small circle of friends and suitable ways to pass one's time, but for those who had been brought up from childhood to observe it, it was little extra effort.

Small wonder if Joscelin Grey was angry with it, even contemptuous after he had seen the frozen bodies on the heights before Sebastopol, the carnage at Balaclava, the filth, the disease and the agony of Scutari.

In the street below a carriage clattered by and someone shouted and there was a roar of laughter.

Suddenly Monk found himself feeling this same strange, almost impersonal disgust Grey must have suffered coming back to England afterwards, to a family who were strangers insofar as their petty, artificial little world was concerned; who knew only the patriotic placebos they read in the newspapers, and had no wish to look behind them for uglier truths.

He had felt the same himself after visiting the 'rookeries', the hell-like, rotting tenements crawling with vermin and disease, sometimes only a few dozen yards from the lighted streets where gentlemen rode in carriages from one sumptuous house to another. He had seen fifteen or twenty people in one room, all ages and sexes together, without heating or sanitation. He had seen child prostitutes of eight or ten years old with eyes tired and old as sin, and bodies riddled with venereal disease; children of five or even less frozen to death in the gutters because they could not beg a night's shelter. Small wonder they stole, or sold for a few pence the only things they possessed, their own bodies.

How did he remember that, when his own father's face was still a blank to him? He must have cared very much, been so shocked by it that it left a scar he could not forget, even now. Was that, at least in part, the fire behind his ambition, the fire behind his relentless drive to improve himself, to copy the mentor whose features he could not recall, whose name, whose station, eluded him? Please God that was so. It made a more tolerable man of him, even one he could begin to accept.

Had Joscelin Grey cared?

Monk intended to avenge him; he would not be merely another unsolved mystery, a man remembered for his death rather than his life.

And he must pursue the Latterly case. He could hardly go back to Mrs Latterly without knowing at least the outline of the matter he had promised her to solve, however painful the truth. And he did intend to go back to her. Now that he thought about it, he realized he had always intended to visit her again, speak with her, see her face, listen to her voice, watch the way she moved; command her attention, even for so short a time.

There was no use looking among his files again; he had already done that almost page by page. Instead he went directly to Runcorn.

'Morning, Monk.' Runcorn was not at his desk but over by the window, and he sounded positively cheerful; his rather sallow face was touched with colour as if he had walked briskly in the sun, and his eyes were bright. 'How's the Grey case coming along? Got something to tell the newspapers yet? They're still pressing, you know.' He sniffed faintly and reached in his pocket for a cigar. 'They'll be calling for our blood soon; resignations, and that sort of thing!'

Monk could see his satisfaction in the way he stood, shoulders a little high, chin up, the shine on his shoes gleaming in the light.

'Yes, sir, I imagine they will,' he conceded. 'But as you said over a week ago, it's one of those investigations that is bound to rake up something extremely unpleasant, possibly several things. It would be very rash to say anything before we can prove it.'

'Have you got anything at all, Monk?' Runcorn's face hardened, but his sense of anticipation was still there, his scent of blood. 'Or are you as lost as Lamb was?'

'It looks at the moment as if it could be in the family, sir,' Monk replied as levelly as he could. He had a sickening awareness that Runcorn was controlling this, and enjoying it. 'There was considerable feeling between the brothers,' he went on. 'The present Lady Shelburne was courted by Joscelin before she married Lord Shelburne—'

'Hardly a reason to murder him,' Runcorn said with contempt. 'Would only make sense if it had been Shelburne who was murdered. Doesn't sound as if you have anything there!'

Monk kept his temper. He felt Runcorn trying to irritate him, provoke him into betraying all the pent-up past that lay between them; victory would be sweeter if it were acknowledged, and could be savoured in the other's presence. Monk wondered how he could have been so insensitive, so stupid as not to have known it before. Why had he not forestalled it, even avoided it altogether? How had he been so blind then when now it was so glaring? Was it really no more than that he was rediscovering himself, fact by fact, from the outside?

'Not that in itself.' He went back to the question, keeping his voice light and calm. 'But I think the lady still preferred Joscelin, and her one child, conceived just before Joscelin went to the Crimea, looks a good deal more like him than like his lordship.'

Runcorn's face fell, then slowly widened again in a smile, showing all his teeth; the cigar was still unlit in his hand.

'Indeed. Yes. Well, I warned you it would be nasty, didn't I? You'll have to be careful, Monk; make any allegations you can't prove, and the Shelburnes will have you dismissed before you've time to get back to London.'

Which is just what you want, Monk thought.

'Precisely, sir,' he said aloud. 'That is why as far as the newspapers are concerned, we are still in the dark. I came because I wanted to ask you about the Latterly case—'

'Latterly! What the hell does that matter? Some poor devil committed suicide.' He walked around and sat down at his desk and began fishing for matches. 'It's a crime for the church, not for us. Have you got any matches, Monk? We wouldn't have taken any notice of it at all if that wretched woman hadn't raised it. Ah – don't bother, here they are. Let them bury their own dead quietly, no fuss.' He struck a light and held it to his cigar, puffing gently. 'Man got in over his head with a business deal that went sour. All his friends invested in it on his recommendation, and he couldn't take the shame of it. Took that way out; some say coward's way, some say it's the honourable way.' He blew out smoke and stared up at Monk. 'Damn silly, I call it. But that class is very jealous of what it thinks is its good name. Some of them will keep servants they can't afford for the sake of appearance, serve six-course meals to guests, and live on bread and dripping the rest of the time. Light a fire when there's company, and perish with cold the rest of the time. Pride is a wicked master, most especially social pride.' His eyes flickered with malicious pleasure. 'Remember that, Monk.'

He looked down at the papers in front of him. 'Why on earth are you bothering with Latterly? Get on with Grey; we need to solve it, however painful it may prove. The public won't wait much longer; they're even asking questions in the House of Lords. Did you know that?'

'No, sir, but considering how Lady Shelburne feels, I'm not surprised. Do you have a file on the Latterly case, sir?'

'You are a stubborn man, Monk. It's a very dubious quality. I've got your written report that it was a suicide, and nothing to concern us. You don't want that again, do you?'

'Yes, sir, I do.' Monk took it without looking at it and walked out.

He had to visit the Latterlys' house in the evening, in his own time, since he was not officially working on any case that involved them. He must have been here before; he could not have met with Mrs Latterly casually, nor expected her to report to the police station. He looked up and down the street, but there was nothing familiar in it.

The only streets he could remember were the cold cobbles of Northumberland, small houses whipped clean by the wind, grey seas and the harbour below and the high moors rising to the sky. He could remember vaguely, once, a visit to Newcastle in the train, the enormous furnaces towering over the rooftops, the plumes of smoke, the excitement running through him in their immense, thrumming power, the knowledge of coal-fired blast furnaces inside; steel hammered and beaten into engines to draw trains over the mountains and plains of the whole Empire. He could still capture just an echo of the thrill that had been high in his throat then, tingling his arms and legs, the awe, the beginning of adventure. He must have been very young.

It had been quite different when he had first come to London. He had been so much older, more than the ten or so years the calendar had turned. His mother was dead; Beth was with an aunt. His father had been lost at sea when Beth was still in arms. Coming to London had been the beginning of something new, and the end of all that belonged to childhood. Beth had seen him off at the station, crying, screwing up her pinafore in her hand, refusing to be comforted. She could not have been more than nine, and he about fifteen. But he could read and write, and the world was his for the labour.

But that was a long time ago. He was well over thirty now, probably over thirty-five. What had he done in more than twenty years? Why had he not returned? That was something else he had yet to learn. His police record was there in his office, and in Runcorn's hate. What about himself, his personal life? Or had he no one, was he only a public man?

And what before the police? His files here went back only twelve years, so there must have been more than eight years before that. Had he spent them all learning, climbing, improving himself with his faceless mentor, his eyes always on the goal? He was appalled at his own ambition, and the strength of his will. It was a little frightening, such single-mindedness.

He was at the Latterlys' door, ridiculously nervous. Would she be in? He had thought about her so often; he realized only now and with a sense of having been foolish, vulnerable, that she had probably not thought of him at all. He might even have to explain who he was. He would seem clumsy, gauche, when he said he had no further news.

He hesitated, unsure whether to knock at all, or to leave, and come again when he had a better excuse. A maid came out into the areaway below him, and in order not to appear a loiterer, he raised his hand and knocked.

The parlour maid came almost immediately. Her eyebrows rose in the very slightest of surprise.

'Good evening, Mr Monk; will you come in, sir?' It was sufficiently courteous not to be in obvious haste to get him off the doorstep. 'The family have dined and are in the withdrawing room, sir. Do you wish me to ask if they will receive you?'

'Yes please. Thank you.' Monk gave her his coat and followed her through to a small morning room. After she had gone he paced up and down because he could not bear to be still. He hardly noticed anything about the furniture or the pleasant, rather ordinary paintings and the worn carpet. What was he going to say? He had charged into a world where he did not belong, because of something he dreamed in a woman's face. She probably found him distasteful, and would not have suffered him if she were not so concerned about her father-in-law, hoping he could use his skills to discover something that would ease her grief. Suicide was a terrible shame, and in the eyes of the church financial disgrace would not excuse it. He could still be buried in unconsecrated ground if the conclusion were inevitable.

It was too late to back away now, but it crossed his mind. He even considered concocting an excuse, another reason for calling, something to do with Grey and the letter in his flat, when the parlour maid returned and there was no time.

'Mrs Latterly will see you, sir, if you come this way.'

Obediently, heart thumping and mouth dry, he followed the maid.

The withdrawing room was medium sized, comfortable, and originally furnished with the disregard for money of those who have always possessed it, but the ease, the unostentation of those for whom it has no novelty. Now it was still elegant, but the curtains were a little faded in portions where the sun fell on them, and the fringing on the swags with which they were tied was missing a bobble here and there. The carpet was not of equal quality with the pie-crust tables or the chaise longue. He felt pleasure in the room immediately, and wondered where in his merciless self-improvement he had learned such taste.

His eyes went to Mrs Latterly beside the fire. She was no longer in black, but dark wine, and it brought a faint flush to her skin. Her throat and shoulders were as delicate and slender as a child's, but there was nothing of the child in her face. She was staring at him with luminous eyes, wide now, and too shadowed to read their expression.

Monk turned quickly to the others. The man, fairer than she and with less generous mouth, must be her husband, and the other woman sitting opposite with the proud face with so much anger and imagination in it he knew immediately; they had met and quarrelled at Shelburne Hall – Miss Hester Latterly.

'Good evening, Monk.' Charles Latterly did not stand. 'You remember my wife?' He gestured vaguely towards Imogen. 'And my sister, Miss Hester Latterly. She was in the Crimea when our father died.' There was a strong accent of disapproval in his voice and it was apparent that he resented Monk's involvement in the affair.

Monk was assailed by an awful thought – had he somehow disgraced himself, been too brash, too insensitive to their pain and added not only to their loss but the manner of it? Had he said something appallingly thoughtless, or been too familiar? The blood burned up his face and he stumbled into speech to cover the hot silence.

'Good evening, sir.' Then he bowed very slightly to Imogen and then to Hester. 'Good evening, ma'am; Miss Latterly.' He would not mention that they had already met. It was not a fortunate episode.

'What can we do for you?' Charles asked, nodding towards

a seat, indicating that Monk might make himself comfortable.

Monk accepted, and another extraordinary thought occurred to him. Imogen had been very discreet, almost furtive in speaking to him in St Marylebone Church. Was it conceivable neither her husband nor her sister-in-law knew that she had pursued the matter beyond the first, formal acknowledgment of the tragedy and the necessary formalities? If that were so he must not betray her now.

He drew a deep breath, hoping he could make sense, wishing to God he could remember anything at all of what Charles had told him, and what he had learned from Imogen alone. He would have to bluff, pretend there was something new, a connection with the murder of Grey; it was the only other case he was working on, or could remember anything at all about. These people had known him, however slightly. He had been working for them shortly before the accident; surely they could tell him something about himself?

But that was less than half a truth. Why lie to himself? He was here because of Imogen Latterly. It was purposeless, but her face haunted his mind, like a memory from the past of which the precise nature is lost, or a ghost from the imagination, from the realm of daydreams so often repeated it seems they must surely have been real.

They were all looking at him, still waiting.

'It is possible . . .' His voice was rough at first. He cleared his throat. 'I have discovered something quite new. But before I tell you I must be perfectly sure, more especially since it concerns other people.' That should prevent them, as a matter of good taste, from pressing him. He coughed again. 'It is some time since I spoke to you last, and I made no notes, as a point of discretion—'

'Thank you,' Charles said slowly. 'That was considerate of you.' He seemed to find it hard to say the words, as if it irritated him to acknowledge that policemen might possess such delicate virtues.

Hester was staring at him with frank disbelief.

'If I could go over the details we know again?' Monk asked, hoping desperately they would fill in the gaping blanks in his mind; he knew only what Runcorn had told him, and that was in turn only what he had told Runcorn. Heaven knew, that was barely enough to justify spending time on the case.

'Yes, yes of course.' Again it was Charles who spoke, but Monk felt the eyes of the women on him also: Imogen anxious, her hands clenched beneath the ample folds of her skirt, her dark eyes wide; Hester was thoughtful, ready to criticize. He must dismiss them both from his mind, concentrate on making sense, picking up the threads from Charles, or he would make a complete fool of himself, and he could not bear that in front of them.

'Your father died in his study,' he began. 'In his home in Highgate on fourteenth of June.' That much Runcorn had said.

'Yes.' Charles agreed. 'It was early evening, before dinner. My wife and I were staying with them at the time. Most of us were upstairs changing.'

'Most of you?'

'Perhaps I should say "both of us". My mother and I

were. My wife was late coming in. She had been over to see Mrs Standing, the vicar's wife, and as it transpired my father was in his study.'

The means of death had been a gunshot. The next question was easy.

'And how many of you heard the report?'

'Well, I suppose we all heard it, but my wife was the only one to realize what it was. She was coming in from the back garden entrance and was in the conservatory.'

Monk turned to Imogen.

She was looking at him, a slight frown on her face as if she wanted to say something, but dared not. Her eyes were troubled, full of dark hurt.

'Mrs Latterly?' He forgot what he had intended to ask her. He was conscious of his hands clenched painfully by his sides and had to ease the fingers out deliberately. They were sticky with sweat.

'Yes, Mr Monk?' she said quietly.

He scrambled for something sensible to say. His brain was blank. What had he said to her the first time? She had come to him; surely she would have told him everything she knew? He must ask her something quickly. They were all waiting, watching him. Charles Latterly cool, disliking the effrontery, Hester exasperated at his incompetence. He already knew what she thought of his abilities. Attack was the only defence his mind could think of.

'Why do you think, Mrs Latterly, that you suspected a shot, when no one else did?' His voice was loud in the silence, like the sudden chimes of a clock in an empty room.

'Were you afraid even then that your father-in-law contemplated taking his life, or that he was in some danger?'

The colour came to her face quickly and there was anger in her eyes.

'Of course not, Mr Monk; or I should not have left him alone.' She swallowed, and her next words were softer. 'I knew he was distressed, we all knew that; but I did not imagine it was serious enough to think of shooting himself – nor that he was sufficiently out of control of his feelings or his concentration that he would be in danger of having an accident.' It was a brave attempt.

'I think if you have discovered something, Mr Monk,' Hester interrupted stiffly, 'you had better ascertain what it is, and then come back and tell us. Your present fumbling around is pointless and unnecessarily distressing. And your suggestion that my sister-in-law knew something that she did not report at the time is offensive.' She looked him up and down with some disgust. 'Really, is this the best you can do? I don't know how you catch anyone, unless you positively fall over them!'

'Hester!' Imogen spoke quite sharply, although she kept her eyes averted. 'It is a question Mr Monk must ask. It is possible I may have seen or heard something to make me anxious – and only realize it now in retrospect.'

Monk felt a quick, foolish surge of pleasure. He had not deserved defending.

'Thank you, ma'am.' He tried to smile at her, and felt his lips grimacing. 'Did you at that time know the full extent of your father-in-law's financial misfortune?'

'It was not the money that killed him,' Imogen replied before Charles could get his own words formed and while Hester was still standing in resigned silence – at least temporarily. 'It was the disgrace.' She bit her lip on all the distress returned to her. Her voice dropped to little more than a whisper, tight with pity. 'You see, he had advised so many of his friends to invest. He had lent his name to it, and they had put in money because they trusted him.'

Monk could think of nothing to say, and platitudes offended him in the face of real grief. He longed to be able to comfort her, and knew it was impossible. Was this the emotion that surged through him so intensely – pity? And the desire to protect?

'The whole venture has brought nothing but tragedy,' Imogen went on very softly, staring at the ground. 'Papa-in-law, then poor Mama, and now Joscelin as well.'

For an instant everything seemed suspended, an age between the time she spoke and the moment overwhelming realization of what she had said came to Monk.

'You knew Joscelin Grey?' It was as if another person spoke for him and he was still distant, watching strangers, removed from him, on the other side of a glass.

Imogen frowned a little, confused by his apparent unreason; there was a deep colour in her face and she lowered her eyes the moment after she had spoken, avoiding everyone else's, especially her husband's.

'For the love of heaven!' Charles's temper snapped. 'Are you completely incompetent, man?'

Monk had no idea what to say. What on earth had Grey to

do with it? Had he known him?

What were they thinking of him? How could he possibly make sense of it now? They could only conclude he was mad, or was playing some disgusting joke. It was the worst possible taste – life was not sacred to them, but death most certainly was. He could feel the embarrassment burning in his face, and was as conscious of Imogen as if she were touching him, and of Hester's eyes filled with unutterable contempt.

Again it was Imogen who rescued him.

'Mr Monk never met Joscelin, Charles,' she said quietly. 'It is very easy to forget a name when you do not know the person to whom it belongs.'

Hester stared from one to the other of them, her clear, intelligent eyes filled with a growing perception that something was profoundly wrong.

'Of course,' Imogen said more briskly, covering her feelings. 'Mr Monk did not come until after Papa was dead; there was no occasion.' She did not look at her husband, but she was obviously speaking to him. 'And if you recall, Joscelin did not return after that.'

'You can hardly blame him.' Charles's voice contained a sharpening of criticism, an implication that Imogen was somehow being unfair. 'He was as distressed as we were. He wrote me a very civil letter, expressing his condolences.' He put his hands in his pockets, hard, and hunched his shoulders. 'Naturally, he felt it unsuitable to call, in the circumstances. He quite understood our association must end; very delicate of him, I thought.' He looked at Imogen with impatience, and ignored Hester altogether.

'That was like him, so very sensitive.' Imogen was looking far away. 'I do miss him.'

Charles swivelled to look at her beside him. He seemed about to say something, and then changed his mind and bit it off. Instead he took his hand out of his pocket and put it around her arm. 'So you didn't meet him?' he said to Monk.

Monk was still floundering.

'No.' It was the only answer he had left himself room to make. 'He was out of town.' Surely that at least could have been true?

'Poor Joscelin.' Imogen appeared unaware of her husband, or his fingers tightening on her shoulder. 'He must have felt dreadful,' she went on. 'Of course he was not responsible, he was as deceived as any of us, but he was the sort of person who would take it on himself.' Her voice was sad, gentle and utterly without criticism.

Monk could only guess, he dared not ask: Grey must somehow have been involved in the business venture in which Latterly Senior lost money, and so ill advised his friends. And it would seem Joscelin had lost money himself, which he could hardly afford; hence perhaps the request to the family estate for an increased allowance? The date on the letter from the solicitor was about right, shortly after Latterly's death. Possibly it was that financial disaster that had prompted Joscelin Grey to gamble rashly, or to descend to blackmail. If he had lost enough in the business he might have been desperate, with creditors pressing, social disgrace imminent. Charm was his only stock in trade; his

273

entertainment value was his passport to hospitality in other people's houses the year round, and his only path to the heiress who might ultimately make him independent, no longer begging from his mother and the brother he scarcely loved.

But who? Who among his acquaintances was vulnerable enough to pay for silence; and desperate, murderous enough to kill for it?

Whose houses had he stayed in? All sorts of indiscretions were committed on long weekends away from the city. Scandal was not a matter of what was done but of what was known to have been done. Had Joscelin stumbled on some well-kept secret adultery?

But adultery was hardly worth killing over, unless there was a child to inherit, or some other domestic crisis, a suit for divorce with all its scandal, and the complete social ostracism that followed. To kill would need a secret far worse, like incest, perversion or impotence. The shame of impotence was mortal, God knew why, but it was the most abhorred of afflictions, something not even whispered of.

Runcorn was right, even to speak of such a possibility would be enough to have him reported to the highest authorities, his career blocked forever, if he were not dismissed out of hand. He could never be forgiven for exposing a man to the ruin which must follow such an abominable scandal.

They were all staring at him. Charles was making no secret of his impatience. Hester was exasperated almost beyond endurance; her fingers were fiddling with the plain cambric handkerchief and her foot tapped rapidly and silently on the floor. Her opinion was in every line of her remarkable face.

'What is it you think you may know, Mr Monk?' Charles said sharply. 'If there is nothing, I would ask that you do not distress us again by raking over what can only be to us a tragedy. Whether my father took his own life or it was an accident while his mind was distracted with distress cannot be proved, and we should be obliged if you allowed those who are charitable enough to allow that it might have been an accident to prevail! My mother died of a broken heart. One of our past friends has been brutally murdered. If we cannot be of assistance to you, I would prefer that you permit us to come to terms with our grief in our own way, and do our best to resume the pattern of our lives again. My wife was quite wrong to have persisted in her hope for some more pleasant alternative, but women are tender-hearted by nature, and she finds it hard to accept a bitter truth.'

'All she wished of me was to ascertain that it was indeed the truth,' Monk said quickly, instinctively angry that Imogen should be criticized. 'I cannot believe that mistaken.' He stared with chill, level eyes at Charles.

'That is courteous of you, Mr Monk.' Charles glanced at Imogen condescendingly, to imply that Monk had been humouring her. 'But I have no doubt she will come to the same conclusion, in time. Thank you for calling; I am sure you have done what you believed to be your duty.'

Monk accepted the dismissal and was in the hall before he realized what he had done. He had been thinking of

275

Imogen, and of Hester's scalding disdain, and he had allowed himself to be awed by the house, by Charles Latterly's self-assurance, his arrogance, and his very natural attempts to conceal a family tragedy and mask it in something less shameful.

He turned on his heel and faced the closed door again. He wanted to ask them about Grey, and he had the excuse for it, indeed he had no excuse not to. He took a step forward, and then felt foolish. He could hardly go back and knock like a servant asking entry. But he could not walk out of the house, knowing they had had a relationship with Joscelin Grey, that Imogen at least had cared for him, and not ask more. He stretched out his hand, then withdrew it again.

The door opened and Imogen came out. She stopped in surprise, a foot from him, her back against the panels. The colour came up her face.

'I'm sorry.' She took a breath. 'I – I did not realize you were still here.'

He did not know what to say either; he was idiotically speechless. Seconds ticked by. Eventually it was she who spoke.

'Was there something else, Mr Monk? Have you found something?' Her voice lifted, all eagerness, hope in her eyes; and he felt sure now that she had come to him alone, trusted him with something she had not confided to her husband or Hester.

'I'm working on the Joscelin Grey case.' It was the only thing he could think of to say. He was floundering in a morass of ignorance. If only he could remember!

Her eyes dropped. 'Indeed. So that is why you came to see us. I'm sorry, I misunderstood. You – you wish to know something about Major Grey?'

It was far from the truth.

'I—' He drew a deep breath. 'I dislike having to disturb you, so soon after—'

Her head came up, her eyes angry. He had no idea why. She was so lovely, so gentle; she woke yearnings in him for something his memory could not grasp: some old sweetness, a time of laughter and trust. How could he be stupid enough to feel this torrent of emotion for a woman who had simply come to him for help because of family tragedy, and almost certainly regarded him in the same light as she would the plumber or the fireman?

'Sorrows do not wait for one another.' She was talking to him in a stiff little voice. 'I know what the newspapers are saying. What do you wish to know about Major Grey? If we knew anything that was likely to be of help, we should have told you ourselves.'

'Yes.' He was withered by her anger, confusingly and painfully hurt by it. 'Of course you would. I – I was just wondering if there was anything else I should have asked. I don't think there is. Good night, Mrs Latterly.'

'Good night, Mr Monk.' She lifted her head a little higher and he was not quite sure whether he saw her blink to disguise tears. But that was ridiculous – why should she weep now? Disappointment? Frustration? Disillusion in him, because she had hoped and expected better? If only he could remember!

'Parkin, will you show Mr Monk to the door.' And without looking at him again, or waiting for the maid, she walked away, leaving him alone.

Chapter Nine

Monk was obliged to go back to the Grey case, although both Imogen Latterly, with her haunting eyes, and Hester, with her anger and intelligence, intruded into his thoughts. Concentration was almost beyond him, and he had to drive himself even to think of its details and try to make patterns from the amorphous mass of facts and suppositions they had so far.

He sat in his office with Evan, reviewing the growing amount of it, but it was all inconclusive of any fact, negative and not positive. No one had broken in, therefore Grey had admitted his murderer himself; and if he had admitted him, then he had been unaware of any reason to fear him. It was not likely he would invite in a stranger at that time in the evening, so it was more probably someone he knew, and who hated him with an intense but secret violence.

Or did Grey know of the hatred, but feel himself safe from it? Did he believe that person powerless to injure, either for an emotional reason, or a physical? Even that answer was still beyond him.

The description both Yeats and Grimwade had given of the only visitor unaccounted for did not fit Lovel Grey, but it was so indistinct that it hardly mattered. If Rosamond Grey's child was Joscelin's, and not Lovel's, that could be reason enough for murder; especially if Joscelin himself knew it and perhaps had not been averse to keeping Lovel reminded. It would not be the first time a cruel tongue, the mockery at pain or impotence had ended in an uncontrolled rage.

Evan broke into his thoughts, almost as if he had read them.

'Do you suppose Shelburne killed Joscelin himself?' He was frowning, his face anxious, his wide eyes clouded. He had no need to fear for his own career – the establishment, even the Shelburnes, would not blame him for a scandal. Was he afraid for Monk? It was a warm thought.

Monk looked up at him.

'Perhaps not. But if he paid someone else, they would have been cleaner and more efficient about it, and less violent. Professionals don't beat a man to death; they usually either stab him or garrote him, and not in his own house.'

Evan's delicate mouth turned down at the corners. 'You mean an attack in the street, follow him to a quiet spot – and all over in a moment?'

'Probably; and leave the body in an alley where it won't be found too soon, preferably out of his own area. That way there would be less to connect them with the victim, and less of a risk of their being recognized.'

'Perhaps he was in a hurry?' Evan suggested. 'Couldn't wait for the right time and place?' He leaned back a little in his chair and tilted the legs.

'What hurry?' Monk shrugged. 'No hurry if it was

Shelburne, not if it were over Rosamond anyway. Couldn't matter a few days, or even a few weeks.'

'No.' Evan looked gloomy. He allowed the front legs of the chair to settle again. 'I don't know how we begin to prove anything, or even where to look.'

'Find out where Shelburne was at the time Grey was killed,' Monk answered. 'I should have done that before.'

'Oh, I asked the servants, in a roundabout way.' Evan's face was surprised, and there was a touch of satisfaction in it he could not conceal.

'And?' Monk asked quickly. He would not spoil Evan's pleasure.

'He was away from Shelburne; they were told he came to town for dinner. I followed it up. He was at the dinner all right, and spent the night at his club, off Tavistock Place. It would have been difficult for him to have been in Mecklenburgh Square at the right time, because he might easily have been missed, but not at all impossible. If he'd gone along Compton Place, right down Hunter Street, 'round Brunswick Square and Lansdowne Place, past the Foundling Hospital, up Guilford Place – and he was there. Ten minutes at the outside, probably less. He'd have been gone at least three quarters of an hour, counting the fight with Grey – and returning. But he could have done it on foot – easily.'

Monk smiled; Evan deserved praise and he was glad to give it.

'Thank you. I ought to have done that myself. It might even have been less time, if the quarrel was an old one – say ten minutes each way, and five minutes for the fight. That's not long for a man to be out of sight at a club.'

Evan looked down, a faint colour in his face. He was smiling.

'It doesn't get us any further,' he pointed out ruefully. 'It could have been Shelburne, or it could have been anyone else. I suppose we shall have to investigate every other family he could have blackmailed? That should make us rather less popular than the ratman. Do you think it was Shelburne, sir, and we'll just never prove it?'

Monk stood up.

'I don't know but I'm damned if it'll be for lack of trying.' He was thinking of Joscelin Grey in the Crimea, seeing the horror of slow death by starvation, cold and disease, the blinding incompetence of commanders sending men to be blown to bits by enemy guns, the sheer stultifying of it all; feeling fear and physical pain, exhaustion, certainly pity, shown by his brief ministrations to the dying in Scutari – all while Lovel stayed at home in his great hall, marrying Rosamond, adding money to money, comfort to comfort.

Monk strode to the door. Injustice ached in him like a gathering boil, angry and festering. He pulled the handle sharply and jerked it open.

'Sir!' Evan half rose to his feet.

Monk turned.

Evan did not know the words, how to phrase the warning urgent inside him. Monk could see it in his face, the wide hazel eyes, the sensitive mouth.

'Don't look so alarmed,' he said quietly, pushing the

door to again. 'I'm going back to Grey's flat. I remember a photograph of his family there. Shelburne was in it, and Menard Grey. I want to see if Grimwade or Yeats recognize either of them. Do you want to come?'

Evan's face ironed out almost comically with relief. He smiled in spite of himself.

'Yes, sir. Yes I would.' He reached for his coat and scarf. 'Can you do that without letting them know who they are? If they know they were his brothers – I mean – Lord Shelburne—'

Monk looked at him sideways and Evan pulled a small face of apology.

'Yes of course,' he muttered, following Monk outside. 'Although the Shelburnes will deny it, of course, and they'll still ride us to hell and back if we press a charge!'

Monk knew that, and he had no plan even if anyone in the photograph were recognized, but it was a step forward, and he had to take it.

Grimwade was in his cubbyhole as usual and he greeted them cheerfully.

'Lovely mild day, sir.' He squinted towards the street. 'Looks as if it could clear up.'

'Yes,' Monk agreed without thinking. 'Very pleasant.' He was unaware of being wet. 'We're going up to Major Grey's rooms again, want to pick up one or two things.'

'Well, with all of you on the case, I 'spec' you'll get somewhere one of these days.' Grimwade nodded, a faint trace of sarcasm in his rather lugubrious face. 'You certainly are a busy lot, I'll give yer that.'

Monk was halfway up the stairs with the key before the significance of Grimwade's remark came to him. He stopped sharply and Evan trod on his heel.

'Sorry,' Evan apologized.

'What did he mean?' Monk turned, frowning. 'All of us? There's only you and me – isn't there?'

Evan's eyes shadowed. 'So far as I know! Do you think Runcorn has been here?'

Monk stood stiffly to the spot. 'Why should he? He doesn't want to be the one to solve this, especially if it is Shelburne. He doesn't want to have anything to do with it.'

'Curiosity?' There were other thoughts mirrored in Evan's face, but he did not speak them.

Monk thought the same thing – perhaps Runcorn wanted some proof it was Shelburne, then he would force Monk to find it, and then to make the charge. For a moment they stared at each other, the knowledge silent and complete between them.

'I'll go and find out.' Evan turned around and went slowly down again.

It was several minutes before he came back, and Monk stood on the stair waiting, his mind at first searching for a way out, a way to avoid accusing Shelburne himself. Then he was drawn to wonder more about Runcorn. How old was the enmity between them? Was it simply an older man fearing a rival on the ladder of success, a younger, cleverer rival?

Only younger and cleverer? Or also harder, more ruthless

284

in his ambitions, one who took credit for other people's work, who cared more for acclaim than for justice, who sought the public, colourful cases, the ones well reported; even a man who managed to shelve his failures onto other people, a thief of other men's work?

If that were so, then Runcorn's hatred was well earned, and his revenge had a justice to it.

Monk stared up at the old, carefully plastered ceiling. Above it was the room where Grey had been beaten to death. He did not feel ruthless now – only confused, oppressed by the void where memory should be, afraid of what he might find out about his own nature, anxious that he would fail in his job. Surely the crack on the head, however hard, could not have changed him so much? But even if the injury could not, maybe the fear had? He had woken up lost and alone, knowing nothing, having to find himself clue by clue, in what others could tell him, what they thought of him, but never why. He knew nothing of the motives for his acts, the nice rationalizations and excuses he had made to himself at the time. All the emotions that had driven him and blocked out judgment were in that empty region that yawned before the hospital bed and Runcorn's face.

But he had no time to pursue it further. Evan was back, his features screwed up in anxiety.

'It was Runcorn!' Monk leaped to the conclusion, suddenly frightened, like a man faced with physical violence.

Evan shook his head.

'No. It was two men I don't recogniz? at all from Grimwade's description. But he said they were from the police, and he saw their papers before he let them in.'

'Papers?' Monk repeated. There was no point in asking what the men had looked like; he could not remember the men of his own division, let alone those from any other.

'Yes.' Evan was obviously still anxious. 'He said they had police identification papers, like ours.'

'Did he see if they were from our station?'

'Yes sir, they were.' His face puckered. 'But I can't think who they could be. Anyway, why on earth would Runcorn send anyone else? What for?'

'I suppose it would be too much to ask that they gave names?'

'I'm afraid Grimwade didn't notice.'

Monk turned around and went back up the stairs, more worried than he wished Evan to see. On the landing he put the key Grimwade had given him into the lock and swung Grey's door open. The small hallway was just as before, and it gave him an unpleasant jar of familiarity, a sense of foreboding for what was beyond.

Evan was immediately behind him. His face was pale and his eyes shadowed, but Monk knew that his oppression stemmed from Runcorn, and the two men who had been here before them, not any sensitivity to the violence still lingering in the air.

There was no purpose in hesitating any more. He opened the second door.

There was a long sigh from behind him almost at his shoulder as Evan let out his breath in amazement.

The room was in wild disorder; the desk had been tipped

over and all its contents flung into the far corner – by the look of them, the papers a sheet at a time. The chairs were on their sides, one upside down, the seats had been taken out, the stuffed sofa ripped open with a knife. All the pictures lay on the floor, backs levered out.

'Oh my God.' Evan was stupefied.

'Not the police, I think,' Monk said quietly.

'But they had papers,' Evan protested. 'Grimwade actually read them.'

'Have you never heard of a good screever?'

'Forged?' Evan said wearily. 'I suppose Grimwade wouldn't have known the difference.'

'If the screever were good enough, I daresay we wouldn't either.' Monk pulled a sour expression. Some forgeries of testimonials, letters, bills of sale were good enough to deceive even those they were purported to come from. At the upper end, it was a highly skilled and lucrative trade, at the lower no more than a makeshift way of buying a little time, or fooling the hasty or illiterate.

'Who were they?' Evan went past Monk and stared around the wreckage. 'And what on earth did they want here?'

Monk's eyes went to the shelves where the ornaments had been.

'There was a silver sugar scuttle up there,' he said as he pointed. 'See if it's on the floor under any of that paper.' He turned slowly. 'And there were a couple of pieces of jade on that table. There were two snuffboxes in that alcove; one of them had an inlaid lid. And try the sideboard; there should be silver in the second drawer.'

'What an incredible memory you have; I never noticed them.' Evan was impressed and his admiration was obvious in his luminous eyes before he knelt down and began carefully to look under the mess, not moving it except to raise it sufficiently to explore beneath.

Monk was startled himself. He could not remember having looked in such detail at trivialities. Surely he had gone straight to the marks of the struggle, the bloodstains, the disarranged furniture, the bruised paint and the crooked pictures on the walls? He had no recollection now of even noticing the sideboard drawer, and yet his mind's eye could see silver, laid out neatly in green-baize-lined fittings.

Had it been in some other place? Was he confusing this room with another, an elegant sideboard somewhere in his past, belonging to someone else? Perhaps Imogen Latterly?

But he must dismiss Imogen from his mind – however easily, with whatever bitter fragrance, she returned. She was a dream, a creation of his own memories and hungers. He could never have known her well enough to feel anything but a charm, a sense of her distress, her courage in fighting it, the strength of her loyalty.

He forced himself to think of the present; Evan searching in the sideboard, the remark on his memory.

'Training,' he replied laconically, although he didn't understand it himself. 'You'll develop it. It might not be the second drawer, better look in all of them.'

Evan obeyed, and Monk turned back to the pile on the

floor and began to pick his way through the mess, looking for something to tell him its purpose, or give any clue as to who could have caused it.

'There's nothing here.' Evan closed the drawer, his mouth turned down in a grimace of disgust. 'But this is the right place; it's all slotted for them to fit in, and lined with cloth. They went to a lot of trouble for a dozen settings of silver. I suppose they expected to get more. Where did you say the jade was?'

'There.' Monk stepped over a pile of papers and cushions to an empty shelf, then wondered with a sense of unease how he knew, when he could have noticed it.

He bent and searched the floor carefully, replacing everything as he found it. Evan was watching him.

'No jade?' he asked.

'No, it's gone.' Monk straightened up, his back stiff. 'But I find it hard to believe ordinary thieves would go to the trouble, and the expense, of forging police identification papers just for a few pieces of silver and a jade ornament, and I think a couple of snuffboxes.' He looked around. 'They couldn't take much more without being noticed. Grimwade would certainly have been suspicious if they had taken anything like furniture or pictures.'

'Well, I suppose the silver and the jade are worth something?'

'Not much, after the fence has taken his cut.' Monk looked at the heap of wreckage on the floor and imagined the frenzy and the noise of such a search. 'Hardly worth the risk,' he said thoughtfully. 'Much easier to have burgled a

289

place in which the police have no interest. No, they wanted something else; the silver and the jade were a bonus. Anyway, what professional thief leaves a chaos like this behind him?'

'You mean it was Shelburne?' Evan's voice was half an octave higher with sheer disbelief.

Monk did not know what he meant.

'I can't think what Shelburne could want,' he said, staring around the room again, his mind's eye seeing it as it had been before. 'Even if he left something here that belonged to him there are a dozen reasons he could invent if we'd asked him with Joscelin dead and not able to argue. He could have left it here, whatever it was, any time, or lent it to Joscelin; or Joscelin could simply have taken it.' He stared around the ceiling at the elaborate plaster work of acanthus leaves. 'And I can't imagine him employing a couple of men to forge police papers and come here to ransack the place. No, it can't have been Shelburne.'

'Then who?'

Monk was frightened because suddenly there was no rationality in it at all. Everything that had seemed to fit ten minutes ago was now senseless, like puzzle parts of two quite different pictures. At the same time he was almost elated – if it were not Shelburne, if it were someone who knew forgers and thieves, then perhaps there was no society scandal or blackmail at all.

'I don't know,' he answered Evan with sudden new firmness. 'But there's no need to tiptoe in this one to find out. Nobody will lose us our jobs if we ask embarrassing questions of a few screevers, or bribe a nose, or even press a fence a little hard.'

Evan's face relaxed into a slow smile and his eyes lit up. Monk guessed that perhaps he had had little taste so far of the colour of the underworld, and as yet it still held the glamour of mystery. He would find its tones dark; grey of misery, black of long-used pain and habitual fear; its humour quick and bitter, gallows laughter.

He looked at Evan's keen face, its soft, sensitive lines. He could not explain to him; words are only names for what you already know – and what could Evan know that would prepare him for the hive of human waste that teemed in the shadows of Whitechapel, St Giles, Bluegate Fields, Seven Dials, or the Devil's Acre? Monk had known hardship himself in childhood; he could remember hunger now – it was coming back to him – and cold, shoes that leaked, clothes that let through the bitter north-east wind, plenty of meals of bread and gravy. He remembered faintly the pain of chilblains, angry itching face when at last you warmed a little; Beth with chapped lips and white, numb fingers.

But they were not unhappy memories; behind all the small pains there had always been a sense of well-being, a knowledge of eventual safety. They were always clean: clean clothes, however few and however old, clean table, smell of flour and fish, salt wind in the spring and summer when the windows were open.

It was sharper in his mind now; he could recall whole scenes, taste and touch, and always the whine of the wind and the cry of gulls. They had all gone to church on Sundays;

he could not bring back everything that had been said, but he could think of snatches of music, solemn and full of the satisfaction of people who believe what they sing, and know they sing it well.

His mother had taught him all his values: honesty, labour and learning. He knew even without her words that she believed it. It was a good memory, and he was more grateful for its return than for any other. It brought with it identity. He could not clearly picture his mother's face; each time he tried it blurred and melted into Beth's, as he had seen her only a few weeks ago, smiling, confident of herself. Perhaps they were not unalike.

Evan was waiting for him, eyes still bright with anticipation of seeing at last the real skill of detection, delving into the heartland of crime.

'Yes.' Monk recalled himself. 'We shall be free there to pursue as we wish.' And no satisfaction for Runcorn, he thought, but he did not add it aloud.

He went back to the door and Evan followed him. There was no point in tidying anything; better to leave it as it was – even that mess might yield a clue, some time.

He was in the hallway, next to the small table, when he noticed the sticks in the stand. He had seen them before, but he had been too preoccupied with the acts of violence in the room beyond to look closely. Anyway, they already had the stick that had been the weapon. Now he saw that there were still four there. Perhaps since Grey had used a stick to walk with, he had become something of a collector. It would not be unnatural; he had been a man to whom appearance mattered: everything about him said as much. Probably he had a stick for morning, another for evening, a casual one, and a rougher one for the country.

Monk's eye was caught by a dark, straight stick, the colour of mahogany and with a fine brass band on it embossed like the links of a chain. It was an extraordinary sensation, hot, almost like a dizziness; it prickled in his skin – he knew with total clarity that he had seen that stick before, and seen it several times.

Evan was beside him, waiting, wondering why he had stopped. Monk tried to clear his head, to broaden the image till it included where and when, till he saw the man who held it. But nothing came, only the vivid tingle of familiarity – and fear.

'Sir?' Evan's voice was doubtful. He could see no reason for the sudden paralysis. They were both standing in the hallway, frozen, and the only reason was in Monk's mind. And try as he might, bending all the force of his will on it, still he could see nothing but the stick, no man, not even a hand holding it.

'Have you thought of something, sir?' Evan's voice intruded into the intensity of his thought.

'No.' Monk moved at last. 'No.' He must think of something sensible to say, to explain himself, a reason for his behaviour. He found the words with difficulty. 'I was just wondering where to start. You say Grimwade didn't get any names from those papers?'

'No; but then they wouldn't use their own names anyway, would they?'

'No, of course not, but it would have helped to know what name the screever used for them.' It was a foolish question to have asked, but he must make sense of it. Evan was listening to his every word, as to a teacher. 'There are a vast number of screevers in London.' He made his voice go on with authority, as if he knew what he was saying, and it mattered. 'And I daresay more than one who has forged police papers in the last few weeks.'

'Oh – yes, of course,' Evan was instantly satisfied. 'No, I did ask, before I knew they were burglars, but he didn't notice. He was more interested in the authorization part.'

'Oh well.' Monk had control of himself again. He opened the door and went out. 'I daresay the name of the station will be enough anyway.' Evan came out also and he turned and closed the door behind him, locking it.

But when they reached the street Monk changed his mind. He wanted to see Runcorn's face when he heard of the robbery and realized Monk would not be forced to ferret for scandals as the only way to Grey's murderer. There was suddenly and beautifully a new way open to him, where the worst possibility was simple failure; and there was even a chance now of real success, unqualified.

He sent Evan off on a trivial errand, with instructions to meet him again in an hour, and caught a hansom through sunny, noisy streets back to the station. Runcorn was in, and there was a glow of satisfaction in his face when Monk came into his office.

'Morning, Monk,' he said cheerfully. 'No further, I see?'

Monk let the pleasure sink a little deeper into him, as one hesitates exquisitely in a hot bath, inching into it to savour each additional moment.

'It is a most surprising case,' he answered meaninglessly, his eyes meeting Runcorn's, affecting concern.

Runcorn's face clouded, but Monk could feel the pleasure in him as if it were an odour in the room.

'Unfortunately the public does not give us credit for amazement,' Runcorn replied, stretching out the anticipation. 'Just because they are puzzled that does not, in their view, allow us the same privilege. You're not pressing hard enough, Monk.' He frowned very slightly and leaned farther back in his chair, the sunlight in a bar through the window falling in on the side of his head. His voice changed to one of unctuous sympathy. 'Are you sure you are fully recovered? You don't seem like your old self. You used not to be so—' He smiled as the word pleased him. 'So hesitant. Justice was your first aim, indeed your only aim; I've never known you to balk before, even at the most unpleasant inquiries.' There was doubt at the very back of his eyes, and dislike. He was balancing between courage and experience, like a man beginning to ride a bicycle. 'You believe that very quality was what raised you so far, and so fast.' He stopped, waiting; and Monk had a brief vision of spiders resting in the hearts of their webs, knowing flies would come, sooner or later: the time was a matter of delicacy, but they would come.

He decided to play it out a little longer; he wanted to watch Runcorn himself, let him bring his own feelings into the open, and betray his vulnerability.

'This case is different,' he answered hesitantly, still putting the anxiety into his manner. He sat down on the chair opposite the desk. 'I can't remember any other like it. One cannot make comparison.'

'Murder is murder.' Runcorn shook his head a trifle pompously. 'Justice does not differentiate; and let me be frank, neither does the public – in fact if anything, they care more about this. It has all the elements the public likes, all the journalists need to whip up passions and make people frightened – and indignant.'

Monk decided to split hairs.

'Not really,' he demurred. 'There is no love story, and the public likes romance above all things. There is no woman.'

'No love story?' Runcorn's eyebrows went up. 'I never suspected you of cowardice, Monk; and never, ever of stupidity!' His face twitched with an impossible blend of satisfaction and affected concern. 'Are you sure you are quite well?' He leaned forward over the desk again to reinforce the effect. 'You don't get headaches, by any chance, do you? It was a very severe blow you received, you know. In fact, I daresay you don't recall it now, but when I first saw you in the hospital you didn't even recognize me.'

Monk refused to acknowledge the appalling thought that had come to the edge of his mind.

'Romance?' he asked blankly, as if he had heard nothing after that.

'Joscelin Grey and his sister-in-law!' Runcorn was

watching him closely, pretending to be hazy, his eyes a little veiled, but Monk saw the sharp pinpoints under his heavy lids.

'Do the public know of that?' Monk equally easily pretended innocence. 'I have not had time to look at newspapers.' He pushed out his lip in doubt. 'Do you think it was wise to tell them? Lord Shelburne will hardly be pleased!'

The skin across Runcorn's face tightened.

'No of course I haven't told them yet!' He barely controlled his voice. 'But it can only be a matter of time. You cannot put it off forever.' There was a hard gleam in his face, almost an appetite. 'You have most assuredly changed, Monk. You used to be such a fighter. It is almost as if you were a different person, a stranger to yourself. Have you forgotten how you used to be?'

For a moment Monk was unable to answer, unable to do anything but absorb the shock. He should have guessed it. He had been overconfident, stupidly blind to the obvious. Of course Runcorn knew he had lost his memory. If he had not known from the beginning, then he had surely guessed it in Monk's careful manoeuvring, his unawareness of their relationship. Runcorn was a professional; he spent his life telling truth from lies, divining motives, uncovering the hidden. What an arrogant fool Monk must have been to imagine he had deceived him. His own stupidity made him flush hot at the embarrassment of it.

Runcorn was watching him, seeing the tide of colour in his face. He must control it, find a shield; or better, a weapon. He straightened his body a little more and met Runcorn's eyes.

'A stranger to you perhaps, sir, but not to myself. But then we are few of us as plain as we seem to others. I think I am only less rash than you supposed. And it is as well.' He savoured the moment, although it had not the sweetness he had expected.

He looked at Runcorn's face squarely. 'I came to tell you that Joscelin Grey's flat has been robbed, at least it has been thoroughly searched, even ransacked, by two men posing as police. They seemed to have had quite competently forged papers which they showed to the porter.'

Runcorn's face was stiff and there was a mottle of red on his skin. Monk could not resist adding to it.

'Puts a different light on it, doesn't it?' he went on cheerfully, pretending they were both pleased. 'I don't see Lord Shelburne hiring an accomplice and posing as a Peeler to search his brother's flat.'

A few seconds had given Runcorn time to think.

'Then he must have hired a couple of men. Simple enough!'

But Monk was ready. 'If it was something worth such a terrible risk,' he countered, 'why didn't they get it before? It must have been there two months by now.'

'What terrible risk?' Runcorn's voice dropped a little in mockery of the idea. 'They passed it off beautifully. And it would have been easy enough to do: just watch the building a little while to make sure the real police were not there, then go in with their false papers, get what they went for, and leave. I daresay they had a crow out in the street.'

'I wasn't referring to the risk of their being caught in the act,' Monk said scornfully. 'I was thinking of the much greater risk, from his point of view, of placing himself in the hands of possible blackmailers.'

He felt a surge of pleasure as Runcorn's face betrayed that he hadn't thought of that.

'Do it anonymously.' Runcorn dismissed the idea.

Monk smiled at him. 'If it was worth paying thieves, and a first-class screever, in order to get it back, it wouldn't take a very bright thief to work out it would be worth raising the price a little before handing it over. Everyone in London knows there was murder done in that room. If whatever he wanted was worth paying thieves and forgers to get back, it must be damning.'

Runcorn glared at the table top, and Monk waited.

'So what are you suggesting then?' Runcorn said at last. 'Somebody wanted it. Or do you say it was just a casual thief, trying his luck?' His contempt for the idea was heavy in his voice and it curled his lip.

Monk avoided the question.

'I intend to find out what it is,' he replied, pushing back his chair and rising. 'It may be something we haven't even thought of.'

'You'll have to be a damn good detective to do that!' The triumph came back into Runcorn's eyes.

Monk straightened and looked levelly back at him.

'I am,' he said without a flicker. 'Did you think that had changed?'

* * *

When he left Runcorn's office Monk had had no idea even how to begin. He had forgotten all his contacts; now a fence or an informer could pass him in the street and he would not recognize him. He would not ask any of his colleagues. If Runcorn hated him, it was more than likely many of them did too and he had no idea which; and to show such vulnerability would invite a *coup de grâce*. Runcorn knew he had lost his memory, of that he was perfectly sure now, although nothing had been said completely beyond ambiguity. There was a chance, a good chance he could fend off one man until he had regained at least enough mixture of memory and skill to do his job well enough to defy them all. If he solved the Grey case he would be unassailable; then let Runcorn say what he pleased.

But it was an unpleasant knowledge that he was so deeply and consistently hated, and with what he increasingly realized was good reason.

And was he fighting for survival? Or was there also an instinct in him to attack Runcorn; not only to find the truth, to be right, but also to be there before Runcorn was and make sure he knew it? Perhaps if he had been an onlooker at this, watching two other men, at least some of his sympathy would have been with Runcorn. There was a cruelty in himself he was seeing for the first time, a pleasure in winning that he did not admire.

Had he always been like this – or was it born of his fear?

How to start finding the thieves? Much as he liked Evan – and he did like him increasingly every day; the man had enthusiasm and gentleness, humour, and a purity of intention Monk envied – even so, he dare not place himself in Evan's hands by telling him the truth. And if he were honest (there was a little vanity in it also), Evan was the only person, apart from Beth, who seemed unaffectedly to think well of him, even to like him. He could not bear to forfeit that.

So he could not ask Evan to tell him the names of informers and fences. He would just have to find them for himself. But if he had been as good a detective as everything indicated, he must know many. They would recognize him.

He was late and Evan had been waiting for him. He apologized, somewhat to Evan's surprise, and only afterward realized that as a superior it was not expected of him. He must be more careful, especially if he were to conceal his purpose, and his inability, from Evan. He wanted to go to an underworld eating house for luncheon, and hoped that if he left word with the potman someone would approach him. He would have to do it in several places, but within three or four days at most he should find a beginning.

He could not bring back to memory any names or faces, but the smell of the back taverns was sharply familiar. Without thinking, he knew how to behave; to alter colour like a chameleon, to drop his shoulders, loosen his gait, keep his eyes down and wary. It is not clothes that make the man; a cardsharp, a dragsman, a superior pickpocket or a thief from the Swell Mob could dress as well as most – indeed the nurse at the hospital had taken him for one of the Swell Mob himself.

Evan, with his fair face and wide, humorous eyes, looked

too clean to be dishonest. There was none of the wiliness of
a survivor in him; yet some of the best survivors of all were
those most skilled in deception and the most innocent of
face. The underworld was big enough for any variation of lie
and fraud, and no weakness was left unexploited.

They began a little to the west of Mecklenburgh Square,
going to the King's Cross Road. When the first tavern
produced nothing immediate, they moved north to the
Pentonville Road, then south and east again into Clerkenwell.

In spite of all that logic could tell him, by the following
day Monk was beginning to feel as if he were on a fool's
errand, and Runcorn would have the last laugh. Then, in a
congested public house by the name of the Grinning Rat, a
scruffy little man, smiling, showing yellow teeth, slid into
the seat beside them, looking warily at Evan. The room was
full of noise, the strong smell of ale, sweat, the dirt of clothes
and bodies long unwashed, and the heavy steam of food. The
floor was covered with sawdust and there was a constant
chink of glass.

''Ello, Mr Monk; I hain't seen you for a long time. W'ere
yer bin?'

Monk felt a leap of excitement and studied hard to hide
it.

'Had an accident,' he answered, keeping his voice level.

The man looked him up and down critically and grunted,
dismissing it.

'I 'ears as yer after som'un as'll blow a little?'

'That's right,' Monk agreed. He must not be too
precipitate, or the price would be high, and he could not

afford the time to bargain; he must be right first time, or he would appear green. He knew from the air, the smell of it, that haggling was part of the game.

'Worf anyfink?' the man asked.

'Could be.'

'Well,' the man said, thinking it over. 'Yer always bin fair, that's why I comes to yer 'stead o' some 'o them other jacks. Proper mean, some o' them; yer'd be right ashamed if yer knew.' He shook his head and sniffed hard, pulling a face of disgust.

Monk smiled.

'Wotcher want, then?' the man asked.

'Several things.' Monk lowered his voice even further, still looking across the table and not at the man. 'Some stolen goods – a fence, and a good screever.'

The man also looked at the table, studying the stain ring marks of mugs.

'Plenty o' fences, guv; and a fair few screevers. Special goods, these?'

'Not very.'

'W'y yer want 'em then? Som'one done over bad?'

'Yes.'

'O'right, so wot are they then?'

Monk began to describe them as well as he could; he had only memory to go on.

'Table silver—'

The man looked at him witheringly.

Monk abandoned the silver. 'A jade ornament,' he continued. 'About six inches high, of a dancing lady with

303

her arms up in front of her, bent at the elbows. It was pinky-coloured jade—'

'Aw, nah that's better.' The man's voice lifted; Monk avoided looking at his face. 'Hain't a lot o' pink jade abaht,' he went on. 'Anyfink else?'

'A silver scuttle, about four or five inches, I think, and a couple of inlaid snuffboxes.'

'Wot kind o' snuffboxes, guv: siller, gold, enamel? Yer gotta give me mor'n that!'

'I can't remember.'

'Yer wot? Don't the geezer wot lorst 'em know?' His face darkened with suspicion and for the first time he looked at Monk. ''Ere! 'E croaked, or summink?'

'Yes,' Monk said levelly, still staring at the wall. 'But no reason to suppose the thief did it. He was dead long before the robbery.'

'Yer sure o' that? 'Ow d'yer know 'e were gorn afore?'

'He was dead two months before.' Monk smiled acidly. 'Even I couldn't mistake that. His empty house was robbed.'

The man thought this over for several minutes before delivering his opinion.

Somewhere over near the bar there was a roar of laughter.

'Robbin' a deadlurk?' he said with heavy condescension. 'Bit chancy to find anyfink, in' it? Wot did yer say abaht a screever? Wot yer want a screever fer then?'

'Because the thieves used forged police papers to get in,' Monk replied.

The man's face lit up with delight and he chuckled richly.

'A proper downy geezer, that one. I like it!' He wiped the

back of his hand across his mouth and laughed again. 'It'd be a sin ter shop a feller wiv that kind o' class.'

Monk took a gold half-sovereign out of his pocket and put it on the table. The man's eyes fastened onto it as if it mesmerized him.

'I want the screever who made those fakements for them,' Monk repeated. He put out his hand and took the gold coin back again. He put it into his inside pocket. The man's eyes followed it. 'And no sly faking,' Monk warned. 'I'll feel your hands in my pockets, and you remember that, unless you fancy picking oakum for a while. Not do your sensitive fingers any good, picking oakum!' He winced inwardly as a flash of memory returned of men's fingers bleeding from the endless unravelling of rope ends, day in, day out, while years of their lives slid by.

The man flinched. 'Now that ain't nice, Mr Monk. I never took nuffink from yer in me life.' He crossed himself hastily and Monk was not sure whether it was a surety of truth or a penance for the lie. 'I s'pose yer tried all the jollyshops?' the man continued, screwing up his face. 'Couldn't christen that jade lady.'

Evan looked vaguely confused, although Monk was not sure by what.

'Pawnshops,' he translated for him. 'Naturally thieves remove any identification from most articles, but nothing much you can do to jade without spoiling its value.' He took five shillings out of his pocket and gave them to the man. 'Come back in two days, and if you've got anything, you'll have earned the half-sovereign.'

'Right, guv, but not 'ere; there's a slap bang called the Purple Duck dahn on Plumber's Row – orf the Whitechapel Road. Yer go there.' He looked Monk up and down with distaste. 'An' come out o' twig, eh; not all square rigged like a prater! And bring the gold, 'cos I'll 'ave summink. Yer 'ealf, guv, an' yers.' He glanced sideways at Evan, then slid off the seat and disappeared into the crowd. Monk felt elated, suddenly singing inside. Even the fast-cooling plum duff was bearable. He smiled broadly across at Evan.

'Come in disguise,' he explained. 'Not soberly dressed like a fake preacher.'

'Oh.' Evan relaxed and began to enjoy himself also. 'I see.' He stared around at the throng of faces, seeing mystery behind the dirt, his imagination painting them with nameless colour.

Two days later Monk obediently dressed himself in suitable secondhand clothes; 'translators' the informer would have called them. He wished he could remember the man's name, but for all his efforts it remained completely beyond recall, hidden like almost everything else after the age of about seventeen. He had had glimpses of the years up to then, even including his first year or two in London, but although he lay awake, staring into the darkness, letting his mind wander, going over and over all he knew in the hope his brain would jerk into life again and continue forward, nothing more returned.

Now he and Evan were sitting in the saloon in the Purple Duck, Evan's delicate face registering both his distaste and his efforts to conceal it. Looking at him, Monk wondered how often he himself must have been here to be so unoffended by it. It must have become habit, the noise, the smell, the uninhibited closeness, things his subconscious remembered even if his mind did not.

They had to wait nearly an hour before the informer turned up, but he was grinning again, and slid into the seat beside Monk without a word.

Monk was not going to jeopardize the price by seeming too eager.

'Drink?' he offered.

'Nah, just the guinea,' the man replied. 'Don' want ter draw attention to meself drinkin' wiv the likes o' you, if yer'll pardon me. But potmen 'as sharp mem'ries an' loose tongues.'

'Quite,' Monk agreed. 'But you'll earn the guinea before you get it.'

'Aw, nah Mr Monk.' He pulled a face of deep offence. ''Ave I ever shorted yer? Now 'ave I?'

Monk had no idea.

'Did you find my screever?' he asked instead.

'I carsn't find yer jade, not fer sure, like.'

'Did you find the screever?'

'You know Tommy, the shofulman?'

For a moment Monk felt a touch of panic. Evan was watching him, fascinated by the bargaining. Ought he to know Tommy? He knew what a shofulman was, someone who passed forged money.

'Tommy?' he blinked.

'Yeah!' the man said impatiently. 'Blind Tommy, least 'e pretends 'e's blind. I reckon as 'e 'alf is.'

'Where do I find him?' If he could avoid admitting anything, perhaps he could bluff his way through. He must not either show an ignorance of something he would be expected to know or on the other hand collect so little information as to be left helpless.

'You find 'im!' The man smiled condescendingly at the idea. 'Yer'll never find 'im on yer own; wouldn't be safe anyhow. 'E's in the rookeries, an' yer'd get a shiv in yer gizzard sure as 'ell's on fire if yer went in there on yer tod. I'll take yer.'

'Tommy taken up screeving?' Monk concealed his relief by making a general and he hoped meaningless remark.

The little man looked at him with amazement.

''Course not! 'E can't even write 'is name, let alone a fakement fer some'un else! But 'e knows a right downy geezer wot does. Reckon 'e's the one as writ yer police papers fer yer. 'E's known to do that kind o' fing.'

'Good. Now what about the jade – anything at all?'

The man twisted his rubber-like features into the expression of an affronted rodent.

'Bit 'ard that, guv. Know one feller wot got a piece, but 'e swears blind it were a snoozer wot brought it – an' you din't say nuffink abaht no snoozer.'

'This was no hotel thief,' Monk agreed. 'That the only one?'

'Only one as I knows fer sure.'

Monk knew the man was lying, although he could not

have said how – an accumulation of impressions too subtle to be analyzed.

'I don't believe you, Jake; but you've done well with the screever.' He fished in his pocket and brought out the promised gold. 'And if it leads to the man I want, there'll be another for you. Now take me to Blind Tommy the shofulman.'

They all stood up and wormed their way out through the crowd into the street. It was not until they were two hundred yards away that Monk realized, with a shudder of excitement he could not control, that he had called the man by name. It was coming back, more than merely his memory for his own sake, but his skill was returning. He quickened his step and found himself smiling broadly at Evan.

The rookery was monstrous, a rotting pile of tenements crammed one beside the other, piled precariously, timbers awry as the damp warped them and floors and walls were patched and repatched. It was dark even in the late summer afternoon and the humid air was clammy to the skin. It smelled of human waste and the gutters down the overhung alleys ran with filth. The squeaking and slithering of rats was a constant background. Everywhere there were people, huddled in doorways, lying on stones, sometimes six or eight together, some of them alive, some already dead from hunger or disease. Typhoid and pneumonia were endemic in such places and venereal diseases passed from one to another, as did the flies and lice.

Monk looked at a child in the gutter as he passed, perhaps five or six years old, its face grey in the half-light, pinched sharp; it was impossible to tell whether it was male or female. Monk thought with a dull rage that bestial as it was to beat a man to death as Grey had been beaten, it was still a better murder than this child's abject death.

He noticed Evan's face, white in the gloom, eyes like holes in his head. There was nothing he could think of to say – no words that served any purpose. Instead he put out his hand and touched him briefly, an intimacy that came quite naturally in that awful place.

They followed Jake through another alley and then another, up a flight of stairs that threatened to give way beneath them with each step, and at the top at last Jake stopped, his voice hushed as if the despair had reached even him. He spoke as one does in the presence of death.

'One more lot o' steps, Mr Monk, from 'ere, an' Blind Tommy's be'ind the door on yer right.'

'Thank you. I'll give you your guinea when I've seen him, if he can help.'

Jake's face split in a grin.

'I already got it, Mr Monk.' He held up a bright coin. 'Fink I fergot 'ow to do it, did yer? I used ter be a fine wirer, I did, w'en I were younger.' He laughed and slipped it into his pocket. 'I were taught by the best kidsman in the business. I'll be seein' yer, Mr Monk; yer owes me anuvver, if yer gets them fieves.'

Monk smiled in spite of himself. The man was a pickpocket, but he had been taught by one of those who make their own living by teaching children to steal for them, and taking the profits in return for the child's keep. It was an apprenticeship in survival. Perhaps his only alternative had been starvation, like the child they had passed. Only the quick-fingered, the strong and the lucky reached adulthood. Monk could not afford to indulge in judgment, and he was too torn with pity and anger to try.

'It's yours, Jake, if I get them,' he promised, then started up the last flight and Evan followed. At the top he opened the door without knocking.

Blind Tommy must have been expecting him. He was a dapper little man, about five feet tall with a sharp, ugly face, and dressed in a manner he himself would have described as 'flash'. He was apparently no more than shortsighted because he saw Monk immediately and knew who he was.

''Evenin', Mr Monk. I 'ears as yer lookin' fer a screever, a partic'lar one, like?'

'That's right, Tommy. I want one who made some fakements for two rampsmen who robbed a house in Mecklenburgh Square. Went in pretending to be Peelers.'

Tommy's face lit up with amusement.

'I like that,' he admitted. 'It's a smart lay, that is.'

'Providing you don't get caught.'

'Wot's it worf?' Tommy's eyes narrowed.

'It's murder, Tommy. Whoever did it'll be topped, and whoever helps them stands a good chance of getting the boat.'

'Oh Gawd!' Tommy's face paled visibly. 'I 'an't no fancy for Horstralia. Boats don't suit me at all, they don't. Men wasn't meant ter go orf all over like that! In't nat'ral. An' 'orrible stories I've 'eard about them parts.' He shivered

dramatically. 'Full o' savages an' creatures wot weren't
never made by no Christian Gawd. Fings wif dozens 'o legs,
an' fings wi' no legs at all. Ugh!' He rolled his eyes. 'Right
'eathen place, it is.'

'Then don't run any risk of being sent there,' Monk
advised without any sympathy. 'Find me this screever.'

'Are yer sure it's murder?' Tommy was still not entirely
convinced. Monk wondered how much it was a matter of
loyalties, and how much simply a weighing of one advantage
against another.

'Of course I'm sure!' he said with a low, level voice. He
knew the threat was implicit in it. 'Murder and robbery.
Silver and jade stolen. Know anything about a jade dancing
lady, pink jade, about six inches high?'

Tommy was defensive, a thin, nasal quality of fear in his
tone.

'Fencin's not my life, guv. Don't do none o' that – don't
yer try an' hike that on me.'

'The screever?' Monk said flatly.

'Yeah, well I'll take yer. Anyfink in it fer me?' Hope
seldom died. If the fearful reality of the rookery did not kill
it, Monk certainly could not.

'If it's the right man,' he grunted.

Tommy took them through another labyrinth of alleys
and stairways, but Monk wondered how much distance they
had actually covered. He had a strong feeling it was more to
lose their sense of direction than to travel above a few
hundred yards. Eventually they stopped at another large
door, and after a sharp knock, Blind Tommy disappeared

and the door swung open in front of them.

The room inside was bright and smelled of burning. Monk stepped in, then looked up involuntarily and saw glass skylights. He saw down the walls where there were large windows as well. Of course – light for a forger's careful pen.

The man inside turned to look at the intruders. He was squat, with powerful shoulders and large spatulate hands. His face was pale-skinned but ingrained with the dirt of years, and his colourless hair stuck to his head in thin spikes.

'Well?' he demanded irritably. When he spoke Monk saw his teeth were short and black; Monk fancied he could smell the stale odour of them, even from where he stood.

'You wrote police identification papers for two men, purporting to come from the Lime Street station.' He made a statement, not a question. 'I don't want you for it; I want the men. It's a case of murder, so you'd do well to stay on the right side of it.'

The man leered, his thin lips stretching wide in some private amusement. 'You Monk?'

'And if I am?' He was surprised the man had heard of him. Was his reputation so wide? Apparently it was.

'Your case they walked inter, was it?' The man's mirth bubbled over in a silent chuckle, shaking his mass of flesh.

'It's my case now,' Monk replied. He did not want to tell the man the robbery and the murder were separate; the threat of hanging was too useful.

'Wotcher want?' the man asked. His voice was hoarse, as

if from too much shouting or laughter, yet it was hard imagining him doing either.

'Who are they?' Monk pressed.

'Now, Mr Monk, 'ow should I know?' His massive shoulders were still twitching. 'Do I ask people's names?'

'Probably not, but you know who they are. Don't pretend to be stupid; it doesn't suit you.'

'I know some people,' he conceded in little more than a whisper. ' 'Course I do; but not every muck snipe 'oo tries 'is 'and at thievin'.'

'Muck snipe?' Monk looked at him with derision. 'Since when did you hand out fakements for nothing? You don't do favours for down-and-outs. They paid you, or someone did. If they didn't pay you themselves, tell me who did; that'll do.'

The man's narrow eyes widened a fraction. 'Oh, clever, Mr Monk, very clever.' He clapped his broad, powerful hands together in soundless applause.

'So who paid you?'

'My business is confidential, Mr Monk. Lose it all if I starts putting the down on people wot comes ter me. It was a moneylender, that's all I'll tell yer.'

'Not much call for a screever in Australia.' Monk looked at the man's subtle, sensitive fingers. 'Hard labour – bad climate.'

'Put me on the boat, would yer?' The man's lip curled. 'Yer'd 'ave ter catch me first, and yer know as well as I do yer'd never find me.' The smile on his face did not alter even a fraction. 'An' yer'd be a fool ter look, 'orrible fings 'appen ter a Peeler as gets caught in the rookeries, if the word goes aht.'

'And horrible things happen to a screever who informs on his clients – if the word goes out,' Monk added immediately. 'Horrible things – like broken fingers. And what use is a screever without his fingers?'

The man stared at him, suddenly hatred undisguised in his heavy eyes.

'An' w'y should the word go out, Mr Monk, seein' as 'ow I aven't told yer nuffink?'

In the doorway Evan moved uncomfortably. Monk ignored him.

'Because I shall put it out,' he replied, 'that you have.'

'But you ain't got no one fer yer robbery.' The hoarse whisper was level again, the amusement creeping back.

'I'll find someone.'

'Takes time, Mr Monk; and 'ow are yer goin' ter do it if I don't tell yer?'

'You are leaping to conclusions, screever,' Monk said ruthlessly. 'It doesn't have to be the right ones; anyone will do. By the time the word gets back I have the wrong people, it'll be too late to save your fingers. Broken fingers heal hard, and they ache for years, so I'm told.'

The man called him something obscene.

'Quite.' Monk looked at him with disgust. 'So who paid you?'

The man glared at him, hate hot in his face.

'Who paid you?' Monk leaned forward a little.

'Josiah Wigtight, moneylender,' the man spat out. 'Find

'im in Gun Lane, Whitechapel. Now get out!'

'Moneylender. What sort of people does he lend money to?'

'The sort o' people wot can pay 'im back, o' course, fool!'

'Thank you.' Monk smiled and straightened up. 'Thank you, screever; your business is secure. You have told us nothing.'

The screever swore at him again, but Monk was out of the door and hurrying down the rickety stairs. Evan, anxious and doubtful, at his heel, but Monk offered him no explanation, and did not meet his questioning look.

It was too late to try the moneylender that day, and all he could think of was to get out of the rookeries in one piece before someone stabbed one of them for his clothes, poor as they were, or merely because they were strangers.

He said good-night briefly and watched Evan hesitate, then reply in his quiet voice and turn away in the darkness, an elegant figure, oddly young in the gaslight.

Back at Mrs Worley's, he ate a hot meal, grateful for it, at once savouring each mouthful and hating it because he could not dismiss from his mind all those who would count it victory merely to have survived the day and eaten enough to sustain life.

None of it was strange to him, as it obviously had been to Evan. He must have been to such places many times before. He had behaved instinctively, altering his stance, knowing how to melt into the background, not to look like a stranger, least of all a figure of authority. The beggars, the sick, the hopeless moved him to excruciating pity, and a deep, abiding anger – but no surprise.

And his mercilessness with the screever had come without calculation, his natural reaction. He knew the rookeries and their denizens. He might even have survived in them himself.

Only afterwards, when the plate was empty, did he lean back in the chair and think of the case.

A moneylender made sense. Joscelin Grey might well have borrowed money when he lost his small possessions in the affair with Latterly, and his family would not help. Had the moneylender meant to injure him a little, to frighten repayment from him, and warn other tardy borrowers, and when Grey had fought back it had gone too far? It was possible. And Yeats's visitor had been a moneylender's ruffian. Yeats and Grimwade had both said he was a big man, lean and strong, as far as they could tell under his clothes.

What a baptism for Evan. He had said nothing about it afterwards. He had not even asked if Monk would really have arrested people he knew to be innocent and then spread the word the screever had betrayed them.

Monk flinched as he remembered what he had said; but it had simply been what instinct directed. It was a streak of ruthlessness in himself he had been unaware of; and it would have shocked him in anyone else. Was that really what he was like? Surely it was only a threat, and he would never have carried it out? Or would he? He remembered the anger that had welled up inside him at the mention of moneylenders, parasites of the desperate poor who clung to respectability, to a few precious standards. Sometimes a man's honesty was his only real possession, his only source of pride and identity in the anonymous, wretched, teeming multitude.

What had Evan thought of him? He cared; it was a miserable thought that Evan would be disillusioned, finding his methods as ugly as the crime he fought, not understanding he was using words, only words.

Or did Evan know him better than he knew himself? Evan would know his past. Perhaps in the past the words had been a warning, and reality had followed.

And what would Imogen Latterly have felt? It was a preposterous dream. The rookeries were as foreign to her as the planets in the sky. She would be sick, disgusted even to see them, let alone to have passed through them and dealt with their occupants. If she had seen him threaten the screever, standing in the filthy room, she would not permit him to enter her house again.

He sat staring up at the ceiling, full of anger and pain. It was cold comfort to him that tomorrow he would find the usurer who might have killed Joscelin Grey. He hated the world he had to deal with; he wanted to belong to the clean, gracious world where he could speak as an equal with people like the Latterlys; Charles would not patronize him, he could converse with Imogen Latterly as a friend, and quarrel with Hester without the hindrance of social inferiority. That would be a delicate pleasure. He would dearly like to put that opinionated young woman in her place.

But purely because he hated the rookeries so fiercely, he

could not ignore them. He had seen them, known their squalor and their desperation, and they would not go away.

Well at least he could turn his anger to some purpose; he would find the violent, greedy man who had paid to have Joscelin Grey beaten to death. Then he could face Grey in peace in his imagination – and Runcorn would be defeated.

Chapter Ten

Monk sent Evan to try pawnshops for the pink jade, and then himself went to look for Josiah Wigtight. He had no trouble finding the address. It was half a mile east of Whitechapel off the Mile End Road. The building was narrow and almost lost between a seedy lawyer's office and a sweatshop where in dim light and heavy, breathless air women worked eighteen hours a day sewing shirts for a handful of pence. Some felt driven to walk the street at night also, for the extra dreadfully and easily earned silver coins that meant food and rent. A few were wives or daughters of the poor, the drunken or the inadequate; many were women who had in the past been in domestic service, and had lost their 'character' one way or another – for impertinence, dishonesty, loose morals, or because a mistress found them 'uppity', or a master had taken advantage of them and been discovered, and in a number of cases they had become with child, and thus not only unemployable but a disgrace and an affront.

Inside, the office was dim behind drawn blinds and smelled of polish, dust and ancient leather. A black-dressed clerk sat at a high stool in the first room. He looked up as Monk came in.

'Good morning, sir; may we be of assistance to you?' His voice was soft, like mud. 'Perhaps you have a little problem?' He rubbed his hands together as though the cold bothered him, although it was summer. 'A temporary problem, of course?' He smiled at his own hypocrisy.

'I hope so.' Monk smiled back.

The man was skilled at his job. He regarded Monk with caution. His expression had not the nervousness he was accustomed to; if anything it was a little wolfish. Monk realized he had been clumsy. Surely in the past he must have been more skilled, more attuned to the nuances of judgment?

'That rather depends on you,' he added to encourage the man, and allay any suspicion he might unwittingly have aroused.

'Indeed,' the clerk agreed. 'That's what we're in business for: to help gentlemen with a temporary embarrassment of funds. Of course there are conditions, you understand?' He fished out a clean sheet of paper and held his pen ready. 'If I could just have the details, sir?'

'My problem is not a shortage of funds,' Monk replied with the faintest smile. He hated moneylenders; he hated the relish with which they plied their revolting trade. 'At least not pressing enough to come to you. I have a matter of business to discuss with Mr Wigtight.'

'Quite.' The man nodded with a smirk of understanding. 'Quite so. All matters of business are referred to Mr Wigtight, ultimately, Mr— er?' He raised his eyebrows.

'I do not want to borrow any money,' Monk said rather more tartly. 'Tell Mr Wigtight it is about something he had mislaid, and very badly wishes to have returned to him.'

'Mislaid?' The man screwed up his pallid face. 'Mislaid? What are you talking about, sir? Mr Wigtight does not mislay things.' He sniffed in offended disapproval.

Monk leaned forward and put both hands on the counter, and the man was obliged to face him.

'Are you going to show me to Mr Wigtight?' Monk said very clearly. 'Or do I take my information elsewhere?' He did not want to tell the man who he was, or Wigtight would be forewarned, and he needed the slight advantage of surprise.

'Ah—' The man made up his mind rapidly. 'Ah – yes; yes sir. I'll take you to Mr Wigtight, sir. If you'll come this way.' He closed his ledger with a snap and slid it into a drawer. With one eye still on Monk he took a key from his waistcoat pocket and locked the drawer, then straightened up. 'Yes, sir, this way.'

The inner office of Josiah Wigtight was quite a different affair from the drab attempt at anonymous respectability of the entrance. It was frankly lush, everything chosen for comfort, almost hedonism. The big armchairs were covered in velvet and the cushions were deep in both colour and texture; the carpet muffled sound and the gas lamps hissing softly on the walls were mantled in rose-coloured glass which shed a glow over the room, obscuring outlines and dulling glare. The curtains were heavy and drawn in folds to keep out the intrusion and the reality of daylight. It was not a matter of taste, not even of vulgarity, but purely the uses of pleasure. After a moment or two the effect was curiously soporific. Immediately Monk's respect for Wigtight rose. It was clever.

'Ah.' Wigtight breathed out deeply. He was a portly man, swelling out like a giant toad behind his desk, wide mouth split into a smile that died long before it reached his bulbous eyes. 'Ah,' he repeated. 'A matter of business somewhat delicate, Mr— er?'

'Somewhat,' Monk agreed. He decided not to sit down in the soft, dark chair; he was almost afraid it would swallow him, like a mire, smother his judgment. He felt he would be at a disadvantage in it and not able to move if he should need to.

'Sit down, sit down!' Wigtight waved. 'Let us talk about it. I'm sure some accommodation can be arrived at.'

'I hope so.' Monk perched on the arm of the chair. It was uncomfortable, but in this room he preferred to be uncomfortable.

'You are temporarily embarrassed?' Wigtight began. 'You wish to take advantage of an excellent investment? You have expectations of a relative, in poor health, who favours you—'

'Thank you, I have employment which is quite sufficient for my needs.'

'You are a fortunate man.' There was no belief in his smooth, expressionless voice; he had heard every lie and excuse human ingenuity could come up with.

'More fortunate than Joscelin Grey!' Monk said baldly.

Wigtight's face changed in only the minutest of ways – a shadow, no more. Had Monk not been watching for it he would have missed it altogether.

'Joscelin Grey?' Wigtight repeated. Monk could see in his face the indecision whether to deny knowing him or admit it as a matter of common knowledge. He decided the wrong way.

'I know no such person, sir.'

'You've never heard of him?' Monk tried not to press too hard. He hated moneylenders with far more anger than reason could tell him of. He meant to trap this soft, fat man in his own words, trap him and watch the bloated body struggle.

But Wigtight sensed a pitfall.

'I hear so many names,' he added cautiously.

'Then you had better look in your books,' Monk suggested. 'And see if his is there, since you don't remember.'

'I don't keep books, after debts are paid.' Wigtight's wide, pale eyes assumed a blandness. 'Matter of discretion, you know. People don't like to be reminded of their hard times.

'How civil of you,' Monk said sarcastically. 'How about looking through the lists of those who didn't repay you?'

'Mr Grey is not among them.'

'So he paid you.' Monk allowed only a little of his triumph to creep through.

'I have not said I lent him anything.'

'Then if you lent him nothing, why did you hire two men to deceive their way into his flat and ransack it? And incidentally, to steal his silver and small ornaments?' He saw with delight that Wigtight flinched. 'Clumsy, that, Mr

Wigtight. You're hiring a very poor class of ruffian these days. A good man would never have helped himself on the side like that. Dangerous; brings another charge into it – and those goods are so easy to trace.'

'You're police!' Wigtight's understanding was sudden and venomous.

'That's right.'

'I don't hire thieves.' Now Wigtight was hedging, trying to gain time to think, and Monk knew it.

'You hire collectors, who turned out to be thieves as well,' Monk said immediately. 'The law doesn't see any difference.'

'I hire people to do my collecting, of course,' Wigtight agreed. 'Can't go out into the streets after everybody myself.'

'How many do you call on with forged police papers, two months after you've murdered them?'

Every vestige of colour drained out of Wigtight's face, leaving it grey, like a cold fish skin. Monk thought for a moment he was having some kind of a fit, and he felt no concern at all.

It was long seconds before Wigtight could speak, and Monk merely waited.

'Murdered!' The word when it came was hollow. 'I swear on my mother's grave, I never had anything to do with that. Why should I? Why should I do that? It's insane. You're crazed.'

'Because you're a usurer,' Monk said bitterly, a well of anger and scalding contempt opening up inside him. 'And usurers don't allow people not to pay their debts, with all the interest when they're due.' He leaned forward towards the man, threatening by his movement when Wigtight was motionless in the chair. 'Bad for business if you let them get away with it,' he said almost between his teeth. 'Encourages other people to do the same. Where would you be if everyone refused to pay you back? Bleed themselves white to satisfy your interest. Better one goose dead than the whole wretched flock running around free and fat, eh?'

'I never killed him!' Wigtight was frightened, not only by the facts, but by Monk's hatred. He knew unreason when he saw it; and Monk enjoyed his fear.

'But you sent someone – it comes to the same thing,' Monk pursued.

'No! It wouldn't make sense!' Wigtight's voice was growing higher, a new, sharp note on it. The panic was sweet to Monk's ear. 'All right.' Wigtight raised his hands, soft and fat. 'I sent them to see if Grey had kept any record of borrowing from me. I knew he'd been murdered and I thought he might have kept the cancelled IOU. I didn't want to have anything to do with him. That's all, I swear!' There was sweat on his face now, glistening in the gaslight. 'He paid me back. Mother of God, it was only fifty pounds anyway! Do you think I'd send out men to murder a debtor for fifty pounds? It would be mad, insane. They'd have a hold over me for the rest of my life. They'd bleed me dry – or see me to the gibbet.'

Monk stared at him. Painfully the truth of it conquered him. Wigtight was a parasite, but he was not a fool. He would not have hired such clumsy chance help to murder a man for a debt, of whatever size. If he had intended murder he would have been cleverer, more discreet about it. A little violence might well have been fruitful, but not this, and not in Grey's own house.

But he might well have wanted to be sure there was no trace of the association left, purely to avoid inconvenience.

'Why did you leave it so long?' Monk asked, his voice flat again, without the hunting edge. 'Why didn't you go and look for the IOU straightaway?'

Wigtight knew he had won. It was there gleaming in his pallid, globular face, like pond slime on a frog.

'At first there were too many real police about,' he answered. 'Always going in and out.' He spread his hands in reasonableness. Monk would have liked to call him a liar, but he could not, not yet. 'Couldn't get anyone prepared to take the risk,' Wigtight went on. 'Pay a man too much for a job, and immediately he begins to wonder if there's more to it than you've told him. Might start thinking I had something to be afraid of. Your lot was looking for thieves, in the beginning. Now it's different; you're asking about business, money—'

'How do you know?' Monk believed him, he was forced to, but he wanted every last ounce of discomfort he could drag out.

'Word gets about; you asked his tailor, his wine merchant, looking into the paying of his bills—'

Monk remembered he had sent Evan to do these things. It would seem the usurer had eyes and ears everywhere. He realized now it was to be expected: that was how he found his customers, he learned weaknesses, sought out vulnerability. God, how he loathed this man and his kind.

'Oh.' In spite of himself his face betrayed his defeat. 'I shall have to be more discreet with my inquiries.'

Wigtight smiled coldly.

'I shouldn't trouble yourself. It will make no difference.' He knew his success; it was a taste he was used to, like a ripe Stilton cheese and port after dinner.

There was nothing more to say, and Monk could not stomach more of Wigtight's satisfaction. He left, going out past the oily clerk in the front office; but he was determined to take the first opportunity to charge Josiah Wigtight with something, preferably something earning a good long spell on the prison treadmill. Perhaps it was hate of usury and all its cancerous agonies eating away the hearts of people, or hate for Wigtight particularly, for his fat belly and cold eyes; but more probably it was the bitterness of disappointment because he knew it was not the moneylender who had killed Joscelin Grey.

All of which brought him back again to facing the only other avenue of investigation. Joscelin Grey's friends, the people whose secrets he might have known. He was back to Shelburne again – and Runcorn's triumph.

But before he began on that course to one of its inevitable conclusions – either the arrest of Shelburne, and his own ruin after it; or else the admission that he could not prove his case and must accept failure; and Runcorn could not lose – Monk would follow all the other leads, however faint, beginning with Charles Latterly.

He called in the late afternoon, when he felt it most likely Imogen would be at home, and he could reasonably ask to see Charles.

He was greeted civilly, but no more than that. The parlour maid was too well trained to show surprise. He was kept waiting only a few minutes before being shown into the withdrawing room and its discreet comfort washed over him again.

Charles was standing next to a small table in the window bay.

'Good afternoon, Mr— er— Monk,' he said with distinct chill. 'To what do we owe this further attention?'

Monk felt his stomach sink. It was as if the smell of the rookeries still clung to him. Perhaps it was obvious what manner of man he was, where he worked, what he dealt with; and it had been all the time. He had been too busy with his own feelings to be aware of theirs.

'I am still inquiring into the murder of Joscelin Grey,' he replied a little stiltedly. He knew both Imogen and Hester were in the room but he refused to look at them. He bowed very slightly, without raising his eyes. He made a similar acknowledgment in their direction.

'Then it's about time you reached some conclusion, isn't it?' Charles raised his eyebrows. 'We are very sorry, naturally, since we knew him; but we do not require a day-by-day account of your progress, or lack of it.'

'It's as well,' Monk answered, stirred to tartness in his hurt, and the consciousness that he did not, and would never, belong in this faded and gracious room with its padded furniture and gleaming walnut. 'Because I could not afford it. It is because you knew Major Grey that I wish to speak to you again.' He swallowed. 'We naturally first considered the possibility of his having been attacked by some chance thief, then of its being over a matter of debt, perhaps gambling, or borrowing. We have exhausted these avenues now, and are driven back to what has always, regrettably, seemed the most probable—'

'I thought I had explained it to you, Mr Monk.' Charles's voice was sharper. 'We do not wish to know! And quite frankly, I will not have my wife or my sister distressed by hearing of it. Perhaps the women of your—' He searched for the least offensive word. 'Your background – are less sensitive to such things: unfortunately they may be more used to violence and the sordid aspects of life. But my sister and my wife are gentlewomen, and do not even know of such things. I must ask you to respect their feelings.'

Monk could sense the colour burning up his face. He ached to be equally rude in return, but his awareness of Imogen, only a few feet from him, was overwhelming. He did not care in the slightest what Hester thought; in fact it would be a positive pleasure to quarrel with her, like the sting in the face of clean, icy water – invigorating.

'I had no intention of distressing anyone unnecessarily, sir.' He forced the words out, muffled between his teeth. 'And I have not come for your information, but to ask you some further questions. I was merely trying to give you the reason for them, that you might feel freer to answer.'

Charles blinked at him. He was half leaning against the

mantel shelf, and he stiffened.

'I know nothing whatsoever about the affair, and naturally neither do my family.'

'I am sure we should have helped you if we could,' Imogen added. For an instant Monk thought she looked abashed by Charles's so open condescension.

Hester stood up and walked across the room opposite Monk.

'We have not been asked any questions yet,' she pointed out to Charles reasonably. 'How do we know whether we could answer them or not? And I cannot speak for Imogen, of course, but I am not in the least offended by being asked; indeed if you are capable of considering the murder, then so am I. We surely have a duty.'

'My dear Hester, you don't know what you are speaking of.' Charles's face was sharp and he put his hand out towards her, but she avoided it. 'What unpleasant things may be involved, quite beyond your experience!'

'Balderdash!' she said instantly. 'My experience has included a multitude of things you wouldn't have in your nightmares. I've seen men hacked to death by sabres, shot by cannon, frozen, starved, wasted by disease—'

'Hester!' Charles exploded. 'For the love of heaven!'

'So don't tell me I cannot survive the drawing room discussion of one wretched murder,' she finished.

Charles's face was very pink and he ignored Monk. 'Has it not crossed your very unfeminine mind that Imogen has feelings, and has led a considerably more decorous life than you have chosen for yourself?' he demanded. 'Really, sometimes you are beyond enduring!'

'Imogen is not nearly as helpless as you seem to imagine,' Hester retorted, but there was a faint blush to her cheeks. 'Nor, I think, does she wish to conceal truth because it may be unpleasant to discuss. You do her courage little credit.'

Monk looked at Charles and was perfectly sure that had they been alone he would have disciplined his sister in whatever manner was open to him – which was probably not a great deal. Personally Monk was very glad it was not his problem.

Imogen took the matter into her own hands. She turned towards Monk.

'You were saying that you were driven to an inevitable conclusion, Mr Monk. Pray tell us what it is.' She stared at him and her eyes were angry, almost defensive. She seemed more inwardly alive and sensitive to hurt than anyone else he had ever seen. For seconds he could not think of words to answer her. The moments hung in the air. Her chin came a little higher, but she did not look away.

'I—' he began, and failed. He tried again. 'That – that it was someone he knew who killed him.' Then his voice came mechanically. 'Someone well known to him, of his own position and social circle.'

'Nonsense!' Charles interrupted him sharply, coming into the centre of the room as if to confront him physically. 'People of Joscelin Grey's circle do not go around murdering people. If that's the best you can do, then you had better give up the case and hand it over to someone more skilled.'

'You are being unnecessarily rude, Charles.' Imogen's

eyes were bright and there was a touch of colour in her face. 'We have no reason to suppose that Mr Monk is not skilled at his job, and quite certainly no call to suggest it.'

Charles's whole body tightened; the impertinence was intolerable.

'Imogen,' he began icily; then remembering the feminine frailty he had asserted, altered his tone. 'The matter is naturally upsetting to you; I understand that. Perhaps it would be better if you were to leave us. Retire to your room and rest for a little while. Return when you have composed yourself. Perhaps a tisane?'

'I am not tired, and I do not wish for a tisane. I am perfectly composed, and the police wish to question me.' She swung around. 'Don't you, Mr Monk?'

He wished he could remember what he knew of them, but although he strained till his brain ached, he could recall nothing. All his memories were blurred and coloured by the overwhelming emotion she aroused in him, the hunger for something always just out of reach, like a great music that haunts the senses but cannot quite be caught, disturbingly and unforgettably sweet, evocative of a whole life on the brink of remembrance.

But he was behaving like a fool. Her gentleness, something in her face had woken in him the memory of a time when he had loved, of the softer side of himself which he had lost when the carriage had crashed and obliterated the past. There was more in him than the detective, brilliant, ambitious, sharp tongued, solitary. There had been those who loved him, as well as the rivals who hated, the subordinates who feared or admired, the villains who knew his skill, the poor who looked for justice – or vengeance. Imogen reminded him that he had a humanity as well, and it was too precious for him to drown in reason. He had lost his balance, and if he were to survive this nightmare – Runcorn, the murder, his career – he must regain it.

'Since you knew Major Grey,' he tried again, 'it is possible he may have confided in you any anxieties he may have had for his safety – anyone who disliked him or was harassing him for any reason.' He was not being as articulate as he wished, and he cursed himself for it.

'Did he mention any envies or rivalries to you?'

'None at all. Why would anyone he knew kill him?' she asked. 'He was very charming; I never knew of him picking a quarrel more serious than a few sharp words. Perhaps his humour was a little unkind, but hardly enough to provoke more than a passing irritation.'

'My dear Imogen, they wouldn't!' Charles snapped. 'It was robbery; it must have been.'

Imogen breathed in and out deeply and ignored her husband, still regarding Monk with solemn eyes, waiting for his reply.

'I believe blackmail,' Monk replied. 'Or perhaps jealousy over a woman.'

'Blackmail!' Charles was horrified and his voice was thick with disbelief. 'You mean Grey was blackmailing someone? Over what, may I ask?'

'If we knew that, sir, we should almost certainly know who it was,' Monk answered. 'And it would solve the case.'

'Then you know nothing.' There was derision back again in Charles's voice.

'On the contrary, we know a great deal. We have a suspect, but before we charge him we must have eliminated all the other possibilities.' That was overstating the case dangerously, but Charles's smug face, his patronizing manner roused Monk's temper beyond the point where he had complete control. He wanted to shake him, to force him out of his complacence and his infuriating superiority.

'Then you are making a mistake.' Charles looked at him through narrow eyes. 'At least it seems most likely you are.'

Monk smiled dryly. 'I am trying to avoid that, sir, by exploring every alternative first, and by gaining all the information anyone can give. I'm sure you appreciate that!'

From the periphery of his vision Monk could see Hester smile and was distinctly pleased.

Charles grunted.

'We do really wish to help you,' Imogen said in the silence. 'My husband is only trying to protect us from unpleasantness, which is most delicate of him. But we were exceedingly fond of Joscelin, and we are quite strong enough to tell you anything we can.'

'"Exceedingly fond" is overstating it, my dear,' Charles said uncomfortably. 'We liked him, and of course we felt an extra affection for him for George's sake.'

'George?' Monk frowned, he had not heard George mentioned before.

'My younger brother,' Charles supplied.

'He knew Major Grey?' Monk asked keenly. 'Then may I speak with him also?'

'I am afraid not. But yes, he knew Grey quite well. I believe they were very close, for a while.'

'For a while? Did they have some disagreement?'

'No, George is dead.'

'Oh.' Monk hesitated, abashed. 'I am sorry.'

'Thank you.' Charles coughed and cleared his throat. 'We were fond of Grey, but to say we were extremely so is too much. My wife is, I think, quite naturally transferring some of our affection for George to George's friend.'

'I see.' Monk was not sure what to say. Had Imogen seen in Joscelin only her dead brother-in-law's friend, or had Joscelin himself charmed her with his wit and talent to please? There had been a keenness in her face when she had spoken of him. It reminded him of Rosamond Shelburne: there was the same gentleness in it, the same echo of remembered times of happiness, shared laughter and grace. Had Charles been too blind to see it – or too conceited to understand it for what it was?

An ugly, dangerous thought came to his mind and refused to be ignored. Was the woman not Rosamond, but Imogen Latterly? He wanted intensely to disprove it. But how? If Charles had been somewhere else at the time, provably so, then the whole question was over, dismissed forever.

He stared at Charles's smooth face. He looked irritable, but totally unconscious of any guilt. Monk tried frantically to think of an oblique way to ask him. His brain was like glue, heavy and congealing. Why in God's name did

Charles have to be Imogen's husband?

Was there another way? If only he could remember what he knew of them. Was this fear unreasonable, the result of an imagination free of the sanity of memory? Or was it memory slowly returning, in bits and pieces, that woke that very fear?

The stick in Joscelin Grey's hall stand. The image of it was so clear in his head. If only he could enlarge it, see the hand and the arm, the man who held it. That was the knowledge that lay like a sickness in his stomach; he knew the owner of the stick, and he knew with certainty that Lovel Grey was a complete stranger to him. When he had been to Shelburne not one member of the household had greeted him with the slightest flicker of recognition. And why should they pretend? In fact to do so would in itself have been suspicious, since they had no idea he had lost his memory. Lovel Grey could not be the owner of that stick with the brass chain embossed around the top.

But it could be Charles Latterly.

'Have you ever been to Major Grey's flat, Mr Latterly?' The question was out before he realized it. It was like a die cast, and he did not now want to know the answer. Once begun, he would have to pursue it; even if only for himself he would have to know, always hoping he was wrong, seeking the one more fact to prove himself so.

Charles looked slightly surprised.

'No. Why? Surely you have been there yourself? I cannot tell you anything about it!'

'You have never been there?'

'No, I have told you so. I had no occasion.'

'Nor, I take it, have any of your family?' He did not look at either of the women. He knew the question would be regarded as indelicate, if not outrightly impertinent.

'Of course not!' Charles controlled his temper with some difficulty. He seemed about to add something when Imogen interrupted.

'Would you care for us to account for our whereabouts on the day Joscelin was killed, Mr Monk?'

He looked carefully, but he could see no sarcasm in her. She regarded him with deep, steady eyes.

'Don't be ridiculous!' Charles snapped with mounting fury. 'If you cannot treat this matter with proper seriousness, Imogen, then you had better leave us and return to your room.'

'I am being perfectly serious,' she replied, turning away from Monk. 'If it was one of Joscelin's friends who killed him, then there is no reason why we should not be suspected. Surely, Charles, it would be better to clear ourselves by the simple fact of having been elsewhere at the time than it would be to have Mr Monk satisfy himself we had no reason to, by investigating our affairs?'

Charles paled visibly and looked at Imogen as if she were some venomous creature that had come out of the carpeting and bitten him. Monk felt the tightness in his stomach grip harder.

'I was at dinner with friends,' Charles said thinly.

Considering he had just supplied what seemed to be an alibi, he looked peculiarly wretched. Monk could not avoid it; he had to press. He stared at Charles's pale face.

'Where was that, sir?'

'Doughty Street.'

Imogen looked at Monk blandly, innocently, but Hester had turned away.

'What number, sir?'

'Can that matter, Mr Monk?' Imogen asked innocently.

Hester's head came up, waiting.

Monk found himself explaining to her, guilt surprising him.

'Doughty Street leads into Mecklenburgh Square, Mrs Latterly. It is no more than a two- or three-minute walk from one to the other.'

'Oh.' Her voice was small and flat. She turned slowly to her husband.

'Twenty-two,' he said, teeth clenched. 'But I was there all evening, and I had no idea Grey lived anywhere near.'

Again Monk spoke before he permitted himself to think, or he would have hesitated.

'I find that hard to believe, sir, since you wrote to him at that address. We found your letter among his effects.'

'God damn it – I—' Charles stopped, frozen.

Monk waited. The silence was so intense he imagined he could hear horses' hooves in the next street. He did not look at either of the women.

'I mean—' Charles began, and again stopped.

Monk found himself unable to avoid it any longer. He was embarrassed for them, and desperately sorry. He looked at Imogen, wanting her to know that, even if it meant nothing to her at all.

She was standing very still. Her eyes were so dark he could see nothing in them, but there did not seem to be the hate he feared. For a wild moment he felt that if only he could have talked to her alone he could have explained, made her understand the necessity for all this, the compulsion.

'My friends will swear I was there all evening.' Charles's words cut across them. 'I'll give you their names. This is ridiculous; I liked Joscelin, and our misfortunes were as much his. There was no reason whatever to wish him harm, and you will find none!'

'If I could have their names, Mr Latterly?'

Charles's head came up sharply.

'You're not going to go 'round asking them to account for me at the time of a murder, for God's sake! I'll only give you their names—'

'I shall be discreet, sir.'

Charles snorted with derision at the idea of so delicate a virtue as discretion in a policeman.

Monk looked at him patiently.

'It will be easier if you give me their names, sir, than if I have to discover them for myself.'

'Damn you!' Charles's face was suffused with blood.

'Their names, please, sir?'

Charles strode over to one of the small tables and took out a sheet of paper and a pencil. He wrote for several moments before folding it and handing it to Monk.

'Thank you, sir.'

'Is that all?'

'No, I'm afraid I would still like to ask you anything further you might know about Major Grey's other friends, anyone with whom he stayed, and could have known well enough to be aware, even accidentally, of some secret damaging to them.'

'Such as what, for God's sake?' Charles looked at him with extreme distaste.

Monk did not wish to be drawn into speaking of the sort of things his imagination feared, especially in Imogen's hearing. In spite of the irrevocable position he was now in, every vestige of good opinion she might keep of him mattered, like fragments of a broken treasure.

'I don't know, sir; and without strong evidence it would be unseemly to suggest anything.'

'Unseemly,' Charles said sarcastically, his voice grating with the intensity of his emotion. 'You mean that matters to you? I'm surprised you know what the word means.'

Imogen turned away in embarrassment, and Hester's face froze. She opened her mouth as if to speak, then realized she would be wiser to keep silent.

Charles coloured faintly in the silence that followed, but he was incapable of apology.

'He spoke of some people named Dawlish,' he said irritably. 'And I believe he stayed with Gerry Fortescue once or twice.'

Monk took down such details as they could remember of the Dawlishes, the Fortescues and others, but it sounded useless, and he was aware of Charles's heavy disbelief, as if he were humouring an uncaged animal it might be dangerous to annoy. He stayed only to justify himself, because he had said to them that it was his reason for having come.

When he left he imagined he could hear the sigh of relief behind him, and his mind conjured up their quick looks at each other, then the understanding in their eyes, needing no words, that an intruder had gone at last, an extreme unpleasantness was over. All the way along the street his thoughts were in the bright room behind him and on Imogen. He considered what she was doing, what she thought of him, if she saw him as a man at all, or only the inhabiter of an office that had become suddenly more than usually offensive to her.

And yet she had looked so directly at him. That seemed a timeless moment, recurring again and again – or was it simply that he dwelt on it? What had she asked of him originally? What had they said to one another?

What a powerful and ridiculous thing the imagination was – had he not known it so foolish, he could have believed there must have been deep memories between them.

When Monk had gone, Hester, Imogen and Charles were left standing in the withdrawing room, the sun streaming in from the French windows into the small garden, bright through the leaves in the silence.

Charles drew in his breath as if to speak, looked first at his wife, then at Hester, and let out a sigh. He said nothing. His face was tight and unhappy as he walked to the door, excused himself perfunctorily, and went out.

A torrent of thoughts crowded Hester's mind. She disliked Monk, and he angered her, yet the longer she watched him the less did she think he was as incompetent as he had first seemed. His questions were erratic, and he appeared to be no nearer finding Joscelin Grey's killer than he had been when he began; and yet she was keenly aware both of an intelligence and a tenacity in him. He cared about it, more than simply for vanity or ambition. For justice's sake he wanted to know and to do something about it.

She would have smiled, did it not wound so deep, but she had also seen in him a startling softness towards Imogen, an admiration and a desire to protect – something which he certainly did not feel for Hester. She had seen that look on several men's faces; Imogen had woken precisely the same emotions in Charles when they first met, and in many men since. Hester never knew if Imogen herself was aware of it or not.

Had she stirred Joscelin Grey as well? Had he fallen in love with her, the gentleness, those luminous eyes, the quality of innocence which touched everything she did?

Charles was still in love with her. He was quiet, admittedly a trifle pompous, and he had been anxious and shorter tempered than customarily since his father's death; but he was honourable, at times generous, and sometimes fun – at least he had been. Lately he had become more sober, as though a heavy weight could never be totally forgotten.

Was it conceivable that Imogen had found the witty, charming, gallant Joscelin Grey more interesting, even if only briefly? If that had been so, then Charles, for all his seeming self-possession, would have cared deeply, and the hurt might have been something he could not control.

Imogen was keeping a secret. Hester knew her well enough, and liked her, to be aware of the small tensions, the silences where before she would have confided, the placing of a certain guard on her tongue when they were together. It was not Charles she was afraid might notice and suspect; he was not perceptive enough, he did not expect to understand any woman – it was Hester. She was still as affectionate, as generous with small trinkets, the loan of a kerchief or a silk shawl, a word of praise, gratitude for a courtesy – but she was careful, she hesitated before she spoke, she told the exact truth and the impetuosity was gone.

What was the secret? Something in her attitude, an extra awareness, made Hester believe it had to do with Joscelin Grey, because Imogen both pursued and was afraid of the policeman Monk.

'You did not mention before that Joscelin Grey had known George,' she said aloud.

Imogen looked out of the window. 'Did I not? Well, it was probably a desire not to hurt you, dear. I did not wish to remind you of George, as well as Mama and Papa.'

Hester could not argue with that. She did not believe it, but it was exactly the sort of thing Imogen would have done.

'Thank you,' she replied. 'It was most thoughtful of you, especially since you were so fond of Major Grey.'

Imogen smiled, her far-off gaze seeing beyond the dappled light through the window, but to what Hester thought it unfair to guess.

345

'He was fun,' Imogen said slowly. 'He was so different from anyone else I know. It was a very dreadful way to die – but I suppose it was quick, and much less painful than many you have seen.'

Again Hester did not know what to say.

When Monk returned to the police station Runcorn was waiting for him, sitting at his desk looking at a sheaf of papers. He put them down and pulled a face as Monk came in.

'So your thief was a moneylender,' he said dryly. 'And the newspapers are not interested in moneylenders, I assure you.'

'Then they should be!' Monk snapped back. 'They're a filthy infestation, one of the more revolting symptoms of poverty—'

'Oh for heaven's sake, either run for Parliament or be a policeman,' Runcorn said with exasperation. 'But if you value your job, stop trying to do both at once. And policemen are employed to solve cases, not make moral commentary.'

Monk glared at him.

'If we got rid of some of the poverty, and its parasites, we might prevent the crime before it came to the stage of needing a solution,' he said with heat that surprised himself. A memory of passion was coming back, even if he could not know anything of its cause.

'Joscelin Grey,' Runcorn said flatly. He was not going to be diverted.

'I'm working,' Monk replied.

'Then your success has been embarrassingly limited!'

'Can you prove it was Shelburne?' Monk demanded. He knew what Runcorn was trying to do, and he would fight him to the very last step. If Runcorn forced him to arrest Shelburne before he was ready, he would see to it that it was publicly Runcorn's doing.

But Runcorn was not to be drawn.

'It's your job,' he said acidly. 'I'm not on the case.'

'Perhaps you should be.' Monk raised his eyebrows as if he were really considering it. 'Perhaps you should take over?'

Runcorn's eyes narrowed. 'Are you saying you cannot manage?' he asked very softly, a lift at the end of his words. 'That it is too big for you?'

Monk called his bluff.

'If it is Shelburne, then perhaps it is. Maybe you should make the arrest; a senior officer, and all that.'

Runcorn's face fell blank, and Monk tasted a certain sweetness; but it was only for a moment.

'It seems you've lost your nerve, as well as your memory,' Runcorn answered with a faint sneer. 'Are you giving up?'

Monk took a deep breath.

'I haven't lost anything,' he said deliberately. 'And I certainly haven't lost my head. I don't intend to go charging in to arrest a man against whom I have a damn good suspicion, but nothing else. If you want to, then take this case from me, officially, and do it yourself. And God help you when Lady Fabia hears about it. You'll be beyond anyone else's help, I promise you.'

'Coward! By God you've changed, Monk.'

'If I would have arrested a man without proof before, then I needed to change. Are you taking the case from me?'

'I'll give you another week. I don't think I can persuade the public to give you any more than that.'

'Give *us*,' Monk corrected him. 'As far as they know, we are all working for the same end. Now have you anything helpful to say, like an idea how to prove it was Shelburne, without a witness? Or would you have gone ahead and done it yourself, if you had?'

The implication was not lost on Runcorn. Surprisingly, his face flushed hotly in anger, perhaps even guilt.

'It's your case,' he said angrily. 'I shan't take it from you till you come and admit you've failed or I'm asked to remove you.'

'Good. Then I'll get on with it.'

'Do that. Do that, Monk; if you can!'

Outside the sky was leaden and it was raining hard. Monk thought grimly as he walked home that the newspapers were right in their criticism; he knew little more now than he had when Evan had first showed him the material evidence. Shelburne was the only one for whom he knew a motive, and yet that wretched walking stick clung in his mind. It was not the murder weapon, but he knew he had seen it before. It could not be Joscelin Grey's, because Imogen had said quite distinctly that Grey had not been back to the Latterlys' house since her father-in-law's death, and of course Monk had never been to the house before then.

Then whose was it?

Not Shelburne's.

Without realizing it his feet had taken him not towards his own rooms but to Mecklenburgh Square.

Grimwade was in the hallway.

'Evenin', Mr Monk. Bad night, sir. I dunno wot summer's comin' ter – an' that's the truth. 'Ailstones an' all! Lay like snow, it did, in July. An' now this. Cruel to be out in, sir.' He regarded Monk's soaking clothes with sympathy. 'Can I 'elp yer wif summink, sir?'

'The man who came to see Mr Yeats—'

'The murderer?' Grimwade shivered but there was a certain melodramatic savouring in his thin face.

'It would seem so,' Monk conceded. 'Describe him again, will you?'

Grimwade screwed up his eyes and ran his tongue around his lips.

'Well, that's 'ard, sir. It's a fair while ago now, an' the more I tries to remember 'im, the fainter 'e gets. 'E were tallish, I know that, but not outsize, as you might say. 'Ard ter say w'en somebody's away from yer a bit. W'en 'e came in 'e seemed a good couple o' hinches less than you are, although 'e seemed bigger w'en 'e left. Can be deceivin', sir.'

'Well, that's something. What sort of colouring had he: fresh, sallow, pale, swarthy?'

'Kind o' fresh, sir. But then that could 'a' bin the cold. Proper wicked night it were, somethin' cruel for July. Shockin' unseasonal. Rainin' 'ard, an' east wind like a knife.'

'And you cannot remember whether he had a beard or not?'

'I think as 'e 'adn't, leastways if 'e 'ad, it were one o' them very small ones wot can be 'idden by a muffler.'

'And dark hair? Or could it have been brown, or even fair?'

'No sir, it couldn't 'a' bin fair, not yeller, like; but it could 'a' bin brahn. But I do remember as 'e 'ad very grey eyes. I noticed that as 'e were goin' out, very piercin' eyes 'e 'ad, like one o' them fellers wot puts people inter a trance.'

'Piercing eyes? You're sure?' Monk said dubiously, sceptical of Grimwade's sense of melodrama in hindsight.

'Yes, sir, more I fink of it, more I'm sure. Don't remember 'is face, but I do remember 'is eyes w'en 'e looked at me. Not w'en 'e was comin' in, but w'en 'e was a-goin' out. Funny thing, that. Yer'd fink I'd 'a' noticed them w'en 'e spoke ter me, but sure as I'm standin' 'ere, I didn't.' He looked at Monk ingenuously.

'Thank you, Mr Grimwade. Now I'll see Mr Yeats, if he's in. If he isn't then I'll wait for him.'

'Oh 'e's in, sir. Bin in a little while. Shall I take you up, or do you remember the way?'

'I remember the way, thank you.' Monk smiled grimly and started up the stairs. The place was becoming wretchedly familiar to him. He passed Grey's entrance quickly, still conscious of the horror inside, and knocked sharply at Yeats's door, and a moment later it opened and Yeats's worried little face looked up at him.

'Oh!' he said in some alarm. 'I—I was going to speak to

you. I—I, er— I suppose I should have done it before.' He wrung his hands nervously, twisting them in front of him, red knuckled. 'But I heard all about the— er— the burglar— from Mr Grimwade, you know – and I rather thought you'd, er— found the murderer— so—'

'May I come in, Mr Yeats?' Monk interrupted. It was natural Grimwade should have mentioned the burglar, if only to warn the other tenants, and because one could hardly expect a garrulous and lonely old man to keep to himself such a thrilling and scandalous event, but Monk was irritated by the reminder of its uselessness.

'I'm – I'm sorry,' Yeats stammered as Monk moved past him. 'I—I do realize I should have said something to you before.'

'About what, Mr Yeats?' Monk exercised his patience with an effort. The poor little man was obviously much upset.

'Why, about my visitor, of course. I was quite sure you knew, when you came to the door.' Yeats's voice rose to a squeak in amazement.

'What about him, Mr Yeats? Have you recalled something further?' Suddenly hope shot up inside him. Could this be the beginning of proof at last?

'Why sir, I discovered who he was.'

'What?' Monk did not dare to believe. The room was singing around him, bubbling with excitement. In an instant this funny little man was going to tell him the name of the murderer of Joscelin Grey. It was incredible, dazzling.

'I discovered who he was,' Yeats repeated. 'I knew I

should have told you as soon as I found out, but I thought—'

The moment of paralysis was broken.

'Who?' Monk demanded; he knew his voice was shaking. 'Who was it?'

Yeats was startled. He began to stammer again.

'Who was it?' Monk made a desperate effort to control himself, but his own voice was rising to a shout.

'Why – why, sir, it was a man called Bartholomew Stubbs. He is a dealer in old maps, as he said. Is it – is it important, Mr Monk?'

Monk was stunned.

'Bartholomew Stubbs?' he repeated foolishly.

'Yes, sir. I met him again, through a mutual acquaintance. I thought I would ask him.' His hands fluttered. 'I was quite shockingly nervous, I assure you; but I felt in view of the fate of poor Major Grey that I must approach him. He was most civil. He left here straight after speaking to me at my doorstep. He was at a temperance meeting in Farringdon Road, near the House of Correction, fifteen minutes later. I ascertained that because my friend was there also.' He moved from one foot to the other in his agitation. 'He distinctly remembers Mr Stubbs's arrival, because the first speaker had just commenced his address.'

Monk stared at him. It was incomprehensible. If Stubbs had left immediately, and it seemed he had, then who was the man Grimwade had seen leaving later?

'Did – did he remain at the temperance meeting all evening?' he asked desperately.

'No, sir.' Yeats shook his head. 'He only went there to

meet my friend, who is also a collector, a very learned one—'

'He left!' Monk seized on it.

'Yes, sir.' Yeats danced around in his anxiety, his hands jerking to and fro. 'I am trying to tell you! They left together and went to get some supper—'

'Together?'

'Yes, sir. I am afraid, Mr Monk, Mr Stubbs could not have been the one to have so dreadfully attacked poor Major Grey.'

'No.' Monk was too shaken, too overwhelmingly disappointed to move. He did not know where to start again.

'Are you quite well, Mr Monk?' Yeats asked tentatively. 'I am so sorry. Perhaps I really should have told you earlier, but I did not think it would be important, since he was not guilty.'

'No – no, never mind,' Monk said almost under his breath. 'I understand.'

'Oh, I'm so glad. I thought perhaps I was in error.'

Monk muttered something polite, probably meaningless – he did not want to be unkind to the little man – and made his way out onto the landing again. He was hardly aware of going down the stairs, nor did he register the drenching weight of the rain when he passed Grimwade and went outside into the street with its gaslight and swirling gutters.

He began to walk, blindly, and it was not until he was spattered with mud and a cab wheel missed him by less than a foot that he realized he was on Doughty Street.

''Ere!' the cabby shouted at him. 'Watch w'ere yer

goin', guv! Yer want ter get yerself killed?'

Monk stopped, staring up at him. 'You occupied?'

'No, guv. Yer want ter go somewhere? Mebbe yer'd better, afore yer get someb'dy into a haccident.'

'Yes,' Monk accepted, still without moving.

'Well, come on then,' the cabby said sharply, leaning forward to peer at him. 'Not a night fer man ner beast ter be out in, it ain't. Mate o' mine were killed on a night like this, poor sod. 'Orse bolted and 'is cab turned over. Killed, 'e were. 'It 'is 'ead on the kerb an' 'e died, jes' like that. And 'is fare were all smashed abaht too, but they say as 'e were o'right, in the end. Took 'im orf ter 'orspital, o' course. 'Ere, are yer goin' ter stand there all night, guv? Come on now, either get in, or don't; but make up yer mind!'

'This friend of yours.' Monk's voice was distorted, as if from far away. 'When was he killed, when was this accident, exactly?'

'July it were, terrible weather fer July. Wicked night. 'Ailstorm wot lay like snow. Swear ter Gawd – I don't know wot the wevver's comin' ter.'

'What date in July?' Monk's whole body was cold, and idiotically calm.

'Come on now, sir?' the cabby wheedled, as one does a drunk or a recalcitrant animal. 'Get in aht o' the rain. It's shockin' wet aht there. Yer'll catch yer death.'

'What date?'

'I fink as it were the fourf. Why? We ain't goin' ter 'ave no haccident ternight, I promises yer. I'll be as careful as if you was me muvver. Jus' make up yer mind, sir!'

'Did you know him well?'

'Yes, sir, 'e were a good mate o' mine. Did yer know 'im too, sir? Yer live 'rahnd 'ere, do yer? 'E used ter work this patch all the time. Picked up 'is last fare 'ere, right in this street, accordin' ter 'is paper. Saw 'im that very night meself, I did. Nah is yer comin', sir, or ain't yer? 'Cos I 'aven't got all night. I reckon w'en yer goes a henjoyin' yerself, yer oughter take someone wiv yer. Yer in't safe.'

On this street. The cabby had picked him, Monk, up on this street, less than a hundred yards from Mecklenburgh Square, on the night Joscelin Grey was murdered. What had he been doing here? Why?

'Yer sick, sir?' The cabby's voice changed; he was suddenly concerned. ''Ere, yer ain't 'ad one too many?' He climbed down off his box and opened the cab door.

'No, no I'm quite well.' Monk stepped up and inside obediently and the cabby muttered something to himself about gentlemen whose families should take better care of them, stepped back up onto the box and slapped the reins over his horse's back.

As soon as they arrived at Grafton Street Monk paid the cabby and hurried inside.

'Mrs Worley!'

Silence.

'Mrs Worley!' His voice was hard, hoarse.

She came out, rubbing her hands dry on her apron.

'Oh my heavens, you are wet. You'd like an 'ot drink. You'll 'ave to change them clothes; you've let yourself get soaked through! What 'ave you bin thinking of?'

'Mrs Worley.'

The tone of his voice stopped her.

'Why, whatever is the matter, Mr Monk? You look proper poorly.'

'I—' The words were slow, distant. 'I can't find a stick in my room, Mrs Worley. Have you seen it?'

'No, Mr Monk, I 'aven't, although what you're thinking about sticks for on a night like this, I'm sure I don't know. What you need is an umbrella.'

'Have you seen it?'

She stood there in front of him, square and motherly. 'Not since you 'ad yer haccident, I 'aven't. You mean that dark reddish brown one with the gold chain like 'round the top as yer bought the day afore? Proper 'andsome it were, although wot yer want one like that fer, I'll never know. I do 'ope as you 'aven't gorn and lorst it. If yer did, it must 'a' bin in yer haccident. You 'ad it with yer, 'cos I remember plain as day. Proud of it. Proper dandy, yer was.'

There was a roaring in Monk's ears, shapeless and immense. Through the darkness one thought was like a brilliant stab of light, searingly painful. He had been in Grey's flat the night he was killed; he had left his own stick there in the hall stand. He himself was the man with the grey eyes whom Grimwade had seen leaving at half past ten. He must have gone in when Grimwade was showing Bartholomew Stubbs up to Yeats's door.

There was only one conclusion – hideous and senseless – but the only one left. God knew why, but he himself had killed Joscelin Grey.

356

Chapter Eleven

Monk sat in the armchair in his room staring at the ceiling. The rain had stopped and the air was warm and clammy, but he was still chilled to the bone.

Why?

Why? It was as inconceivably senseless as a nightmare, and as entanglingly, recurringly inescapable.

He had been in Grey's flat that night, and something had happened after which he had gone in such haste he had left his stick in the stand behind him. The cabby had picked him up from Doughty Street, and then barely a few miles away, met with an accident which had robbed him of his life, and Monk of all memory.

But why should he have killed Grey? In what connection did he even know him? He had not met him at the Latterlys'; Imogen had said so quite clearly. He could imagine no way in which he could have met him socially. If he were involved in any case, then Runcorn would have known; and his own case notes would have shown it.

So why? Why kill him? One did not follow a complete stranger to his house and then beat him to death for no reason. Unless one were insane?

Could that be it – he was mad? His brain had been

357

damaged even before the accident? He had forgotten what he had done because it was another self that had enacted such a hideousness, and the self he was in now knew nothing of it, was unaware even of its lusts and compulsions, its very existence? And there had been feeling – inescapable, consuming, and appalling feeling – a passion of hate. Was it possible?

He must think. Thought was the only possible way of dealing with this, making some sense, finding an escape back into reason and an understandable world again, following and examining it, piece by piece – but he could not believe it. But then perhaps no clever, ambitious man truly believes he is mad? He turned that over in his mind too.

Minutes turned into hours, dragging through the night. At first he paced restlessly, back and forth, back and forth, till his legs ached, then he threw himself into the chair and sat motionless, his hands and feet so cold he lost all sensation in them, and still the nightmare was just as real, and just as senseless. He tormented his memory, scrambling after tiny fragments, retelling himself everything he could remember from the schoolroom onward, but there was nothing of Joscelin Grey, not even his face. There was no reason to it, no pattern, no vestige of anger left, no jealousy, no hatred, no fear – only the evidence. He had been there; he must have gone up when Grimwade had taken Bartholomew Stubbs up to see Yeats and been absent for a moment on his other errand.

He had been in Joscelin Grey's flat for three quarters of an hour, and Grimwade had seen him going out and presumed he was Stubbs leaving, whereas in truth Stubbs must have passed him on the stair, as Stubbs left and he arrived. Grimwade had said that the man leaving had seemed heavier, a little taller, and he had especially noticed his eyes. Monk remembered the eyes he had seen staring back at him from the bedroom mirror when he had first come from the hospital. They were unusual, as Grimwade had said, level, dark, clear grey; clever, almost hypnotic eyes. But he had been trying to find the mind beyond, a flash of the memory – the shade was irrelevant. He had made no connection of thought between his grave policeman's gaze – and the stare of the man that night – any more than had Grimwade.

He had been there, inside Grey's flat; it was incontrovertible. But he had not followed Grey; he had gone afterwards, independently, knowing where to find him. So he had known Grey, known where he lived. But why? Why in God's name did he hate him enough to have lost all reason, ignored all his adult life's training and beliefs and beaten the man to death, and gone on beating him when even a madman must have seen he was dead?

He must have known fear before, of the sea when he was young. He could dimly remember its monumental power when the bowels of the deep opened to engulf men, ships, even the shore itself. He could still feel its scream like an echo of all childhood.

And later he must have known fear on the dark streets of London, fear in the rookeries; even now his skin crawled at the memory of the anger and the despair in them, the hunger and the disregard for life in the fight to survive. But he was

359

too proud and too ambitious to be a coward. He had grasped what he wanted without flinching.

But how do you face the unknown darkness, the monstrosity inside your own brain, your own soul?

He had discovered many things in himself he did not like: insensitivity, overpowerful ambition, a ruthlessness. But they were bearable, things for which he could make amends, improve from now on – indeed hc had started.

But why should he have murdered Joscelin Grey? The more he struggled with it the less did it make any sense. Why should he have cared enough? There was nothing in his life, no personal relationship that called up such passion.

And he could not believe he was simply mad. Anyway, he had not attacked a stranger in the street, he had deliberately sought out Grey, taken trouble to go to his home; and even madmen have some reason, however distorted.

He must find it, for himself – and he must find the reason before Runcorn found it.

Only it would not be Runcorn, it would be Evan.

The cold inside him grew worse. That was one of the most painful realizations of all, the time when Evan must know that it was he who had killed Grey, he was the murderer who had raised such horror in both of them, such revulsion for the mad appetite, the bestiality. They had looked upon the murderer as being another kind of creature, alien, capable of some darkness beyond their comprehension. To Evan it would still be such a creature, less than quite human – whereas to Monk it was not outward and foreign, where he could sometimes forget it, bar it out, but the deformed and obscene within himself.

Tonight he must sleep; the clock on the mantel said thirteen minutes past four. But tomorrow he would begin a new investigation. To save his own mind, he must discover why he had killed Joscelin Grey; and he must discover it before Evan did.

He was not ready to see Evan when he went into his office in the morning, not prepared; but then he would never be.

'Good morning, sir,' Evan said cheerfully.

Monk replied, but kept his face turned away, so Evan could not read his expression. He found lying surprisingly hard; and he must lie all the time, every day in every contact from now on.

'I've been thinking, sir.' Evan did not appear to notice anything unusual. 'We should look into all these other people before we try to charge Lord Shelburne. You know, Joscelin Grey may well have had affairs with other women. We should try the Dawlishes; they had a daughter. And there's Fortescue's wife, and Charles Latterly may have a wife.'

Monk froze. He had forgotten that Evan had seen Charles's letter in Grey's desk. He had been supposing blithely that Evan knew nothing of the Latterlys.

Evan's voice cut across him, low and quite gentle. It sounded as though there were nothing more than concern in it.

'Sir?'

'Yes,' Monk agreed quickly. He must keep control, speak sensibly. 'Yes I suppose we had better.' What a hypocrite he was, sending Evan off to pry the secret hurts out of people in the search for a murderer. What would Evan think, feel, when he discovered that the murderer was Monk?

'Shall I start with Latterly, sir?' Evan was still talking. 'We don't know much about him.'

'No!'

Evan looked startled.

Monk mastered himself; when he spoke his voice was quite calm again, but still he kept his face away.

'No, I'll try the people here: I want you to go back to Shelburne Hall.' He must get Evan out of the city for a while, give himself time. 'See if you can learn anything more from the servants,' he elaborated. 'Become friendly with the upstairs maids, if you can, and the parlour maid. Parlour maids are on in the morning; they observe all sorts of things when people are off their guard. It may be one of the other families, but Shelburne is still the most likely. It can be harder to forgive a brother for cuckolding you than it would be a stranger – it's not just an offence, it's a betrayal – and he's constantly there to remind you of it.'

'You think so, sir?' There was a lift of surprise in Evan's voice.

Oh God. Surely Evan could not know, could not suspect anything so soon? Sweat broke out on Monk's body, and chilled instantly, leaving him shivering.

'Isn't that what Mr Runcorn thinks?' he asked, his voice husky with the effort of seeming casual. What isolation this was. He felt cut off from every human contact by his fearful knowledge.

'Yes, sir.' He knew Evan was staring at him, puzzled, even anxious. 'It is, but he could be wrong. He wants to see you arrest Lord Shelburne—' That was an understanding he had not committed to words before. It was the first time he had acknowledged that he understood Runcorn's envy, or his intention. Monk was startled into looking up, and instantly regretted it. Evan's eyes were anxious and appallingly direct.

'Well, he won't – unless I have evidence,' Monk said slowly. 'So go out to Shelburne Hall and see what you can find. But tread softly, listen rather than speak. Above all, don't make any implications.'

Evan hesitated.

Monk said nothing. He did not want conversation.

After a moment Evan left and Monk sat down on his own chair, closing his eyes to shut out the room. It was going to be even harder than it had seemed last night. Evan had believed in him, liked him. Disillusionment so often turned to pity, and then to hate.

And what about Beth? Perhaps far up in Northumberland she need never know. Maybe he could find someone to write to her and say simply that he had died. They would not do it for him; but if he explained, told them of her children, then for her?

'Asleep, Monk? Or dare I hope you are merely thinking?' It was Runcorn's voice, dark with sarcasm.

Monk opened his eyes. He had no career left, no future.

But one of the few reliefs it brought was that he need no longer be afraid of Runcorn. Nothing Runcorn could do would matter in the least, compared with what he had already done to himself.

'Thinking,' Monk replied coldly. 'I find it better to think before I face a witness than after I have got there. Either one stands foolishly silent, or rushes, even more foolishly, into saying something inept, merely to fill the chasm.'

'Social arts again?' Runcorn raised his eyebrows. 'I would not have thought you would have had time for them now.' He was standing in front of Monk, rocking a little on his feet, hands behind his back. Now he brought them forward with a sheaf of daily newspapers displayed belligerently. 'Have you read the newspapers this morning? There has been a murder in Stepney, a man knifed in the street, and they are saying it is time we did our job, or were replaced by someone who can.'

'Why do they presume there is only one person in London capable of knifing a man?' Monk asked bitterly.

'Because they are angry and frightened,' Runcorn snapped back. 'And they have been let down by the men they trusted to safeguard them. That is why.' He slammed the newspapers down on the desk top. 'They do not care whether you speak like a gentleman or know which knife and fork to eat with, Mr Monk; but they care very much whether you are capable of doing your job and catching murderers and taking them off the streets.'

'Do you think Lord Shelburne knifed this man in Stepney?' Monk looked straight into Runcorn's eyes. He was pleased to be able to hate someone freely and without feeling any guilt about lying to him.

'Of course I don't.' Runcorn's voice was thick with anger. 'But I think it past time you stopped giving yourself airs and graces and found enough courage to forget climbing the ladder of your own career for a moment and arrested Shelburne.'

'Indeed? Well, I don't, because I'm not at all sure that he's guilty,' Monk answered him with a straight, hard stare. 'If you are sure, then you arrest him!'

'I'll have you for insolence!' Runcorn shouted, leaning forward towards him, fists clenched white. 'And I'll make damned sure you never reach senior rank as long as I'm in this station. Do you hear me?'

'Of course I hear you.' Monk deliberately kept calm. 'Although it was unnecessary for you to say so, your actions have long made it obvious; unless of course you wish to inform the rest of the building? Your voice was certainly loud enough. As for me, I knew your intentions long ago. And now . . .' He stood up and walked past him to the door. 'If you have nothing else to say, sir; I have several witnesses to question.'

'I'll give you till the end of the week,' Runcorn bellowed behind him, his face purple, but Monk was outside and going down the stairs for his hat and coat. The only advantage of disaster was that all lesser ills are swallowed up in it.

By the time he had reached the Latterlys' house and been shown in by the parlour maid, he had made up his mind to do the only thing that might lead him to the truth. Runcorn had given him a week. And Evan would be back long before that. Time was desperately short.

He asked to see Imogen, alone. The maid hesitated, but it was morning and Charles was quite naturally out; and anyway, as a servant she had not the authority to refuse.

He paced backwards and forwards nervously, counting seconds until he heard light, decisive footsteps outside and the door opened. He swung around. It was not Imogen but Hester Latterly who came in.

He felt an immediate rush of disappointment, then something almost resembling relief. The moment was put off; Hester had not been here at the time. Unless Imogen had confided in her she could not help. He would have to return. He needed the truth, and yet it terrified him.

'Good morning, Mr Monk,' she said curiously. 'What may we do for you this time?'

'I am afraid you cannot help me,' he replied. He did not like her, but it would be pointless and stupid to be rude. 'It is Mrs Latterly I would like to see, since she was here at the time of Major Grey's death. I believe you were still abroad?'

'Yes I was. But I am sorry, Imogen is out all day and I do not expect her return until late this evening.' She frowned very slightly and he was uncomfortably aware of her acute perception, the sensitivity with which she was regarding him. Imogen was kinder, immeasurably less abrasive, but there was an intelligence in Hester which might meet his present need more readily.

'I can see that something very serious troubles you,' she

said gravely. 'Please sit down. If it is to do with Imogen, I would greatly appreciate it if you would confide in me, and I may help the matter to be dealt with with as little pain as possible. She has already suffered a great deal, as has my brother. What have you discovered, Mr Monk?'

He looked at her levelly, searching the wide, very clear eyes. She was a remarkable woman and her courage must be immense to have defied her family and travelled virtually alone to one of the most dreadful battlefields in the world, and to have risked her own life and health to care for the wounded. She must have very few illusions, and that thought was comforting now. There was an infinity of experience between himself and Imogen: horror, violence, hatred and pain outside her grasp to think of, and which from now on would be his shadow, even his skin. Hester must have seen men in the very extremity of life and death, the nakedness of soul that comes when fear strips everything away and the honesty that loosens the tongue when pretence is futile.

Perhaps after all it was right he should speak to her.

'I have a most profound problem, Miss Latterly,' he began. It was easier to talk to her than he had expected. 'I have not told you, or anyone else, the entire truth about my investigation of Major Grey's death.'

She waited without interruption; surprisingly, she did know when to keep silent.

'I have not lied,' he went on. 'But I have omitted one of the most important facts.'

She was very pale. 'About Imogen?'

'No! No. I do not know anything about her, beyond what

367

she told me herself – that she knew and liked Joscelin Grey, and that he called here, as a friend of your brother George. What I did not tell you is about myself.'

He saw the flash of concern in her face, but he did not know the reason for it. Was it her nurse's professional training, or some fear for Imogen, something she knew and he did not? But again she did not interrupt.

'The accident I suffered before beginning the Joscelin Grey case is a severe complication which I did not mention.' Then for a hideous moment he thought she might imagine he was seeking some kind of sympathy, and he felt the blood burn up his skin. 'I lost my memory.' He rushed to dispel the idea. 'Completely. When I came to my senses in the hospital I could not even think of my own name.' How far away that minimal nightmare seemed now! 'When I was recovered enough to go back to my rooms they were strange to me, like the rooms of a man I had never met. I knew no one, I could not even think how old I was, or what I looked like. When I saw myself in the mirror I did not recognize myself even then.'

There was pity in her face, gentle and quite pure, without a shadow of condescension or setting herself apart. It was far sweeter than anything he had expected.

'I'm deeply sorry,' she said quietly. 'Now I understand why some of your questions seemed so very odd. You must have had to learn everything over again.'

'Miss Latterly – I believe your sister-in-law came to me before, asked me something, confided – perhaps to do with Joscelin Grey – but I cannot remember. If she could tell me everything she knows of me, anything I may have said—'

'How could that help you with Joscelin Grey?' Then suddenly she looked down at the hand in her lap. 'You mean you think Imogen may have something to do with his death?' Her head came up sharply, her eyes candid and full of fear. 'Do you think Charles may have killed him, Mr Monk?'

'No – no, I am quite sure he did not.' He must lie; the truth was impossible, but he needed her help. 'I found old notes of mine, made before the accident, which indicate I knew something important then, but I can't remember it. Please, Miss Latterly – ask her to help me.'

Her face was a little bleak, as if she too feared the outcome.

'Of course, Mr Monk. When she returns I will explain the necessity to her, and when I have something to tell you I shall come and do so. Where may I find you that we can talk discreetly?'

He was right: she was afraid. She did not wish her family to overhear – perhaps especially Charles. He stared at her, smiling with a bitter humour, and saw it answered in her eyes. They were in an absurd conspiracy, she to protect her family as far as was possible, he to discover the truth about himself, before Evan or Runcorn made it impossible. He must know *why* he had killed Joscelin Grey.

'Send me a message, and I shall meet you in Hyde Park, at the Piccadilly end of the Serpentine. No one will remark two people walking together.'

'Very well, Mr Monk. I shall do what I can.'

'Thank you.' He rose and took his leave, and she watched

his straight, very individual figure as he walked down the steps and out into the street. She would have recognized his stride anywhere; there was an ease in it not unlike a soldier's who was used to the self-discipline of long marches, and yet it was not military.

When he was out of sight she sat down, cold, unhappy, but knowing it was unavoidable she should do exactly as he had asked. Better she should learn the truth first than that it should be dragged out longer, and found by others.

She spent a solitary and miserable evening, dining alone in her room. Until she knew the truth from Imogen she could not bear to risk a long time with Charles, such as at a meal table. It was too likely her thoughts would betray her and end in hurting them both. As a child she had imagined herself to be marvellously subtle and capable of all sorts of deviousness. At about twenty she had mentioned it quite seriously at the dinner table. It was the only occasion she could recall of every member of her family laughing at once. George had begun, his face crinkling into uncontrollable delight and his voice ringing out with hilarity. The very idea was funny. She had the most transparent emotions any of them had seen. Her happiness swept the house in a whirlwind; her misery wrapped it in a purple gloom.

It would be futile, and painful, to try to deceive Charles now.

It was the following afternoon before she had the opportunity to speak alone with Imogen for any length of time. Imogen had been out all morning and came in in a swirl of agitation, swinging her skirts around as she swept into the hallway and deposited a basket full of linen on the settle at the bottom of the stairs and took off her hat.

'Really, I don't know what the vicar's wife is thinking of,' she said furiously. 'Sometimes I swear that woman believes all the world's ills can be cured with an embroidered homily on good behaviour, a clean undershirt and a jar of homemade broth. And Miss Wentworth is the last person on earth to help a young mother with too many children and no maid-servant.'

'Mrs Addison?' Hester said immediately.

'Poor creature doesn't know whether she is coming or going,' Imogen argued. 'Seven children, and she's as thin as a slat and exhausted. I don't think she eats enough to keep a bird alive – giving it all to those hungry little mouths forever asking for more. And what use is Miss Wentworth? She has fits of the vapours every few minutes! I spend half my time picking her up off the floor.'

'I'd have fits of the vapours myself if my stays were as tight as hers,' Hester said wryly. 'Her maid must lace them with one foot on the bedpost. Poor soul. And of course her mother's trying to marry her off to Sydney Abernathy – he has plenty of money and a fancy for wraithlike fragility – it makes him feel masterful.'

'I shall have to see if I can find a suitable homily for her on vanity.' Imogen ignored the basket and led the way through to the withdrawing room and threw herself into one of the large chairs. 'I am hot and tired. Do have Martha bring us some lemonade. Can you reach the bell?'

It was an idle question, since Hester was still standing. Absently she pulled the end. 'It isn't vanity,' she said, still referring to Miss Wentworth. 'It's survival. What is the poor creature to do if she doesn't marry? Her mother and sisters have convinced her the only alternative is shame, poverty and a lonely and pitiful old age.'

'That reminds me,' Imogen said, pushing her boots off. 'Have you heard from Lady Callandra's hospital yet? I mean the one you want to administer?'

'I don't aim quite so high; I merely want to assist,' Hester corrected.

'Rubbish!' Imogen stretched her feet luxuriously and sank a little further into the chair. 'You want to order around the entire staff.'

The maid came in and stood waiting respectfully.

'Lemonade, please, Martha,' Imogen ordered. 'I'm so hot I could expire. This climate really is ridiculous. One day it rains enough to float an ark, the next we are all suffocated with heat.'

'Yes, ma'am. Would you like some cucumber sandwiches as well, ma'am?'

'Oh yes. Yes I would – thank you.'

'Yes, ma'am.' And with a whisk of skirts she was gone.

Hester filled the few minutes while the maid was absent with trivial conversation. She had always found it easy to talk to Imogen and their friendship was more like that of sisters than of two women related only by marriage, whose patterns of life were so different. When Martha had brought the sandwiches and lemonade and they were alone, she turned at last to the matter which was pressing so urgently on her mind.

'Imogen, that policeman, Monk, was here again yesterday—'

Imogen's hand stopped in the air, the sandwich ignored, but there was curiosity in her face and a shadow of amusement. There was nothing that looked like fear. But then Imogen, unlike Hester, could conceal her feelings perfectly if she chose.

'Monk? What did he want this time?'

'Why are you smiling?'

'At you, my dear. He annoys you so much, and yet I think part of you quite likes him. You are not dissimilar in some ways, full of impatience at stupidity and anger at injustice, and perfectly prepared to be as rude as you can.'

'I am nothing like him whatever,' Hester said impatiently. 'And this is not a laughing matter.' She could feel an irritating warmth creep up in her cheeks. Just once in a while she would like to take more naturally to feminine arts, as Imogen did as easily as breathing. Men did not rush to protect her as they did Imogen; they always assumed she was perfectly competent to take care of herself, and it was a compliment she was growing tired of.

Imogen ate her sandwich, a tiny thing about two inches square.

'Are you going to tell me what he came for, or not?'

'Certainly I am.' Hester took a sandwich herself and bit into it; it was lacily thin and the cucumber was crisp and cool. 'A few weeks ago he had a very serious accident, about the time Joscelin Grey was killed.'

'Oh – I'm sorry. Is he ill now? He seemed perfectly recovered.'

'I think his body is quite mended,' Hester answered, and seeing the sudden gravity and concern in Imogen's face felt a gentleness herself. 'But he was struck very severely on the head, and he cannot remember anything before regaining his senses in a London hospital.'

'Not anything.' A flicker of amazement crossed Imogen's face. 'You mean he didn't remember me – I mean us?'

'He didn't remember himself,' Hester said starkly. 'He did not know his name or his occupation. He did not recognize his own face when he saw it in the glass.'

'How extraordinary – and terrible. I do not always like myself completely – but to lose yourself! I cannot imagine having nothing at all left of all your past – all your experiences, and the reason why you love or hate things.'

'Why did you go to him, Imogen?'

'What? I mean, I beg your pardon?'

'You heard what I said. When we first saw Monk in St Marylebone Church you went over to speak to him. You knew him. I assumed at the time that he knew you, but he did not. He did not know anyone.'

Imogen looked away, and very carefully took another sandwich.

'I presume it is something Charles does not know about,' Hester went on.

'Are you threatening me?' Imogen asked, her enormous eyes quite frank.

'No I am not!' Hester was annoyed, with herself for being clumsy as well as Imogen for thinking such a thing. 'I didn't know there was anything to threaten you with. I was going to say that unless it is unavoidable, I shall not tell him. Was it something to do with Joscelin Grey?'

Imogen choked on her sandwich and had to sit forward sharply to avoid suffocating herself altogether.

'No,' she said when at last she caught her breath. 'No it was not. I can see that perhaps it was foolish, on reflection. But at the time I really hoped—'

'Hoped what? For goodness' sake, explain yourself.'

Slowly, with a good deal of help, criticism and consolation from Hester, Imogen recounted detail by detail exactly what she had done, what she had told Monk, and why.

Four hours later, in the golden sunlight of early evening, Hester stood in the park by the Serpentine watching the light dimple on the water. A small boy in a blue smock carrying a toy boat under his arm passed by with his nursemaid. She was dressed in a plain stuff dress, had a starched lace cap on her head and walked as uprightly as any soldier on parade. An off-duty bandsman watched her with admiration.

Beyond the grass and trees two ladies of fashion rode along Rotten Row, their horses gleaming, harnesses jingling and hooves falling with a soft thud on the earth. Carriages rattling along Knightsbridge towards Piccadilly seemed in another world, like toys in the distance.

She heard Monk's step before she saw him. She turned when he was almost upon her. He stopped a yard away; their eyes met. Lengthy politeness would be ridiculous between them. There was no outward sign of fear in him – his gaze was level and unflinching – but she knew the void and the imagination that was there.

She was the first to speak.

'Imogen came to you after my father's death, in the rather fragile hope that you might discover some evidence that it was not suicide. The family was devastated. First George had been killed in the war, then Papa had been shot in what the police were kind enough to say might have been an accident, but appeared to everyone to be suicide. He had lost a great deal of money. Imogen was trying to salvage something out of the chaos – for Charles's sake, and for my mother's.' She stopped for a moment, trying to keep her composure, but the pain of it was still very deep.

Monk stood perfectly still, not intruding, for which she was grateful. It seemed he understood she must tell it all without interruption in order to be able to tell it at all.

She let out her breath slowly, and resumed.

'It was too late for Mama. Her whole world had collapsed. Her younger son dead, financial disgrace, and then her husband's suicide – not only his loss but the shame of the manner of it. She died ten days later – she was simply broken—' Again she was obliged to stop for several minutes. Monk said nothing, but stretched out his hand and held hers, hard, firmly, and the pressure of his fingers was like a lifeline to the shore.

In the distance a dog scampered through the grass, and a small boy chased a penny hoop.

'She came to you without Charles's knowing – he would not have approved. That is why she never mentioned it to you again – and of course she did not know you had forgotten. She says you questioned her about everything that had happened prior to Papa's death, and on successive meetings you asked her about Joscelin Grey. I shall tell you what she told me—'

A couple in immaculate riding habits cantered down the Row. Monk still held her hand.

'My family first met Joscelin Grey in March. They had none of them heard of him before and he called on them quite unexpectedly. He came one evening. You never met him, but he was very charming – even I can remember that from his brief stay in the hospital where I was in Scutari. He went out of his way to befriend other wounded men, and often wrote letters for those too ill to do it for themselves. He often smiled, even laughed and made small jokes. It did a great deal for morale. Of course his wound was not as serious as many, nor did he have cholera or dysentery.'

Slowly they began to walk, so as not to draw attention to themselves, close together.

She forced her mind back to that time, the smell, the closeness of pain, the constant tiredness and the pity. She pictured Joscelin Grey as she had last seen him, hobbling away down the steps with a corporal beside him, going down to the harbour to be shipped back to England.

'He was a little above average height,' she said aloud. 'Slender, fair-haired. I should think he still had quite a limp – I expect he always would have had. He told them his name, and that he was the younger brother of Lord Shelburne, and of course that he had served in the Crimea and been invalided home. He explained his own story, his time in Scutari, and that his injury was the reason he had delayed so long in calling on them.'

She looked at Monk's face and saw the unspoken question.

'He said he had known George – before the battle of the Alma, where George was killed. Naturally the whole family made him most welcome, for George's sake, and for his own. Mama was still deeply grieved. One knows with one's mind that if young men go to war there is always a chance they will be killed, but that is nothing like a preparation for the feelings when it happens. Papa had his loss, so Imogen said, but for Mama it was the end of something terribly precious. George was the younger son and she always had a special feeling for him. He was—' She struggled with memories of childhood like a patch of sunlight in a closed garden. 'He looked the most like Papa – he had the same smile, and his hair grew the same way, although it was dark like Mama's. He loved animals. He was an excellent horseman. I suppose it was natural he should join the cavalry.

'Anyway, of course they did not ask Grey a great deal about George the first time he called. It would have been very discourteous, as if they had no regard for his own friendship, so they invited him to return any time he should find himself free to do so, and would wish to—'

'And he did?' Monk spoke for the first time, quietly, just

an ordinary question. His face was pinched and there was a darkness in his eyes.

'Yes, several times, and after a while Papa finally thought it acceptable to ask him about George. They had received letters, of course, but George had told them very little of what it was really like.' She smiled grimly. 'Just as I did not. I wonder now if perhaps we both should have? At least to have told Charles. Now we live in different worlds: and I should be distressing him to no purpose.'

She looked beyond Monk to a couple walking arm in arm along the path.

'It hardly matters now. Joscelin Grey came again, and stayed to dinner, and then he began to tell them about the Crimea. Imogen says he was always most delicate, he never used unseemly language, and although Mama was naturally terribly upset, and grieved to hear how wretched the conditions were, he seemed to have a special sense of how much he could say without trespassing beyond sorrow and admiration into genuine horror. He spoke of battles, but he told them nothing of the starvation and the disease. And he always spoke so well of George, it made them all proud to hear.

'Naturally they also asked him about his own exploits. He saw the Charge of the Light Brigade at Balaclava. He said the courage was sublime: never were soldiers braver or more loyal to their duty. But he said the slaughter was the most dreadful thing he had ever seen, because it was so needless. They rode right into the guns; he told them that.' She shivered as she remembered the cartloads of dead and wounded, the labour all through the night, the helplessness, all the blood. Had Joscelin Grey felt anything of the overwhelming emotions of anger and pity that she had?

'There was never any chance whatsoever that they could have survived,' she said quietly, her voice so low it was almost carried away by the murmur of the wind. 'Imogen said he was very angry about it. He said some terrible things about Lord Cardigan. I think that was the moment I most thought I should have liked him.'

Deeply as it hurt, Monk also most liked him for it. He had heard of that suicidal charge, and when the brief thrill of admiration had passed, he was left with a towering rage at the monumental incompetence and the waste, the personal vanity, the idiotic jealousies that had uselessly, senselessly squandered so many lives.

For what, in heaven's name, could he have hated Joscelin Grey?

She was talking and he was not listening. Her face was earnest, pinched for the loss and the pain. He wanted to touch her, to tell her simply, elementally, without words that he felt the same.

What sort of revulsion would she feel if she knew it was he who had beaten Joscelin Grey to death in that dreadful room?

'—as they got to know him,' she was saying, 'they all came to like him better and better for himself. Mama used to look forward to his visits; she would prepare for them days before. Thank heavens she never knew what happened to him.'

He refrained at the last moment, when it was on the tip of his tongue, from asking her when her mother had died. He remembered something about shock, a broken heart.

'Go on,' he said instead. 'Or is that all about him?'

'No.' She shook her head. 'No, there is much more. As I said, they were all fond of him; Imogen and Charles also. Imogen used to like to hear about the bravery of the soldiers, and of the hospital in Scutari, I suppose at least in part because of me.'

He remembered what he had heard of the military hospital – of Florence Nightingale and her women. The sheer physical labour of it, quite apart from the social stigma. Nurses were traditionally mostly men; the few women were of the strongest, the coarsest, and they did little but clean up the worst of the refuse and waste.

She was speaking again. 'It was about four weeks after they first met him that he first mentioned the watch—'

'Watch?' He had heard nothing of a watch, except he recalled they had found no watch on the body. Constable Harrison had found one at a pawnbroker's – which had turned out to be irrelevant.

'It was Joscelin Grey's,' she replied. 'Apparently it was a gold watch of great personal value to him because he had been given it by his grandfather, who had fought with the Duke of Wellington at Waterloo. It had a dent in it where a ball from a French musket struck it and was deflected, thus saving his grandfather's life. When he had first expressed a desire to be a soldier himself, the old man had given it to him. It was considered something of a talisman. Joscelin

Grey said that poor George had been nervous that night, the night before the Battle of the Alma, perhaps something of a premonition, and Joscelin had lent him the watch. Of course George was killed the next day, and so never returned it. Joscelin did not make much of it, but he said that if it had been returned to them with George's effects, he would be most grateful if he might have it again. He described it most minutely, even to the inscription inside.'

'And they returned it to him?' he asked.

'No. No, they did not have it. They had no idea what could have happened to it, but it was not among the things that the army sent them from George's body, nor his personal possessions. I can only presume someone must have stolen it. It is the most contemptible of crimes, but it happens. They felt quite dreadful about it, especially Papa.'

'And Joscelin Grey?'

'He was distressed, of course, but according to Imogen he did his best to hide it; in fact he hardly mentioned it again.'

'And your father?'

Her eyes were staring blindly past him at the wind in the leaves. 'Papa could not return the watch, nor could he replace it, since in spite of its monetary value, its personal value was far greater, and it was that which really mattered. So when Joscelin Grey was interested in a certain business venture, Papa felt it was the very least he could do to offer to join him in it. Indeed from what both he and Charles said, it seemed at the time to be, in their judgment, an excellent scheme.'

'That was the one in which your father lost his money?'

Her face tightened.

'Yes. He did not lose it all, but a considerable amount. What caused him to take his life, and Imogen has accepted now that he did so, was that he had recommended the scheme to his friends, and some of them had lost far more. That was the shame of it. Of course Joscelin Grey lost much of his own money too, and he was terribly distressed.'

'And from that time their friendship ceased?'

'Not immediately. It was a week later, when Papa shot himself. Joscelin Grey sent a letter of condolence, and Charles wrote back, thanking him, and suggesting that they discontinue their acquaintance, in the circumstances.'

'Yes, I saw the letter. Grey kept it – I don't know why.'

'Mama died a few days after that.' She went on very quietly. 'She simply collapsed, and never got up again. And of course it was not a time for social acquaintance: they were all in mourning.' She hesitated a moment. 'We still are.'

'And it was after your father's death that Imogen came to see me?' he prompted after a moment.

'Yes, but not straightaway. She came the day after they buried Mama. I cannot think there was ever anything you could have done, but she was too upset to be thinking as deeply as she might, and who can blame her? She just found it too hard then to accept what must have been the truth.'

They turned and began walking back again.

'So she came to the police station?' he asked.

'Yes.'

'And told me everything that you have told me now?'

'Yes. And you asked her all the details of Papa's death: how he died, precisely when, who was in the house, and so on.'

'And I noted it?'

'Yes, you said it might have been murder, or an accident, although you doubted it. You said that you would make some investigation.'

'Do you know what I did?'

'I asked Imogen, but she did not know, only that you found no evidence that it was other than it seemed, which was that he took his own life while in deep despair. But you said you would continue to investigate it and let her know if you discovered anything further. But you never did, at least not until after we saw you again in the church, more than two months later.'

He was disappointed, and becoming frightened as well. There was still no direct connection between himself and Joscelin Grey, still less any reason why he should have hated him. He tried a last time.

'And she does not know what my investigations were? I told her nothing?'

'No.' She shook her head. 'But I imagine, from the questions you asked her about Papa and the business, such as she knew it, that you inquired into that.'

'Did I meet Joscelin Grey?'

'No. You met a Mr Marner, who was one of the principals. You spoke of him; but you never met Joscelin Grey so far as she knows. In fact the last time she saw you you said quite plainly that you had not. He was also a victim of the same misfortune, and you seemed to consider Mr Marner the author of it, whether intentionally or not.'

It was something, however frail; a place to begin.

'Do you know where I can find Mr Marner now?'

'No, I am afraid not. I asked Imogen, but she had no knowledge.'

'Did she know his Christian name?'

Again she shook her head. 'No. You mentioned him only very briefly. I'm sorry. I wish I could help.'

'You have helped. At least now I know what I was doing before the accident. It is somewhere to begin.' That was a lie, but there was nothing to be gained in the truth.

'Do you think Joscelin Grey was killed over something to do with the business? Could he have known something about this Mr Marner?' Her face was blank and sad with the sharpness of memory, but she did not evade the thought. 'Was the business fraudulent, and he discovered it?'

Again he could only lie.

'I don't know. I'll start again, from the beginning. Do you know what manner of business it was, or at least the names of some of the friends of your father who invested in it? They would be able to give me the details.'

She told him several names and he wrote them down, with addresses. He thanked her, feeling a little awkward, wanting her to know, without the embarrassment for both of them of his saying it, that he was grateful – for her candour, her understanding without pity, the moment's truce from all argument or social games.

He hesitated, trying to think of words. She put her hand

very lightly on his sleeve and met his eyes for an instant. For a wild moment he thought of friendship, a closeness better than romance, cleaner and more honest; then it disappeared. There was the battered corpse of Joscelin Grey between him and everyone else.

'Thank you,' he said calmly. 'You have been very helpful. I appreciate your time and your frankness.' He smiled very slightly, looking straight into her eyes. 'Good afternoon, Miss Latterly.'

Chapter Twelve

The name Marner meant nothing to Monk, and the following day, even after he had been to three of the addresses Hester had given him, he still had no more than a name and the nature of the business – importing. It seemed no one else had met the elusive Mr Marner either. All inquiries and information had come from Latterly, through Joscelin Grey. The business was for the importing of tobacco from the United States of America, and a very profitable retailing of it was promised, in alliance with a certain Turkish house. No one knew more than that; except of course a large quantity of figures which indicated the amount of capital necessary to begin the venture and the projected increase to the fortunes of those who participated.

Monk did not leave the last house until well into the afternoon, but he could not afford time for leisure. He ate briefly, purchasing fresh sandwiches from a street seller, then went to the police station to seek the help of a man he had learned investigated business fraud. He might at least know the name of dealers in tobacco; perhaps he could find the Turkish house in question.

'Marner?' the man repeated agreeably, pushing his fingers through his scant hair. 'Can't say as I've ever heard of him.

You don't know his first name, you say?'

'No, but he floated a company for importing tobacco from America, mixing it with Turkish, and selling it at a profit.'

The man pulled a face.

'Sounds unpleasant – can't stand Turkish myself – but then I prefer snuff anyway. Marner?' He shook his head. 'You don't mean old Zebedee Marner, by any chance? I suppose you've tried him, or you wouldn't ask. Very sly old bird, that. But I never knew him mixed up with importing.'

'What does he do?'

The man's eyebrows went up in surprise.

'Losing your grip, Monk? What's the matter with you?' He squinted a little. 'You must know Zebedee Marner. Never been able to charge him with anything because he always weasels his way out, but we all know he's behind half the pawnbrokers, sweatshops and brothels in the Limehouse area right down to the Isle of Dogs. Personally I think he takes a percentage from the child prostitutes and the opium as well, although he's far too downy to go anywhere near them himself.' He sighed in disgust. 'But then, of course, there's a few who wouldn't say as far as that.'

Monk hardly dared hope. If this were the same Marner, then here at last was something that could lead to motive. It was back to the underworld, to greed, fraud and vice. Reason why Joscelin Grey should have killed – but why should he have been the victim?

Was there something in all this evidence that could at last convict Zebedee Marner? Was Grey in collusion with Marner?

But Grey had lost his own money – or had he?

'Where can I find Marner?' he asked urgently. 'I need him, and time is short.' There was no time to seek out addresses himself. If this man thought he was peculiar, incompetent at his job, he would just have to think it. Soon it would hardly matter anyway.

The man looked at Monk, interest suddenly sharpening in his face, his body coming upright.

'Do you know something about Marner that I don't, Monk? I've been trying to catch that slimy bastard for years. Let me in on it?' His face was eager, a light in his eyes as if he had seen a sudden glimpse of an elusive happiness. 'I don't want any of the credit; I won't say anything. I just want to see his face when he's pinched.'

Monk understood. He was sorry not to be able to help.

'I don't have anything on Marner,' he answered. 'I don't even know if the business I'm investigating is fraudulent or not. Someone committed suicide, and I'd like to know the reasons.'

'Why?' He was curious and his puzzlement was obvious. He cocked his head a little to one side. 'What do you care about a suicide? I thought you were on the Grey case. Don't tell me Runcorn's let you off it – without an arrest?'

So even this man knew of Runcorn's feelings about him. Did everyone? No wonder Runcorn knew he had lost his memory! He must have laughed at Monk's confusion, his fumbling.

'No.' He pulled a wry face. 'No, it's all part of the same thing. Grey was involved in the business.'

'Importing?' His voice rose an octave. 'Don't tell me he was killed over a shipment of tobacco!'

'Not over tobacco; but there was a lot of money invested, and apparently the company failed.'

'Oh yes? That's a new departure for Marner—'

'If it's the same man,' Monk said cautiously. 'I don't know that it is. I don't know anything about him but his name, and only part of that. Where do I find him?'

'Thirteen Gun Lane, Limehouse.' He hesitated. 'If you get anything, Monk, will you tell me, as long as it isn't the actual murder? Is that what you're after?'

'No. No, I just want some information. If I find evidence of fraud I'll bring it back for you.' He smiled bleakly. 'You have my word.'

The man's face eased into a smile. 'Thank you.'

Monk went early in the morning and was in Limehouse by nine o'clock. He would have been there sooner had there been any purpose. He had spent much of the time since he woke at six planning what he would say.

It was a long way from Grafton Street and he took a hansom eastward through Clerkenwell, Whitechapel and down towards the cramped and crowded docks and Limehouse. It was a still morning and the sun was gleaming on the river, making white sparkles on the water between the black barges coming up from the Pool of London. Across on the far side were Bermondsey – the Venice of the Drains – and Rotherhithe, ahead of him the Surrey Docks, and along the shining Reach the Isle of Dogs. On the far side were

Deptford and then the beautiful Greenwich with its green park and trees and the exquisite architecture of the naval college.

But his duty lay in the squalid alleys of Limehouse with beggars, usurers and thieves of every degree – and Zebedee Marner.

Gun Lane was a byway off the West India Dock Road, and he found Number 13 without difficulty. He passed an evil-looking idler on the pavement and another lounging in the doorway, but neither troubled him, perhaps considering him unlikely to give to a beggar and too crisp of gait to be wise to rob. There was other, easier prey. He despised them, and understood them at the same time.

Good fortune was with him: Zebedee Marner was in, and after a discreet inquiry, the clerk showed Monk into the upper office.

'Good morning, Mr – Monk.' Marner sat behind a large, important desk, his white hair curled over his ears and his white hands spread on the leather-inlaid surface in front of him. 'What can I do for you?'

'You come recommended as a man of many businesses, Mr Marner,' Monk started smoothly, gliding over the hatred in his voice. 'With a knowledge of all kinds of things.'

'And so I am, Mr Monk, so I am. Have you money to invest?'

'What could you offer me?'

'All manner of things. How much money?' Marner was watching him narrowly, but it was well disguised as a casual cheerfulness.

'I am interested also in safety, rather than quick profit,' Monk said, ignoring the question. 'I wouldn't care to lose what I have.'

'Of course not, who would?' Marner spread his hands wide and shrugged expressively, but his eyes were fixed and blinkless as a snake's. 'You want your money invested safely?'

'Oh, quite definitely,' Monk agreed. 'And since I know of many other gentlemen who are also interested in investment, I should wish to be certain that any recommendation I made was secure.'

Marner's eyes flickered, then the lids came down to hide his thoughts. 'Excellent,' he said calmly. 'I quite understand, Mr Monk. Have you considered importing and exporting? Very nourishing trade; never fails.'

'So I've heard.' Monk nodded. 'But is it safe?'

'Some is, some isn't. It is the skill of people like me to know the difference.' His eyes were wide again, his hands folded across his paunch. 'That is why you came here, instead of investing it yourself.'

'Tobacco?'

Marner's face did not change in the slightest.

'An excellent commodity.' He nodded. 'Excellent. I cannot see gentlemen giving up their pleasures, whatever the economic turns of life. As long as there are gentlemen, there will be a market for tobacco. And unless our climate changes beyond our wit to imagine' – he grinned and his body rocked with silent mirth at his own humour – 'we will be unable to grow it, so must need import it. Have you any special company in mind?'

'Are you familiar with the market?' Monk asked, swallowing hard to contain his loathing of this man sitting here like a fat white spider in his well-furnished office, safe in his grey web of lies and façades. Only the poor flies like Latterly got caught – and perhaps Joscelin Grey.

'Of course,' Marner replied complacently. 'I know it well.'

'You have dealt in it?'

'I have, frequently. I assure you, Mr Monk, I know very well what I am doing.'

'You would not be taken unaware and find yourself faced with a collapse?'

'Most certainly not.' Marner looked at him as if he had let fall some vulgarity at the table.

'You are sure?' Monk pressed him.

'I am more than sure, my dear sir.' Now he was quite pained. 'I am positive.'

'Good.' Monk at last allowed the venom to flood into his voice. 'That is what I thought. Then you will no doubt be able to tell me how the disaster occurred that ruined Major Joscelin Grey's investment in the same commodity. You were connected with it.'

Marner's face paled and for a moment he was too confused to find words.

'I— er— assure you, you need have no anxiety as to its happening again,' he said, avoiding Monk's eyes, then looking very directly at him, to cover the lie of intent.

'That is good,' Monk answered him coolly. 'But hardly

393

of more than the barest comfort now. It has cost two lives already. Was there much of your own money lost, Mr Marner?'

'Much of mine?' Marner looked startled.

'I understand Major Grey lost a considerable sum?'

'Oh – no. No, you are misinformed.' Marner shook his head and his white hair bounced over his ears. 'The company did not precisely fail. Oh dear me no. It simply transferred its operation; it was taken over. If you are not a man of affairs, you could not be expected to understand. Business is highly complicated these days, Mr Monk.'

'It would seem so. And you say Major Grey did not lose a great deal of his own money? Can you substantiate that in any way?'

'I could, of course.' The smug veils came over Marner's eyes again. 'But Major Grey's affairs are his own, of course, and I should not discuss his affairs with you, any more than I should dream of discussing yours with him. The essence of good business is discretion, sir.' He smiled, pleased with himself, his composure at least in part regained.

'Naturally,' Monk agreed. 'But I am from the police, and am investigating Major Grey's murder, therefore I am in a different category from the merely inquisitive.' He lowered his voice and it became peculiarly menacing. He saw Marner's face lighten. 'And as a law-abiding man,' he continued, 'I am sure you will be only too happy to give me every assistance you can. I should like to see your records in the matter. Precisely how much did Major Grey lose, Mr Marner, to the guinea, if you please?'

394

Marner's chin came up sharply; his eyes were hot and offended.

'The police? You said you wanted to make an investment.'

'No, I did not say that – you assumed it. How much did Joscelin Grey lose, Mr Marner?'

'Oh, well, to the guinea, Mr Monk, he— he did not lose any.'

'But the company dissolved.'

'Yes— yes, that is true; it was most unfortunate. But Major Grey withdrew his own investment at the last moment, just before the – the takeover.'

Monk remembered the policeman from whom he had learned Marner's address. If he had been after Marner for years, let him have the satisfaction of taking him now.

'Oh.' Monk sat back, altering his whole attitude, almost smiling. 'So he was not really concerned in the loss?'

'No, not at all.'

Monk stood up.

'Then it hardly constitutes a part of his murder. I'm sorry to have wasted your time, Mr Marner. And I thank you for your cooperation. You do, of course, have some papers to prove this, just for my superiors?'

'Yes. Yes, I have.' Marner relaxed visibly. 'If you care to wait for a moment—' He stood up from his desk and went to a large cabinet of files. He pulled a drawer and took out a small notebook ruled in ledger fashion. He put it, open, on the desk in front of Monk.

Monk picked it up, glanced at it, read the entry where Grey had withdrawn his money, and snapped it shut.

'Thank you.' He put the book in the inside pocket of his coat and stood up.

Marner's hand came forward for the return of the book. He realized he was not going to get it, debated in his mind whether to demand it or not, and decided it would raise more interest in the subject than he could yet afford. He forced a smile, a sickly thing in his great white face.

'Always happy to be of service, sir. Where should we be without the police? So much crime these days, so much violence.'

'Indeed,' Monk agreed. 'And so much theft that breeds violence. Good day, Mr Marner.'

Outside he walked briskly along Gun Lane and back towards the West India Dock Road, but he was thinking hard. If this evidence was correct, and not fiddled with by Zebedee Marner, then the hitherto relatively honest Joscelin Grey had almost certainly been forewarned in time to escape at the last moment himself, leaving Latterly and his friends to bear the loss. Dishonest, but not precisely illegal. It would be interesting to know who had shares in the company that took over the tobacco importing, and if Grey was one of them.

Had he uncovered this much before? Marner had shown no signs of recognition. He had behaved as if the whole question were entirely new to him. In fact it must be, or Monk would never have been able to deceive him into imagining him an investor.

But even if Zebedee Marner had never seen him before, it was not impossible he had known all this before Grey's death, because then he had had his memory, known his contacts, who to ask, who to bribe, who could be threatened, and with what.

But there was no way yet to find out. On the West India Dock Road he found a hansom and sank back for the long ride, thinking.

At the police station he went to the man who had given him Zebedee Marner's address and told him of his visit, gave him the ledger and showed him what he thought the fraud would be. The man positively bubbled with delight, like someone who contemplates a rich feast only hours away. Monk had a brief, fierce glow of satisfaction.

It did not last.

Runcorn was waiting for him in his own office.

'No arrest yet?' he said with black relish. 'No one charged?'

Monk did not bother to reply.

'Monk!' Runcorn slammed his fist on the table.

'Yes, sir?'

'You sent John Evan out to Shelburne to question the staff?'

'Yes I did. Isn't that what you wanted?' He raised sarcastic eyebrows. 'Evidence against Shelburne?'

'You won't get it out there. We know what his motive was. What we need is evidence of opportunity, someone who saw him here.'

'I'll start looking,' Monk said with bitter irony. Inside himself he was laughing, and Runcorn knew it, but he had not the faintest idea why, and it infuriated him.

'You should have been looking for the last month!' he shouted. 'What in hell is the matter with you, Monk? You were always a hard, arrogant devil, with airs beyond your station, but you were a good policeman. But now you're a fool. This crack on the head seems to have impaired your brain. Perhaps you should have some more sick leave?'

'I am perfectly well.' Misery was black inside Monk; he wanted to frighten this man who hated him so much and was going to have the last victory. 'But maybe you ought to take over this case? You are right, I am getting nowhere with it.' He looked straight back at Runcorn with wide eyes. 'The powers that be want a result – you should do the job yourself.'

Runcorn's face set. 'You must take me for a fool. I've sent for Evan. He'll be back tomorrow.' He held up his thick finger, wagging it in Monk's face. 'Arrest Shelburne this week, or I will take you off it.' He turned and strode out, leaving the door squealing on its hinges.

Monk stared after him. So he had sent for Evan to return. Time was even shorter than he had feared. Before much longer Evan must come to the same conclusion as he had, and that would be the end.

In fact Evan came back the next day, and Monk met him for luncheon. They sat together in a steamy public house. It was heavy and damp with the odour of massed bodies, sawdust, spilled ale and nameless vegetables stewed into soup.

'Anything?' Monk asked as a matter of form. It would have seemed remarkable had he not.

'Lots of indication,' Evan replied with a frown. 'But I wonder sometimes if I see it only because I'm looking for it.'

'You mean invent it for yourself?'

Evan's eyes came up quickly and met Monk's. They were devastatingly clear.

'You don't honestly believe he did it, do you, sir?'

How could he know so quickly? Rapidly Monk flew in his mind through all the possible things he might say. Would Evan know a lie? Had he seen all the lies already? Was he clever enough, subtle enough, to be leading Monk gently into trapping himself? Was it conceivable the whole police department knew, and were simply waiting for him to uncover his own proof, his own condemnation? For a moment fear engulfed him and the cheerful rattle of the alehouse became a din like bedlam – witless, formless and persecutory. They all knew; they were merely waiting for him to know, to betray himself, and then the mystery would end. They would come out in the open, with laughter, handcuffs, questions, congratulations at another murder solved; there would be a trial, a brief imprisonment, and then the tight, strong rope, a quick pain – and nothing.

But why? Why had he killed Joscelin Grey? Surely not because Grey had escaped the crash of the tobacco company – probably even profited from it?

'Sir? Sir, are you all right?' It was Evan's voice cutting across his panic, Evan's face peering at him anxiously. 'You look a little pale, sir. Are you sure you are all right?'

Monk forced himself to sit upright and meet Evan's eyes. If he were to be given one wish now, it would be that Evan

399

would not have to know. Imogen Latterly had never really
been more than a dream, a reminder of the softer self, the
part of him that could be wounded and could care for
something better than ambition – but Evan had been a
friend. Maybe there had been others, but he could not
remember them now.

'Yes,' he said carefully. 'Yes, thank you. I was just
thinking. No, you are right; I am not at all sure it was
Shelburne.'

Evan leaned forward a little, his face eager.

'I'm glad you say that, sir. Don't let Mr Runcorn push
you.' His long fingers were playing with the bread, too
excited to eat. 'I think it's someone here in London. In fact I
have been looking at Mr Lamb's notes again, and ours, and
the more I read them the more I think it could have something
to do with money, with business.

'Joscelin Grey seems to have lived fairly comfortably,
better than the allowance from his family supported.' He put
down his spoon and abandoned all pretence of the meal. 'So
either he was blackmailing someone, or else he gambled
very successfully, or, most likely of all, he had some business
we know nothing about. And if it were honest, we ought to
have found some record of it, and the other people concerned
should have come forward. Similarly, if he borrowed money,
the lenders would have put in some claim against the estate.'

'Unless they were sharks,' Monk said automatically, his
mind cold with fear, watching Evan draw closer and closer
to the thread that must lead him to the truth. Any moment
now and his fine, sensitive hands would grasp it.

'But if they were sharks,' Evan said quickly, his eyes alight, 'they would not have lent to someone like Grey. Sharks are exceedingly careful about their investments. That much I've learned. They don't lend a second sum out before they have the first back, and with interest, or a mortgage on property.' A lock of his heavy hair fell forward over his brow and he ignored it. 'Which brings us back to the same question: Where did Grey get the repayment, not to mention the interest? He was the third brother, remember, and he had no property of his own. No, sir, he had some business, I'm sure of it. And I have some thoughts where to start looking for it.'

He was coming closer with every new idea.

Monk said nothing; his mind was racing for a thought, any thought to put Evan off. He could not avoid it forever, the time would come; but before that he must know why. There was something vital so close, a finger's length out of his reach.

'Do you not agree, sir?' Evan was disappointed; his eyes were shadowed with it. Or was it disappointment that Monk had lied?

Monk jerked himself back, dismissing his pain. He must think clearly just a little longer.

'I was turning it over,' he said, trying to keep the desperation out of his voice. 'Yes, I think you may very well be right. Dawlish spoke of a business venture. I don't recall how much I told you of it; I gathered it had not yet begun, but there may easily have been others already involved.' How he hated lying. Especially to Evan – this betrayal was the worst of all. He could not bear to think what Evan would feel when he knew. 'It would be a good thing if we investigated it far more thoroughly.'

Evan's face lit up again.

'Excellent. You know I really believe we could yet catch Joscelin Grey's murderer. I think we are near it; it will only take just one or two more clues and it will all fall into place.'

Did he know how appallingly near he was to the truth?

'Possibly,' Monk agreed, keeping his voice level with an effort. He looked down at the plate in front of him, anything to avoid Evan's eyes. 'You will still have to be discreet, though. Dawlish is a man of considerable standing.'

'Oh, I will, sir, I will. Anyway, I do not especially suspect him. What about the letter we saw from Charles Latterly? That was pretty chilly, I thought. And I found out quite a lot more about him.' He took a spoonful of his stew at last. 'Did you know his father committed suicide just a few weeks before Grey was killed? Dawlish is a business affair in the future, but Latterly could have been one from the past. Don't you think so, sir?' He was ignoring the taste and texture of the food, almost swallowing it whole in his preoccupation. 'Perhaps there was something not quite right there, and the elder Mr Latterly took his life when he was implicated, and young Mr Charles Latterly, the one who sent the letter, was the one who killed Grey in revenge?'

Monk took a deep breath. He must have just a little more time.

'That letter sounded too controlled for a man passionate enough to kill in revenge,' he said carefully, beginning to eat his own stew. 'But I will look into it. You try Dawlish, and you might try the Fortescues as well. We don't know very much about their connection either.' He could not let Evan pursue Charles for his, Monk's, crime; also the truth was too close for Charles to deny it easily. He had no liking for him, but there was something of honour left to cling to – and he was Hester's brother.

'Yes,' he added, 'try the Fortescues as well.'

In the afternoon when Evan set off full of enthusiasm after Dawlish and Fortescue, Monk went back to the police station and again sought out the man who had given him Marner's address. The man's face lit up as soon as Monk came in.

'Ah, Monk, I owe you something. Good old Zebedee at last.' He waved a book in the air triumphantly. 'Went down to his place on the strength of the ledger you brought, and searched the whole building. The rackets he was running.' He positively chortled with delight and hiccupped very slightly. 'Swindling left and right, taking a rake-off from half the crime and vice in Limehouse – and the Isle of Dogs. God knows how many thousands of pounds must have gone through his hands, the old blackguard.'

Monk was pleased; it was one career other than his own he had helped.

'Good,' he said sincerely. 'I always like to imagine that particular kind of bloodsucker running his belly off in the treadmills for a few years.'

The other man grinned.

'Me too, and that one especially. By the way, the tobacco importing company was a sham. Did you know that?' He hiccupped again and excused himself. 'There was a company, but there was never any practical chance it could have done any trading, let alone make a profit. Your fellow Grey took his money out at precisely the right moment. If he wasn't dead I should be wishing I could charge him as well.'

Charge Grey? Monk froze. The room vanished except for a little whirling light in front of him, and the man's face.

'Wishing? Why only wishing?' He hardly dared ask. Hope hurt like a physical thing.

'Because there's no proof,' the man replied, oblivious of Monk's ecstasy. 'He did nothing actually illegal. But I'm as sure as I am that Hell's hot, he was part of it; just too damned clever to step over the law. But he set it up – and brought in the money.'

'But he was taken in the fraud,' Monk protested, afraid to believe. He wanted to grab the man and shake him; he resisted only with difficulty. 'You're sure beyond doubt?'

'Of course I am.' The other raised his eyebrows. 'I may not be as brilliant a detective as you are, Monk, but I know my job. And I certainly know a fraud when I see one. Your friend Grey was one of the best, and very tidy about it.' He hitched himself more comfortably in his seat. 'Not much money, not enough to cause suspicion, just a small profit, and no guilt attached to him. If he made a habit of it he must have done quite nicely. Although how he got all those people to trust him with their money I don't know. You should see the names of some of those who invested.'

404

'Yes,' Monk said slowly. 'I also should like to know how he persuaded them. I think I want to know that almost as much as I want to know anything.' His brain was racing, casting for clues, threads anywhere. 'Any other names in that ledger, any partners of Marner's?'

'Employees – just the clerk in the outer office.'

'No partners; were there no partners? Anyone else who might know the business about Grey? Who got most of the money, if Grey didn't?'

The man hiccupped gently and sighed. 'A rather nebulous "Mr Robinson", and a lot of money went on keeping it secret, and tidy, covering tracks. No proof so far that this Robinson actually knew exactly what was going on. We've got a watch on him, but nothing good enough to arrest him yet.'

'Where is he?' He had to find out if he had seen this Robinson before, the first time he had investigated Grey. If Marner did not know him, then perhaps Robinson did?

The man wrote an address on a slip of paper and handed it to him.

Monk took it: it was just above the Elephant Stairs in Rotherhithe, across the river. He folded it and put it in his pocket.

'I won't spoil your case,' he promised. 'I only want to ask him one question, and it's to do with Grey, not the tobacco fraud.'

'It's all right,' the other man said, sighing happily. 'Murder is always more important than fraud, at least it is when it's a lord's son that's been killed.' He sighed and hiccupped together. 'Of course if he'd been some poor shopkeeper or chambermaid it would be different. Depends who's been robbed, or who's been killed, doesn't it?'

Monk gave a hard little grimace for the injustice of it, then thanked him and left.

Robinson was not at the Elephant Stairs, and it took Monk all afternoon to find him, eventually running him down in a gin mill in Seven Dials, but he learned everything he wanted to know almost before Robinson spoke. The man's face tightened as soon as Monk came in and a cautious look came into his eyes.

'Good day, Mr Monk; I didn't expect to see you again. What is it this time?'

Monk felt the excitement shiver through him. He swallowed hard.

'Still the same thing—'

Robinson's voice was low and sibilant, and there was a timbre in it that struck Monk with an almost electric familiarity. The sweat tingled on his skin. It was real memory, actual sight and feelings coming back at last. He stared hard at the man.

Robinson's narrow, wedge-shaped face was stiff.

'I've already told you everything I know, Mr Monk. Anyway, what does it matter now Joscelin Grey is dead?'

'And you told me everything you knew before? You swear it?'

Robinson snorted with a faint contempt.

'Yes I swear it,' he said wearily. 'Now will you please go away? You're known around 'ere. It don't do me no good to 'ave the police nosing around and asking questions. People think I 'ave something to 'ide.'

Monk did not bother to argue with him. The fraud detective would catch up with him soon enough.

'Good,' he said simply. 'Then I don't need to trouble you again.' He went out into the hot, grey street milling with pedlars and waifs, his feet hardly feeling the pavement beneath. So he had known about Grey before he had been to see him, before he had killed him.

But why was it Grey he had hated so much? Marner was the principal, the brains behind the fraud, and the greatest beneficiary. And it seemed he had made no move against Marner.

He needed to think about it, sort out his ideas, decide where at least to look for the last missing piece.

It was hot and close, the air heavy with the humidity coming up from the river, and his mind was tired, staggering, spinning with the burden of what he had learned. He needed food and something to drink away this terrible thirst, to wash the stench of the rookeries from his mouth.

Without realizing it he had walked to the door of an eating house. He pushed it open and the fresh smell of sawdust and cider engulfed him. Automatically he made his way to the counter. He did not want ale, but fresh bread and sharp, homemade pickle. He could smell them, pungent and a little sweet.

The potman smiled at him and fetched the crusty bread, crumbling Wensleydale cheese, and juicy onions. He passed over the plate.

''Aven't seen yer for a w'ile, sir,' he said cheerfully. 'I s'pose you was too late to find that fellow you was looking for?'

Monk took the plate in stiff hands, awkwardly. He could not draw his eyes from the man's face. Memory was coming back; he knew he knew him.

'Fellow?' he said huskily.

'Yes.' The potman smiled. 'Major Grey; you was looking for 'im last time you was 'ere. It was the same night 'e was murdered, so I don't s'pose you ever found 'im.'

Something was just beyond Monk's memory, the last piece, tantalizing, the shape of it almost recognizable at last.

'You knew him?' he said slowly, still holding the plate in his hands.

'Bless you, 'course I knew 'im, sir. I told you that.' He frowned. ''Ere, don't you remember?'

'No.' Monk shook his head. It was too late now to lie. 'I had an accident that night. I don't remember what you said. I'm sorry. Can you tell me again?'

The man shook his head and continued wiping a glass. 'Too late now, sir. Major Grey was murdered that night. You'll not see 'im now. Don't you read the newspapers?'

'But you knew him,' Monk repeated. 'Where? In the army? You called him "Major"!'

'That's right. Served in the army with 'im, I did, till I got invalided out.'

'Tell me about him! Tell me everything you told me that night!'

'I'm busy right now, sir. I got to serve or I'll not make me livin',' the man protested. 'Come back later, eh?'

Monk fished in his pocket and brought out all the money he had, every last coin. He put it on the counter.

'No, I need it now.'

The man looked at the money, shining in the light. He met Monk's eyes, saw the urgency in them, understood something of importance. He slid his hand over the money and put it rapidly in the pocket under his apron before picking up the cloth again.

'You asked me what I knew of Major Grey, sir. I told you when I first met 'im and where – in the army in the Crimea. 'E were a major, and I were just a private o' course. But I served under 'im for a long time. 'E were a good enough officer, not specially good nor specially bad; just like most. 'E were brave enough, as fair as most to 'is men. Good to 'is 'orses, but then most well-bred gents is.'

The man blinked. 'You didn't seem terribly interested in that,' he went on, still absently working on the glass. 'You listened, but it didn't seem to weigh much with you. Then you asked me about the Battle o' the Alma, where some Lieutenant Latterly 'ad died; an' I told you as we wasn't at the Battle o' the Alma, so I couldn't tell you about this Lieutenant Latterly—'

'But Major Grey spent the last night before the battle with Lieutenant Latterly.' Monk grabbed at his arm. 'He lent him his watch. Latterly was afraid; it was a lucky piece, a talisman. It had belonged to his grandfather at Waterloo.'

'No, sir, I can't say about any Lieutenant Latterly, but Major Grey weren't nowhere near the Battle o' the Alma, and 'e never 'ad no special watch.'

'Are you sure?' Monk was gripping the man's wrist, unaware of hurting him.

'O' course I'm sure, sir.' The man eased his hand. 'I was there. An' 'is watch were an ordinary gold plate one, and as new as 'is uniform. It weren't no more at Waterloo than 'e were.'

'And an officer called Dawlish?'

The potman frowned, rubbing his wrist. 'Dawlish? I don't remember you asking me about 'im.'

'I probably didn't. But do you remember him?'

'No, sir, I don't recall an officer o' that name.'

'But you are sure of the Battle of the Alma?'

'Yes, sir, I'd swear before God positive. If you'd been in the Crimea, sir, you'd not forget what battle you was at, and what you wasn't. I reckon that's about the worst war there's ever been, for cold and muck and men dyin'.'

'Thank you.'

'Don't you want your bread an' cheese, sir? That pickle's 'omemade special. You should eat it. You look right peaked, you do.'

Monk took it, thanked him automatically, and sat down at one of the tables. He ate without tasting and then walked out into the first spots of rain. He could remember doing this before, remember the slow building anger. It had all been a lie, a brutal and carefully calculated lie to earn first acceptance from the Latterlys, then their friendship, and finally to deceive them into a sufficient sense of obligation, over the lost watch, to repay him by supporting his business scheme.

Grey had used his skill to play like an instrument first their grief, then their debt. Perhaps he had even done the same with the Dawlishes.

The rage was gathering up inside him again. It was coming back exactly as it had before. He was walking faster and faster, the rain beating in his face now. He was unaware of it. He splashed through the swimming gutters into the street to hail a cab. He gave the address in Mecklenburgh Square, as he knew he had done before.

When he got out he went into the building. Grimwade handed him the key this time; the first time there had been no one there.

He went upstairs. It seemed new, strange, as if he were reliving the first time when it was unknown to him. He got to the top and hesitated at the door. Then he had knocked. Now he slipped the key into the lock. It swung open quite easily and he went in. Before Joscelin Grey had come to the door, dressed in pale dove, his fair face handsome, smiling, just a little surprised. He could see it now as if it had been only a few minutes ago.

Grey had asked him in, quite casually, unperturbed. He had put his stick in the hall stand, his mahogany stick with the brass chain embossed in the handle. It was still there. Then he had followed Grey into the main room. Grey had been very composed, a slight smile on his face. Monk had told him what he had come for: about the tobacco business, the failure, Latterly's death, the fact that Grey had lied, that he had never known George Latterly, and there had been no watch.

He could see Grey now as he had turned from the sideboard, holding out a drink for Monk, taking one himself. He had smiled again, more widely.

'My dear fellow, a harmless little lie.' His voice had been light, very easy, very calm. 'I told them what an excellent fellow poor George was, how brave, how charming, how well loved. It was what they wanted to hear. What does it matter whether it was true or not?'

'It was a lie,' Monk had shouted back. 'You didn't even know George Latterly. You did it purely for money.'

Grey had grinned.

'So I did, and what's more, I shall do it again, and again. I have an endless stream of gold watches, or whatever; and there's not a thing you can do about it, policeman. I shall go on as long as anyone is left who remembers the Crimea – which will be a hell of a long time – and shall damned well never run out of the dead!'

Monk had stared at him, helpless, anger raging inside him till he could have wept like an impotent child.

'I didn't know Latterly,' Grey had gone on. 'I got his name from the casualty lists. They're absolutely full of names, you've no idea. Although actually I got some of the better ones from the poor devils themselves – saw them die in Scutari, riddled with disease, bleeding and spewing all over the place. I wrote their last letters for them. Poor George might have been a raving coward, for all I know. But what good does it do to tell his family that? I've no idea what he was like, but it doesn't take much wit to work out what they wanted to hear! Poor little Imogen adored him,

412

and who can blame her? Charles is a hell of a bore; reminds me a bit of my eldest brother, another pompous fool.' His fair face had become momentarily ugly with envy. A look of malice and pleasure had slid into it. He looked at Monk up and down knowingly.

'And who wouldn't have told the lovely Imogen whatever she would listen to? I told her all about that extraordinary creature, Florence Nightingale. I painted up the heroism a bit, certainly, gave her all the glory of "angels of mercy" holding lamps by the dying through the night. You should have seen her face.' He had laughed; then seeing something in Monk, a vulnerability, perhaps a memory or a dream, and understanding its depth in a flash: 'Ah yes, Imogen.' He sighed. 'Got to know her very well.' His smile was half a leer. 'Love the way she walks, all eager, full of promise, and hope.' He had looked at Monk and the slow smile spread to his eyes till the light in them was as old as appetite and knowledge itself. He had tittered slightly. 'I do believe you're taken with Imogen yourself.'

'You clod, she'd no more touch you than carry out her own refuse.'

'She's in love with Florence Nightingale and the glory of the Crimea!' His eyes met Monk's, glittering bright. 'I could have had her any time, all eager and quivering.' His lip curled and he had almost laughed as he looked at Monk. 'I'm a soldier; I've seen reality, blood and passion, fought for Queen and country. I've seen the Charge of the Light Brigade, lain in hospital at Scutari among the dying. What do you imagine she thinks of grubby little London policemen

413

who spend their time sniffing about in human filth after the beggars and the degenerate? You're a scavenger, a cleaner up of other people's dirt – one of life's necessities, like the drains.' He took a long gulp of his brandy and looked at Monk over the top of the glass.

'Perhaps when they've got over that old idiot getting hysterical and shooting himself, I shall go back and do just that. Can't remember when I've fancied a woman more.'

It had been then, with that leer on his mouth, that Monk had taken his own glass and thrown the brandy across Grey's face. He could remember the blinding anger as if it were a dream he had only just woken from. He could still taste the heat and the gall of it on his tongue.

The liquid had hit Grey in his open eyes and burned him, seared his pride beyond bearing. He was a gentleman, one already robbed by birth of fortune, and now this oaf of a policeman, jumped above himself, had insulted him in his own house. His features had altered into a snarl of fury and he had picked up his own heavy stick and struck Monk across the shoulders with it. He had aimed at his head, but Monk had almost felt it before it came, and moved.

They had closed in a struggle. It should have been self-defence, but it was far more than that. Monk had been glad of it – he had wanted to smash that leering face, beat it in, undo all that he had said, wipe from him the thoughts he had had of Imogen, expunge some of the wrong to her family. But above all, towering in his head and burning in his soul, he wanted to beat him so hard he would never feed on the gullible and the bereaved again, telling them lies of invented debt and robbing the dead of the only heritage they had left, the truth of memory in those who had loved them.

Grey had fought back; for a man invalided out of the army he had been surprisingly strong. They had been locked together struggling for the stick, crashing into furniture, upsetting chairs. The very violence of it was a catharsis, and all the pent-up fear, the nightmare of rage and the agonizing pity poured forth and he barely felt the pain of blows, even the breaking of his ribs when Grey caught him a tremendous crack on the chest with his stick.

But Monk's weight and strength told, and perhaps his rage was even stronger than Grey's fear and all his held-in anger of years of being slighted and passed over.

Monk could remember quite clearly now the moment when he had wrested the heavy stick out of Grey's hands and struck at him with it, trying to destroy the hideousness, the blasphemy he saw, the obscenity the law was helpless to curb.

Then he had stopped, breathless and terrified by his own violence and the storm of his hatred. Grey was splayed out on the floor, swearing like a trooper.

Monk had turned and gone out, leaving the door swinging behind him, blundering down the stairs, turning his coat collar up and pulling his scarf up to hide the abrasion on his face where Grey had hit him. He had passed Grimwade in the hall. He remembered a bell ringing and Grimwade leaving his position and starting upstairs.

Outside the weather was fearful. As soon as he had opened the door the wind had blown it against him so hard it

415

had knocked him backwards. He had put his head down and plunged out, the rain engulfing him, beating in his face cold and hard. He had his back to the light, going into the darkness between one lamp and the next.

There was a man coming towards him, towards the light and the door still open in the wind – for a moment he saw his face before he turned and went in. It was Menard Grey.

Now it all made obvious and tragic sense – it was not George Latterly's death, or the abuse of it, which had spurred Joscelin Grey's murder, it was Edward Dawlish's – and Joscelin's own betrayal of every ideal his brother believed.

And then the joy vanished just as suddenly as it had come, the relief evaporated, leaving him shivering cold. How could he prove it? It was his word against Menard's. Grimwade had been up the stairs answering the bell, and seen nothing. Menard had gone in the door Monk had left open in the gale. There was nothing material, no evidence – only Monk's memory of Menard's face for a moment in the gaslight.

They would hang him. He could imagine the trial now, himself standing in the dock, the ridiculousness of trying to explain what manner of man Joscelin Grey had been, and that it was not Monk, but Joscelin's own brother Menard who had killed him. He could see the disbelief in their faces, and the contempt for a man who would try to escape justice by making such a charge.

Despair closed around him like the blackness of the night, eating away strength, crushing with the sheer weight of it. And he began to be afraid. There would be the few short weeks in the stone cell, the stolid warders, at once pitying and contemptuous, then the last meal, the priest, and the short walk to the scaffold, the smell of rope, the pain, the fighting for breath – and oblivion.

He was still drowned and paralysed by it when he heard the sound on the stairs. The latch turned and Evan stood in the doorway. It was the worst moment of all. There was no point in lying, Evan's face was full of knowledge, and pain. And anyway, he did not want to.

'How did you know?' Monk said quietly.

Evan came in and closed the door. 'You sent me after Dawlish. I found an officer who'd served with Edward Dawlish. He didn't gamble, and Joscelin Grey never paid any debts for him. Everything he knew about him he learned from Menard. He took a hell of a chance lying to the family like that – but it worked. They'd have backed him financially, if he hadn't died. They blamed Menard for Edward's fall from honour, and forbade him the house. A nice touch on Joscelin's part.'

Monk stared at him. It made perfect sense. And yet it would never even raise a reasonable doubt in a juror's mind.

'I think that is where Grey's money came from – cheating the families of the dead,' Evan continued. 'You were so concerned about the Latterly case, it wasn't a great leap of the imagination to assume he cheated them too – and that is why Charles Latterly's father shot himself.' The eyes were soft and intense with distress. 'Did you come this far the first time too – before the accident?'

So he knew about the memory also. Perhaps it was all far

more obvious than he believed; the fumbling for words, the unfamiliarity with streets, public houses, old haunts – even Runcorn's hatred of him. It did not matter any more.

'Yes.' Monk spoke very slowly, as if letting the words fall one by one would make them believable. 'But I did not kill Joscelin Grey. I fought with him, I probably hurt him – he certainly hurt me – but he was alive and swearing at me when I left.' He searched Evan's countenance feature by feature. 'I saw Menard Grey go in as I turned in the street. He was facing the ligh˙ ˙nd I was going away from it. The outer door was still open in the wind.'

A desperate, painful relief flooded Evan's face, and he looked bony and young, and very tired. 'So it was Menard who killed him.' It was a statement.

'Yes.' A blossom of gratitude opened wide inside Monk, filling him with sweetness. Even without hope, it was to be treasured immeasurably. 'But there is no proof.'

'But—' Evan began to argue, then the words died on his lips as he realized the truth of it. In all their searches they had found nothing. Menard had motive, but so had Charles Latterly, or Mr Dawlish, or any other family Joscelin had cheated, any friend he had dishonoured – or Lovel Grey, whom he might have betrayed in the cruellest way of all – or Monk himself. And Monk had been there. Now that they knew it, they also knew how easily provable it was, simply find the shop where he had bought that highly distinctive stick – such a piece of vanity. Mrs Worley would remember it, and its subsequent absence. Lamb would recall seeing it in Grey's flat the morning after the murder. Imogen Latterly would have to admit Monk had been working on the case of her father's death.

The darkness was growing closer, tighter around them, the light guttering.

'We'll have to get Menard to confess,' Evan said at last.

Monk laughed harshly. 'And how do you propose we should do that? There's no evidence, and he knows it. No one would take my word against his that I saw him, and kept silent about it till now. It will look like a rather shabby and very stupid attempt to shift the blame from myself.'

That was true, and Evan racked his mind in vain for a rebuttal. Monk was still sitting in the big chair, limp and exhausted with emotions from terror through joy and back to fear and despair again.

'Go home,' Evan said gently. 'You can't stay here. There may be—' Then the idea came to him with a flutter of hope, growing and rising. There was one person who might help. It was a chance, but there was nothing left to lose. 'Yes,' he repeated. 'Go home – I'll be there soon. I've just got an errand. Someone to see—' And he swung on his heel and went out of the door, leaving it ajar behind him.

He ran down the stairs two at a time – he never knew afterwards how he did not break his neck – shot past Grimwade, and plunged out into the rain. He ran all the way along the pavement of Mecklenburgh Square along Doughty Street and accosted a hansom as it passed him, driver's coat collar up around his neck and stovepipe hat jammed forward over his brow.

'I ain't on duty, guv!' the driver said crossly. 'Finished, I am. Goin' 'ome ter me supper.'

Evan ignored him and climbed in, shouting the Latterlys' address in Thanet Street at him.

'I told you, I ain't goin' nowhere!' the cabby repeated, louder this time. ''Ceptin 'ome fer me supper. You'll 'ave ter get someone else!'

'You're taking me to Thanet Street!' Evan shouted back at him. 'Police! Now get on with it, or I'll have your badge!'

'Bleedin' rozzers,' the cabby muttered sullenly, but he realized he had a madman in the back, and it would be quicker in the long run to do what he said. He lifted the reins and slapped them on the horse's soaking back, and they set off at a brisk trot.

At Thanet Street Evan scrambled out and commanded the cabby to wait, on pain of his livelihood.

Hester was at home when Evan was shown in by a startled maid. He was streaming water everywhere and his extraordinary, ugly, beautiful face was white. His hair was plastered crazily across his brow and he stared at her with anguished eyes.

She had seen hope and despair too often not to recognize both.

'Can you come with me!' he said urgently. 'Please? I'll explain as we go. Miss Latterly— I—'

'Yes.' She did not need time to decide. To refuse was an impossibility. And she must leave before Charles or Imogen came from the withdrawing room, impelled by curiosity, and discovered the drenched and frantic policeman in the hall. She could not even go back for her cloak – what use would it be in this downpour anyway? 'Yes— I'll come now.' She walked past him and out of the front door. The wall of rain hit her in the face and she ignored it, continuing across the pavement, over the bubbling gutter and up into the hansom before either Evan or the driver had time to hand her up.

Evan scrambled behind her and slammed the door, shouting his instructions to drive to Grafton Street. Since the cabby had not yet been paid, he had little alternative.

'What has happened, Mr Evan?' Hester asked as soon as they were moving. 'I can see that it is something very terrible. Have you discovered who murdered Joscelin Grey?'

There was no point in hesitating now; the die was cast.

'Yes, Miss Latterly. Mr Monk retraced all the steps of his first investigation – with your help.' He took a deep breath. He was cold now that the moment came; he was wet to the skin and shaking. 'Joscelin Grey made his living by finding the families of men killed in the Crimea, pretending he had known the dead soldier and befriended him – either lending him money, paying the debts he left, or giving him some precious personal belonging, like the watch he claimed to have lent your brother, then when the family could not give it back to him – which they never could, since it did not exist – they felt in his debt, which he used to obtain invitations, influence, financial or social backing. Usually it was only a few hundred guineas, or to be a guest at their expense. In your father's case it was to his ruin and death. Either way Grey did not give a damn what happened to his victims, and he had every intention of continuing.'

'What a vile crime,' she said quietly. 'He was totally

despicable. I am glad that he is dead – and perhaps sorry for
whoever killed him. You have not said who it was?' Suddenly
she was cóld also. 'Mr Evan—?'

'Yes, ma'am – Mr Monk went to his flat in Mecklenburgh
Square and faced him with it. They fought – Mr Monk beat
him, but he was definitely alive and not mortally hurt when
Mr Monk left. But as Monk reached the street he saw
someone else arrive, and go towards the door which was still
swinging open in the wind.'

He saw Hester's face pale in the glare of the streetlamps
through the carriage window.

'Who?'

'Menard Grey,' he replied, waiting in the dark again to
judge from her voice, or her silence, if she believed it.
'Probably because Joscelin dishonoured the memory of his
friend Edward Dawlish, and deceived Edward's father into
giving him hospitality, as he did your father – and the money
would have followed.'

She said nothing for several minutes. They swayed and
rattled through the intermittent darkness, the rain battering
on the roof and streaming past in torrents, yellow where the
gaslight caught it.

'How very sad,' she said at last, and her voice was tight
with emotion as though the pity caused a physical pain in
her throat. 'Poor Menard. I suppose you are going to arrest
him? Why have you brought me? I can do nothing.'

'We can't arrest him,' he answered quietly. 'There is no
proof.'

'There—' She swivelled around in her seat; he felt her

rather than saw her. 'Then what are you going to do? They'll think it was Monk. They'll charge him— They'll—' She swallowed. 'They'll hang him.'

'I know. We must make Menard confess. I thought you might know how we could do that? You know the Greys far better than we could, from the outside. And Joscelin was responsible for your father's death – and your mother's, indirectly.'

Again she sat silent for so long he was afraid he had offended her, or reminded her of grief so deep she was unable to do anything but nurse its pain inside her. They were drawing close to Grafton Street, and soon they must leave the cab and face Monk with some resolution – or admit failure. Then he would be faced with the task he dreaded so much the thought of it made him sick. He must either tell Runcorn the truth, that Monk fought with Joscelin Grey the night of his death – or else deliberately conceal the fact and lay himself open to certain dismissal from the police force – and the possible charge of accessory to murder.

They were in the Tottenham Court Road, lamps gleaming on the wet pavements, gutters awash. There was no time left.

'Miss Latterly.'

'Yes. Yes,' she said firmly. 'I will come with you to Shelburne Hall. I have thought about it, and the only way I can see success is if you tell Lady Fabia the truth about Joscelin. I will corroborate it. My family were his victims as well, and she will have to believe me, because I have no interest in lying. It does not absolve my father's suicide in the eyes of the church.' She hesitated only an instant. 'Then if you proceed to tell her about Edward Dawlish as well, I think Menard may be persuaded to confess. He may see no other avenue open to him, once his mother realizes that he killed Joscelin – which she will. It will devastate her – it may destroy her.' Her voice was very low. 'And they may hang Menard. But we cannot permit the law to hang Mr Monk instead, merely because the truth is a tragedy that will wound perhaps beyond bearing. Joscelin Grey was a man who did much evil. We cannot protect his mother either from her part in it, or from the pain of knowing.'

'You'll come to Shelburne tomorrow?' He had to hear her say it again. 'You are prepared to tell her your own family's suffering at Joscelin's hands?'

'Yes. And how Joscelin obtained the names of the dying in Scutari, as I now realize, so he could use them to cheat their families. At what time will you depart?'

Again relief swept over him, and an awe for her that she could so commit herself without equivocation. But then to go out to the Crimea to nurse she must be a woman of courage beyond the ordinary imagination, and to remain there, of a strength of purpose that neither danger nor pain could bend.

'I don't know,' he said a trifle foolishly. 'There was little purpose in going at all unless you were prepared to come. Lady Shelburne would hardly believe us without further substantiation from beyond police testimony. Shall we say the first train after eight o'clock in the morning?' Then he remembered he was asking a lady of some gentility. 'Is that too early?'

'Certainly not.' Had he been able to see her face there might have been the faintest of smiles on it.

'Thank you. Then do you wish to take this hansom back home again, and I shall alight here and go and tell Mr Monk?'

'That would be the most practical thing,' she agreed. 'I shall see you at the railway station in the morning.'

He wanted to say something more, but all that came to his mind was either repetitious or vaguely condescending. He simply thanked her again and climbed out into the cold and teeming rain. It was only when the cab had disappeared into the darkness and he was halfway up the stairs to Monk's rooms that he realized with acute embarrassment that he had left her to pay the cabby.

The journey to Shelburne was made at first with heated conversation and then in silence, apart from the small politeness of travel. Monk was furious that Hester was present. He refrained from ordering her home again only because the train was already moving when she entered the carriage from the corridor, bidding them good-morning and seating herself opposite.

'I asked Miss Latterly to come,' Evan explained without a blush, 'because her additional testimony will carry great weight with Lady Fabia, who may well not believe us, since we have an obvious interest in claiming Joscelin was a cad. Miss Latterly's experience, and that of her family, is something she cannot so easily deny.' He did not make the mistake of claiming that Hester had any moral right to be there because of her own loss, or her part in the solution. Monk wished he had, so he could lose his temper and accuse him of irrelevance. The argument he had presented was extremely reasonable – in fact he was right. Hester's corroboration would be very likely to tip the balance of decision, which otherwise the Greys together might rebut.

'I trust you will speak only when asked?' Monk said to her coldly. 'This is a police operation, and a very delicate one.' That she of all people should be the one whose assistance he needed at this point was galling in the extreme, and yet it was undeniable. She was in many ways everything he loathed in a woman, the antithesis of the gentleness that lingered with such sweetness in his memory; and yet she had rare courage, and a force of character which would equal Fabia Grey's any day.

'Certainly, Mr Monk,' she replied with her chin high and her eyes unflinching, and he knew in that instant that she had expected precisely this reception, and come to the carriage late intentionally to circumvent the possibility of being ordered home. Although of course it was highly debatable as to whether she would have gone. And Evan would never countenance leaving her on the station platform at Shelburne. And Monk did care what Evan felt.

He sat and stared across at Hester, wishing he could think of something else crushing to say.

She smiled at him, clear-eyed and agreeable. It was not so much friendliness as triumph.

They continued the rest of the journey with civility, and gradually each became consumed in private thoughts, and a dread of the task ahead.

When they arrived at Shelburne they alighted onto the platform. The weather was heavy and dark with the presage of winter. It had stopped raining, but a cold wind stirred in gusts and chilled the skin even through heavy coats.

They were obliged to wait some fifteen minutes before a trap arrived, which they hired to take them to the Hall. This journey too they made huddled together and without speaking. They were all oppressed by what was to come, and the trivialities of conversation would have been grotesque.

They were admitted reluctantly by the footman, but no persuasion would cause him to show them into the withdrawing room. Instead they were left together in the morning room, neither cheered nor warmed by the fire smouldering in the grate, and required to wait until Her Ladyship should decide whether she would receive them or not.

After twenty-five minutes the footman returned and conducted them to the boudoir, where Fabia was seated on her favourite settee, looking pale and somewhat strained, but perfectly composed.

'Good morning, Mr Monk. Constable.' She nodded at Evan. Her eyebrows rose and her eyes became icier. 'Good morning, Miss Latterly. I assume you can explain your presence here in such curious company?'

Hester took the bull by the horns before Monk had time to form a reply.

'Yes, Lady Fabia. I have come to inform you of the truth about my family's tragedy – and yours.'

'You have my condolences, Miss Latterly.' Fabia looked at her with pity and distaste. 'But I have no desire to know the details of your loss, nor do I wish to discuss my bereavement with you. It is a private matter. I imagine your intention is good, but it is entirely misplaced. Good day to you. The footman will see you to the door.'

Monk felt the first flicker of anger stir, in spite of the consuming disillusion he knew this woman was shortly going to feel. Her wilful blindness was monumental, her ability to disregard other people total.

Hester's face set hard with resolve, as granite hard as Fabia's own.

'It is the same tragedy, Lady Fabia. And I do not discuss it out of good intentions, but because it is a truth we are all obliged to face. It gives me no pleasure at all, but neither do I plan to run away from it—'

Fabia's chin came up and the thin muscles tightened in her neck, suddenly looking scraggy, as if age had descended on her in the brief moments since they entered the room.

'I have never run from a truth in my life, Miss Latterly, and I do not care for your impertinence in suggesting I might. You forget yourself.'

'I would prefer to forget everything and go home.' A ghost of a smile crossed Hester's face and vanished. 'But I cannot. I think it would be better if Lord Shelburne and Mr Menard Grey were to be present, rather than repeat the story for them later. There may be questions they wish to ask –

Major Grey was their brother and they have some rights in knowing how and why he died.'

Fabia sat motionless, her face rigid, her hands poised halfway towards the bell pull. She had not invited any of them to be seated, in fact she was on the point of asking again that they leave. Now, with the mention of Joscelin's murderer, everything was changed. There was not the slightest sound in the room except the ticking of the ormolu clock on the mantelpiece.

'You know who killed Joscelin?' She looked at Monk, ignoring Hester.

'Yes, ma'am, we do.' He found his mouth dry and the pulse beating violently in his head. Was it fear, or pity – or both?

Fabia stared at him, demanding he explain everything for her, then slowly the challenge died. She saw something in his face which she could not overcome, a knowledge and a finality which touched her with the first breath of a chill, nameless fear. She pulled the bell, and when the maid came, told her to send both Menard and Lovel to her immediately. No mention was made of Rosamond. She was not a Grey by blood, and apparently Fabia did not consider she had any place in this revelation.

They waited in silence, each in their separate worlds of misery and apprehension. Lovel came first, looking irritably from Fabia to Monk, and with surprise at Hester. He had obviously been interrupted while doing something he considered of far greater urgency.

'What is it?' he said, frowning at his mother. 'Has

something further been discovered?'

'Mr Monk says he knows at last who killed Joscelin,' she answered with masklike calm.

'Who?'

'He has not told me. He is waiting for Menard.'

Lovel turned to Hester, his face puckered with confusion. 'Miss Latterly?'

'The truth involves the death of my father also, Lord Shelburne,' she explained gravely. 'There are parts of it which I can tell you, so you understand it all.'

The first shadow of anxiety touched him, but before he could press her further Menard came in, glanced from one to another of them, and paled.

'Monk finally knows who killed Joscelin,' Lovel explained. 'Now for heaven's sake, get on with it. I presume you have arrested him?'

'It is in hand, sir.' Monk found himself more polite to them all than previously. It was a form of distancing himself, almost a sort of verbal defence.

'Then what is it you want of us?' Lovel demanded.

It was like plunging into a deep well of ice.

'Major Grey made his living out of his experience in the Crimean War—' Monk began. Why was he so mealymouthed? He was dressing it in sickening euphemisms.

'My son did not "make his living" as you put it!' Fabia snapped. 'He was a gentleman – there was no necessity. He had an allowance from the family estates.'

'Which didn't begin to cover the expenses of the way he liked to live,' Menard said savagely. 'If you'd ever looked at him closely, even once, you would have known that.'

'I did know it.' Lovel glared at his brother. 'I assumed he was successful at cards.'

'He was – sometimes. At other times he'd lose – heavily – more than he had. He'd go on playing, hoping to get it back, ignoring the debts – until I paid them, to save the family honour.'

'Liar,' Fabia said with withering disgust. 'You were always jealous of him, even as a child. He was braver, kinder and infinitely more charming than you.' For a moment a brief glow of memory superseded the present and softened all the lines of anger in her face – then the rage returned deeper than before. 'And you couldn't forgive him for it.'

Dull colour burned up Menard's face and he winced as if he had been struck. But he did not retaliate. There was still in his eyes, in the turn of his lips, a pity for her which concealed the bitter truth.

Monk hated it. Futilely he tried again to think of any way he could to avoid exposing Menard even now.

The door opened and Callandra Daviot came in, meeting Hester's eyes, seeing the intense relief in them, then the contempt in Fabia's eyes and the anguish in Menard's.

'This is a family concern,' Fabia said, dismissing her. 'You need not trouble yourself with it.'

Callandra walked past Hester and sat down.

'In case you have forgotten, Fabia, I was born a Grey. Something which you were not. I see the police are here. Presumably they have learned more about Joscelin's death –

431

possibly even who was responsible. What are you doing here, Hester?'

Again Hester took the initiative. Her face was bleak and she stood with her shoulders stiff as if she were bracing herself against a blow.

'I came because I know a great deal about Joscelin's death, which you may not believe from anyone else.'

'Then why have you concealed it until now?' Fabia said with heavy disbelief. 'I think you are indulging in a most vulgar intrusion, Miss Latterly, which I can only presume is a result of that same wilful nature which drove you to go traipsing off to the Crimea. No wonder you are unmarried.'

Hester had been called worse things than vulgar, and by people for whose opinion she cared a great deal more than she did for Fabia Grey's.

'Because I did not know it had any relevance before,' she said levelly. 'Now I do. Joscelin came to visit my parents after my brother was lost in the Crimea. He told them he had lent George a gold watch the night before his death. He asked for its return, assuming it was found among George's effects.' Her voice dropped a fraction and her back became even stiffer. 'There was no watch in George's effects, and my father was so embarrassed he did what he could to make amends to Joscelin – with hospitality, money to invest in Joscelin's business enterprise, not only his own but his friends' also. The business failed and my father's money, and all that of his friends, was lost. He could not bear the shame of it, and he took his own life. My mother died of grief a short while later.'

432

'I am truly sorry for your parents' death,' Lovel interrupted, looking first at Fabia, then at Hester again. 'But how can all this have anything to do with Joscelin's murder? It seems an ordinary enough matter – an honourable man making a simple compensation to clear his dead son's debt to a brother officer.'

Hester's voice shook and at last her control seemed in danger of breaking.

'There was no watch. Joscelin never knew George – any more than he knew a dozen others whose names he picked from the casualty lists, or whom he watched die in Scutari— I saw him do it – only then I didn't know why.'

Fabia was white-lipped. 'That is a most scandalous lie – and beneath contempt. If you were a man I should have you horsewhipped.'

'Mother!' Lovel protested, but she ignored him.

'Joscelin was a beautiful man – brave and talented and full of charm and wit,' she plunged on, her voice thick with emotion, the joy of the past, and the anguish. 'Everyone loved him except those few who were eaten with envy,' Her eyes darted at Menard with something close to hatred. 'Little men who couldn't bear to see anyone succeed beyond their own petty efforts.' Her mouth trembled. 'Lovel, because Rosamond loved Joscelin; he could make her laugh – and dream.' Her voice hardened. 'And Menard, who couldn't live with the fact that I loved Joscelin more than I loved anyone else in the world, and I always did.'

She shuddered and her body seemed to shrink into itself as if withdrawing from something vile. 'Now this woman has come here with her warped and fabricated story, and you stand there and listen to it. If you were men worthy of the name, you would throw her out and damn it for the slander it is. But it seems I must do it myself. No one has any sense of the family honour but me.' She put her hands on the arms of her chair as if to rise to her feet.

'You'll have no one thrown out until I say so,' Lovel said with a tight, calm voice, suddenly cutting like steel across her emotion. 'It is not you who have defended the family honour; all you've defended is Joscelin – whether he deserved it or not. It was Menard who paid his debts and cleaned up the trail of cheating and welshing he left behind—'

'Nonsense. Whose word do you have for that? Menard's?' She spat the name. 'He is calling Joscelin a cheat, no one else. And he wouldn't dare, if Joscelin were alive. He only has the courage to do it now because he thinks you will back him, and there is no one here to call him the pathetic, treacherous liar he is.'

Menard stood motionless, the final blow visible in the agony of his face. She had hurt him, and he had defended Joscelin for her sake for the last time.

Callandra stood up.

'You are wrong, Fabia, as you have been wrong all the time. Miss Latterly here, for one, will testify that Joscelin was a cheat who made money deceiving the bereaved who were too hurt and bewildered to see him for what he was. Menard was always a better man, but you were too fond of flattery to see it. Perhaps you were the one Joscelin deceived most of all – first, last and always.' She did not flinch now, even from Fabia's stricken face as she caught sight at last of a fearful truth. 'But you wanted to be deceived. He told you what you wished to hear; he told you you were beautiful, charming, gay – all the things a man loves in a woman. He learned his art in your gullibility, your willingness to be entertained, to laugh and to be the centre of all the life and love in Shelburne. He said all that not because he thought for a moment it was true, but because he knew you would love him for saying it – and you did, blindly and indiscriminately, to the exclusion of everyone else. That is your tragedy, as well as his.'

Fabia seemed to wither as they watched her.

'You never liked Joscelin,' she said in a last, frantic attempt to defend her world, her dreams, all the past that was golden and lovely to her, everything that gave her meaning as it crumbled in front of her – not only what Joscelin had been, but what she herself had been. 'You are a wicked woman.'

'No, Fabia,' Callandra replied. 'I am a very sad one.' She turned to Hester. 'I assume it is not your brother who killed Joscelin, or you would not have come here to tell us this way. We would have believed the police, and the details would not have been necessary.' With immeasurable sorrow she looked across at Menard. 'You paid his debts. What else did you do?'

There was an aching silence in the room.

Monk could feel his heart beating as if it had the force to shake his whole body. They were poised on the edge of truth, and yet it was still so far away. It could be lost again by a single slip; they could plunge away into an abyss of fear, whispered doubts, always seeing suspicions, double meanings, hearing the footstep behind and the hand on the shoulder.

Against his will, he looked across at Hester, and saw that she was looking at him, the same thoughts plain in her eyes. He turned his head quickly back to Menard, who was ashen-faced.

'What else did you do?' Callandra repeated. 'You knew what Joscelin was—'

'I paid his debts.' Menard's voice was no more than a whisper.

'Gambling debts,' she agreed. 'What about his debts of honour, Menard? What about his terrible debts to men like Hester's father and brother – did you pay them as well?'

'I— I didn't know about the Latterlys,' Menard stammered.

Callandra's face was tight with grief.

'Don't equivocate, Menard. You may not have known the Latterlys by name, but you knew what Joscelin was doing. You knew he got money from somewhere, because you knew how much he had to gamble with. Don't tell us you didn't learn where it came from. I know you better than that. You would not have rested in that ignorance – you knew what a fraud and a cheat Joscelin was, and you knew there was no honest way for him to come by so much. Menard—' Her face was gentle, full of pity. 'You have behaved with such honour so far – don't soil it now by lying. There is no point, and no escape.'

He winced as if she had struck him, and for a second Monk thought he was going to collapse. Then he straightened up and faced her, as though she had been a long-awaited execution squad – and death was not now the worst fear.

'Was it Edward Dawlish?' Now her voice also was barely above a whisper. 'I remember how you cared for each other as boys, and your grief when he was killed. Why did his father quarrel with you?'

Menard did not evade the truth, but he spoke not to Callandra but to his mother, his voice low and hard, a lifetime of seeking and being rejected naked in it finally.

'Because Joscelin told him I had led Edward into gambling beyond his means, and that in the Crimea he had got in over his head with his brother officers, and would have died in debt – except that Joscelin settled it all for him.'

There was a rich irony in that, and it was lost on no one. Even Fabia flinched in a death's-head acknowledgment of its cruel absurdity.

'For his family's sake,' Menard continued, his voice husky, his eyes on Callandra. 'Since I was the one who had led him to ruin.'

He gulped. 'Of course there was no debt. Joscelin never even served in the same area as Edward – I found that out afterwards. It was all another of his lies – to get money.' He looked at Hester. 'It was not as bad as your loss. At least Dawlish didn't kill himself. I am truly sorry about your family.'

'He didn't lose any money.' Monk spoke at last. 'He

didn't have time. You killed Joscelin before he could take it. But he had asked.'

There was utter silence. Callandra put both her hands to her face. Lovel was stunned, unable to comprehend. Fabia was a broken woman. She no longer cared. What happened to Menard was immaterial. Joscelin, her beloved Joscelin, had been murdered in front of her in a new and infinitely more dreadful way. They had robbed her not only of the present and the future, but all the warm, sweet, precious past. It had all gone; there was nothing left but a handful of bitter ash.

They all waited, each in a separate world in the moments between hope and the finality of despair. Only Fabia had already been dealt the ultimate blow.

Monk found the nails of his hands cutting his palms, so tightly were his fists clenched. It could all still slip away from him. Menard could deny it, and there would be no proof sufficient. Runcorn would have only the bare facts, and come after Monk, and what was there to protect him?

The silence was like a slow pain, growing with each second.

Menard looked at his mother and she saw the movement of his head, and turned her face away, slowly and deliberately.

'Yes,' Menard said at last. 'Yes I did. He was despicable. It wasn't only what he had done to Edward Dawlish, or me, but what he was going to go on doing. He had to be stopped – before it became public, and the name of Grey was a byword for a man who cheats the families of his dead comrades-in-arms, a more subtle and painful version of those who crawl over the battlefield the morning after and rob the corpses of the fallen.'

Callandra walked over to him and put her hand on his arm.

'We will get the best legal defence available,' she said very quietly. 'You had a great deal of provocation. I think they will not find murder.'

'We will not.' Fabia's voice was a mere crackle, almost a sob, and she looked at Menard with terrible hatred.

'I will,' Callandra corrected. 'I have quite sufficient means.' She turned back to Menard again. 'I will not leave you alone, my dear. I imagine you will have to go with Mr Monk now – but I will do all that is necessary, I promise you.'

Menard held her hand for a moment; something crossed his lips that was almost a smile. Then he turned to Monk.

'I am ready.'

Evan was standing by the door with the manacles in his pocket. Monk shook his head, and Menard walked out slowly between them. The last thing Monk heard was Hester's voice as she stood next to Callandra.

'I will testify for him. When the jury hears what Joscelin did to my family, they may understand—'

Monk caught Evan's eye and felt a lift of hope. If Hester Latterly fought for Menard, the battle could not easily be lost. His hand held Menard's arm – but gently.

Half Moon Street

To
Carol Ann Lee
in appreciation

Chapter One

❦

The wraiths of mist curled up slowly from the grey and silver surface of the river, gleaming in the first light from the sun. To the right the arch of Lambeth Bridge rose dark against a pearly sky. Whatever barges followed the tide down towards the Port of London and the docks were still invisible in the dark and the September fog.

Superintendent Thomas Pitt stood on the stormy wet ledge of Horseferry Stairs and looked at the punt which nudged gently against the lowest step. It was moored now, but an hour and a half ago, when the constable had first seen it, it had not been. Not that a drifting boat was of any interest to the head of the Bow Street Police Station – it was what lay in it, grotesque, like some obscure parody of Millais' painting of Ophelia that captured his attention.

The constable averted his eyes, keeping them studiously on Pitt's face.

'Thought we should report it to you, sir.'

Pitt looked down at the body reclining in the punt, its wrists encased in manacles chained to the wooden sides, its ankles apart, chained also. The long green robes looked like a dress, but so torn and distorted it was impossible to tell its original shape. The knees were apart, the head thrown back, mimicking ecstasy. It was a feminine pose, but the body was unmistakably male. He had been in his mid-thirties, fair-haired, with good features and a well-trimmed moustache.

'I don't know why,' Pitt said quickly as the water slurped against the steps below him, perhaps the wash from some passing boat invisible in the coils of mist. 'This is not Bow Street area.'

The constable shifted uncomfortably. 'Scandal, Mr Pitt.' He still did not look at the boat or its occupant. 'Could get very nasty, sir. Best you're in at the beginning.'

Very carefully, so as not to slip on the river-wet stone, Pitt went further down. The melancholy sound of a foghorn drifted across the water, and from some unseen cargo barge a man's voice called out a warning. The answer was lost in the cloying vapour. Pitt looked again at the figure lying in the punt. It was impossible from this angle to see how he had died. There was no apparent wound, no weapon, and yet if he had died of a heart attack, or a seizure, then someone else had certainly had a grotesque part in leaving his corpse in such a way. Some family was going to begin a nightmare today. Perhaps life would never be quite the same for them again.

'I suppose you've sent for the surgeon?' Pitt asked.

'Yes sir. Due any time now, I should think.' The constable swallowed and moved his feet, scraping his boots a little on the stone. 'Mr Pitt – sir.'

'Yes?' Pitt was still staring at the punt scraping its wooden prow on the steps and juggling a little with the wash of another boat.

'Weren't only the way 'e is that I called yer.'

Pitt caught something in the man's voice and swivelled to look up. 'Oh?'

'No sir. I think as I might know 'oo 'e is, sir, which is goin' ter be very nasty, an' all.'

Pitt felt the river cold seep into him. 'Oh. Who do you think it is, Constable?'

'Sorry, sir. I think it might be a Monsewer Bonnard, 'oo was reported missing day afore yesterday, an' the French won't 'alf kick up a fuss if this is 'im.'

'The French?' Pitt said warily.

'Yes sir. Missing from their embassy, 'e is.'

'And you think this is him?'

'Looks like it, Mr Pitt. Slender, fair 'air, good-lookin', small moustache, about five feet nine inches tall, an' a gent. Eccentric, by all accounts. Likes a bit of a party, theatricals an' the like.' His voice was heaving with incomprehension and disgust. 'Mixes with them aesthetes, as they calls 'emselves . . .'

Pitt was saved further comment by the clatter of hooves and the rattle of wheels on the road above them, and a moment later the familiar figure of the police surgeon, top hat a trifle askew, came down the steps, bag in his hand. He looked beyond Pitt to the body in the punt, and his eyebrows rose.

'Another one of your scandals, Pitt?' he said drily. 'I don't envy you unravelling this one. Do you know who he is?' He let out a sigh as he reached the bottom step, standing precariously only a foot above the sucking water. 'Well, well. Didn't think there was much about human nature I didn't know, but I swear it's beyond me what some men will do to entertain themselves.' Very carefully he balanced his weight and moved over to stand in the punt. It rocked and pitched him forward, but he was ready for it. He kneeled down and started to examine the dead man.

Pitt found himself shivering, in spite of the fact that it was

3

not really cold. He had sent for his assistant, Sergeant Tellman, but he had not yet arrived. Pitt looked back at the constable.

'Who found this, and what time?'

'I found it meself, sir. This is my beat along 'ere. I were goin' ter sit on the steps an' 'ave a bite to eat when I saw it. That were about 'alf-past five, sir. But o' course it could 'a bin there a lot longer, cause in the dark no one'd 'ave seen it.'

'But you saw it? Dark then, wasn't it?'

'More like 'eard it, bumpin', an' went ter see what it was. Shone me light on it, an' near 'ad a fit! I don't understand the gentry, an' that's a fact.'

'You think he's gentry?' Pitt was vaguely amused in spite of himself.

The constable screwed up his face. 'Where'd a working bloke get fancy clothes like that dress? It's velvet. An' you look at 'is 'ands. Never done a day's work wi' them.'

Pitt thought there was a strong element of prejudice in the constable's deductions, but it was good observation. He told him so.

'Thank you, sir,' the constable said with pleasure. He had aims of being a detective one day.

'You had better go to the French Embassy and fetch someone to see if they can identify him,' Pitt went on.

'Who – me, sir?' The constable was taken aback.

Pitt smiled at him. 'Yes. After all, you were the one alert enough to see the likeness. But you can wait and see what the surgeon says first.'

There were a few moments' silence, then the punt rocked a little, scraping against the stone. 'He was hit on the head with something very hard and rounded, like a truncheon,' the surgeon said distinctly. 'And I very much doubt it was an accident. He

4

certainly didn't tie himself up like this.' He shook his head. 'God knows whether he put the clothes on, or someone else did. They're torn enough to indicate a struggle. Very difficult to do anything much with a dead body.'

Pitt had been expecting it, but it still came as a blow. Some part of him had been hoping it was an accident, which would be ugly and stupid, but not a crime. He also hoped profoundly it was not the missing French diplomat.

'You'd better see for yourself,' the surgeon offered. Pitt clambered inelegantly into the rocking punt and in the now clear, white light of sunrise, bent to examine the dead man carefully, detail by detail.

He was very clean and well-nourished but without any surplus flesh. He was a trifle flabby, fat on his limbs rather than muscle. His hands were fine and soft. He wore a gold signet ring on his left hand. There were no calluses, no marks of ink, but there was a fine scar on the first finger of the left hand, as if a knife or similar blade might have slipped in his grasp. His face was expressionless in death and it was hard to judge anything of his character. His hair was thick and finely barbered, far better than Pitt's had ever been. Unconsciously he put his hand up and pushed the fall of hair off his own brow. It fell back immediately. But then it was probably six inches longer than that of the man on his back in the punt.

Pitt looked up.

'Be diplomatic, Constable. You won't get the ambassador himself, but ask for a senior attaché, not a clerk. Just say we've found a body and would like his help in identifying it. There is some urgency.'

'Do I tell 'im it's murder, sir?'

'Not unless you have to, but don't lie. And for heaven's

sake don't tell him any of the details. This will have to be handled with some care.'

'Yes sir. You don't think, in view o' the . . . the dress, and the like, that mebbe Sergeant Tellman should go?' he asked hopefully.

Pitt knew Tellman very well. 'No, I don't,' he replied.

''E's 'ere!'

'Good. Send him down. And take a hansom to the French Embassy. Catch!' He tossed up a shilling for the fare. The constable caught it and thanked him, hesitating a moment longer in the vain hope that Pitt would change his mind, then reluctantly obeyed.

The mist was lifting off the river. Here and there water shone silver, and the dark shapes of barges were no longer softened and blurred, but sharp, mounded with bales of goods bound for all the corners of the earth. Up river on Chelsea Reach the parlour maids would be setting breakfast tables, valets and kitchen maids would be carrying bath-water and putting out clothes for the day. Down river all the way to the Isle of Dogs dockers and boatmen would be lifting, hauling, guiding. The first markets at Bishopsgate would have started hours ago.

Tellman came down the stairs, lantern jaw set, hair slicked back, his disgust written already in his expression.

Pitt turned back to the body and started to look more carefully at the extraordinary clothes the man was wearing. The green dress was torn in several places. It was impossible to tell if it had happened recently or not. The silk velvet of the bodice was ripped across the shoulders and down the seams of the arms. The flimsy skirt was torn up the front.

There were several garlands of artificial flowers strewn around. One of them sat askew across his chest.

Pitt looked at the manacle on the man's right wrist, and moved it slightly. There was no bruising or grazing on the skin. He examined the other wrist, and then both ankles. They also were unmarked.

'Did they kill him first?' he asked.

'Either that, or he put the manacles on willingly,' the surgeon replied. 'If a guess will do, I'd say after death.'

'And the clothes?'

'No idea. But if he put them on himself, he was pretty rough about it.'

'How long do you think he's been dead?' Pitt had little hope of a definite answer. He was not disappointed.

'No idea beyond what you can probably deduce for yourself. Some time last night, from the rigor. Can't have been floating around the river for long like this. Even a bargee would notice this is a little odd.'

He was right. Pitt had concluded it would have to have been after dark that the boat was floated out. There had been no mist on the river yesterday evening, and on a fine day, even up to dusk, there would be people out in pleasure boats, or strolling along the embankment.

'Any signs of struggle?' he asked.

'Nothing I can see so far.' The surgeon straightened up and made his way back to the steps. 'Nothing on his hands, but I dare say you saw that. Sorry, Pitt. I'll look at him more closely, of course, but so far you've got an ugly situation which I am only going to make even uglier, I imagine. Good day to you.' And without waiting for a reply, he climbed up the steps to the top of the Embankment where already a small crowd had gathered, peering curiously over the edge.

Tellman looked at the punt, his face puckered with

7

incomprehension and contempt. He pulled his jacket a little tighter around himself. 'French, is he?' he said darkly, his tone suggesting that that explained everything.

'Possibly,' Pitt answered. 'Poor devil. But whoever did this to him could be as English as you are.'

Tellman's head came up sharply and he glared at Pitt.

Pitt smiled back at him innocently.

Tellman's mouth tightened and he turned and looked up the river at the light flashing silver on the wide stretches clear of mist and the dark shadows of barges materialising from beyond. It was going to be a beautiful day. 'I'd better find the river police,' Tellman said grimly. 'See how far he would have drifted since he was put in.'

'Don't know when that was,' Pitt replied. 'There's very little blood here. Wound like that to the head must have bled quite a lot. Unless there was some kind of blanket or sail here which was removed after, or he was killed somewhere else, and then put here.'

'Dressed like that?' Tellman said incredulously. 'Some kind of a party, Chelsea sort of way? Some . . . thing . . . went too far, and they had to get rid of him? Heaven help us, this is going to be ugly!'

'It is,' Pitt agreed. 'But it would be a good idea to see the river police anyway, and get some idea how far he could have drifted if he went in around midnight, or an hour or two either side of it.'

'Yes sir,' Tellman said with alacrity. That was something he was willing to do, and was a great deal better than waiting around for anyone from the French Embassy. 'I'll find out everything I can.' And with an air of busyness he set off, taking the steps two at a time, at considerable risk, given the slipperiness of the wet stone.

Pitt returned his attention to the punt and its cargo. He examined the boat itself more closely. It was lying low in the water and he had not until then wondered why. Now he realised on handling and touching the wood that it was old and many of the outer boards were rotted and waterlogged. It had foundered against the stairs rather than simply caught against them. It was obviously not a pleasure boat which anyone currently used on the river, and would therefore miss. It must have lain idle somewhere for a considerable time.

Pitt looked again at the body with its manacled wrists and chained ankles, its grotesque position. An overriding passion had driven this murderer; a love, or hate, a terror or need, had made this disposition of the corpse as much part of his crime as the killing itself. It must have been a tremendous risk to wait long enough to take off whatever clothes the dead man was wearing, dress him in this torn silk and velvet gown and chain him on to the punt in this obscene position, then set the boat adrift out in the water, getting himself wet in the process. Why had anyone bothered?

The answer to that might be the answer to everything.

He stood in the faintly rocking stern, adjusting his balance to keep upright as the wash of a string of barges reached him. Had the murderer brought the green dress and the manacles and chains with him, and the artificial flowers cast around? Or had they already been to hand wherever he had killed? Certainly he had not brought the boat. That would have been impossible to move far.

Which also meant it had not come more than a few miles at most now.

His thoughts were interrupted by the noise of a carriage up

on the Embankment, horses' hooves on the stone, and footsteps to the top of the stairs.

He moved across to the bottom step, which was now slimy and well clear of the water as the tide receded. He looked up to see an immaculate and very anxious man, his polished boots gleaming in the early sun, his head bent, his face very pale.

'Good morning, sir,' Pitt said quietly, climbing up towards him.

'Good morning,' the man replied with scarcely the trace of an accent. 'Gaston Meissonier,' he introduced himself, deliberately keeping his eyes on Pitt's face and averted from the figure in the boat.

'Superintendent Pitt. I'm sorry to bring you out so early in the morning, Monsieur Meissonier,' Pitt replied, 'but your embassy reported one of your diplomats missing, and unfortunately we have found the body of a man who answers the description you gave us.'

Meissonier turned and stared at the punt. The skin across his face tightened, his lips drawn a little closer together. For several moments he did not speak.

Pitt waited.

The last mist was evaporating from the river and the far bank was now clearly visible. The sound of traffic increased along the Embankment above them.

'"Unfortunate" is hardly an adequate word, Superintendent,' Meissonier said at last. 'What an extremely distressing circumstance.'

Pitt stood aside and Meissonier came gingerly down the steps until he was only a couple of feet above the tide. He stopped and stared across at the body.

'That is not Bonnard,' he said fiercely. 'I am afraid I do not know this man. I cannot help you. I'm sorry.'

Pitt studied his face, reading not only the distaste but a certain tension that was not eased by his denial of recognition. He may not have been lying, but he was certainly not telling the entire truth.

'Are you sure, sir?' Pitt pressed.

Meissonier swivelled towards him. 'Yes, I am quite sure. The man does bear some resemblance to Bonnard, but it is not he. I had not really thought it would be, but I wished to be certain beyond doubt.' He drew in his breath. 'I am sorry you were misinformed. Bonnard is not missing, he is on leave. An overzealous junior has not read his instructions fully and leaped to a wrong conclusion. I must find who it was and admonish him for raising a false alarm and – as it has turned out – wasting your time.' He bowed courteously and turned to go back up the steps.

'Where has Monsieur Bonnard taken his leave, sir?' Pitt asked, raising his voice a little.

Meissonier stopped. 'I have no idea. We do not require such information from junior diplomats. He may have friends here in England, or have gone to visit a place of beauty or interest on his own, or, for all I know, he may have returned to Provence, to his own family.'

'But you came to look at the body,' Pitt persisted.

Meissonier raised his eyebrows a little, and not enough for sarcasm, just sufficient to indicate that the question was unnecessary.

'I wished to assure myself that he had not met with an accident while leaving for his holiday. It was unlikely, but not impossible. And of course I wished to be courteous to all officials of Her Majesty's Government, with whom we enjoy the most cordial relations, and whose guests we are.' It was a polite but unmistakable reminder of his diplomatic standing.

There was nothing Pitt could do but concede. 'Thank you, Monsieur Meissonier. It was most gracious of you to come, and at this hour. I am pleased it was not your countryman.' That at least was true. The last thing Pitt wished was an international scandal, and were the body that of a French diplomat, such a scandal would be almost impossible to avoid, although it would have been his unenviable task to try.

Meissonier gave the same little bow as before, and then climbed up the rest of the steps and disappeared. A moment later Pitt heard his carriage move away.

The mortuary wagon came and Pitt watched as the manacles were removed, and the body was lifted up and carried away for the surgeon to examine in more detail at the morgue.

Tellman returned with the river police, who took the punt to safeguard it. It would have to remain on the water, but moved somehow to sufficiently shallow a place that it did not sink altogether.

'Was it the Frenchie?' Tellman asked when he and Pitt were alone on the Embankment. The traffic was now heavy and moving in both directions past them. The wind had risen a little and carried the smell of salt and mud and fish, and although the day was bright, it was definitely chilly.

'He said not,' Pitt replied. He was hungry and longing for a hot cup of tea.

Tellman grunted. 'Well, he would, wouldn't he?' he said darkly. 'If he's lying, can we prove it? I mean if he's French, and he gets all the Embassy to cover for him, what can we do? We can hardly fetch all Paris over here to take a look!' He pulled his face into an expression of disgust.

Pitt had already had his own doubts. The thought was increasingly unpleasant.

'It'll be hard enough to find out who did this,' Tellman went on, 'without not knowing who he is either!'

'Well, he's either Bonnard, or he's someone else,' Pitt said drily. 'We'd better assume he's someone else, and start looking. The punt, in the state it is, won't have come more than a couple of miles down the river . . .'

'That's what the river police said,' Tellman agreed. 'Somewhere up Chelsea, they reckoned.' He wrinkled his nose. 'I still think it's the Frenchman, and they just don't want to say so.'

Pitt was not disposed to argue with Tellman's prejudices, at least not yet. Personally he would very much prefer it to be an Englishman. It was going to be ugly enough without working with a foreign embassy.

'You had better go with the river police and see the sorts of places the punt could have been kept within a mile or two of the Chelsea Reach. And see if by any extraordinary chance anyone saw it drifting . . .'

'In the dark?' Tellman said indignantly. 'In that mist? Anyway, barges passing up river, if here before dawn, will be way beyond the Pool by now.'

'I know that!' Pitt sighed sharply. 'Try the shore. Someone may know where the punt is usually moored. It's obviously been lying in water for some time.'

'Yes sir. Where'll I find you?'

'At the morgue.'

'Surgeon won't be ready yet! He's only just gone.'

'I'm going home for breakfast first.'

'Oh.'

Pitt smiled. 'You can get a cup of tea from the stall over there.'

Tellman gave him a sideways look, and went, back stiff, shoulders square.

Pitt unlocked his front door and went into a silent house. It was full daylight as he took his coat off and hung it in the hall, then his boots, leaving them behind him, and padded in his stocking feet along to the kitchen. The stove was about out. He would have to riddle it, carry out the dead ash, and nurture the last of the embers into flame again. He had seen Gracie do it often enough he should know the idiosyncrasies of this particular grate, but there was something peculiarly desolate about a kitchen without a woman busy in it. Mrs Brady came in every morning and attended to the heavy work, the laundry and ordinary house-cleaning. She was a good-hearted soul and quite often also brought him a pie or a nice piece of roast beef, but she would not make up for the absence of his family.

Charlotte had been invited to go to Paris with her sister, Emily, and Emily's husband, Jack. It was only for three weeks, and it had seemed to Pitt to have been mean-spirited for him to forbid her going, or to behave with enough resentment that it would effectively ruin her pleasure. In marrying a man so far beneath her own financial and social status she would have been the first to say she had gained enormously in freedom to become involved in all manner of pursuits impossible to ladies of her mother or sister's situation. But it also denied her many things, and Pitt was wise enough to realise that however much he missed her, or would like to have been the one to take her there, the greater happiness of both of them rested in his agreeing to her going with Emily and Jack.

14

Gracie, the maid who had been with them now for seven and a half years – in fact since she was thirteen – he considered almost as family. She had taken the children, Jemima and Daniel, to the seaside for a fortnight's holiday. They had all three of them been beside themselves with excitement, fervently packing boxes and chattering about everything they intended to see and to do. They had never been to the coast before, and it was an enormous adventure. Gracie felt her responsibility keenly and was very proud that she should be given it.

It left Pitt at home with no company except the two cats, Archie and Angus, now curled up together in the clothes basket where Mrs Brady had left the clean linen.

Pitt had grown up on a large country estate, and for some time his mother had worked in the kitchens of the big house. He was perfectly capable of looking after himself, although since his marriage he had lost the knack for it. He missed the comfort of all the small things Charlotte did for him, but these were nothing compared with the loneliness. There was no one to talk to, with whom to share his feelings, to laugh or simply to speak of the day.

And he missed the sound of the children's voices, giggling, their running footsteps, their incessant questions and demands for his attention or approval. No one interrupted him to say, 'Look at me, Papa' or, 'What is this for?' or, 'What does this mean?' or the favourite, 'Why?' Peace was not peace any more, it was simply silence.

It took over ten minutes for the stove to begin to draw properly, and another ten after that before the kettle boiled and he was able to make himself a pot of tea and toast some bread for breakfast. He considered frying a pair of kippers as well, and then thought of the fishy smell, and the trouble of washing

15

the dishes and the frying pan, and abandoned the idea.

The first post came, bringing only a bill from the butcher. He had been hoping there would be a letter from Charlotte. Perhaps it was too soon to expect one, but he was surprised how disappointed he was. Fortunately he was going to the theatre this evening, with his mother-in-law, Caroline Fielding. After Charlotte's father, Edward Ellison, had died, and a decent period of mourning had passed, Caroline had met and fallen in love with an actor, considerably younger than herself. She had scandalised Edward's mother, Mariah, by marrying again, and mortified her by being apparently very happy. She had also adopted a rather more liberal way of life, which was another point of conflict. Old Mrs Ellison had absolutely refused to live under the same roof with Caroline and her new husband. As a result she had been obliged to move in with Emily. But then Jack Radley was a Member of Parliament and eminently respectable compared to an actor, even if he had rather too much charm than was good for him, and no title, or breeding worth mentioning.

Emily suffered it with fortitude most of the time. Occasionally she was just as forthright back to the old lady, who then retreated into icy rage, until she got bored and sallied out for the next attack.

However, since Emily and Jack were in Paris, and taking the opportunity of their absence to have the plumbing in the house redone, Grandmother was once again staying with Caroline. Pitt hoped profoundly that she was not well enough to come to the theatre this evening. He had every cause to be optimistic. The sort of play that Caroline attended these days was not what old Mrs Ellison considered fit entertainment and, even consumed with curiosity as she might be, she would not allow herself to be seen there.

By late morning Pitt was at the morgue listening to the police surgeon summing up the very little of use he had found.

'Exactly what I said! Hit on the head with something round and heavy, wider than a poker, more regular than a branch from a tree.'

'What about an oar, or a punting pole?' Pitt asked.

'Possible.' The surgeon thought about it for a moment. 'Very possible. Have you got one?'

'We don't know where he was killed yet!' Pitt protested.

'Of course it might be floating in the river.' The surgeon shook his head. 'Probably never find it, or if you do all the blood will be long since washed off it. You may surmise but you won't prove anything.'

'When did he die?'

'Late last night, as near as I can tell.' He shrugged his thin shoulders. 'By the time I saw him he'd certainly been dead five or six hours. Of course when you find out who he is – if you do – then you may be able to narrow it down better than that.'

'What do you know about him?'

'Between thirty and thirty-five, I should say.' The surgeon considered carefully. 'Seemed in very good health. Very clean. No calluses on his hands, no dirt. No parts of his body exposed to the sun.' He pursed his lips. 'Certainly didn't work manually. He either had money of his own, or he did something with his mind rather than his hands. Or could be an artist of some sort, or even an actor.' He looked sideways at Pitt. 'Hope I'm not saying that because of the way the dratted fellow was found?' He sighed. 'Ridiculous!'

'Couldn't he have lain like that himself, and been struck where he was?' Pitt asked, although he knew the answer.

'No,' the surgeon said decisively. 'Blow struck him on the back of the head. Couldn't have been in the boat unless he was sitting up and he wasn't. Those manacles are too short. He couldn't sit up like that. If you don't believe me, try it! Not enough blood there anyway.'

'Are you sure he wasn't wearing that dress when he was killed?' Pitt pressed.

'Yes I am.'

'How can you tell?'

'Because there are no bruises on him from having been held or forced,' the surgeon explained patiently. 'But there are tiny scratches, as if someone had caught him with a fingernail while trying to force the dress over his head and get it straight on his body. It's damned difficult to dress a dead body, especially if you're trying to do it by yourself.'

'It was one person?' Pitt said quietly.

The surgeon drew in his breath between his teeth. 'You are right,' he conceded. 'I was making assumptions. I simply cannot imagine this sort of . . . lunacy . . . being a dual affair. There is something essentially solitary about obsession – and obsessive, dear God, this is, if anything in the world is. I suppose some alternative is conceivable, but you'll have to prove it to me before I'll believe it. In my opinion one solitary man did this because of a perverse passion, a love or a hatred so strong that it broke all the bounds of sense, even of self-preservation, and not only did he strike that man and kill him, he then was compelled to dress him like a woman and set him adrift on the river.' He swivelled to look at Pitt sharply. 'I can't think of any sane reason for doing that. Can you?'

'It obscures his identity . . .' Pitt said thoughtfully.

'Rubbish!' the surgeon snapped. 'Could have taken his own clothes off and wrapped him in a blanket to do that! Certainly didn't have to set him out like the Lady of Shalott – or Ophelia, or whoever it is.'

'Didn't Ophelia drown herself?' Pitt asked.

'All right – Lady of Shalott then,' the surgeon snapped. 'She was stricken by a curse. Does that suit you better?'

Pitt smiled wryly. 'I'm looking for something human. I don't suppose you can tell if he was French, can you?'

The surgeon's eyes opened very wide. 'No – I cannot! What do you expect – "Made in France" on the soles of his feet?'

Pitt pushed his hands into his pockets. He felt self-conscious now for having asked. 'Signs of travel, illnesses, past surgery . . . I don't know.'

The surgeon shook his head. 'Nothing helpful. Teeth are excellent, one small scratch on the finger, just an ordinary dead man wearing a green dress and chains. Sorry.'

Pitt gave him a long, level stare, then thanked him and left.

Early afternoon found Pitt at the French Embassy – after he had eaten a sandwich in a public house, with a pint of cider. He did not wish to see Meissonier again. He would only repeat what he had said at Horseferry Stairs, but Pitt was not convinced that the man in the boat was not the diplomat Bonnard. So far it was the only suggestion he had, and Meissonier had been acutely uncomfortable. There had been relief in his face when he had seen the body more closely, but his anxiety had not vanished altogether. Had it been only because there was nothing that could be traced to him, and he was free to deny it was Bonnard?

How could Pitt now question anyone else at the embassy?

He would appear to be calling Meissonier a liar, which considering he was a foreign diplomat – a guest in England, as he had pointed out – would be sufficient to cause an unpleasant incident for which Pitt would rightly get the blame.

The answer was that he must find some other excuse to call. But what could that be? Meissonier had denied all connection with the corpse. There could be no further questions to ask him.

He was already at the door. He must either knock, or continue along the street. He knocked.

It was opened by a footman in full livery.

'Yes sir?'

'Good afternoon,' Pitt said hastily. He produced a card and handed it to the footman, speaking at the same time. 'One of your diplomats was reported missing, I now believe in error, according to Monsieur Meissonier. However, before I alter the police record I should like to speak to the person who made the original report. It would look better if he were the person to withdraw it. Tidier . . .'

'Indeed? Who would that be, sir?' The footman's expression did not change in the slightest.

'I don't know.' He had only just thought of the excuse. He should have asked the constable at Horseferry Stairs, but it had not mattered then. 'The gentleman reported missing is Monsieur Bonnard. I imagine it would be whoever he works with, or is his friend.'

'That will be Monsieur Villeroche, I dare say, sir. If you care to take a seat I shall ask when he is able to see you.' And he indicated several hard-backed leather benches, and left Pitt to make himself if not comfortable, at least discreet.

The footman returned within minutes.

'Monsieur Villeroche will see you in a quarter of an hour, sir. He is presently engaged.' He said no more, and left Pitt to make up his own mind if he wished to wait.

As it turned out Monsieur Villeroche must have finished with his visitor earlier than expected. He came out into the hallway himself to find Pitt. He was a dark, good-looking young man dressed with great elegance, but at the moment he was obviously perturbed. He looked in both directions before approaching Pitt.

'Inspector Pitt? Good. I have a small errand to run. Perhaps you would not mind walking with me? Thank you so much.' He did not give Pitt time to refuse. He ignored the footman and went to the door, leaving Pitt to follow behind. 'Most civil of you,' he said as he stepped outside.

Pitt was obliged to walk smartly to keep up with him until they were round the corner of the next street where Villeroche stopped abruptly.

'I . . . I'm sorry.' He spread his hands in a gesture of apology. 'I did not wish to speak where I might be overheard. The matter is . . . delicate. I do not mean to cause embarrassment for anyone, but I am concerned . . .' He stopped again, uncertain how to continue.

Pitt had no idea whether he knew of the body at Horseferry Stairs or not. The midday newspapers had carried it, but possibly none of them had reached the embassy. It would not appear to be a matter to concern France.

Villeroche lost patience with himself. 'I apologise, Monsieur. I reported to your excellent police that my friend and colleague Henri Bonnard has disappeared . . . that is to say he is not where we would expect to find him. He is not at his work, he is not at his apartment. None of his friends have seen him in several days, and he has missed appointments of business as well as social functions at which he was expected.' He shook his head quickly. 'That is most unlike him! He does not do these things! I fear for his welfare.'

'So you reported him missing,' Pitt concluded. 'Monsieur Meissonier has told us that he is on leave. Is it possible he went without the courtesy of informing you?'

'Possible, of course,' Villeroche agreed, not taking his eyes from Pitt's face. 'But he would not have missed his duties. He is an ambitious man who values his career, at least . . . at least he would not jeopardise it for a trivial matter. He might . . . er . . .' He was obviously at a loss how to explain himself without saying more than he intended, and driven to speak at all only by the most acute anxiety.

'What sort of man is he?' Pitt asked. 'What does he look like? What are his habits, his pastimes? Where does he live? What parties were these that he missed?' His mind pictured the man in the punt and the extraordinary green velvet dress. 'Does he enjoy the theatre?'

Villeroche was patently uncomfortable. His gaze did not waver from Pitt's, as if he willed him to understand without the necessity of words.

'Yes, he was fond of . . . of . . . entertainment. Perhaps not always . . . what His Excellency the Ambassador would have best approved. Not that he is . . .'

Pitt rescued him. 'Did you hear that we found the body of a man in a boat in the river this morning, at Horseferry Stairs? He answers the description of Henri Bonnard. Monsieur Meissonier was good enough to come to look at it, and he said it was not he. He seemed quite certain. But he also said Monsieur Bonnard was on leave.'

Villeroche looked wretched. 'I had not heard it. I am most sorry. I do hope . . . I profoundly hope it is not Henri, but I am equally sure that he is not on leave.' His eyes were still steady on Pitt's face. 'He had an invitation to attend a play by Oscar Wilde, and to dine with Monsieur Wilde and his friends afterwards. He did not go. That is not a thing he would do without the most abject apology and an explanation to satisfy an examining magistrate, let alone a playwright!'

Pitt felt a sinking in his stomach.

'Would you like to go to the morgue and see if this man is Bonnard, and be certain in your own mind?' he offered.

'The morgue!'

'Yes. It is the only way you will satisfy yourself.'

'I . . . I suppose it is necessary?'

'Not to me. Monsieur Meissonier has said Bonnard is not missing. I have to accept that. Therefore it cannot be him.'

'Of course. I will come. How long will it take?'

'In a hansom we can be there and back in less than an hour.'

'Very well. Let us make haste.'

Ashen-faced and deeply unhappy, Villeroche stared at the face of the dead man, and said it was not Henri Bonnard.

'It is most like him.' He coughed and held his handkerchief to his face. 'But I do not know this man. I am sorry for having taken your time. You have been most civil. Please, in no circumstances, mention to Monsieur Meissonier, or anyone else, that I came here.' And he turned and all but ran out of the morgue and scrambled up into the hansom again, directing it back to the embassy so hastily Pitt had to jump after him not to be left on the pavement.

'Where does Bonnard live?' he asked, flinging himself into

the seat as the cab pulled away.

'He has rooms in Portman Square,' Villeroche replied. 'But he isn't there . . .'

'More precisely?' Pitt persisted. 'And names of one or two other friends or associates who might know more?'

'Second floor of number fourteen. And I suppose you could ask Charles Renaud, or Jean-Claud Aubusson. I'll give you their addresses. They . . . they don't work at the embassy. And of course there are Englishmen also. There is George Strickland, and Mr O'Halloran.' He fumbled in his pocket but did not find what he wanted.

Pitt habitually carried all sorts of things. It had been the despair of his superiors when they saw him more frequently, and even now Commissioner Cornwallis, who had been in the Navy before taking up his present appointment, found Pitt's untidiness hard to tolerate. Pitt pulled out string, a pocket knife, sealing wax, a pencil, three shillings and sevenpence in coins, two used French postage stamps he was saving for Daniel, a receipt for a pair of socks, a note to remind himself to get his boots mended and buy some butter, two boiled humbugs covered in fluff, and a small pad of paper. He handed the pencil and paper to Villeroche, and put the rest back.

Villeroche wrote the names and addresses for him, and when they reached the corner nearest the embassy, stopped the cab, said goodbye and then ran across the road and disappeared up the steps.

Pitt called upon all of the men Villeroche had named. He found two of them at home and willing to talk to him.

'Ah, but he's a fine man,' O'Halloran said with a smile. 'But I haven't seen him in a week or more, which is surely a shame. I expected him at Wylie's party last Saturday night, and

I would have bet my shirt he'd have been at the theatre on Monday. Wilde was there himself, and what a night we had of it, for sure.' He shrugged. 'Not that I'd swear I can remember everything of it myself, mind!'

'But Henri Bonnard was not there?' Pitt pressed him.

'That I do know,' O'Halloran said with certainty. He looked at Pitt narrowly out of vivid blue eyes. 'Police, you said you are? Is there something wrong? Why for are you wanting Bonnard?'

'Because at least one of his other friends believes he is missing,' Pitt replied.

'And they're sending a superintendent to look for him?' O'Halloran asked wryly.

'No. There was a body found in the Thames at Horseferry Stairs this morning. There was a question it might be he, but two men from the French Embassy have both said it is not.'

'Thank God for that!' O'Halloran said with feeling. 'Although it's some poor devil. Surely you don't think Bonnard is responsible? Can't imagine it. Harmless sort of fellow, he is. A bit wild in his tastes, maybe, all for enjoying himself, but no malice in him, none at all.'

'That was never in question,' Pitt assured him.

O'Halloran relaxed, but he could say nothing more of use, and Pitt thanked him and left.

The other person willing to see him was Charles Renaud.

'Actually I rather assumed he'd gone to Paris,' he said with surprise. 'I seem to remember him saying something about having to pack, and he mentioned the time the Dover train left. It was all rather in passing, you know? I made the assumption. I'm afraid I wasn't especially interested. I'm sorry.'

* * *

Tellman went to the river police eagerly, not because he had any great fondness for them, but questioning about tides and hours was infinitely preferable to trying to extract embarrassing truths from foreigners who were protected by diplomatic immunity. What the man in the punt had been doing that provoked his murder it was beyond Tellman's power, or desire, even to guess. Tellman had seen a great deal of the sordid and tragic sides of life. He had grown up in extreme poverty, and knew crime and both the need and the viciousness which drove it. But there were things some so-called gentlemen did, especially those connected with the theatre, which no decent person should have a guess at, far less observe.

Men who wore green velvet dresses were among them. Tellman had been brought up to believe there were two sorts of women: good women, such as wives, mothers and aunts, who did not show passions, and probably did not have them; and the sort who did publicly and embarrassingly. A man who would dress up as the second was beyond his comprehension.

Thinking of women, and love, brought Gracie to his mind. Without intending to, he could see her bright little face, the angle of her shoulders, the quick way she moved. She was tiny – all her dresses had to be taken up – and too thin for most men's tastes, with not much shape to her, no more than a suggestion. He hadn't thought he liked women like that himself. She was all spirit and mind, a sharp tongue, all courage and wit.

Tellman had no idea what she really thought of him. He sat on the omnibus going along the Embankment and remembered with curiously painful loneliness how her eyes had shone when she spoke of that Irish valet at Ashworth Hall. He did not want to name the pain inside him. It was something he preferred not to recognise.

He would point his mind to what he should ask the river police about tides, and where the boat must have started, in order to finish at Horseferry Stairs by dawn.

Tellman reported his findings to Pitt in the late afternoon, at his home in Keppel Street. It was warm and clean, but it seemed very empty without the women in the kitchen, or busying about upstairs. There were no children's voices, no light, quick feet, no one singing to themselves. He even missed Gracie's orders, telling him to watch his boots, not to bump anything or make a mess.

He sat across the kitchen table from Pitt, sipping at his tea and feeling strangely empty.

'Well?' Pitt prompted.

'Not very helpful, actually,' Tellman answered. There was no home-made cake, only a tin of bought biscuits. It was not nearly the same. 'Low water was at three minutes past five at London Bridge, and it gets later the higher you go up the river. Like it would be near quarter-past six up at Battersea.'

'And high tide?' Pitt asked.

'Quarter-past eleven last night at London Bridge.'

'And an hour and ten minutes later at Battersea . . .'

'No . . . that's the thing. Only twenty minutes, more like twenty-five to midnight.'

'And the rate of flow? How far would the punt have drifted?'

'That's the other thing,' Tellman explained. 'The ebb tide takes six and three-quarter hours, near enough. The flood tide takes only five and a quarter. River police bloke reckoned the punt could go as much as two and a half miles an hour, but on the other hand, on ebb tide there are mud shoals and sand banks it could get stuck on . . .'

'But it didn't,' Pitt pointed out. 'If it had, it wouldn't have come off till the flood again.'

'Or it could have got caught up by passing barges in the dark, or anything else,' Tellman went on. 'Caught on the piles of a bridge and then loosed again if something bumped into it . . . a dozen things. All they can say for sure is that it most likely came from up river, because no one'd carry that extra weight against the tide, and there's no place likely anyone'd keep a boat like that, which is a private sort of pleasure boat, down river from Horseferry Stairs. It's all city, docks and the like.'

Pitt remained silent for several minutes, thinking it over.

'I see,' he said at length. 'So time and tide don't really help at all. It could have been as far as eleven or twelve miles, at the outside, and as close as one mile, or wherever the nearest house is with an edge on the water. Or even nearer, if anyone kept that punt moored in the open. It'll just be a matter of questioning.'

'It would help to find out who he is!' Tellman pointed out. 'I still think it could be that French fellow, and they're embarrassed to say so. I'd disown him if any Englishman did that in France!'

Pitt looked at him with a faint smile. 'I found a friend of his who thought he had gone to Dover, on the way to Paris. I'd like to know if that's true.'

'Across the Channel?' Tellman said with mixed feelings. He was not very keen on the idea of foreign travel, but on the other hand it would be quite an adventure to go in a packet boat or a steamer, over to Calais, and then perhaps even to

Paris itself. That would be something to tell Gracie! 'I'd better find out if he did,' he said hopefully. 'If he isn't the body, he might be the one who killed him!'

'If it isn't him, there's no reason to suppose he has anything to do with it,' Pitt pointed out. 'But you are right, we need to know whose body it is. We've got nothing else.'

Tellman stood up. 'So I'll go to Dover, sir. Shipping company ought to know whether he went over to France or not. I'll go and find out.'

Chapter Two

The last post arrived just as Tellman left, and Pitt felt a surge of excitement as he recognised Charlotte's handwriting on a thick envelope addressed to him. He ignored the others and went back to the kitchen, tearing hers open and pulling out six or seven sheets of notepaper as he went. He sat down at the table and read.

My dearest Thomas,

I spent the whole of the train journey to Dover swapping the latest news and gossip with Emily, and poor Jack was so bored with us he read his political papers. Dover, of course, was much like any other town, as far as I can remember. I admit I spent most of my time worrying about baggage and whether we would be in the right place at the right time.

However it was all excellently arranged, and we had a very uneventful crossing to Calais. I was very pleased that the weather was calm, and I was not adversely affected in the slightest. But I am not sure sailing would be my choice! It was chilly, even in the sun.

The journey from Calais to Paris was more steam and

31

noise and not at all unlike any English train journey, except that everyone spoke French, of course. I used to study it in the schoolroom at home, but I have forgotten so much! I hope it will return to me over the next few days.

Paris is marvellous. What a beautiful city! I miss you, but I am enjoying myself. There is simply so much to see, to listen to, to learn. I have never been in a place so buzzing with life and ideas. Even the posters on the walls are by real artists, and quite different from anything in London. They have such a flair they invite interest straight away – even if it might not be of a kind one would be willing to own.

The streets, or should I say 'boulevards', for they are all relatively new and very wide and grand, are lined with oceans of trees. Light dances on fountains in all directions. 'Or blew the silver down-baths of her dreams/To sow futurity with seeds of thought/And count the passage of her festive hours'. Elizabeth Barrett Browning said it so well.

Everyone I see seems to be filled with a kind of excitement.

Jack plans to take us to the theatre, but one hardly knows where to begin. There are over twenty in the city, so we are told, and of course that does not include the opera. I should love to see Sarah Bernhardt in something – anything at all. I hear she has even played Hamlet! Or intends to. One knows she is unique. If she is on the stage, one can look at nobody else.

Actually what I think might be even more fun, if Jack will allow it, would be to go to a café concert, where everyone sits around drinking and talking, and then there is entertainment. It is a very Parisian thing, and I believe some of it is terribly daring and controversial. One may see all sorts of people there, famous, very modern artists. I have heard Monet, Renoir and Cézanne mentioned, to name but a few, and politicians, society gentlemen and *demi-mondaines* ladies of uncertain reputation but great wit, and in most cases, beauty and flair. I should love to observe them!

Our host and hostess here are very charming and do everything to make us welcome. But I do miss my own house. Here they have no idea how to make a decent cup of tea, and chocolate first thing in the morning is horrible!

Some things are so different, and others so much the same. There is great talk about a young man who is on trial for murder. He swears he was elsewhere at the time, and could prove it, if only the friend he was with would come forward. No one believes him. But the thing which is interesting is that he says he was at the Moulin Rouge! That is a famous, or perhaps notorious, dance hall. It is in the Boulevard de Clichy at the foot of Montmartre. I asked Madame about it, but she seemed rather scandalised, so I did not pursue the matter. A very strange artist called Henri Toulouse-Lautrec paints wonderful posters for it. I saw one when we were out on the street yesterday. It was rather vulgar, but so full of life I had to look. I felt as if I could hear the music just by seeing it. He may not be nice, but he is extremely clever.

Today we went for a trip on the river. Thomas, it is the most exquisite city! There is a grace, an elegance to it which is quite wonderful. I love you for being so generous in allowing me to come, and without casting the least shadow over it. I look forward the more to telling you about it face to face when I come home.

Tomorrow we go to see M. Eiffel's tower, which is enormous, and I am not at all sure if I like it. I saw it from the river today, and it seemed quite out of place to me. Perhaps I shall think differently if I see it closer to? I must be very conservative! Who would have thought I would ever say such a thing? Actually, I believe there is a water closet at the very top, whose windows would have the very best view in Paris – could one see out of them!

I miss you all, and realise how much I love you, because you are not here with me. When I come home I shall be so devoted, obedient and charming – for at least a week!

    Yours always,
     Charlotte

Pitt sat with the paper in his hand, smiling. Reading her words, written enthusiastically, scrawled across the page, was almost like hearing her voice. Again he was reminded how right he had been to let her go with grace, rather than grudgingly. It was only for three weeks. Every day of it dragged, but it would come to an end. Then he realised with a start that the time today was actually flying by on wings, and he needed to prepare to go out to the theatre with Caroline. He folded up Charlotte's letter and slid it back in the envelope, put it in his jacket pocket and went upstairs to wash and change into the only evening suit he possessed. It was something he had been obliged to purchase when going to stay, on police duty, at Emily's country home.

He worked hard at looking tidy and sufficiently respectable not to embarrass his mother-in-law. He was fond of Caroline, quite apart from their family relationship. He admired her courage in seizing her happiness with Joshua regardless of the social risks involved. Charlotte had done the same in marrying him, and he did not delude himself that the costs were not real.

He surveyed himself in the glass. The reflection he saw was not entirely satisfactory. His face was intelligent and individual rather than handsome. No matter what he did with his hair it was always unruly. Of course a good barber could have cut two or three inches off it and helped a lot, but short hair made him uncomfortable, and he somehow never remembered to make time. His shirt collar was straight, for a change, if a little high, and its dazzling white was becoming to him. He would have to do.

He walked briskly to Bedford Square and caught a cab to the theatre in Shaftesbury Avenue. The street was milling with people, the sombre black and white of gentlemen, the brilliant colours of women, the glitter of jewels. Laughter mixed with the sound of hooves and the rattle of harness as carriages fought for room to move. The gaslight was bright and the theatre front had huge posters advertising the performance, the leading actress's name above the title of the play. Neither meant anything to Pitt, but he could not help being infected by the excitement. It was sharp and brittle in the air, like moonlight on a frosty night.

Everyone was surging forward, all pressing to get inside, to see and to be seen, call to people they knew, take their seats, anticipate the drama.

Pitt found Caroline and Joshua in the foyer. They saw him, perhaps because of his height, before he saw them. He heard Joshua's voice, clear and carrying, with the perfect diction of an actor.

'Thomas! Over to your left, by the pillar!'

Pitt turned and saw him immediately. Joshua Fielding had the sort of face perfectly designed for conveying emotion: mobile features, heavy-lidded, dark eyes, a mouth quick to humour, or as easily to tragedy. Now he was simply pleased to see a friend.

Beside him Caroline looked remarkably well. She had the same warm colouring as Charlotte, hair with auburn lights in it, touched with grey, the proud carriage of her head. Time had dealt kindly with her, but the mark of pain was there for anyone perceptive enough to see. She had not been unscathed by life, as Pitt knew very well.

He greeted them with real pleasure, and then followed them up the steps and around the long, curving corridor to the box which Joshua had reserved. It had an excellent view of the stage, quite uninterrupted by other people's heads, and they were at a broad angle so they could see everyone except in the wings on their own side.

Joshua held the chair for Caroline, then both men seated themselves.

Pitt told them of Charlotte's letter, omitting the part about the young man's trial and the question of visiting places like the Moulin Rouge.

'I hope she is not going to come home with radical ideas,' Caroline said with a smile.

'The whole world is changing,' Joshua replied. 'Ideas are in flux all the time. New generations want different things from

36

life and expect happiness in new ways.'

Caroline turned towards him, looking puzzled. 'Why do you say that?' she asked. 'You made odd remarks at breakfast also.'

'I am wondering if I should have told you more about tonight's play. Perhaps I should. It is very . . . avant-garde.' He looked a little rueful, his face gentle and apologetic in the shadows from the box curtains and the glare of the chandeliers.

'It's not by Mr Ibsen, is it?' Caroline asked uncertainly.

Joshua smiled widely. 'No, my dear, but it's just as controversial. Cecily Antrim would not play in something by an unknown author unless it was fairly radical, and espoused views she shared.' There was a warmth in his voice as he spoke and a humour in his eyes.

Pitt thought Caroline looked uncertain, even though she replied immediately, but before either of them could pursue the subject their attention was caught by people they knew in one of the boxes opposite.

Pitt settled back in his seat and watched the colour and excitement around him, the fashionable women parading, heads high, more conscious of each other than any of the men. It was not romance which motivated them, but rivalry. He thought of Charlotte, and imagined how well she would have read them and understood the finer nuances he could only observe. He would try to describe it to her when she came back, if she stopped talking long enough to listen.

The lights dimmed and a hush fell over the auditorium. Everyone straightened up and looked towards the stage.

The curtain rose on a domestic scene in a beautiful withdrawing room. There were half a dozen people present, but the spotlight caught only one of them. The rest seemed drab compared with the almost luminous quality she possessed. She was unusually tall and extremely slender, but there was a grace in her even when motionless. Her fair hair caught the light and the strong, clean bones of her face were ageless.

She spoke, and the drama began.

Pitt had expected to be entertained, perhaps as much by the occasion as by the play. That was not what happened. He found himself drawn in from the moment he saw Cecily Antrim. There was an emotional vitality in her which conveyed loneliness and a devastating sense of need, so that he ached for her. He became unaware of his own surroundings. For him reality was the withdrawing room on the stage. The people playing out their lives were of intense importance.

The character played by Cecily Antrim was married to an older man, upright, honest, but incapable of passion. He loved her, within his own limits, and he was loyal and possessive. Certainly he did not ignore her, and it would have been beyond his comprehension to betray her. Yet he was slowly killing something inside her which, as they watched, was beginning to fight for life.

There was another man, younger, with more fire and imagination, more hunger of the soul. From the time they met their mutual attraction was inevitable. That issue was not what the playwright wished to explore, nor what would occupy the vast majority of the audience. The question was what would each of the characters do about it. The husband, the wife, the young man, his fiancée, her parents – all had fears and beliefs which governed their reactions, inhibitions which distorted the truth they might otherwise have spoken, expectations taught them by their lives and their society. Above all, was there any avenue of escape for the wife, who could not institute divorce, as could the husband, had their rites been reversed?

As Pitt watched he found himself reconsidering his own assumptions about men and women, what each expected of the other, and of the happiness marriage might afford, or deny. He had expected passion and fulfilment, and he had found it. Of course there were times of loneliness, misunderstanding, exasperation, but on the whole he could only feel a deep and abiding happiness. But how many others felt the same? Was it something one had the right to expect?

More urgently and far more painfully, had any man the right to expect the loyalty to conceal and endure his inadequacies that the character on stage demanded of his wife? The audience were intensely aware of her loneliness, of the weight of his inability which was crushing her, but no one else was, except the young lover, and he understood only a part of it. The flame that burned within her was too great for him also. In the end one feared he, too, would be charred by it.

The wife had duties towards the husband, physical duties on the rare occasions he wished, duties of obedience, tact, domestic responsibility, and always to behave with discretion and decorum.

Legally he had no such duties towards her – what about morally? Unquestionably to provide her with a home, to be sober and honest, to take his pleasures, whatever they may be, with a corresponding discretion. But had he a duty of physical passion? Or was the need for it unbecoming in a decent woman? If he had given her children, should that be enough?

Cecily Antrim, in every movement of her body, inflexion of her voice, showed that it was not enough. She was dying of an inner loneliness which consumed her being. Was she unreasonable, overdemanding, selfish, even indecent? Or was she only voicing what a million other silent women might feel?

It was a disquieting thought. As the curtains drew closed and the lights blazed up again, Pitt turned to look at Caroline.

Caroline herself was as deeply disturbed by the first act of the play as Pitt had been, but in different ways. It was not the questions of hunger and loyalty which disturbed her most, at least it was not the answer to them, it was the fact that they should be raised at all! Such matters were intensely private. They were the thoughts one had alone, in darker moments of confusion and self-doubt, and dismissed when common sense prevailed.

She did not even look across at Joshua, embarrassed to meet his eyes. Nor did she wish to look at Pitt. In showing her emotions so nakedly on the stage, Cecily Antrim had, in a very real sense, stripped the decent clothes of modesty and silence from all women. Caroline could not forgive her easily for that.

'Brilliant!' Joshua's voice came softly beside her. 'I've never seen anyone else who could combine such a delicacy of touch with such power of feeling. Don't you think so?'

Caroline felt the movement as he looked towards her.

'She is extraordinary,' she answered with honesty. She never doubted for an instant that he was referring to Cecily Antrim. No one in the entire theatre would have needed assurance on that. She hoped her voice had not sounded as cool as she felt. He had made no secret of how profoundly he admired Cecily. Caroline wondered now if the regard was personal as well as professional. It brushed by her with a coldness she preferred to dismiss.

'I knew you would love her,' Joshua went on. 'She has a moral courage which is almost unique. Nothing deters her from fighting for her beliefs.'

Caroline made herself smile. She refused to ask what those beliefs were. After watching the first act of the play, she greatly preferred not to know.

'You are quite right,' she said with as much enthusiasm as she could manage. She was no actress at all. 'I always admire courage . . . more than almost any other quality . . . except perhaps kindness.'

Joshua's reply was cut short by a knock at the door of the box. He stood up to reply, and a moment later a man in his late forties came in, tall and slim with a mild, rather austere face. The woman beside him was almost beautiful. Her features were regular, her eyes wide, deep-set and very blue. There was perhaps a lack of humour in her which robbed her of the final magic.

They were a Mr and Mrs Marchand. Caroline had known them for over a year and enjoyed their company on many occasions. She was pleased they had called. Without question they would feel as she did regarding the play. In fact she was surprised they had come to see it. Like her, they could not have known its content.

Their first remarks after being introduced to Pitt proved her correct.

'Extraordinary!' Rafe Marchand said quietly, his face reflecting his puzzlement. He avoided Caroline's eyes, as if he had not yet overcome his embarrassment at the subject, and could not easily discuss it in a woman's company.

Joshua offered Mrs Marchand his seat and she accepted it, thanking him.

'Remarkable woman,' Mr Marchand went on, obviously referring to Cecily Antrim. 'I realise, of course, that she is merely acting what the playwright has written, but I am sorry a woman of such talent should lend herself to this. And frankly I am surprised that the Lord Chamberlain permitted it a licence to be performed!'

Joshua leaned gracefully against the wall near the edge of the red, plush-padded balcony, his hands in his pockets. 'Actually I should be very surprised if she didn't have considerable sympathy with the character,' he replied. 'I think it was a part she chose to play.'

Mr Marchand looked surprised, and Caroline thought also disappointed.

'Really? Oh . . .'

'I cannot understand the Lord Chamberlain either,' Mrs Marchand said sadly, her blue eyes very wide. 'He is lacking in his duties that he has not exercised his power to censor it. He is supposed to be there for our protection! That, after all, is his purpose, isn't it?'

'Of course it is, my dear,' her husband assured her. 'It seems he does not appreciate the harm his laxity is doing.'

Caroline glanced at Joshua. She knew his views on censorship and she was afraid he would say something which would offend the Marchands, but she did not know how to prevent it without in turn hurting him. 'It is a difficult decision,' she said tentatively.

'It may require courage,' Mrs Marchand replied without hesitation. 'But if he accepts the office then we have the right to expect that much of him.'

Caroline could understand exactly what she meant. She knew instinctively her concerns, and yet she was equally sure Joshua would not. She was surprised how moderate his answer was when he spoke.

'Protection is a double-edged sword, Mrs Marchand.' He did not move his relaxed position against the corner of the balcony, but Caroline could see the more angular lines of his body as his muscles tensed.

Mrs Marchand looked at him guardedly. 'Double-edged?' she enquired.

'What is it you would like to be protected from?' Joshua kept his voice level and gentle.

Mr Marchand moved his position slightly, only a changing of weight.

'From the corruption of decency,' Mrs Marchand replied, anger and certainty ringing in her tone. Unconsciously she put her hand towards her husband. 'From the steady destruction of our way of life by the praising of immorality and selfishness. The teaching of young and impressionable people that self-indulgence is acceptable, even good. The exhibiting in public of emotions and practices which should remain private. It cheapens and demeans that which should be sacred . . .'

Caroline knew what she meant and she more than half agreed with her. The Marchands had a young son, about fifteen or sixteen years old. Caroline could remember when her daughters were that age, and how hard she had worked to guide and protect them. It had been less difficult then.

She looked at Joshua, knowing he would disagree. But then he had never had children, and that made the world of difference. He had no one to protect in that passionate way that demanded all commitment.

'Is self-denial better than self-indulgence?' Joshua questioned.

43

Mrs Marchand's dark eyebrows rose. 'Of course it is. How can you need to ask?'

'But is not one person's self-denial only the reverse side, the permission, if you like, for another's self-indulgence?' he asked. He leaned forward a little. 'Take the play, for example. When the wife denied herself, was she not making it possible for the husband to delude and indulge himself?'

'I . . .' Mrs Marchand began, then stopped. She was convinced she was right, but not sure how to explain it.

Caroline knew what she meant. The husband's suffering was public, his wife's had been private, one of the many things one did not speak of.

'She is disloyal,' Mr Marchand said for her. His voice was not raised in the slightest, but there was a ring of unshakeable conviction in it. 'Disloyalty can never be right. We should not portray it as such and seek sympathy for it. To do so confuses people who may be uncertain. Women may be led to feel that the wife's behaviour is excusable.'

The smile stayed fixed on Joshua's face. 'And on the other hand, men may be led to question if perhaps their wives have as much need, even right, to happiness as they have,' he countered. 'They may even realise that life would be better for both of them if they were to understand that women cannot be married and then safely considered to be purchased, for use when desired, like a carpet sweeper or a clothes mangle.'

Mr Marchand looked confused. 'A what?'

'A clothes mangle,' Joshua replied with a sudden shift to lightness. 'A machine for wringing the excess water out of laundry.'

'I have no idea what you mean!' Marchand looked at Caroline.

But it was Pitt who interpreted for him. 'I think what Mr Fielding is saying is that one person's protection may be another person's imprisonment; or one person's idea of freedom another's idea of licence,' he explained. 'If we refuse to look at anyone else's pain because it is different from ours, and makes us feel uncomfortable – or because it is the same, and embarrasses us – then we are neither a liberal nor a generous society, and we will slowly suffocate ourselves to death.'

'Good heavens!' Mr Marchand said softly. 'You are very radical, sir.'

'I thought I was rather conservative!' Pitt said with surprise. 'I found the play distinctly uncomfortable as well.'

'But do you think it should be suppressed?' Joshua said quickly.

Pitt hesitated. 'That's a harsh step to take . . .'

'It subverts decency and family life,' Mrs Marchand put in, leaning forward over her taffeta skirts, her hands folded.

'It questions values,' Joshua corrected. 'Must we never do that? Then how can we grow? We shall never learn anything or improve upon anything! Worse than that, we shall never understand other people, and perhaps not ourselves either.' His face was keen, the emotion naked now as he forgot his intended moderation. 'If we do that we are hardly worth the nobility of being human, of having intelligence, freedom of will or the power of judgement.'

Caroline could see the imminent possibility of the discussion becoming ugly and a friendship being lost.

'It is a matter of how they are questioned,' she said in haste.

Joshua regarded her seriously. 'The image that has the power to disturb is the only one that has the power to change. Growth is often painful, but not to grow is to begin to die.'

'Are you saying everything perishes sooner or later?' Mr Marchand asked him. He sounded almost casual, but there was a rigidity in his hands, in his body, which belied any ease. 'I don't believe that. I am sure there are values which are eternal.'

Joshua straightened up. 'Of course there are,' he agreed. 'It is a matter of understanding them, and that is more difficult. One must test the truth often, or it will become polluted by ignorance and misuse.' He smiled, but his eyes were steady. 'It's like the dusting in a good household. It has to be done every day.'

Hope Marchand looked puzzled. She glanced at Caroline, then away again.

Mr Marchand offered her his arm. 'I think it is time we returned to our seats, my dear. We don't wish to spoil other people's enjoyment by disturbing them when the performance has begun.' He turned to Caroline. 'So nice to see you again, Mrs Fielding.' Then to Pitt and to Joshua he added, 'And to meet you, Mr Pitt. I hope you enjoy the evening.' A moment later they were gone.

Caroline took a deep breath and let it out slowly.

Joshua grinned at her. It lit his face with warmth and laughter, and her fear evaporated. She wanted to warn him how close he had come to confusing and hurting people, to explain why they were afraid, but her anger evaporated, and instead she simply smiled back.

The lights dimmed and the curtain rose for the second act.

Caroline directed her attention to the stage where the drama continued to develop. It could only end in tragedy. The character played by Cecily Antrim hungered for more passion in life than the society in which she was could either give or understand.

She was trapped among people who were increasingly disturbed and frightened by her.

Her husband would not divorce her, and she had no power to divorce him, and no justification to leave. Even her misery was from no cause she could explain to anyone who did not share it.

Whether she could ever have behaved differently was a question not yet raised, but Caroline was asking herself this even while the scene was playing itself out in front of her. She did not wish to identify with Cecily Antrim. She was a creature of ungovernable emotions, wayward, indiscreet, allowing far too much of herself to be known, and in so doing betraying the inner thoughts of all women.

Caroline was angry for the sense of embarrassment. She wanted to turn away, as one does if accidentally intruding on someone in a private moment. One says nothing, and both parties pretend it did not happen. It was the only way to make civilised living possible. There are things one does not see, words one does not voice, and if they slip out in a moment of heat, they are never repeated. Secrets are necessary.

And here was this actress stripping the coverings of discretion from her very soul and showing the need and the pain, the laughter and the vulnerability to everyone with the price of a ticket to watch.

The character of the husband was well acted, but he was there to be torn apart, to evoke anger and frustration, and in the end Caroline knew it would be pity as well.

The fiancée also evoked a certain compassion. She was an ordinary girl who could not begin to fight against the woman, all but twice her age, whose subtlety and fire swept away the man she thought she had won. The audience knew the battle for him was lost before the first blow was struck.

The fiancée's brother was more interesting, not as a character in the play, but because the actor who portrayed him had a remarkable presence, even in so relatively minor a part. He was tall and fair. It was difficult to tell his real age, but it must have been no more than twenty-five. He had a sensitivity which came across the footlights, an emotion one was aware of even though he gave it few words. It was an inner energy, something of the mind. He in no sense played to the gallery, but there can have been few in the audience who would not remember him afterwards.

When the second act ended and the lights went up again Caroline did not look at Joshua or Pitt. She did not want to know what they had thought or felt about it, but more than that, she did not wish to betray her own feelings, and she was afraid they would be too readable in her eyes.

There was a knock on the door of the box again, and Joshua went to open it.

Outside was one of Joshua's fellow actors whom Caroline knew slightly, a man named Charles Leigh. Beside him stood a second man of completely different countenance, taller, a little heavier. There was an intelligence in his face and a humour which lit his eyes even before he spoke, but it was his resemblance to her first husband which for a moment made the breath catch in her throat.

'I should like you to meet my visitor from America, Samuel Ellison. Mr and Mrs Fielding, and . . .' Leigh began.

'Mr Pitt,' Joshua supplied. 'How do you do?'

'How do you do, sir?' Samuel Ellison replied, bowing very slightly, glancing at the others, but his eyes resting on Caroline. 'Pardon me for the intrusion, ma'am, but when Mr Leigh told me that you were named Ellison before you married Mr Fielding, I could not wait to meet you.'

'Indeed?' Caroline said uncertainly. It was ridiculous, but she felt a nervousness inside herself, almost alarm. This man was so like Edward she could not doubt some relationship. They were of a height, and their features were not at all unlike. The same longish nose, blue eyes, line of cheeks and jaw. She was uncertain what to say. The play had disoriented her until her usual composure had vanished.

He smiled widely. There was nothing overfamiliar in it. Only a most foolish person would have taken offence.

'I fear I am being much too forward, ma'am,' he apologised. 'You see I hoped we might be related. My mother left these shores a short while before I was born, a matter of weeks, and I heard my father had married again.'

Caroline knew what he would say. The resemblance was too remarkable to deny. But she had had no idea of any such person, still less that her father-in-law had had a wife prior to his marriage to Grandmama. Her thoughts whirled wildly – had the old lady herself known? Was this going to shatter her world – assuming Caroline told her?

A flicker of anxiety crossed Joshua's brow.

Samuel was still gazing at Caroline. 'My father was Edmund Ellison of King's Langley, in Hertfordshire . . .'

Caroline cleared her throat. 'My husband's father,' she answered. 'You must be . . . half-brothers.'

Samuel beamed with unaffected delight. 'How marvellous! Here am I come all the way from New York, to the biggest city in the world, and within a month I have run into you, and at the theatre of all places!' He glanced around him. 'Who is to say the hand of destiny is not in it? I am happy beyond words to

49

have found you, ma'am. I hope I may have the privilege of making your further acquaintance in due course, and that I shall conduct myself in such a manner that we may become friends. Relatives can become mighty tedious, but can any person in the world have too many friends?'

Caroline smiled in spite of herself. It was impossible not to warm to his enthusiasm. And mere good manners required that she make a courteous reply.

'I hope we shall, Mr Ellison. Are you planning to stay in London for some time?'

'I have no plans, ma'am,' he said airily. 'I am my own master, and shall do whatever I wish, as opportunities arise. So far I am having such an excellent time that I could not possibly think of leaving.' Again his eyes wandered around the crowded auditorium. 'I feel as if the whole world and all its ideas are here, and if I wait I shall see them all sooner or later.'

Caroline smiled. 'I have heard it said that if you stand in Piccadilly Circus long enough, everyone who is anyone will pass by.'

'I can believe it,' he agreed. 'But I should probably be arrested for loitering. I had far rather go out and look for people than wait for them to come to me.'

'Do you live in New York, Mr Ellison?' Joshua enquired, making room for Samuel and Leigh to be more comfortable, allowing Samuel to have his chair.

'I've lived in all sorts of places,' Samuel answered pleasantly, sitting down and crossing his legs. 'I was born in New York. My mother landed there from the ship, and it took her quite some time to get a start. What with being alone, and expecting a child, life wasn't easy for her. She was a brave woman, and a likeable one, and she found friends who were generous enough to care for her when I was born.'

Caroline tried to imagine it, and failed. She thought of what she knew of her father-in-law.

Why had Samuel's mother leave him? She racked her memory and could recall no mention of her at all. She was certain beyond any question that Grandmama had never said a word about her husband having had a previous wife. Had she run off with another man?

From what Samuel was now saying, she had reached New York alone. Had he abandoned her? Had Edmund Ellison thrown her out for some unforgivable offence?

'It must have been appalling,' she said sincerely 'How did she manage? Was there no one to . . .'

'You mean kin, relatives?' Samuel seemed amused. He leaned back a little, relaxing. 'Not at first, but so many people were making new lives, beginning again with nothing, it didn't seem so odd. And there were opportunities. She was handsome, and willing to work hard.'

'Doing what?' Caroline asked, then blushed at her clumsiness. Perhaps it was not something he was comfortable to discuss. 'I mean . . . she had a baby to care for . . .'

'Oh, I was passed around from hand to hand,' Samuel replied cheerfully. 'By the time I was two I could have said "Mama" or "I'm hungry", in a dozen different languages.'

'What amazing courage,' Joshua said quietly. 'You must have witnessed some remarkable events, Mr Ellison?'

'Indeed,' Samuel agreed with feeling. 'And history made. But I'll wager, so have you. And heard great ideas discussed, and seen a heap of beautiful things I haven't yet.' He looked around. 'There's got to be all kinds of life in this city, everything a man has ever thought of. Crossroads to the nations of the

51

earth. Makes me feel like a boy from the backwoods. And here I thought New York was getting sophisticated, after all our adventures.'

'Adventures?' Caroline asked with as much real curiosity as good manners.

He grinned. 'Oh, New York after the war was something else, ma'am. You never saw a town like it in your life! Not a place for ladies then, but proper civilised now, compared with the past, that is. Mind if you want the real gentry, maybe Boston is the town to be.'

'Have you travelled further west, Mr Ellison?' Pitt spoke to him for the first time.

Samuel regarded him with interest. 'I've been some – you mean like Indian country? I could tell a few tales, but a lot of them'd be sad, to my way of thinking. But maybe not every man'd agree with me.'

'Who would disagree with you?' Joshua asked with interest.

A shadow passed over Samuel's face. 'The march of progress is not always a pretty sight, sir, and it leaves an awful lot of dead bodies in its wake. Sometimes the best part of a nation and its dreams get trodden under. I guess maybe the strongest wins, but the weaker can be very beautiful, and their passing can leave you with an emptiness inside there's nothing left that can fill.'

Caroline glanced at Pitt. His face was away from the light, and the shadows threw his features into relief. In listening to Samuel he had caught a vision of some kind of bereavement, and the mark of it was plain to see.

'You speak with great feeling, Mr Ellison,' Joshua said quietly. 'You make us wish to hear more, and learn what it is that moves you so deeply. I hope that we shall make your closer acquaintance.'

Samuel rose to his feet. 'You are very generous, Mr Fielding. I'll surely take you up on it. But I guess that's my cue to go back to my own box before the lights go down, so I don't inconvenience you all by not being in my seat in time. Quite apart from manners, this is a play no one should miss the end of. I don't think in all my days I've ever seen a woman like that leading lady of yours. She could light a fire just by looking at dry wood!' He turned to Caroline. 'I'm delighted to make your acquaintance, ma'am. A man can choose his friends, but not his family. It's a rare blessing to find nature's pick for you coincides with your own!' And after bidding them all good evening, he turned, accompanied by Charles Leigh, and went out of the door, closing it softly behind him.

Joshua stared at Caroline. 'Can he be?'

'Oh yes!' she said without hesitation. She turned to Pitt, but it was not really a question.

Pitt nodded. 'He bears a remarkable resemblance to Edward Ellison. It is too great to be coincidence.' He frowned slightly. 'Did you know your father-in-law had an earlier wife?'

'No! I'm astounded!' she admitted. 'I have never heard a single word about her. I am not even sure if Grandmama knows!' Years of hidden battles with the old lady were sharp in her mind – the criticism, the comparisons of the present with the past, always to the detriment of Caroline and her daughters. She could not help a little bubble of satisfaction rising inside her, as she turned to the stage ready to watch the drama there reach its climax.

She was immediately drawn into the tragedy again. Cecily Antrim's character was the vehicle for such passion it was impossible to remain apart from it. Even the coming of Samuel Ellison into Caroline's life with his revelations was forgotten as the unfolding emotions captured her and she felt the pain and the urgency as if it were her own life.

Part of her resented the laying bare of feelings within herself she would rather not have recognised. Another part found a kind of release in the amazing knowledge that she was not alone. Other women felt the same hunger, disillusion, sense of having betrayed their dreams, and that some part of life was a disappointment they had not known how to deal with, only to deny.

Should such things be said? Was there something indecent in the exposure of feelings so intimate? To know it herself was one thing, to realise that others also knew was quite different. It was being publicly naked rather than privately.

Usually when she visited the theatre with Joshua she looked at him often, wishing to share the laughter or the tragedy with him. It was a great part of her pleasure. Tonight she wished to remain alone. She was afraid of what she would see in his face, and even more what he would see in hers. She was not yet ready to be quite so close; perhaps she never would be. There must be some privacy in even the deepest love, some secrets left, some things one did not wish to know. It was part of respect, the room to be oneself, a wholeness.

When the tragedy was complete and the final curtain descended, Caroline found there were tears on her cheeks and her voice was choked in her throat. She sat motionless, staring at the folds of the curtains. The last bows had been taken again and again, flowers presented, the applause had died away.

'Are you all right?' Pitt asked softly, close to her elbow.

She turned and smiled at him, and blinked, feeling the tears roll down her face. She was glad it was he who had asked, not Joshua. Just at the moment she felt remote from theatre people, actors who could look at this professionally, as an art. It was too real for that, too much the stuff of life.

'Yes . . . yes, thank you, Thomas. Of course I am. It was just . . . very moving.'

He smiled. He did not say anything else, but she could see in his eyes that he understood the thoughts it raised as well, the questions and the confusions that would live on long after tonight.

'Superb!' Joshua breathed out, his face glowing. 'I swear she's never been better! Even Bernhardt could not have exceeded this. Caroline – Thomas – we must go backstage to tell her. I couldn't miss this opportunity. Come!' Without waiting for a reply he moved towards the door of the box, so consumed in his enthusiasm it never occurred to him either of the others could think differently.

Caroline glanced at Pitt.

Pitt shrugged very slightly, smiling.

Together they followed after Joshua's already retreating figure. He led them unhesitatingly through a door marked 'Private' and along a bare passage, down a flight of steps lit only by a single gas bracket, and through another door on to a landing off which were several dressing rooms, each marked with someone's name. The one with 'Cecily Antrim' on it was half open and the sound of voices came from inside quite clearly.

Joshua knocked, then went in, Caroline and Pitt on his heels.

Cecily was standing by the mirrors, the table spread with greasepaints and powders. She was still wearing the gown from the last act, and her hair was quite obviously her own and not a wig. Despite her youthful figure, at this distance it was

55

possible to see that she was in her early forties, not thirties as she had appeared on stage. Caroline needed only a glance to know she was one of those women to whom age is irrelevant. Her beauty was in her bones, her magnificent eyes, and above all the fire inside her.

'Joshua! Darling!' she said with delight, spreading her arms wide to embrace him.

He walked forward and hugged her, kissing her on both cheeks.

'You have excelled even yourself!' he said ardently. 'You made us feel everything, and care passionately. And now we have no choice but to think . . .'

She pulled back, her arms still around his neck. Her smile was radiant. 'Really? You mean that? You think we may succeed?'

'Of course,' he responded. 'When have I ever lied to you? If it had been merely good I should have said it was good . . .' He pulled a slight face. 'I should have been exquisitely vague. As to whether it will succeed or not – that is in the lap of the gods.'

She laughed. 'I'm sorry, darling. I shouldn't have doubted you. But I do care so much. If we can only make people see the woman's side.' She waved a hand in a wide gesture. 'Freddie may be able to get his bill passed in the House. Change the climate, then the law. Ibsen has already achieved miracles. We are going to build on it. People will see there must be rights in divorce for women also. Isn't it marvellous to live in an age when there is such work to be done – new battles – chances?'

'Indeed it is,' he agreed, still staring at her. Then suddenly he seemed to remember the others present. 'Cecily, you haven't met my wife, Caroline; and her son-in-law, Thomas Pitt.'

Cecily smiled charmingly and acknowledged the introductions. There was no question she looked just a moment longer at Pitt than at Caroline. Then she turned back to Joshua.

Caroline looked at the other people in the tiny room. Just behind Cecily there was the man she had indicated as Freddie. He had a powerful face, broad-bridged nose and sensuous mouth. He seemed very relaxed, even slightly amused, and his eyes moved constantly back to Cecily. His admiration was unmistakable.

Lounging in the other chair was the young man whom Caroline had noticed had such presence in the play. Closer to, he bore more of a resemblance to Cecily, and Caroline was not surprised when a few moments later he was introduced as Orlando Antrim, and she gathered from the reference that he was Cecily's son.

There was a couple named Harris and Lydia, and the man so close to Cecily was Lord Frederick Warriner. His presence was partially explained by the reference to a private member's bill before Parliament, apparently to liberalise divorce proceedings for women.

Joshua and Cecily were still talking, with only the occasional glance at anyone else. Perhaps they did not mean to exclude others, but their exuberance carried them along, and their professional appreciation was on a different level of understanding from that of those who were merely watchers.

'I tried the scene in rehearsal at least three different ways,' Cecily was saying earnestly. 'You see, we might have played it as near hysteria, emotions crowding to break through, high tones in the voice, knife-edge sharp, jerking movements.' She demonstrated with gestures which somehow excluded Caroline and Pitt, simply because it extended too close to them, as if to a screen on a wall. 'Or with tragedy,' she went on, 'as if in her heart she already knew what was inevitable. Do you think she did, Joshua? What would you have done?'

'Unaware of it,' he said immediately. 'She was beyond such consideration of thought. I am sure if you asked the playwright he'd have said she was far too driven, too honest in emotion to have been aware of what would happen eventually.'

'You're right!' she agreed, swinging round to Orlando.

He grinned. 'Wouldn't dream of arguing, Mother. More than my role is worth!'

She glared at him in mock anger, then threw her hands up and laughed. She turned to Caroline. 'Did you enjoy the play . . . Caroline? What did you think of it?' Her wide eyes were unwavering, grey-blue, dark-lashed, impossible to lie to.

Caroline felt cornered. She would far rather not have answered, but now everyone was looking at her, including Joshua. What should she say? Something polite and flattering? Should she try to be perceptive, explain some of the impressions it created? She was not even sure if she knew what they wanted to hear.

Or should she tell the truth, that it was disturbing, intrusive, that it raised questions she thought were perhaps better not asked? That it would hurt, maybe waken unhappiness best left sleeping, because there was no cure for it? The play had ended in tragedy. Was it good for life to follow the same path? No one could bring the curtain down on it, and go home to something else.

What would Joshua expect her to say? What would he want? She must not look at him, as if she were expecting a cue. She did not want to hurt or embarrass him. She was suddenly overwhelmed by how much she cared, and how inadequate she was to match up to these people. Cecily Antrim was radiant, so absolutely certain of what she thought and felt. The power of her feeling lent an incandescence to her beauty. It was at least half the reason the entire audience had watched her.

Cecily laughed. 'My dear, are you afraid to say, in case you hurt my feelings? I assure you, I can bear it!'

Caroline found her tongue at last, and smiled back. 'I'm sure you can, Miss Antrim. But it is not an easy play to sum up in a few words, and be even remotely honest, and I don't believe you are looking for an easy reply. Even if you are, the work does not deserve one . . .'

'Bravo!' Orlando said from the background, holding his hands up in silent applause. 'Please tell us what you really think, Mrs Fielding. Perhaps we need to hear an honest opinion from outside the profession.'

There was complete silence.

Caroline felt her throat tighten. She swallowed. They were all staring at her. She had to speak.

'I think it asks a great many questions,' she said through dry lips. 'Some of the answers we may need to know, but there are others I think perhaps we don't. There are griefs one has to live with, and the thought that they are borne in private is all that makes them endurable.'

Cecily looked startled. 'Oh dear! A cry from the heart! Joshua?' Her meaning was plain, even as it was also plain she was only teasing.

Joshua blushed slightly. 'By heaven, I hope not!'

Everyone else laughed, except Pitt.

Caroline felt her face flame. She should have been able to laugh too, but she could not. She felt clumsy, unsophisticated, conscious of her hands and feet as if she were a schoolgirl again.

And yet she was older than anyone else here! Was that what was wrong? Another three or four years older and she could have been Cecily Antrim's mother! For that matter, she was seventeen years older than Joshua! Standing as he was beside Cecily, he must be aware of that.

How could she retain a shred of dignity, and not look ridiculous and make him ashamed of her? They must wonder why on earth he had chosen to marry a woman like her anyway, so staid by comparison with them, so unimaginative, a stranger in their world unable even to pass a clever or witty comment, let alone behave with an air of glamour and a magic as they did.

They were waiting for her to say something. She must not let them down. She had no wit to invent. There was nothing for it but to say what she thought.

She looked straight at Cecily, as if there were no one else in the crowded room.

'I am sure as an actress you are used to speaking for many people, and feeling the emotions of women quite unlike yourself.' She phrased it as a certainty, but left it half a question by her intonation.

'Ah!' Orlando said instantly. 'How perceptive, Mrs Fielding. She has you there, Mama! How often do you think of the vulnerable, as well as the passionate, those afflicted with doubts or wounds that are better hidden? Perhaps they have a right to privacy?'

The man named Harris looked shocked. 'What are you suggesting, Orlando? Censorship?' He said the word in the tone of voice he would have used if he had said 'treason'.

'Of course not!' Cecily retorted sharply. 'That's absurd! Orlando has no more love of censorship than I have. We'll both fight to the last breath for the freedom to speak the truth, to ask questions, to suggest new ideas, or restate old ones nobody wants to hear.' She shook her head. 'For God's sake, Harris, you know better than that! One man's blasphemy is another man's religion! Take that far enough, and we'll end up back burning people at the stake because they worship different gods from us – or even the same God but in different words.' She lifted her shoulders exaggeratedly. 'We'll be back to the Dark Ages, or the Inquisition!'

'There has to be some censorship, darling,' Warriner spoke for the first time. 'Shouldn't shout "Fire!" in a crowded theatre – especially if there isn't one. And even if there is, panic doesn't help. Gets more people crushed in the stampede than burned by the flames.' He looked slightly amused as he said it, but the smile did not go as far as his eyes.

Cecily's mood changed abruptly. 'Of course!' she said with a laugh. 'Shout "Fire!" in church if you must, but never, never in the theatre – at least not while there's a performance on!'

Everyone else laughed as well.

Caroline was looking at Joshua.

It was Pitt who spoke.

'And perhaps we should be careful about libel? Unless, of course one is a theatre critic . . .'

'Oh!' Cecily drew in her breath sharply and swung round to face him. 'My goodness! I didn't realise you had been listening so carefully. I should have paid you more attention. You're not a critic, are you?'

He smiled. 'No, ma'am, I'm a policeman.'

Her eyes widened. 'Good God! Are you really?'

Pitt nodded.

'How perfectly grim! Do you arrest people for picking pockets, or causing an affray?' She tossed the idea away.

'I'm afraid more often it is something as serious as murder,' he replied, the light gone from his voice.

Orlando stood up. 'Which is probably exactly what Mrs Fielding meant about questions we shouldn't ask, because we don't want the answers,' he said in the silence which had followed. 'Freedom of speech has to include the freedom not to listen. I never thought of that until these last few days.' He walked to the door. 'I'm fearfully hungry. I'm going to find something to eat. Good night, everyone.'

'A good idea,' Cecily said quickly. It was the first time she seemed in the slightest out of composure. 'Champagne supper, everyone?'

Joshua declined politely, excusing them, and after repeating their congratulations, they withdrew.

Pitt offered his thanks again and wished them good night. Caroline and Joshua rode home making polite and rather stiff conversation about the play, speaking of the characters, not once mentioning Cecily Antrim herself. Caroline was filled with an increasing sense of being an outsider.

The following morning Joshua left early to see a playwright, and Caroline took a late breakfast alone. She was sitting staring at her second cup of tea, which she had allowed to go cold, when Grandmama came in, leaning heavily on her stick. She had been handsome in her youth, but age and ill temper had marked her features now, and her sharp eyes were almost black as she stared at Caroline with disfavour.

'Well, you look as if you lost sixpence and found nothing!' she said tartly. 'Face like a jar of vinegar.' She glanced at the teapot. 'Is that fresh? I don't suppose it is.'

'You are quite right,' Caroline replied, looking up.

'Not much use admitting I'm right,' the old lady said, pulling out a chair and sitting down opposite her. 'Do something about it! No man likes a wife with a sour expression, particularly if she's older than he is in the first place. Ill temper is displeasing enough in the young and pretty! In those past their best it is intolerable.'

Caroline had spent her adult life curbing her tongue in order to be civil to her mother-in-law. This latest rudeness was beyond bearing, because it was so close to the truth. Her self-control snapped.

'Thank you for giving me the benefit of your experience,' she retorted. 'I am sure you are in a position to know.'

Mariah was surprised. Caroline had never been so blunt before.

'I presume it was a bad play,' she said deliberately.

'It was a very good play,' Caroline contradicted. 'In fact it was brilliant.'

Grandmama scowled at the teapot. 'Then why are you sitting here by yourself over a cup of cold tea, and with an expression like a bad egg?' she demanded. 'I suppose you have a servant of some sort you can ring for to get a fresh pot? I know this is not Ashworth Hall, but I assume that the young actor you have elected to live with earns sufficient to afford the basic amenities?'

Caroline was so angry, and her sense of hurt so deep, she said the first thing that came into her head.

'I met a most interesting and charming gentleman yesterday evening.' She stared at the old lady unflinchingly. 'From America, over here on a visit, and hoping to trace his family.'

'Is that supposed to be an answer?' Grandmama enquired. 'If you want some more tea, ring the bell and the maid will

63

come,' Caroline replied. 'Tell her what you wish. I did not explain that to you because I thought you could work it out for yourself. I mentioned Mr Ellison because I thought you would wish to know. After all, he is more closely related to you than to me.'

The old woman froze. 'I beg your pardon?'

'Mr Ellison is more closely related to you than to me,' Caroline repeated distinctly.

'Does this – ' she opened her eyes very wide – 'person claim that he is part of my family? You are no longer an Ellison. You have chosen to become a . . . a . . . whatever he is!'

'A Fielding,' Caroline said for the umpteenth time. It was part of the old woman's offence that she pretended to forget Joshua's name. 'And yes, he does claim it. And his likeness to Edward is so remarkable I could not doubt him.'

The old lady sat very still. Even the bell for the maid was forgotten.

'Really? And what manner of man is he? Who does he claim to be, exactly?'

Now Caroline was not so certain how much she enjoyed the revelation. It had not had quite the effect she had expected; however, there was no alternative now but to go on.

'Apparently Papa-in-law was married before . . . before he met you.'

The old woman's face remained like stone.

'Samuel is his son,' Caroline finished.

'Is he indeed?' the old woman replied. 'Well . . . we'll see. You did not answer my question . . . what manner of man is he?'

'Charming, intelligent, articulate, and to judge by his clothes, very comfortably situated,' Caroline answered. 'I found him most agreeable. I hope he will call upon us.' She took a deep breath. 'In fact I shall invite him to.'

Grandmama said nothing, but reached across for the bell and rang it furiously.

Chapter Three

❧

Pitt was in his office in Bow Street early the next morning. There was little pleasure in staying at home alone, and there had been no letter from Charlotte in the first post. As soon as he had eaten breakfast and fed the cats he was happy to leave Keppel Street and be on his way.

It was too early to hear word from Tellman in Dover, but he did not expect him to find anything conclusive. Was the grotesquely placed body at Horseferry Stairs that of the French diplomat, or some other unfortunate eccentric who had indulged one taste too many? He profoundly hoped it was the latter. A scandal with the French Embassy would be most unpleasant, and possibly not one which could be contained so it did not strain relations between the two countries.

The play last night had left him disturbed by the power of its emotions. He was not as uncomfortable as Caroline had obviously been by the portrayal of the hungers of a woman married to a man who did not satisfy her passions or her dreams. He was a generation younger than she, and also he was of a different social class, one which felt freer to express their feelings. And he had also grown up in the country, far closer to nature.

Even so, the nakedness of the emotions he had seen on the stage had provoked deep thought in him, and a new perception of what lies behind even the most outwardly serene faces. He wished intensely that Charlotte were home so he could have discussed it with her. The emptiness of the house was like an ache inside him, and he was pleased to return to the problem of the body in the punt.

In the middle of the morning, while he was combing through reports of missing persons, there was a knock on his door and a sergeant came in looking pleased with himself.

'What is it, Leven?' Pitt asked.

'Woman come to the desk, sir, sayin' as 'er employer is missin'. 'Ain't bin 'ome fer a couple o' days, like. She says it's not like 'im at all. Most partic'lar, 'e is, bein' a professional gent, an' all. Never misses an appointment. 'Is reputation dependin' on it, dealin' with the gentry an' so on. Can't keep lords and ladies waitin', or they won't come again.'

'Well, make a note of it, Leven,' Pitt said impatiently. 'There's not a great deal we can do about it. Tell Inspector Brown, if you think it's serious enough.'

Leven stood his ground. 'No sir, that in't the point. Point is, she told us what 'e looks like. Matches the poor soul as yer found at 'Orseferry Stairs just about exact. I were reckoning yer'd want ter talk to 'er, an' mebbe even take 'er ter see the poor feller.'

Pitt was annoyed with himself for not having understood.

'Yes I would, Leven. Thank you. Bring her up, will you?'

'Yes sir.'

'And, Leven . . .'

'Yes sir?'

'That was well thought of. I'll tell you if it's him.'

'Thank you, sir.' Leven went out beaming with satisfaction, closing the door very gently behind him.

He was back in five minutes with a small, sturdy woman behind him, her face puckered with anxiety. The moment she saw Pitt she started to speak.

'Are you the gentleman what I should talk ter? Yer see 'e's bin gorn two days now . . . least this is the second . . . an' I got messages askin' where 'e is!' She was shaking her head. 'An' I in't got the faintest, 'ave I? I jus' know it in't like 'im, all the years I bin doin' the 'ouse fer 'im, 'e never let nothing get in the way of 'is work. That partic'lar, 'e is. I seen 'im make time fer folks when 'e's bin 'alf out on 'is feet. Always oblige. That's 'ow 'e got where 'e is.'

'Where is that, Mrs . . . ?' Pitt asked.

'That's wot I'm sayin'!' she protested. 'Nobody knows where 'e is! Vanished. That's why I come ter the po-liss. Summink's 'appened, sure as eggs is eggs.'

Pitt tried again. 'Please sit down, Mrs . . . ?'

'Geddes. I'm Mrs Geddes.' She sat down in the chair opposite him. 'Ta.' She rearranged her skirts. 'Yer see I bin cleanin' an' doin' fer 'im fer near ten years now, an' I knows 'is ways. There's summink not right.'

'What is his name, Mrs Geddes?'

'Cathcart – Delbert Cathcart.'

'Could you describe Mr Cathcart for me, please?' Pitt requested. 'By the way, where does he live?'

'Battersea,' she replied. 'Right down on the river. Lovely 'ouse, 'e 'as. Nicest one as I does for. What's that got ter do wif 'im not bein' there?'

'Perhaps nothing, Mrs Geddes. What does Mr Cathcart look like, if you please?'

'Sort o' ordinary 'ight,' she replied gravely. 'Not very tall, not very short. Not 'eavy. Sort o' . . .' She thought for a moment. 'Sort o' neat-lookin'. Got fair 'air an' a moustache, but not wot yer'd call real whiskers. Always dressed very well. Sort o' good-lookin', I suppose yer'd say. But 'ow will yer know 'im from that?'

'I'm not sure that we will, Mrs Geddes.' Pitt had had to tell people about deaths countless times before, but it never became any easier or pleasanter. At least this was not a relative. 'I am afraid there was a man found dead in a small boat on the river, yesterday morning. We don't know who he is, but he looks very much as you describe Mr Cathcart. I'm sorry to ask this, Mrs Geddes, but would you come and look at this man and see if you know him?'

'Oh! Well . . .' She stared at him for several moments. 'Well I s'pose I better 'ad, 'adn't I? Better me than one o' them society ladies as 'e knows.'

'Does he know a lot of society ladies?' Pitt asked curiously. He did not even know if the man in the punt was Cathcart or not, but he was interested to learn what he could about him before Mrs Geddes saw the body, in case she was so shocked she found herself unable to think coherently afterwards.

'O' course 'e does!' she said with wide eyes. ''E's the best photographer in London, in't 'e?'

Pitt knew nothing of photographers, except the odd bit he had heard in passing conversation. Someone had referred to it as the new form of portraiture.

'I didn't know that,' he admitted. 'I should like to learn more about him.'

'Real beautiful, they are. Yer never seen anyfink like it. People was that thrilled wif 'em.'

70

'I see.' Pitt rose to his feet. 'I'm sorry, Mrs Geddes, but there's no alternative to going to the morgue and seeing if it is Mr Cathcart we have. I hope it's not.' He said it as a matter of sympathy for her, but he realised immediately that it was less than true. It would be a great deal easier if the body proved to be an English society photographer than a French diplomat.

'Yes,' Mrs Geddes said quietly. She stood up and smoothed her jacket. 'Yes o' course. I'm comin'.'

The morgue was close enough to walk to, and there was so much noise in the street that conversation would have been difficult. Hansom cabs, omnibuses, wagons and brewers' drays clattered past them. Street pedlars shouted, men and women argued, and a costermonger roared with laughter at an old man's joke.

It was utterly different inside the morgue. The silence and the clinging, damp smell closed over them and suddenly the world of the living seemed far away.

They were conducted through to the ice house where bodies were stored. The sheet was taken off the face of the man from Horseferry Stairs.

Mrs Geddes looked at it and drew in her breath in a little gasp.

'Yes,' she said with a catch in her voice. 'Oh dear . . . that's Mr Cathcart, poor soul.'

'Are you quite sure?' Pitt pressed.

'Oh yes, that's 'im.' She turned away and put her hand up to her face. 'Whatever 'appened to 'im?'

There was no need to tell her about the green velvet dress, or the chains, at least not yet, perhaps not at all.

'I am afraid he was struck on the head,' Pitt answered.

71

Her eyes widened. 'Yer mean on purpose, like? 'E were murdered?'

'Yes.'

'Why'd anyone wanna murder Mr Cathcart? Were 'e robbed?'

'It seems very unlikely. Do you know of anyone who might have quarrelled with him?'

'No,' she said straight away. ''E weren't that sort.' She kept her face averted. 'It must be someb'dy very wicked wot done it.'

Pitt nodded to the morgue attendant, who covered the body again.

'Thank you, Mrs Geddes. Now I would appreciate it very much if you would take me to his house and allow me to find out whatever I can there. We'll get a hansom.' He waited a moment while she composed herself, then walked beside her out of the morgue and into the sunlight again. 'Are you all right?' he asked, seeing her ashen face. 'Would you like to stop for a drink, or a place to sit down?'

'No thank you,' she said stoically. 'Very nice o' yer, I'm sure, but I'll make us a proper cup o' tea when we get there. No time ter be sittin' down. Yer gotta find them as done this, an' see 'em on the end of a rope.'

He did not reply, but continued beside her until he saw a hansom and hailed it. He asked her for the address, and gave it to the cabbie, then settled down for the ride. He would like to have questioned her further about Cathcart, but she sat with her hands clenched in her lap, her eyes fixed, every now and then giving a little sigh. She needed time to absorb what had happened and come to terms with it in her own way.

The hansom rumbled across the Battersea Bridge and down

the other side, turning left along George Street, and stopped outside an extremely handsome house whose long garden backed on to the water. Pitt alighted, helping Mrs Geddes out. He paid the driver and gave him a message to take to the local police station, requesting a constable to come.

Mrs Geddes sniffed hard, and with a little shake of her head, walked up the long driveway and, taking a key from her pocket, opened the front door. She did it without hesitation. It was obviously a regular thing for her.

The moment he was inside Pitt stared around him. The entrance hall was long, with stairs down one side. It was excellently lit from a very large window extending the length of the stairwell. On one wall were several photographs of groups of people, half a dozen ragged urchins playing in the street, beside it society ladies at Ascot, lovely faces under a sea of hats.

'I told you 'e were good,' Mrs Geddes said sadly. 'Poor soul. I dunno wot yer wanter see 'ere. There in't nuffink missin', nuffink stole, so far as I can see. 'E must 'a bin set on in the street. 'E didn't never 'ave them sort o' people 'ere!'

'What sort of people did he have?' Pitt asked, following her through to the sitting room, which was surprisingly small for such a house. It was very elegant with Sheraton table and chairs in gleaming wood, and a Bokhara rug which would have cost Pitt at least a year's wages.

The windows looked on to a long lawn set with trees, sloping down to the water beyond. A willow made a cavern of green and reflected like lace on the barely moving current. A pergola was covered with rose trees, its latticed arches white through the leaves.

Mrs Geddes was watching him.

'Used that a lot, 'e did.' She sighed. 'Folks like ter 'ave their pictures took in beautiful places. Specially ladies. Makes 'em look good . . . kind o' romantic. Gentlemen prefer summink grand. Like ter dress up in uniforms, they do.' Her tone of voice conveyed her opinion of people who wore clothes that made them look more important than they were. ''Ad one daft 'aporth as dressed 'isself up as Julius Caesar!' She sniffed vigorously. 'I ask yer!'

'But Mr Cathcart had no objection?' Pitt tried to imagine it.

'O' course 'e didn't. 'Elped 'im, an' all. Then that's 'is job, in't it? Take pictures o' people so they looks like they wanter see 'emselves. Daft, I call it. But that don't matter. I dunno wot yer wanter see 'ere, but this is all there is.'

Pitt looked around, uncertain himself what he wanted to ask. Had Cathcart been killed here? The answer to that might matter a great deal. This house was in an excellent place for a punt to float from, down as far as Horseferry Stairs. But then so were scores of other houses that backed on to the river.

'Did he entertain here?' Pitt asked. 'Have parties?'

She stared at him with total incomprehension.

'Did he?' he repeated. Although the neatness of the rooms in the house he had seen so far made a party in which clothes such as the green velvet dress might be worn seem unlikely, certainly not before Mrs Geddes had very thoroughly cleaned and tidied up.

'Not as I know of.' She shook her head, still puzzled.

'You never had anything to clear up, a lot of dishes to wash?'

'No, I never did, not as yer'd call a lot. Not more'n three or four people'd use. Why yer askin', Mr Pitt? Yer said as 'e were murdered. That don't 'appen at parties. Wot yer on about?'

'He decided to tell her a half-truth. 'He was dressed for a

party . . . fancy dress. It seems unlikely he was out in the street in such clothes.'

''Is clients dressed daft,' she responded hotly. ''E never did! More sense, even if 'e catered ter some as 'adn't.'

There was probably a great deal Mrs Geddes did not know about Mr Cathcart, but Pitt forbore from saying so.

'Does he have a boat, perhaps moored up the river at the bottom of the garden?' he asked instead.

'I dunno.' A look of misery filled her face. 'You said summink about a boat before. 'E were found in a boat, were 'e?'

'Yes, he was. Did you do any tidying yesterday when you came?'

'There weren't nuffink ter do. Just cleaned as usual. Did a bit o' tidying, like. Same as always . . . 'ceptin' the bed weren't slept in, which was unusual, but not like it never 'appened before.' She narrowed her lips a trifle.

Pitt read the gesture as one of disapproval.

'He occasionally spent the night elsewhere? He has a lover, perhaps?' Remembering the green dress he was careful not to attribute a gender.

'Well, I can't see as she murdered 'im!' Mrs Geddes said angrily. 'That's not ter say I approve o' carryin's on, 'cos I don't! But she in't a bad sort, that excepted. Not greedy, and not too flashy, if yer know what I mean.'

'Do you know her name?'

'Well I s'pose as she'll 'ave ter be told an' all. 'Er name's Lily Monderell. Don' ask me 'ow she spells it, as I got no idea.'

'Where will I find Miss Monderell?' he asked.

'Over the bridge, in Chelsea. I 'spec 'e's got it writ down somewhere.'

'I'd like you to come with me through the rest of the house to tell me if anything's different from the way it usually is,' he requested.

'I dunno wot you think yer gonna find!' she said, blinking hard. Suddenly the awareness of Cathcart's death seemed to have overtaken her again, now that police were walking through his house as if he no longer possessed it. They were going to be looking through his belongings, in his absence and without asking him. 'If there were anyfink wrong I'd 'a seen it!' she added with a sniff.

'You weren't looking before,' he soothed her. 'Let us begin down here and work upwards.'

'Yer wastin' yer time,' she retorted. 'Yer should be out there.' She jerked her head towards some unknown beyond. 'That's where yer'll find murderers an' the like.' Still she led the way into the next room and he followed after her.

It was a well-proportioned house and furnished in extravagant taste, as if Cathcart had had an eye to curtains and ornaments he might use in photographs at some future date. However, the whole created a place of distinction and considerable beauty. An alabaster Egyptian cat of clean and elongated lines contrasted with an ornate red, black and gold painted Russian icon.

A minor Pre-Raphaelite painting of a knight in vigil before an altar hung on the upstairs landing, curiously highlighting the simplicity of an arrangement of sword-shaped leaves. It was highly individual, and Pitt had a sharp sense of personality, of a man's tastes, his dreams and ideals, perhaps something of the life which had shaped him. Oddly, the knowledge of loss was greater than when he had stared at the body in the boat as it knocked against Horseferry Stairs, or again in the morgue, when he had been thinking more of Mrs Geddes, and the question of identification.

She showed him through every room and each was immaculate. Nothing was out of the place one would expect to find it, no chairs or tables were crooked, no cushions or curtains disturbed. Everything was clean. It was impossible to believe there had been a fancy-dress party here which had indulged in the sort of excesses the green velvet dress suggested, and certainly no violence in which two men had fought, and one been killed.

The last room they reached was up a flight of stairs from a second, smaller landing, and it extended the length of the top storey, with windows and skylights giving the light an excellent clarity. It was immediately obvious that this was the studio where Cathcart took many of his photographs. One end was furnished as an elegant withdrawing room, one side overlooked the river, and a person seated would appear to have nothing but the sky behind them. The nearest end was cluttered like a storeroom with what seemed at a glance to be scores of objects of wildly varied character.

'I don't come up 'ere much,' Mrs Geddes said quietly. '"Just sweep the floor," 'e says. "Keep it clean. Don't touch nuffink".'

Pitt regarded the conglomeration with interest. Without moving anything he recognised a Viking horned helmet, half a dozen pieces from a suit of armour, uncountable pieces of velvet of a variety of shades. There was an ostrich-feather fan, two stuffed pheasants, a round Celtic shield with metal bosses, several swords, spears, pikes, and bits and pieces of military and naval uniform. What lay hidden beneath them was beyond even guessing.

77

Mrs Geddes answered his unspoken thoughts. 'Like I said, some of 'em likes ter dress daft.'

A closer examination of the room discovered nothing in which Pitt could see any connection with Cathcart's death. In a large wardrobe there were a number of other dresses of varying degrees of ornateness. But then since Cathcart frequently photographed women, that was to be expected. There were also men's clothes from many historical periods, both real and fanciful.

There were four cameras carefully set up on tripods, with black cloths for obscuring the light. Pitt had never seen a camera before so closely, and he looked at them with interest, being careful not to disturb them. They were complicated boxes in both metal and wood, with pleated leather sides, obviously to telescope back and forth. In size they were roughly a cubic foot or a little less, and on two of them brass fittings shone freshly polished.

There were also a number of arc lights on the floor. There was no gas supply to them, but heavy cables.

'Electric,' Mrs Geddes said with pride. 'Got 'is own machine wot drives 'em. Dynamo, it's called. 'E says as yer can't get proper light fer pictures 'ceptin' in the summer, not inside the 'ouse, like.'

Pitt regarded it with interest. It was increasingly apparent that Cathcart had taken great thought and trouble to make an art of his work. Neither time nor expense had been spared.

'Special room 'e 'as fer doin' the pictures, in the basement, like,' Mrs Geddes said. 'Full o' chemicals. Smells 'orrible. But 'e never lets me in there, case I 'urts meself wif anyfink. Spill some o' them things an' yer'll never be the same again.'

'Did he keep any of the pictures here?' he asked, looking

78

around curiously. 'Recent or current ones?'

'In them drawers,' she pointed to a large cabinet a little to his left.

'Thank you.' He opened it and studied the prints inside, going through them one by one. The first was of a very striking woman dressed in a highly exotic gown with ropes of beads around her neck. By her feet was a beautifully wrought raffia basket, out of which trailed a very live-looking snake. It was an arresting image, not principally for its suggestions of classical Egypt, which was presumably what the subject had intended, but for the lighting of the face, showing its power and sensuality.

In a second picture a young man posed as whom Pitt took to be St George. He was complete with polished armour, sword and shield. The helmet was balanced on a table beside him. The light caught the sheen on the points and curves of the metal breastplate and reflected in his pale eyes and through his fair hair, making an aureole of it. It was the portrait not of a knight at war, but of a dreamer who fights battles of the soul.

A third photograph caught the essential vanity of a face, a fourth the sweetness, a fifth the self-indulgence, although they were so disguised by the trappings of fantasy or wealth as to be hidden from the less perceptive eye. By now, Pitt had a far deeper respect for the photographer than he had begun with, and a realisation that such skill in judging the human character and portraying it so tellingly, might earn him enemies as well as friends.

He closed the drawer and turned back to Mrs Geddes. As he did so he heard the front doorbell ring.

'S'pose I'd better go an' answer that,' Mrs Geddes said, looking at him, as if for permission. 'Do I tell 'oever it is as Mr Cathcart's dead, or not?'

'No, please don't do that yet,' he said quickly. 'But I hope it is a constable from the local station. At least as a matter of courtesy I have to inform them what has happened, and if the murder actually happened here, then it is in their jurisdiction.' If he were fortunate, local police would insist they took over the case. It now seemed quite certain the French Embassy was in no way involved, and there was no reason why Pitt should remain in charge.

It was indeed the local constable, a plain-faced, agreeable man of middle years named Buckler. Pitt explained to him briefly what had occurred so far. Even the more lurid details were necessary, although he excused Mrs Geddes before describing them. If Buckler were to assist in the further search, he must know what might be relevant.

'Well, I'm very surprised, sir, an' that's a fact,' he said when Pitt had finished. 'Mr Cathcart was an artist an' a bit eccentric, like, but we always found 'im a very decent gentleman. Not what you'd call the best standards – no churchman or the like – but good as most gentlemen, an' better'n many. It's a very ugly business, an' that's no mistake.'

'Indeed,' Pitt agreed, not yet sure whether he believed Buckler as to Cathcart's character. 'Mrs Geddes has shown me through the house, and says there is nothing out of place, and no signs of any other presence here.'

Buckler glanced around. 'D'you think 'e were killed 'ere then? Although I can't see anyone gettin' around the streets dressed like you say. Not even at night! Most likely was 'ere, an' 'e were put in the boat an' turned loose. Could easy fetch up any place between 'ere an' the Pool.'

Pitt led him back through the house towards the side door to the garden, passing Mrs Geddes in the sitting room.

'Watch out for that rug,' she called after him. 'Edge is frayed an' it's easy ter catch yer boot in it. I keep tellin' Mr Cathcart as 'e should get it mended.'

Pitt glanced at the floor. It was smoothly polished and quite bare.

'Mrs Geddes!'

'Yes sir?'

'There's no rug here.'

'Yes, there is, sir.' Her voice came quite clearly. 'Smallish green one wi' red in it. Edge is frayed, like I said.'

'No there isn't, Mrs Geddes. There's nothing on the floor at all.'

He heard the sound of her footsteps and a moment later she appeared in the doorway. She stared at the polished floor.

'Well, I'll go to the foot of our stairs! There should be one there, sir. It's gorn!'

'When did you last see it?'

'Now . . . let me see.' She looked bewildered. 'Yes, the day before Mr Cathcart . . . got . . . well, the day before. It was there then, because I sort o' nagged 'im about gettin' it mended. I gave 'im the name o' someone as does that kind o' thing. Cobbler 'e is, actually, but stitch anything up pretty good.'

'Could Mr Cathcart have taken it to him?'

'No sir,' she said firmly. ''Cos 'e don't do that kind o' thing 'isself. 'E'd a' gave it ter me ter take. I reckon it's bin stole. But why anyone'd wanna take summink like that I'm blessed if I know.' She was staring as she spoke, her brow puckered, but not at the floor, rather at the blue and white vase which sat on the jardinière by the wall.

'What is it, Mrs Geddes?' Pitt asked her.

81

'An' that's not the right jar for there neither. Wrong colour. Mr Cathcart'd never a' put a blue and white jar there, 'cos o' the curtains along at the end bein' red, like. Big red and gold jar 'e 'ad. Twice the size o' that one.' She shook her head. 'I dunno, Mr Pitt. 'Oo'd take a great big jar like that, an' then go an' stick the wrong one in its place?'

'Someone who wished to conceal the fact that anything was gone,' Pitt replied softly. 'Someone who did not realise how good your memory is, Mrs Geddes.'

She smiled with satisfaction. 'Thank yer—' She stopped abruptly, her face paling, her eyes wide. 'Yer mean as 'e were killed 'ere? Oh my . . .' She swallowed convulsively. 'Oh . . .'

'A possibility, no more,' Pitt said apologetically. 'Maybe you should go and put the kettle on . . . make that tea you didn't have before.' He kneeled down on the wooden floor and ran his fingers gently along the edge by the skirting board. It was not long before he felt a sharp prick, and picked up a tiny sliver of porcelain. He examined it carefully. One smooth side was dark red.

'That it?' Buckler asked, leaning a little over to look also.

'Yes . . .'

'You reckon 'e was killed 'ere, sir?'

'Probably.'

'There's no blood,' Buckler pointed out. 'Did they wash it all out? Not leave even a mark?'

'No, it was probably on the rug that's missing.'

Buckler looked around. 'What did 'e do with it? 'Ave yer looked in the garden? In the rubbish? I suppose 'e more likely took it away with 'im. Though I can't think why. What difference'd it make? Doesn't tell us 'oo 'e is.'

'No, I haven't looked in the garden yet,' Pitt replied, climbing to his feet. 'If I find something there, I would rather have a local man with me when I do.'

Buckler straightened his tunic coat and breathed out gently. 'Right, sir. Then we'd better be about it, 'adn't we?'

Pitt opened the side door and stepped out. The autumn trees were still in full leaf but the chestnuts were beginning to turn gold. The asters and Michaelmas daisies were a blaze of varying purples, blues and magentas, and the last marigolds were still spilling brightly over the edge of the borders. A few roses glowed amber and pink, fading quickly, but with a luminous tone richer than that of summer.

Beyond the evergreens the light danced on the river and as Pitt and Buckler walked across the grass it was easier to see the dark shadow where the willow made a cavern over the bank and about twenty yards of the stream.

They moved more slowly, eyes to the ground, looking for footprints, signs of anyone passing recently.

'There, sir,' Buckler said between his teeth. 'I reckon that's 'cos something was dragged. See where it's all bent? Some o' their stalks is broke.'

Pitt had seen it. Something heavy had fallen, and then been pulled along.

'I expect he carried Cathcart as far as he could, then dropped him here and hauled him the rest of the way.' He stepped forward, leading Buckler to the edge of the river. Here the weed was deeply scored, but the tide had risen and fallen four times in the last two days, and the marks were obliterated below the high-water line. There was a post where a boat could be tied, and the ridges worn on its sides made its use apparent.

Pitt stood staring at the water, rippling, dark peat browns

83

reflecting the sun. It was several moments before he noticed the white edge of another chip of porcelain, and then another. It was Buckler who saw the mass of the rolled-up rug half sunken under the willow, brushed by the branches. At first it had looked like a drifting log, and he had ignored it.

Loath to wade into the river, or ask Buckler to do it, Pitt went up to the garden shed and fetched a long-handled rake, and together they managed to pull the mass ashore. They unrolled it and looked at it carefully, but it had been in the mud and water too long for them to tell if any of the marks were blood or not.

'It was done in the 'ouse, and then 'e were carried out 'ere and put in the boat,' Buckler said grimly. 'An' 'ooever done it broke the jar an' threw the bits down 'ere, an' took the rug up 'cos o' the blood. Mebbe they 'oped as it'd 'ide the fact 'e were dead, an' we'd think 'e jus' upped an' took off somewhere.'

Pitt was inclined to agree with him, and said so. The longer an investigation was delayed the more difficult it was. But it did not answer whether the crime had been spontaneous or premeditated, simply that the killer had been in sufficient possession of his wits to act with self-preservation afterwards.

'Must a' bin quite a big feller,' Buckler said doubtfully. 'Ter carry 'im down 'ere from the 'ouse, an' put 'im in the boat.'

'Or else he had help,' Pitt pointed out, although he did not believe that. There was too much emotion, too much that was violent and twisted for a collaboration between two people, unless both were affected with the same madness.

'There's nothing more for us here.' Pitt looked around at the quiet garden and the fast-flowing river. The tide had risen inches even while they stood there. 'We'd better go back to your station. This is your patch.'

But Superintendent Ward had no desire to take the case, and told Pitt in no uncertain terms that since the body had been found at Horseferry Stairs, and Pitt had already started to investigate, he should continue to do so.

'Besides,' he pointed out forcefully, 'Delbert Cathcart was a very important photographer. Done a lot of high society. This could be a very nasty scandal indeed. Needs to be handled with a great deal of discretion!'

Tellman returned from Dover hot and tired, and after a cup of tea and a sandwich at the railway station, he went to Bow Street and reported to Pitt.

'No sign of Bonnard in Dover now,' he said with a mixture of relief at not having to arrest a French diplomat, and disappointment because he had been denied a trip to France. 'But he was there. Booked a passage across to Calais, then never turned up to go. I questioned them up and down about that, but they were absolutely certain. Wherever he is, he's still in England.'

Pitt leaned back in his chair, looking at Tellman's dour face and reading the anxiety in him.

'The body in the boat wasn't him,' he said. 'It's a society photographer called Delbert Cathcart. He lived in Battersea, just across the bridge from Chelsea, where he had a very nice house backing on to the river.' He told him about finding the place where Cathcart had been carried down to the punt, and the broken jar and the stained rug.

Tellman sat in the other chair, frowning. 'Then where's

Bonnard? Why did he take off to Dover, and then disappear? Do you suppose he's the one who killed what's his name . . . Cathcart?'

'There's no reason to think they are connected,' Pitt said with a wry smile. He knew Tellman's opinion of foreigners. 'We'll go and see Lily Monderell this evening.'

'His mistress?' Tellman invested the word with considerable scorn. There was a deep-rooted anger inside him against all sorts of things – privilege, injustice, greed, being patronised or ignored – but although he would have denied it hotly, he was a very moral man and his beliefs on marriage were conservative, as were his ideas about women.

'We have to begin somewhere,' Pitt answered. 'There were no signs of anyone having broken into the house, so we must presume that whoever killed him was someone he knew, and let in himself. He knew of no reason to fear them. Mrs Geddes says she has no idea who it could be. Perhaps Miss Monderell will know more.'

'Other servants?' Tellman asked. 'Does this Mrs Geddes do everything?'

'Apparently. Cathcart very often ate out, and didn't care to have a manservant. Someone came in to do the scrubbing two days a week, and there was a gardener, but no one who knew him any better than Mrs Geddes.'

'Then I suppose we'd best go and see this mistress,' Tellman conceded grudgingly. 'Is there time for a proper dinner first?'

'Good idea,' Pitt said willingly. He would far rather find a warm, noisy public house and eat with Tellman than go home to the silence of Keppel Street and eat something alone at the kitchen table. The sight of the familiar room with its polished copper and the smell of linen and clean wood only made him more aware of Charlotte's absence.

Tellman had formed a picture of Lily Monderell in his mind. She would be the sort of woman a man took to bed, but did not marry. There would be something essentially vulgar about her, and of course greedy. She would have to be handsome, or she would not succeed in her purpose, especially with someone who was an artist, of sorts. Without any reason, he had seen her as fair-haired and rather buxom, and that she would be dressed flamboyantly.

When he and Pitt were shown into her sitting room in Chelsea, he was disconcerted, and yet he could not have said why. Apart from the fact that she was dark, she answered his imagined description very well. She was extremely handsome, with bold eyes, wide, sensuous mouth and masses of shining, dark brown hair. Her figure was very rich, and the gown she wore displayed it to fine advantage. It was a trifle ostentatious, but that might have been because she had so much to show. On a thinner woman it would have been more modest.

What upset his composure was that he did not find her unattractive. Her face was full of laughter, as if she knew some joke she was waiting to share. From the moment they stepped into the warm room with its rose-shaded lamps, she flirted with Pitt.

'I'm very sorry,' Pitt said after he had told her the news of Cathcart's death, but sparing her the details.

She sat on the sofa, her rose-red skirts billowing around her. She leaned back a little, more from habit than thought, showing off her generous body.

'Well, poor Delbert,' she said with feeling. She shook her head. 'I can't think who would want to do something so . . . vicious,' she sighed. 'He made enemies, of course! That's natural when you're really good at what you do, and he was brilliant. In some ways there was no one to touch him.'

'What sort of enemies, Miss Monderell?' Pitt asked. 'Professional rivals?'

'Not who'd kill him, love,' she said with a wry smile.

Tellman noticed a slight northern accent. He was not sure where to place it, but he thought Lancashire. He did not know much about the cities outside London.

Pitt kept his gaze steady on her. 'What sort?' he repeated.

'You ever seen any of his pictures?' She looked back at him without wavering.

'A few. I thought they were extremely good. Were some of his clients dissatisfied?'

Her smile widened, showing excellent teeth. 'Well, I dare say you don't know the clients,' she answered. 'Did you see the lady dressed as Cleopatra . . . with the snake?'

'Yes.'

Tellman was startled, but he said nothing.

'What did you think of it?' she asked, still looking at Pitt.

A flicker of uncertainty crossed Pitt's face.

Tellman was fascinated. He wished he had seen the pictures. He wondered fleetingly if the lady in question had been fully dressed.

'Come on, love! What did you think of it?' Lily Monderell repeated. 'Tell the truth and shame the devil! Poor Delbert deserves that.'

'I thought it was extremely powerful,' Pitt replied, the faintest colour rising to his cheeks.

88

Lily Monderell threw her head back and roared with laughter.

Tellman was shocked. Her lover was newly dead, she had heard the news only moments before, and here she was laughing! He tried to frown to convey his disapproval, and found he could not. There was a warmth about her which enveloped him in spite of himself.

She glanced at him, and her mirth died away.

'Don't look like that, love,' she said gently. 'You didn't know Delbert. He had a good life, enjoyed it. He wouldn't want anyone standing around with a face like the milk had gone off. He'd expect us to go on . . . me especially. I knew him, you see. You never did.'

Tellman could not think how to answer her. She looked like all the images he had in his mind of such women, but inside she was different, more alive, more disturbing, and it confused him.

But she was finished with Tellman. She turned back to Pitt, her face sharp with interest and amusement.

'Powerful?' she said curiously. 'How carefully you choose your words, Superintendent. Is that all?'

Tellman watched Pitt, wondering what he would say. He knew Pitt had seen far more than that in it.

'Go on! Be honest!' Lily urged. 'What kind of woman is she?'

A half-smile hovered around Pitt's mouth. 'In the picture – a sensuous, selfish woman,' he replied. 'Impetuous, ruthless, very confident. A doubtful friend and a bad enemy.'

She nodded her head very slowly, satisfaction bright in her eyes. 'You see? It's all there in the picture. You look at it once, and you know her better than she wants to be known.' There was considerable pride in her. 'That was his genius. He could do that time and time again. A light here or there, a shadow, something in the setting. You'd be surprised how often people like the sort of thing that shows up their real character. They forget that a photograph is taken in a very private place, but the picture when it's finished may be shown anywhere.'

Pitt leaned forward a little. 'What sort of things did he add?'

Tellman could not see any reason for knowing. He thought Pitt was interested for himself.

'Well, the snake, of course,' she started to recall. 'And I remember some butterflies for one young society woman. She thought they were beautiful . . . which they were. They also reflected her nature rather too well.' She was smiling as she spoke. 'And a looking-glass, knives, fruit, wine glasses, stuffed animals, different kinds of flowers . . . all sorts of things. And where he put the lights made a lot of difference. A face lit from below doesn't look anything like the same one as lit from the side, or above.'

Pitt was thoughtful. 'And he made enemies with this perception?'

'You can't understand how strong vanity is if you have to ask that,' she answered, shaking her head at him. 'Don't you know people at all? And you supposed to be a detective!'

'As you said before, Miss Monderell, you knew Mr Cathcart and I did not.'

'You're right, love, of course.' A sadness filled her for a moment, and Tellman was startled to see tears in her eyes. He did not know why, but he was pleased. A decent person grieved for death.

Pitt suddenly changed his line of enquiry. 'Did he inherit

his wealth, or earn it with his photography?'

She looked momentarily startled. 'He never spoke about it. He was generous, but I didn't need him for that.' She said it quite casually, but Tellman felt she wished them to know it.

Pitt looked down at his hands. 'You weren't dependent on him financially?' he said curiously. 'Were you lovers, or just friends?'

She smiled at him, shaking her head a little and the tears spilling over her cheeks. 'I know what you're saying, and you're wrong. We were lovers. He liked women, and I never imagined I was the only one . . . but with me it was different. It was never a grand affair, but we liked each other. He was fun; that is more than you can say of everyone. I'll miss him.' She wiped her cheek, 'I . . . I'd like to think it was quick . . . that he didn't suffer . . .'

'I should think he didn't even know it,' Pitt replied gently.

She glanced at Tellman. He thought she was afraid Pitt was being kind rather than honest.

'Back of the head,' Tellman confirmed. 'Probably went out straight away.' He startled himself by wanting to comfort her. She was everything he disapproved of, and as unlike Gracie as possible. Gracie was small and thin with a wide-eyed, quick little face and as spiky a nature as he had ever met. She was careful, sharp-witted, and as brave as anyone he'd ever known. In fact she was altogether the opposite of the sort of woman he had always been drawn to and imagined one day he would marry. Liking her was reasonable enough, respecting her certainly was, but they disagreed about so many things, important things like social justice and people's places in society, it would be ridiculous to think of anything more than a pleasant association.

Of course it was ridiculous! Gracie didn't even like him! She tolerated him because he worked with Pitt, no more. She probably wouldn't have done that, had she a choice. But she would have given tea and home-made cakes to the devil, if Pitt had asked her to, and she thought it would help him in a case.

Pitt was still talking to Lily Monderell, asking about Delbert Cathcart's life, his clothes, his trips to the theatre, his parties, the sort of people with whom he spent his time when not seeking clients.

'Of course he went to parties,' she said quickly. 'All sorts, but he liked theatre best. It was almost part of what he does.'

'Did he dress up himself?'

'You mean fancy dress, for society balls and the like? Probably. Most of those folks do.' She frowned. 'Why? What's that got to do with who killed him?'

'He was . . . in fancy dress,' Pitt replied.

She looked surprised, a little puzzled.

'That wasn't usual. He preferred to be . . . ordinary. He said what you picked for fancy dress gave away too much of who you were inside.'

'What would he dress as . . . if he did?' Pitt asked.

She thought for a moment or two. 'Only time I remember, he went all in black, and he carried a pen and a looking-glass. Kind of clown, I thought he was. What was he wearing when he died?'

Pitt hesitated.

Her face darkened. 'What?'

Pitt looked up at her. 'A green velvet dress,' he answered.

'Dress? What do you mean?' She was obviously at a loss.

'I mean a woman's gown,' Pitt elaborated.

She stared at him in disbelief. 'That's . . . silly! He'd never

wear that kind of thing! Somebody else did that to him . . . after
. . .' She shivered and blinked hard.

'I was hoping you might be able to tell us who it might be,'
Pitt pressed.

Her voice was higher pitched, sharper. 'Well I can't!
Colourful, a bit wild, spend a lot on their pleasures, but not to
do that! Poor Delbert.' She looked beyond Pitt to something
within her own imagination, her eyes troubled. 'I'd help you if
I could, but it isn't any one of his friends I've met.' She focused
on Pitt again. 'I want you to find him, Mr Pitt. Delbert didn't
deserve that. He was a bit too clever sometimes, and he didn't
always know when to keep his observations quiet . . . and that
can make enemies. And he saw too clearly . . . but he wasn't a
bad man. He liked a good joke, and a good party, and he was
generous. Find out who did that to him . . .'

'I'll do everything I can, Miss Monderell,' Pitt promised.
'If you would give me a list of Mr Cathcart's friends, we'll see
if any of them can help us also.'

She stood up in a graceful movement and walked over to
the bureau, skirts rustling, a wave of perfume teasing Tellman,
warm and sweet, and confusing him all over again.

93

Chapter Four

◄❧►

Grandmama was nervous. That made her angry because nervousness was something she had managed to avoid for more years than she could remember, and that was now a great many. She had kept control of events so that she was very seldom placed at a disadvantage. It was one of the privileges of age.

This was entirely Caroline's fault. A great deal that was presently disagreeable was Caroline's fault. Imagine marrying an actor! The woman had taken leave of her wits! Not that she had ever had very many. But she had seemed sensible enough when she had married Edward, the old lady's only son. Poor Edward. How he would grieve to see what a state his widow had fallen into – taking up with theatrical people, and then marrying one young enough to be her own son! Edward's death must have unhinged her mind, that was the most charitable explanation one could offer. Not made of stern enough stuff, that was her trouble. Grandmama had not fallen into pieces like that when Edward's father had died and left her a widow at much the same age. But then Mariah Ellison was of a different generation from Caroline, and had a backbone of steel!

Who was this Samuel person she had gone and invited to tea so hastily? Apparently she had written a note this very morning and dispatched an errand boy with it to the hotel where Mr Ellison was staying during his time in London. The acceptance had come by return. He would be delighted to call upon them at three o'clock.

Grandmama had debated whether to invite anyone else to come, or not. He could be any sort of a person! Caroline had said he was charming, but then her marriage was witness enough as to her judgement! Heaven only knew what else she might admire these days.

In the end the old lady had sent a note around to Mrs Blanie to explain why she could not visit her today as she had planned, but to invite her to come here instead, and a similar note to Mrs Hunter-Jones, adding to each the tantalising mention that a long-lost relative from America was due to call. Of course curiosity would be bound to bring them. With a piece of information like that offered, nothing short of war or plague would keep them away.

Naturally she had brought her own maid, Mabel, with her from Ashworth Hall. That was the least comfort they could afford her. Accordingly it was Mabel who looked out Mariah's best black afternoon gown – she was a widow and, like the Queen, had refused to wear anything but black for the last twenty-five years.

Mabel helped her dress, to a constant stream of instruction and criticism, of which she took little notice.

'There you are, ma'am,' she said at last. 'You look very nice – fit to meet anyone.'

The old lady grunted and surveyed herself in her glass for the final time, straightened her lace collar and went to the bedroom door.

Who was this Samuel Ellison person? Of course she knew

her husband had been married before. She had never told Caroline because she did not need to know, and it was not a matter Mariah desired to discuss with anyone. She had not known there was a son. It was perfectly possible this man was an impostor, but if he really resembled Edward so closely, then presumably he was genuine. She would know as soon as she saw him.

She opened the door and stepped out on to the landing. There was no need to be disquieted, even if the man was who he claimed to be. If he were she would be pleasant to him, and the afternoon would pass agreeably enough. After all, he was American, she could hardly be held responsible if he were not socially desirable. She could apologise, disclaim all connection, and not invite him again.

And if he was charming, interesting, amusing, so much the better.

If he were an impostor she would ring for the butler and have him shown out, abruptly. Mrs Blanie and Mrs Hunter-Jones would understand. Everyone had relatives they did not care to own. It happened even in the best families.

She went down the stairs and into the withdrawing room.

Caroline was standing by the window looking out. As the old lady came in she turned around. She was very handsome for her age, one might almost say beautiful, except that she had a light in her eye and a flush to her cheek which was unbecoming in a mature woman. She should know how to behave with more discretion. And that shade of burgundy was much too rich.

'You are overdressed,' the old lady remarked critically. 'He will think he has come to dinner! It is barely three o'clock in the afternoon.'

'Well, if he looks at you, he will expect baked meats!'

Caroline retorted. 'You seem to be dressed for a funeral!'

The old lady straightened to total rigidity. 'I am a widow! As are you, or you were – until you went off and married that actor! I would have thought in deference to the fact that this man is apparently a member of our family, and his brother is dead, you might have worn something more in keeping with the occasion.' She sat down solidly in the best chair.

Caroline looked at her closely. 'You never told us that Grandpapa had been married previously.'

The old lady avoided her eyes. 'It is not your concern,' she said coldly. 'She was a woman of . . .' For once she was uncertain. Dark memories brushed the edge of her mind and she refused to allow them closer. 'She ran away.' Her voice grew sharper. 'She abandoned him. Went off with some worthless adventurer . . .' That was a lie, but it was easier to believe, and to understand. 'Naturally we did not speak of it. No one would.' That was true.

'Edward might have wished to know he had a half-brother,' Caroline said quite gently.

'No one knew,' the old lady replied, her voice steadier. That also was true. She had no idea whatever that Alys had been with child. Edmund would not have let her go so easily if he had known. To lose a son would be altogether a different matter.

Caroline started as there was a sound outside, but no one came to the door.

Grandmama deliberately unclenched her hands. They were cold and a little clammy with tension. Memories long forgotten were stirring in her mind, shapeless pain, things denied so long they were only darkness now, no sharp edges, just the ache. Why didn't someone arrive, so she did not have to work so hard at not thinking?

There it was! A carriage outside. The footsteps across the hall, the murmur of voices. Thank heaven. It would be Mrs Blanie, her curiosity overwhelming her.

She came bustling in, also dressed in black, with far too many bows, as if her afternoon gown were made of dozens of pieces of silk all tied together rather than stitched. But she had pretty hair and a common sense face.

They greeted each other with the same reticence as always, and mentioned something trite about the weather. A moment later Mrs Hunter-Jones arrived. She was a large woman who cared very much about correct appearance, and seemed quite unaware that blue did not become her, but then her voice was unusually attractive, especially when she laughed.

'How exciting for you,' she said enthusiastically. 'It is so tedious to know all one's relatives, and find that most of them are quite interchangeable, for any interest they may offer in conversation. I haven't a single one who comes from any further away than Berkshire! Isn't it dreadful?'

'If they came from Berkshire, at least they can go home again quite quickly,' Mrs Blanie responded. 'Mine come from Edinburgh, which obliges them to stay for weeks. And they say the same thing every year anyway. I don't know why they bother.'

Another few moments of similar conversation came to an end when the door opened and the butler announced Mr Samuel Ellison.

As one person they all turned to face him. He was tall, well built and dressed in the latest cut of waistcoat and jacket, but all this was nothing to Grandmama. Her breath almost stopped in her throat as she saw his face. He was so like her own son a wave of loss overtook her like a physical pain. It was not that she and Edward had been friends, or shared ideas or confidences, it was the bond of years of knowledge, of memories of childhood intimacy, the very fact that he was part of her. And here was this man of whose existence she had been unaware until this morning, and he had the same eyes, the same shape of head, the same manner of moving.

Caroline was welcoming him in and before she was ready for it, presenting him to Grandmama.

He bowed, smiling at her, his expression full of interest as he looked at her face.

'How do you do, Mrs Ellison? It is charming of you to receive me with almost no notice at all. But after so long, hoping to meet my English family, I simply could not wait another day.'

'How do you do, Mr Ellison?' she replied. It was difficult to say the name, her own name, to a stranger. 'I hope your stay in England will be a pleasant one.'

Mrs Blanie and Mrs Hunter-Jones were fascinated. They gave him the same welcome, and they all sat down to exchange small talk of the usual innocuous and meaningless kind. However, almost immediately it took another turn. Mrs Blanie had made some trivial enquiry about Samuel's youth, and he replied with a vivid description of New York, where apparently his mother had landed from the ship which had taken her across the Atlantic.

'Alone?' Mrs Blanie said in amazement. 'Poor creature! However did she manage?' Perhaps it was an intrusive question. The answer may not have been one he was willing to give, but it was made from instinctive sympathy.

'Oh, there were many of us in the same circumstances,' Samuel replied easily. 'We helped one another, as I was telling Mrs Fielding yesterday evening.' He glanced at her with a smile.

'And my mother was a woman of remarkable courage, and never afraid to work hard.'

Grandmama barely heard their murmured replies. Her mind was filled with thoughts of this woman she had never seen, who had been Edmund's first wife, and fled to America alone, without a friend or ally in the world, according to Samuel, and carrying Edmund's child. Why had she gone if not with some lover? The answer to that lay like a dark and ugly threat just out of reach, but close . . . far too close!

'And did you remain in New York?' Mrs Hunter-Jones enquired.

'Oh no!' Samuel replied with a wide smile. 'In '48, when I was twenty, I decided to journey westward, just to go and see it, you understand?'

'And leave your poor mother?' Mrs Blanie's eyebrows rose.

'Oh, believe me, ma'am, my mother was well able to care for herself by then,' he assured her, leaning back more comfortably in his chair. 'She had a nice little business going in dressmaking, and employed several girls. She had made friends and knew a great many people. She missed me, I hope, but she did not mind when I packed up and went west, first to Pittsburgh, then up to Illinois.'

'Oh, my gracious!' Mrs Hunter-Jones breathed in, her face pink with excitement. 'Did you see Indians . . . wild men?'

'Surely I did!' he replied with a broad grin. 'As close as I see you. Beautiful, they were, with high cheekbones and long black hair with feathers stuck in it.' He glanced at Caroline, and Grandmama thought she saw him wink.

Mrs Blanie was not sure if he were joking. She waited for him to continue, which he did with marvellous descriptions of the great plains that stretched for a thousand miles westwards to the foothills of the Rocky Mountains.

Grandmama began to relax. He was merely entertaining, after all. He had an audience, and they were enraptured. Like most men, he loved to be the centre of attention. Unlike most, he had a great gift for anecdote, and a very ready sense of humour. The ladies were enthralled, including Caroline. Her face was quite flushed and she had barely taken her eyes off him since he began.

Tea was brought, poured and passed. This was a good idea, after all. The afternoon would be spoken of with great relish. Mrs Waterman would regret being so dismissive. Her uncle who had been to Berlin was very tame compared with this.

'But you returned to New York?' Mrs Blanie was saying, sipping her tea carefully.

'I came back east when my mother was taken ill,' Samuel answered her.

'Of course,' she nodded. 'Of course. You would naturally want to take care of her. She never married again?'

A curious expression crossed Samuel's face, a mixture of pity and something which could have been anger.

Grandmama felt the chill of warning shiver through her. It was not over. She wanted to say something to cut off Mrs Blanie's intrusive enquiries, but for once she could think of nothing which would not simply make it worse.

It was Caroline who saved the issue, albeit unintentionally.

'I hope she recovered. She must still have been quite young.'

'Oh, yes,' Samuel responded cheerfully. 'It proved to be no more than a passing thing, thank heaven.'

'You must have been close,' Caroline said gently, 'having endured so much together.'

His face softened and there was a great tenderness in his

102

eyes. 'We were. Much as I wished to find my English family as well, I don't think I would ever have left America while she was alive. I never knew a person, man or woman, with more courage and strength of will to follow their own mind and be their own person, whatever it cost.'

Mrs Blanie looked slightly puzzled.

'Well, well,' Mrs Hunter-Jones said meaninglessly.

Caroline smiled; there was a sweetness in her, almost a glow, as if the words held great value for her.

'It does cost,' she agreed, looking intently at Samuel. 'One can be so uncertain, so filled with doubts and loneliness, and the way cannot always be retraced. Sometimes it is too late before you even realise what you have paid.'

Samuel looked at her with quite open appreciation, as though she had offered him a profound compliment.

'I see you understand very well, Mrs Fielding. I believe you would have liked her, and she you. You seem to be of one mind.'

Grandmama stiffened. What was he talking about? The woman had left her husband and run off to America! He was speaking as if it were some kind of a virtue! How much did he know? Surely she would never have – could never . . . no woman would! The coldness hardened inside her, like ice. Old memories of pain returned, things forgotten years ago, pushed into the oblivion at the edges of her mind.

She must do something, now, before it was too late.

'I suppose you were there during that miserable war?' she said abruptly. 'It must have been most disagreeable.'

'That hardly begins to describe it, Mrs Ellison,' Samuel said gravely. 'Any war is dreadful, but one among people of one nation, who are even known to each other, perhaps brothers, fathers and sons, is the most terrible. The violence and the hatred has a bitterness which does not fade.'

Neither Mrs Blanie nor Mrs Hunter-Jones seemed to understand.

He perceived it quickly and his expression changed. The sense of tragedy was wiped away; compassion and a wry humour replaced it.

'I can't say I enjoyed being a soldier, but looking back on it, I think it is something I couldn't regret.'

'Really?' Mrs Blanie remarked with surprise. 'Perhaps you would explain?'

More tea was sent for. No one even thought of leaving. Grandmama would dearly like to have brought the afternoon to a decent conclusion, but it was very apparent that neither of her guests had any intention of leaving. Samuel himself was charming, and his tales were quite the most interesting they were likely to hear in years of afternoon calls. At least while he was discussing the Civil War, he was not speaking of his mother.

He judged it very well. He mentioned battles by name, but he avoided describing any fighting or the horror of injuries, cold or disease. And yet neither did he allow it to seem as if there had been any glory without loss. He told them of individual episodes, his voice expressing laughter or sorrow, his face reflecting everything he felt.

None of the women spoke. Mrs Blanie's eyes were fixed on his face, her hand halfway to her mouth, her tea forgotten. Mrs Hunter-Jones's cake slipped from her lips and landed unnoticed in her lap.

Grandmama felt a certain satisfaction that this tea party would be the talk of her friends for months to come, perhaps even years, certainly long after Samuel Ellison had returned home to America.

'I couldn't rightly say I was proud of any part of that war,' Samuel said quietly. 'It was too big a tragedy for a country I can't help loving. Too many men died – and women too – and there's a bitterness left I'll not live to see the end of.' He was looking at them very steadily. 'But when men see fearful things together, share a terror and a hope, know each other's pain and the sorrow that comes when you see a land destroyed, and brother fighting brother, you learn to laugh at little things, because it's the only way for sanity. Otherwise you'd just break apart. Sometimes it's the silly things that hold you together.' His voice dropped even lower. 'If you'd ever been really sick with fear till your stomach knotted up like a fist, you'd understand that.'

A wave like a prickle of heat swept over Grandmama's skin as memory washed around her in a tide, followed by a chill that left her shaking as if she had swallowed ice. How dare he make her feel like this? How dare he arrive out of nowhere and awaken the past?

It was Caroline's voice which cut across the silence and jerked her back to this pleasant, modest room with its well-worn, comfortable furnishings, the afternoon light streaming in through the windows on to the carpet.

'You speak of it with such passion we can feel something of what you know,' she said softly.

Samuel turned to look at her, and moved momentarily as if he would have put out his hand to touch her, had he not remembered in time that it would be too familiar.

'What did you do after the war?' she asked. She heard the hard edge in her own voice, but it was beyond her control. 'You must have made a living at something!'

'And what about your poor mother?' Mrs Blanie added.

105

'Who cared for her – all this time?'

His face filled with a softness which changed him profoundly. For the first time the confidence was gone, and in its place one saw for a moment a more vulnerable man, one with more knowledge of his own need, and the understanding that much of his strength came from another source. Grandmama wanted to like him for it, and could not because she was afraid of what he was going to say.

'My mother cared for herself, ma'am,' he answered, and he could not keep the pride out of his voice. 'And for a good many others also. She had all the courage in the world. She never thought twice about fighting for what she believed to be right – win or lose.' He lifted his chin a little. 'She taught me all I know of how to face an enemy, no matter how you feel or what you fear the cost will be. I've often thought, in my worst moments, how I'd like to be worthy of her. I dare say there's many a man the same.'

Grandmama felt the misery tighten inside her, like an iron band, never to be escaped again. Damn him for coming! Damn Caroline for letting him. It's easy to talk about courage and fighting when the battle is an honourable one, and everybody understands! When you aren't so ashamed you could die of it!

Was that what he was talking about? Did he guess – even know? She stared at his charming, humorous face, so like her own son's in its features, but she could not read it! There was no one she could turn to, certainly never Caroline! She must not know, ever. All those times they had quarrelled, the times over the years, even more often recently, when she had told her what a fool she was . . . marrying a man two-thirds her age instead of retiring decently into widowhood. It was bound to end in disaster, and she had told her that. It was no less than the truth. It would be unbearable now, unliveable with, if Caroline were to know all her long-buried darkness. She would rather be dead, and respectably buried somewhere . . . even beside Edmund. That was probably what they would do. It was what she had told them she wanted – but what else could she say?

But one did not die merely of wanting to. She knew that well enough.

They were talking again. The noise buzzed around her like a jar full of flies.

'. . . back in New York?' Mrs Blanie was saying.

'Was it very different after the war?' Caroline asked. She was bent forward a little, the deep burgundy silk of her dress pulled tight across her shoulders, her face intent. She was very individual, the intelligence and will in her, the unusual shape of her mouth. The old lady had thought her beautiful in the beginning. Now they were too familiar for her to think in such terms. And beauty belonged to the young.

'Changed beyond belief,' Samuel was answering her. A curious expression crossed his face, laughter in his eyes and something which could have been excitement, and both sadness and distaste in his mouth. 'The war had left everything in a flux. New York was not a big city.' He gave a little shrug. 'Not compared with London . . . but well over three-quarters of a million people, and I've heard it said thirty thousand of them thieves, and twenty thousand women of . . . I don't know any way of putting it delicately . . .'

They understood. Mrs Blanie sighed. Mrs Hunter-Jones moved a little in her seat, rustling the silk of her dress. Caroline hid a smile. But then lately, she thought, she had lost all the sense of decorum she had once possessed!

'And how do you know that?' Grandmama enquired. 'I would not have the faintest idea how many thieves there are in London.'

Samuel shook his head, the swift amusement lighting his face again.

'I'm sure you would not, Mrs Ellison, even were you a young man in his late thirties recently returned from the fear and hardship of war, and the strange tragedies of victory, which were far more bitter in the mouth than any of us had foreseen. New York was nothing like London, although I've seen wealth side by side with poverty here too. But there is a respectability here, a maturity, which has a far different flavour. New York then was raw and jumping, like an open wound. There was nothing secret in the corruption. It came right from the top, Boss Tweed himself, and ran through every channel of government and police like veins through flesh. Prick it anywhere, and it bled graft and violence. The police were little better than the mobs – less open about it, that's all.' He drew in a long breath. 'Perhaps that makes them worse?'

Caroline nodded her agreement. She was regarding him with fascination. As if any of this mattered! Still, it was a safe enough subject, and Mrs Blanie and Mrs Hunter-Jones seemed almost as interested. This party would be the talk of the neighbourhood, and the envy.

'There is no "perhaps" about it!' Grandmama said waspishly. 'One may not especially admire the police . . .' She thought of Charlotte, and her marriage to Pitt: Caroline should not have allowed that. Charlotte was awkward enough, heaven knew, but something better could have been managed! 'Or wish to associate with them,' she continued. 'But at least one ought to be able to trust them.'

Samuel turned to her, his eyes wide. 'I met your granddaughter's husband at the theatre,' he said with a smile.

How stupid! She had forgotten that.

'Indeed! Then you know precisely what I mean!' she said ungraciously. At that moment the thought of Pitt's probing eyes was peculiarly unwelcome.

'I imagine he is a good detective,' Samuel said generously. 'But he would hardly be the man to have tackled the gangs in New York after the war. You can't imagine men like the Bowery Boys, or the Slaughter Housers.' He spread his hands expressively. 'There were three hundred saloons in the city in those days. I saw a few.' He made a little gesture of apology. 'I was in McGurk's Suicide Hall, and the Tub of Blood more than once. I remember Wreck Donovan, and Eddie the Plague, One-Lung Curren, Baboon Dooley, Slops Connally. I was in the saloon the night before Happy Jack Mulraney killed the saloon keeper for laughing at him. Happy Jack had a twitch . . .' He imitated it, jerking his eye and cheek very slightly till Caroline and Mrs Blaine both dissolved in giggles, in spite of themselves.

'The poor devil thought Jack was laughing at him,' he went on. 'And he laughed back. It was the last thing he ever did.' He sighed. 'And there were others: Boiled Oysters Malloy – I never knew why they called him that – Ludwig the Bloodsucker. He was the hairiest man I ever saw. I met him face to face one night, when I confess I was more than a little drunk. He had hair growing out of every possible place and it was easy enough to imagine he was not entirely human. Not that I believe in vampires, of course! But I did that night!'

Caroline was laughing, not completely certain if he was serious, or at least half teasing them.

Mrs Blanie was shaking her head, but she never for an instant took her eyes from his face.

'And there were pirates up and down the Hudson River,' he resumed. 'They used to terrorise the poor farmers. Scotchy Lavelle was one, and of course the worst of them all was Sadie the Goat, who led her gang out of an old gin mill on the East Side waterfront.'

'Sadie the Goat?' Grandmama said witheringly. 'It sounds like a farmyard animal.'

Samuel was leaning forward, his elbows on his knees. 'Oh, she was a woman all right,' he said. 'They called her that because she used to attack people by lowering her head and charging them in the stomach, and when the wind was knocked out of them and they were on the floor, her partner would rob them of anything they fancied.' He raised both his hands. 'But she met her match in Gallus Mag, who kept the Hole-in-the-Wall saloon.'

He stopped. He was obviously enjoying telling the story. If there were memories in it that hurt him, they were long since absorbed or healed over. He glanced from one to another of them, but more often at Caroline, and the brilliance in her eyes suggested she knew it.

'Yes?' she asked.

His face broke into a smile. 'Gallus Mag used to bite the ears off people she didn't like. She kept them in vinegar in a pickle jar behind the bar. When she and Sadie fell out, she won – and put Sadie's ear with the rest.'

'You're joking . . . aren't you?' Mrs Blanie said tentatively, her face very pink.

'No! I swear!' he answered her, laughing now. 'They made up the quarrel later, and Gallus Meg gave Sadie her ear back.

She put it on a pendant and wore it around her neck.'

Caroline burst into laughter. 'Oh really!'

'Really!' he assured them, his eyes dancing. 'It was an extraordinary time, bursting with violence and life, all kinds of men dispossessed, all the old certainties gone, hundreds of soldiers trying to return to homes and lives that no longer existed. There are always profiteers in war, and afterwards.' A note of rage sharpened his voice, as sudden as it was unexpected. He had hidden most of his feelings, recounted things at the core of his life as if they had been merely history he had happened to observe.

Then the glimpse of nakedness was gone. His face resumed its mask of good-humoured interest.

'Did you remain in New York?' Caroline asked. She did not mean to be intrusive, but she was enthralled by him. He reminded her of Edward, of past years which were at times very ordinary, lacking in understanding or imagination, but looking back now had a warmth she had almost forgotten. How easy it was to mistake safety for boredom! There had been so much that was good . . . unspoken, perhaps, but then not everyone believed in the necessity for words. There was a familiarity that did not require them.

Samuel was looking at her curiously, as if he realised for a moment her thoughts had been elsewhere, far from this moment or this room.

'No, I didn't,' he replied. 'In '69 I went west again . . . much further this time. The country was opening up. People were driving the railroad right across the continent from one ocean to the other. I had a hunger to see what it was all about.' He made a tiny, self-deprecating gesture.

'Aren't there savages all over the west?' Mrs Hunter-Jones

said guilelessly. 'Don't they cut the heads off people, or something terrible?'

'You're thinking of scalps, ma'am,' he corrected her. 'It's Europeans who cut people's heads off. And come to think of it, it was white men who first started cutting scalps off too, then the Indians just copied them, and I guess did it rather better.'

'Better!' Mrs Blanie said in amazement. 'What can you mean?'

'I suppose I mean the idea caught on,' he replied. 'And they used to beat us at our own game.' He looked beyond her, into some distance he alone could see. 'About the only thing they did beat us at. We had the guns, the whisky and the measles – and that's what counted in the end.'

Grandmama glared at him. 'I don't understand you. I thought you said "measles".'

'I did, ma'am. Indians can't take whisky, and they can't take the measles. Killed thousands of them.'

'Why didn't it kill the white men as well?' Caroline asked with a shiver, trying not to picture in her mind the ravages of disease.

'I guess we're used to it,' Samuel replied, turning again to her with something like relief. 'Sometimes we think all people are made the same. Other times we see how different they are.'

'Well, I never imagined I was anything like a savage with a bow and arrow!' Mrs Hunter-Jones said swiftly.

'You're not so different from a squaw, underneath,' Samuel replied.

Mrs Hunter-Jones froze.

Samuel blushed.

Caroline found herself bursting with laughter. She took a

look at Samuel's flaming cheeks and allowed herself to let it erupt.

He looked at her with intense gratitude.

Grandmama was furious. She opened her mouth to say something crushing. Then she changed her mind and swallowed whatever it had been. Her hands were clenched together in her lap, nails biting her palms. Caroline realised with amazement that the old lady was labouring under some emotion far fiercer than simple irritation or embarrassment. Her whole body, under her black silk and jet beads, was rigid, the muscles of her neck corded as if she were waiting for a blow to strike her.

Caroline ought to care. She ought to want to defend her, but the old woman had exercised so many years of criticism and carping complaint she had no pity left. If Samuel's arrival troubled her, if the remembrance of some earlier marriage, before Grandpapa even knew her, disturbed her, then she would just have to accommodate herself to it. Samuel was here, and Caroline was delighted. She liked his company. He made her laugh, and he was most certainly interesting. He was a relation and they would make him welcome.

'I'm sure we all are,' she said aloud. 'We might suffer differently from illnesses, but I imagine we all feel the same about our children, and our husbands, our homes. We probably have many of the same dreams, especially when we are young.'

Mrs Hunter-Jones looked at her as if she had spoken in Chinese. 'You must speak for yourself, my dear Mrs . . . Fielding . . .'

Caroline looked at Samuel. 'Don't Indian girls dream of falling in love with somebody handsome and brave, who will love them above all others, who will look after them and be gentle, and make them laugh? And that in time they will have children, and watch them grow up, and be strong, and happy?'

Again he reached out his hand as if to touch her, then let it fall to the edge of her skirt where it lay on the chair.

'I think so,' he said softly. 'I think all the world depends upon its women dreaming of those things, and having the will to make them happen, or something as close to it as possible. I am afraid we men don't always live up to it.' There was a sadness in him, and his hand tightened for a moment on the red silk of her skirt, then withdrew.

Grandmama let out a strange, choking little sound between her teeth, as if she were aching to speak, but dared not. Such a restraint was unthinkable in her. She had never held her tongue for anyone – all the years Caroline had known her, which was nearly forty now. She had never cared in the slightest what effect her words might have on others.

She caught Caroline looking at her, and glared back, then suddenly turned away.

'Well, I suppose if you put it like that . . .' Mrs Hunter-Jones said awkwardly.

Samuel recovered himself. Caroline could see that it cost him a little effort of concentration, but she imagined no one else observed it.

'The men and women who took the wagon trains through were among the finest and bravest I've ever known,' he resumed his tale. 'The hardships they endured, without complaint, were enough to make you weep. And they were all sorts: Germans, Italians, Swedes and French, Spaniards, Irish and Russians, but so many from right here. I came across one group of English people who were pushing all their worldly possessions in handcarts, women walking beside, some with babes in arms, going all the way to the Salt Lake Valley. God knows how many died on the way.'

'I cannot imagine it,' Mrs Blanie said softly. 'I don't know how people have the courage.'

The parlour-maid brought yet more fresh tea and cakes. It was far too interesting for anyone to think of excusing themselves to leave. This was the afternoon call of a lifetime. In recounting it Mrs Blanie and Mrs Hunter-Jones could be the centres of attention for the next five years.

Caroline watched Samuel and thought of yesterday evening at the theatre, and how utterly different that had been. She could see perfectly in her mind's eye Cecily Antrim's vivid figure illuminated on the stage, her hair like a halo in the lights, her every gesture full of passion and imprisoned despair. She wanted so much more than she had. Would that woman ever conceive of what it would be like to struggle simply to survive?

Or were the emotions much the same, only the object of the hunger different? Did one long for love, for the freedom to be yourself, unrestrained by social expectations, with the same fierceness as one hungered for religious or political freedom, and set out to walk on foot into a vast and unknown land, inhabited only by an alien race who saw you as an invader?

Cecily Antrim was fighting a complex and sophisticated society in order to win the freedom to say anything she wished. Caroline felt threatened by her. Sitting here watching Samuel and less than half listening to him, she could admit that. She was used to a world where certain things were not said. It was safer. There were things she did not want to know, about others and about herself. There were emotions she did not want to think others understood. It made her naked in a dangerous way, and far too vulnerable.

115

Cecily Antrim was very brave. Nothing seemed to frighten her sufficiently to deter her. That was part of what Joshua admired so much; that, and her beauty. It was unique, not a prettiness at all, far too strong, too passionate and uncompromising for that. Her face had a symmetry from every angle, a balance in the smoothness of the bones, the wide, unflinching eyes. She moved with extraordinary grace. She made Caroline feel very ordinary, sort of brown and old, like a moth instead of a butterfly.

And the worst thing of all was that it was not merely physical. Cecily had such vigour and courage to fight for whatever she believed in, and Caroline was increasingly unsure of what she thought was right or wrong. She wanted to agree with Joshua – that censorship was wrong. The only way to freedom and growth, to the just equality of one person's faith with another's, was for ideas to be expressed and questions to be asked, comfortable or not. And for laws to be changed, people's emotions had to be awoken, sympathies for passions and beliefs outside their own experience. That was what her mind told her.

Deeper, woven into her being, was the conviction that there are things that should never be spoken, perhaps not even known.

Was that cowardice?

She was quite certain Cecily Antrim would think so, and would despise her for it, though that hardly mattered. It was what Joshua thought that would hurt. Would he also find a gulf opening up between them, between the brave of heart and mind, those strong enough to look at everything life had to offer, and those like Caroline, who wanted to stay where it was safe, where ugly things could be hidden away and denied?

Samuel was still talking, but he was looking mostly at her. Mrs Blanie and Mrs Hunter-Jones were merely onlookers he

116

was too polite to ignore. And Grandmama sat straight-backed, her black eyes fixed, her face set in lines so rigid one might have thought she was battling some kind of pain.

For the first time Caroline wondered how much the old lady had known of the first Mrs Ellison. Presumably when they were married she must have been aware that she had had a predecessor. There would have been legal necessities, and perhaps religious ones also. What kind of a woman was Samuel's mother that she had bolted from Edmund Ellison, from England altogether, and gone across the Atlantic by herself?

Socially a disaster. In England in 1828 it had been a crime for a woman to leave her husband, whatever he had done, or failed to do, whatever she had wished. The law, had he chosen to invoke it, could have brought her back to him by force. Presumably he had not wished that. Perhaps he had even been glad to be relieved of her, though from all that Samuel had said, she had been an excellent mother to him, and his love for her shone in his face every time he spoke of her. He had never mentioned her name with indifference. Perhaps he knew nothing of the circumstances? Or whatever she had told him had been the facts as she saw them, but less than the truth.

He was watching Caroline now as he spoke of his journey in the steamship across the Atlantic and of his docking in Liverpool, and later his first sight of London. His eyes were dancing with it, and she could not help smiling in return.

His company was remarkably pleasant. He was most interesting to listen to, he had seen so much and recounted it vividly and with a generous spirit. Yet she did not feel threatened as she had yesterday in Cecily Antrim's dressing room. She was sufficiently experienced in the difference between good manners and friendship to be certain that he liked her, and it was a most pleasing feeling. There was admiration in his eyes as he regarded her and it was like warmth after a sense of deep chill. He would not find her boring or conventional in her ideas. She did not feel left behind by more daring minds, quicker and more agile, and – she said the word to herself at last – younger.

Was that at the core of it, not just sophistication and physical beauty, but age? She was seventeen years older than Joshua. It was like poking at an unhealed wound just to say it to herself. Perhaps the old woman, with her vindictive, all-seeing eyes, was right, and she had been a fool to marry a man she was absurdly in love with, who made her laugh and cry, but who in the end would not be able to protect himself from finding her boring!

That would be the ultimate pain – loyalty through pity.

'. . . and of course at the theatre my host told me of his acquaintance with Mrs Fielding,' Samuel was saying. 'And that she had been Mrs Ellison until her recent marriage. You can imagine how delighted I was! Well . . . no, you can't,' he amended. 'I feel as if in a sense I have come back to my roots, a homecoming.'

'I am glad you find London so entertaining,' Grandmama said rather curtly. 'I am sure your new friends will wish to show you all manner of things: the Tower, the parks, riding in Rotten Row, perhaps Kew Gardens? There are all sorts of sights to see, not to mention Society, to meet. I am afraid we no longer know anyone.' She gave a sideways look at Caroline, then back to Samuel. It was a dismissal, and so phrased as to make it clear he need not look to return in the near future. Duty had been satisfied.

Caroline was furious, and unreasonably disappointed. Damn

118

Grandmama. She turned a radiant smile on Samuel as he rose to his feet.

'Thank you so much for giving us one of the most delightful and interesting afternoons I can ever recall,' she said warmly. 'It has been a journey into another land without the dangers and inconvenience of travel. I know you must have a thousand things to see, but I do hope you will come again. We may lay some superior claim to you, since we are family, and we must not lose each other now.'

'Don't be ridiculous!' the old lady snapped, swivelling around to glare at her. 'Mr Ellison has called upon us, which is all we could possibly expect of him. We cannot suppose that a man who has fought in a war and ridden with savages, not to mention drunk with people like Slops Molloy, or whatever he was called, and women who bite people's ears off and pickle them, will find himself entertained taking tea with old women in a withdrawing room.'

'I do not judge people by their age, Mrs Ellison,' he replied immediately. 'Some of the most interesting people I have ever met have been on the upper side of seventy, and have learned wisdom far greater than mine. It is a mistake of the young to assume that only they have passion or beauty, and I am far too old myself to fall into that error any more. I hope I shall be invited to call again.' He glanced at Caroline, then away. His meaning did not need elaboration.

Grandmama's face pinched, her lips tightened and she said nothing.

Caroline rose also and moved towards the door to accompany him at least as far as the hall when he had bidden the others farewell. 'And as for being invited,' she said warmly, 'please consider that you are always welcome.'

He accepted instantly, and after wishing each of the ladies goodbye, he took his leave. Mrs Blanie and Mrs Hunter-Jones left too. It had been an extraordinarily long afternoon and they would be late for dinner as it was.

When Caroline returned to the withdrawing room her maid informed her that the old lady had retired to her room, and she did not reappear all evening, nor send further word.

Chapter Five

~❧~

In the morning Pitt and Tellman returned to the area of Battersea near Cathcart's house. It was a grey day with a fine mist swirling in from the river, and Pitt had turned his coat collar up against it. Tellman trudged along with his head down, his face set in lines of disapproval.

'I don't know what you think we can find,' he said morosely. 'It was probably some time in the middle of the night when all decent folk were asleep anyway.'

Actually Pitt agreed with him, but Tellman's perversity was irritating and he refused to let him win.

'This is the neighbourhood where Cathcart lived,' he replied. 'Since we don't know exactly when he was killed, and we certainly don't know why or by whom, can you think of anything better?'

Tellman grunted. 'How's Mrs Pitt getting on in Paris?' he asked in retaliation. He glanced sideways at Pitt's face, then away again. He read him too well.

'Enjoying it,' Pitt answered. 'Says it's a beautiful city and very exciting. The women have a flair for dress and are extremely elegant. They look as if they achieve it without any effort at all. She says it's infuriating.'

'Well, they're French, aren't they?' Tellman asked reasonably. 'One would expect them to be infuriating,' he added.

In spite of himself Pitt grinned.

'If Cathcart was half as clever as that woman said he was,' Tellman returned to the subject in hand, 'then he probably got above himself with someone, and maybe tried a touch of blackmail. I dare say photographers are like servants, and they get to see a lot of things. Maybe people think they don't matter, and speak in front of them. He moved around in plenty of big houses, sort of there, but not there, if you know what I mean? He might have found it out only by accident, but took his chance.'

The road was wet underfoot, heavy dew glistening in the hedges. The mournful sound of a foghorn drifted up from the water.

Pitt pushed his hands hard into his pockets. 'That leaves us a pretty wide field,' he said thoughtfully. 'I'd like to know how much he earned with his photography, and what he spent.'

Tellman did not bother to ask why.

'And how much of that house and its furnishings he inherited,' Pitt went on, thinking of the works of art he had seen, and trying to make some mental assessment of their value.

Tellman was looking at him. 'Worth a lot?' he asked, curiously. He knew forgery of banknotes and letters of credit, and the disposal of ordinary household goods and silver, but not art of that quality.

Pitt had not doubted that what he had seen in Cathcart's house was genuine – probably even the vase which had been smashed, and almost certainly the once beautiful rug that they had fished out of the river.

'Yes . . .'

'More than you'd earn taking photographs of the gentry?'

'I wouldn't be surprised.'

Tellman's chin came up a little. 'Right!' he said more cheerfully. 'Then we'd better see what we can find out about Mr Cathcart!'

They parted company, Tellman going to the local shops and generally asking around. Pitt returned to Cathcart's house and, with Mrs Geddes looking on proprietorially, made what assessment he could of the value of the works of art he could see. Then went through Cathcart's desk, looking at such bills and receipts as were there. They covered approximately the last three months. It seemed Cathcart did not stint himself for anything that took his fancy. His tailor's bills were enormous, but all receipted within days of being presented. His appointments diary noted several trips to various other cities within a comfortable train journey: Bath, Winchester, Tunbridge Wells, Brighton, Gloucester. There was no indication whether he was going on business or pleasure.

Pitt leaned back in the elegant chair and read the list of clients Cathcart had photographed in the previous six months. He made notes of those for the last five weeks. It seemed Cathcart worked hard on preparation before he finally made his portraits. He took time to learn about his subject, and to suggest several possibilities to them.

Next he went through Cathcart's professional receipts for photographic materials, which were surprisingly expensive. The margin for profit was not nearly as large as he had supposed. And then there were all the pieces of stage dressing he used, not to mention the generator for the lights.

He must find out if Cathcart had inherited this house and its beautiful carpets, pictures, furniture, vases, and so on. Even if he had, it seemed he must live to the limit of his income, unless there were another source.

He should also find out if Cathcart had left a will. He certainly had much to bequeath. He searched the desk again to find a note of who was his man of affairs, who would surely know.

He found it only just before Tellman returned, looking less than pleased.

'Didn't shop much around here,' he said, sitting down gingerly on a Sheraton chair, as if he were afraid he might break its beautiful legs. 'Mrs Geddes seems to have bought most of the household necessities. Sent his stuff out to be laundered – linens, clothes, all of it. Expensive.' He grunted. 'Still, I suppose keeping a staff would cost a bit too, and it may be he preferred not to have anyone around too much.'

'What's the gossip?' Pitt leaned back in the desk chair.

'Not a lot,' Tellman replied. 'Beyond the impression that he's got money and is a bit odd. Some have a less charitable word for it, but comes to the same thing. Local chap comes in twice a week and does the garden, but seems Cathcart liked it all overgrown and artistic, like. Can't bear rows of things, and can't be bothered with vegetables or anything useful.'

'Perhaps in his profession flowers are more use?' Pitt suggested. 'Roses on the arches and pergolas, the willow trailing over the water.'

Tellman refrained from comment. 'You find anything?' He had always resented calling Pitt 'sir', and for some time now had abandoned it altogether, except when he was being sarcastic.

'He went through a lot of money,' Pitt replied. 'More than he earned as a photographer, unless his books are fiddled. But

I need to know if he inherited the house, and the things in it . . . which are probably worth more than it is.'

Tellman looked around, his brows drawn together. 'Reckon he was killed for it? People have killed for a lot less, but not dressed them up and chained them like that. That's . . . personal.'

'Yes I know,' Pitt said quietly. 'But we need to find out all the same.'

'Now what?' Tellman asked, his eyes going surreptitiously to the Chinese vase on the mantelpiece, and then across to a blue plaque with raised white figures of dancing children on it, which Pitt guessed to be Italian Renaissance, either della Robbia, or a good copy. He had seen something like it once recovered from a burglary.

'Is it really worth a lot?' Tellman asked.

'I think so. We'll find out if he inherited it. And who inherits it now.' Pitt folded up the paper he had been writing on and put it in his pocket with the usual variety of things already there, and stood up. 'We'll go and find Mr Dobson of Phipps, Barlow & Jones, Cathcart's solicitors. He should be able to answer both questions for us.'

Mr Dobson was a mild-mannered man with a long, distinguished face which fell very naturally into lines of the gravity appropriate to his calling.

'Police, you say?' He regarded Pitt's untidy figure dubiously. Tellman he seemed to have no doubt of.

Pitt produced his card and offered it.

'Ah!' Dobson let out a sigh, apparently satisfied. 'Come in, gentlemen.' He indicated his office and followed after them, closing the door. 'Please be seated. What can I do for you?'

'We are here regarding Mr Delbert Cathcart. I believe he

is a client of yours,' Pitt replied.

'Indeed he is,' Dobson agreed, sitting down and inviting his visitors to do the same. 'But of course his business is confidential, and to the very best of my knowledge, completely honest, and even praiseworthy.'

'You are not aware of his recent death?' Pitt asked him, watching the man's face closely.

'Death?' Dobson was clearly taken aback. 'Did you say death? Are you perfectly sure?'

'I am afraid so,' Pitt replied.

Dobson's eyes narrowed. 'And what brings you here, sir? Is there something questionable about the manner of it?'

Obviously the newspapers had not yet been informed that the body from Horseferry Stairs had been identified, but it could only be a matter of time. Briefly Pitt told him the essentials.

'Oh dear. How extremely distressing.' Dobson shook his head. 'In what manner may I assist you? I knew nothing of it, nor do I know anything which would seem to be relevant. It must be some madman responsible. What is the world coming to?'

Pitt decided to be completely frank. 'It happened in Mr Cathcart's house, Mr Dobson, which would make it probable it was someone he knew.'

Dobson's face expressed misgiving, but he did not interrupt.

'Did Mr Cathcart inherit his house in Battersea?' Pitt asked.

Whatever Dobson had been expecting, his face betrayed that it was not this. 'No! Good heavens, why do you ask?'

'He purchased it himself?'

'Certainly. About, let me see, eight years ago, August of '83, I think. Why? There was nothing irregular in it, I assure you. I handled the matter myself.'

'And the objects of art in it, the furnishings?'

'I have no idea. Are they . . . questionable?'

'Not so far as I know. Who inherits them, Mr Dobson?'

'Various charities, sir. No individual.'

Pitt was surprised, although he had not seriously thought Cathcart had been killed for property, any more than Tellman did. But it cast a new light on Cathcart's income that he had purchased both house and works of art himself. He was aware of Tellman shifting uncomfortably in his chair.

'Thank you,' he sighed, looking at Dobson. 'Did he receive any bequests that you are aware of, from an appreciative client, perhaps? Or a deceased relative?'

'Not so far as I know. Why do you ask, sir?'

'To exclude certain possibilities as to why he may have been killed,' Pitt answered somewhat obliquely. He did not wish to tell Dobson his suspicions as to Cathcart's sources of income.

There was little more to learn, and five minutes later they excused themselves and left.

'Do you think they could be stolen?' Tellman asked as soon as they were in the street. 'If he goes into the houses of all those fancy people and talks to them before he takes their pictures,' he'd be in an ideal position to know what they had and where it was kept!'

'And when they came to his studio to be photographed they'd be in an ideal position to see it again,' Pitt pointed out, stepping round a pile of manure as they crossed the road.

Tellman skipped up on to the kerb on the far side and grunted acknowledgement. He had to stride to keep up with Pitt. He was used to it, but it still annoyed him. 'I suppose those sort all know each other!'

'Probably,' Pitt agreed. 'Couldn't take a risk, anyway. But I suppose we should still check if there've been any robberies. I've got a list of his clients.'

But the enquiries produced nothing, as he had expected. Nor were there reports from anywhere else of objects of art or furniture missing which answered the descriptions of any of the pieces he had seen in Battersea. He was drawn back to the conclusion that Cathcart had a second, and probably larger source of income than his photography, excellent as that was.

He ate a good dinner at the nearest public house, but with little enjoyment, and went home to sit by the stove at the kitchen table for a while. There were no letters from Paris. He went to bed early and was surprised to sleep well.

The following two days he and Tellman spent further investigating Cathcart's life, and visiting his clients listed for the five weeks prior to his death.

Lady Jarvis, whom Pitt called on in the middle of the afternoon of the first day, was typical. She received them in a heavily ornate withdrawing room. Brocade curtains fell almost from ceiling to well below floor length, gathered up in the rich swathes that demonstrated wealth. Pitt thought with some envy that they would also be excellent at keeping out winter drafts, even if now they also excluded some of the golden autumn light. The furniture was massive and where the wood showed it was deeply carved oak, darkened by generations of overpolishing. The surfaces were cluttered with small photographs of various ages of people, all posed solemnly to be immortalised in sepia tint. Several were gentlemen in stiff uniforms, staring earnestly into space.

Lady Jarvis herself was about thirty-five, handsome in a conventional way, although her eyebrows were well marked, like delicate wings, giving her face rather more imagination than a first glance betrayed. Her clothes were expensive and rigidly fashionable, with a very slight bustle, perfect tailoring, big sleeves full at the shoulder. Pitt would dearly liked to have bought Charlotte such a gown. And she would have looked better in it, because he would have chosen a warmer colour, something a little less ordinary than this pedestrian blue.

'You said it was about Mr Cathcart, the photographer?' she began, obvious interest in her face. 'Has somebody brought a complaint?'

'Do you know who might?' Pitt asked quickly.

For her the chance to savour a little of the spice of gossip was too pleasant to pass by, even if it was dangerous.

'It could be Lady Worlingham,' she said half questioningly. 'She was very offended by the portrait he took of her younger daughter, Dorothea. Actually I thought it caught her rather well, and she herself was delighted with it. But I suppose it was a trifle improper.'

Pitt waited.

'All the flowers,' Lady Jarvis went on, waving her hand delicately. 'A bit . . . lush, I suppose. Hid her dress until its existence was left to the imagination . . . in places.' She almost laughed, then remembered herself. 'Has she complained? I wouldn't have thought it was a police matter. There's no law, is there?' She shrugged. 'Anyway, even if there is, I don't have any complaint.' A look of wistfulness crossed her face, just for an instant, as if she would like to have had, and Pitt glimpsed a life of unrelenting correctness where a photograph with too many flowers would have been exciting.

'No, there is no law, ma'am,' he replied quietly. 'And so far as I know Lady Worlingham has not complained. Did Mr Cathcart take your photograph?' He let his glance wander around the room to indicate that he did not see it.

'Yes.' There was no lift in her voice. Apparently this was not a matter of flowers. 'It is in my husband's study,' she answered. 'Do you wish to see it?'

Pitt was curious. 'I should like to very much.'

Without saying anything more she rose and led the way out across the chilly hall to a study perfectly in keeping with the sombre grandeur of the withdrawing room. A massive desk dominated everything else. A bookcase was crammed full of matching volumes. A stag's head hung high on one wall, glass eyes staring into space, a bit like the military photographs on the table in the other room.

On the wall opposite the desk hung a large photographic portrait of Lady Jarvis dressed in a formal afternoon gown. Her features were lit softly from the window she was facing, her eyes clear and wide, her winged brows accentuated. There was no furniture visible, no ornaments, and the shadow of the Georgian panes fell in a pattern of bars across her.

Pitt felt a sudden chill inside him, an awareness of Cathcart's brilliance which was both frightening and sad. The picture was superb, beautiful, fragile, full of emptiness, of a creature just beginning to realise it was imprisoned. And yet it was also no more than the portrait of a lovely woman in a manner which might be intended only to strengthen the awareness of the character in her face. One might see the deeper meaning, or miss it. There were no grounds for complaint, only a matter of taste.

He felt a pervading, quite personal sense of loss that Cathcart was dead and could no longer practise his art.

Lady Jarvis was watching him, her face puckered in curiosity. What should he say? The truth? It would be intrusive, and serve no purpose. Could she and Cathcart have been lovers? The murder definitely sprang from some form of passion. He turned to the portrait again. It was not the picture a man created of a woman he loved. The perception was too sharp, the compassion impersonal.

'It's remarkable,' he said tactfully. 'It is unique, and very beautiful. He was an artist of genius.'

Her face lit with pleasure. She was about to reply when they both heard the front door close and footsteps across the hall. The door opened behind them. Automatically they turned.

The man standing there was slight, of medium height, and at this moment his pleasant, rather bland face was filled with alarm.

'Is something wrong?' he demanded, turning from one to the other of them. 'My butler says you are from the police! Is that true?'

'Yes sir,' Pitt answered him. 'I am here regarding the death of Delbert Cathcart.'

'Cathcart?' Jarvis's face was blank. Certainly there was no guilt or dismay in it, no anger, not even comprehension. 'Who is Cathcart?'

'The photographer,' Lady Jarvis supplied.

'Oh!' Enlightenment came in a word. 'Is he dead? Pity.' He shook his head sadly. 'Clever fellow. Quite young. How can we help you?' His face darkened again. He did not understand.

'He was murdered,' Pitt said boldly.

'Was he? Good heavens. Why? Why would anyone murder a photographer?' He shook his head. 'Are you sure?'

'Certain.' Pitt did not know whether to bother pursuing the matter. He had never seen anyone look less guilty than Jarvis.

Yet if he did not, there would always be the faint, prickling knowledge that he had left something undone. 'You didn't happen to see him last Tuesday evening, did you?'

'Tuesday? No, I'm afraid not. I was at my club. Stayed rather late, I'm afraid. Got into a game of . . . well, a game.' He stared at Pitt with wide eyes. 'Was playing, you see, and suddenly looked up and realised it was gone two in the morning. Freddie Barbour. Too damned good. Certainly didn't see Cathcart. Not a member, actually. Old club. A trifle particular.'

'I see. Thank you.'

'Not at all. Sorry to be of no use.'

Pitt thanked him and left. It would be easy enough to check, if he ever needed to, but there was no doubt in his mind that Jarvis had neither cause nor passion to have murdered Cathcart.

It was growing late, and Pitt was happy to return home and leave the rest of the client list until the following day. He was tired, he did not really believe that he would learn anything of value, and there might be another letter from Paris waiting for him.

He opened the door trying not to expect too much, squashing down the hope inside himself in case there was nothing. It was only three days since the last letter. She was enjoying herself in a strange and exciting city. She should make everything of it that she could. She would have little time for writing home, especially when she would certainly tell him everything when she returned.

He looked down. There it was; he would know her exuberant writing anywhere. He was grinning as he picked it up and tore it open, pushing the door closed behind him with his foot. He read:

Dearest Thomas,

I am having a marvellous time. It is so very beautiful along the Bois de Boulogne, so desperately fashionable and terribly French. You should see the clothes! Even Emily was impressed, and that is not an easy feat. Visiting costumes are almost as ornate as evening gowns. You've never seen so much lace and velvet, silk, fur, flowers and braids. Sleeves and bustles are quite moderate and it is all very elegant. I can imagine how long it takes to look after it! It is all such fun to see, like watching a very long play without the inconvenience of having to sit down all the time. And yet for me there is the same sense of unreality, and the knowledge that I can leave it all without becoming involved. None of it is my life.

Which brings me to the Moulin Rouge again. One keeps hearing whispers of terrible gossip. The artist Henri Toulouse-Lautrec goes there often. He sits at one of the tables and makes sketches of the women. He is a dwarf, you know – at least his legs have never grown, and he is terribly short. Apparently the cancan that the chorus girls do is inexpressibly vulgar and exciting. The music is marvellous, the costumes outrageous, and they have no undergarments, even when they kick their legs right over their heads – or so I'm told. That is why Jack has said we absolutely cannot go. No decent woman would even mention the place. (Of course we all do! How could we not? We simply don't do it in the hearing of the gentlemen – just as they don't within ours! Isn't it all silly? But we have nothing else to do but play games. The less we have to do that matters, the more complicated the rules become.) Reputations are made and lost!

I heard the oddest story from Madame yesterday when the gentlemen were out. Apparently up to '64 the public morgue on the Quai du Marche-Neuf used to be a place ordinary people could go to look at the bodies – just as spectators, not because they expected to identify anyone. It was a tourist attraction – can you imagine it? Here is this lovely city with its ancient cathedral, its palaces and marvellous houses, its river with arching bridges and light on the water, steeped in so much history – where there are theatres and operas, balls and salons how can anyone want to go and stare at dead bodies on slabs? And yet apparently they did, even up to twenty-seven years ago! They would applaud, joke or catcall, as if in a theatre. Aren't people odd?

I think of you all so often, wonder how you are. How is Gracie managing at the seaside and are the children enjoying it? They were so keen to go. I hope it is living up to all their dreams. My trip is, in every way. Best of all because I shall be ready to come home when the time arrives.

I sit here at the end of my long day and wonder what you are doing with your body in the punt. I suppose all cities have their crimes and their scandals. Here everyone is talking about the case I mentioned to you before – the young gentleman who is accused of murder, but swears he was somewhere else, and so could not be guilty. But the trouble is that the 'somewhere else' is the Moulin Rouge – at the very hour when La Goulou, the infamous dancer, was doing the cancan. No one else is willing to say they saw him because they dare not admit they were there! I suppose most people know it, but saying it is different. Then we 'ladies' cannot pretend not to know, and if we know of course we have to react. We cannot be seen to approve, so we have to disapprove. I wonder how many issues are like that? I wish you were here to talk to. There is no one else to whom I could say exactly what I think, or who will tell me what they think so honestly.

And yet I suppose there is something to be said for tact? (Don't tell me I have none – I do have a little!) I don't want to know what everybody really thinks. Then I would have to keep everyone updated any time I changed my mind, or learned that I had been wrong.

Dear Thomas – I miss you. I shall have so much to say when I get home. I hope you are not too bored staying in London. Dare I wish you an interesting case? Or is that tempting fate?

Either way, be well, be happy – but miss me! I shall see you soon.

With my true love,

   Charlotte

Pitt folded the last page, still smiling, and held on to the letter as he went along the corridor to the kitchen. She must have stayed up very late writing that. He did miss her terribly; it would probably be foolish to tell her how much. And yet in a way he was pleased she had gone. It was good to realise how much he valued her. The silence of the house was all around him, but in his mind he could hear her voice.

And sometimes when parted one would write the deeper feelings one did not express in words when the daily business of living intruded. Certainly that had been so lately.

135

He left the letter out on the table as he stoked up the stove and put the kettle on to make himself a pot of tea. Archie and Angus were both purring and winding themselves around his legs, leaving hairs on his trousers. He spoke to them conversationally, and fed them.

He did not bother to meet with Tellman before going to see Lord Kilgour, another of Cathcart's clients.

'Yes! Yes – it's in the newspapers,' Kilgour agreed, standing in the sunlight in his magnificent withdrawing room in Eaton Square. He was a handsome man, tall and very slim, with delicate, aquiline features and a fair moustache. It was a fine-boned face but without real strength. However the lines of humour were easily apparent and there was intelligence in his light blue eyes. 'Happened five or six days ago, so they say. What can I tell you of use? He took my photograph. Wonderful artist with a camera. Don't imagine it was professional rivalry, do you?' A quick smile lit his face.

'Do you think that is possible?' Pitt asked.

Kilgour's eyebrows rose sharply. 'I've never heard of photographers murdering each other because one was better than the rest. But it would certainly cut down the competition. I suppose anyone who wants a portrait in future will have to go to Hampton, or Windrush, or anybody else they like. Certainly they cannot go to Cathcart, poor devil.'

'Was he the best?' Pitt was curious as to Kilgour's opinion.

There was no hesitation. 'Oh, undoubtedly. He had a knack of seeing you in a particular way.' He shrugged and the humour was back in his face. 'No doubt as you would most like to see yourself – whether you had realised it or not. He had an eye for the hidden truths. Not always flattering, of course.' He looked at Pitt quizzically, assessing how much he understood.

Having seen Cathcart's portrait of Lady Jarvis, Pitt understood it exactly. He allowed Kilgour to perceive as much.

'Would you like to see his picture of me?' Kilgour asked, his eyes bright.

'Very much,' Pitt answered.

Kilgour led the way from the withdrawing room to his own study, threw open the door and invited Pitt to view.

Immediately Pitt saw why the portrait was hung here and not in one of the reception rooms. It was superb, but bitingly perceptive. Kilgour was in fancy dress, if one could call it such. He wore the uniform and robes of an Austrian Emperor of the middle of the century. It was ornate, magnificent, almost overpowering his slender face and fair colouring. The crown sat on a table to his right and half behind him. One side of it was resting on an open book, so it sat at a tilt and looked as if it might slide off altogether on to the floor. On the wall beyond it was a long looking-glass, reflecting a blurred suggestion of Kilgour, and the light and shadows of the room behind him, invisible in the picture. There was an illusory quality to the whole, as if he were surrounded by the unknown. Kilgour himself was facing the camera, his eyes sharp and clear, a half-smile on his lips, as if he understood precisely where he was, and could both laugh and weep at it. As a photographic work it was brilliant, as portraiture it was a masterpiece. Words to describe it were both inadequate, and superfluous.

'Yes, I see,' Pitt said quietly. 'An artist to inspire passionate feelings.'

'Oh, quite,' Kilgour agreed. 'I could name you half a dozen others he did just as fine as this. Some people were thrilled, but then they were not the sort who would have done him any harm were they not. I suppose that is self-evident, isn't it? It is the ones with flawed characters who would think of killing him for his revelations, not the charming or the brave, the funny or the kind.'

Pitt smiled. 'And his rivals?' he pressed.

'Oh, I'm sure they hated him.' Kilgour moved back out of the study into the hallway and closed the door. 'I keep that picture where I work. I have enough sense of the absurd to enjoy it, and when I get delusions of my own importance it is a very salutary reminder. My wife likes it, because she does not see my weaknesses, and has not a very quick eye to understand what Cathcart was saying. But my sister understands, and advised me to keep it out of general sight.' He shrugged ruefully. 'As if I couldn't see it for myself! But then she is my elder sister – so what may one expect?'

They returned to the withdrawing room and spoke a little longer. Pitt finally left with several names written on a list, both clients and rivals of Cathcart.

He spent the rest of the day visiting them, but learned nothing else that furthered his knowledge of Cathcart's life.

In the morning he met with Tellman and over a cup of tea in the kitchen they discussed the matter.

'Not a thing,' Tellman said dismally. He kept glancing at the door as if he half expected Gracie to come in any moment. He heard the marmalade cat, Archie, come trotting along the passage and saw him look up hopefully at Pitt, then seeing he was unresponsive, go over to the laundry basket and hop in. He curled up half on top of his brother, and went to sleep.

'Nor I,' Pitt replied. 'He was brilliant, and I saw one of his competitors who acknowledged as much, but he was doing well enough.'

'You don't murder someone because they've got a talent you haven't,' Tellman said gloomily. 'You might spread lies about them, or criticise their work.' He shook his head, staring at his half-empty cup. 'But this was personal. It wasn't a matter of money, I'd swear to that.'

Pitt reached for the teapot and refilled Tellman's cup. 'I know,' he said quietly. 'Someone who merely wanted him out of the way wouldn't do this. But I couldn't find anything in his life to provoke this sort of emotion. We aren't looking in the right place.'

'Well, I've been all around his day-to-day business,' Tellman said defensively, straightening his shoulders a little. 'He lived pretty high! He's got to have spent a lot more than he made taking pictures. And he bought that house, we know that. Where'd the money come from? Blackmail, if you ask me.'

Pitt was inclined to agree. They had already investigated the possibility of theft, using Cathcart's knowledge of art and of the possessions of his clients. But none of them admitted to any losses.

'You must have talked to enough people,' he looked up at Tellman. 'What did they say about him?'

Tellman reached for the teapot. 'Spent a lot of money but paid his bills on time,' he sighed. 'Liked good things – the best – but he wasn't awkward to suit, like some folk. Always pleasant enough to the few that saw him, that is. Sent for a lot of things, or had them on regular order. Seems he worked pretty hard.'

'How hard?' Pitt asked, his mind turning over the clients he knew of from Cathcart's list.

Tellman looked puzzled.

'Hours?' Pitt prompted. 'He only took about one client a week, on average. Visited them maybe twice or three times, then had them to his studio for the actual photograph. That's not ten hours a day, by any means.'

'No, it isn't.' Tellman frowned. 'Doesn't exactly account for the time he seems to have been away, and people assumed he was working. Perhaps he wasn't? Could have been doing anything. Wouldn't be the first man that said he was working when he wasn't.'

'Whatever he was doing, it made him money,' Pitt said grimly. 'We need to know what it was.' He drank the last of his tea and stood up. 'It's about the only thing we've got.'

'Unless it was really the Frenchman and not Cathcart at all,' Tellman answered, standing as well. 'That would explain everything.'

'Except where Cathcart is.' Pitt poured a little milk for Archie and Angus, and made sure they had food. Angus smelled the milk in his sleep and woke up, stretching and purring.

'Well, if it is Cathcart, where is the Frenchman?' Tellman continued. 'He didn't go on the boat from Dover, he came back on the train to London, but he's not here now!'

'And as long as the French Embassy maintain that they know where he is, that is not our problem.' Pitt made sure the back door was locked. 'Let's go and see Miss Monderell again. Maybe she knows where Cathcart spent the rest of his time.'

The door was opened to them by a startled maid who told them very firmly that Miss Monderell was not yet receiving visitors, and if they cared to come back in an hour she would enquire whether Miss Monderell would see them then.

Tellman drew in his breath sharply, and only with difficulty waited for Pitt to speak. It was quarter to ten. In his opinion, plain already in his face, anyone who was not ill should have been out of bed long ago.

A flicker of humour hovered around Pitt's mouth. 'Will you please inform Miss Monderell that Superintendent Pitt would like to speak with her in the matter of Mr Cathcart's death, and unfortunately I cannot afford the time to wait upon her convenience.' His tone of voice made it clearly an order.

She looked startled; his mention of his police rank, and a death she now knew to be murder, robbed her of all argument. However, she left them to wait in the hall, not the withdrawing room.

Lily Monderell came down the stairs twenty minutes later, dressed in a beautiful morning gown of russet red trimmed with black braid, which showed off her extremely handsome figure to full advantage. The sleeves were barely exaggerated at all, and the skirt swept back to a slight bustle. It reminded Pitt of the fashions Charlotte had described in her letter. There was not the slightest crease or blemish in it, no sign of wear at all, and he wondered if it were new.

'Good morning, Mr Pitt,' she said with a dazzling smile. She looked at Tellman, to his renewed discomfort. 'Morning, love. You look as if you've been rode hard an' put away wet. Have a cup of tea and a sit-down. Cold outside, is it?'

In spite of himself, Pitt stifled a laugh at Tellman's expression of conflicting fury and dismay. He plainly wanted to be outraged, and she had denied him the chance. She refused to be intimidated or offended, she refused to see his disapproval, instead she swept around the bottom of the stairs and led the way to the dining room with her back to him, her silk skirts rustling, a waft of perfume filling the air.

The dining room was quite small, but extremely elegant. It

was papered entirely in warm yellow with a golden wood floor and mahogany furniture which could have been original Adam, or else was an excellent copy. There were tawny bronze chrysanthemums in a vase on the sideboard, and the maid was already laying two extra places at the table.

Lily Monderell invited them to sit down. Tellman accepted gingerly, Pitt with interest.

The maid came in with an exquisite Georgian silver teapot, gently steaming at the spout. She set it down admiringly, and Pitt had the strong impression that it also was new.

'There now,' she said with satisfaction. 'Looks real good, doesn't it!'

Pitt realised that one of the pictures he had noticed while waiting in the hall was new since they had been here before, or else moved from a different room. But did one keep pictures of that quality in a room not seen by guests? Lily Monderell was doing very well for herself since Cathcart's death. And yet she had not been mentioned in the will. Did she know that? Was she spending on credit, and expectation? It was ridiculous to feel sorry for her, and yet he did.

He looked at the teapot. 'It's very handsome. Is it new?' He watched her face closely to see the shadow of a lie before it reached her lips.

She hesitated so slightly he was not sure if he saw it or not. 'Yes.' She smiled, reaching for it to pour.

'A gift?' He kept his eyes on hers.

She had already decided what to say. 'No. Unless you count a gift to myself?'

Should he say something, rather than allow her to buy herself into debt on false hopes? It was none of his business. And yet where she obtained her money might very well be his business.

If Cathcart had blackmailed his clients, or anybody else, then perhaps she knew of it. She might even have shared the information and have taken over since his death. It was his duty to prevent a crime, whether it was continued blackmail, or another murder. And the thought of Lily Monderell lying grotesquely, half naked, in a punt drifting down the cold Thames in the morning mist was peculiarly repellent. Whatever she had done, or was doing, to provoke it. She was so vital it would be a denial of life itself to allow her to be destroyed.

He sipped the tea she had given him. It was fragrant and very hot. 'I have been to see Mr Cathcart's man of affairs,' he said almost casually.

'To find out when he bought the house?' she asked.

'Among other things,' he replied, hiding his respect for her sharp intuition. 'Also to see how he had bequeathed it, and his works of art, and whatever money he had.'

She lifted her cup and drank delicately. Hers too was very hot. 'Charity,' she said after a moment. 'At least that's what he always said he would do.'

He felt a wave of surprise, and then relief. He should have been disappointed. Her spending was not based on any expectation of profit from Cathcart's death, at least not by inheritance! There was still blackmail.

She was watching him now, waiting.

'Yes, exactly,' he replied. He let his gaze rest on the teapot. 'That's a nice new watercolour of cows that you have in the hall. I've always liked pictures of cows. They seem so supremely restful.'

Did he imagine the tightening of her shoulders under the silk?

'Thank you,' she answered. 'I am pleased you like it, love.

Would you care for some toast? Have you had any breakfast, or have you been walking around the streets asking questions all morning?' Her voice was warm, rich, as if she was really concerned for them.

Tellman cleared his throat uncomfortably. He was almost certainly hungry, and equally certainly did not want to accept her hospitality. He would find it confusing to be obliged to her, even for so small a thing.

'Thank you,' Pitt accepted, because he would like it, but primarily because it would give him an easy excuse to remain here talking to her.

She rang a small crystal bell on the table, and when the maid came, she requested toast, butter and marmalade for all of them. Tellman's discomfort amused her; it was there in the curve of her lips and the sparkle in her eyes. By the standards of the day, she was not beautiful: her features were too large, especially her mouth. There was nothing modest or fragile about her. But she was one of the most attractive women Pitt had ever met, full of laughter and vitality. He admired Cathcart for his taste with regard to her even more than for the beauty of his house.

'We haven't learned very much,' he said thoughtfully. 'We've spent several days asking questions and discovered almost nothing except that Mr Cathcart spent a great deal more money than he earned in his art.' He was watching her eyes for the smallest flicker, and even so he was not certain whether he saw it or not. And then he did not know how to interpret it. Had she loved him? Was it grief, or only a decent distaste for the violence and waste of his death? Surely she had been fond of him? She had liked him, whether she had loved him or not.

She lowered her eyes. 'He was very clever. He wasn't just a photographer, you know, he was a real artist.'

'Yes, I do know.' He meant that every bit as much as she did. 'I've seen several of his portraits. I don't think genius would be too powerful a word.'

She looked up quickly, smiling again. 'He was, wasn't he?' There were tears in her eyes.

Neither like nor dislike should overrule his judgement.

'He had a gift I've never seen equalled for catching the essence of a person and symbolising it in an image,' he continued. 'Not only what they would like to have seen in themselves, but a great deal they could not have wished shown so clearly. I saw not only faces portrayed, but the vanity or emptiness inside them, the weaknesses as much as the beauty or the strength.'

'That's portraiture,' she said softly.

'Perhaps it's also dangerous,' Pitt observed. 'Not everyone wishes to have their characters stripped so naked to the eyes of strangers, and perhaps still less to the eyes of those they love, or to whom they are vulnerable.'

'You think he was killed by a client?' She was startled.

'I'm sure he was killed by someone who knew him,' Pitt answered. 'And who felt passionately about him.'

She said nothing.

'Had you thought it was a crime of greed?' he asked her. 'It was hardly self-defence. Unless he was blackmailing someone . . .' He stopped, waiting to see her reaction.

Her eyes widened so little the moment after he was not sure he had seen it at all. Why? She should have been startled, even offended. He had just suggested her friend was guilty of one of the ugliest of crimes.

'Over what?' she asked, measuring her words. 'What makes you think he knew anything about . . . anyone?'

'Did he?'

'If he did – he certainly didn't tell me . . .'

'Would he have?'

She was definitely uncomfortable now. It was very well hidden, only a tightening of her hand on the delicate porcelain of the cup, a very slight shaking so the tea in it dimpled on the surface. She knew he was working his way towards asking if she knew the secret which had cost Cathcart his life, and if she was also using it the same way, which might in the end cost her her life also.

'I don't know.' She made herself smile. 'He didn't! But then I don't know for sure if there was anything to tell.'

Was that true? Where had his money come from? Where had she suddenly found sufficient to purchase the painting in the hall, and the silver teapot? It was a great deal of money to spend in the space of one week. Had she acquired a new and extremely generous lover?

Or had she been back to Cathcart's house and abstracted a few keepsakes, with or without Mrs Geddes's knowledge? It could even be that with no heir to be particular, Mrs Geddes had collaborated, keeping a few small things for herself. Would anyone know? Probably not, unless Cathcart kept a list of his possessions somewhere, and from what Pitt had seen of his life, that was unlikely. Certainly there had been no such list among his papers.

He did not wish to think of Lily Monderell going in among Cathcart's possessions and taking what she fancied. He could understand it well enough, but it was still not a pleasant thought.

His silence bothered her.

'Like some more tea, love?' she asked, reaching for the beautiful pot.

146

'Thank you,' he accepted, looking at the light gleam on its satin surface. It was almost as if she were provoking him into the very questions she least wanted.

'Have you been back to his house since he was killed?' he asked.

Her hand clenched and she had to reach up the other hand to steady the pot.

He waited. Even Tellman sat motionless, toast and marmalade halfway to his mouth.

'Yes,' she admitted.

'What for?'

She poured his tea, and some more for Tellman also, and lastly for herself, until she had delayed all she could. She looked up again and met Pitt's eyes.

'He promised me some of his pictures that he was going to sell. I went to get them. That's where the money came from.'

'You sold them already?'

'Why not? They were good. I know where to go.'

She was nervous. He did not know why. He was not sure if she was telling the truth, but it was reasonable enough. She had been his mistress. Men gave gifts to their mistresses, often very expensive ones. He had been surprised that Cathcart had not bequeathed her anything in a more formal way. He had no dependants, and it would be logical enough that the pictures in question would be her legacy.

Why was she nervous? What were the pictures? The means of his blackmail? Had she sold them back to the victims? Or kept them as further source of income? Most people would do the latter. It was an ugly thought.

But Lily Monderell needed to survive, and her looks would not last indefinitely. She had no husband to care for her, probably no skills but those of a mistress, certainly none which would keep her in the manner she now enjoyed, and had become accustomed to.

And all of those arguments were excuses, not reasons.

'Pictures of whom?' he asked, not expecting an honest answer, only to see something in her face.

Her eyes did not flicker. She was prepared for the question; he could see it unspoken in her.

'Artists' models,' she replied. 'No one you would know, I should think. They were just beautiful pictures. He used them as practice for when he was going to do a client . . . to get the costume and lighting right. But people like them . . . they're so well done they're worth a lot.' She sighed and glanced at the teapot again.

Should he ask her who she had sold them to? And if she told him would he follow up to make sure it was the truth? Could he? It might have been the sort of cash transaction of which there was no written record, a quick profit in the works of a man now dead.

Or on the other hand she might have sold them back to the people Cathcart had blackmailed, and any written record would be worthless.

Or she might simply have collected more blackmail money. Probably he would never be able to prove any of those possibilities.

'Miss Monderell,' he said gravely, 'you were close to Cathcart. Perhaps he trusted you with more intimate knowledge of his business, even of his clients. He was murdered by someone who hated him in a very personal way, and with an intensity beyond their ability to control.'

The colour drained from her face.

'Be careful, Miss Monderell.' He lowered his voice even further. 'If you have any knowledge about his death, any at all, you would be very unwise not to tell me what it is . . . as fully as you are able. I don't want to be investigating your death next week . . . or the week after.'

She stared at him in silence, her bosom rising and falling as she strove to control her breathing.

He stood up. 'Thank you for your hospitality.'

'I don't know anything about his death.' She looked up at him.

He would like to have believed her, but he did not.

Chapter Six

While Pitt was trying to learn more about Delbert Cathcart's life, Caroline had invited Samuel Ellison to call again, and was delighted when he accepted. This much was obvious to Grandmama as Caroline came into the room with Samuel almost at her heels. She looked pleased with herself.

'Good afternoon, ma'am,' Samuel said to the old lady, inclining his head a little. 'I'm glad to see you looking well. It's very kind of you to receive me again so soon.'

It *was* soon, far too soon in the old lady's opinion, although it would be unacceptable to say so. However, she could not let her displeasure go entirely unmarked.

'Good afternoon, Mr Ellison,' she replied coolly, looking him up and down with a flutter inside she could not suppress. He was so like her own son, Edward, it was almost as if his ghost had returned to her. Perhaps more disconcerting at the moment, he was also markedly like his father. He could not know that, but she did. It was as if parallel with this autumn afternoon in 1891, there were hundreds of other afternoons in other years when Edmund Ellison had walked in, courteous as this man, sounding as he did now, with heaven knew what going on in his mind.

'I dare say you wish to make the most of whatever time you have in London,' she continued. She must leave him in no doubt that he could not keep coming here. 'There must be many calls upon it. And then you will go back to America. No doubt you have obligations there.'

'Not an obligation in the world,' he said airily.

'Please sit down,' Caroline invited. 'Tea will be served shortly.'

He took the chair she indicated, crossing his legs comfortably and reclining. The old lady thought he looked offensively at ease.

'It is unfortunate you could not have come when Mr Fielding was at home!' she said sharply. She wished to make Caroline sensible of a certain disloyalty to her husband in inviting Samuel, who was far nearer her own age, and much too obviously found her attractive, at an hour when Joshua was out doing whatever it was he did. She did not know what he occupied his time with, and had never thought to ask. It was probably something she would prefer not to know. Men should keep their indiscretions to themselves, and a woman with the least sense did not ask. 'I am sure he also would have liked to see you,' she added, to prevent it being obvious she was not pleased to see him. Criticising Caroline was one thing; she did not wish to appear rude, if it could be avoided.

'I had hoped he would be,' Samuel replied with a quick smile. 'I thought the afternoon quite a good time. It seems I misjudged.'

There was a slight flush on Caroline's cheek. 'Usually it is. He has gone to see a friend who is writing a play, and wants his advice on stage directions.'

Samuel's face lit up with interest. 'What a fascinating thing to do! To know what instructions to give to create the perfect illusion and draw in people's emotions and understanding, to form a world which lies open to observation, and yet is perfectly contained within itself. Do you know the play?'

It seemed that Caroline did. She answered with a detailed description of the setting and the plot. Grandmama sat back in her chair, still upright, but in a sense, by her posture, expressing her exclusion from the conversation. They were discussing the theatre again, and she did not approve. Certainly marrying an actor was a social catastrophe no decent woman would even consider. But now that Caroline had made her bed, she must lie in it. She owed Joshua some loyalty, and sitting here smiling and hanging on every word of Samuel Ellison was disloyal.

Samuel was talking about Oscar Wilde of all people! Caroline was listening intently, her eyes alight. Grandmama's mind raced on what she could do to get rid of Samuel before he said something which woke Caroline's suspicion of what the old lady least wished her to know, and she started to think, to ask.

She had already tried hints so direct any decent man would have taken them! It was perfectly obvious to anyone, except a fool, that he was attracted to Caroline, and she was thoroughly enjoying it! It was intolerable!

'I've just read *The Picture of Dorian Gray*, and I was fascinated,' Samuel said with enthusiasm. 'The man is truly brilliant. But of course meeting him would be the real thing.'

'Really?' Grandmama said icily. She had not meant to join the conversation, but this was too much to allow to pass. 'I would not have thought he was the sort of person any respectable man, and any woman at all, would care to associate with. I believe "decadent" is the term applied to him and his like.'

'I believe it is,' Samuel agreed, turning away from Caroline to face her mother-in-law. 'I'm afraid my desire to experience as much of life as I can has led me to some very questionable places, and most certainly into some company you would not approve of, Mrs Ellison. And yet I have found honour, courage, and compassion in some places you would swear there was nothing good to see . . . maybe not even any redemption to hope for. It's a great thing to see beauty in the darkness of what seems to be lost.'

There was a kind of light in his face which defied her to go on disapproving. He was so like Edward it was deeply disturbing, and also unlike him, and that disturbed her as well, because it was inappropriate, and yet it was also kind. She wished with a fierceness that nearly choked her that he had never come.

Caroline saved her the necessity of replying.

'Please tell us the sort of thing you mean,' she asked eagerly. 'I shall never go to America myself, and certainly even if I did I would never go westwards. Is New York like London . . . I mean now? Do you have theatres and operas and concerts? Do people care about Society, and fashion, who is being seen with whom? Or are they beyond that sort of silly concern?'

He laughed outright, then proceeded to tell her about New York society. 'The original "400" is superb,' he said with a laugh. 'Although the word is now that there are at least fifteen hundred, if one were to believe all those who claim to be descendants.'

'I don't see how that bears any resemblance to us!' Grandmama said acidly. 'I don't know anyone at all who claims to have arrived on a ship from anywhere. I cannot imagine why they should wish to.' She fervently desired him to change the subject away from America and ships altogether. If she could freeze him out of it she would.

'William the Conqueror!' Caroline said instantly.

'I beg your pardon?'

'Or, I suppose, if you want to be even grander and older still, Julius Caesar,' Caroline explained.

Had they been alone the old lady could have disclaimed all knowledge of what she was talking about, and indeed of the conversation at all. But ignorance was not a satisfactory riposte to Samuel Ellison. He would only believe her, and then she would have to explain, probably at length.

'I have no idea whether my ancestors came over with William the Conqueror, or Julius Caesar, or were here before either of them,' she replied, drawing in a deep breath. 'Half a dozen generations should be sufficient for anyone.'

'I agree with you wholeheartedly!' Samuel said with great feeling, leaning towards her a little. 'It is who a man is that matters, not who his father was. Good men have had bad sons, and bad men good ones.'

Grandmama wanted to say something to end this subject before it became catastrophic, but suddenly her throat was too dry to speak.

Caroline was regarding Samuel with gentleness and concern. She had caught a deeper note of meaning in what he said, or else Grandmama had imagined it. The old lady shivered. This was appalling! What did he know? How much was possible? Anything! Everything! What would a woman tell her son? A decent woman, nothing at all! How could she? It was unspeakable – literally – beyond the power of being put into speech. She must get rid of him! Out of the house for ever. Caroline must be made to see the unsuitability of this – immediately even.

But for now, she must make her heart calm down, cease choking her. This was all unnecessary. His choice of words was unfortunate, but it was accidental, no more. Face him down.

Caroline was talking again. 'I suppose Society in New York has pastimes similar to ours?' she said in as casual a tone of voice as she could manage.

'Oh indeed,' he agreed. 'Just last year they opened Madison Square Gardens for the Horse Show. We get English experts over to do the judging.'

'Have you been?' Caroline asked as the maid brought in the tea. She thanked her but declined her help in pouring and serving it.

'Me? No.' Samuel shook his head. 'I've been to the bicycle display, which was enormous fun.'

'Bicycles!' Caroline said with delight. 'How interesting! Have you ridden on one?'

'But of course! They're wonderful, and incredibly fast,' he enthused. 'Naturally I'm speaking of gentlemen's machines.'

'I'm sure ladies' could be very fast as well, if we wore the correct clothing,' she countered. 'I believe they are known as bloomers.'

'Bloomers are hardly "correct clothing" for anything at all!' Grandmama snapped. 'Really! What will you think of next? As if your theatrical antics are not sufficient, you want to dress like a man and career around the streets on wheels? Even Joshua would not allow that!' Her voice rose sharp and high. 'Presuming you care what Joshua likes? You used to be besotted enough upon him, I think you would have jumped off Brighton

Pier into the sea, if you thought he wished it.'

Caroline looked at her with wide eyes, perfectly steady and unblinking. For a moment the old lady was quite alarmed at the boldness of them.

'I think that might be a pleasant thought, on a hot summer afternoon – a tedious one, when everybody is gossiping and talking essentially nonsense,' Caroline replied deliberately. 'Not to please Joshua, to please myself.'

That was so outrageous, so perfectly idiotic, that for a moment the old lady was robbed of a reply adequate to the occasion.

Samuel was only too apparently entertained by the notion, and that Caroline should not only think it but say it. But then he did not have to live with her!

Then the perfect answer sprang to her tongue.

'If you act to please yourself, Caroline,' she glared at her daughter-in-law, 'then you may very well end up pleasing no one else! And that, for a woman in your situation, would be catastrophic.' She pronounced the last word with relish.

She was rewarded by a look of startling vulnerability in Caroline's face, almost as if she had seen an abyss of loneliness opening in front of her. The satisfaction to the old lady was not what she had expected. This was nearly victory, and yet isolation, inadequacy, guilt and the burning sense of shame were too familiar, and she wanted to put them behind her for ever, so far behind she would never see them or think of them again, not in Caroline, not in anyone. It was intolerable that Caroline, of all people, should remind her.

'It is vulgar to speak so much of oneself!' she said quickly. She turned to Samuel. 'Is this garden for horse shows agreeable?'

'Oh most.' He looked at her very directly, his eyes wide with surprise. 'At least . . . there was one scandalous aspect to it. There was a very high tower, nearly three hundred and fifty feet high, and on top of it a statue of the Greek goddess Diana . . .'

'I do not perceive what is scandalous about that.'

'Unclothed . . .'

She decided to be perverse. 'At three hundred and fifty feet I hardly see that that matters. If one takes a telescope to it one deserves to see all one gets.'

'My sentiment exactly,' he agreed with enthusiasm. 'If one wants something to disapprove of, there are far better things. There are—'

'Well – we have undoubtedly learned something,' she cut him off completely. 'Like my daughter-in-law, I shall never go to America, so it is interesting to hear of it from someone who is familiar with its life. How long do you intend to remain in London? You will surely wish to see the rest of the country. I believe Bath is still very attractive. It used to be. And highly fashionable. Anyone who had the slightest aspirations to be anyone would take the waters, in the right season.'

'Oh yes.' He must have been aware it was a dismissal, but he refused to go. 'Roman baths, aren't they?'

'They were, yes. Now they are entirely English, if anything can be said to be.'

'Please tell us more of your own country?' Caroline poured more tea and offered the sandwiches again. She seemed oblivious to decency. 'How far west did you go? Did you really see Indians?'

A sadness came into his face. 'Indeed I did. How far west? All the way to California and the Barbary Coast. I met men who panned for gold in the Rush of '49, men who saw the great buffalo herds that darkened the plains, and made the earth tremble when they stampeded.' His eyes were very far away, his face marked deep with emotion. 'I know men who made the desert blossom, and men who murdered the old inhabitants and tore up what was wild and beautiful, and can't ever be replaced. Sometimes it was done in ignorance, and sometimes it was done in greed. I watched the white man strengthen and the red man die.'

Caroline drew breath to say something, then changed her mind. She sat silently, watching him, knowing it was not a time to intrude.

He turned and smiled at her.

The understanding between them was tangible in the quiet room.

'Caroline, will you pour me more tea!' Grandmama demanded. How could she make him leave? If she claimed a headache she would have to retire, and he might well be gauche enough to remain even so – alone with Caroline! And she was stupid enough to let him! Couldn't see a foot beyond the end of her own nose! Ever since poor Edward had died it had been one disaster after another.

'Of course,' Caroline said willingly, reaching for the pot and obeying. 'Samuel, would you care for another sandwich?'

He accepted, although he was doing far more talking than eating or drinking. He was showing off, and enjoying it thoroughly. Could Caroline not see that? He probably did the same to every woman who was fool enough to listen! And here was Caroline simpering and hanging on his every word as if he were courting her. Joshua would be disgusted – and then she would lose even what little she had, which now she had let the world know about it by marrying him, was at least better than nothing. Then where would she be? A disgraced woman! Put out for immorality – at her age – with no means and no reputation!

Caroline was looking at Samuel again.

'The way you speak of it makes me feel as if there is much tragedy attached. I had always heard of it as brave and exciting, filled with hardship and sacrifice, but not dishonour.' She sensed in him a real wound and she wished to understand, even to share a fraction of it. There was an emotion driving her she did not realise, but there was a need for reassurance, to find her own balance and certainties, and she was drawn to Samuel's pain. If one could not gain comfort, one could at least give it. And she could not remember when she had liked anyone so quickly and easily before, except perhaps Joshua, and that was not something she wished to think about just at the moment.

She watched his face for an answer, avoiding Grandmama's eyes. The old lady was in a strange frame of mind, even for her. If Caroline did not know such a thing was impossible, she would have said she was afraid. Certainly she was angry, but then Caroline had never known her when there was not an underlying emotion in her which she realised now was a kind of fury. She had always been quick to find fault, to criticise, to strike out, as if hurting another person released something within her.

But today was different. Was it loneliness, the grief she referred to every so often because she had been a widow so long? Did she really mourn Edmund still? Was her anger at the world because they went on with their own lives regardless of the fact that Edmund Ellison was dead?

Caroline had loved her own husband, but when he had died her grief was not inconsolable. Time had not robbed her of the need for affection. Occasionally she still missed him. But shock had certainly healed, and the momentary numbing loneliness without him.

Now, of course, there was Joshua, and that was a whole new world: exciting – sometimes too much so – exhilarating and threatening, full of laughter deeper than any she had known before, and disturbing new ideas – perhaps not all good ones, not ones she could keep up with, or wanted to.

She liked Samuel Ellison very much. Was it for himself, or because he reminded her of everything that had been good in Edward, and of a past which was so much less threatening, less dangerous to her safety, her self-esteem, to keeping the ideas and values she had grown accustomed to?

Samuel was talking to her, his face puckered with concern, perhaps because he knew she was not really listening.

' – all about land,' he was saying. 'You see Indians don't see land as we do, to be owned by one individual or another. They hold it in common to the tribe, to hunt, to live on and to preserve. We didn't understand their way of life and we didn't want to. They didn't understand ours. Their tragedy was that they believed us when we said we would feed and protect them in return for allowing us to settle.'

'You didn't?' she asked, knowing the answer already from his face.

'Some would have.' He was not looking at her but somewhere into the distance of his memory. 'But more moved west, and then more again. Once we saw the rich land we were greedy to keep it, put fences around it and let no one else in. The story of the Indians is a tale of one tragedy after another.'

Caroline did not interrupt as he recounted the betrayal of the Modoc tribe. She did not know whether Grandmama was listening or not. She sat with her black eyes half closed, her mouth thin and narrow, but whether it was the Indian Wars which she disapproved of, or Samuel Ellison, or something else altogether, it was impossible to say.

Caroline was startled, and deeply moved, to see tears on his cheeks. Without thinking she stretched out her hand and touched him, but she said nothing. Words would have been pointless, a mark of failure to understand, an attempt to communicate the incommunicable.

He smiled. 'I'm sorry. That really wasn't a teatime story. I forgot myself.'

'This is not an ordinary teatime call,' Caroline said instinctively. 'If one cannot speak to one's family of things that matter, then who can one speak to? Should it be strangers, so we don't have to think of it again, or live with those who know what we have said, and felt?'

Grandmama ached to agree, the words throbbed inside her, but fear held them in. It would be too much, too precipitate. Once out they could not be withdrawn, and they might give her away.

Samuel smiled. 'Of course not,' he answered Caroline. 'But I do speak too much.'

'It is customary in England to discuss less personal things,' Grandmama said with emphasis. 'Not to disturb people, or cause them embarrassment or distress. Teatime is supposed to be pleasant, a small social interlude in the day.'

Samuel looked uncomfortable. It was the first time Caroline had seen him disconcerted, and she felt instantly protective.

'And criticism of other people's behaviour or remarks is an excellent thing to avoid!' she said sharply.

'As is family unpleasantness,' Grandmama retorted.

'Disrespect,' she went on. 'Or any form of unseemly familiarity or clumsiness.' She did not look at Samuel but at Caroline. 'It makes people wish they had not come, and desire to leave as soon as they decently may.'

Samuel glanced from one to the other of them uncertainly.

Caroline did not know what to say. Even for Grandmama this was extraordinary behaviour.

The old lady cleared her throat. She was sitting rigidly upright, her shoulders so tight they strained the black bombazine of her dress. The jet beads hanging from her mourning brooch shivered slightly. Caroline was torn by conflicting loathing and loyalty. She had no idea what emotions raged inside the old woman. She had known her for almost forty years, and never understood her except superficially, and they equally disliked each other.

'Thank you for coming to see us, Mr Ellison,' Grandmama said stiffly. 'It is good for you to spare us the time when you must have many other commitments. You must not rob yourself of the opportunity to go to the theatre and see the sights of London, or wherever else you may care to go.'

Samuel rose to his feet. 'It was my pleasure, Mrs Ellison,' he replied. He turned to Caroline and bade her farewell, thanking them both again for their hospitality, then took his leave.

When he had gone, and before Caroline could speak, the old lady stood up also, leaning heavily on her cane as if she needed it to support herself, and half turned her back. 'I have a fearful headache. I am going to my room,' she announced. 'You may have the maid bring my dinner upstairs to me. You would be well advised to spend the rest of the afternoon considering your behaviour, and your loyalties to the husband you have elected to marry. Not that you ever took advice! But you have made your bed . . . you had best learn to lie in it before you fall out and have no bed at all! You are making a complete fool of yourself. In the privacy of your own home is one thing, but if you throw yourself upon him like this in public, you will cause scandal – and rightly so. A woman who has lost her reputation has lost everything!' She lowered her voice and stared at Caroline intently. 'You had better hope that your husband does not learn of it! Consider your situation!' And with that as a parting shot she stumped out of the room and Caroline heard her heavy footsteps cross the hall to the stairs.

She felt cold inside . . . and angry.

There was nothing to say. Not that she was sure what she would have said, were the old lady listening. Actually she was glad to be alone. The words stung precisely because she realised she was thinking all sorts of things which a few days ago had seemed unquestionable – matters of loyalties and beliefs and a sense of belonging.

She half turned and caught sight of herself in the glass over the mantel. At this distance she was handsome, dark hair with a warmth of colour in it, only a little grey, slender neck and shoulders, features still almost beautiful, perhaps a trifle too individual to please the strictest taste. But closer to she knew she would see the telltale signs of age, the fine lines around eyes and mouth, the less-than-perfect sweep of jaw. Did Joshua see that every time he looked at her as well?

He would not be here until this evening. He was performing on stage, and she was going alone to dine with the Marchands. She did not feel in the least like going out and making pleasant conversation about trivia, but it would be better than staying here alone and wondering about herself, about Joshua, and how he saw her compared with someone like Cecily Antrim.

Had she really made as big a fool of herself as the old woman said? Would it all have been better, easier, far more honest if she had married someone her own age, with the same memories and beliefs, even someone like Samuel Ellison?

She hadn't! She had fallen in love with Joshua, and believed it when he had said he returned her feelings. She had wanted it so much, it had been the most important thing in the world to her. Was she utterly blind, like a schoolgirl, as the old lady said? Could she lose everything?

She turned away from the glass impatiently and went upstairs to her room to consider what she should wear for dinner. Nothing would make her feel beautiful, charming or young. Attempting to be so was simply a charade she had made unavoidable.

The Marchands greeted Caroline with great pleasure. They were charming, supremely civilised people who would never wittingly have made any guest less than welcome, but it was impossible not to see the genuineness of their feelings.

'How very nice to see you,' Mrs Marchand said, coming forward from where she had been standing near a small table of flowers in the withdrawing room. The evening was not cold, but there was a fire burning in the grate and the room was warm with the glow of flames reflected on the copper fender and scuttle, and the brass and copper fire tongs. The heavy curtains were old rose and the furniture massive and obviously comfortable. Embroidered cushions and samplers and an open book of cards and scraps gave the room a look of having long been the heart of a family home, albeit a very orthodox one.

'I'm so glad you were prepared to come even without Joshua,' Mr Marchand added from in front of the largest armchair where he had obviously risen to his feet. He was smiling broadly. He was a shy man, and this was an unusually outspoken remark for him.

Caroline felt enfolded by familiarity and its comfort. It was people like these she had known and understood all her life. There was no need to make any pretence with them, any effort to keep up with bright conversation or forward-thinking opinions.

'I really am very happy to come,' she answered, quite honestly. 'It is so relaxing to be able to converse without wondering when the theatre bell will go, or who else one really ought to speak to.'

'Isn't it!' Mrs Marchand agreed quickly. 'I love the theatre, and concerts and soirees and so on, but there is nothing like the quiet company of friends. Do come and sit for a little while and tell us how you are.'

Caroline did as she was bidden, and they spoke for a little while, of fashion, gossip, mutual acquaintances, and other agreeable and unimportant things.

A little before dinner was served the door opened and a youth of about sixteen came in. He was already tall and lean, as if outgrowing his strength. He had his mother's wide blue eyes and dark hair. His skin was still soft; it would be some time before he needed to shave. He was composed, but his slightly awkward silence, the uncertainty what to do with his hands, betrayed his shyness. That much at least was sharply reminiscent of his father, and Caroline could so easily imagine Rafe Marchand at the same age.

'How do you do, Mrs Fielding,' he replied when they were introduced. She wanted to engage him in conversation so he would not have to search for something to say to her. What manner of subject would interest a boy of his age? She must not seem condescending, or intrusive, or make him feel as if he were being examined.

He looked at her steadily, because he had been taught it was rude not to meet people's eyes when you spoke to them, but she could see he was highly uncomfortable doing so, only awaiting the moment he could disengage himself.

She smiled. Complete candour was the only thing that came to her mind.

'I am very pleased you joined us, Lewis, but at a loss to know what to say to you. I'm sure you are not the least interested in the latest births, deaths and marriages in Society, or the fashions either. I do not know sufficient of politics to discuss them with anyone except in the most superficial manner. I am afraid I have become rather singular in my interests lately, and that may make me very tedious.'

He drew in his breath to make the denial courtesy called for, and she cut him off. 'Please don't feel the need to be polite. Instead, tell me what you would most like to speak of, were you to initiate the conversation, and not I.'

'Oh!' He looked startled, and a little flattered. A warm colour flushed up his cheeks, but he did not seek to move away.

'Papa tells me Mr Fielding is an actor. Is that really so?'

'Are you still being courteous?' she said, teasing him very gently. 'You really would wish to speak of the one thing I am obsessed with myself? Or are you trying to make me feel at ease, just as I am with you? If so, you are remarkably sophisticated for one so early in his career. You will be an enormous success in Society. Ladies will love you.'

He blushed scarlet. He opened his mouth to say something, and quite obviously could think of nothing adequate. His eyes

167

were shining, and it was a moment before she realised he was making an intense effort to look only at her face, not even for an instant to allow his gaze to slide as far as her neck or shoulder, let alone the smooth skin above her bosom.

Mr Marchand cleared his throat, as if about to speak, then said nothing.

Mrs Marchand blinked.

Caroline was aware of an oppressive silence. The sudden crackling of the fire was almost explosive.

'Yes, he is an actor,' she said more abruptly than she intended. 'Do you like the theatre? I expect you are studying plays in your schoolwork?'

'Oh yes,' he agreed. 'But mostly Shakespeare, I'm afraid. Nothing very modern. That is all very . . . well, some of it is outrageous – parts of *Hamlet* . . . Ophelia . . . Oh! I'm sorry. I didn't mean to imply that Mr Fielding—'

'Of course you didn't,' she agreed quickly. 'I expect Shakespeare was considered outrageous in his time, at least by some.'

'Do you think so?' He looked hopeful. 'It all seems so . . . historical! Sort of . . . safe. The histories happened . . . and we know they did.'

She laughed. 'I expect even Mr Ibsen will be a classic one day, and perfectly "safe" as well.' She knew that was what Joshua would have said. 'And we don't know what really happened in the histories, only what Shakespeare told us, for the sake of his drama.'

He was surprised. 'Do you think it wasn't true?' It was obviously a new thought to him. 'I suppose it doesn't have to be, does it? Maybe there was no one to stop libel and blasphemy then.' He was frowning. 'Only it wasn't, of course . . . I mean not Shakespeare. Maybe all the things that were, have been stopped . . . either by some censorship, or because we learned they were untrue, so we didn't watch them any more.'

'I should think it is more likely we became so used to them, we now believe they are the truth,' she replied, and then instantly wondered if perhaps she was speaking too freely. He was only a child, after all. 'You may well be right,' she amended. 'In the long run we are fairly competent judges of what is good.' She hoped Joshua would forgive her for such arrant nonsense. 'What are you studying?'

'*Julius Caesar*,' he said instantly.

'Marvellous!' she responded. 'My favourite . . . except that all the characters that matter are men.'

He looked confused.

She knew she was repeating Joshua's words now even as she said them. 'You should try the Greeks some time. They have marvellous women as well, full of passion and courage, love and hate. Read *Antigone*, or *Women of Troy*.'

He was startled. '*Women* . . . is that . . .' He was clearly embarrassed. The idea of women as central on a stage seemed to confuse him. 'Surely . . . I mean . . . I don't think . . .' He glanced at his mother, then away again, his eyes lowered. 'Surely it wouldn't be seemly . . . Women are . . .' He stopped altogether.

Rafe Marchand moved very slightly.

Caroline sensed she was treading on ground full of unknown fears and assumptions, far too dangerous to continue when she knew him so little.

'Perhaps in the future,' she said lightly. She turned to Mrs Marchand. 'I hear there is a new political satire. I am not sure whether I wish to see it or not. Sometimes they are so obvious there is no point, and other times they are so abstruse I have no idea what the point is!'

The tension dissipated. They talked for a few minutes longer on harmless subjects. Lewis having paid his respects to the visitor, excused himself, leaving the adults to go in to dinner.

It was a very traditional meal, unsurprising, but excellently cooked. It took Caroline into the safety of the past when so much had been familiar with all the reassurance of the knowledge that she understood it, that she knew the questions and the answers and was certain of her own place. Now there were countless situations where she had to think harder, weigh her responses. She seemed to spend half her time struggling to say something appropriate, trying to keep her balance between being true to her beliefs and yet not sounding insensitive, old-fashioned and exhibiting precisely that bigotry her new friends despised. Although it was Joshua who really mattered. How much did she disappoint him? He was too innately kind to look for fault or to express criticism where it could do no good. The very knowledge of that brought a sudden closing of her throat, and she rushed into speech to drive it away.

Mrs Marchand was talking about censorship. Behind her, her husband's face was dark, his body tense as he listened.

'. . . and we have to protect the innocent from the darkness of mind which can so easily injure them permanently,' she was saying.

'Darkness of mind?' Caroline had not heard the beginning and did not know to what she referred.

Mrs Marchand leaned forward a little across the table, the pearl embroidery on her gown catching the light. 'My dear, take that play we saw the other evening, just for one example. It is amazing what can become acceptable if one sees it often enough, and in public. There are ideas which you and I would find appalling, and which undermine all the values we most cherish, and if we were among our trusted friends we would all feel free to express our outrage when they are mocked or violated.' Her face was creased with earnestness. 'And yet when it is done with wit and we are made to laugh, it feels different. No one wishes to seem without humour, to be pompous or out of date. We all laugh. No one looks at anyone else. No one knows who is really embarrassed or offended. And sooner or later we become used to whatever it is, and it no longer offends us. It becomes more and more difficult to say anything. We feel isolated, as if the whole tide of what everyone thinks has moved on and left us behind, alone.'

Caroline knew precisely what she meant. She was correct. One grows less sensitive to vulgarity, to coarseness of thought or perception, even to the witnessing of other people's pain. The initial shock wears off. Anger finally dies.

And yet she heard herself saying what she knew Joshua would have, were he here.

'Of course it does. That is why we must constantly explore the boundaries and find new ways to say things, precisely so people will not become used to them and no longer care.'

Mrs Marchand frowned. 'I am not sure that I follow you. What new things must we say?'

Her husband set down his wine glass, his expression tightly controlled, his eyes very steady. 'I admit to being old-fashioned. I believe the ideals of my father and grandfather were high, and I have no desire to see them questioned, let alone flouted,' he replied. 'They believed a man was bound by his honour, and his word, once given, was unbreakable.' His voice warmed. 'They held duty sacred, thought of others before self, regarded

171

service the highest calling. They treated all women with gentleness, and those of their family they were not only bound to protect from all violence, coarseness of thought or word, or vulgarity, but it was their pleasure as well. Surely that is what love is, the desire above all things, no matter at what cost to oneself, to protect and make life joyous and rich, and safe for them?' He looked at her earnestly, his blue eyes unclouded.

Caroline thought of Edward, and of Samuel Ellison, and heard Joshua's voice in her ears. Oddly enough, she also heard Pitt.

'It is a kind of love,' she answered gently. 'Is it what you would wish for yourself?'

A shadow crossed his face. 'I beg your pardon?'

'Is it the kind of love you would wish extended towards yourself?'

'My dear, our circumstances are entirely different,' he said patiently. 'It is my place to protect, not to be protected. Women are uniquely vulnerable. If they become coarsened by what is violent and destructive in life, what devalues innocence, reverence for the beautiful and precious, for intimacy and the finer emotions, they pass it on to our children, and then what is there left for anyone? There must be some hallowed place where there is no mockery of the sacred, no belittling of tenderness, no willingness to injure or take advantage, where the spiritual always outweighs the carnal.'

Caroline felt a strange, painful mixture of shame and frustration, and at the same time, of comfort.

'Of course there must,' she agreed wholeheartedly. 'I wish I knew how to keep it without at the same time closing my eyes to everything that is uncomfortable or questioning. How can I keep innocence, and yet also grow up rather than remain a child?

How can I fight for what is good if I have no idea what is evil?'

'You should not have to fight, my dear,' he said with intense feeling, leaning towards her, his face very earnest. 'You should be protected from such things! That is society's duty, and if those whose charge and whose privilege it is were honouring their callings, then the question would never arise. As it is, the Lord Chamberlain is gravely remiss, and there is all manner of dangerous – deeply dangerous – material around.' He stared intently at Caroline, faint spots of colour in his cheeks. 'You can have no concept of how terrible some of it is. I pray God you never do!' His face tightened. 'The damage is irreparable.'

'The Lord Chamberlain certainly does not do enough!' Mrs Marchand agreed, turning to him with a pucker between her brows. 'I think you should write to him, my dear, say that many of us are deeply concerned about the openness of very private emotions expressed on the stage, which may suggest to susceptible minds that women in general may be possessed of the kind of . . . of appetites indicated by Miss Antrim's character—'

'I already have, my dear,' he interrupted.

She relaxed a little, her shoulders easing, a slight smile returning to her lips. 'I'm so glad. Think of the kind of effect, the fearful notions, that could place in the minds of young men . . . like . . . like Lewis! How could he, or they, grow up with the tenderness and respect towards their wives and daughters, not to say mothers, that one would desire?'

Caroline understood only too easily what she meant. It was not herself she thought of, but her own daughters. She remembered with grief, even now so many years afterwards, how Sarah had suffered, before her death, the fear and the disillusion in her husband because of his behaviour. Any censorship at all was better than the misery they had endured then.

'Of course,' she concurred, but there was a small voice nagging at the back of her mind, one that condemned cowardice and told her she was sacrificing honesty for comfort. She quelled it, and continued with her dinner, although she was aware that Mrs Marchand had been far more easily reassured than her husband. He had been gentle with her, wanting to give her a comfort he himself could not share.

When Caroline arrived home Joshua was in the withdrawing room, sitting in the large chair he liked best, a book open in his lap and the gaslight turned high so he could read. It caught the few strands of silver in his brown hair, and the shadows of weariness around his eyes. He closed the book and smiled at her, rising to his feet slowly.

'Nice evening with the Marchands?' He came towards her and kissed her lightly on the cheek. She felt the warmth of him and the very slight smell of stage make-up, and that indefinable odour of the theatre – sweat, excitement, fabric, paint. Ten years ago it would have been as alien to her as a foreign land. Now it had familiarity, a host of memories of laughter and passion. She realised with a rush of confusion how much she was still as sharply in love with Joshua as if she were a girl and this were her first real romance. It was absurd, ludicrous in a woman of her age. It made her unbearably vulnerable.

'Yes, very pleasant,' she answered, forcing herself to smile brightly, as if it were all quite casual. 'I met their son for the first time. A very shy boy.' She walked on past him towards the fire. It was not really cold outside, but she was shivering a little. And she was unprepared for the intimacy of retiring to bed. Her mind was still busy with conflicting thoughts: Edward and the past; Samuel Ellison's smile, his stories; Hope Marchand's fear of the depiction of new ideas, the passion to protect the young from the intrusion of violence and degradation of things they needed to believe in as pure; and Rafe Marchand's longer sight and far deeper fear of things to come. He was right in saying that when you lost the ability to feel reverence, you lost almost everything.

She thought of her own daughters when they had been young. Joshua would not understand that; he had no children. The need to protect was so deep it was far more elemental than thought or reason, it was at the core of life. And it was so much more than merely physical . . . it was a need to nurture all that was of beauty in the heart, that gave happiness. Who wanted their child alive, but incapable of faith in the essential value of love, honour or joy?

'Caroline?' There was an edge of anxiety in Joshua's voice. He had sensed the distance she had placed between them.

She swung round to face him, and emotion overtook her. She saw confusion in him also, and tiredness after the mental and physical effort of a performance, and yet his concern was for her. She felt utterly selfish. What did the issues of censorship matter tonight, or what the Marchands thought about it?

'Silly dinner conversation.' She dismissed it with a smile, stepping forward into his arms. It was still easier to hold him than to meet his eyes. She felt his slightness, and his strength. He was very gentle. It was far too late to wonder about whether she had made the right decision in marrying him, whether she was absurd or not. She could either go with her heart, or deny it. Nothing would change the commitment inside her.

But in the morning censorship mattered very much. She saw

it in Joshua's face even before her eye caught it in the newspapers.

'What is it?' she asked, a lurch of alarm inside her. 'What has happened?'

He held up the paper. 'They've taken off Cecily's play! Banned it!' He sounded stunned, defeated. There were pink spots of colour in his cheeks.

She did not understand. 'How can they? The Lord Chamberlain gave it a licence . . .' She stopped. She did not understand the details of the process, but the principle was clear. Something in his face held her. 'What?'

'It isn't quite . . . like that.' He bit his lip. 'He would never have given it a licence,' he admitted, 'because it would raise questions, make some people uncomfortable.' He shrugged very slightly. 'There are ways around that – submit the script late and hope he'll not read it carefully . . . That seldom works because he's clever enough to suspect anything presented that way, and read it extra carefully. The other is to perform a new play under the title of an old one that already has a licence. That's what they did this time . . .'

'But they'd all have to know!' she protested. 'The theatre manager in particular!'

'They do. Bellmaine is as keen as Cecily. He's prepared to take the chance, pay the fine if he has to. It's worth it, to say the things you really believe in, to ask the questions, shake the damnable complacency! If we could stir public opinion, we could reform all manner of laws that are antiquated, unjust.' He leaned forward a little, the flush in his cheeks deepening. 'More than that, alter the attitudes that are beyond the law, the prejudices that wound . . . and cripple! Can't you see how . . . how terrible this is? Some censorship is absurd! Did you know we aren't even allowed to represent a clergyman on stage – at all! Not even sympathetically! How can we question anything?'

'Will it change Lord Warriner's bill?' she asked quietly.

'Ever the practical,' he said with a rueful little smile. 'Do you want women to be able to institute divorce for neglect, or unhappiness?' His face was unreadable, wry, humorous, sad, uncertain.

'I don't know,' she said honestly. 'I never even thought about it until I saw the play. But surely that's the point! I should have.'

He stretched across the table and laid his hand lightly over hers, barely touching her. 'Yes it is the point. And yes, it probably will affect it. Warriner may well lose his nerve. Too many of his friends will lose theirs. They will have felt which way the wind blows, and retreat.'

'I'm sorry,' she said quietly, turning her head upwards and closing her fingers over his. She remained like that for a moment, then withdrew and picked up the newspaper where he had left it.

Further down on the page from the article on the closure of the play was a letter from Oscar Wilde, eloquent, witty and informed, with the same outrage as Joshua felt. He wrote of censorship as an act of oppression of the mind, performed by cowards who were as much afraid of what was within themselves as anything others might say.

'The thing I resent most of all,' Joshua said, his eyes still on her, 'is not the restriction in what I may or may not say, but what I may or may not listen to! What monumental arrogance makes the Lord Chamberlain believe he has the right to dictate whether I shall listen to this or that man's views on faith and religion? I may find I agree with him! Where does the whole concept of blasphemy come from?'

'From the Bible,' she replied quietly. 'There are many people to whom it is a very real offence to speak mockingly or vulgarly of God.'

'Whose God?' he asked, searching her eyes.

For a moment she was at a loss.

'Whose God?' he repeated. 'Yours? Mine? The vicar's? The man next door? Anybody's?'

She drew in her breath to reply, thinking she knew exactly what she was going to say, then realised like a shaft of light in darkness, that she did not. There were probably as many ideas of God as there were people who gave the matter a thought. It had never occurred to her before.

'Isn't there . . . some sort of consensus . . . at least . . .' She tailed off. They had never discussed religion before. She knew his morality, but not his faith, not the deep, unspoken part that governed his heart. They had never even discussed his heritage of Judaism, even though he made little outwardly of it now. But perhaps it was still part of him, if you touched a nerve?

As if reading her thoughts, he looked at her with a twisted smile. 'Didn't they crucify Christ for blasphemy?' he said softly. 'I would have thought as a Christian you would have a certain tolerance towards blasphemers.'

'No you wouldn't,' she contradicted him, a little catch in her voice. Suddenly they were speaking of such fierce reality. 'You know better than that: we have almost no tolerance at all. We are perfectly happy to burn one another for a difference of opinion, let alone outsiders of a different religion altogether!'

'You are more likely to burn each other than outsiders,' he pointed out. 'But new ideas do find their way in every now and then, through the bloodshed, the smoke and the fury. It used to be a sin unto death for ordinary people to read the Bible; now

178

we are encouraged to. Somebody had to be the first to challenge that monumental piece of censorship. Now we all accept that the whole concept of denying God's word was monstrous.'

'Well . . . perhaps I don't mind about blasphemy,' she said reluctantly, thinking of the Marchands again. 'But what about obscenity? As well as the good that new ideas can do, what about the harm?'

Before he could answer her the door flew open and the old lady stumped in, banging her cane on the floor.

Joshua rose to his feet automatically. 'Good morning, Mrs Ellison. How are you?'

She drew in her breath deeply. 'As well as can be expected,' she replied.

He pulled her chair out and assisted her to be seated before returning to his own place.

Caroline offered her tea and toast, which she accepted.

'What harm are you talking about?' She reached for the butter and black cherry preserve. Her appetite was excellent, although this morning she did look a little paler than usual.

Joshua's eyes barely flickered to Caroline before he answered. 'There is an article about censorship in the newspapers—' he began.

'Good!' she interrupted, swallowing her toast half chewed in order to speak. 'Far too much is said without regard to decency these days. It never was when I was young. The world today is filled with vulgarity. It degrades all of us. I am glad I am at the end of my life.' She reached for the butter and helped herself. 'At least someone cares enough to fight for standards of a sort.'

'It is a protest against censorship,' Caroline corrected her, and then instantly wondered if it would not have been a great

179

deal wiser to have allowed the subject to drop.

'Some actress, I suppose.' Grandmama raised her eyebrows. 'There seems to be nothing women will not say or do these days, and in public for all to see.' She looked at Caroline meaningfully. 'Morality is on the decline everywhere – even where one would least expect!'

'You agree with censorship?' If Joshua were angry he masked it so well no one would have guessed it. But then acting was his profession, and he was very good at it. Caroline reminded herself of that quite often.

The old lady stared at him as if he had questioned her sanity.

'Of course I do!' she responded indignantly. 'Any sane and civilised person knows there are some things you cannot say without corrupting our entire way of life. Where there is no reverence for things which are sacred, for the home and all it embodies, no safety for the mind, then the entire nation begins to crumble. Did they not teach you history wherever you come from? You must have heard of Rome?'

Joshua kept his temper superbly. There was even a shadow of amusement in his eyes.

'London,' he replied. 'I come from London, the other side of the river, five miles away from here. And certainly I have heard of Rome, and of Egypt, and Babylon, and Greece, and Inquisitorial Spain. So far as I know, Greece had the best theatre, although Egypt had some excellent poetry.'

'They were heathens.' The old lady dismissed them with a flick of her hand, perilously close to the milk jug. 'The Greeks had all sorts of gods who behaved appallingly, if the stories we hear are to be believed. And the Egyptians were worse. They worshipped animals! If you can imagine such a thing!'

'There was one pharaoh who set up his own new religion

believing in and worshipping only one God,' Joshua told her with a smile.

She looked startled. 'Oh . . . well, I dare say that is a step forward. It didn't last, though, did it?'

'No,' he agreed. 'They accused him of blasphemy, and obliterated everything he had done.'

She glared at him. It was a moment before she recovered her thought. 'You weren't talking about blasphemy. Caroline said "obscene".'

'That's a matter of view as well,' he argued. 'What is beautiful to one may be obscene to another.'

'Nonsense!' Her face was flushed pink. 'Every decent person knows what is obscene: intrusion into other people's private lives and feelings, and where it is unforgivable to trespass, and only the most vulgar and depraved would wish to.'

'Of course there are—' he began.

'Good!' The word was like a trap closing. 'Then that is the end of the subject. My tea is cold. Will you be good enough to send for some more.' It was a command, not a request.

Caroline rang the bell. She could see the anger inside Joshua, barely suppressed by a thin veneer of courtesy because of the old lady's age, and because she had been Caroline's mother in-law, and she was a guest in their home, however unwillingly.

Caroline found herself saying what she knew Joshua wished to. 'Everybody agrees there are things which should not be said, the disagreement is as to which things they are.'

'All things that flout morality and disregard the decent sensibilities of men and women,' Grandmama said flatly. 'You may have lost sight of what they are, but most of us have not. Ask any of those who used to be your friends. Thank God the Lord Chamberlain knows.'

Caroline held her tongue with difficulty, and only because she knew the pointlessness of arguing any further.

The maid came and was sent for fresh tea. Joshua rose and excused himself, kissing Caroline on the cheek and wishing the old lady a pleasant day.

Caroline picked up the newspaper again and looked at an article about Cecily Antrim. There was a sketch of her from a playbill above it, looking beautiful and intense. It was that which first caught her attention.

Yesterday Miss Cecily Antrim protested vigorously against the Lord Chamberlain's censorship of her new play, *The Lady's Love*, which is not now to be performed because of its indecency, and the tendency to degrade public morality and cause distress and outrage.

Miss Antrim marched up and down the Strand carrying a placard and causing a nuisance, until the police were called to oblige her to desist. She claimed afterwards that the play was a valid work of art questioning misconceptions about women's feelings and beliefs. She said that refusing to allow it to be performed was to deny women the freedom granted men to explore a far better understanding of those sides of their nature which are profound, and often the wellspring of controversial acts.

Mr Wallace Albright, for the Lord Chamberlain's office, said the play would be likely to undermine the values upon which our society is founded, and it would not be in the public good for it to be performed.

Miss Antrim has not been charged with affray, and was permitted to return to her home.

Caroline sat staring at the page. She was filled with an unreasonable anger, but it was confused, veering one way and then the other. Why should one man be able to decide what people may see, or not see? Who was he? What manner of man? What were his prejudices and secrets, his fears or dreams? Did he see threat where there was simply intelligent enquiry, a challenge to bigotry and to one person's dominion over another's thoughts and beliefs?

Or was he protecting the young or vulnerable against the assaults of pornography and violence, the coarsening effects upon sensibility of seeing abuse of others portrayed as acceptable, the eroding of values because they were mocked and made fun of, until it took more courage to espouse gentleness and reverence than it did to deny it?

She looked across the table at the old lady's face, set in lines of bitterness, and saw also something she thought for a moment was fear. It was profoundly disturbing; it aroused in her fears of her own, and something far too like pity.

Chapter Seven

The constable stood in front of Pitt in his office, very much to attention.

'Yes sir, that's wot 'e said.'

It was early morning, the sun hazy gold outside, warm on the walls and the stones of the street, only a little dimmed by the smoke of countless chimneys. The air was dry and mild, pungent with the smells of the city.

'He saw Orlando Antrim and Delbert Cathcart quarrelling, the day of Cathcart's death,' Pitt repeated. 'You are sure?'

'Yes sir, I am. That's wot 'e said, an' seems there were no shaking 'im from it.'

'Presumably he is acquainted with both men, this . . . what's his name?'

'Hathaway, sir. Peter Hathaway. I dunno, sir, 'cept I reckon 'e must be, or 'ow would 'e know 'oo they are? Two gents quarrellin' could be anybody!'

'Precisely. Where do I find this Mr Hathaway?'

'Arkwright Road, sir, 'Ampstead. Number twenty-six.'

'And he reported this to Bow Street?' Pitt was surprised.

'No sir, 'Ampstead. They told us . . . by telephone.' The constable lifted his head a little higher. He was proud of new technology and had great hopes of its use in catching criminals, even in preventing crime before it occurred.

'I see.' Pitt rose to his feet. 'Well, I suppose I had better go and talk to Mr Hathaway.'

'Yes sir. Maybe this Mr Antrim is our man, sir, seein' as 'ow they was quarrellin' real violent, like.' He looked hopeful, his eyes wide and bright.

'Perhaps,' Pitt agreed with a sharp sense of disappointment. He had admired Orlando Antrim, and there was something likeable about him, a sensitivity, an acuteness of perception. But it would not be the first time Pitt had liked someone who was capable of killing another person. 'Inform Sergeant Tellman where I've gone, will you?' he said from the door.

When Pitt reached Arkwright Road he was told by the housemaid that young Mr Hathaway was not at home. It was a fine day, and he had gone out with his camera, no doubt to his club, and if the gentlemen were on a field trip, that could be anywhere at all. However, after a little probing, she gave him the address of the place where they met, and the doorman there in turn told him that today the members of the club had taken a trip to the nearby Heath in order to practise photographing natural scenery.

'Very big on natural scenery, they are,' he added approvingly. 'Take some lovely pictures. Fair lifts yer spirits to see them.'

Pitt thanked him and walked back towards Hampstead Heath to begin the search for the Camera Club, and Mr Peter Hathaway. Of course whatever he had seen was only indicative. People could quarrel without it leading to violence of any sort, let alone to murder. But Cathcart's death was a melodramatic crime, one perpetrated by a person of high emotion and a great deal of imagination, and presumably a familiarity with art, to mimic Millais' painting of Ophelia so closely. Unless that had been accidental, not a copying so much as another person with the same passion expressing it in the same, fairly elemental way.

It was pleasant walking in the sun over the dry, springy grass, the wind barely rustling the leaves, the smell of earth in the air instead of smoke and manure and dusty stone. There were birds singing, not the ever-present sparrows but what sounded like a blackbird, high, persistent and sweet.

He saw a young man and woman half lying on the ground, her skirts billowing around her, a picnic basket near them, as yet unopened. They had been laughing together, she flirting, he showing off a little. They stopped and looked up as Pitt approached them.

'Excuse me,' Pitt apologised. He would far rather have been doing as they were – savouring the last echoes of summer, enjoying the moment with no thought of yesterday or tomorrow – than caring who killed Delbert Cathcart, or why.

When Charlotte came home from Paris he would take a day off, and the two of them would go out into the country sunshine, just wander around doing nothing in particular. It would not be difficult, and trains were cheap if you did not go too far.

'Yes?' the young man asked, politely enough.

'Have you seen a group of men go past carrying cameras?' Pitt enquired.

It was the girl who answered. 'About half an hour ago. Ever so serious they was, all talking together.'

'Which way did they go?'

She looked at him to see if he were carrying a camera as well, and was puzzled when there was none visible.

'I'm looking for a friend,' Pitt said somewhat lamely. 'Which way did they go?'

She was not sufficiently interested to pursue her curiosity. 'That way.' She pointed across the swell of grass towards a clump of trees, gnarled roots writhing above the earth in intricate and beautiful form.

'Thank you.' He nodded briefly and set off as directed.

It took him twenty minutes longer and he was hot and out of breath when he saw the group of a dozen young men dressed in jackets, waistcoats, trousers, and all but two in bowler hats as well. Every one of them had his share of equipment, including a variety of leather cases and boxes from less than a cubic foot in size to ones large enough to have carried clothes for a weekend, and boots to go with them. Tripods straddled the grass with a strange, angular kind of elegance. Cameras balanced on top of them with lenses pointing intently at a bough or a branch, or some interesting formation of wood and leaf.

'Good morning,' Pitt interrupted their concentration.

No one answered.

'Excuse me!' he tried a little more loudly.

The nearest young man turned, startled by the intrusion. 'Sir!' he said, holding up his hand as if to stop traffic. 'Unless you are in urgent need of assistance, pray do not interrupt this moment. The light is just so.'

Pitt looked to where they all seemed to be staring, and indeed the rays of the sun shone through the leaves of a great oak with a remarkable luminescence, but he doubted it would translate into anything so spectacular without the green and gold of reality. How could mere sepia tint be worth anything after what the eye had seen? Nevertheless he waited while twelve cameras clicked and squeaked and generally recorded the instant.

'Yes sir!' the young man said at last. 'Now, what may we do for you? Do you wish your photograph taken? Or you are perhaps an enthusiast yourself, and you wish to join us? Bring us some of your work, and we will make our decision. We are very generous, I assure you. We desire only to increase our art, enlarge the boundaries of what may be achieved. Colours will be next, you know.' His voice rose excitedly. 'I mean real colours! Reds – blues – greens – everything!'

'Will it?' For a moment Pitt's mind was taken with the idea. First he thought of the beauty of it, then hard on its heels he thought of the police use. If photographs could be taken of things shown in the colour they really were, then the possibilities were limitless, not just for identification of people, but of stolen goods, paintings, works of art, all the sort of things in Delbert Cathcart's home. Verbal descriptions never did justice to them. Police constables were not meant to be poets. 'That will be marvellous,' he agreed. 'But I came to speak to Mr Hathaway. He is a member, I believe?'

'Oh yes, very good, he is, in fact most talented.' He very nearly asked what Pitt wanted, and curbed his inquisitiveness only just in time. He inclined his head towards a young man with rather long fair hair, who was still gazing with rapt attention at the light on the branches. 'That's Hathaway over there.'

'Thank you,' Pitt acknowledged, and strode off before he could be further drawn into enthusiasm for the photographic inventions of the future.

Hathaway looked up as Pitt's shadow fell across his camera.

'I'm sorry,' Pitt apologised. 'Are you Peter Hathaway?'

'Yes. Is there something I can do for you?'

'Superintendent Pitt, from the Bow Street Police Station,' Pitt explained, handing him his card.

189

'Oh!' Hathaway looked serious. He swallowed hard. 'Is it about that report I made to the local police? Look, could we discuss it a little further off?' He gestured rather wildly with his free arm. 'It is sort of . . . well . . . delicate . . . with Cathcart dead, and all that . . . you know?' A flicker of distress crossed his face. 'He was a damn decent photographer. Almost the best, I'd say. Can't let him be killed and do nothing about it . . . not when I saw the quarrel.'

'Tell me exactly what you did see, Mr Hathaway,' Pitt encouraged him. 'First of all, where did this happen? Set the scene for me, if you like.'

'Ah . . . yes. Well, it was the Tuesday, as I said.' Hathaway thought hard, re-creating it in his mind, his eyes almost closed. 'We were by the Serpentine, trying to catch the early light on the water, so we were there about eight o'clock. A bit inconvenient, certainly, but one has to follow nature; you can't lead it. We did some excellent work, really excellent.' He looked away quickly. 'You've no idea how blind one can be to the glories of light and shade, the intricacies of form, until you see them through a lens! You really do see the world through a new eye. Pardon the obvious, but it's true. You should take up photography, sir, you really should! Bit expensive, I suppose, but most pleasures are, and without the artistic merit or the truly spiritual uplift of catching a moment of nature's glory and immortalising it to share with all mankind.' His voice increased in enthusiasm. 'It's a window in time, sir! A kind of immortality!'

Pitt could not help catching a glimpse of what he meant. It was true, a photograph far more than any painting caught the moment and made it, if not eternal, at least of unimaginable duration. But Delbert Cathcart had been a great photographer, and an ordinary, mortal man, and he was dead. It was Pitt's duty to find out how and why, and by whose hand. There might be time for thoughts of capturing beauty later on.

'It is marvellous,' he agreed. 'I don't suppose you took any photographs of Mr Cathcart and Mr Antrim while they were there?'

For a moment Hathaway's face fell with disappointment that Pitt should think of something so mundane, but he was too much of an enthusiast to miss the point. Interest flared up in his eyes and his face brightened. 'Oh, if only I had! What a wonderful thing that would be, wouldn't it? Unarguable evidence! It will come, sir! It will come! The camera is a witness whose testimony no one can doubt! Oh, the future is full of wonders we can barely imagine! Just think of—'

'What was Mr Cathcart doing at the Serpentine?' Pitt interrupted. Speculation on the marvels of the future could go on indefinitely and, fascinating as it was, it was a luxury he could not afford now.

'Er . . . I don't know.' Hathaway sounded surprised. 'Actually, when I think of it, it was quite odd. As far as I know he only takes portraits. He wasn't here to teach us . . . which would have been marvellous, of course! But he didn't speak to us at all. He had his camera with him, though. I imagine he was looking at places to use for backdrop. That's all that would make sense.'

'But you did see him?'

'Oh yes, quite clearly.'

'Did you speak to him?'

'No. No, it would have been . . . intrusive. He is a – was a – very great man . . . something of an idol to an amateur like me.' He flushed slightly as he said it. 'It is a most awful thing that he should have been killed, an act of barbarism. That's what makes it so hard to understand. But great artists can be volatile. Perhaps it was over a woman?'

'Maybe. What was Orlando Antrim doing here? Is he an amateur photographer?'

'Oh yes, really quite good, you know. Of course he also prefers figures, but one would expect that. After all, drama is his art.'

'Tell me exactly what you saw, Mr Hathaway.'

A couple of young men walked past them, carrying their cameras and tripods and talking to each other excitedly, their voices raised, trying to gesticulate with arms weighed down by their equipment. The bowler hat of one of them had been knocked to a rakish angle, but he seemed quite unaware of it. They disappeared into the shade of a tree, propped their tripods and began looking at the area with interest.

'I saw them arguing,' Hathaway answered, frowning. 'Antrim seemed to be pleading with Cathcart, trying to persuade him of something. He appeared very emphatic about it, waving his hands around.'

'Did you hear what he said?'

'No.' His eyes widened. 'No, that's the odd thing. Neither of them raised his voice at all. I knew they were quarrelling because of the furious gestures and the anger in their faces. Antrim was trying to persuade Cathcart to do something, and Cathcart kept refusing more and more vehemently, until finally Antrim stormed off in a rage.'

'But Cathcart remained?'

'Only for a few moments. Then he picked up his camera, snapped his tripod closed and went off as well.'

'In the same direction?'

192

'More or less. But then they would. It was towards the road and the natural way out.'

'Did anyone else observe this exchange?'

'I don't know. One does tend to get rather absorbed in what one is doing. I'm afraid I have lost a few friends because of my obsession. I noticed them because I was at that moment casting my eye around for a particular pattern against which to take a picture of one of my friends, a young lady with fair hair. I imagined clothing her in white, and having her stand looking—'

Pitt smiled, but interrupted his explanation. 'Yes, I understand. You have been very helpful, Mr Hathaway. Is there anything else you can tell me about this encounter? Have you seen the two together on any other occasion? Do you know either of them personally, as members of the club, perhaps?'

Hathaway lifted his shoulders in a shrug. 'I'm so sorry. I've only been a member a short time. I know perhaps three or four of the other fellows: Crabtree, Worthing, Ullinshaw, Dobbs, that's about all. Dobbs has the most wonderful knack with light on stones and fences and things, and he's so good with birds.' His voice rose again with excitement. 'He's the first one who showed me film on a roll, rather than plates. It was absolutely marvellous. You have no idea! A Mr Eastman in America invented it. Twenty feet long.' He gestured with his hands. 'All wound up so you can take a hundred pictures one after the other! Imagine it! One after the other . . . just like that. They are round, almost two and a half inches in diameter.'

'Round?' Pitt said quickly. All the pictures he had seen in Cathcart's house had been rectangular, as had been the portraits in the houses of his clients.

'Yes,' Hathaway smiled. 'Of course that's amateurs. I know

the professionals use the square ones, but these are pretty good, you know. When they are all done you send the whole camera back to them and they process the film, and return you the camera reloaded. It all costs about five guineas.' He looked a trifle uncomfortable. 'As I said, it is rather expensive. But I'd rather do that than any other pastime I can think of.' He jutted his chin out defiantly, daring Pitt to say he was wasting money.

'That is most interesting,' Pitt said quite sincerely. 'Thank you for your candour, Mr Hathaway, and your instruction. If anything else occurs to you, please let me know. Good day.'

Pitt spoke to other members of the Camera Club, but no one else could help. One young man had seen the quarrel, but could only describe the participants; he did not know them by name.

'Oh yes,' he agreed vehemently. 'Very heated. I thought at one moment they would come to blows, but the taller young man stalked off, leaving the other very red in the face and mighty uncomfortable.'

Nothing Pitt asked could elicit anything more, except numerous details on the marvels of photography, the newest technical advances, the miracle of Mr Eastman's roll of film – although it could apparently be used only outside and in natural daylight, which explained largely why Delbert Cathcart, who frequently worked in subdued light or inside a room, still worked with the old-style plates.

The club members were all male, and it had not occurred to them as worthy of comment that there were no women among them, but they were ardent in their admiration for female photographers, and not the least hesitant in accounting them great artists in their field, and indeed possessing an excellent and comprehensive grasp of the techniques involved as well. It did not advance Pitt's detection in the slightest, but in spite of himself he was interested.

From Hampstead Pitt went to seek Orlando Antrim. The next necessary step would be to ask him what the quarrel had been about and where and when he had last seen Cathcart. Pitt was dreading the moment when he might have to accuse him of the murder. But some confrontation was unavoidable.

He found Orlando at the theatre rehearsing his part in *Hamlet*, which he was due to play within a week, now that the controversial drama had been banned.

Pitt was required to explain himself to the doorman and prove his identity before he was allowed in.

'They're in rehearsal!' the old man said, fixing Pitt with a gimlet eye. 'Don't you go interruptin' 'em, now! You wait till yer spoke to. Mr Bellmaine'll tell you when it's your turn. Mustn't upset actors, isn't fair. Plainer than that, it isn't right.'

Pitt acknowledged the stricture, and obediently tiptoed along the dusty passages as he had been directed. After a few false starts, he eventually ended up in the wings of the huge stage, bare except for two embroidered screens and a chair. A tall lean man stood towards the front, perhaps a couple of yards from the orchestra pit and a little to the left. His cadaverous face was fired with emotion and he held one arm high as if hailing someone in the distance.

Then Pitt saw her, coming from the shadows of the wings opposite him into the light of the stage: Cecily Antrim, dressed in very ordinary grey-blue, a simple blouse and skirt with a slight bustle. Her hair was caught up untidily in a few pins, and yet it was extraordinarily flattering. It looked casual and youthful, full of energy.

195

'Ah, my dear!' the tall man said warmly. 'Ready for Polonius' death. From the top. Where's Hamlet? Orlando!'

Orlando Antrim emerged from the wings behind his mother. He too was dressed in the most ordinary of clothes: trousers, a collarless shirt and a waistcoat which matched nothing. His boots were dusty and scuffed and his hair tousled. A look of fierce concentration darkened his face.

'Good. Good,' the tall man said. Pitt assumed he was the Mr Bellmaine the doorman had referred to. 'Hamlet, from the right. Gertrude, you and I from the left. This is the arras in question. Let us begin.' He led the way off the stage, his footsteps echoing across the boards, then he turned and walked back beside Cecily.

'"A will come straight",' he began. '"Look you lay home to him . . ."' His voice sounded no more than a conversational level, and yet it filled the stage and the auditorium beyond. '"Pray you, be round."'

'"Mother, mother, mother!"' Orlando called from the wings.

Cecily turned to Bellmaine. '"I'll warrant you, fear me not. Withdraw, I hear him coming."'

In a single, oddly graceful movement for one aping age, Bellmaine slipped behind the screen.

Orlando came on to the stage. '"Now, mother, what's the matter?"'

'"Hamlet, thou hast thy father much offended,"' Cecily answered, her voice carrying the same considered music.

Orlando's face was strained, his eyes wide and dark. There was a harshness in him of emotion so tightly held in, and yet so tormented, he was at the edge of breaking. '"Mother, you have my father much offended."'

Pitt watched in fascination as people he had seen in totally

196

different characters took on the roles familiar to every generation for nearly three hundred years. He had studied *Hamlet* in the schoolroom on Sir Arthur Desmond's estate. He had read the great soliloquy himself with Matthew, and pulled it apart to its separate elements. Yet in front of him the play became a story of people with lives as real as his own. He watched the Queen's guilt, Polonius' death, Hamlet's torture, all created with voice and gestures on a bare stage, and then shattered in an instant as the actors stopped, threw parts aside and became themselves again.

'Too quick,' Bellmaine criticised, looking at Orlando. 'Your accusation blurs the words. Hamlet is in fury and indignation, but the audience still needs to hear the substance of his charge. You are too realistic.'

Orlando smiled. 'Sorry. Should I hesitate before "Heaven's face doth glow"?'

'Try it,' Bellmaine agreed with enthusiasm. He turned to Cecily. 'You are pleading. Guilt is angrier. You are trying too hard to win the audience's sympathy.'

She shrugged an apology.

'Again,' he ordered. 'From Hamlet's entrance.'

Pitt watched them go through it a second time, and a third, and a fourth. He marvelled at their patience, and even more at the emotional energy that invested it with the passion each time, picking up halfway through a scene with its changing moods, and throwing themselves into it. Only twice did anyone need prompting, and then their continuance was immediate. They seemed able to create the illusion of an entire world by the power of their own belief, and yet to remember someone else's words and speak them as if they were their own.

Finally Bellmaine allowed them some respite, and for the

first time Pitt noticed that several other actors and actresses had appeared ready to rehearse their parts. He tried to imagine them in the costumes of a far earlier period, and see them as they would be in character. A young woman with fair hair and a high forehead he thought to be Ophelia, and as soon as the recognition came to him, he saw Delbert Cathcart obscenely splayed out in the punt, dressed in the green velvet gown in parody of ecstasy and death.

He rose to his feet from where he had been sitting on a pine box.

'Excuse me . . .'

'My dear fellow,' Bellmaine said straight away, 'I can't be doing auditioning now. Go and see Mr Jackson. He'll talk with you. If you can be prompt, come and go exactly as you are told, stay sober and only speak when you are spoken to, a guinea a week and you have begun your career on the stage.' He smiled and his whole countenance was illuminated with sudden charm. 'You never know where it will lead. Tour with us in the provinces, get a small part and we'll pay you up to twenty-five shillings . . . thirty-five in time. Now be a good chap and go and look for Jackson. He's probably around at the back somewhere, scenery and lighting, don't you know!'

Pitt smiled back in spite of himself. 'I'm not looking for a career on the stage, Mr Bellmaine. I am from the Bow Street Police Station . . . Superintendent Pitt . . .'

Cecily looked up from the edge of the stage where she was sitting. 'My goodness, it's the policeman friend of Joshua's! Polonius is alive and well, I assure you!' Since Bellmaine was standing between them that was incontestable.

'I should hardly arrest Hamlet, ma'am,' he promised. 'The nation would never forgive me.'

'The world would not, Mr Pitt,' she answered. 'But I am delighted you have such an excellent sense of priorities. We fluffed a few lines but our performance was hardly a crime!' She sat back a little, hugging one knee. 'What brings you here? Not my protest against the Lord Chamberlain, surely? Now if you read my mind as to what I would like to do to the wretch, which may well be arrestable.'

'I cannot arrest you until after you have done it, Miss Antrim,' he pointed out, trying to hide his amusement. It was not a time for it, and yet it rose unbidden within him.

She understood far too quickly. Her face broke into a lovely smile. 'How very kind of you! Thank you so much!'

Bellmaine stepped between them. 'You have come for something, sir. Pray what is it? We cannot afford to stop for long. This may not appear much to you, but it is our living, and far harder than it seems.'

Pitt turned to him. 'It seems extremely hard, Mr Bellmaine,' he said honestly. 'I have to speak to Mr Antrim. I shall keep it as brief as possible. Is there a scene you can rehearse without him?'

'Hamlet without the prince? You jest, sir? Ah . . . I suppose so. A little. Laertes, Ophelia! Come! We have no time to idle. Act One Scene Three. From the top, if you please. Begin "My necessaries are embarked" . . . Pay attention!'

Pitt walked across the boards towards Orlando, his footsteps loud and solitary for a moment until the arrival of Laertes and Ophelia muffled them, and the drama began instantly with well-schooled voices and passion lit as if the whole story leading to it were barely dismissed the moment before.

'What is it?' Orlando asked with a frown. 'Is it to do with

the censorship thing? I protested, but quite peacefully,'

'No, Mr Antrim, it has nothing to do with censorship at all. As far as I know, you have broken no laws in this matter.' He walked beside Orlando further into the wings and behind the stage where bare brick walls stretched up into the darkness out of sight, and huge painted backdrops for a dozen different worlds hung or were stacked in layers.

'Then what?' Orlando faced him, standing with grace so deeply learned he did it without thought.

'Do you belong to a gentlemen's camera club near Hampstead?' Pitt asked.

'What?'

Pitt began to repeat the question.

'Yes!' Orlando interrupted. 'Yes I do . . . At least I go there occasionally, not very often, but I do belong. Why?'

'Did you join them near the Serpentine Tuesday of last week, quite early in the morning?' He watched Orlando's face, and was not sure in the uncertain light whether he saw him pale or not.

'Yes . . .' Orlando said guardedly. He swallowed and coughed. 'Yes I did. Why? Nothing unusual happened, so far as I am aware.'

'You met Mr Cathcart there, and had a heated disagreement with him.'

'No.' He looked startled, as if the question had taken him completely by surprise. 'You – you mean the photographer who was killed? If he was there I certainly didn't see him.'

'But you were there?'

'Yes, of course I was there. It was an excellent morning, clear early light, with a sort of whiteness to it, and not many people about. I didn't have to rehearse and I hadn't been too late the night before. Who told you Cathcart was there?'

'Do you know him?'

'No.' The answer was very quick. Orlando's eyes did not leave Pitt's and they were unnaturally steady. But then he knew Cathcart had been murdered. Any normal man would be nervous. 'No I don't,' he repeated. 'He was a professional, one of the best, so everyone says. I am completely amateur. I just enjoy it. But I think I'll have to give it up. I haven't time.'

Pitt could believe that without the slightest difficulty. He could not even imagine the amount of mental and emotional energy needed to play a role like Hamlet, let alone the physical endurance.

'You quarrelled with someone that morning, and left in some heat. If it was not Cathcart, who was it?' he asked.

Orlando flushed. He hesitated several moments before replying, and when he did so he looked away first.

'A friend,' he said, a touch defiantly. 'A fellow I've known for a little while. I'd rather not get him concerned in this. It was a simple disagreement, that's all. I dare say it looked more violent than it was. There was no ill will, just a . . . a difference of opinion as to what was right. Not the sort of thing you would lose a friendship over, let alone come to blows.'

Pitt disliked what he had to do, but to omit it would be irresponsible, even though he half believed Orlando.

'Others have identified the man as Cathcart, Mr Antrim. If it was not he, then I need to verify that. The name of your friend?'

Orlando hesitated again, then his face set. 'I'm sorry.' He waited for a moment to gauge Pitt's reaction. He must have seen no yielding. 'Actually he is out of town anyway, and I couldn't get in touch with him. So there would be no point in

201

my giving you his name . . . or address.'

'If he is out of the town, Mr Antrim, there would be no harm either, would there?' Pitt resumed.

'Well, yes there would. It might do his reputation some damage, and he would not be there to protect it.'

'Mr Antrim, all I wish to do is confirm that it was he you quarrelled with the morning of the day Mr Cathcart was killed, no more than that.'

'Well you cannot, because he is not here. But surely if a man of Cathcart's standing and reputation had been in the presence of the Camera Club, some other member would be able to confirm it?'

That was unarguably true. It was also true that they ought to be able to tell him the identity of the man Orlando Antrim had spoken with so passionately. Why should he wish to hide it, supposing Hathaway had been mistaken?

'Then I shall have to ask them,' Pitt accepted, looking very directly at Orlando. 'No doubt they saw you as well, and if he is a member they will know his name. It would be a great deal easier if you were to tell me, but if I must draw it out by questioning other members, then I will do so.'

Orlando looked acutely unhappy. 'I see you are not going to let it go. It has no bearing on your case, I swear. The subject of our disagreement was photography. It was a diplomat with the French Embassy . . . The situation is delicate . . .'

'Henri Bonnard,' Pitt supplied.

Orlando stiffened, his chin jerking up a little, his eyes wide, but he did not speak.

'Where is he, Mr Antrim?'

'I am not at liberty to say.' Orlando's face set, hard and miserable, but completely resolute. It was apparent that he was not going to say anything further, no matter how hard pressed. 'I have given my word.'

Nothing Pitt said would change his mind.

Bellmaine was apparently through with the scene to his satisfaction, or else was no longer prepared to remain in ignorance as to what Pitt wanted with his principal actor. He came around the corner into the cluttered space where they were standing, his face sharp, his eyes first to Orlando, then to Pitt.

'Art is long and life is short, Superintendent,' he said with a wry half-smile. 'If we really can be of help, then of course we are at your disposal. But if, on the other hand, it is not a matter of urgency or importance, perhaps we could now continue with *Hamlet*?' He looked very carefully at Orlando, perhaps to assess if he were in any way disturbed sufficiently to damage his concentration. He seemed moderately satisfied with what he saw. He turned back to Pitt, waiting for his answer.

Orlando seemed vaguely relieved that Bellmaine had come. Perhaps unconsciously, he moved a step closer to him.

Bellmaine put a hand on his shoulder. 'Work, my prince,' he said, still facing Pitt. 'If the superintendent will allow?'

There was nothing further to be gained. Pitt was breaking their rhythm of creation for no good reason. 'Of course,' he yielded. 'Thank you for your time.'

Orlando shrugged his thanks off.

Bellmaine spread his hands in an eloquent and graceful gesture, then led the way back to the stage where everyone was waiting for them. Pitt took one last look at the actors as they took up their own world again and lost themselves in it, then he turned and walked away.

* * *

He saw Tellman briefly and told him what little he had learned.

'That embassy's hiding something,' Tellman replied, sitting in the chair at the other side of Pitt's paper-strewn desk. 'I still think it's got something to do with them. There's only Mrs Geddes that says the body was Cathcart. Maybe it isn't? Maybe it *is* the Frenchman. The whole thing looks more like actors and foreigners anyway.'

'It looks more like passion than greed,' Pitt answered. 'But all sorts of people are capable of that, not only Frenchmen and eccentrics.'

Tellman gave him a look of silent disdain.

'We'll go back to the embassy in the morning,' Pitt conceded. 'We need to know what happened to Henri Bonnard, even if it is only to exclude him from the investigation.'

'Or what happened to Cathcart,' Tellman added.

'I think we know what happened to him,' Pitt said sadly. 'He was murdered in his own house, and then sent down the Thames on a last, obscure journey. What I don't know is by whom, and exactly why.'

Tellman did not answer.

Monsieur Villeroche was just as adamant as he had been the first time Pitt saw him, only on this occasion he managed to conduct the meeting in the privacy of his own neat office.

'No! No, absolutely!' he repeated. 'He has not returned, nor sent any word, so far as I know, and I am at my wits' end to know what has happened to him.' His face was pink and he waved his hands jerkily to emphasise his distress. 'It is now well over a week and there is no account of him at all. His work is piling up, and I am simply told not to worry! I am worried sick! Who would not be?'

'Have you been in contact with his family in France?' Pitt asked him.

'In France? No. They live in the south – Provence, I believe. He would hardly go all the way there without telling me. If a crisis arose it would be simple enough to ask for leave. The ambassador is not unreasonable.'

Pitt did not pursue it, although, of course, Tellman had already ascertained that Bonnard had not taken the packet boat across the Channel but had returned from Dover to London.

'Could it be a romantic affair?' he said instead.

Villeroche shrugged. 'Then why not simply say so?' he asked reasonably. 'He has not taken a normal leave of absence, a holiday, that is certain. What kind of a man pursues a secret romantic affair by abandoning his position, where he is trusted and respected, and disappears into . . . God knows where – and without a word to anyone?'

'A man who is pursuing someone he should not be,' Pitt said with a slight smile. 'A man in the grasp of a passion so intense he loses all sense of propriety, or duty towards his colleagues.'

'A man who does not desire to keep his position,' Villeroche responded. 'And thus be in a situation to afford to marry this secret love.' He bit his lip. 'So I suppose we must speak of an illicit affair, a woman who is already married, or is the daughter of someone who does not find him an acceptable suitor. Or, I suppose, a woman of low class he could not marry? Or . . .' He did not name the last alternative, but both Pitt and Tellman knew what he was thinking.

'Is that likely?' Pitt asked, avoiding Tellman's eye. The green velvet gown was sharp in his memory.

Villeroche frowned. 'No!' He was obviously surprised that it should even be considered. 'Not in the least. I know that one seldom understands a person as well as one imagines, but Bonnard seemed as natural a man as any I know.' He shook his head slightly. 'But I wish you could find him. He was distressed before he left, labouring under some . . . some difficulty, some pressure, although I have no idea what. I am afraid some harm has come to him.'

Pitt obtained a list of clubs or other places Bonnard frequented, and where he would almost certainly call were he in London. Then he thanked Villeroche, and he and Tellman took their leave.

'Well, what do you reckon, then?' Tellman said as soon as they were out in the windy street again.

An omnibus clattered past them, women on the open top deck clasping their hats. A man on the footpath jammed his bowler on more firmly.

A newspaper seller shouted headlines about a government bill, and the forthcoming visit of some minor royalty to London, doing his best to make it sound interesting. An elderly man smiled at him good-naturedly and shook his head, but he bought a newspaper and tucked it under his arm.

'Bless yer, guv!' the seller called after him.

Tellman was waiting, his face keen.

'I think we've got to look a good deal harder for Bonnard,' Pitt said reluctantly. 'It may be a romance that for some reason he had to keep in complete secrecy.'

'You don't believe that!' Tellman looked at him with scorn. 'Villeroche is his friend. He'd know if there were something like that going on. Anyway, what kind of a man just drops everything and goes off after a woman without telling anyone, however he feels? He's not a poet or an actor – this is a man supposed to deal with governments. I know he's French, but even so!'

Pitt agreed with him but there was no reasonable alternative. Together they set off to visit the places on Villeroche's list, asking questions as discreetly as possible without being so vague as to be meaningless.

No one knew where Bonnard was, or had heard him make any mention at all of leaving London. Certainly no one knew of any romantic interest in particular. He had given them all the impression that he enjoyed the company of a number of young ladies, more than a few of whom were of questionable reputation. Marriage was the last thing on his mind at the moment. Romantic pleasure was something that lay far in the future.

'Not Henri,' one young man said vehemently as they sat around a café table, then added, with a slightly nervous laugh, 'he's far too ambitious to marry badly, let alone chase after another man's wife, and when he's on foreign soil as well. Oh no.' He glanced from Pitt to Tellman and back again. 'He was – is – the sort of man to enjoy himself, perhaps not always with the discretion one would wish in a diplomat, but only . . . convivially, if you like? Temporarily . . . I don't really know how to put it . . .' He trailed off.

'He likes to wine and dine but make no commitment,' Pitt interpreted.

'Precisely,' the other man agreed. 'A man of the world . . . or perhaps I should say a man of the city, the bright lights and the music, and yet not so worldly-wise as might be.'

Pitt smiled in spite of himself. They were all trying so hard to avoid the blunter way of expressing Bonnard's indulgences.

'Thank you. I believe I understand. You have been very helpful. Good day, sir.'

They visited several more of the people whose names Villeroche had given them, but no one added anything new. By the middle of the evening they had begun to call in at the various clubs he was known to frequent.

It was half-past nine, they were tired and discouraged when they came to Ye Olde Cheshire Cheese in an alleyway next to a tailor and a barber's shop.

'Is it worth it?' Tellman protested, wrinkling his nose in distaste as they stood together on the step, the gaslight making their shadows long across the stones.

'Probably not,' Pitt answered. 'I'm beginning to accept that he's either gone into the country somewhere after a romance which he managed to keep so well hidden even his closest friends didn't know about it, or he is involved in something darker, perhaps illegal, perhaps even Cathcart's murder, although I still don't see any connection. Come on, we'll make this the last place. The fellow is probably in a warm bed somewhere with someone unsuitable, and thoroughly enjoying himself, while we tramp around half London wondering what's happened to him.' He turned and pushed the door open, and was immediately inside a warm, close atmosphere smelling of wine and tobacco smoke. A score of young men and a few older sat around in groups with glasses or tankards at their elbows, many talking eagerly, others listening, leaning forward to catch every word.

Pitt must have looked a trifle Bohemian with his untidy clothes and hair seriously in need of a barber's attention, because no one questioned his presence. He was not sure whether that pleased him or not. He was certain it would not have pleased his superiors.

Tellman drew a few glances, but since he was obviously with Pitt, he was suffered to pass without question. He took a deep breath, ran his fingers around inside his collar, as if it were too tight and restricted his breath, and plunged in.

Pitt passed the first table, the conversation being so earnest he thought interrupting it would earn him no favour. At the second, where the company was far more relaxed, he saw a face he thought in some way familiar, although he was not sure from where. It was heavy-set with thick, dark hair and dark eyes.

'Lesser men will always criticise what they do not understand,' the man said vehemently. 'It is their only way of feeling that they have in some way made themselves masters of the subject, whereas in truth they have only displayed their failure to match it. It is a ceaseless source of amazement to me that the greater the fool, the more he is compelled to acquaint everyone with his shortcomings.'

'But doesn't it anger you?' a fair young man asked, his eyes wide and bright.

The darker man raised his eyebrows. 'My dear fellow, what would be the point? For some men, another man's work of art is simply a mirror. They see a reflection of themselves in it, according to their obsession of the moment, and then criticise it for all they are worth, which admittedly is very little, because they do not like what it shows them. So Mr Henley believes I am advocating the love of beauty above all things, precisely because he has no love for it. It frightens him. It is clear, yet ungraspable; it taunts him by its very elusiveness. In attacking *The Picture of Dorian Gray* he is, in some way of his own, finding a weapon to attack his personal enemy.'

Another of the company seemed fiercely interested. 'Do you believe that, Oscar? You could reduce him to pieces, if you wanted to! You have everything with which to do it – the wit, the perception, the vocabulary . . .'

'But I don't want to,' Oscar argued. 'I admire his work. I refuse to allow him to turn me into something I do not wish to be – namely an artist who has lost sight of art, and will descend to criticising in public, for retaliation's sake, what he truly admires in private. Or even worse, to deny myself the pleasure of enjoying what he has created because he is foolish enough to deny himself the enjoyment of what I have made. That, my dear friend, is a truly stupid thing to do. And when an ignorant or frightened man calls me immoral it hurts me, but I can tolerate it, but were an honest man to call me stupid, I should have to consider the possibility that he was right, and that would be awful!'

'We live in an age of Philistines,' another young man said wearily, pushing back a heavy quiff of hair. 'Censorship is a creeping death, the beginning of a necrosis of the soul. How can a civilisation grow except with new ideas, and any man who suffocates a new idea is a murderer of thought, and the enemy of the generations who follow him, because he has robbed them of a little of their lives. He has diminished them.'

'Well said!' Oscar applauded generously.

The young man blushed with pleasure.

Oscar smiled at him.

'Excuse me, Mr Wilde,' Pitt seized the lull in the conversation to interrupt.

Wilde looked up at him curiously. There was no hostility in his eyes, not even a guardedness as to a stranger.

'You agree, sir?' he asked warmly. He looked Pitt up and

down, his eyes resting a moment on Pitt's untidy hair and on his crooked shirt collar, less well cared for than usual in Charlotte's absence. 'Let me assay a guess! You are a poet whom some narrow and grubby-minded critic has censored? Or are you an artist who has painted his view of the reality of the soul of man, and no one will hang it in public because it challenges the comfortable assumptions of Society?'

Pitt grinned. 'Not quite right, sir. I am a policeman who has misplaced a French diplomat, and wondered if you might know where he is.'

Wilde looked thunderstruck, then he burst into a roar of laughter, thumping his fist on the table. It was several moments before he controlled himself.

'Good heavens, sir, you have a dry sense of the absurd. I like you. Please, sit down and join us. Have a glass of wine. It's dreadful, like vinegar and sugar, but it cannot dampen our spirits, and if you take enough of it, it will no longer matter. Bring your lugubrious friend as well.' He waved his arm towards an empty chair a few feet away, and Pitt drew it up and sat with them. Tellman obeyed also.

A pale young Irishman addressed by his fellows as Yeats, stared moodily into the distance. The newcomers' inclusion seemed to displease him.

'Take no notice at all,' Wilde gave them his full attention. 'Personally or professionally, may one ask?'

Pitt felt vaguely uncomfortable. He knew Wilde's reputation, and he did not wish to be misunderstood.

Tellman was quite obviously confused and it showed in the pinkness of his cheeks and the stubborn set of his mouth.

'Professionally,' Pitt replied, keeping his eyes steadily on Wilde's.

'Will any French diplomat do?' the young man with the quiff asked, then giggled cheerfully. 'Or do you want a particular one?'

Tellman sneezed.

'I would like a particular one,' Pitt replied. 'Henri Bonnard, to be exact. One of his friends has reported him missing, and it seems that if he does not reappear soon he may be in jeopardy of losing his position, which makes me fear he has met with harm.'

'Harm?' Wilde looked from one to another of them around the table. He turned back to Pitt. 'I know Bonnard, slightly. I had no idea he was missing. I confess, I haven't seen him in . . .' he thought for a moment, 'oh . . . a couple of weeks, or nearly as long.'

'He was last seen nine days ago,' Pitt said. 'In the morning near the Serpentine. He had an altercation with a friend, and left rather heatedly.'

'How do you know?' Wilde asked.

'It was observed by a number of people,' Pitt explained. 'There was a camera club out taking pictures in the early light. Both men were members.'

Tellman shifted uncomfortably in his seat.

'I prefer my visions in words.' Yeats lost interest and turned away.

'A poetry of light and shade,' the man with the quiff observed. 'An enormous number of pictures in black and white and shades of grey. Better than Whistler, what?'

'But not as good as Beardsley,' someone else said sharply. 'A photograph will catch only the obvious, the outside! Beardsley's drawings will catch the soul, the essence of good and evil, the eternal questions, the paradox of all things.'

Pitt had no idea what he was talking about. From the look on Tellman's face he was no longer even trying to understand.

'Of course,' the man with the quiff agreed. 'The brush, in the hands of a genius with the courage to draw whatever he wants – and no bigoted, frightened little censor to stop him – can mirror the torment or the victory within. Anything you dare to think, he can show.'

Someone else leaned forward enthusiastically, almost knocking a glass of wine off the table with his elbow. 'The immediacy of it!' he declaimed, looking at Wilde. 'Your *Salome*, his drawings, the ideas of black, gold and red were brilliant! Bernhardt would have adored it! Can't you just imagine her? We would have broken into a new age of the mind and of the senses. The Lord Chamberlain should be shot!'

'The man's a policeman!' a handsome man warned, waving at Pitt, then banging his fist on the table top and making the glasses jump.

'He won't arrest you for expressing a civilised opinion,' Wilde assured him, glancing at Pitt with a smile. 'He's a good fellow, and I know he goes to the theatre because I remember now where I saw him before. When that wretched judge was murdered in his box – Tamar MacAuley was on the stage, and Joshua Fielding.'

'That's right,' Pitt agreed. 'You actually supplied me with the pieces of information that indicated the truth.'

Wilde was obviously delighted. 'I did? How marvellously satisfying. I wish I could help you find poor Henri Bonnard, but I have no idea where he is, or why he should have gone.'

'But you do know him?'

'Certainly! A charming fellow . . .'

'Here or in Paris?' the man with the quiff enquired.

213

'Did you know him in Paris?' Pitt asked quickly.

'No, not at all,' Wilde dismissed it with amusement. 'I just went for a short trip. Visited around a little. Superb city, lovely people . . . at least most of them. Went to see Proust. Awful!' He waved his arms sweepingly. 'He was late for our appointment at his own home – and it was the ugliest house I ever saw. Dreadful! I don't know how anyone could choose to live in such a place. Anyway, Bonnard didn't come from Paris. I think his family is in the south somewhere.'

'Have you any idea why he might suddenly leave London?' Pitt looked around the table at each of them.

Tellman straightened to attention again.

Yeats frowned. 'Could be anything from a woman to a bad debt,' he answered. He seemed about to say something more, then changed his mind.

'He had plenty of money.' The man with the quiff dismissed that idea.

'Not the sort of man to throw up everything on a romance either,' someone else offered.

'How sad,' Wilde murmured. 'There should always be at least one thing in life for which one would sacrifice everything else. It gives life a sort of unity, a wholeness. And then you spend your time soaring and plunging between hope and terror that you never have to. To know that you will not would be as dreadful as to know you will. Have a glass of wine, Mr Pitt.' He picked up the bottle. 'I'm afraid we can't help you. We are poets, artists and dreamers . . . and occasionally great political theorists – of the socialist order, of course – except Yeats who is tangling his soul in the troubles of Ireland, and that has no names an Englishman could pronounce. We have no idea where Bonnard is, or why he went there. I can only say I hope he returns safe and well, and if you have to go and look for him, that it is somewhere with an agreeable climate, people who have new ideas all the time, and the last censor died of boredom at least a hundred years ago.'

'Thank you, Mr Wilde,' Pitt said graciously. 'I wish I could begin in Paris, but I'm afraid we know he did not take the Dover packet he was booked on, and I regret I have something uglier and more urgent to attend to than pursuing this any further.'

'Another judge?' Wilde enquired.

'No, a man found dead in a punt at Horseferry Stairs.'

Wilde looked sad. 'Delbert Cathcart. I am very sorry. When you find who killed him don't forget to charge him with vandalism as well as murder. The unwitting fool destroyed a genius.'

Tellman winced.

'That kind of vandalism is not a crime, Mr Wilde,' Pitt said quietly. 'Unfortunately.'

'Did you know Mr Cathcart well, sir?' Tellman spoke for the first time, his voice sounding a little hoarse and very different from those of the group around the table.

They stared at him in amazement, as if one of the chairs had spoken to them.

Tellman flushed, but he would not lower his eyes.

Wilde was the first to recover his composure. 'No . . . only saw him once, at a party somewhere or other. But I've seen quite a lot of his work. You don't have to meet a man who is an artist in order to know his soul. If it is not there in what he creates then he has cheated you, and worse than that, he has cheated himself.' He was still holding the wine bottle. 'Perhaps that, and cruelty, are the greatest sins of all. I never spoke to him – or he to me – in the sense you mean.'

Tellman looked confused and crestfallen.

Pitt thanked them again and, finally declining the offer of wine, excused them both.

Outside in the dark alley Tellman drew in a deep breath and wiped his hand over his face.

'I heard he was odd,' he said quietly. 'Can't say that I know what to make of him. Do you think that lot have anything to do with Bonnard and Cathcart?'

'I don't even know that Bonnard and Cathcart have got anything to do with each other,' Pitt said grimly, and pulled his coat collar up as he turned along the alley, Tellman's footsteps sounding hollowly after him.

Chapter Eight

❧

The nightmare was so real that even when the old lady woke up the room around her seemed to be the one in which she had spent her married life. It was a moment before her vision cleared and she realised there was no door to the left leading to Edmund's room. There was no need to be afraid. It would not open because it was smooth, patterned wall. She could see the light on the paper, unbroken. But it was shades of deep rose pink! It should be yellow. She was used to yellow. Where was she?

Her feet were cold. There was light coming through a crack in the curtains. She heard footsteps outside, quick and firm.

She grasped the covers and pulled them up to her chin, hiding her shoulders. She saw her hands on the sheet, knuckles swollen and clenched, an old woman's hands, blue-veined, thin-skinned with dark patches on them, the gold wedding ring slipping around easily. They had once been slim and smooth.

The past receded. But where was she? This was not Ashworth Hall!

Then she remembered. Emily and her husband were away in Paris, gadding around again. They were having the plumbing altered in Ashworth Hall and she was obliged to stay with

Caroline. She hated being dependent! It was the worst part of being a widow. In fact in some respects perhaps it was the only part that was really hard to bear. Now she was answerable to no one. There was a certain degree of sympathy and respect for a widow, the last one of her generation alive in her family.

Of course all that could change – now that Samuel Ellison had arrived from America. Who in all the green earth could have imagined that that would happen? Alys had had a son. Edmund had never known that. He would have been . . . She stopped. She had no idea how he would have felt about it. It hardly mattered now. In fact there was only one thing which did matter, and control over that was fast slipping away from her.

Where was Mabel? What was the use of bringing a maid all the way from Ashworth Hall if the woman was not there when she was needed? The old lady reached out and yanked on the bell rope at the side of the bed so hard she was fortunate it did not come away in her hand.

It seemed for ever until Mabel came, but when she did she was carrying a tray with hot tea. She set it down on the small table by the bed, then opened the curtains and let in the sunlight. There was a sort of sanity in it, a reassuring, pedestrian busyness in the very ordinary sounds of the day, footsteps, horses' hooves in the street, someone calling out, a bucket dropped and a girl somewhere laughing.

Perhaps she would find a way to keep control of the situation after all?

It was eight days since Caroline had come back from the theatre saying Samuel Ellison had turned up.

Breakfast was satisfying, if a meal taken in near silence, and alone except for Caroline, could be said to be satisfactory. Caroline was even more self-absorbed than usual. Sometimes she looked thoroughly miserable, which was very unbecoming in a woman of her age who had little to offer except good temper, knowledge of how to behave in any company whatsoever, and the ability to run a household. Since Caroline had no household to speak of, and she no longer mixed in public society, an equable nature was her only asset.

Her mood this morning was one of excitement and unattractive smugness, as if she knew something amusing which she refused to share. That was even more unbecoming. It was enough in a young girl, who could not be expected to know better, and had to be taught. In a woman with grandchildren it was ridiculous.

The reason for her satisfaction manifested itself in the middle of the afternoon. Samuel Ellison arrived yet again. Caroline had not had the sense to put him off, even after all Grandmama had said, and it seemed he was totally insensitive to all hint or suggestion, however plain! This time he brought flowers and a box of Belgian sweetmeats. They were ostensibly for Grandmama, but she knew perfectly well they were really for Caroline; etiquette forbade her to be so open about it.

The old lady accepted them in a matter-of-fact manner, and even considered having the maid take them up to her room straight away, so Caroline would not have them at all. She did not do it, and then was annoyed with herself for her failure of nerve. It would have served them both right.

Before tea was sent for and he was made thoroughly welcome, the old lady considered excusing herself. A headache or any other such thing would have served. Certainly neither

Samuel nor Caroline would have tried to persuade her to stay!
They might be only too delighted were she to retreat! It would
leave them unchaperoned, of course. But would they have the
decency to care? She could not even rely on that. Family honour
required she remain, and so did a certain sense of self-
preservation. At least if she were present she might exercise
some degree of control over events. Samuel would hardly speak
about her if she were sitting right in front of him. Yes, painful
as it was, it was definitely better to stay. She could not afford
the luxury of running away.

After the usual exchange of pleasantries Caroline asked
Samuel about his early days in New York.

'I cannot imagine what it must have been like for you and
your mother, completely alone in a city teeming with
immigrants, many of them with nothing but hope,' she said
earnestly.

'Hope, and a will to work,' he answered. 'To work all day
and as much of the night as one could stay awake. They spoke
a hundred different languages . . .'

'Babel,' the old lady said distinctly.

'Absolutely,' he agreed with a smile towards her. Then he
looked again at Caroline. 'But it is amazing how much you can
understand what people mean, when you share the same
emotions. We all felt the hope and the fear, the hunger
sometimes, the exhilaration, the sense of being miles away from
anything familiar . . .'

'I thought you were born there!' the old lady snapped.

'I was,' he agreed. 'But for my mother it was a terrible
wrench to leave all that she was used to and begin again, with
nothing, and among strangers.'

Grandmama could have kicked herself. How incredibly

220

stupid of her! She had found a dangerous situation and turned it into a disaster. Ice gripped her stomach. She gulped as fear overcame her. Did her face show it? Did he know?

He looked as perfectly smug and bland as usual. She did not want to meet his eyes.

Caroline was talking, and for once Mariah was glad of it.

'I cannot say how much I admire her courage,' Caroline said warmly. 'It is both frightening and uplifting at once to hear of such people. I admit it makes me feel as if I have done very little.'

Damn Caroline! How dare she be so perceptive? How dare she put so exquisitely into words the comparison between Alys and other women, Alys and Grandmama?

The room seemed to blur around her. Her face was hot, her hands and stomach cold.

'Thank you,' Samuel said softly, his eyes on Caroline's face. 'I think she was marvellous. I always thought so . . . but then I loved her.' He blinked quickly. 'But I'm sure much happened here that was extraordinary and exciting too. I seem to have talked endlessly about myself.' He shook his head a little. 'Please tell me something about England in all these years. I dare say your news of us was more than ours of you. We tend to be rather absorbed in our own affairs. I am American by birth – just – and by upbringing, but I'm English by heritage.' He leaned back in his chair and turned to face Grandmama. 'What was it like here at the heart of things when I was growing up in New York, out on the edge of the world?'

He was waiting for her to answer. She must do so, take control of the conversation. Remember all the things that were going on outside in the city, in the country. Think of nothing in the house, only of history. That should be easy enough.

'You were born in '28?' She cleared her throat. 'Well, two years later the old King died.'

'And Victoria became Queen?' he said quickly.

'Nonsense! George IV died,' she corrected. 'William became King . . . William IV. He didn't go until '37. All sorts of things happened before that.' She thought of meeting Edmund, of their courtship and marriage, how satisfied her mother had been. She found her throat full of tears. She sniffed and restrained herself with difficulty. She was overwhelmed with anger for their ignorance, and her own; and then most painfully with pity. Of course her mother had never known! Mariah would have been dragged along the ground by a runaway horse before she would have told her!

Samuel was waiting with interest.

She coughed and cleared her throat again. 'Lots of reform bills,' she said. 'Catholic emancipation, for one.'

He looked uncertain.

'Roman Catholics were allowed to enter Parliament,' she explained impatiently. 'After that they could hold almost any public office. A police force was created in the city later in the same year. Actually it was the year before the old king died and the new one was crowned, and the Duke of Wellington resigned.'

'I didn't know dukes could resign,' he said. 'I thought it was for life.'

'Not as Duke,' she said contemptuously. 'As Prime Minister!'

Samuel coloured. 'Oh . . . yes, of course. Wasn't he the general who fought at Waterloo?'

'Certainly he was,' she agreed. She made herself smile. This, after all, was as safe a subject as possible. It was a matter of history. Even Americans knew about that. It had changed the world. 'A most exceptional man,' she continued. 'I was very young, but I can remember when the news of the victory came through, the excitement, the pride, the relief, the terror that a father, a brother or a son might be among the dead. The slaughter had been terrible. But war was over, Napoleon defeated at last, no more threat of invasion. Peace! And there has been peace at home ever since.' It was a staggering thought. She found herself smiling, lifting her chin a little.

Samuel was watching her, his face alight with interest, waiting for her to go on.

But that was her youth, a time it was painful to think of. It was another life, another person. Then she had been a girl full of hope and an innocence, which was unbearable to look back on, knowing what came after. It had not occurred to her until this moment to wonder what secrets too awful to touch lay in other women's lives, behind their composed outward faces. Maybe none! Maybe she was as alone as she felt.

The silence grew heavy. She became aware of outside sounds, horses in the street. It was Caroline who broke the tension.

'All I know of the reign of William IV was a lot of Acts of Parliament to do with the Irish. That's what I learned at school. Just as the first ten years of the Queen's reign seems to have been all repeal of the Corn Laws. It's terribly tedious. And of course the Irish potato famine. But I expect you know about that? Tens of thousands of people left Ireland for America. You will have known some of them, I dare say.'

There was a sharp compassion in his face. 'Of course. I couldn't count how many of them fetched up in New York, haggard-faced, their clothes hanging off them as if they were

223

made of sticks underneath, their eyes full of weariness, trying to hope, and yet not hope too much, bewildered and home-sick.'

'Your mother must have felt like that too,' Caroline said gently, and it was clear in her face how vividly she was imagining what that unknown woman felt, trying to put herself in her place and understand.

Samuel must have seen it too. His smile was touched with grief. The loss of her still hurt him and he found no need to disguise it here among those who were also his family.

Mariah tried to imagine it. She knew nothing of Alys, except that she had gone. Edmund had never described her. Mariah did not know if she had been beautiful or homely, fair or dark, slender or buxom. She knew nothing of her personality or tastes.

But Alys had gone. That was the one thing that rose like a mountain in her mind, and it made her as different from Mariah as if she had been of another species. That was why she had hated her all these years, and envied her, why it choked in her throat to say she admired her, because it was the truth.

Did she want to know more about her? Did she want to be able to see her in the mind's eye as a real woman, flesh and blood, laughter and pain, as vulnerable as anyone else? No – because then she would have to stop hating her. She would be forced to think of the differences between them, and ask herself why she had stayed.

Samuel was talking about her. Caroline had asked him, of course. Caroline – it was always Caroline!

'. . . I suppose a little taller than average,' he was saying. 'Fair brown hair.' He smiled a little self-consciously. 'I know I am prejudiced, but I was far from the only one who thought she was beautiful. There was a grace about her, a kind of inner

224

repose, as if she never doubted what she held dearest, and she'd fight like a tiger to protect it. She could get terribly angry, but I never heard her raise her voice. I think she taught me more than anybody else what it means to be a gentleman.'

There was nothing to say that sounded appropriate, and Caroline held her peace.

Grandmama knew the familiar bitterness that rose up inside her. How could Alys have been such a perfect lady? Wasn't she broken inside as well, broken and crying like a hurt child, alone in the dark? Why was her anger only a fleeting thing, acted upon and then forgotten, so that she kept her temper and behaved with such sublime dignity . . . and was loved? Mariah's anger was deep, inward, lacerating until there was no dignity left, and she seldom ever tried to keep her temper these days. What had made Alys so golden, so bright and brave? Was she just a better woman? Was it as simple as that? What had given her the courage?

'. . . but I want to know more about all of you,' Samuel was saying, looking earnestly at Caroline.

'Well, the Queen married Prince Albert in 1840,' Grandmama said quickly, before Caroline could reply. That was a nice, safe subject. 'And they introduced a postage stamp. One penny.' She said that with some pride. 'And in 1851 there was the Great Exhibition in Hyde Park. People came from all over the world to see it. And Lord Palmerston was dismissed for interfering with the French. The year after that the old Duke died.'

Samuel looked bemused. 'All the French?' There was a quiver of laughter in his voice.

'How should I know?' Grandmama said coldly. 'He did something to them he should not have. All very silly, if you ask me. He was Foreign Secretary. Why shouldn't he meddle in France? Anyway, three years later we began the war in the Crimea. I dare say you know all about that?'

'I have heard something, yes. The most terrible losses, I believe. And of course we all know of Miss Nightingale.'

'Of course,' she agreed. 'Even America cannot be as far away as that. I presume you do know of the death of Prince Albert from typhoid fever, in '61.'

'Yes,' he said quickly. 'A terrible thing. But please tell me more of yourselves. It is you I really care about. Where did you live? What happened to you? Where did you go and what did you do? What did you talk about to each other? You are my only link with a father I never knew. It is like losing part of myself.'

Grandmama drew in her breath sharply and it caught in her throat, making her choke. It was several moments before she could speak.

'Nonsense!' she coughed violently. Caroline was staring at her. 'What I mean . . .' she tried again, '. . . is that you are who you are, regardless of your father.' This was terrible. She must say something that would not make him suspicious. Her mind raced futilely.

Caroline came to the rescue.

'Papa-in-law had great dignity,' she said gently, as if she thought the old lady's coughing were to hide emotion – as it was – but she assumed grief, not cold, gripping fear. 'He was tall, about the height you are, I should think,' she went on. 'And he dressed beautifully. He had a gold watch, and he wore the chain across his waistcoat. He liked very good boots, and always had them perfectly polished till you could see your reflection in them.' There was a faraway look in her eyes. 'He did not smile very often, but he had a way of listening that gave you his complete attention. You never felt as if he were merely waiting for you to stop so he could say something himself.'

It was all true. Grandmama could picture Edmund as Caroline was speaking. She could almost hear his voice. It surprised her after all this time that she could recall it so perfectly. In her mind she imagined his step across the hall, brisk and firm. Whenever she smelled snuff she thought of him, or when she felt the faint scratch of good tweed. He used to stand in front of the fire, warming himself, and keeping the heat from other people. Edward had done just the same. She wondered if Caroline had noticed it as she had, and if it had annoyed her as much. She had never said so, but then one did not.

Caroline was talking about Edmund again, telling Samuel some of the stories he used to enjoy, and how he sang sometimes, and how fond he was of the girls, Sarah, Charlotte and Emily, especially Emily because she was so pretty and she laughed easily when he teased her.

Was that really how Caroline remembered him, how she had seen him when he was alive? Why not? It was true, it was all exactly true. What did anyone really know of somebody else?

And Samuel sat there listening with his eyes on hers as if he believed every word of it! 'I never knew,' he said at last.

'Your mother must have spoken of him,' Caroline exclaimed ingenuously. 'Whatever her reasons for leaving, she knew he was your father, and therefore you had to care about him.' She did not add that he must have asked her, but the implication hung in the air between them.

Grandmama could hear her own heart beating. She was holding her breath, as if that could somehow stop him from answering. This was her worst nightmare come back no longer a dream, but as real as tea and toast, the maid's footsteps on the stairs, and the smells of soap and lavender or the morning newspapers. It would become part of life, as inescapable as the past, only worse, because the wound had healed over. This would be a second time, without escape ever, and she had not the strength any more. The first time you don't know what is coming, and ignorance shields you. This time she did know, and the fear before would be as bad as the fact, and the morning afterwards. Except there would be no afterwards. It would never stop. As long as Caroline knew, it would be there in her eyes every time they met.

And she would tell Emily, and Charlotte, and that would make life unbearable. Emily might tell Jack! She could picture the pity and then the revulsion in his wide, dark-lashed eyes.

Samuel was talking about his mother again, about Alys. His face was lit with the same tenderness as before, his eyes shining.

'. . . people made the mistake of thinking that because she carried herself like a lady that she hadn't the courage to speak out, or stick to her beliefs,' he said urgently. 'But I never knew a woman with more courage. She endured things most people don't even guess at, and fought against what was wrong . . .'

Grandmama cringed inside as if he had struck her. He knew! He must do. It was there in his words, just under the surface. If it were true of Alys, then it was true of Mariah. He would know that, anyone would. People don't change.

What possessed Alys to have told him? How could she?

Grandmama imagined telling Edward! Her face burned at the very idea of it. Would he even have believed her? If it repelled him as it did her, then he would be unable to accept it, and he would consider her not only mad but dangerous.

But then if that same hideous seed were in him, he would have believed, and he would never have looked at her in the same way again. The image of 'mother' would be gone and that other terrible one would have replaced it.

And that is how Caroline would be now. The old lady refused to think about it. Every shred of dignity, of human worth or value, would be stripped from her, leaving her grotesquely naked, as no living thing should be. It would be better to be dead. Except that she had not the courage. That was at the core of it, she was a coward – not like Alys.

They were still talking about Alys, how beautiful she was, how brave, how everyone admired her, liked to be in her company. She was different – breathtakingly, unbearably different – and the knowledge of it was like a red-hot knife twisting in an old wound, gouging deeper until it touched the bone.

They were still talking about the past, Caroline recounting some anecdote that had happened thirty years ago. She made it sound as immediate as yesterday. It could not go on. It was only a matter of time before the truth was said. That must be prevented – at any cost.

But nothing she could say now made the slightest difference. The only means of stopping this conversation would be to make it necessary for Samuel to leave. If she retired from the room, surely he would go? He said he admired his mother so much, he would attempt to behave like a gentleman.

'Excuse me,' she interrupted, rather more loudly than she had intended. 'I feel a little faint. I think if you will ring for my maid, Caroline, I will go to my room. At least until dinner. I shall see how I feel then.' She forced herself to look at Samuel. 'Pardon me for ending your visit so abruptly. I have not the good health I used to.'

Caroline looked crestfallen. 'I am sorry, Mama-in-law. Would you like a tisane sent up?' She reached for the bell as she spoke.

'No thank you. I think a little lavender will suffice. It is one of the disadvantages of age: one has not the stamina one used to have.'

Samuel rose to his feet. 'I hope I have not bored you, Mrs Ellison. It was very thoughtless of me to have remained so long.'

She stared at him and said nothing. The man seemed impervious to suggestion.

The parlour-maid opened the door and Caroline asked her to send the old lady's maid to assist her upstairs.

Samuel took his leave – he had no alternative – but even as she was climbing the stairs slowly, not having to ape the stiffness or fumbling hands on the banister – they were all too real – the old lady could hear Caroline inviting him to return and resume their conversation, and his acceptance. It was that which finally sealed the decision in her mind.

Since she had said she was ill, she was obliged to stay upstairs for the remainder of the afternoon, which was irritating because she had nothing to do, and would either have to lie down and pretend to be resting, which would leave her thoughts free to torment her, or else create some task or other and affect to be busy with it. She did not want to face her decision – not yet.

Mabel was a good woman, both competent and tactful, which was the only reason she had survived in the old lady's service for so long. She made no comment on the situation, simply brewed her a camomile tisane, without asking, and brought her a lavender pillow. Both were refreshing, and had Mariah suffered from the headache she professed, would have helped her immensely.

She lay on the bed for nearly an hour, quite long enough to have recovered, then feeling lonely and oppressed with useless thoughts and memories, she went to the small upstairs room where the maids mended the household linen and did a little dressmaking as was necessary. Most reasonably well-to-do women had three or four bought gowns for afternoon wear, the same again for evening, and they had their maids sew the others. It was cheaper, and if the maid were good, quite as effective. She knew Mabel was making something for her, because it was a permanent state of affairs. Emily was generous with supplying fabric, beads, braid and other trimmings.

'Are you feeling better, ma'am?' Mabel asked, looking up from her needle. 'Can I get you anything else?'

'No thank you,' the old lady replied, closing the door behind her. She sat down in the other chair. Mabel resumed stitching. It was growing dusk outside and the lamps were lit. The gaslight caught in the silver needle, making it look like a flash of light itself, weaving in and out of the cloth, in the thimble. Mabel was getting old too. Her knuckles were swollen, rheumatic. She did not walk as easily as she used to either. As always, the cloth she sewed was black. The old lady had worn black ever since Edmund had died. Like the Queen, she was conspicuous in her mourning. It had seemed the right thing to do at the time. Grief was an acceptable emotion, very appropriate. Everyone understood and sympathised. It was so much better than guilt, although to onlookers it could appear the same. She could weep, retreat to privacy, or ask for anything, which was freely granted. She was the centre of attention and no questions were asked.

She very easily fell into the habit of being 'bereaved'. There never seemed a suitable time to come out of black, and then it was too late. People assumed she was devastated by Edmund's death. It became impossible to do anything but agree. She told people what she wanted them to believe, which in time she tried to believe herself. It was better that way.

Now Samuel Ellison had turned up out of God knew where, and everything was crashing in ruins.

Mabel was threading black beads on to her needle, stitching them on to the bosom of the new dress. Why in damnation should Mariah wear black for the rest of her life for Edmund's sake? He must be laughing in whatever hell he had gone to. It had never suited her, and did so even less now that she was old, and sallow-skinned. And to put rouge on her face would make her look like a painted corpse! A painted corpse! That was how she felt – dead inside but still hurting, and ridiculous.

She wanted to tell Mabel to throw it away, make something of another colour – maybe purple: that was half-mourning. But lavender would not suit her either, in fact it would look even worse.

She was afraid to change. Everyone would ask why, and she did not want to mention Edmund at all, let alone offer any explanations. So she sat in silence, idle-fingered. Her head really did ache now.

She did not go down to dinner, but had a tray brought up to her room. She dreaded listening to Caroline wittering on about Samuel Ellison, and far worse, she might talk about Edmund, ask questions, bring back memories. Of course what she recalled of him was the face everyone knew, the one the old lady herself had perpetuated deliberately. She would talk about his kindness, his charm, his ability to tell a story and bring it to life. She would recall Christmas when they walked together through the snow to church on Christmas Eve, how he sung the old songs with such a rich voice.

Her throat ached. Tears spilled and ran down her cheeks. If only it could all have been like that!

Who was wrong? Was it her? Was she the one who was different, out of step, cold, stuck in some childish fantasy of the world, a woman who had grown old but had never grown up?

Then that was how it would be! She could not change now.

But this was unendurable. She would rather be dead.

Mabel came and removed the tray, the food half eaten. She said nothing. But then she would not. She had served the old lady for twenty years. They knew all kinds of intimate things about each other, physical things, habits, footsteps, a cough, the texture of skin and hair. And yet at heart they were also strangers. Mariah had never asked what Mabel thought or hoped for in life, what kept her awake at night, and Mabel had no idea now what dread clutched inside her like a cold hand.

She could not go on like this. She must do something, now before it was too late. Caroline must never know. Mariah was left with no choice. All the old panic and despair was back, the familiar darkness inside her, eating away at her heart, closing her in, unutterably alone.

Damn Samuel Ellison for coming from America where he was safely out of her life! Damn Alys for being beautiful and brave and in control of everything! She had gone – just left! But there was nowhere for Mariah to go. She was not young and healthy with a lovely face. She was old, stiff, bone weary and terrified. What would so lovely, so clever Alys do if she were here now?

She would do something! She would not sit waiting for the axe to fall, helpless! Then not only would the old lady be despised for what was known, she would despise herself for letting it happen! That was the worst of it, the self-loathing.

But would that stop it? Would it work?

It took all the resolve she possessed to come down to the breakfast table, but she could not spend the rest of her life in her bedroom. She had to appear sometime. Joshua would be present at this hour of the day, and that would prevent Caroline chattering on and on endlessly about Samuel Ellison, and somehow Mariah would contrive to speak to Joshua alone. She must. She dare not leave it any longer.

The usual greeting and enquiries dealt with, she forced herself to take tea and toast.

'Have you heard from Thomas lately?' Joshua said, turning to Caroline.

'Not for over a week,' she replied. 'I imagine he is very busy with the death of the man they found at Horseferry Stairs. It was mentioned in the newspapers again. It seems he was a famous society photographer.'

'Delbert Cathcart,' he said, taking more toast and reaching for the apricot preserve. 'He was brilliant.'

'One wonders why anyone should wish to kill him,' Caroline continued, pushing the butter dish across the table for Joshua. 'Envy? Perhaps jealousy over some private matter . . .'

'Do you mean a lover?' he asked with a smile. 'Why are you being so delicate?'

She flushed very slightly. 'That sort of thing,' she conceded.

It was an opening. The old lady did not hesitate.

'When people practise immorality it very often ends in disaster,' she said distinctly. 'If people would remember that, we should be able to get rid of half the misery in the world!' She was startled to hear the bitterness in her own voice. She had meant it for Caroline, but waves of loathing were thick in it as well, carrying a passion she would rather not have revealed.

Joshua was staring at her. He had heard it and was puzzled. She looked away.

'It may simply have been robbery,' Caroline said calmly. 'The poor man was out late, and what was intended merely to take his watch or money became more violent than expected. Perhaps he fought.'

'Are you suggesting he brought it upon himself?' Mariah demanded. 'He fought, so he deserved to be murdered?' She did not want this line of thought. 'Sometimes your ideas of right and wrong confuse me.' She aimed that remark at Caroline.

'I am not talking about right or wrong,' Caroline said impatiently. 'Only about probability.'

'That should not surprise me,' the old lady retorted. She did not explain what she meant. Their looks of confusion satisfied her.

'Warriner has withdrawn his bill,' Joshua said finally.

Mariah had no idea what he was talking about, but from his expression it displeased him intensely. She did not ask.

'I'm sorry,' Caroline said quietly. 'I suppose it was to be expected.'

Joshua grimaced. 'Part of me says it is providence. They should wait for a better time. The other part says it is cowardice, and we should make our own time. We could wait for ever.'

Mariah's curiosity was piqued. On a different occasion she would have asked what they were talking about. Now other matters were crowding far too urgently in her mind. She must contrive to speak to Joshua alone. One thing he had said was true – one must make one's own time. One might wait for other people to offer it for ever, and still fail.

Her mind raced. What excuse could she make for speaking with Joshua alone? She could hardly ask him for financial advance. She obtained that from Jack. A family matter she would have spoken about to Caroline; a loss or a threat of any sort she would have called Pitt. A chore she would have called a servant. She barely knew Joshua. She had never hidden her disapproval of him personally and of the marriage in general. What reason could she use?

Maybe she could get Caroline to leave? A domestic duty. But what? Anything usual she would leave it until Joshua was gone.

She must go herself, and then catch Joshua in the hall. Not very satisfactory, but she could not wait for something better. She stood up, placing her napkin across her plate. She was leaving half her tea, but that could not be helped.

'Excuse me,' she said, her voice a little high-pitched. It was ridiculous. She must control her nerves. 'I have a small errand to do.' And without struggling for further explanation she went. No one commented. They were not curious as to what she was doing in such a hurry. This realisation made her feel bitterly alone.

She must govern her thoughts. This was a time for action. Soon Joshua would leave and she must take the opportunity to catch him alone. If Caroline came into the hall to wish him goodbye, she, Mariah, would have no chance, unless she actually went outside altogether! It would appear excessive. There would be no way in which she could claim it was an accidental encounter. But she could not afford to wait another day. Samuel Ellison must not come back to the house! Once he spoke it would be too late for ever. It could never be withdrawn. One cannot undo knowledge.

She went to the front door and opened it. The air was brisk, the sun warm, smelling of dust and horses. In the park a hundred yards away the leaves were beginning to turn. The grass was still damp. An errand boy was whistling. There was a woman on a bicycle, wearing most unsuitable clothes, travelling far too quickly. Mariah envied her. She looked so completely free, and happy.

She turned her attention back to her task. How long would he be? She had not actually made certain that he was going out at all this morning, but he usually did, though not early like most men, because he had been late the previous evening. The whole household rose late.

She paced back and forth on the pavement, feeling more and more conspicuous. Then suddenly he was there, coming down the path, and she had had her back to him and not seen. She turned and hurried towards him.

'Mrs Ellison!' He looked startled. He seemed about to say something, and then decided against it.

She must seize the chance, no matter how awkward to find the words, or how foolish he thought her. Her survival depended on it.

'Joshua! I . . . I must speak with you . . . in confidence.'

'Is something wrong?' he asked, catching her emotion.

'Yes,' she said hastily. 'I fear it is. But it may be addressed, and more damage prevented.'

He did not look sufficiently alarmed. How should she phrase it so as to be believed? She had rehearsed this through the restless hours of the night, but still it did not sound right yet.

'What is the matter?' he asked her, quite gently, without alarm.

She wanted to be away from the front door, in case Caroline should chance to look out of one of the windows and see them. She started to walk, and he moved with her, keeping step. She must begin.

'It is Samuel Ellison,' she said, finding herself oddly breathless. 'No doubt you know he has been calling quite regularly at the house, in the afternoons. He stays for far longer than merely a social call.'

'He is family,' Joshua replied. 'Is that not natural enough?'

'Natural, maybe.' She heard the sharpness in her voice and tried to steady it. 'But he is . . . behaving in an unfortunate manner.'

'Really?' There was no change in his expression.

This was worse than she expected. Damn him for being so obtuse. Now she would have to be too frank. Why couldn't the man use his imagination? He was supposed to be an actor! Couldn't he think?

'He is overfamiliar!' she said sharply.

'With you?' His eyebrows rose as if he found it incredible. 'Well, if you feel he is rude, and you cannot curtail it yourself, you had better ask Caroline to speak to him.'

'Not with me!' she snapped. She only just avoided adding 'you fool!' 'With Caroline! He very obviously finds her attractive, and feels no need to disguise it. It is . . . it is worse than unsuitable, it is cause for concern.'

He stiffened slightly. 'I am sure Caroline is quite able to remind him of appropriate behaviour,' he said a little coolly. 'He is American. Perhaps over there manners are freer.'

'If he is anything to go by, then they are very free indeed,' she said with a note of desperation. 'I speak because I am concerned for Caroline's reputation! And for your welfare . . .' For heaven's sake, could he not see what she was saying? Was he totally stupid? Or perhaps he did not care? What a terrible thought . . . It filled her with ice as if someone had opened a door on to midwinter. Maybe theatre people behaved that sort of way, and expected others to. Immorality might mean nothing to him.

No! That could not be true. It must not be.

Joshua smiled very slightly, a small curve of the lips. 'I am sure Caroline will rebuff him, gently, if he should trespass. But thank you for speaking on her behalf. I'm glad you are there, which will assure no one has room to speak ill of her. Good morning.' And with a nod of his head, he passed her and continued on his way towards the end of the street, where presumably he was going to look for a hansom.

The old lady stood on the pavement alone, furious and defeated. But that was temporary. It must be! She could not afford to surrender. Samuel Ellison would be back, and next time, or the time after, he would finally say something which Caroline would understand, some thread which she would unravel until it reached the truth, and nothing would be left any more, nothing safe or clean, no light, nothing but the darkness consuming everything.

She turned and walked back up the path, climbed the steps and went into the house. Her mind raced. She had tried, and it had not been enough. She had been delicate, subtle, laying no blame, except upon Samuel, and it had not worked.

She crossed the hall past the housemaid carrying one of those new sweeping machines. Time had been when there were half a dozen maids, and carpets had been sprinkled with damp tea leaves, and swept and beaten two or three times a week. Then households had been run properly!

She went upstairs to her room and closed the door. She must be alone to think. There was no time to waste. Whatever she did, it must be today. Another visit could bring ruin.

There was still only one way she could think of to ensure that Samuel Ellison never returned. If Joshua would not be told and believe her, then he must be shown in such a way he could not disbelieve. He had left her no choice.

The question now was how to achieve it. There were many details to be considered with great care. She could afford no mistakes. Since she had tried and failed this morning, there was now only one chance left. This must succeed.

She sat by the window in the autumn sun, with a piece of paper and a pen and ink, and worked it out to the last detail. The timing must be perfect. She knew what the cost would be. She regretted it would be so high. If Joshua left Caroline she would be alone, reputation ruined and without means of her own, but Emily would see that she was not homeless. She would be provided for to that extent. If she were to live in Ashworth Hall it would be highly uncomfortable, but it was large enough that she and Mariah would be able to avoid each other. If necessary one of them could live in the Hall in the country. Probably Caroline, since she would be socially ostracised. It was a pity, it was not what Mariah would have wanted, but survival made it necessary. There was no decision to consider.

It was best to begin immediately. Long thinking might weaken her resolve. Now that the times for everything had been planned – precisely, written in a neat, crabbed hand, but unwaveringly – there was nothing else to prepare. She already knew Caroline's plans for the next two days. She would be in this evening, and Joshua would be at rehearsal. It was perfect, as if it were meant to be.

She wrote the first letter.

Dear Samuel,

You can have little idea how intensely I have enjoyed your company and the friendship you have offered me. You have brought into my life much that I had not even realised I was missing so deeply. Your stories of America are not only thrilling, but far more than that, you have the eyes to see beauty where other people might miss it, to see laughter and to feel compassion in a rare and wonderful way, which wakens in me an appreciation of life I hardly knew I possessed.

Was that too strong. Or not plain enough? Surely he would understand? She had seen Caroline's handwriting often enough over the years to find it easy to copy. They had never written letters to each other; there had been no occasion. The style she had to invent. But then Caroline, to her knowledge, had not written to Samuel Ellison either, so he would not know differently.

He must not mistake her meaning. She must leave no doubt, or the whole plan would fail. There was only this one chance. It was win or lose everything.

She continued:

Before you leave London and go to see the rest of the country I should like to visit with you as often as you can spare the time. I shall miss you extraordinarily when you return to New York. Life will seem so pedestrian again.

Surely that was forward enough, even for an American?

Please call upon us this afternoon, at about five o'clock, if you are at all able. I realise I am behaving with unbecoming urgency, but I can talk with you as I can with no one else. You are family, a link with the past which for me is gone everywhere else I turn. We have so much in common which no one else shares. As you may have observed, and I am sure you have, I find my mother-in-law difficult to speak with, except about trivialities.

Should she add anything about loneliness? No. It was explicit. She must not sound hysterical, it might put him off, and that was the last thing she wished, unless it were completely! And she doubted she could do that. This was her only chance, like one throw of the dice. Win – or lose it all.

I hope to see you,
    Yours most affectionately,
        Caroline

Should she read it over? Or would she lose her nerve and fail at the last minute? No. She had spontaneity. Fold it up and post it! Now.
    Or maybe she should read it?
    She hesitated, sitting with it in her hands.

Once it was gone it was irretrievable.

But the situation was irretrievable anyway. It had been ever since Samuel Ellison had come through the door.

She folded it, put it in the envelope, addressed it and attached the stamp.

She stood up and walked downstairs and out of the front door into the warm sun. The pillar box was at the end of the street. The post would be collected in half an hour. If Samuel returned to his hotel in time, he would have the letter long before five o'clock.

Again she hesitated, standing with it in her hand next to the red pillar box.

But if she did not post it he would come one afternoon, perhaps with other people there, and the conversation would turn to Alys, as it had every other time. Caroline would ask about her, and it would all come spilling out, now, or tomorrow, or the day after. Here in the bright sunlight she grew cold as remembered pain filled her – the struggle, the anger swelled back like a tide, the helplessness, the knowledge she could not fight, could not escape, could not refuse, could not even slip into the mercy of oblivion. She had tried that, tried to die, but one did not die of misery.

She let go of the letter and heard it thump on the others lying inside the box. It was done. Now to return home and carry out the rest of her plan. Alys would have done something like this – to protect herself!

Then there was nothing to do but wait. Caroline had already said that she did not intend to go out. Perhaps she was hoping Samuel Ellison would call! That was possible.

The old lady spent a wretched day. She thought it must be the most tense and miserable time of her life. She had no more excuses to remain upstairs, unless she pretended to be ill, and she did not want to behave in any way other than usual in case it aroused suspicion. No one must ever know what she had done.

She could hardly bear to look at Caroline. Her own thoughts consumed her. Perhaps it would be easier if she called on someone else, but she must be here, in case he came early, or Caroline should change her mind and decide to go out. She might need all her wits to counter such a thing.

This afternoon would make up for all the years of the past when she had done nothing but endure, like a coward. It would wipe all that away, cancel it as if it had never been. She would be rid of it. The thought of that freedom was like a crushing burden lifted. She would not despise herself any more, nor feel that weight of shame like a stone inside her.

She would have liked to have talked about something trivial, to keep her thoughts occupied, but she could think of nothing, and, anyway, it would be out of character. She and Caroline never chatted in friendly, inconsequential fashion. So she sat in silence while Caroline wrote to Charlotte in Paris, and there was no sound in the room but the flames in the hearth, the occasional fall of ash as the coals collapsed, and the scratch of Caroline's pen over the paper.

Then suddenly it happened. The maid was at the door.

'Mr Ellison has called, ma'am. Shall I say you are receiving?'

Caroline looked surprised. 'Oh! Yes, please tell him we are.' She was smiling. She looked very elegant in her afternoon dress and there was a slight flush to her cheeks.

The door opened again and Samuel came in, his eyes going straight to Caroline. He could not keep the pleasure from his face. He barely glanced at Mariah.

'How nice to see you,' Caroline said courteously. 'It is a little late for tea. Would you care for some other refreshment?'

'Thank you,' he accepted, coming further into the room. 'I hope it is not an inconvenient hour?' At last he acknowledged the old lady. 'Good afternoon, Mrs Ellison.'

This was going extremely well. She could hardly have orchestrated it better. She rose to her feet.

'If you will excuse me,' she said, grasping her stick. 'I shall return directly.' And without further explanation she left the room. She must send the other letter immediately. It was already written. There was an all-purpose manservant. He would deliver it, if she gave him the necessary cab fare. She had that ready also.

She went up to her room and fetched the letter. She knew it by heart. It was very simple.

Dear Joshua,
     Will you please return home the moment you receive this. Do not hesitate. The situation is serious, and only your presence may avert disaster.
     I am very sorry,
          Mariah Ellison

She took the envelope and several shillings and gave them to the manservant.

He looked startled.

'Will you take this to Mr Fielding immediately, please?' she requested. 'It is most urgent, a matter of the utmost importance.'

''E's in rehearsal, ma'am,' he protested. ''E won't want to be interrupted.'

'Of course he won't,' she agreed. 'But he will want even less for the disaster which will happen if you do not deliver this to him at once, and see that he reads it. If you have any loyalty to him at all, do as you are told!'

'Yes, ma'am.' Looking puzzled and unhappy, he obeyed.

Mariah went back upstairs, checking the clock on the landing, wondering how long she would have to wait.

Perhaps she should go downstairs again, in case Samuel was aware of being unchaperoned, and left? Or Caroline perceived the impropriety of it, and asked him to go!

She turned and walked back, still uncertain.

She stood at the top of the stairs and saw the parlour-maid go across the hall with a salver with a decanter of whisky and a glass. Excellent! At least he would remain until he had drunk that!

She would go down in five minutes, or maybe ten. How long would it take the servant to go to the theatre, and Joshua to read the letter, and come back? He would come, surely? If he didn't it would only be because he already suspected something, and did not care. That was not true. He was certainly an actor, but he was a decent man, gentle, unusually honest. She had noticed that about him. He had unfortunately liberal ideas about some things, but he was essentially loyal, and kind. He would care very much. No one could be betrayed without pain.

She refused to think of that. She was stupid to have allowed her mind to wander to such thoughts.

She watched the clock. Eight minutes and she could not bear the tension. She went down the stairs again slowly, gripping the banister. She reached the bottom and crossed the hall.

What if he had mentioned the letter, even shown it to her,

and she had denied it? What if they had guessed the truth, and he was this moment telling her all about his mother, and why she had gone! The hall swam around Mariah. She struggled for breath.

She could not go in. She couldn't bear it! There was nowhere to run to. Her heart was pounding so violently her body shook. She could hear it in her ears.

She stood there paralysed. Seconds ticked by. Or was it minutes?

She had to know. Nothing could be worse than this. It was as bad as knowing, and yet every so often there was this hope so sharp it was like sickness, leaving her dizzy. Knowledge, even despair, would be worse.

She walked towards the withdrawing-room door and opened it. It was like a dream, like moving underwater.

Samuel was sitting in the chair Joshua usually chose, and Caroline was very upright in the one opposite. Her colour was high, and they both turned rather quickly as they heard the door.

Mariah looked at Samuel. She did not want to meet Caroline's eyes. He did not look any different. He seemed puzzled, but not contemptuous, not angry, certainly not knowing. He did not understand . . . not yet.

She took a deep breath and let it out slowly.

'I have . . . a slight . . . headache,' she said with difficulty. She had meant it to sound casual, quite natural, but she had not the control of her voice she had wished.

Samuel murmured something.

'If you don't mind,' she went on. 'I shall go into the garden for a little while. I shall be just round the corner. The air might do me good.' And without waiting for either of them to reply, she crossed the room and went out of the French doors on to the small patch of grass, and down the steps out of sight.

It was another endless fifteen minutes before she heard the voices, and came back up the steps to eavesdrop at the French doors.

Samuel was by the fireplace and Caroline was in between them. Even from where she stood, Mariah could see the colour high and bright in her neck and staining her cheeks.

'Caroline, please leave us,' Joshua said softly. From his tone and his gestures he was repeating himself.

She said something, a protest. She had her back to the window and Mariah did not hear her words.

Joshua did not answer but stood very still, his cold eyes steady.

Caroline walked to the door and went out, closing it behind her.

'You were made welcome in my home, Mr Ellison,' Joshua said in a tight low voice. 'But your behaviour in visiting so frequently, and spending your time alone with my wife, is inappropriate, and is compromising her reputation. I regret I must ask you not to call again. You have left me no room to do anything else. Good day, sir.'

Samuel stood perfectly still, his face scarlet. Once he made as if to speak, hesitated, then walked past Joshua to the door. Again he seemed about to say something.

'Good day, sir,' Joshua repeated.

'Good day,' Samuel answered, and opened the door.

It was done, accomplished. Samuel Ellison had left and he would not return. He had been prevented from saying anything.

But Mariah did not feel any sense of elation. She was cold in the afternoon sun, and she could not bear to go into the withdrawing room. She turned, walked the distance round to the areaway and in at the scullery door, through the kitchen without looking to right or left, and up to her own room where she sat down on the bed with the tears running down her face.

Chapter Nine

Caroline stood at the top of the landing confused and wretched. The whole scene with Samuel had been acutely embarrassing and she had no idea what had produced the change in his attitude. He had been friendly and open from the beginning, much less formal than an Englishman would in the same circumstances. She had found it refreshing and not in the least out of place. She had not misunderstood it for forwardness, and she felt that she had responded only appropriately.

Then today he had arrived at an unusual hour, and behaved as if she had invited him, more than that, as if there had been something peculiarly intimate about it, and urgent.

She racked her brain to think of anything she could have said which could be so misinterpreted, but nothing came. She had listened to all his stories with interest, perhaps more than courtesy demanded. But they were extraordinary and fascinating. Anyone else would have done the same. It was immeasurably more than drawing-room chatter. And he was a relative turned up from nowhere, a brother-in-law she did not know she had. At a glance, before he spoke, he was so like Edward, perhaps she had offered a friendship more instant and natural than was normal, but surely she had not implied anything else.

Had she?

She was touched by guilt as she realised how much she had enjoyed his company. No, not just his company, the way he had flattered her by liking her so much, by the unspoken suggestion that he found her equally interesting, charming, attractive. It was such a welcome contrast to Cecily Antrim's subtly patronising air. Caroline had been made to feel feminine, in control of herself, and the situation again.

Now it was completely out of control, out of even her attempts to understand what had gone so disastrously wrong.

What did Joshua believe she had done? Why had he come racing home from a rehearsal in the middle of the late afternoon, and in such ice-cold anger commanded her to leave the room, and then seemingly ordered Samuel from the house? Did he really not know her better than to believe she had . . . what? Had an assignation of some sort, here in her own house? In his house! That was absurd! It was only the merest coincidence that Grandmama had not been in the room with them the entire time, as usual. And the old lady missed nothing; she was as quick as a ferret, and twice as vicious.

Should she try to explain? Samuel had left, but her courage failed at the thought of going down to Joshua. She had never seen him really angry before, and it hurt her more than she could have imagined. No, hurt was the wrong word. It frightened her. Suddenly she caught a glimpse of what she might lose, not to Cecily Antrim, but because of her own behaviour, something stupid, unintentionally immoral she had done. It would not be that he had found Cecily more alluring, more exciting, but that he found Caroline contemptible, not to be trusted to behave with honour, with inner cleanness of spirit.

That cut to the heart.

And it was not true. Not really. If it were true at all, it was by omission, carelessness, misunderstanding . . . never intent.

She went down the first step, but Joshua came out of the withdrawing room and went straight across the hall and out of the front door without looking back. He had not even tried to speak with her. It was as if he no longer cared what she thought.

A new kind of darkness had begun, a pain inside she could not believe would ever heal.

She turned back up and went to her room – not her bedroom she shared with Joshua, but her sitting room upstairs where she could be alone. She could not eat dinner, and she certainly could not face the prying, jubilant eyes of the old woman. She had warned her this would happen. She would be triumphant now that it had.

Caroline went to bed a little after ten o'clock. Joshua had not come home. She had thought for a moment whether she wanted to wait up for him, however long it was, but she dreaded the confrontation. What would she say? It might only make things worse. He would be tired. They could neither of them pretend that nothing had happened.

She might have considered sleeping in the spare bedroom, and perhaps he might also, but Grandmama was in it, so that was impossible.

Of course the worst probability was that he would not come home at all! That was too painful to hold in her mind. She thrust it away. This might be the death of trust . . . for a while, even a long while . . . but it could not be the end of the marriage! He could not believe she had done anything but be indiscreet, surely?

She lay in the dark, longing for sleep, starting at every sound in case it were his footsteps. Eventually about midnight she drifted into oblivion.

She woke again with no idea what time it was, and knew instantly that he was there beside her. He had come in and gone to bed and to sleep without disturbing her, without speaking or touching her.

She lay listening to him breathing. He was on the far side of the bed. She could barely feel the weight or the warmth of him. He was as separate from her as if they were strangers, together by chance in the crowd in some public place. She had never felt more crushingly alone.

Part of her wanted to waken him now, and end the terrible tension, provoke a resolution, for better or worse. Her stomach was sick at the thought of what the worst would be. Could he really think that of her? Did he not know her better than that? She remembered the moments of tenderness, the laughter, the quick understanding, the vulnerability in him, and the hot tears filled her eyes.

Don't waken him now. It was childish. Wait. Perhaps in the morning it would be better, there would be some sense in it? He would speak to her and explain. But when she woke headachy and still tired, he was already gone and she was alone.

The old lady also slept little, in spite of her triumph. Nothing would warm the coldness inside her. She drifted in and out of nightmare. She was alone in an icy swamp. She cried out and no one heard her. Blind, inhuman faces peered and did not see. Hate. Everything was drenched and dark with hate. Guilt brought her out in a sweat, and then froze, leaving her shuddering under the bedclothes.

When Mabel finally came at half-past eight with hot tea, the old lady had dozed into a fitful sleep again and was actually grateful to be startled into wakefulness in a sunlit room and see the familiar, plump figure of the lady's maid whose ordinary face held no alarm and no accusation.

The tea had never been more welcome. Even almost scalding as it was, it was clean and fragrant, and it eased her dry mouth and pounding head. She had no desire to get up and get dressed and face the morning, but to lie here in bed alone with her thoughts would be unendurable.

'Are you all right, Mrs Ellison?' Mabel said with concern.

'I . . . I didn't sleep well. I think I may have to remain upstairs.'

'Oh dear.' Mabel looked suitably sympathetic.

The old lady wondered suddenly what Mabel really thought of her. Was Mariah Ellison anything more than the source of a good position to her, someone to look after until she died, because Mabel was secure in Ashworth Hall, always warm enough, always well fed and treated with respect? Did she have any personal feelings for her? Perhaps it would be better not to know. They might be of dislike. And if she were to think of it honestly, she had given Mabel very little cause to feel anything else. One did not treat servants like friends; they did not expect it or want it; it would be embarrassing. But there were always degrees of consideration, and of the occasional word of thanks. Usually a lady's maid could expect as part of her remuneration to receive her mistress's clothes when they were past her best use of them. However, since Grandmama had worn black for the last quarter of a century, that was of less value to Mabel than might have been foreseen. But she never complained, at least not as far as the old lady knew.

'Thank you,' she said aloud.

Mabel looked startled.

'For your care!' the old lady said tartly. 'Don't look like that at me, as if I'd spoken to you in Greek!' She moved to get up, impatiently, and a stab of pain brought her up with a gasp.

'Would you like a doctor, ma'am?' Mabel asked helpfully.

'No thank you, I would not! Here, give me your arm!' She took it and hauled herself heavily out of bed and stood up, steadying herself with difficulty. She really did feel unwell. She had had no idea it would leave her with this kind of reaction. She should have felt the weight lifted, not added to. After all, Samuel Ellison was gone. She was safe. She had achieved what she wanted to – no, needed to! It was a matter of survival!

He had threatened to destroy her, unwittingly perhaps, but destroy her nevertheless.

But that did not relieve the darkness. In fact it hardly seemed even to matter!

She dressed with Mabel's help. Pity about the black. There would be nothing decent for Mabel to inherit when the time came. Perhaps that would not be long. What was she clinging on to life for? She was old, worn out and unloved. Maybe she would wear something lavender, or dark blue.

'Mabel!'

'Yes, Mrs Ellison?'

'I want three new dresses . . . or perhaps two new dresses and a costume . . . a skirt and jacket.'

'I'm making one now, ma'am. Is that three including that?'

'Not that one!' she said impatiently. 'Three more. Put that aside for now. I want one in dark blue, one in lavender and . . . one in green! Yes . . . green.'

'Green! Did you say one in green, ma'am?'

'Are you losing your hearing, Mabel? I would like a green dress, a dark blue one, and a lavender one. Unless you don't care for lavender, in which case make it something else . . . burgundy, perhaps.'

'Yes, Mrs Ellison.' The incredulity was high in her voice. 'I'll fetch some designs for you to look at.'

'Don't bother, just do whatever you think is becoming. I trust your judgement.' Heaven forfend she chose something outlandish, and the old lady lived long enough she had to wear them! But an unbecoming dress was really the least of her worries now. Yesterday it would have been merely irritating, two weeks ago it would have been a major catastrophe. Now it was nothing at all. 'See to it,' she added firmly. 'I shall give you the money immediately.'

'Yes, Mrs Ellison,' Mabel said quietly, her eyes wide.

But it was a wretched morning. It was impossible to concentrate on anything, not that she had any tasks of importance to do. She never had! Her entire life was a round of domestic trivialities that did not matter in the slightest.

She did not want to spend the morning with Caroline. She could not bear to see her, and sooner or later she would be bound to say something about yesterday's disastrous events. And what answer was there? She had thought she could cope with it, be evasive, or even tell her she had brought it upon herself. But now that it was accomplished, she felt nothing but a black despair, and a weight of guilt that was like a physical pain.

She busied herself doing small domestic chores, to the considerable irritation of the maids. First she gathered several pieces of used string and undid the knots, all the while instructing the youngest maid how to do it herself in the future.

'Never throw away good string!' she said imperiously.

'It's full o' knots!' the girl pointed out. 'I can't get them undone! It's more'n me fingers is worth!'

'That is simply because you don't know how,' the old lady pointed out. 'Here. Fetch me a wooden spoon. Quickly!'

'A wooden spoon?' The girl, who was perhaps thirteen, was nonplussed.

'Are you deaf, child? Do as you are told! And quickly! Don't stand there all day.'

The girl vanished and returned in a few moments with a large wooden spoon. She offered it, handle first.

'Thank you. Now watch and learn.' The old lady took the first piece of knotted string, placed it on the table in front of her and turning the knot over as she went, struck it hard several times with the spoon. Then she took a tiny pair of scissors from her pocket and inserted the points into the middle of the knot. Gradually she eased it open. 'There you are!' she said triumphantly. 'Now you do the next one.'

The girl obeyed with enthusiasm, pounding the knots, and gouging them undone. It was a considerable victory.

Next she taught the child how to clean the cane stand in the hall with lemon juice and salt, then how to shine the brass in the withdrawing room with olive oil, and sent her to find beer from the servants' hall, and have cook set it on the hearth for a few minutes to warm it. With that she instructed her how to clean the dark wood of the mantel.

'I'd teach you how to clean diamonds in gin,' she said tartly, 'if Mrs Fielding had any diamonds!'

'Or any gin,' the child added. 'I never met anyone afore wot knows so much!' Her eyes were wide with admiration. 'D'yer

know 'ow ter get rid o' scorch marks an' all? We got a terrible
one on the master's shirt yesterday, an' the mistress'll be proper
tore up when she knows.'

'If she were any use she'd know how to get it out herself!'
Grandmama said with satisfaction. Here at the back of the house
she could not hear every carriage that passed, or footsteps
coming and going. She would not see Caroline, or Joshua, if he
came home. She would not have to hear them, the confusion,
the pain. 'Vinegar, fuller's earth, washing soda and a small onion
chopped fine,' she went on. 'You should know that! Can't throw
out a good piece of linen just because there's a scorch mark on
it. Make a paste, spread it on the stain and let it dry. Brush it off
the next day.'

''Ow much vinegar?' the girl asked.

'What?'

''Ow much vinegar, please, ma'am?'

She took a deep breath and told her the proportions.

The rest of the morning passed with other minor duties,
excuses to fill the time. She ate no luncheon. It was as if her
throat had closed.

By mid-afternoon she could no longer avoid Caroline
without some very good excuse. She considered saying she was
ill, or even that she had fallen downstairs and was in too much
pain to remain out of her bed. But then Caroline would send
for the doctor, whether she wanted it or not, and that might
provoke all sorts of worse things. She would be proved a liar.
No. Far better she exercise courage and self-mastery. She was
going to have to for the rest of her life. This afternoon was an
excellent time to begin.

She changed into a suitable black bombazine afternoon dress
with jet beading on the bodice, and put on a smart brooch she

had not worn for thirty years. It was not a mourning brooch, with carefully preserved coil or braid of hair. It was a handsome crystal piece with pearls.

She went down to the withdrawing room, and there was no one there.

Caroline's morning began equally wretchedly, but she was looking for something to do to keep her mind from turning over and over the same miserable thoughts. She had stopped in the hall when she half overheard the manservant talking with the housemaid.

'How could I?' he said indignantly. They were standing by the sideboard in the dining room and the maid was regarding the silver with distaste. 'That old devil sent me out in a rush like the house was on fire. Had to go. She said it was urgent, life an' death, as you might say.'

'Sent you?' she said with her eyebrows raised. 'Where?'

'To fetch Mr Fielding, of course,' he replied. 'And he came home hotfoot, and threw out that American gentleman that's been here so often. Then went right back out hisself.'

'Pity.' She shook her head. 'He was very nice spoken, but I s'pose he was here a bit much, like. Anyway, I've got no time to stand here gossiping, and neither have you. You'd best get those knives done now, and quick, or Cook'll be after you. You're all behind!'

'So would you be if you'd been all the way to the theatre an' back!' he retorted, picking up the knives and going out, leaving the door open.

Caroline stood still, her mind racing. Joshua had not come home by chance. The old lady had sent for him, knowing Samuel was here. Why? And what had she said?

What else had she done? Had she somehow caused Samuel to come at five in the afternoon, uninvited? And then he had behaved as if Caroline had summoned him.

As she stood in the hall, her thoughts racing, there was a certainty growing in her mind which she did all she could to suffocate, drive out of existence. She must learn the truth, and that must be from Samuel himself.

If only Charlotte or Emily were here, she would take one of them with her. As it was she would have to go alone. She dreaded it so much it must be done immediately, before she could think about it and lose her courage. Joshua would never understand. This might make it all even worse. He would think she was chasing after Samuel, after he had forbidden him to come to the house!

And what would Samuel himself think? That made her cold to the pit of her stomach.

Yet to leave it as it was would be worse. There was no point in asking the old lady. She would never tell the truth.

She put on her hat and coat, informed the parlour-maid she was going out, and left.

The journey was terrible. Half a dozen times she nearly lost her nerve and told the hansom driver to take her home again, but the knowledge of the days and weeks ahead of loneliness, of never being able to understand, or tell Joshua the truth, was enough to spur her on.

She arrived at the hotel where Samuel was staying and went to the desk. She asked for him and was told he was in the lounge. She allowed the bellboy to conduct her through.

Samuel was sitting reading the newspaper. There were three other men in the room, all equally absorbed. She forced herself to be calm, and walked over to him.

261

He glanced up, then recognised her and the colour burned up his face.

It was too late to run, as she would have liked. For a moment she could hardly breathe.

He stood up. 'Good morning, Mrs Fielding,' he said stiffly.

She could feel her face flame. 'Good morning, Mr Ellison. I am sorry to intrude on your time in this way, most particularly after our last parting.' That was an extraordinary understatement of events. 'But there are too many things that I do not understand, and I fear my mother-in-law may have been meddling with the intention of causing trouble. I do not yet know why.'

He looked confused and more than a little embarrassed. 'I . . . If . . . Of course. If you believe it will help?'

'I do.' She sat down without waiting to be invited, smoothing her skirt self-consciously. She was intensely aware of his presence within a few feet of her. She wondered if he felt as aware of her.

'I'm sorry.' He apologised for the oversight in his manners, then sat down sharply himself.

This was dreadful.

They both started to speak at once, then both stopped.

'I'm sorry . . .' He coloured deeply, but he did not move his eyes from her face.

She looked down at her hands. 'Why did you come yesterday afternoon? I had the impression you thought I expected you?'

'You had the impression?' His voice rose in disbelief.

'Yes.' She avoided looking up. 'Was I mistaken?'

She heard the crinkle of paper and saw it in front of her. It was held in his hand, pushed forward.

She read it with horror that crawled over her skin and left

her cold. She found her voice hoarse when she tried to speak.

'I didn't write that!' Dear God, he had to believe her! And yet her first thought was to pray that Joshua had not seen it. He would be so hurt, so . . . betrayed. 'I did not write that!' She looked up and met his eyes. She was angry now, not for herself but for Joshua. 'It was my mother-in-law who sent the manservant for Joshua to come home. I believe it was she who wrote that as well.' She kept it in her hand and stood up. 'I am very sorry. Please believe me, I am! I like you, I enjoy your company, but whatever I had felt, I would never have written a letter like that. I apologise that you were misled by a member of my family, and for the embarrassment it has occasioned. But I am about to go home and address the matter.' She did not ask if she could keep the letter. She had no intention whatsoever of giving it up. 'Thank you for seeing me,' she added. She was about to say something about a good day, and abandoned it as absurd. She glanced at him once again, then turned and left.

Mariah was sitting alone in the withdrawing room, telling herself that the danger had passed, and she had only done what was necessary, when the door opened and Caroline came in. She looked very pale and there were shadows around her eyes. The pain in her face needed no explanation.

At that moment the old lady would have given all she possessed to have undone yesterday, but she knew nothing can ever be undone. A last thought flickered out somewhere inside her, and the darkness was complete.

'We are not at home,' Caroline said to the maid somewhere behind her. 'Not to anyone. Do you understand?'

'Yes, Mrs Fielding, not to anyone.'

'Good. Now do not interrupt us.'

'No, ma'am.'

Caroline closed the door and faced the old lady.

'Now!' she said grimly. 'You are going to explain this!' She held out the slightly crumpled letter in her hand.

The old lady stared up at her. There was no yielding in her face, her eyes did not waver, no softening.

'Explain?' Mariah repeated through dry lips.

'Don't pretend you don't know,' Caroline said grimly. 'Samuel received this letter inviting him to call yesterday. It is a highly suggestive letter, and he came expecting . . . heaven knows what! Then you sent Joseph to the theatre to fetch Joshua so he would arrive and misread the situation.' She held up the letter. 'Someone used my name. That could only have been you.'

Denial sprang to the old lady's lips, and she saw in Caroline's face that she would not be believed. There was a kind of finality in the moment. A black void of hate opened up in front of her. There was nothing left to lose now. The pain was not where she had expected it. It was not the past after all, it was the present – the loss now. It was the knowledge of having destroyed it all herself.

'I am waiting!' Caroline said sharply. 'This requires an explanation! Why did you send Samuel this letter in my name?'

Could she disclaim any knowledge? Say she sent the letter to prevent Caroline becoming involved in an affair, and ruining her marriage? Would Caroline believe her? No. It was a travesty, and they both knew it.

The ultimate nightmare was real at last. This was the moment when the truth would begin. She might delay it, push it before her in bits and pieces into the future, but in the end it would all be known. It would be clearer to tell it now, like a quick kill.

There was nothing left to lose; it was only the manner of it that was in question.

Caroline was still staring at her, implacable.

The old lady took a long, deep breath. 'Yes, I sent him the letter in your name, to get him here. I knew he would come, for you . . .'

At any other time Caroline's blush would have given her satisfaction. Now she barely noticed it.

'I assume you will tell me why,' Caroline said coldly.

'Of course!' The old lady gulped air and felt it painful inside her. 'I intended Joshua to find you together and throw him out, and forbid him ever to come here again.'

Caroline sat down as if her legs had given way, her skirts all squashed around her.

'Why? What has he ever done that you should even dislike him, let alone do something . . . so . . .' She was lost for words and her voice trailed off helplessly. She looked as if all understanding had fled from her.

There was no alternative. She had to know. It would only be harder if Mariah left it. Now was the time. Half a century of secret pain was about to be opened up without comfort or mercy.

'Because he knew,' she said hoarsely. 'I thought I couldn't live with that. Now I am going to have to.'

'Knew?' Caroline shook her head a little. 'Knew what? What could he possibly know that would be worth . . . that?'

Finally the nightmare was real, something no longer private. It was fixed inescapably, dragged from the darkness of the inner soul and spread wide open. Then even if the old lady could forget it, even for a day, others would always remember. Somehow she would have lost control of it.

Caroline leaned forward in her chair, crushing her skirt

further. 'Mama-in-law! What does Samuel know?' She moistened her lips. 'Were you not married to Grandpapa?'

The old lady wanted to laugh. That would have been shameful – of course it would – and it would mean both her children would be illegitimate! But somehow it looked almost trivial compared with what she would have to tell her.

'Yes, I was married to him. He divorced Alys perfectly legally, and I knew of her existence. My father saw to all that.'

'Then what?' Caroline demanded. 'It obviously has to do with Alys, or Samuel would not know about it.'

'Yes it has. It has to do with why she left. Have you never wondered why she did something so extreme, so dangerous, and both legally and socially unacceptable?'

'Yes, of course I have!' Caroline said instantly. 'But I could hardly ask! I assumed she ran off with someone, and then he abandoned her, and of course she would not then go back to Grandpapa. She must have left before she knew she was with child. No one could doubt Samuel is Grandpapa's.'

'That is what one would assume,' Mariah agreed very quietly. 'It is not what happened.'

There must have been something in her voice which struck Caroline in a new way, more deeply, and with a stab of tragedy. She barely moved, but there was a gentleness in her eyes, an attention which no longer made judgements.

'Why did she go?' she said in little more than a whisper.

This was the moment. It was like plunging into black, stinking water, ice-cold to take the breath away.

'Because he forced her into unnatural practices – painful, degrading things no human should do . . .' It was like hearing someone else's voice.

Caroline drew in her breath as if she had been struck. Her

face was white to the lips, her eyes hollow. She started to speak, then faltered and fell silent. She began to shake her head in short, sharp little movements.

'I thought you wouldn't believe me,' the old lady said quietly. 'No one would. It is not something you can tell . . . not anyone . . . not ever.'

'But . . . but you didn't know Alys!' Caroline protested. 'Samuel didn't tell you . . .' Again she stopped. She stared fixedly into the old lady's eyes. In all the years they had known each other they had never met in a look so honest. Caroline took in a long, shaking breath and let it out in a sigh. 'You mean . . .' She put her hand up to her lips as if to stifle the next words. 'You mean he . . . you . . .'

'Don't say it!' Mariah pleaded. This was absurd, futile! She ached to be believed, and here she was begging Caroline not to give words to the truth.

'Un . . . natural?' Caroline struggled with the word.

Mariah shut her eyes. 'I believe men do it to each other . . . at least some men do. It is known as sodomy. It is more painful than you can imagine . . . against your will. It is your pain which . . . which gives him pleasure.' The rage and humiliation of it poured back over her, bringing her body out in sweat. 'He made me strip naked, on my hands and knees, like an animal . . .'

'Stop it!' Caroline's voice was high and shrill. 'Stop it! Stop it!' She put up her hands, palms outward to push it away.

'You can't imagine your father-in-law like that, can you?' Mariah whispered. 'Or me? Together on the floor like dogs, me weeping with pain and humiliation, wishing I could die, and him more and more excited, shouting, unable to control himself until he was finished.'

'Stop it!' Caroline moved her fingers to her mouth. 'Don't!'

'You can't listen?' The old lady was shaking so violently with the memory of it she could hardly speak without stuttering. 'I l-lived with it . . . for years . . . all my married life. He died of a stroke like that, naked, on the floor, without his clothes. I'd prayed for him to d-die . . . and he did! I crept away from him and washed myself – he often made me bleed – then went back to look at him. He was still dead, lying on the floor on his face. I washed him, and put his nightshirt on him before I called anyone.'

There was horror in Caroline's eyes, but denial was slowly being replaced by the beginning of pity.

'You always said . . . you said you loved him . . .' she began. 'He was so . . . such a wonderful man . . . you said you were so happy!'

The old lady felt the bitter heat of shame in her cheeks. 'What would you have said?' she asked. 'The truth?'

'No . . .' There were tears in Caroline's voice. 'Of course not. I don't know . . . I don't know what I would have done. I can't imagine it . . . I can't . . . I don't know. It . . .' She did not say it was not true, but it was there in her voice, her face, the stiff, tight angle of her shoulders.

'You can't believe it!' It was a challenge, laying bare her own humiliation and her cowardice all those years. No one would believe that Alys left, her courage, her dignity, and Mariah remained, to be used, like an animal.

'I . . .' Caroline stopped, lifting her hands helplessly.

'Why didn't I go . . . as Alys did?' The words were torn out. 'Because I am a coward.' There it was, the lowest ugliness of all, the loathing, the self-disgust, not just that she had been reduced to bestiality, her human dignity stripped from her, but that she had stayed and allowed it to go on happening. She made no excuses. There were none. Whatever Caroline thought of her, it could not equal the contempt she had for herself.

Caroline looked at the old woman's face in front of her, tight and crumpled with pain and years of bitterness. The self-hatred was naked in her eyes, and the despair.

She rejected the idea. It was obscene. And yet it made a hideous sense. Part of her believed it already. But if it were true, it shattered so much of her world, the ideals and the people she had trusted. If behind the self-composed manner, the smile and the Sunday prayers, Edmund Ellison had been a sexual sadist, submitting his wife to humiliating cruelties in the secrecy of their own bedroom, then who, anywhere, was what they seemed? If even his familiar face hid ugliness so appalling her imagination refused to grasp it, then what was safe . . . anywhere?

And yet looking at the old woman in front of her, Caroline could not push the truth of it away. Something terrible had happened to Mariah. Something had precipitated the years of anger and cruelty she had exercised on her family. The hatred she seemed to feel for the world anyone and everyone – was really for herself. She saw the worst in others because she saw it in her own heart. And for years she had despised her inability to fight against it, to defend her humanity from degradation and pain. She was a coward, and she knew it. She had submitted, and endured, rather than run away into the dangerous and unknown as Alys had done, alone, penniless, with nothing but her courage and her desperation. No wonder Samuel admired his mother so profoundly.

Mariah had stayed here in England, living with it, night after night, putting on a brave, smooth face every day, then going up to her bedroom knowing what would happen . . . and it had, year after year, until he had finally died and set her free. Except that she was not free, she was as much imprisoned by it as when he had been alive, because the memory and the loathing were still there, locked inside her.

'Did you really think Samuel would tell anyone?' she said gently, not knowing why these words came to her lips.

There were tears in the old lady's eyes – grief, rage, or self-pity.

'He knew – that was enough,' she replied. 'He might have told. I couldn't live with that. But . . . but . . .'

Caroline waited.

The old lady sniffed. 'I'm sorry for what I did to you. You didn't deserve that. I . . . I wish I hadn't.'

Caroline reached forward and very tentatively touched the ancient hand lying on the black skirt. It was stiff and cold under her fingers.

'There are many kinds of courage,' she said softly. 'Running away is one of them. Remaining is another. What would have happened to Edward and Suzannah if you had gone? You could not have taken them with you, over to America. It would be illegal. The police would have come after you.'

'I could have tried!' The words were angry, grating.

'And made it worse for yourself,' Caroline pointed out. 'To go was brave – but to stay and make the best of it you could, for your children, that was brave too.'

A tiny spark lit in the old lady's black eyes, a flare of hope.

They had cordially disliked each other for years, living under the same roof, circling around each other with chill, occasionally with open, hostility. Now all that seemed unimportant. This was a consuming reality which overrode all the past. The

270

moment was now, in a new light, with new knowledge.

'No, it wasn't. I was afraid to go.' The old lady said the words carefully, looking at Caroline all the time.

Caroline spoke honestly. It was not difficult, which surprised her.

'Perhaps Alys was afraid to stay.'

The old lady hesitated. It was obvious she had not thought of that. In her mind Alys had always been the one who was brave, the one who did the right thing. This was hope from a quarter she had never expected.

Caroline smiled very faintly, just an instant. 'It takes strength to endure, and tell no one, never to run away, simply give up. Did you ever allow Edward or Suzannah to know?'

The old lady stiffened. 'Of course not! What a monstrous question!'

'You hid it from them for yourself . . . but for them also.'

'I . . . I hid it . . .' The struggle for honesty was so plain it was painful for Caroline to see. 'I don't know. I hid it for myself . . . I couldn't bear my children to know I had . . . I had been . . . to see me like . . .' At last the tears spilled over on to her cheeks and she began to shudder uncontrollably.

Caroline was horrified. For a moment she was paralysed. Then pity swept away everything else. She could not like the old woman – there was too much cruelty, too many years of criticism and complaint to forget – but she could feel the wrenching sorrow inside her, the guilt and the self-loathing, the unbearable loneliness. She leaned forward and put her arms around the old woman's shoulders and held her gently.

They stayed like that, motionless, neither one of them speaking, until Caroline felt a kind of peace settle over them, perhaps no more than a temporary emotional exhaustion. Then she let go, and sat back in her own chair for a moment.

Was there something else she should say, of comfort, or honesty, something which if left silent now could not be recaught later? Should they agree on some story to tell Joshua? He had to know.

For a moment she was cold, frightened.

She looked at the old woman in front of her, head still bent, face hidden. How could she explain the letter? It had to have been someone in the house, using her name? She and Samuel had never been seen together in public, except at the theatre the night they met. No woman in Samuel's life, presuming there were one, could be jealous enough to do such a thing. Caroline was his brother's widow. Who more natural for him to call on in a strange city?

But she must explain yesterday to Joshua. That was insistent, at the front of her mind.

She looked at the old lady, and pity ground hard with a unique pain, but she had brought that upon herself, her own actions had made it inevitable. Caroline was not going to wound Joshua, and herself, to save her from it. That Samuel himself knew of her humiliation was almost unendurable. How could Alys have told her son such a thing? But he was leaving, taking his understanding with him. Joshua would remain. What should she say?

Perhaps Alys had needed to explain why she had left Edmund and set out on such a dangerous and lonely journey. To make Samuel understand that he was legitimate, that he had a legal father and a mother who had left because she had no alternative, not a flighty or irresponsible woman who cared only for herself, and so he should not blame her for their poverty and the hardship of their lives.

272

Maybe she had not ever intended to tell him, and kept silent for years, then he had said something, either some complaint or accusation, and that had prompted her to speak. Perhaps she had been exhausted, lonely, at her wits' end to find food and clothes, a little warmth, and the truth had come spilling out. Who could blame her? Caroline might have done the same.

Her own decision was made. She rose to her feet and went quietly out of the room, closing the door. In the hall she saw the maid.

'Mrs Ellison would like a little time alone,' she said to the girl. 'Please see that she is not disturbed for a while, half an hour at least. Unless, of course, she rings for you.'

'Yes, ma,'am.'

Caroline went upstairs deep in thought. It would be very difficult to tell Joshua. Perhaps she could avoid the details. She had never kept a secret from him before. She had been used to discretion all her married life with Edward, but Joshua was different . . . or he had been, before this.

Perhaps she could tell him that there was an agonising, humiliating secret, but not what it was? Maybe he would not ask.

She crossed the landing to her bedroom. She had no particular purpose in going there, simply to be alone. She closed the door and sat down in the dressing chair with its pretty chintz flowers. She loved this room. It was what she had wanted for years, since Edward's time, but he would have disliked it. He would have found the flowers too large, too bright, and the whole thing not dignified enough.

She tried to remember him clearly, bring back his presence into her mind, everything that was good and gentle about him, the reality of his feelings. How he had grieved for Sarah! He had disliked Pitt so much, to begin with. He had never really come to know him well. But then like a lot of men, he had loved his daughters deeply, even if he had not often shown it, and no man was good enough to marry them and care for them as they should have been. Emily's first husband had had the money and the breeding, but Edward had always worried that he would not necessarily be faithful to her.

And of course Pitt had no money to speak of, and no social background at all! How could he ever give Charlotte all Edward thought she was worthy of?

And how Dominic had treated his beloved Sarah was an old pain best forgotten now. Sarah was dead, and nothing could retrieve that.

Then her thoughts skipped to Edward himself, and Mrs Attwood, whose lovely face Caroline could still picture quite easily, even after all these years. She remembered exactly how she had felt when she had first realised she was Edward's mistress, not the invalid widow of an old friend, as he had claimed. She had discovered a part of Edward she had not known. What else might there have been she never knew?

She was beginning to feel a coldness inside her. Her hands were trembling. She had been totally duped by her father-in-law. She had seen him only as the dignified man she met in the withdrawing room, or presiding at the dining table, saying the family prayers. The other man, the creature Grandmama described, was a monster living in the same skin, and she had neither seen nor felt anything of him at all. How could she have been so utterly blind, so insensitive?

What else was she blind to? It was not only that she had been wrong about her father-in-law, it was that she had been so wrong about herself! All that cruelty, that misery and humiliation, even physical pain, had been there behind the daily masks, and she had seen nothing of them.

In who else's face had she seen only what she wanted to? What had Edward asked of Mrs Attwood that he had never asked of Caroline? How much did she really know about anyone? Even Joshua . . . ?

Caroline did not feel in the least like going out that evening, but it was the first night of Joshua's new play. Normally she would be there, whatever the circumstances. Not to go would make a statement she could never retrieve.

She ate a light supper alone – the old lady remained upstairs – then she dressed with great care in a magnificent royal-blue gown. She added the cameo pendant that Joshua had given her, and a long, velvet cloak, then took the carriage to the theatre, feeling cold, shivering and uncertain. Joshua could not be more afraid of this evening than she was. He could not have as much riding on its success, or failure.

For a while the buzz of excitement carried her along and she had no chance to think of anything other than greeting friends and those who wished her well. They congratulated her for Joshua and were filled with anticipation of the audience's reaction. She desperately wished him to succeed, to be praised, and yet not to portray any of the disturbing passions she saw in Cecily Antrim.

At last the lights dimmed, the audience fell silent and the curtain rose.

The play was superb – subtle, intelligent, and funny. Many times she found herself laughing aloud. During the first interval she glanced across and saw Mr and Mrs Marchand, smiling and at ease. She was too far away to read their expressions in detail, but their gestures made their pleasure evident.

Suddenly Caroline was aware of hurt, even defensiveness. She did not want them to be disturbed; she liked them and understood them, she wanted their friendship, and perceived both its values and its limitations. And yet complacency was a kind of death. Something that did not stir thought, awaken new emotions or challenge preconceptions was agreeable, but no more than that. And she knew that Joshua would despise himself if that was all he did. He did not wish merely to entertain. That was at least in part why he admired Cecily Antrim so profoundly. She had the courage to say what she believed, whether one agreed with it or not.

The second act was swifter moving than the opening, and it was almost over before Caroline realised there were deeper emotions drawn from her than in the first, and becoming more complex. It was painful, and it was also a kind of relief. She began to think again of Grandmama, and how the sudden knowledge of her suffering and anger over all these years had changed her own life.

Twenty-four hours ago she would not have believed that civilised people would even think of the things the old lady had said Edmund Ellison had forced on her, most nights of her married life. And yet even sitting here in this exquisite theatre, watching drama so perfectly performed, acted, pretended with consummate skill, surrounded in the half-dark by hundreds of exquisitely dressed people, she did believe it. That darkness might lie behind any number of these calm, smoothly groomed faces. She would never know.

She thought of the old lady sitting in growing terror every time Samuel called, then at last planning her terrible, destructive escape. Had she thought that if Joshua left Caroline, threw her out for immorality, just what that would mean? Surely she did? And yet she had known nothing but bitterness and humiliation in marriage, and she could not live with the thought that her family to whom she had perpetuated the tie for so many years, would at last know that!

What terrible isolation, what loneliness and fear all the time that Caroline had never guessed, horror that had never entered her imagination.

Perhaps some of these things needed to be said, emotions stirred and disturbed, painful questions asked, so a thread of understanding could be woven between people who would never experience for themselves the things that tortured others who sat only a few feet away.

She leaned forward to watch the third and final act of the play.

Afterwards she went backstage to Joshua's dressing room, as she always did after a major performance. She was as nervous as if she herself were to step out in front of the audience and she did not know her lines.

She had rehearsed a dozen times what she was going to say to him, but what if he would not see her? What if he would not listen? She would have to make him . . . insist. She could be as determined as Cecily Antrim, or anyone else. She loved Joshua, wholly and completely, and she was not going to lose him without fighting with every skill and strength she possessed.

The dressing-room door was closed. She could hear laughter inside. How could he laugh, when he had left her in the morning without speaking?

She knocked. She would not go in uninvited. She might see something she would prefer not to. That thought was like ice inside her. It made her feel sick.

There were footsteps and the door opened. Joshua stood there in a robe, half changed from his costume. He looked startled, then his face softened a little. He pulled the door wide without saying anything. There were two other people inside, a man and a woman.

Relief flooded over Caroline, and guilt. He had not been alone with anyone.

They were people she knew from other plays, and they welcomed her. She congratulated them all on the performance, quite honestly. She could hardly believe how normal her voice sounded.

They seemed to talk endlessly. Would they never leave? Could she say anything to suggest they did? No, that would be unforgivably rude.

Then the words were out. 'I'm so glad I came. It was so much richer than I could have guessed,' she said distinctly. 'There is something about a first night that can never be repeated exactly. And I nearly didn't.' She avoided Joshua's eyes. 'My mother-in-law is staying with us at the moment, and she was not at all well today. Something . . . happened . . . which distressed her more than I would have thought possible.'

The others expressed their concern.

'Should you be home early?' the man asked.

Caroline looked at Joshua at last.

'Is she ill?' he said. His voice was unreadable.

The other two excused themselves, graciously, and left.

'Is she?' Joshua repeated.

'No,' Caroline replied. He was tired and the mood was too fragile between them to play with words. 'She did something wicked; and today I discovered it, and when I faced her she told me why.'

He looked puzzled. He did not really want to know. He tolerated the old lady because he felt he should, perhaps for Caroline's sake.

'Wicked?' he said dubiously.

She must continue. 'Yes, I think so. She wrote a very forward letter to Samuel Ellison, inviting him to call yesterday afternoon, and signed it with my name.' Why did he not say something? She hurried on. 'When he arrived she deliberately left the room, which she has never done before, then sent Joseph to fetch you.'

'Why?' he said slowly. 'I know she disapproves of me, because I am an actor and a Jew, but as much as that?'

The tears stung her eyes and she felt her throat ache. 'No!' She wanted to touch him, but it would be wrong now. He might see it as pity. 'No! It has nothing to do with you! Samuel knew something about his own mother which must be true about Mariah also, something dreadful, of which she was so ashamed she could not bear anyone else to know. She was afraid he would tell me, and so she wanted you to throw him out so he would never return. Then her secret would be safe. She was so terrified of it she did not care if she ruined my happiness. She would do anything to stop me knowing, and of course the rest of the family as well. She felt she could not live if we did.'

He stared at her in amazement. He was very pale, but it was not anger in his face, it was horror.

'I know what it is,' she said quietly. 'And I think I can forgive her for what she has done. If you don't mind, I would rather not tell you what she suffered, but I will if I must.'

His face relaxed. He was too tired, perhaps too shaken to smile, but there was a gentleness in him she did not mistake.

'No,' he said softly. 'No, I don't want to know. Let her keep her secret.'

The tears spilled down her cheeks and she found herself sniffing and swallowing hard. 'I love you,' she whispered, and sniffed again.

He stood up and reached out a little tentatively. Suddenly she realised how much he had been hurt. He had doubted . . . feared.

She put her arms around him and held him so hard she felt him wince. 'I'm sorry I didn't behave so you knew that,' she said into his shoulder.

His arms tightened until he was holding her just as closely as she held him. He did not say anything, just moved his lips over her hair, slowly.

Chapter Ten

❧

Pitt and Tellman still pursued the matter of Henri Bonnard and his quarrel with Orlando Antrim. Frankly Pitt was not certain that they would learn anything useful from it, even if they were to discover the entire truth of the matter. If Bonnard had disappeared of his own volition it might well be worrying, and extremely irritating to the French Embassy, but it was not a police matter. The only real connection with Cathcart's death was photography. The two men's resemblance to each other was coincidental and Pitt could see no importance in it. He was perfectly certain that the body at Horseferry Stairs was Cathcart, and it was Bonnard with whom Orlando Antrim had quarrelled.

'Do you think it was really about pictures?' Tellman said dubiously as they rode in a hansom towards Kew, where they had been told the Camera Club was photographing interesting foliage in the tropical glasshouses. 'Would anyone really commit murder over a photograph? I mean,' he added hastily, 'a photograph that wasn't of somebody doing something they shouldn't!'

'I doubt it,' Pitt admitted. 'But I suppose it could have been the start of a quarrel which got out of hand.'

Tellman sat forward morosely. 'I think I'm just getting to understand people and know why they do what they do, then I get on a case like this, and I feel as if I know nothing!'

Pitt looked at his angular shoulders and dour, lantern-jawed face, and saw the confusion in him. Tellman had such set ideas about society and people, about what was just and what was not. It sprang from the poverty of his youth, the underlying anger that fuelled his desire to change things, to see labour rewarded and find some greater equality among people who worked and those who, as far as he could see, did not, and yet possessed so much. Investigating the private tragedies of their lives constantly upset his preconceptions, and obliged him to feel a pity and an understanding he did not wish to, where it would have been so much easier, and more comfortable, simply to have hated.

Now the photographs, which these privileged young men obviously cared about so much, seemed to him both beautiful and trivial, but not a comprehensible motive for murder.

Pitt was inclined to agree with him. But at the moment they had little better to pursue. No one in the area where Cathcart lived had observed anything helpful, and Lily Monderell was telling nothing more about the photographs she had removed and sold almost immediately at such an excellent profit. Once again they were back to photographs. It seemed the motive lay somewhere within them.

They travelled the rest of the way to Kew Gardens and went in to find the tropical house, a magnificent tower of glass containing giant palm trees with fronds more than a yard across, exotic ferns, trailing vines with flowers and bromeliads blooming in pale, lustrous colours.

Tellman drew in his breath deeply, smelling the heat and the damp, the rich humus. He had never experienced anything like it before.

Pitt saw the photographers first, balancing their tripods carefully on the uneven surfaces of the earth, angling cameras up to tangled vines or intricate patterns of branches, trying to catch the light on the surface of a leaf. He knew they would be furious to be interrupted. He also knew that unless he forced his way into their attention he would stand waiting until the light faded at the end of the day.

He approached a fair-haired young man with a keen face, at that moment shading his eyes with his hand as he stared at the crown of a soaring palm.

Pitt craned his neck upward and saw a tracery of vines across the roof, erratic circles and curves against the geometry of the paned glass. It was a pity to interrupt, but necessary. Beauty and imagination would have to wait.

'Excuse me!'

The young man waved his other hand to ward off the disturbance.

'Later, sir, you may have my entire attention. Come back in half an hour, if you would be so good.'

'I'm sorry, I have not half an hour to spare,' Pitt apologised. He meant it. 'I am Superintendent Pitt of the Bow Street Police Station, and I am investigating the murder of a photographer.'

That captured the young man's concentration. He abandoned the palm and stared at Pitt with wide blue eyes. 'One of our club? Murdered. My God! Who?'

'Not one of your club, Mr . . . ?'

'McKellar, David McKellar. You said a photographer?'

'Delbert Cathcart.'

'Oh!' He seemed vaguely relieved. 'Oh yes, of course. I

read about that. Robbed and thrown into the river, so it seems. I'm terribly sorry. He was brilliant.' He coloured faintly. 'I'm sorry, I didn't mean that to sound callous. Of course a death is terrible whoever's it is. From his point of view, I dare say his talent is irrelevant. But I know nothing about it! What could I tell you?'

'On the morning of the day Mr Cathcart was killed there was a quarrel between Orlando Antrim, the actor, and Mr Henri Bonnard of the French Embassy,' Pitt explained.

McKellar looked startled.

'Do you know anything about it?' Pitt pressed. 'It was apparently on the subject of photographs.'

'Was it?' McKellar seemed perplexed, but not entirely at a loss, as he might have been were the subject to make no sense to him at all.

'Do people quarrel over photographs?' Pitt asked.

'Well . . . I suppose so. What has that to do with poor Cathcart?'

'Do you sell your pictures?' Tellman said suddenly. 'I mean is there money in it?' He glanced around at the cameras and their tripods.

McKellar coloured a little more deeply. 'Well, sometimes. It – it helps funds, you know. Costs a bit, all this stuff. Not that . . .' he trailed off and stopped, standing a little uncomfortably.

Pitt waited.

'I mean . . .' McKellar fidgeted. 'Look, I think I may be speaking a trifle out of turn, you know? I've just sold the odd picture here and there, that's all.'

'Of vines and leaves?' Tellman said incredulously. 'People pay for that?'

McKellar avoided his eyes. 'No . . . no, I shouldn't think so. Mostly a nice picture of a young lady, perhaps a few flowers . . . more . . . more personal, more charm, that sort of thing.'

'A young lady with perhaps a few flowers,' Pitt repeated, raising his eyebrows a little. 'And a gown, or not?'

McKellar looked wretched. 'Well, I dare say. Sometimes . . . not.' He met Pitt's eyes and this time he was quite vehement. 'Just a bit – artistic. Not vulgar!'

Pitt smiled. He carefully avoided Tellman's glance. 'I see. And these sales supplement your funds for the expense of films and so on?'

'Yes.'

'And do the young ladies in question receive part of this profit?'

'They get copies of . . . of one or two of the pictures.'

'And are they aware that the rest are sold – to be bought, I presume, by the general public?' Pitt enquired.

McKellar was silent for a moment. 'I . . . I think so,' he said unhappily. 'I mean . . . the reason's clear, isn't it?'

'Perfectly,' Pitt agreed. 'You wish to make some money in order to finance your hobby.' His voice was colder than he had meant it to be.

McKellar flushed bright pink.

'And where are these photographs sold?' Pitt pressed. 'Sergeant Tellman will take down the names and addresses of all the dealers you have business with.'

'Well . . . I . . .'

'If you can't remember them then we'll accompany you to wherever you have the information, and take it from there.'

McKellar gave up. He swallowed convulsively. 'It's all quite innocent, you know!' he protested. 'Just . . . just pictures!'

In the afternoon Pitt and Tellman began visiting the dealers in postcards.

To begin with all they saw were pretty pictures of a variety of young women in fairly conventional poses, their gentle faces looking out at the camera, some awkwardly, self-conscious, others boldly, with a smile, even a challenge. There was nothing to be offended by, except the possibility that they had been denied a share of the profits. But then considering the cost of cameras, film, development and so on, the profits were probably extremely small. The postcards themselves sold for a few pence, and they were of a good quality. The greatest gain from them was the pleasure in the creation and the possession.

'Is that all you have?' he asked, without hope of learning anything further that was of value; it was a matter of habit. They were in a small tobacconist and bookseller's in Half Moon Street, just off Piccadilly, its shelves crowded, wooden floor creaking at every step. The smells of leather and snuff filled the air.

'Well . . .' the dealer said dubiously. 'More the same, others much like these. That's all.'

There was something in the way he said it, a directness that caught Pitt's attention. He was not certain it was a lie, but he felt it was.

'I'll see them,' he said firmly.

Several dozen more cards were produced and he and Tellman went through them fairly rapidly. They were of a wide variety, some quiet country scenes with pretty girls in the foreground, some almost domestic, some artificial and carefully posed. Many had a kind of innocence about them and were obviously amateur. Pitt recognised the round form and the type of foliage

286

and patterns of light and shade he had seen the young men of the Camera Club study. He thought he even recognised parts of Hampstead Heath.

There were others more skilled, with subtler uses of light and shade, effects less obviously contrived. These were taken by enthusiasts with more practice and considerably more ability.

'I like the round ones,' Tellman observed, fingering through the cards. 'I mean I like the shape of the picture. But it does waste space, and on the whole I'd say the square ones were better, in a way. Sort of different, not like the girl you might meet in the street, more like . . . I don't know . . .'

'Square ones?' Pitt interrupted.

'Yes, here. There's half a dozen or so.' Tellman passed over four of them.

Pitt looked. The first was well done, but ordinary enough. The second was very good indeed. The girl had dark, curly hair blowing untidily around her face and she was laughing. In the background was a distant scene of the river, with light on the water and figures out of focus, no more than suggestions. She looked happy, and as if she were ready for anything that might be fun, the sort of girl most men would love to spend a day with, or longer. The photographer had caught her at the perfect moment.

The next was equally good, but extremely different. This girl was fair, almost ethereal. She gazed away from the camera, the light made an aureole of her hair, and her pale shoulders gleamed like satin where her gown had slipped a little low. It was a brilliant mixture of innocence and eroticism. She was leaning a little on a pedestal, either of stone or plaster, and there was a vine growing around it.

It stirred a memory in Pitt, but he could not place it.

The last picture was of a very formal beauty reclining on a chaise longue. He had seen a photograph of Lillie Langtry in a similar pose. Only this girl was looking directly at the camera and there was a slight smile on her lips, as if she were aware of a hidden irony. The longer he looked at it the more attractive it became, because of the intelligence in her face.

Then he remembered where he had seen the pillars in the photograph before, because the chaise longue came from the same place. They belonged to Delbert Cathcart; he had seen them in his studio.

'These are very good,' he said thoughtfully.

'You like them?' the dealer asked with interest, scenting a possible sale. 'I'll make you a fair price.'

'Did you buy them legitimately?' Pitt said, frowning a little.

The man was indignant. 'Of course I did! Do all my business fair and legal!'

'Good. Then you can tell me where you bought these. Was it from Miss Monderell?'

'Never 'eard of 'er. Bought 'em from the artist 'isself.'

'Did you? That would be Mr Delbert Cathcart.'

'Well . . .' He regarded Pitt nervously.

Pitt smiled. 'Actually it is Mr Cathcart's murder I am investigating.'

The man blanched visibly, and swallowed. He shifted his weight from one foot to the other. 'Oh? Yeah?'

Pitt continued to smile. 'I'm sure you would be eager to help as much as possible, Mr Unsworth. I think if you have these pictures of Mr Cathcart's then you may have others as well, worth more money, perhaps. And before you make an error by denying that, I must advise you that I can very easily remain here to talk to you about the matter while Sergeant

Tellman goes to fetch a warrant to search your premises. Or I could call the local constable to wait, and Sergeant Tellman and I could both go . . .'

'No . . . no!' The thought of a constable in uniform was enough to settle Unsworth's mind completely. It would be very bad for custom, particularly among those gentlemen who had rather private tastes. 'I'll show you the rest meself. Course I will. A bit o' colour in life is one thing, but I draw the line at murder. That's quite diff'rent – quite diff'rent. Come wi' me, gents. This way!' He led the way up rickety, twisting stairs.

The pictures that he had in the room above were a good deal more explicit than those in the front of the shop. Many women had abandoned gowns altogether and were posed with little more than a few wisps of fabric, a feathered fan or a posy of flowers. They were handsome women in early or middle youth with firm, high breasts and rich thighs. Some of the poses were more erotic than others.

'All quite harmless, really,' Unsworth said, watching Pitt guardedly.

'Yes, they are,' Pitt agreed, conscious of Tellman at his elbow exuding disapproval. In the sergeant's opinion, women who sold themselves for this kind of picture were of the same general class as those who sold themselves in prostitution, only these girls were young and well fed and far from any outward sign of poverty or despair.

Unsworth relaxed. 'Y'see?'

Pitt looked at them more carefully. He saw half a dozen or so which could have been Cathcart's. The quality was there, the subtlety of light and shade, the more delicate suggestion of something beyond the mere flesh. One woman had a bunch of lilies in her hands half obscuring her breasts. It was a highly evocative mixture of purity and licence. Another woman with rich dark hair lay sprawled on a Turkish carpet, a brass hookah behind her, as if she were about to partake of the smoke from some pungent herb. The longer he looked at it, the more certain Pitt became that it was Cathcart's work. The symbolism was there, the skill of suggestion, as well as the practised use of the camera itself.

But none of these, good as they were, was worth the price of Lily Monderell's teapot, let alone the watercolour.

'Yes, I see,' he said aloud. 'Now how about the others, the expensive ones? Do you bring them to me, or do I have to look for them myself?'

Unsworth hesitated, clearly torn as to how much he could still hope to get away with.

Pitt turned to Tellman. 'Sergeant, go and see if you can find . . .'

'All right!' Unsworth said loudly, his face dark, his voice edged with anger. 'I'll show 'em to yer meself! Yer an 'ard man! Wot's the 'arm in a few pictures? Nobody's 'urt. Nobody's in it as doesn't wanter be. It ain't real!'

'The pictures, Mr Unsworth,' Pitt said grimly. He would not argue realities of the mind with him.

Ungraciously Unsworth produced the pictures, slamming them down on the table in front of Pitt, then stood back, his arms folded.

These were different. Innocence was gone completely. Pitt heard Tellman's intake of breath between his teeth and did not need to turn sideways to know the expression on his face, the revulsion, the hurt inside. Some of them still possessed an art, albeit a twisted one. In the first four the women were leering, their bodies in attitudes of half-ecstasy already, but vulgar, totally physical. There was no suggestion of tenderness, only appetite.

He flipped through them quickly. He would rather not have looked at all. Each one of these women had not so long ago been a child, searching for love, not lust. They may have been used rather than cared for, they may have been lonely or frightened, or bored, but they had still been outside the adult world of selfish, physical use of one person by another, merely to relieve a hunger.

Except of course, for those who long knew abuse from the very people whom nature had intended to protect. And looking at some of these sad, worldly eyes, that might have described a few of them. There was already a self-disgust in some that was harsher than any of the physical degradations.

Others were worse again, mimicking pain inflicted for pleasure, with the implication that it held some kind of secret joy, reached only by breaching all the barriers. Some were obscene, some blasphemous. Many women were dressed in mockery of those in holy orders – nuns with skirts torn open, hurled to the ground, or over the banisters of stairs – as if rape were on a level with martyrdom, and a kind of religious ecstasy was achieved by submission to violence.

Pitt felt a sickness churn in his stomach. The moment he looked he wished he had not seen. How did one erase from the mind such images? He would not want it to, but the next time he saw a nun this would return to him, and he would be unable to meet her eyes, in case she saw what was in his mind. Something was already soiled for him.

And there were others equally ugly, some involving men also, and children. Satanic rituals were suggested with emblems of death, sacrifice. In two or three the shadow of a goat's head, goblets of blood and wine, light shining on the blade of a knife.

Tellman gave a little grunt. It was a short sound, barely audible, but Pitt heard the distress in it as if it had been a scream. He wished there were a way he could excuse them both, but there was not.

Among the pictures he recognised one beautiful face, not a young one, not lovely with the untouched flower of youth, but older, the beauty was that of the clean sweep of throat and cheek, the perfect balance of bone delicate yet strong, the halo of fair hair. It was Cecily Antrim, dressed as a nun, her head back, her arms tied by the wrists to a wheel, her body bent over it. A man dressed as a priest kneeled in front of her, his face reflecting ecstasy. It was a curious picture, half pornographic, half blasphemous, as if the two, in the figure of the priest, came together. It was a powerful and profoundly disturbing image, far less easy to forget than those which were simply erotic. This raised questions in the mind as to the nature of religious practice and the honesty or dishonesty of what purported to be service of God.

Pitt looked at a few more, another dozen or so. He was almost at the bottom of the pile when he saw it. He knew from the stifled gasp beside him that Tellman had seen at the same instant.

It was Cecily Antrim again, in a velvet gown lying on her back in a punt, surrounded by drifting flowers. Her knees were half drawn up. Her wrists and ankles were very obviously manacled to the boat. It was the parody of Ophelia again, making it seem as if the imprisonment of the chains was what excited her, and the beginning of ecstasy was sharp and real in her face.

'That's disgusting!' Tellman said with a half-sob. 'How could any woman like that sort of thing?' He was glaring at Pitt. 'What kind of idea does that give a man, eh?' He jabbed his thin finger at the shiny card. 'A man looking for that is going to . . . to think . . . God knows! What's he going to do, tell me that?'

'I don't know,' Pitt said quietly. 'Maybe he's going to think that's the sort of thing women like.'

'Exactly!' Tellman's voice cracked. 'It's revolting. It's got to be stopped! What would happen if some young lad came in here?'

'I don't sell to young lads!' Unsworth cut in. 'That sort of thing's only for special customers, ones I know!'

Pitt swung around on him, his eyes blazing, his voice raw. 'And of course you know exactly what they do with them, don't you! You know that every one of them is safely locked up by some sane and responsible person, who treats his own wife like a precious friend, a lady, the mother of his children?' His voice was getting louder and he could not help it. 'No one ever feeds his own dreams with them, and then acts them out? No one even sells them on to curious and ignorant boys who don't even know what a naked woman's body looks like, and is aching to find out?'

He remembered his own first awakenings of curiosity with surprising sharpness, and his ideas, his realisations of boundless, terrifying and wonderful possibilities.

'Well . . .' Unsworth spluttered. 'Well, you can't hold me responsible for . . . I'm not my brother's keeper!'

'Just as well for him!' Pitt snapped. 'The way you're going about it he's on that high road to that misery where he destroys everything he sees, because he no longer believes in the

293

possibility of worth. No, Mr Unsworth, perhaps it is people like Sergeant Tellman and me who are his keeper, and we are now going to set about doing exactly that. You have a choice. You can either give us a list of your clients who buy these pictures – a complete list . . .'

Unsworth shook his head violently.

'Or,' Pitt continued, 'I shall presume you have these here for your own pleasure, and since one of them is evidence in a murder, that you are protecting the person who committed it . . .'

Unsworth gasped and waved his hands in denial.

'Or that you committed it yourself,' Pitt finished. 'Which is it to be?'

'I . . . eh . . . I,' Unsworth ground his teeth, 'I'll give you a list. But you'll ruin me! You'll put me in the workhouse!'

'I hope so,' Pitt said.

Unsworth shot him a venomous look, but he went and fetched a piece of paper and a pen and ink, and wrote a long list of names for Pitt, but no addresses.

Pitt read through it and saw none he recognised. He would get a list of members of the Camera Club and compare them, but he held little hope that there would be any in common.

'Tell me something about each of these men,' he said grimly to Unsworth.

Unsworth shook his head. 'They're customers! They buy pictures! What do I know about them?'

'A great deal,' Pitt replied without shifting his gaze. 'If you didn't, you'd not risk selling pictures like these to them. And I want a list of the men who supply these pictures as well.' He watched Unsworth's face. 'And before you deny that too, one of these pictures prompted the murder of Cathcart. The

murderer saw it, and laid Cathcart's body in the exact image.'
He was satisfied to see Unsworth pale considerably and a sweat
break out on his brow. 'Coincidence would be unbelievable,'
he went on. 'Especially since Cathcart took the photograph. I
need to know who else saw it. Do you understand me, Mr
Unsworth? You are the key to a murder which I intend to solve.
You can tell me now or I can close down your business until
you do. Which will it be?'

Unsworth looked at him with hatred, his eyes narrow and
dark.

'You tell me which picture it is, I'll tell yer 'oo brought it
an' 'oo I sold it to,' he said grudgingly.

Pitt indicated the photograph of Cecily Antrim in the punt.

'Oh. Well, like yer said yerself, Cathcart brought me that
one.'

'Sole rights?' Pitt asked.

'Wot?' Unsworth hedged.

'Do you have sole rights to the picture?' Pitt snapped.

'Wake up an' dream! O' course I don't!'

It was a lie. Pitt knew it from the fixed steadiness of his
eyes.

'I see. And you wouldn't know the names of the other dealers
who have it, because you wouldn't have sold it to them?' Pitt
agreed.

Unsworth shifted his weight again. 'That's right.'

'So tell me all you can about those people you did sell to.'

'That'd take all day!' Unsworth protested.

'Probably,' Pitt agreed. 'But Sergeant Tellman and I have
all day.'

'Maybe you bleedin' 'ave – but I 'aven't! I've got a livin'
ter make!'

'Then you had better start quickly, hadn't you, and not waste your valuable time in arguing?' Pitt said reasonably.

But even though they spent several hours in the small upstairs room and the shop was closed for business all the time, Pitt and Tellman learned nothing that appeared to be of use to guide them any further in Cathcart's murder. They left as it was growing dusk and went out on to the gaslit pavements with a heavy feeling of oppression.

Tellman drew in a long breath, as though the foggy air with its slight damp, the smell of horses, wet roads, soot and chimneys was still cleaner than the air inside the closed shop.

'That's poison,' he said quietly, his voice husky with misery and rage. 'Why do we let people make things like that?' It was not a rhetorical question. He wanted and needed an answer. 'What good are we doing if we can only arrest people after they do things wrong, if we can't stop them?' He jerked his head back towards the shop. 'We could arrest someone if they put poison in a sack of flour!'

'But people don't want to buy sacks of flour with poisons in them,' Pitt answered him. 'They want to buy these things. That's the difference.'

They walked in silence for a while, crossing the street amid rumbling drays and wagons, fast-moving carriages, light hansoms, all with lamps gleaming. The sound of hooves was sharp, as was the hiss of wheels, the smell of fog in the nostrils and an increasing chill as darkness closed in. Wreaths of mist shrouded the lamps, diffusing the light.

'Why do they do it?' Tellman demanded suddenly, striding out to keep up with Pitt who, in his own anger, had unconsciously been going faster and faster. 'I mean, why does a woman like Miss Antrim let anyone take pictures like that?

She doesn't need the money! She isn't starving, desperate, can't pay the rent! She must make hundreds as it is. Why?' He waved his arms around in a wild gesture of incomprehension. 'She's quality! She knows better than that!'

Pitt heard the confusion in him, and more than that, the disappointment. He understood it sharply. He felt it also. What perversity led a beautiful and brilliant woman to such degradation?

'Was she blackmailed into it, do you suppose?' Tellman asked, swerving to avoid banging into a lamppost.

'Maybe.' Pitt would have to ask. He half hoped that was the answer. The weight of disillusion inside him was heavier than he would have imagined. A dream had been broken, a brightness gone.

'Must be,' Tellman said, trying to convince himself. 'Only answer.'

For Caroline it was not quite the end of the matter with Samuel Ellison. She had liked him very much, not for his resemblance to Edward, or because he liked her or found her attractive, but for his enthusiasm, and for the gentleness and the complexity with which he saw his own country. She did not wish to part from him with anger remembered.

She looked across the breakfast table. She and Joshua were alone. The old lady had remained in her room.

'May I write to Samuel and tell him that we have solved the mystery of the letter, and we apologise for the mischief caused? I cannot quite see how to do it without telling him the reasons, and I would prefer not to do that.'

'No,' Joshua said clearly, but his eyes were soft, and he was smiling. 'He still behaved a trifle improperly. He admires you,

297

which shows excellent taste, but he was too forward about it.'

'Oh . . .'

'I shall write to him,' he continued. 'I shall tell him what happened, as much as I know. I cannot tell him the old lady's reason because I don't know it. And I shall apologise for her appalling behaviour, and invite him out to dinner . . .'

She smiled, delight flooding through her.

'. . . at my club,' he finished, looking amused and a trifle smug. 'Then I shall take him to the theatre, if he accepts, and introduce him to Oscar Wilde. I know him passably well, and he is a very agreeable fellow. I am not having him here. Grandmama may be a mischief-making woman, but Samuel is still too fond of my wife for my peace of mind.'

Caroline felt the colour burn up her cheeks, but this time it was pleasure, sharp and delicious. 'What an excellent idea,' she said, looking down at the toast on the plate. 'I am sure he will enjoy that enormously. Please give him my best wishes.'

'Certainly,' he replied, reaching for the teapot. 'I shall be happy to.'

After Joshua had left Caroline went upstairs and asked if the old lady was well. She was told by Mabel that so far she had not arisen, and it seemed she had no desire to get up today. Mabel was concerned that perhaps the doctor should be called.

'Not yet,' Caroline replied firmly. 'I dare say it is no more than a headache, and will pass without treatment – except what you can give, of course.'

'Are you sure, ma'am?' Mabel asked anxiously.

'I think so. I shall go and see her.'

'She didn't want to be disturbed, ma'am!'

'I shall tell her you said so,' Caroline assured her. 'Please don't worry.' And without arguing the point any further she went along the landing to the old lady's room and knocked briskly on the door.

There was no answer.

She knocked again, then opened it and went in.

The old lady was sitting propped up against the pillows, her grey-white hair spread around her, her face pale, with dark shadows under her eyes, making the sockets look enormous.

'I did not give you permission to come in!' she said tartly. 'Please have the decency to leave. Do I not even have the privilege of being allowed to be alone?'

'No, you don't.' Caroline closed the door behind her and walked over to the bed. 'I came to tell you that I spoke with Joshua yesterday evening.'

Mariah stared at her, misery draining her face of all life.

Caroline wanted to be furious with her, but pity overtook justified anger and every shred of the satisfaction in revenge that she had expected.

'I told him you had written the letter to Samuel.'

Mariah winced as if Caroline had struck her. She seemed to grow smaller, huddled into herself.

'But I did not tell him why,' Caroline went on. 'I said it was something that had hurt you greatly, and he did not ask what it was.'

There was total silence in the room. Slowly the old lady let out her breath and her shoulders sagged. 'He didn't . . . ?' she whispered with disbelief.

'No.'

Again there was silence. Caroline searched for words to tell her that the wound would heal, the damage was not irreparable after all, but perhaps it was unnecessary.

The old lady started to say something, then stopped. Her eyes did not move from Caroline's face. She was grateful – her gratitude was there somewhere in the depths – but to put it into words would make it real, a solid thing between them, and she was not ready to yield that yet.

Caroline smiled briefly, then stood up and left.

She did not see the old lady again that day.

In the evening, when Joshua had left to visit a friend after a very brief supper, the maid announced Superintendent Pitt, and Caroline was delighted to see him. The pleasure of having Joshua at home during parts of the day was paid for in far too many lonely evenings.

'Thomas! Come in,' she said with pleasure. 'How are you? My dear, you look awfully tired. Sit down.' She gestured to the big armchair near the fire. 'Have you eaten?' She was very aware that with Charlotte in Paris he too was alone. He looked even more crumpled than usual and had a forlorn air about him. It was not until he had done as he was bidden and the gaslight caught his face more closely that she realised he was also deeply unhappy.

'Thomas, what is it? What has happened?'

He gave a very small smile, rueful and a trifle self-conscious.

'Can I be so easily read?'

It had been a day of honesty. 'Yes.'

He relaxed into the chair, letting the warmth seep into him.

'I suppose it's Joshua I really wanted to speak to. I did not realise he wouldn't be here at this hour.' He stopped.

She could see he wanted to talk about something. Whatever it was that had distressed him, he needed to speak of it, and Charlotte was not there.

'I can tell Joshua when he comes home,' she said almost

casually. 'What is it about? The theatre, I presume. Is it to do with the murder of the photographer?'

'Yes. It is really not something to discuss with a woman.'

'Whyever not? Are you embarrassed?'

'No!' He hesitated. 'Well . . .'

She thought bitterly of what Grandmama had told her. Whatever Pitt had to say, it could hardly be more obscene than that, or more intimately degrading.

'Thomas, I do not need to be protected from life. If you are afraid I cannot keep a confidence, then—'

'That is not it at all!' he protested, running his hand through his hair and leaving it even more rumpled. 'It is simply . . . intensely unpleasant!'

'I can see that much in your face. Do you believe that Cathcart's murder has something to do with the theatre?'

'I think it may. He certainly knew Cecily Antrim . . . very well.'

'You mean they were lovers?' She was amused at his delicacy.

'Not necessarily. That would hardly matter.' He stretched out his legs a little more comfortably. His face was screwed up. It was obviously still difficult for him to say to her what it was that filled his mind. She thought of herself this morning trying to find words to tell Samuel about Grandmama, and she waited.

The fire flickered pleasantly in the grate. There was no other noise in the room except the clock.

'I found photographs of Cecily Antrim in a postcard shop,' he said at last. 'We didn't tell the newspapers how Cathcart was found, except that it was in a boat.' He avoided her eyes and there was a faint colour in his cheeks. 'Actually he was wearing a green velvet dress . . . pretty badly torn . . . and he was manacled by the wrists and ankles . . . into a sort of obscene parody of Millais' painting of Ophelia. Flowers thrown around . . . artificial ones.' He stopped.

She controlled her amazement with difficulty, and an idiotic desire to laugh.

'What has that to do with Cecily Antrim?'

'There were several obscene or blasphemous pictures of her in the shop,' he replied. 'One of them was almost exactly like that. It couldn't be a coincidence. It was the same dress, the same garlands of flowers. It looked to be even the same boat. Cathcart was killed, and then placed in exactly that pose. Whoever did it had to have seen the photograph.'

A cold prickle ran through her. 'You think she was involved?' She thought how it would hurt Joshua. He admired her so much – her courage, her passion, her integrity. How could such a woman lend herself to pornography? It could not be for something as paltry as mere money. Surely it had to be a willingness in the mind?

Pitt was looking at Caroline, watching her face, her eyes, the hands now closed tightly in her lap.

'Were there a lot of these pictures?' she asked. 'I mean could they have been sold to many people or used for blackmail?'

'Some of the activities were . . . illegal.' He did not elaborate, but she guessed his meaning.

'The dealer gave me a list of his customers,' he went on, 'but there is nothing to say it is a complete list. We'll investigate it.' His face was sad and tired in the gaslight. 'Some of them will be dealers who sell them on. God knows where they'll end.'

She felt tired herself, a little beaten by the cruelty and the squalor that she had quite suddenly encountered, invading her warm, bright world with dirt she could not dismiss. Most of all it was in the old lady's wounds, so deep they had become woven into her nature. But this that Pitt told her of was part of the same thing, the same sickness of the mind and heart that took pleasure in pain.

'The trouble is,' Pitt went on quietly, 'they could end up in anyone's hands – young people, boys keen to learn a little about women . . . knowing nothing . . .'

Caroline could see in his eyes that he was thinking of himself long ago, remembering his own first stirrings of curiosity and excitement, and crippling ignorance. How appalling it would be if it were something like the brutality Grandmama had described, or the pictures Cecily Antrim had posed for. Young men would grow up seeing women like that . . . willingly chained – just as young Lewis Marchand must have thought of Ophelia, twisted and repellent in her desire for pain, her acceptance of humiliation.

Had that blush in his face been for anything he had conjured out of *Hamlet*, the parts he had considered outrageous, such as the taunting of Ophelia from Shakespeare's text . . . or from Delbert Cathcart's photograph? She had no moral choice but to go to the Marchands and warn them. The misery that could follow did not allow her the luxury of evading it, however embarrassing it might be.

'You must stop it, if you can,' she said aloud. 'Thomas, you really must!'

'I know,' he replied. 'We've taken all the pictures, of course. But that won't prevent him from buying more. You can't ever prevent it. A man with a camera can photograph anything he pleases. A man with a pencil or a paintbrush can draw whatever he likes.' His voice was dark, his lips delicate with revulsion.

'Almost all we can do is see he doesn't display them publicly. Unless the people photographed are abused, then of course we could act on that.' There was no lift in his voice and she knew he felt beaten by it.

She thought of Daniel and Jemima, their innocent faces still looking at the world with no idea of cruelty, no knowledge of the ravages of physical appetite or how it could become so depraved that it consumed all honour or pity, or in the end even preservation of self.

She thought of Edmund Ellison, and Grandmama in her youth, terrified, crouching in the dark, waiting for the pain which would come, if not tonight, then tomorrow, or the next night, and the next, as long as he was alive.

If anyone had done that to one of her own daughters she would have killed them. If they did it to Jemima, or Daniel, she would now, and answer even to God, without regret.

She did not know what connection the pictures had to the act, whether they prompted it, excused it, excited it – or replaced it! She was confused and tired and uncertain how to help. She was sure only that above all things that she needed to.

She sat in the silence with Pitt. There was no sound in the room but the fire and the clock, and neither of them felt compelled to break the understanding with words that were unnecessary. It was a long time before they at last spoke of Charlotte in Paris, her ecstatic account of her visit to the Latin Quarter, breakfast at St-Germain, poets in pink shirts, and another day of a leisurely walk under the horse chestnut trees along the Champs-Elysées.

Chapter Eleven

❦

The old lady did not come down to breakfast the following morning either. Caroline lost her taste for toast and preserves, even though the apricots were delicious.

Joshua looked up. 'What is it? What's wrong?'

She had told him nothing so far. He was absorbed in his own work. She knew by now how exhausting the first few nights of a new play were. Everyone worried how it would be received, how the audience would react, what the critics would say, whether the theatre bookings would remain good, even what others in the profession would think. And if all those things went well, then they worried about their own performances, and always about health, most especially the voice. A sore throat, which was merely unpleasant to most people, to an actor was ruinous. His voice was the instrument of his art.

At first she had found it difficult to understand and know how to help. She had experienced nothing like it in her life with Edward. Now she knew at least when to remain silent, when encouragement was appropriate and when it was not, and what to say that was intelligent. It was the one area in which Joshua had no patience with less than honesty. He could not bear to think he was being patronised. It was at those moments

305

she caught a rare glimpse not only of his temper, but of his vulnerability.

'Thomas was here yesterday evening. Of course he is missing Charlotte . . . and the case he is on is giving him concern.'

'Isn't it always?' He took another slice of toast. 'What good would he be if it didn't worry him? I'm sorry about Cathcart, he was a brilliant photographer. I suppose Thomas is no nearer finding out what happened?'

How much of the truth did he want to know? Not all of it – not until he had to.

'I don't think so. You didn't know him, did you?'

He was surprised. 'Cathcart? No. Just by repute. But I know his work. Everyone does . . . well, I suppose people in the theatre do more than most.' He looked at her narrowly. 'Why?'

She was not as good at deceiving him as she'd thought. He sensed she was telling him less than she knew. She hated the feeling of concealment, the barrier she was creating between them, but to have told him would be a small selfishness, exposing him to unhappiness just for her own peace of mind. And he had already been hurt so deeply by Samuel Ellison, even if it was healed now.

She made her smile more spontaneous, more direct.

'Poor Thomas is trying hard to learn about him, because it seems such a personal crime, a matter of hate or ridicule. If you know anything about him other than reputation it might help.' That sounded reasonable, more like her usual self.

He smiled back and resumed his breakfast.

She made her excuses and went upstairs. The matter of Lewis Marchand had to be addressed, but not until this afternoon. Grandmama should be seen now.

As yesterday, she was still in bed.

'I am not receiving visitors,' she said coldly when Caroline went in.

'I am not a visitor,' Caroline replied, sitting on the edge of the bed. 'I live here.'

The old lady glared at her. 'Are you reminding me that I have no home?' she enquired. 'That I am dependent upon the charity of relations in order to have a roof over my head?'

'That would be quite unnecessary,' Caroline answered her levelly. 'You have complained about it often enough I could hardly imagine you were unaware – or had ever forgotten.'

'It's not something one forgets,' Grandmama retorted. 'One is never allowed to, in a dozen subtle ways. You will learn that one day for yourself, when you are old and alone and everyone else of your generation is dead.'

'Since I have married a man young enough to be my son, as you never tire of telling me, I shall be unlikely to outlive him at all, let alone by long,' Caroline pointed out.

The old lady stared at her, her eyes narrow, her mouth tight shut in a thin, miserable line. She had been bested at her own game, and it thoroughly disconcerted her. She was not sure how to retaliate.

Caroline sighed. 'If you are still not well enough to get up, I shall send for the doctor. We can tell him whatever you please, but whether he believes you is another matter. It is not good for you to lie there. Your system will become sluggish.'

'I am perfectly able to get up! I don't want to!' Grandmama glared at her, daring her to argue.

'What has wanting got to do with it?' Caroline asked. 'The longer you delay it, the more difficult it will be. Do you wish to cause speculation?'

She raised her eyebrows. 'What is there to speculate about? Who cares what I do, or do not do?'

Caroline did not speak. All sorts of thoughts crowded her mind. How close the old lady had come to destroying the happiness she held so precious. She still mentally cringed at the memory of her own misery, and the fear which had darkened everything inside her.

'Please go away. I am exhausted and I prefer to be alone.' The old lady's face set in a mask of loneliness and despair, shutting out Caroline, and everyone else. 'You don't understand. You have not the faintest idea. The least you can afford me is the privacy of suffering without being stared at. I do not want you here. Have the decency to go.'

Caroline hesitated. She could feel her pain as if it were a living thing in the room, but it was beyond her power to touch. She longed to reach out and give it some comfort, some beginning of healing, but she did not know how. For the first time she realised its depth. The scars were woven through her life, not only for the humiliation itself but for how she had dealt with it over the years. It was not just what Edmund had done to her, but what she had done to herself. She had hated herself for so long she did not know how to stop.

'Get out of my room!' the old lady said between her teeth.

Caroline looked at her where she lay hunched up in the bed, her gnarled hands gripping the covers, her face blind with misery, the tears running down her cheeks. She was helpless to do anything about it, even to reach out to her, because the barrier between them was built over the years, reinforced with a thousand daily cuts and abrasions until the scars were impenetrable.

She turned and went out, closing the door behind her, startled to find that the tears were thick in her throat also.

She went to call on the Marchands as early as it was decent to do so, perhaps even a little earlier. Mrs Marchand was surprised to see her, but appeared to be delighted. They sat in the heavy, comfortable withdrawing room for several minutes, making idle conversation, before Mrs Marchand became aware that Caroline had some purpose in coming other than a pleasant way to fill an otherwise empty afternoon. She stopped in the middle of a sentence about some small event, and what people had said about a particular soiree.

Caroline was aware that she had not been listening. Now that she was faced with putting into words what she feared, it was much harder than she had imagined. She looked at Mrs Marchand's wide blue eyes, her direct, almost challenging stare, and her pretty features. She was so sure of her world, of its conventions and its rules. She had conscientiously taught them to her son. Caroline was certain it had never crossed her imagination that he would venture outside its values. She cared almost as passionately as her husband about censorship so the innocent would not be tainted. She would have put fig leaves on all the great classical statues, and blushed to look at the Venus de Milo in the presence of men. She would have seen in it not naked perfection but the indecent display of a woman's breasts.

'Are you quite well, my dear?' Mrs Marchand asked with concern, leaning forward a little, her brow furrowed. 'You look a trifle pale.' Of course what she meant was: You are not listening. What is disturbing you so much you have forgotten your usual manners?

There would never be a better opening. Caroline must take it.

'To tell you the truth, I have been worried lately on a number of matters,' she began awkwardly. 'I am so sorry my attention wandered. I had no wish of being so . . . discourteous.'

'Oh, not at all!' Mrs Marchand disclaimed immediately. 'Can I help, even if it is only to listen? Sometimes a trouble shared seems a little lighter.'

Caroline looked at her earnest face and saw only kindness in it. This was worse than she expected. Mrs Marchand was so vulnerable. It occurred to her to invent something, evading the link altogether. Perhaps she was quite wrong. Maybe Lewis's remarks about Ophelia, the look she had seen in his eyes, was only her own imagination, fuelled since by Grandmama's story, and what Pitt had told her.

But what if it were not? What if Lewis had Cathcart's photographs, lots of them, images which could twist his dreams and cause untold pain in the future, to him, and to some young girl as unknowing as Mariah Ellison had been half a century ago?

'My son-in-law is a policeman, as you know . . .' She ignored the slight flicker of distaste and plunged on. 'He is working on a matter at the moment, to do with a photographic club . . .' That was a ridiculous euphemism! She swallowed and plunged on. 'From something Lewis said when I was here the other day, I believe he may have stumbled on a piece of information which could help. May I have your permission to speak with him?'

'Lewis?' Mrs Marchand was incredulous. 'How on earth could he? He is only sixteen! If he had seen anything . . . wrong . . . he would have told me, or his father.'

'He could not know it was wrong,' Caroline said hastily. 'It is merely information. I am not even sure if I am correct. But if I am, then it would greatly serve justice if he would tell me. I don't believe it would be necessary for him to do more than that. Please, may I speak with him . . . confidentially, if that is possible?'

Mrs Marchand looked uncertain.

Caroline nearly spoke again, then changed her mind. To press too hard might awaken suspicion. She waited.

'Well . . . yes, of course,' Mrs Marchand said, blinking several times. 'I'm sure my husband would wish Lewis to be of any help he can. We all would. A photographic club? I did not know he was interested in photography.'

'I don't know that he is,' Caroline answered quickly. 'It is just that I think he may have seen a particular photograph, and he could tell me where, and I would tell Thomas, without mentioning how I learned.'

'Oh. I see.' She rose to her feet. 'Well, he is upstairs with his tutor. I am sure we could interrupt them for something so important.' She rang the bell for the maid, and Lewis was sent for.

He arrived within minutes, having been going over some of the more abstruse irregular Latin verbs, from which he was delighted to be distracted. He went quite willingly with Caroline into the library and faced her with interest. Anything she had to say, however tedious or pedestrian, had to be better than the eccentricities of the past tense of words he would never in his life have any cause to use. It had been explained to him many times that it was not the practicality but the mental discipline of the exercise which benefited him, but he remained unconvinced.

311

'Yes, Mrs Fielding?' he said politely.

'Please sit down, Lewis,' she replied, sitting herself in the worn, leather armchair in front of the fireplace. 'It is kind of you to spare me your time. I would not have interrupted you were it not an issue of great importance.'

'Of course, Mrs Fielding.' He sat opposite her. 'Whatever I can do.'

She wished now that she had had sons as well as daughters. She had no acquaintance with sixteen-year-old boys. Her own brothers had been older than she, and their adolescence had been an impenetrable mystery to her. But there was no retreat now, except complete failure . . . cowardice. She could hardly send Pitt to do this, although he would certainly have been better at it. He was not the one who had heard Lewis's remarks about Ophelia, or seen the look in his eyes.

She must somehow continue to be direct enough to allow no misunderstanding, and yet spare him as much embarrassment as possible. She had no desire to humiliate him, and no need to. It might even destroy the very purpose for which she had come. Looking into his earnest young face, polite, not really interested, smooth-cheeked still, guileless, she had no words ready that would be subtle.

'Lewis, I did not tell your mother the whole truth, that is up to you, if you wish. The matter my son-in-law is investigating is very serious indeed. It is murder.'

'Is it?' He was not shocked or alarmed. There was a quick flare of interest in his grey eyes. But then he almost certainly had no conception of what that word meant in reality. He would know the facts, not the loss, the horror, the fear that it brought, the sense of pervading darkness.

'I'm afraid so.'

He straightened up a little and his voice lifted. 'What can I do to help, Mrs Fielding?'

She felt a twinge of guilt for what she was about to do, and also the certainty that she must destroy in him the illusion of adventure that filled him at the present.

'When I was here a few days ago and we were speaking, you made a remark from which I now believe you might know something of use,' she said.

He nodded to indicate he was listening.

'In order for you to help,' she went on, 'I need to tell you something about this crime . . . something which is not known to anyone except the police, and the person who committed the murder . . . and to me, because I was told by the police. It is confidential, do you understand?'

He nodded more eagerly. 'Yes, yes, of course I do. I won't tell anyone, I swear.'

'Thank you. I am afraid this is very distressing . . .'

'That's all right!' he assured her, taking a deep breath and sitting very stiffly. 'Please don't worry about it.'

She wanted to smile, but it would have been too easily misunderstood. He was so very young, and unaware.

'The murdered man was struck on the head,' she began solemnly, watching his face. 'Then he was dressed in a velvet gown . . . a woman's gown . . .' She saw him flinch and a look of incomprehension filled his eyes. 'Then he was laid in a small, flat-bottomed boat, a punt, and his wrists and ankles were chained to the boat.'

The colour drained out of the boy's skin leaving him white. His breathing was audible.

'And it was scattered with flowers,' she finished. 'Only his knees were drawn up a little, in a parody of sexual pleasure.'

There was no need to go on. It was painfully apparent from the scarlet of his cheeks and the hot misery in his eyes that he had seen the picture and it was indelible in his memory.

'Where did you see it, Lewis?' she said softly. 'I need to know. I'm sure you must realise that the murderer also saw it, and it is not the kind of picture that is easily found.'

He swallowed, his throat jerking.

'I think you know that,' she went on. 'It is carefully posed. It is not the way women really behave. It is a pretend thing, for people who take pleasure in hurting others . . .' She saw him wince but she did not stop. 'There are people whose appetites are sick, who are not capable of fulfilment in the way most of us are, and they do these sorts of things, cruel and terrible things, regardless of how they torture others.' She stopped, realising she was thinking more of Grandmama and Edmund than of the picture of Cecily Antrim, but they were closely intertwined in her belief. 'Where did you see the picture, Lewis?'

He started to shake his head. He was having difficulty controlling his voice, and above everything he did not want to humiliate himself by weeping in front of a woman he barely knew. He felt cornered. There was no way of escape.

'I would not ask you if it were not connected with murder, Lewis,' she said gently. 'The man who took that photograph is the one who is dead. You can see why it is so important to know everybody who has seen it.'

He gulped. 'Y-yes. I . . . I bought it from a shop. I can tell you where it is . . . if you want?'

'Yes, please.'

'In Half Moon Street, off Piccadilly, about halfway along. It's a shop that sells books, and tobacco, and that sort of thing. I don't remember the name.'

She nearly asked him how he knew of it. Such pictures would not be in the window. But she was afraid of pursuing too far and losing his co-operation altogether. It did not matter.

'That's all right,' she said instead. 'I'm sure they'll find it.'

He kept his eyes lowered. She had the feeling there was something else he wanted to say. And almost as important to her as finding the information for Pitt, was reaching out to this boy and making him believe that what he had seen was an aberration, not the way normal people thought or felt. He had seen the Ophelia picture; she had no idea what other pictures he might also have seen. But how could she do it without betraying his trust to his parents whose rigid ideas had led him to such a way of learning what very little he knew of women and intimacy?

'I suppose they had other pictures as well?' she said.

He avoided her eyes. 'Yes.'

'Were they similar – of women?'

'Well . . . sort of.' His face was scarlet. 'Some . . . were . . . men . . . doing . . .' He could not say it.

She ignored it, for both their sakes. 'Would you prefer to see something a little . . . gentler?' she asked. 'Something more like the kind of woman one day you would like to know yourself?'

His eyes flew open and he stared at her in utter dismay. 'You . . . you mean . . . decent women . . . ?' He blushed crimson and stammered to a halt.

'No, I don't,' she said, trying not to be embarrassed herself. 'I mean . . . I'm not sure what I mean. Decent women certainly don't have photographs like these taken. But we all need to know certain things about men and women.' She was

315

floundering. 'This sort of thing . . . what you've seen . . . is very ugly, and has more to do with hate than with love. I think you need to begin at the beginning, not at the end.'

'My parents would never allow that!' He said it with absolute conviction. 'My father hates –' he gulped – 'pornography. He has spent his whole life fighting against it. He says people who make that and sell it should be hanged!'

She did not argue. She knew it was true.

'If you will allow me to mention these pictures, I think I may be able to persuade them.'

'No!' His voice was shrill with desperation.

'Please don't! You promised you wouldn't tell!'

'I won't,' she said instantly. 'Unless you give me permission.' She leaned towards him earnestly. 'But don't you think, in the long view, it would be better? One day your father is going to have to tell you certain things. Aren't you ready for it to be soon?'

'Well . . . I . . .' He was obviously acutely uncomfortable. He looked everywhere but at her. A moment ago she had been a friend; now, overwhelmingly she was a woman.

'You already know,' she concluded, then wished she had not. Perhaps he did not know? Perhaps it was his burning imagination which had driven him to buy such pictures? Then seeing his agonised face she was certain he did not know. He was confused, hideously embarrassed by his ignorance and his curiosity, and so self-conscious he was crimson to the tips of his ears.

'I think you should speak to your father yourself,' she said gently. 'What you feel is common to all of us. He'll understand exactly.' She hoped to heaven that was true. She was far less certain of Rafe Marchand now than she had been even an hour ago. She stood up and left the room without saying anything more, and almost tiptoed across the hall to the study. She knocked on the door.

'Come in.'

She went in and saw a startled Rafe Marchand facing her across the large desk where he was apparently reading a mound of papers. The ink stand was open. There were pens, knives, sand, wax, and a candle all very much in evidence.

She closed the door as he stood up.

'Mrs Fielding? Is something wrong?' He looked concerned.

'Nothing, I think, that cannot be mended,' she replied, going over to the chair nearest to the desk and sitting down uninvited. 'I have been speaking with Lewis who has been most helpful to me. He is a charming boy, but he is deeply in need of your counsel. I cannot tell you in what regard because it would be breaking a confidence to do so, but if you ask him, I believe he will tell you.'

'My counsel?' He looked completely bewildered. 'About . . . you cannot tell me? Then how can I— What is wrong, Mrs Fielding?'

What should she say? She had given her word to Lewis. She must not break it. Trust should never be broken. And yet he needed help he might be incapable of asking for.

Mr Marchand was staring at her with growing anxiety.

She plunged in. 'Explaining to my daughters the . . . the relations of marriage.' She could feel her own face burn. 'The relationship between men and women . . . was one of the most difficult things I have ever had to do. But if I had not, I would have left them open to all manner of misconceptions which might have caused unhappiness through the years afterwards.' She was babbling. 'It was not merely the . . . details . . . it was the nature of love, and of giving, the kind of tenderness they

317

might give . . . and hope to receive.'

'Mrs Fielding . . . I . . .' He too was very pink.

She looked down at her hands, then up at him quickly. 'If those who love us do not answer the questions burning in our minds, then there is always the risk that we will seek answers elsewhere – and they may not be good ones. One can be . . . too delicate . . . too modest . . .'

He looked at her with confusion, not as to understanding but how to answer. A mixture of emotions crowded his face and she could not read them, only that they were profound.

'Mr Marchand . . . there is a great deal around that is ugly, and true, thank God, of only a very small minority . . .'

He leaned forward across the desk, his hands clenched so the knuckles were white, the colour draining from his face.

'Are you . . . ?' His voice shook. 'Are you saying Lewis has seen . . . this . . . this tide of . . .' there was anguish in his eyes, '. . . filth?'

She did not hesitate to lie. She did not even have to think about it.

'Of course not! But my son-in-law is a policeman; I know it exists, and is more available than we would wish. The best protection against lies and distortions, perhaps the only one, is the truth. Show him what is good, and he will not want what is evil.'

He sat motionless for so long she thought he was not going to reply at all. Then at last he spoke.

He nodded. 'Yes . . . yes, of course. I – I think you may be right.' He smiled at her faintly, still embarrassed, but there was a warmth in his eyes he did not try to hide. 'Forgive me . . . I . . . find the subject of pornography so painful I have not the control of myself I would wish. The damage it can do . . . it is far more than a material robbery. The wound doesn't heal. It is a blasphemy.'

He stopped, acutely self-conscious. He had allowed far too much emotion to intrude. He had exposed some vulnerability of his own, a kind of nakedness.

She understood it, and did the only thing possible: she pretended she had not. She smiled as if it had been a very ordinary remark. 'Thank you so much for allowing me to trouble you.' She rose to her feet. 'Of course it is a most difficult subject to speak of, particularly to the young, but it is one of those gifts one must give . . .'

'Yes . . .' He stood also, relief in his eyes. 'Thank you, so much . . .' He half offered his hand, and then changed his mind, as if it were too formal. 'Thank you,' he said again, and moved to open the door for her.

She girded up her courage to return to the withdrawing room with its comfortable safety, decently dressed statues, and say nothing to Mrs Marchand that would disturb her. Her husband would have to do that, in a time of his own choosing.

She had dealt as well as possible with the issue of the photographs. She would send the address of the dealer to Bow Street for Pitt, then she would have to face the old lady again. The situation she had brought about could not go unresolved indefinitely.

But the damage was so deep, how did she reach it? It had years ago become part of the old lady's character; the anger was consumed into her view of everything. If that were removed, was there anything left?

It was a cool, clear autumn day, the streets full of hazy sunlight, traffic moving swiftly, apart from the occasional crushes at corners where everyone seemed to be a rule to themselves. At a glance she could see a score of people walking, as she was, simply for the pleasure of it. She was not yet ready to look for a cab. Perhaps that was as much because she dreaded returning home as anything to do with the weather.

The situation could not continue like this, day after day. Emily would be home in just over a week. It must be dealt with before then. Which raised another question she had been avoiding. What should she tell Emily, or Charlotte?

She smiled and nodded to two women passing her. She was sure she had met them somewhere, but could not think where. They had the same polite, slightly confused looks on their faces. Presumably they were thinking exactly the same.

She could hardly tell Emily nothing. She had to offer some explanation for the change in the old lady. And whatever she told Emily she would have to tell Charlotte also.

She pictured Edmund Ellison as she remembered him. He was her father-in-law, a relation by marriage, but to them he was Grandfather, a relation by blood, in a sense part of who they were. That made it different. They would find it far harder to bear.

And what thoughts would it awaken about Edward also? It had disturbed Caroline herself, made her view certain memories differently, and she had known him in that regard. She had all the knowledge with which to dismiss all doubts, see them for the slander they were.

Honesty was not the only thing that mattered, surely?

She wished there were someone else she could speak to, someone whose advice she could seek, without laying upon them a burden it was unfair to ask them to carry. She certainly could not ask Joshua, especially not now, with a new play just beginning. Even at any time it would not be right. He had not been warned before. He had no experience of this kind of family problem in all its complicated ugliness and ever-widening circles of pain.

She could not even ask Charlotte, and certainly not Pitt. It was really not a problem she wished to discuss with a man at all, let alone one a generation younger than herself, and with whom she had a continuing family relationship.

A handsome carriage and four swept by with a crest on the door, liveried coachman on the box and footman behind. It was a pleasure to watch them.

Lady Vespasia Cumming-Gould – that was the answer. Of course she might not be in! She might consider this something of an impertinence, a familiarity not warranted by their very slight acquaintance. But on the other hand she might help Caroline as she had helped Charlotte so many times.

She hailed the next hansom and gave the driver Vespasia's address. It was quite an acceptable hour for afternoon calls.

Vespasia received her with both interest and pleasure, and did not indulge the pretence that it was merely a usual courtesy call.

'I am sure you did not come to discuss Society or the weather. You are plainly concerned about something,' she said when they were seated alone in the light sitting room looking into the garden. It was one of the most restful rooms Caroline had been in. The sense of space and air, the cool tones were calming, and she found herself sitting more comfortably in the chair. 'I hope nothing is going badly with Charlotte or Emily?'

'No, far from it,' Caroline assured her. 'I believe Charlotte is enjoying herself enormously.'

Vespasia smiled. The light was silver on her hair, and warm

on her face, which was beautiful as much because of her age as in spite of it. All the lines were upward, the faint prints of time left by courage and laughter, and an inner certainty no one had seen waver.

'Then you had better tell me what it is,' she offered. 'I have instructed my maid that I am not at home to anyone else, but I have no taste to play games with words. I have reached the age when life seems too short as it is, I do not wish to spend any of it uselessly . . . unless it is fun? And from your face, this is not so.'

'No, I am afraid it is not. But I should greatly appreciate your advice,' Caroline admitted. 'I am not sure what I should do for the best.'

Vespasia looked at her steadily. 'What have you done so far?'

As succinctly as possible Caroline told her of meeting Samuel Ellison at the theatre and of his visits to the house and Grandmama's increasing tension.

Vespasia listened without interruption until Caroline reached the point where she had retrieved the letter and confronted Mariah and demanded to know the truth. Then she found it unexpectedly difficult to repeat the obscenity of what the old lady had finally recounted.

'I think you had better tell me,' Vespasia said quietly. 'I presume it was extremely unpleasant, or she would hardly have gone to such lengths to keep it concealed.'

Caroline looked down at her hands locked together in her lap.

'I did not know people behaved in such ways. I have always disliked my mother-in-law. I have never admitted that before, but it is true.' She was embarrassed to confess it. 'She is a bitter and cruel woman. All my married life I have watched her look for ways to hurt people. Now I find myself sorry for her . . . and angry with myself because I can't think of any way to help. She is dying of rage and humiliation, and I can't touch her. She won't let me, and I can't break the barrier.' She looked up. 'I ought to be able to! I'm not the one who has been abused and degraded!'

Vespasia sat silently for so long Caroline began to think she was not going to reply. Perhaps Vespasia was too old to deal with such things and Caroline should not have trespassed.

'My dear,' Vespasia said at last, 'wounds such as you imply can sometimes be healed, if they are reached soon enough. A gentle man, a tender man might have taught her differently, and she would have learned what love can be. In time she might have put the past to the back of her mind, where it could do no more harm. I think for your mother-in-law it is far too late. She has hated herself so long she can find no way back.'

Caroline felt herself go cold, her hands stiff. It was not what she wanted to hear.

'It is pointless to blame yourself for not being able to ease her pain,' Vespasia went on. 'It is not your fault, but more to the point, self-blame will help neither of you. I do not mean to be harsh, but it is a kind of self-indulgence. The most you can do for her is to treat her with some nature of respect, and not allow your new knowledge of her to destroy what little dignity she has left.'

'That's not very much!' Caroline said angrily. 'That sounds like self-preservation.'

'My dear,' Vespasia said gently, 'I have found that when something very dreadful happens, and has to be faced, that it is wisest to consider the matter in the most practical terms. What is fair or unfair no longer really matters, only what is or is not. It is a waste of energy you will desperately need to expend anger on injustice you cannot alter. Concentrate your attention on the pain you can reach, and weigh very carefully what is the most likely result of your actions, and if it is what you wish for. When you have made the wisest judgement you can, then do it. Let the rest take care of itself.'

Caroline knew she was right, and yet she could not help a last protest. 'Is that really all? I feel so . . . There ought to be . . .'

Vespasia shook her head very slightly. 'You cannot heal her, but you can allow her time, and room to heal herself a little . . . if she wants to. After these years of anger it would take a miracle . . . but miracles do happen, from time to time.' She gave a very slight smile. 'I have seen a few. Never give up hope. If she can believe that you have hope, she may learn to have it herself.'

'It doesn't sound a great deal,' Caroline said reluctantly.

Vespasia moved very slightly, the light silver on her hair.

'The damage done by that kind of abuse is very, very deep. The physical is nothing, in comparison. It is the wound to the faith, to what one believes of oneself that may be irrevocable. If you cannot love yourself, and believe you are worth loving, then it is impossible to love anyone else.' She gave a tiny shrug, the sun shimmering on the silk of her gown. 'When Christ commanded us to love our neighbour as ourselves, the "self" part is just as important. We forget that at a terrible price.'

Caroline considered it for several minutes. She thought also of Pitt, and the photographs of Cecily Antrim, and young Lewis Marchand's face. In stilted words she told Vespasia about that also.

When she had finished Vespasia was smiling.

'That must have been very difficult for you,' she said with approval. 'Please do not chastise yourself over what you cannot change. There is a limit to what any of us can do, and sometimes we take the blame for things far beyond our power to affect. We each have our own agency to choose how we will react to our circumstances. We cannot take that from anyone, nor should we wish to, even if we have the arrogance to believe we know better than they do how they should behave, or what judgements they should make. We may beg, plead, argue, we may pray — and we should — but in the end the only person anyone can change is themselves. Please be content with that. It is all you will receive, I promise you. And it is all you should. It is sufficient.'

'And what about pictures?' Caroline asked. 'We talk very freely about not censoring art! But the people who say that don't think of the damage they can do! If they had seen young Lewis Marchand's face, they wouldn't have thought their freedom worth so much. They aren't the people with children. They—' She stopped, realising how wrong she was. 'Yes they are . . . at least Cecily Antrim is.' She frowned. 'Am I old-fashioned, repressed, backward-thinking? She would say I am boring and getting old!' The words hurt as she said them. Spoken aloud they were even worse than silent in her mind.

'I am not getting old,' Vespasia replied vigorously. 'I most assuredly have arrived there. It is not as bad as you may fear. In fact it has distinct pleasures. Go and read your Robert Browning, and have a little more faith in life, my dear. And so far as being boring is concerned, kindness and honesty are never tedious. Cruelty, hypocrisy and pretentiousness always are . . .

excruciatingly so. A fool may not be interesting, but if he or she is generous and interested in you, you will find you like him, however limited his wit.'

'Why would Cecily Antrim pose for such pictures?' Caroline followed her thoughts. 'When Joshua finds out he is going to be so distressed . . . I think . . .'

Then suddenly she was terribly afraid he would not be. It would be she herself he thought out of step, critical, imprisoned in old thought.

Vespasia was looking at her very steadily, her eyes silver-grey in the soft light of this clear, uncluttered room. The sun was bright on the grass beyond the windows, the trees motionless against the blue sky.

Caroline felt transparent, all her thoughts, her fears naked.

'I think you are being a trifle unfair to him,' Vespasia said frankly. 'Of course he will be hurt, and wish to judge her more kindly than may prove possible. Disillusion cuts very deep. He will need you to be sure of yourself. I think you should consider long and carefully what it is you hold most dear, and then do not let go of it.'

Caroline said nothing. She already knew that was true. Samuel Ellison had taught her that.

Vespasia leaned forward a fraction. It was just a slight gesture, but it gave an impression of closeness. 'You are older than he is, and it troubles you.' That was a statement, not a question. 'My dear, you always were. He chose you for who you are. Don't destroy it by trying to be someone else. If he loses a friend he has admired in this miserable business, he is going to need you to be strong, to remain honest and fight for the values you have represented to him. Years are accidents of nature, maturity is very precious. He may very much need you to be older than he is . . . for a little while.' The flicker of a smile touched her mouth. 'The time will come when you can reverse the roles, and allow him to be stronger, or wiser, or even both! Just be subtle about it, that's all. Sometimes when we most need help, we least like to know we are receiving it. Set your own doubts aside for a little while. Fight as you would for your children, without thought for yourself. Just don't lose your temper. It is terribly unbecoming.'

In spite of herself Caroline laughed.

Vespasia laughed also. 'May I lend you a pen and paper, then you may send a note to Thomas to give him the address of this dealer? I shall have my coachman take it to Bow Street. I confess I find it most irritating that Charlotte has gone to Paris. I have no idea what Thomas is doing, and I am bored to doll-rags!' She gave a self-deprecating shrug, pulling the dove-grey silk of her gown. 'I have become addicted to police life and I find Society infinitely tedious. It is merely a new generation of people doing exactly what we did, and convinced they are the first to think of it. How on earth do they imagine they came into the world?'

Caroline found herself overtaken with laughter; the blessed release of it was marvellous. The tears ran down her cheeks and she did not even try to stop, she had no desire to at all. Suddenly she was warm again, and surprisingly hungry. She would like tea . . . and cakes!

While Caroline was worrying about Grandmama and trying in vain to think of some way to comfort her, Pitt was sitting at the table in the kitchen reading the latest letter from Charlotte. He was so absorbed in it he let his tea go cold.

Dearest Thomas,

I am enjoying my last few days here in a unique kind of way. It has been a marvellous holiday, and no doubt the moment I leave I shall wish I could recapture it better in my memory. Therefore I am looking at everything especially closely, so I can print it in my mind . . . the way the light falls on the river, the sun on the old stones . . . some of the buildings are quite frighteningly beautiful and so steeped in history. I think of all the things that have happened here, the people who have lived and died, the great battles for liberty, the terror and the glory . . . and, of course, the squalor as well.

I wonder, do other people come to London and look at it with the same bursting sense of romance? Do foreigners come to our city and see the great ghosts of the past: Charles I going calmly to his death after years of civil war, Queen Elizabeth leaving to rally the troops before the Armada, Anne Boleyn . . . ? Why is it always executions? What's the matter with us? Riot, bloodshed and glorious deaths. I suppose it is the ultimate sacrifice?

By the way, talking about ultimate sacrifice – well, not ultimate, I suppose – but a young French diplomat, Henri Bonnard by name, has just made a conspicuous sacrifice on behalf of his friend. It is in all the newspapers, so Madame says. Apparently he is posted in London and has come back to Paris to testify in this case I was telling you about – the man who said he could not have killed the girl because he was at the Moulin Rouge at the time? Well, so he was – and the diplomat was with him – all night! It seems they went there quite respectably, like anyone else, stayed until after the most infamous of the dancers, La Goulou, had done the cancan – and then went on to even more disreputable pursuits. But together! He swears to it – very reluctantly, I might add. His ambassador will not be pleased. All Paris is laughing about it today. I imagine London will know of it by the time you read this. At least some of London will, the people the ambassador cares about. Poor Monsieur Bonnard, a high price to pay to rescue a friend. I hope he does not lose his job.

We are going to the opera tonight. It should be great fun. Everyone will be dressed to kill. It's just like London, the very best courtesans parade at the back, and pick up custom, only of course I'm not supposed to know that!

All this is marvellous to watch, but nothing on earth could persuade me to live this way permanently. It is the best thing of all to know that I shall be home in a few days, and with you all again.

I don't suppose you have heard from Gracie? I don't think she is sure enough of her writing yet, and of course Daniel and Jemima wouldn't think to write. I hope they are building sand castles, finding crabs and little fish in the rock pools, eating sweets, getting wet and dirty and having an unforgettable time.

I imagine you are working hard. The case you describe sounds macabre. There must be a tragedy behind it. I hope you are eating properly, and finding where I put everything you'll need. Is the house horribly silent without us all? Or wonderfully peaceful? I trust you are not neglecting Archie and Angus? I don't imagine they will allow you to.

I miss you, and shall be happy to be home soon,
    Yours always,
        Charlotte

Pitt read it again carefully, not that he had missed any part of it, but it gave him a sense of her nearness. He could almost hear her quick footsteps down the passage and half expected her to push the door open and come in.

It also finally solved the question of what had happened to Henri Bonnard. He found himself smiling at that. It was a pleasant thought, among the miseries, that when he had finally found the courage to go, it had been for the most generous of reasons. Pitt hoped the ambassador in London viewed his loyalty to his friend as a quality far outweighing the indiscretion of having attended a nightclub of exceedingly dubious reputation. Even if it was as sordid as gossip would have, it was still the sort of thing young men did, even if largely out of curiosity and a certain bravado.

Was that what he and Orlando Antrim had quarrelled about? Not photographs at all? Orlando had been trying to persuade him to go? It seemed finally he had acquiesced.

Pitt finished the last of his tea, grimacing at its coldness – he liked his tea as hot as he could bear it – and stood up, forgetting that Archie was on his lap.

'Sorry,' he apologised absently. 'Here, Archie, have some more breakfast. I hope you realise you'll go back to rations when your mistress comes home? There'll be no extras then. And you'll have to go back to your own bed as well . . . you and Angus!'

Archie wound around his legs, purring, leaving white and ginger hairs on his trousers.

Pitt knew he had no alternative but to confront Cecily Antrim with the photographs. He would like to have avoided it so he could keep his illusions about her and imagine in his mind that she could produce an explanation which would make it understandable and somehow not her fault. She had been blackmailed into it, to save someone else – anything that would not mean she was a willing participant. That was not a great leap of the imagination. Some of the other photographs had certainly been blackmail material, had any of the people in them gone on to more respectable careers. And the money so obtained would explain Cathcart's style of life, and Lily Monderell's.

But he could not so easily imagine Cecily Antrim as anyone's victim. She was too vibrant, too courageous, too willing to follow her own belief even to destruction.

He found her in the early afternoon in the theatre rehearsing *Hamlet*. Tellman was with him, reluctant to the last step.

'Shakespeare!' he said between set teeth. He made no further remark but the expression on his face was eloquent.

As before they were allowed in grudgingly and had to wait in the wings until a suitable break came when the person they wished to see was not necessary to the performance. Today they were rehearsing Act V, in the churchyard. Two men were digging a grave and speaking of the suicide who was to be buried in it, even though it was hallowed ground. After a little joking, one departed, leaving the other alone, singing to himself.

Hamlet and Horatio entered, this time in costume. It was not long until the first night, and Pitt noticed immediately how much more polished they were. There was an air of certainty about them as if they were absorbed in the passions of the story and no longer aware of direction let alone of the world beyond.

Pitt glanced at Tellman and saw the light reflected in his face as he listened, the words washing over him, not in familiar cadence as they did for so many, for Pitt himself, but heard for the first time.

"'Alas, poor Yorick. I knew him, Horatio, a fellow of infinite jest, of most excellent fancy . . .'"

Tellman's eyes were wide. He was unaware of Pitt. He stared at the plaster skull in Orlando Antrim's hand, and saw the emotions within him.

"'Now get you to my lady's chamber,'" Orlando said with irony hard-edged in his voice, harsh with pain, "'. . . and tell her, let her paint an inch thick, to this favour must she come. Make her laugh at that, – Prithee, Horatio, tell me one thing.'"

"'What's that, my lord?'" the other actor enquired.

Tellman leaned forward a little. His face was like a mask, not a muscle moved, nor did his eyes ever leave the small pool of light on the stage. The words poured around him.

"'To what base uses we may return, Horatio! Why, may not imagination trace the noble dust of Alexander till a find it stopping a bung-hole?'"

Someone moved in the wings. A look of annoyance crossed Tellman's face but he did not turn to see who it was.

"'Imperious Caesar, dead and turned to clay".' Orlando spoke the words softly, filled with centuries of wonder and music, as if they wove a magic for him.

'. . . Might stop a hole to keep the wind away.
O that that earth which kept the world in awe
Should patch a wall t'expel the winter's flaw.
But soft, but soft awhile. Here comes the King.'

And from the wing moved a slow, sad procession in sombre, magnificent garments. Priests, the coffin of Ophelia followed by her brother, then the King, and Cecily Antrim, beautiful as Gertrude. It was extraordinary how she could hold the attention, even when the scene was not about her at all. There was a light in her face, a force of emotion in her that could not be ignored.

The drama played itself out and neither Pitt nor Tellman moved until it was over. Then Pitt stepped forward.

Tellman was still transfixed. In a space of less than fifteen minutes he had glimpsed a new world which had thrown aside the old. The still water of his preconceptions had been disturbed by a wave whose ripples were going to reach to the very outer edges, and already he felt it.

Pitt walked alone across the stage to Cecily Antrim.

'I apologise for interrupting you, but there is a matter I need to discuss which will not wait.'

'For God's sake, man!' Bellmaine shouted in outrage, his voice raw-edged with tension. 'Have you no soul, no sensibilities at all? The curtain goes up in two days! Whatever you want, it can wait!'

Pitt stood quite still. 'No, Mr Bellmaine, it cannot wait. It will not take a great deal of Miss Antrim's time, but it will be even less if you permit me to begin straight away, rather than stand here and argue about it.'

Bellmaine swore colourfully and without repeating himself, but he also waved his hands in dismissal, indicating the general direction of the dressing rooms. Tellman remained rooted to the spot, spellbound for the next scene.

Cecily Antrim's room was filled with rails hung with velvets and embroidered satins. A second wig rested on a stand on the long table beneath the mirror amid a clutter of pots, brushes, bowls, powders and rouges.

'Well?' she asked with a wry smile. 'What is it that is so urgent that you dare to defy Anton Bellmaine? I am consumed with curiosity. Even a live audience would not have kept me from coming with you to find out. I assure you, I still do not know who killed poor Delbert Cathcart, or why.'

'Nor do I, Miss Antrim,' he replied, digging his hands into his coat pockets. 'But I know that whoever it was saw a particular photograph of you which is not available to most people, and it mattered to him very much.'

She was intrigued, and the smile on her mouth was too filled with amusement for him to believe she had any idea what he was going to show her. The laughter went all the way to her clear, sky-blue eyes.

'There are scores of photographs of me, Superintendent. My career is longer than I wish to admit! I couldn't begin to tell you who has seen which.' She did not say he was naive, but her voice carried the implication quite plainly, and it entertained her.

He did not like what he had to do next. He pulled out the postcard with the *Ophelia* travesty and held it out.

Her eyes widened. 'Good God! Where did you get that?' She looked up at him. 'You are quite right. That is one of Delbert's. You are never going to say he was killed for that! That's preposterous. You can probably buy them from half a dozen backstreet shops. I certainly hope so! It will have been a lot of discomfort for nothing if you can't! The wet velvet was revolting on the skin, and abysmally cold!'

Pitt was stunned. For a moment he could think of nothing to say.

'But it is effective, don't you think?'

'Effective,' he repeated the word as if it were in an unfamiliar language. He looked at her vivid face with its fine, delicate mouth and wonderful bones. 'Yes, Miss Antrim, I have never known a picture have more effect.'

She heard the emotion in his voice.

'You disapprove, Superintendent. That may be just as well. At least you will remember it, and it might make you think. The image that has no power to disturb probably has no power to change either.'

'To change?' he asked, his voice a little hoarse. 'To change what, Miss Antrim?'

She looked at him very steadily. 'To change the way people think, Superintendent. What else is worth changing?' Her expression filled with disgust. 'If the Lord Chamberlain had not taken off the play you came to, then Freddie Warriner might not have lost his nerve, and we would have started a bill to make the divorce laws more equal. We wouldn't have succeeded this time, but maybe next or the one after! You must begin by making people care!'

He drew in breath to make a dozen replies, then saw her smile and understood what she meant.

'If you can change thought, you can change the world,' she said softly.

He pushed his hands further into his pockets, his fists clenched tight. 'And what thought was it you intended to change with this picture, Miss Antrim?'

She seemed faintly amused. He saw the flicker in her eyes.

'The thought that women are content with a passive role in love,' she replied. 'We are imprisoned in other people's ideas of who we are and what we feel, what makes us happy . . . or

335

Anne Perry

what hurts. We allow it to happen. To be chained by your own beliefs is bad enough, heaven knows; but to be chained by other people's is monstrous.' Her face was alight as she spoke. There was a kind of luminous beauty in her, as if she could see far beyond the physically jarring image on the paper to the spiritual freedom she was seeking, not for herself so much as for others. If it was a lonely crusade, she was prepared for it and her courage was more than equal.

'Don't you understand?' she said urgently to his silence. 'Nobody has the right to decide what other people want, or feel! And we do it all the time, because it's what we need them to want.' She was close to him. He could feel the warmth of her, see the faint down on her cheek. 'We feel more comfortable, it feeds our preconceptions, our ideas about who we are,' she went on fiercely. 'Or else it is what we can give them, so we decide it is what they want. They should be grateful! It is for their good. It is for somebody's good! It is what is right or natural . . . or most of all, it is what God wants! What monumental arrogance that we should decide that what is comfortable for us is what Almighty God wants! And we should make it so.'

'All of the pictures?' Pitt asked with the very faintest sarcastic edge to his voice, but he had to struggle to find it. 'Some of them seemed blasphemous to me.'

'To you?' Her marvellous eyes widened. 'My dear, pedestrian Superintendent. Blasphemous to you! What is blasphemy?'

He jammed his hands further still into his pockets, straightening his arms. He could not allow her to intimidate him because she was beautiful and articulate and supremely sure of herself.

336

'I think it is jeering at other people's beliefs,' he replied quietly. 'Making them doubt the possibility of good and making reverence appear ridiculous. Whose God it is doesn't matter. It isn't a question of doctrine, it's a matter of trying to destroy the innate idea we have of deity, of something better and holier than we are.'

'Oh . . . Superintendent!' She let her breath out in a sigh. 'I think I have just been bested by a policeman! Please don't tell anyone. I shall never live it down! I apologise. Yes, that is what blasphemy is . . . and I did not mean to commit it. I meant to make people question stereotypes and look again at us as individuals, every one different, never again say, "She's a woman, so she feels this . . . or that . . . and if she doesn't, then she ought to!" Or, "He's a priest, he must be good, what he says must be right, he doesn't have this weakness, or that passion . . . if he does he's wicked."' Her eyes widened. 'Do you understand me?'

'Yes, I understand you, Miss Antrim.'

'But you disagree with me! I can see it in your face. You think I shock people, and it is painful. I am breaking something, and you hate breakage. You are here to keep order, to protect the weak, to prevent violent change, or any change that is not by consent of the masses.' She spread her hands wide – strong, beautiful hands. 'But art must lead, Superintendent, not follow! It is my work to upset convention, to defy assumptions, to suggest that disorder out of which progress is born. If you were to succeed . . . entirely . . . we would not even have fire, let alone a wheel!'

'I am all for fire, Miss Antrim, but not for burning people. Fire can destroy as well as create.'

'So can everything that has real power,' she responded.

'Have you seen *A Doll's House*?'

'I beg your pardon?'

'Ibsen! The play – *A Doll's House*!' she repeated impatiently.

He had not seen it, but he knew what she was talking about. The playwright had dared to create a heroine who had rebelled against everything that was expected of her, most of all by herself, and in the end left her husband and home for a dangerous and lonely freedom. It had created a furore. It was condemned passionately by some as subversive and destructive of morality and civilisation. Others praised it as honest and the beginning of a new liberation. A few simply said it was brilliant and perceptive art, most particularly since it was written with such sensitivity and insight of a woman's nature – by a man. He had heard Joshua praise it with almost the same burning enthusiasm as Cecily Antrim now showed.

'Well?' she demanded, the light in her face fading with exasperation as she began to believe she was confusing him.

'There are some differences,' he said tentatively. 'One chooses to go to the theatre. These pictures are on sale to the public. What if young people are there . . . boys who know no better?'

She waved it aside. 'There are always risks, Superintendent. There can be no gain without a certain cost. To be born at all is to risk being alive! Dare it! Shame the devil of the real death – the death of the will, of the spirit! Oh . . . and don't bother to ask me who saw that picture. I would tell you if I could. I am deeply sorry Delbert Cathcart is dead – he was a great artist – but I can't tell you because I haven't the slightest idea!' And with that she turned and walked out of the door, leaving it wide open behind her, and he heard her footsteps dying away along the passage.

He stood alone in the dressing room and looked around at the trappings of illusion, the paint and the costumes which help the imagination. They were wrought with skill, but they were a minuscule part of the real magic. That sprang from the soul and the will, the inner world created with such passion it poured through and no material aids were needed to make it leap from one mind to another. Words, movement, gesture, the fire of the spirit made it real.

He looked at the photograph again. How many people were chained by other people's beliefs of them? Did he expect Charlotte to be something that was not her true nature, or what she really wished? Then he thought back to his first meeting with Caroline. In some ways she had been imprisoned . . . but by family, society, her husband – or herself? The prisoner who loves his bonds is surely also responsible for their continuance?

He would rather Jemima, with her sharp, inquisitive mind, did not ever see a picture like this . . . certainly not until she was at least Charlotte's present age.

What kind of a man would she marry? That was a preposterous thought! She was a child. He could see her bright little face in his mind's eye so easily, so vividly, her child's slender body, but already growing taller, legs longer. One day she would marry someone. Would he be gentle with her, allow her some freedom, and still protect her? Would he be strong enough to wish her happiness, in whatever path it lay? Or would he try to make her conform to his own view of what was right? Would he ever see her as herself, or only what he needed her to be?

So much of him agreed with what Cecily Antrim was trying to do, and yet the picture offended him, and not only because he had seen it mimicked in death but because of the innate violence in it.

Was that necessary, in order to shatter complacency? He did not know.

But he would have to send Tellman to establish beyond doubt where Cecily Antrim had been on the night of Cathcart's death, even though he did not believe she had killed him. There had been no fear in her, no shock, no sense of personal involvement at all.

He would also send Tellman to find out precisely where Lord Warriner had been that night, just in case his love for her was less casual than it appeared. But that was a formality, simply something not to be overlooked. She had posed willingly for the picture – in fact from what she had said, this had been her idea. She wanted them sold. The last thing she intended was for such a performance to be without an audience.

He pushed the picture back into his pocket and went to the door. He found his way out past piled screens and painted trees and walls, and several pieces of beautifully carved wood, to the stage door.

Chapter Twelve

❧

Caroline returned home with new heart and went straight upstairs, before she could think better of it. She knocked on the old lady's door, and when there was no answer, she opened it and went in.

Mariah was lying half reclined in bed. The curtains were pulled to keep the light out and she looked to be asleep. If Caroline had not seen her eyelids flicker she would have believed she was.

'How are you?' she enquired conversationally, sitting on the edge of the bed.

'I was asleep,' Mariah replied coldly.

'No, you weren't,' Caroline contradicted her. 'Nor are you going to be until tonight. Would you like to come to the theatre with us?'

The old lady's eyes flew open. 'Whatever for? I haven't been to the theatre in years. You know that perfectly well. Whatever should I do there?'

'Watch the play?' Caroline suggested. She smiled. 'And watch the audience. Sometimes that can be more fun. The drama on the stage is seldom the only one.'

Mariah hesitated for just an instant. 'I don't go to the theatre,'

341

she said sullenly. 'It's usually nonsense they are performing anyway: cheap, modern rubbish!'

'It's *Hamlet.*'

'Oh.'

Caroline tried to remember Vespasia's words.

'Anyway,' she said honestly, 'the actress who plays the Queen is very beautiful, talented and frightfully outspoken. I am terrified of her. I always feel as if I shall say something foolish, or naive, when I see her afterwards, which we will because Joshua is bound to go and congratulate her. They are great friends.'

The old lady looked interested. 'Are they? I thought the Queen in *Hamlet* was his mother! She's hardly the heroine, is she!'

'Joshua likes older women! I thought you had appreciated that!' Caroline said drily.

Mariah smiled in spite of herself. 'And you are jealous of her.' It was a statement, but for once there was no edge of unkindness to it, rather something that could even have been a sympathy.

Caroline decided to tell the truth. 'Yes – a little. She seems to be so certain of herself . . . of everything she believes in.'

'Believes in? I thought she was an actress!' Mariah hitched herself a little higher in the bed. 'What can she believe in?'

'All sorts of things!' Caroline pictured in her mind Cecily's passionate face, her vivid eyes and the fire in her voice. 'The absolute evil of censorship, the freedom of the mind and will, the values of art . . . She makes me feel terribly old-fashioned and . . . dull.'

'Poppycock!' Mariah said vehemently. 'Stand up for yourself. Don't you know what you believe in any more?'

'Yes, I think so . . .'

'Don't be such a milksop! There must be something you are sure of! You can't live to your age without having at least one certainty. What is it?'

Caroline smiled. 'That I don't know as much as I thought I did. I gather facts and make judgements about people, and things, and so often there is one thing more that I didn't know, and if I had it I would have changed everything.' She was thinking of the old lady, and Grandpapa, but there were other things too, stretching back over the years, issues, decisions, stories only half known.

Mariah grunted, but some of the anger had drained out of her.

'Then you are wiser than this woman, who imagines she knows so much,' she said grudgingly, 'Go and tell her so.'

Caroline did not ask again if the old lady would come. They both knew she would not, and to have made the offer again would have broken the fragile thread of honesty between them.

She stood up and went to the door. Her hand was on it when the old lady spoke again.

'Caroline!'

'Yes?'

'Enjoy yourself.'

'Thank you.' She turned away.

'Caroline!'

'Yes?'

'Wear the red dress. It becomes you.'

She did not look back and spoil the moment by making too much of it. 'Thank you,' she accepted. 'Good night.'

Caroline dressed very carefully for the first night of *Hamlet*.

She hesitated some time before having her maid put out the red dress Grandmama had mentioned. It was actually a rich wine colour, very warm, but definitely dramatic. She was uncertain about being so conspicuous. She sat in the chair in front of her looking-glass and stared at her own face while her maid dressed her hair. She was still slender – she had not lost her shape at all – but she knew all the signs of ageing that were there: the differences between her skin now, and how it had been a few years ago, the slight blurring of the smooth line of her jaw, the fine lines on her neck, not to mention her face!

She had not Cecily Antrim's glowing vitality, the confidence inside which gave her such grace. That was not only youth, it was part of her character. She would always command attention, admiration, a kind of awe because she carried part of the magic of life in her mind.

Caroline still felt dull compared with her – sort of brown . . . compared with gold.

She thought of what Vespasia had said, and Grandmama. But it was the thought of Grandmama's despair which finally made her sit up with a straight back, almost jerking the pins out of the maid's hands.

'I'm sorry,' she murmured, wincing.

'Did I hurt you, ma'am?'

'My own fault. I shall sit still.'

She was as good as her word, but her thoughts still raced, wondering how she should conduct herself, what she should say to be honest, generous and yet not gushing. She cringed inwardly at the picture of appearing to seek favour, push herself forward with too much wordiness in praise she could not mean, because she did not really know what she was talking about. They would listen from good manners, wishing she would stop before she embarrassed everyone further. Her face was hot merely imagining it.

Every instinct was to retreat into quiet dignity, say very little. Then she would appear to be sulking, and make herself even more excluded.

Either way Joshua would be ashamed for her. And suddenly it was not about how she felt at all, but how miserable he would be, that mattered, and how the change would spill over into all their lives afterwards.

The maid was finished. It was beautiful; she had always had lovely hair.

'Thank you,' she said appreciatively. Now she was ready for the dress. She hated having to go alone, but Joshua's own performance would not be over until shortly before the end. Thank goodness *Hamlet* was such a long play. He would be there in time for the last act.

The theatre was so crowded she had to push her way forward, nodding one way and another to people she knew, or thought she recognised. She was quite aware, several times, of smiling graciously at complete strangers whose looks wavered in confusion for a moment, then dutifully smiled back.

She made the deliberate decision to treat that as a joke. She refused to be self-conscious.

She found her way to the box Joshua had reserved for her. It was far easier not to come too late and thus disturb no one else, even if she might feel rather more lonely sitting there so obviously by herself. She spent the time watching others arrive. It was such a parade of character. At a glance she could see status, income, social aspiration, confidence or lack of it, taste, and so often what a woman thought of herself. There were those who were diffident, dressed in sombre colours, dark blues and greens, modest and well cut. She wondered if they would rather have been more daring, had they had the nerve. Was the sobriety their own choice, or from fear of displeasing their husbands – or even their mothers-in-law? How much did anyone dress to conform with what others expected?

And there were those in vivid colours, aching to be noticed. Was her own red like that, a dramatic gown to disguise an undramatic woman?

No. As Vespasia had said, she was free to choose to be whatever she wished. If she were undramatic, overshadowed by Cecily Antrim, then that was her own decision to retreat, to conceal her beliefs in order to please others and conform to what they expected of her. There was no need to be offensive, too forceful; there was never excuse to be intentionally or carelessly unkind. But she could be true to her own values.

And she liked the red dress. It became her colouring and lent a certain glow.

And of course there were those young girls in pale colours, looking innocent and virginal, self-conscious, but fully intending to be looked at.

Almost everyone she saw was acting, in their own way, as much as most of the players would be. It was only that the storyline was obscure. The onlooker saw only one scene.

The lights dimmed at last and there was a breathless expectation. The curtain rose on the battlements at Elsinore. Caroline found she was nervous for Orlando Antrim. This was by far the largest role he had ever played. But then Hamlet was surely the largest role anyone would play. Was it not every actor's dream?

From the moment he entered in the second scene, she sat forward a little, willing him to succeed, to remember all his lines, to pour into them the passion and the grief and the confusion the role demanded.

At the very first he seemed hesitant. Her heart sank. Would he, as always, be overshadowed by his mother who seemed to dominate every stage on which she stepped?

Then the others left, except Orlando. He stepped forward into the light. His face was pale, even haggard, although presumably it was from paint. But the gestures of his body no one else could have imposed upon him, nor the agony in his voice.

> 'O! that this too too solid flesh would melt,
> Thaw, and resolve itself into a dew; . . .
> Or that the Everlasting had not fix'd
> His canon 'gainst self-slaughter!'

He gave the whole speech without hesitation. It poured from him so naturally it sounded as if he must have been the first to say it, not as learned and rehearsed, not brilliant acting, but torn from a young man's soul.

'"But break, my heart, for I must hold my tongue."'

For a moment after the curtain descended there was silence. The stalls forgot they were an audience; they had seemed more like unseen, individual intruders in someone else's tragedy.

Then suddenly they remembered and the applause boomed like thunder roaring around the vast space, filling the high ceiling.

From then on there was an electricity in the air, a charge of emotion so high the entire performance was lifted. The tragedy unfolded itself relentlessly, the doomed relationships progressed from one step to the next as if no one had the power to prevent

347

them. Hamlet's pain seemed a palpable thing in the air, the king's duplicity, Polonius' wise counsel fell on deaf ears, but its words had become familiar down the ages, and Bellmaine's marvellous voice filled the heart and the mind. For those moments he dominated the stage. Even Hamlet was forgotten. "'This above all: to thine ownself be true/And it must follow as the night the day/Thou canst not then be false to any man.'"

Ophelia drifted helplessly into madness, and death, an innocent sacrifice to others' ambition, greed or obsession. Joshua tiptoed in and sat down silently, merely touching Caroline's shoulder. Queen Gertrude wrought her own fate, still blind to it to the very last sip of the poisoned cup.

In spite of the skill and the personality of every actor on the stage, Hamlet ultimately towered above them all. It was his pain, and in the end his light extinguished, which left them in darkness when the last curtain came down.

As Caroline rose to her feet to applaud, Joshua beside her, there were tears running down her cheeks and she was too full of emotion even to think of speaking.

When at last the applause had faded, the house lights were blazing again, and people began to gather themselves to leave, Caroline turned to Joshua.

There was a mixture of joy and sorrow in his face. The joy was by far the greater – the excitement and the admiration – but she saw the faint shadow also, and knew in her heart how he would love to have played Hamlet himself, to have had a gift that far transcended mere talent and soared to genius. But he knew that he had not that. His art lay in wit and compassion, in making people laugh, often at themselves, and feel a new gentleness towards one another. In years to come he might play Polonius, but he would never be Hamlet.

She tried to think what to say that was honest, and held no trace of condescension. That would be unbearable for him, just as it was for her.

The silence needed words and she could not find them.

'I feel as if I've never really seen *Hamlet* before,' she admitted. 'I would never have thought anyone so young could have such a comprehension of – of betrayal. His rage with the Queen was so raw . . . and so close to love as well. Disillusion can destroy you.' She thought of Grandmama, and Edmund Ellison. How does one go on when dreams are shattered so totally there is nothing left to rebuild? How does one continue living with things soiled beyond retrieval?

She longed to share that with Joshua. She knew, looking at his face now, that he would feel only tenderness for the old lady, no judgement, no revulsion.

But was it a breaking of trust to speak of it? The old lady would certainly know, because she would see it in his eyes, hear it in his voice. And she would be looking for it! She would be waiting for Caroline to betray her.

Then Caroline must keep silent. Maybe one day Grandmama would allow it, and then it would be all right.

'Are you going to speak to Cecily?' she said.

His face broke into a smile. 'Oh yes! I wouldn't miss it. She was good – but he was better! This is the first time she has been eclipsed by anyone, except perhaps Bellmaine – long ago when she was just beginning. She will be feeling . . .' he lifted one shoulder very slightly, 'a great mixture of pride in Orlando – surely one has to be proud of one's children.'

She remembered with a stab that he had no children, and he was far too young to regard any of her daughters in that light. He barely knew them. He might have had children, if he had married someone younger. She forced that thought away. This was no time for pity of any sort, least of all self-pity, or for doubt where he had given her cause for none.

'It's not always easy,' she replied frankly. 'You can envy them their youth, and be exasperated by it. And you agonise for their mistakes, especially when you can see them even at the time. And of course you never cease to feel guilt for everything they do that turns out badly. Every flaw of character is directly attributable to something you did, or failed to do, or did the wrong way, or at the wrong time.'

He put his arm around her. 'Come! We'll go and congratulate Cecily . . . and commiserate with her – or whatever seems best.' But he was smiling as he said it, and the faint lines had eased out from round his mouth.

The dressing room was already crowded when they arrived, but this time Orlando was not there. He was the centre now, not peripheral to his mother's star.

Cecily stood with her back to the dressing table and the looking-glass. She was still wearing the gorgeous gown of the last act. Her face was radiant, her fair hair spreading a halo around her. At first glance Caroline thought she was miscast as Hamlet's mother – she looked too young, too vibrant. Then she remembered with a jolt that Cecily was in life Orlando's mother, so she could not be wrong, except to the imagination.

Lord Warriner was not there this time. It was as if he had chosen deliberately to distance himself from the theatre for a while, or at least from Cecily. Two other minor players stood at the edge of the centre, looking tired and happy. A woman in a black gown and a magnificent diamond necklace was enthusing, and a middle-aged man with ribbons on his chest was agreeing with her.

Cecily saw Joshua almost immediately.

'Darling!' She came forward, arms wide to embrace him. 'I'm so glad you could be here. Did you catch the end?' She allowed him to kiss her on both cheeks before she stepped back and acknowledged Caroline. 'And Mrs Fielding . . . Caroline, isn't it? How generous of you to come as well.'

'Generosity had nothing to do with it,' Caroline replied with a smile she hoped was warmer than she felt. 'I came because I wished to see . . . for myself . . . from the beginning. And I am delighted I did. It is by far the best Hamlet I have ever seen.'

Cecily's eyes widened. She hesitated only a moment. 'Really? And have you seen so many?'

Caroline kept her smile sparklingly in place. 'Certainly. From the schoolroom onward. Almost every actor who is remotely suitable has played him at one time or another, and some who are not. I dare say I have seen twenty or more. Your son brought a new life and truth to the role. You must be very proud of him.'

'Of course. How kind of you to say so.' Cecily turned back to Joshua. 'He was rather marvellous, wasn't he? It is the strangest sensation to see your own child begin his first stumbling performance, then progress to minor parts on stage, and ultimately have the whole theatre at his feet.' She gave a slight laugh. 'Can you imagine how I feel?'

Caroline saw the shadow in Joshua's face, only for an instant. A week ago she might have felt crushed by it for her own inability to give Joshua children. Tonight she felt only anger that Cecily should have chosen to focus attention on herself by hurting him this way.

Before Joshua could reply she stepped in.

'It is always surprising to find one's children have grown

up,' she said sweetly. 'And that quite suddenly they can outshine you in the very area you thought yourself always superior . . .'

Cecily's face froze.

'. . . but of course you are thrilled for them,' Caroline continued blithely. 'How could one not be? Apart from the role of Lady Macbeth, all Shakespeare's tragedies seemed to be based around men as the protagonists. But I am sure you could be unsurpassable by anyone in some of the great roles in classical Greek drama. I for one would queue all night for a ticket to see you play Clytemnestra, or Medea.'

There was total silence in the room. Everyone was staring at Caroline.

No one had heard the door open and Orlando come in.

'Clytemnestra!' he said distinctly. 'What a brilliant idea! How extraordinarily clever of you, Mrs Fielding. Mama has never done the Greeks. That would be a whole new career, and superb! And there is also Phaedra!' He turned to Cecily. 'You are too old for Antigone, but you could always do Jocasta . . . but Mrs Fielding is right, Clytemnestra would be the sublime vehicle for you. Who would want Gertrude after that?'

Cecily looked at Caroline, her head high, her eyes bright.

'Perhaps I should be obliged to you, Mrs Fielding. I admit, I am surprised. I should never have thought of you as being so . . . liberal in your views of art. You must tell me, why do you think I might do Clytemnestra well?' She laughed. 'I hope it is not merely because she has adult children?'

Caroline looked back at her with just as much bright candour.

'Of course not although that does make a difference to one's life. But I was thinking of the fact that she is central to the play, not secondary. She is the character whose passions drive the plot. And she has been profoundly wronged in the sacrifice of her daughter. Her murder of her husband is not a sympathetic action, yet it is one most mothers could identify with. It needs an actress of extraordinary power to carry the audience with her and neither play to their pity and lose her own dignity, nor yet become unattractive because of her power and her willingness to take the ultimate step.' She took a deep breath. No one had interrupted her by so much as a movement.

She plunged on. 'It should leave one emotionally wrung out, and yet deepened in experience, and perhaps with more compassion and understanding than before.' Unwittingly the old lady came to her thoughts again. Horror for endless pain could change one's own life immeasurably, cast so much in a different view.

For the first time Cecily looked at her directly and without any mask of emotion. 'You are most surprising,' she said at length. 'I could have sworn you had not a revolutionary idea in your head, much less your heart. And here you are recommending that we stir up the complacent society out there by making them feel Clytemnestra's passions!' She smiled. 'You will provoke letters to *The Times*, and thunder from the Archbishop, not to mention disfavour from the Queen, if you suggest that to murder your husband can ever be acceptable!' The edge of mockery was back in her voice again.

She swivelled around. 'Joshua darling, you had better be careful how you treat your wife's daughters!' She gestured to Caroline. 'You do have daughters, don't you? Yes, of course you do – One of them is married to that policeman with all the hair! I remember him. For heaven's sake, darling, don't sacrifice them to the gods, or you may end your life abruptly, with a knife in your heart. There sleeps a tiger inside that calm and dignified-looking wife of yours.'

'Yes, I know,' Joshua said distinctly smugly. He placed his hand very lightly on Caroline's arm just for a second, but it was a gesture of possession, and Caroline felt the warmth ripple through her. The door opened and Bellmaine came in, still dressed in his Polonius robes, the smudges of greasepaint on his face lending him greater gravity rather than detracting from it.

'Wonderful!' he said radiantly. He spoke to all of them, but it was Orlando his eyes rested on. 'Wonderful, my dears. You surpassed yourselves. Cecily, you had Gertrude to perfection! I had never seen her in such a sympathetic light before. You made me believe in her unawareness of what she had done – until it was too late – a woman caught in the mesh of her own passions. I wept for her.'

'Thank you,' she accepted graciously, smiling at him, but there was a curious brittleness in her stare. 'If I can move you to tears for Gertrude, I feel as if I can do anything.'

Bellmaine turned to Orlando. His expression softened to one of pure joy. 'And you, my dear boy, were sublime. I hardly know what to say. I feel as if I have never really seen Hamlet before tonight. You have taken me along a new path, shown me a madness and a sense of betrayal that transcend the magic of Shakespeare's words and take me into a reality of feeling that has left me exhausted. I am a different man.' He spread his hands as if he could say no more.

Caroline knew exactly what he meant. She too had been shown a new and wider experience. She found herself nodding her agreement. It was born of honesty; she could do no less.

Cecily turned to her, an edge to her voice. 'So you are happy to be harrowed up in such a way, Mrs Fielding? I thought from your previous visit that you were in favour of at least some censorship. Excluding the irresponsibility of shouting "Fire!" where there is none, and causing a panic, or of advocating crime or falsely speaking of someone else, would you agree that the limiting of ideas is an unmitigated evil? Art must be free, if man is to be free. Not to grow is the beginning of death, albeit slow death, perhaps taking a generation or more.' She looked very directly at Caroline. It was a challenge no one in the crowded room mistook. Perhaps it was made because of Orlando's success, a need to assert herself. One did not give up centre stage easily.

Everyone was waiting for Caroline.

She glanced at Joshua. He was smiling. He would not step in and take away her chance to answer. She must speak honestly. She hoped he would not be disappointed in her, or embarrassed, but to say other than what she believed would lay a foundation for misery later. She thought of her daughters, of Jemima, of the old lady sitting hunched up in bed at home.

'Of course not to grow is death.' She felt for the right words. 'But we grow at different speeds, and sometimes in different ways. Don't try to make the argument in general as justification for doing it your way in particular.'

'Oh! You have been preparing this!' Cecily said quickly. 'You will give me a game for my money after all! So what are you going to censor . . . in general, and in particular? You have already said you will allow husband murder in Clytemnestra, a child murder in Medea, and a man to marry his mother and beget children upon her in Oedipus. Great heavens, my dear, what can it be you disapprove of?'

Caroline felt her face flush hot.

'These are all tragedies, and depicted as such. One feels a terrible pity for the protagonist, an insight into how such things could have come about, and perhaps an admiration for the courage or the honesty with which in the end they meet their fate – good or bad.'

'So it is all right, so long as the values are kept?' Cecily said with wide eyes.

Caroline saw the trap. 'Whose values?' she asked. 'Is that not what you are going to say?'

Cecily relaxed in a smile. 'Exactly. If you are going to answer me that it is Society, Civilisation, or even God, then I will ask you whose God? Which part of Society? Mine? Yours? The beggar's in the street? The old Queen, God bless her? Or Mr Wilde . . . whose society is certainly different from most people's!'

'That is your own judgement,' Caroline replied. 'But the values we adopt will be the ones the next generation will live by. I am not sure if anyone can decide for you. But no one can relieve you of the responsibility of what you say, in whatever form. And the better you are at it, the more beautiful or powerful your voice, the greater the burden upon you to use it with wisdom and a great deal of care.'

'Oh my God!' Cecily said a trifle too loudly.

'Bravo!' Orlando gave a little salute of praise.

Caroline turned to look at him. His face startled her, it was so full of emotion – his eyes wide, his lips slightly parted, a kind of rigidity in his body.

Joshua was staring at her.

Bellmaine stood motionless but his face was filled with amazement and a kind of painful relief it was impossible to interpret. Caroline was startled to see his eyes filled with tears.

'The greatest power sometimes lies in not doing a thing,' she finished, her voice suddenly dropped, but she would not leave it unsaid. 'It is so easy to use a skill, simply because you have it, and not look two, three steps ahead to see what it will cause. People listen to you, Miss Antrim. You can move our emotions and make us reconsider all kinds of beliefs. That is very clever. It is not always wise.'

Cecily drew in her breath to say something in rebuttal, then looked at Joshua's face, and changed her mind. She turned to Caroline with a dazzling smile.

'I apologise for having thought too little of you.' She said it with utmost sincerity. There was no doubting that she meant it. 'I think I should have listened to you rather better. I promise I shall in future.' She turned to the others now filling the room. 'Now, shall we send for the champagne and toast Orlando? He has deserved all the praise we can give, and all the rejoicing. Tomorrow the world will be congratulating him. Let us be the first, and do it tonight!'

Bellmaine agreed fervently. He raised his hand. 'Orlando!'

'Hear, hear! Orlando!' everyone responded eagerly. Only Orlando himself seemed still bemused. Caroline looked across at him and wondered how exhausted he was. His young face was pale and his eyes still held the look of Hamlet's haunted madness. It was not a role one could assume so wholly, live its passions and be destroyed by them, and then cast it off as if it had been a garment and not a skin.

She would like to have comforted him, but she had no idea how. This was his world, not hers. Perhaps all great actors felt like this? Could one give such a performance merely on technique and skill, rather than by also pouring oneself into it until it became, for a time, one's own reality?

She looked to Joshua, but he was speaking to one of the other actors and she could not interrupt.

357

There was a knock on the door, and someone came in with champagne and a tray of glasses.

On the way home through the quiet streets, sitting beside Joshua in the hansom, Caroline was tired, but there was a degree of peace inside her that she had not felt in a long time. She realised now, with surprise, how long it had been. She had spent far too much time looking in the mirror and seeing what she disliked, being frightened of it, and projecting on to Joshua emotions born of that fear.

He had been very patient enduring her self-centredness. Or perhaps he had not noticed? That was a far uglier thought. Could she hurt so much, and he be oblivious to it?

Of course! Why not? She had been oblivious to his feelings. Had she for an instant wondered how hard it was for him to be the newcomer in her family, to see her children and grandchildren and know he could never have his own? They might learn to love him, but that was not the same. There was an essence of belonging that . . . that what? Grandmama belonged, and she had lived all her adult life imprisoned in an icy hell of loneliness beyond anything Caroline could imagine. She had glimpsed its horror, but she had no concept of what it would do to her over time. Time was a dimension one could not create in the mind. It was change, exhaustion, the slow dying of hope.

She understood so much more of why the old lady had become the person she was. What had made Edmund Ellison seek his pleasures in cruelty? What devils had crawled into his soul and warped it out of human shape?

She would never know. It was buried with him, and best let go now, let it drift into the darkness of the past and become covered over with other memories.

'He was brilliant, wasn't he?' Joshua's voice came softly out of the shadows beside her. Through the weight of her cloak and his coat she could feel his stiff body.

'Oh yes,' she agreed honestly. 'But I wonder if it will make him happy.'

He was silent for several minutes before finally asking her. 'What do you mean?'

She must word this exactly as she meant it, no carelessness, no fumbling for the right way and missing it.

'He conveyed a dreadful understanding of Hamlet's pain,' she began. 'As if he had looked at a kind of madness and seen its face. I am not sure if I believe one can portray that simply from imagination. Turn one horror into the image of another, probably, but not call it up without a kind of experience, some taste of its reality. It was still there in him long after the curtain had fallen.'

They were moving faster through the darkness, only occasional lights from other vehicles moving past and disappearing.

'Do you think so?' There was no denial in his voice.

She moved closer to him, so slightly only she was aware of it.

'What my mother-in-law told me made me see many things I had not understood before. One of them is the kind of damage that cruelty can inflict, especially when it is held secret where it cannot heal. To be clever is a great gift, and certainly the world needs its clever people, but to be kind is what matters. To be clever, or gifted, will make people laugh, and think, and perhaps grow in certain ways; but to be generous of spirit is what will bring happiness. I would not wish anyone I loved to be a success as an artist, if it meant that they were a failure as a human being.'

He reached out his hand and slid it over hers, gently, then tightened it.

The hansom swayed round the street corner and straightened again.

He turned in his seat and leaned forward. Very gently he kissed her lips. She felt his breath warm on her cheek, and put up her gloved hand to touch his hair.

He kissed her again. and she clung tighter to him.

Chapter Thirteen

❧

Pitt received Caroline's letter with the address of what turned out to be a second seller of photographs and postcards, also in Half Moon Street, and with a deep anger inside him, he went with Tellman to see the man.

'No!' the man protested indignantly, standing behind his counter and staring at the two policemen who had intruded into his place of business and were already costing him good custom. 'No I don't sell no pictures except proper, decent ones as yer could show to a lady!'

'I don't believe you,' Pitt said tersely. 'But it will be easy enough to find out. I shall post a constable here at the door and he can examine every one you sell. And if they are as good as you say, then in four or six weeks we'll know that.'

The man's face went white, his eyes small and glittering.

'And then I'll apologise to you,' Pitt finished.

The man swore venomously, but under his breath so the words were barely audible.

'Now,' Pitt said briskly, 'if you will take another look at this picture you can tell me when you got it in, how many copies you have sold and to whom, Mr . . . ?'

'Hadfield. An' I can't remember 'oo I sold 'em ter!' His

361

voice rose to a squeal of indignation.

'Yes you can,' Pitt insisted. 'Pictures like that are only sold to people you know. Regular customers. But of course if you can't remember who likes this sort of thing, then you'll just have to give me a list of all of them, and I'll go and question them.'

'All right! All right!' Hadfield's eyes burned with fury. 'Yer're a vicious man, Inspector.'

'Superintendent,' Pitt corrected him. 'It was a vicious murder. I want the names of all your customers who like this sort of picture. And if you leave any out, I shall presume you are doing it to protect them, because you know them to be involved. Do you understand me?'

'O' course I understand yer! D'yer take me fer a bleedin' fool?'

'If I take you at all, Mr Hadfield, it will be for accessory to murder,' Pitt replied. 'While you are making me a list, I shall look through the rest of your stock to see if there is anything else that might tell me who killed Cathcart, and who knew about it . . . possibly even why.'

The man flung his arms out angrily. 'Well, there y' are! Seein' as I can't stop yer. An Englishman's 'ome not bein' 'is castle, like, any more, yer'd best 'elp yerself. Cheap way o' gettin' yer 'ands on pictures, an' lookin' at 'em for nothin', if yer ask me!'

Pitt ignored him and began to go through the drawers and shelves of pictures, postcards and slim volumes of drawings. Tellman started at the other end.

Many of them were fairly ordinary, the sort of poses he had seen a hundred times before in the last week, pretty girls and a variety of flattering clothes.

He glanced at Tellman and saw the concentration in his face, and now and again a slight smile. Those were the sort of girls he would like. He might well be too shy to approach them, but he would admire them from a distance, think them attractive and decent enough.

He bent back to the task, and pulled out a new drawer with small books in it. He opened the first one, more out of curiosity than the belief that it would be relevant to Cathcart's death. They were drawings in black and white. There was a kind of lush, imaginative beauty about them, and the draughtsmanship was superb. They were also obscene, figures with leering faces, and both male and female organs exposed.

He closed it again quickly. Had they been more crudely drawn, they would have been less powerful, and less disturbing. He had heard that nature could become so distorted as to do this to people, but this was not the representation of the tragedy of deformity, it was a salacious artistic comment on appetite, and he felt soiled by it. He understood why men like Marchand crusaded so passionately against pornography, not for the offence to themselves, but the strange erotic disturbance to others as well, the degrading of all emotional value. In some way it robbed all people of a certain dignity because it touched upon humanity itself.

He did not bother to open the other books of drawings. Cathcart dealt only in photographs. He moved to the next drawer of cards.

Tellman grunted and slammed a drawer shut.

Pitt looked up and saw the distress in his face. His eyes were narrowed and his lips drawn back a little as if he felt an inward pain. In spite of his experience, this confused him. He expected something higher of artists. Like many of little learning, he admired education. He believed it lifted men above the lowest in them and offered a path out of the trap of ignorance and all the ugliness that went with it. This was a disillusionment he did not expect or understand.

There was nothing for Pitt to say. It was a private distress, at least for the moment better not put into words. In fact Tellman would find it easier to deal with if he did not even realise Pitt was aware of it.

The next drawer of photographs was much the same as the last, pleasant, a few rather risqué, but nothing more than the art of young men seeing how far they dare go in putting their fantasies into expression. Some were the usual rectangular professional plates – slick, showing the same, rather repetitive use of light and shade, angle or exposure.

There were also several of the round pictures which held considerably more individuality, although they were also less skilled than the professional pictures. Sometimes the form was not as sharp, the balance less well disposed. These were amateur, taken by the like of the Camera Club members Pitt had interviewed.

One or two of them were good, if a trifle theatrical. He recognised poses that seemed to be taken directly from the stage. There was a fairly obvious Ophelia, not like Cecily Antrim but alive and disturbingly frantic, on the borders of madness. And yet it was a fascinating picture. The girl looked no more than twenty at the most, with dark hair and wide eyes. Her lips were parted and faintly erotic.

A couple more were rather Arthurian, reminding Pitt of the Pre-Raphaelite painters – definitely romantic. Something in the background of one of them caught his attention, a use of lighting rather than a specific article. In the centre was a young girl kneeling in vigil. On the altar were a chalice and a knight's sword. It made him think of Joan of Arc.

In another a woman in despair leaped to her feet as if fleeing from a mirror, presumably intended as the Lady of Shalott.

A third came from the classical Greek theatre, a young girl about to be sacrificed. The same length of carved wood was used in all three, very cleverly. It gave them a richness of texture as the light and shade accentuated the repeated pattern.

Pitt had seen it before but it took him a moment or two to remember where. Then it came to him. He had passed by it as he had gone from Cecily Antrim's dressing room to the back door.

'Where did you buy these pictures?' he asked.

Hadfield did not even look up from the list he was writing. 'What's the matter now?' he said wearily. 'What crime are you trying to tie them up with?'

'Where did you get them?' Pitt repeated. 'Who brought them to you?'

Hadfield put down his pen, splattering ink over the page, and swore. He came over to Pitt irritably and stared over his shoulder at the photographs.

'I dunno. Some young photographer who thinks he can make a few bob. Why?' His voice was laden with sarcasm. 'What terrible offence ter 'umanity and civilisation can yer see in these? Got a dirty mind, you 'ave. Looks as innocent as a cup o' tea ter me.'

'Who brought them to you?' Pitt repeated, a steel edge of anger to his voice, although it was misery he was feeling inside. He did not want the answer he was almost certain would come.

'I dunno! Do you think I ask the name and address of every young amateur who comes here with an 'andful o' pictures?

365

They're good pictures. Nothin' wrong wif 'em. I bought 'em. Fair sale. Nothin' more ter say.'

'Describe him!'

'Describe 'im! Yer crazy, or summink?' He was thoroughly aggrieved. ''E was a young man wot fancies 'isself as a photographer, an' 'e in't bad.'

'Tall or short? Dark or fair? Describe him!' Pitt said between closed teeth.

'Tall! Fair! But there's nothin' wrong wif 'em! You can find pictures like this all over London . . . all over England! Wot's the matter wif yer?'

'Did he see your other pictures? Like the one of Ophelia chained up in the boat?'

The man hesitated. In that instant Pitt knew that it was Orlando who had brought the photographs, and seen Cathcart's picture of his mother. Until then he had been clinging on to the hope that it had been Bellmaine, or even by some obscure chance, Rafe Marchand, pursuing his crusade against pornography.

'Sergeant Tellman!' Pitt turned sideways, his voice sharp.

Tellman stood up, letting the postcards fall on to the floor. 'Yes sir?'

'Go and find the nearest constable to stand guard here. I think we should continue this discussion at Bow Street.'

'All right!' Hadfield snapped. ''E could 'ave! I dunno!'

'What was his name?'

'I'll 'ave ter look at me records.'

'Then do it!'

Muttering under his breath Hadfield went back to his desk and it was several silent, painful minutes before he returned, waving a piece of paper. There was no name on it, simply the amount of money, a brief description of the photograph, and the date – two days before Cathcart's death.

'Thank you,' Pitt said quietly.

Hadfield's face conveyed the words he did not dare to say.

Pitt wrote him a receipt in exchange for the photographs he was sure were bought by Orlando Antrim; also the sales receipt with its date.

Outside the air seemed cold.

Tellman looked at him questioningly.

'Orlando Antrim,' Pitt answered. 'He was here two days before Cathcart's death. If he saw that picture of his mother, and perhaps some of the others, how do you suppose he felt?'

Tellman's face was pinched with misery, and there was an emotional conflict in him that was painfully apparent. 'I don't know,' he said, stumbling a little as he stepped off the pavement on to the road to cross. 'I don't know.'

Pitt tried to imagine himself in Orlando's place. Cecily was an actress. It was her profession to portray emotion in public and behave in such a way as to stir any of a score of passions. He must be used to it. But could anything make this acceptable to him?

Pitt could see the grotesque picture of Ophelia in his mind's eye so clearly there was no need to pull it out of his pocket to remind himself. It was a woman bound by literal, physical chains, but appearing to be in a paroxysm of sexual ecstasy, as if the bondage she experienced excited her as no freedom could. It suggested that she hungered to be overpowered, forced into submission. It was lust that lit her face as she lay there, knees apart, skirts raised. There was nothing of tenderness in it, certainly nothing that could be thought of as love.

If Pitt had seen his own mother like that, for any reason at all, it would have revolted him beyond measure. Even now, striding along the footpath at an increasing speed, he could not allow his mind to touch such an idea. It polluted the very wellspring of his life. His mother was not that kind of woman. His intelligence told him she had loved his father. He had heard them laughing together often enough, long ago, and seen them kiss, seen the way they looked at each other. He knew the nature and the acts of love.

But that picture had nothing to do with love, nor the things men and women do in private, in generosity, hunger and intimacy. It was a mockery of them all.

Of course the world was full of people whose ideas were different, whose acts he would have found offensive if he had considered them. But within one's own family it was different.

Had he seen Charlotte portrayed that way . . . he felt the blood rise in his face and his muscles lock, his fists clench. If any man were ever to speak coarsely to her he would be tempted to violence. If anyone actually touched her he would probably strike them, and consider the consequences afterwards.

For anyone to think of Jemima in that way, and then use her so, would break his heart.

Cecily Antrim had such profound understanding of so many different kinds and conditions of people, how could she fail to grasp the distress any man must feel to see his own mother in such a way? Had she no conception of the grief and the confusion that had to follow?

He thought of Orlando. If he had seen that picture, or any of them, he would have walked away from the shop like a blind man, the world of footpath and stones and sky, soot in the air, clatter of people, smell of smoke and drains and horses would make no mark on him at all. He would be consumed by the inner pain, and perhaps hatred.

And above all he would be asking the same questions as Pitt was – *why*? Was any cause worth fighting in such a way? Pitt could ask it, and still be hurt by the disillusion over a woman whose glorious talent he had admired, who had made him think, and above all, care about her on the stage. How infinitely more must Orlando have felt?

Pitt had been convinced from the beginning that Cathcart's death was a crime of passion, not simply escape, even from the life-draining clutches of blackmail. That would induce hatred, and fear; but there was more than either of those in the way Cathcart had been laid in the mockery of the Millais painting, the exact replica, a soul-deep injury that could not be undone.

'D'you think he knew who took that picture?' Tellman's voice cut across Pitt's thoughts, harsh yet so quiet he barely heard it.

'No,' Pitt replied, as they both stopped at the next kerb while a heavy wagon rolled past, horses leaning forward into the harness, the wheels rumbling over the cobbles. 'No. He saw it two days before Cathcart's death. I think it took him that long to find out.' He started forward across the street. He did not even know where he was going, at the moment he simply needed to put in a physical effort because he could not bear to keep still.

'How could he do that?' Tellman asked, running a couple of steps to keep up. 'Where would he begin? He can't have asked her. In fact if I were in his place I couldn't even have spoken to her!'

'He's an actor,' Pitt replied. 'I presume he is better at masking his feelings than either of us.' He walked a few yards in silence. 'He would know it was a professional photograph ... the square

369

exposures. Professionals don't use the round ones. No good except in daylight. And he'd hardly have the film manufacturer develop them, which is what the amateurs do.'

Tellman grunted with profound disgust. His emotions were too raw to find words. He walked with his shoulders tight and hunched, his head forward.

'He'd have started to consider the different professionals it might be,' Pitt continued with his thoughts. 'He'd do it very discreetly. He would have been thinking of murder already . . . or at the very least a confrontation. Where would he begin?'

'Well, if he's trying to keep it secret, he'll hardly ask anyone,' Tellman retorted. 'Not that you would ask anyone about pictures like that, anyway!'

'He'd narrow it down to professional photographers who use that kind of scenery,' Pitt answered his own question. 'He'd study them for style. He takes photographs himself. He knows how an artist puts things one way, then another, trying to get exactly the right effect. It's like a signature.'

'So how would he see the style of Cathcart's photographs?' Tellman turned to look at him. 'There must be dozens! How would he even know where to look?'

'Well he did!' Pitt pointed out. 'He found him in less than two days, so whatever he did was effective.'

'Or lucky!'

Pitt shot him a sideways glance.

Tellman shrugged.

'Exhibition,' Pitt said abruptly. 'He'd look to see if there was an exhibition of photography anywhere. Wherever he could see the largest collection of different people's work.'

Tellman quickened his pace a trifle. 'I'll find out! Give me half an hour and I'll know where there are any.'

Nearly two hours later Pitt and Tellman stood side by side in a large gallery in Kensington, staring at photograph after photograph of lovely scenery, handsome women, magnificently dressed men, animals and children with wide, limpid eyes. Some of the pictures were hauntingly beautiful, a world reduced to sepia tints, moments of life caught for ever, a gesture, a smile.

Pitt stopped in front of one. Ragged children huddled together on a doorstep in some alley, dresses with holes in, trousers held up by string, no shoes. And yet the childish curve of their cheeks held a timeless innocence.

In others sunlight slanted across a ploughed field, bare trees filigree against the sky. A flight of birds scattered in the wind, like leaves thrown up.

He was looking for style, use of water, someone who saw symbolism in ordinary objects. Of course Pitt knew he was looking for Delbert Cathcart. Orlando had had no idea of who he was trying to find, or why the man would have used his mother. Had he believed it was blackmail, some kind of force or coercion that had made her do this? He would have to believe that. Anything else was unbearable.

He looked at Tellman, who was standing a few yards away, unaware that he was blocking the view of a large woman in lavender and black, and her dutiful daughter who was quite obviously bored silly, and longing to be almost anywhere else. Tellman was staring at a photograph of a young girl, a housemaid, caught momentarily distracted from beating a rug slung over a line in the areaway. She was small and slight with a humorous face. Pitt knew she reminded him of Gracie, and he was startled that anyone should think of her as a subject for art. He was proud that ordinary people were considered important enough to be immortalised, and it confused him because it was unexpected, and made him self-conscious. They represented his own life caught and displayed for its interest, its uniqueness.

He stopped sharply and turned away, only just missing bumping into the large lady. He muttered an apology and rejoined Pitt. 'This isn't getting us anywhere,' he said quietly. 'Can't learn a thing from this lot.'

Pitt forbore from making any comment.

The next room was more useful, and in the one after they saw some pictures which Pitt knew immediately were Cathcart's. The light and shade, the accentuation of focus, were all similar to the work he had seen both in Cathcart's own house, and in those of his clients. There were even two with the river for background.

'That's his,' Tellman said bluntly. 'But how would Antrim know that? It doesn't prove anything, except that Cathcart's work is exhibited. You'd expect it to be.'

'We've got to prove the link,' Pitt said unnecessarily. 'Antrim found out who he was. This is probably how.'

Tellman said nothing.

Pitt looked carefully at the other pictures until he had found several more showing water, two with small boats, one with a garden and half a dozen using artificial flowers, and one with a long velvet gown.

'Who took these?' Tellman asked.

'According to the card there, Geoffrey Lyneham.'

'Wonder if Antrim went to see him?' Tellman thought aloud. 'Or if he went to Cathcart first? If he did it will be harder to prove, seeing Cathcart can't tell us anything, and Mrs Geddes doesn't know, or she'd have said so.'

'He went to Lyneham first,' Pitt assumed. 'And probably

somewhere else as well. It took him two days to find Cathcart. I don't think he waited any longer than he had to.'

'I wouldn't!' Tellman said with narrowed lips. 'Where do we find this Lyneham?'

It was late afternoon and already growing dusk, the gaslamps coming on in the streets and the air crisp and cold when they went up the stairs of Geoffrey Lyneham's house in Greenwich. Wood smoke drifted on the damp air from a bonfire in someone's garden nearby, and the smell of earth and leaves was sweet.

Lyncham was a small man with a sharp, intelligent face. He was at least fifty, probably more, his hair white at the temples. He was startled when Pitt told him who they were.

'Police? Why? As far as I know I haven't infringed any laws.'

Pitt forced himself to smile. None of the horror was Lyneham's fault, and he would very much sooner discuss the matter in the warmth of Mr Lyneham's sitting room by the fire than out here on the step.

'It is a matter of importance, sir,' he replied. 'About photography.'

'Ah!' Lyneham's face lit with instant enthusiasm. He pulled the door wide and stood back. 'Come in, gentlemen, come in! Anything I can tell you, I should be delighted. What is it you would like to know?' He led the way inside, to the sitting room, still waving his hands energetically, leaving Tellman to close the front door and follow behind.

'I saw several of your photographs in the Kensington exhibition,' Pitt began courteously.

'Oh yes . . . yes?' Lyneham nodded, waiting for the inevitable comments.

'Excellent use of light on water,' Pitt said.

Lyneham looked startled. 'You like that? I find it most interesting to work with. Gives the whole thing an extra dimension, don't you think?'

'Yes . . .'

'Funny you should say that,' Lyneham went on, standing with his back to the fire. 'Young fellow here a couple of weeks ago, said almost exactly the same.'

Pitt felt his stomach tighten. He tried to keep his face blank.

'Really? Who was it? Maybe someone I know.'

'Said his name was Harris.'

'Tall, fair young man, about twenty-five?' Pitt asked. 'Very dark blue eyes?'

'Yes, that's right! You do know him!' Lyneham said eagerly. 'Most interested he was. Keen photographer himself. Very good eye, judging by his remarks. Amateur of course.' He waved a deprecating hand. 'But very keen. Wished to know what localities I thought best, and that kind of thing. Asked about the use of boats. Bit tricky, actually. They tend to move about. Any wind and you're sunk, so to speak. Essence of good photography, light, focus, and position!'

'Yes, I see. And what localities did you recommend? Or is it a secret of your profession?'

'Oh no, not at all! Norfolk broads, myself. Lovely light in East Anglia. Don't have so many painters there for no reason, you know?'

'Always the Broads?' Pitt asked, although he was certain he had the answer.

'Personally, yes,' Lyneham replied. 'Got a house up there. Makes it easy, convenient for taking advantage of the weather. Moment's notice, and there you are. Damned nuisance if you have to go a distance from home and trust to chance. Can get rained on just as you arrive. Carting tripods and things around, very heavy . . . awkward. Much better to have it right there to hand. I've got some lovely shots of swans. Beautiful creatures. Light on white wings.'

'I can imagine,' Pitt agreed. 'Never on the Thames?'

Lyneham pushed out his lip and shook his head. 'No, not personally. Some people have – very well too. Fellow called John Lawless, does some excellent work. Specialises in pictures of children and the poor. People washing, people playing, pleasure boats and so on.' His face darkened. 'And of course poor Cathcart. He actually had a house on the river. Opportunity right there!' He frowned. 'Why do you want to know, sir? Has this to do with Cathcart's death?'

'Yes, I am afraid it has,' Pitt admitted. He produced a theatre bill with Orlando's picture on it, and showed it to Lyneham.

Lyneham looked at it only a moment, then up again at Pitt. 'Yes,' he said quietly. 'That is the young man. I hope he is not seriously involved. He was such a . . . a decent-seeming fellow.'

'What was his mood? Please think carefully.'

'Upset. Very upset,' Lyneham said unhesitatingly. 'Oh, he hid it well, but there was obviously something that troubled him. Didn't say what, of course. But I really can't imagine anyone killing another man over photography – even passionate about it as some of us are. He just wanted to know about styles, that kind of thing . . . nothing else. And he never mentioned Cathcart.'

'I'm sure he didn't. I don't believe at that point he even knew his name. Where did you direct him, Mr Lyneham?'

Lyneham looked at him very steadily, his eyes troubled, his mouth pinched a little.

'To the exhibition in Warwick Square,' he replied. 'Prints, but very good. I thought there he would get the chance to see some of the best uses of water, light and so on. Did I . . . contribute to the . . . crime, sir? I regret that profoundly.'

'No,' Pitt assured him. 'If he had not learned from you, then he would have from someone else. Don't chastise yourself for ordinary civility.'

'Oh dear.' Lyneham shook his head. 'Oh dear. He seemed such an agreeable young man. I'm so sorry!'

Pitt and Tellman arrived at the exhibition in Warwick Square just before it closed for the night. It took them only twenty minutes to walk around the half-dozen rooms used and see the array of photographs. Those which mattered were the pictures of women, stretches of water and the use of symbols and romanticism.

'That's like whatshisname's paintings, isn't it?' Tellman said presently, nodding towards one photograph of a girl sitting in a rowing boat, her long hair loose about her shoulders, flowers drifting in the water.

'Millais,' Pitt supplied. 'Yes it is.'

'Except she's alive, and sitting up,' Tellman added.

'Same flavour,' Pitt walked away. It would not be difficult for Orlando Antrim to have found Cathcart's name here. It was written out on a neat placard under half a dozen of the photographs, with his address underneath it, in case anyone should wish to purchase his professional skills. All the pictures were powerful, characteristic, and one of them even used the same velvet gown, but untorn, and on a slender girl with long, dark hair.

Pitt tried to imagine how Orlando had felt when he knew at

376

last not only who had taken the photograph, but exactly where he lived. Seeing that same dress he can have had no doubts left. What would he do then?

'It's it, isn't it.' Tellman made it a statement, not a question. 'Poor devil.' His voice was thick with pity.

'Yes,' Pitt agreed quietly.

'Do we need to ask if anyone saw him?'

Pitt pushed his hands deep into his pockets. 'Yes.'

There was a guard on duty, to make sure no one damaged any of the exhibits, and perhaps that they did not steal them. He remembered Orlando Antrim, although of course he did not know his name. It was sufficient.

Outside in the cold, walking to find a hansom and go home for the night, Pitt tried to put himself in Orlando's place. What would he do? His mind would be in turmoil, the wound would hurt intolerably, the sense of betrayal. He might not blame Cecily. He would still be fighting to excuse her. She must have been frightened or coerced into such a thing. It could not be her fault. It had to be Cathcart's.

He knew where to find him. Now he would have to resolve in his mind what he meant to do about it. He intended to harm him, perhaps already to kill him. He would be careful.

He would find out all he could about Cathcart – but discreetly now. He might even have searched for what was more or less public knowledge from newspaper advertisements for photographic skills. He might even have made an appointment to be certain of finding Cathcart at home. If he had, he had destroyed the record of it.

'Tomorrow we'll have to find if he asked anyone local about Cathcart, and his habits,' Pitt said aloud.

'And where he got the weapon,' Tellman added. 'Someone

may have seen him. I suppose it's just a matter of being thorough.'

'Yes . . . I suppose it is.' There was no pleasure in it, no satisfaction in the solution, only a sense of tragedy.

Tellman did not bother to reply.

Pitt spent a restless and unhappy night. The house seemed cold without Charlotte and the children, even though he had kept the kitchen stove alight. It was a sense of darkness, and he expected no more letters from her because in a couple of days she would be home, the weather across the Channel permitting. He had not actually put words to it in his mind until now, but he would be glad when she was safely on land again in England. And Gracie would be back with the children two days after that. The house would be bright and warm again, full of the sound of voices and footsteps, laughter, chattering, the smells of wax polish, baking, clean laundry.

In the meantime he had to follow the steps of Orlando Antrim and find the proof of exactly how he had murdered Cathcart, and then when he had it, go and arrest him. There was an anger against Cecily Antrim inside him like a stone, heavy and hard. Her arrogant certainty that she knew best how to pursue her cause, without thought for the consequences, had destroyed her son. He was angry with her for what she had done, and because she also woke in him a terrible pity. Could he ever, unthinkingly, pursuing what he believed to be justice, or truth, do the same to his own children? His emotions were as strong, perhaps their consequences as profound.

He met Tellman in Battersea at the far end of the bridge, just after nine o'clock. Tellman was there before him, a forlorn figure standing in the early morning river mist, his coat collar turned up, his hat pulled forward and down over his eyes. Pitt wondered if he had had any breakfast.

'I've been thinking,' Tellman said as he heard Pitt's footsteps and looked up. 'He didn't need to ask about where he lived, he knew that already. And he wouldn't want to be too open in trying to find out about the household.'

'Household?' Pitt asked.

'Yes!' Tellman was impatient, shivering a little. 'You don't go attacking someone if you think there's a resident manservant that'll come to his rescue, or even a maid who'll remember you, maybe scream the place down! First thing, he'd go and see if there are near neighbours, and how he's going to get there, and away again.'

'Yes, you're right,' Pitt agreed quickly, increasing his pace. He was wondering if Orlando had intended to use the dress and the chains right from the beginning, or if it had been an inspiration only when he realised they were still there, but he did not say so aloud.

'And what weapon did he mean to use?' Tellman went on morosely as they walked together along the road towards the river and Cathcart's house. 'Or did it go too far and turn into murder?'

Pitt had not wanted to face that question, but it was inevitable. 'The time he chose the weapon would answer that.'

'We don't know what it was,' Tellman reminded him. 'It's probably at the bottom of the river by now, anyway. That's what I would have done with it, wouldn't you?'

'Unless I dropped it by mistake, in the dark,' Pitt replied. 'I should have asked Mrs Geddes if there was anything missing besides the rug and the vase.' He blamed himself. That was an oversight.

'We could still do that. We know where she lives.' Tellman was half offering.

It should be done. Pitt accepted.

'Right!' Tellman squared his shoulders. 'I'll meet you at the Crown and Anchor at one.' He set off at a smart pace, leaving Pitt to pursue the less clear objective of tracing Orlando's investigation into Cathcart's daily life and domestic arrangements.

He turned and went back towards the Battersea Bridge Road, away from the river and the soft mist curling up from it with the smell of the incoming tide. Autumn was in the air, and the smell of turned earth, wood smoke, chrysanthemums, the last mowing of the grass. When Orlando had come this way did he really think only to quarrel with Cathcart, and then walk away? Why? He had no threat against him, no way to stop him doing such a thing again as often as he wished to, until Cecily was no longer worth photographing, if that time ever came.

He would not have trusted to finding a weapon when he got there, he would have obtained it first. Pitt reached the centre of the village, the shops and public houses, places where Orlando might have made enquiries, or purchased something to use as a weapon.

It must have been something of considerable weight to land a blow sufficiently hard to kill a man. A length of plumbing pipe would do, or perhaps the handle of a garden implement.

He walked past a chemist's shop with blue glass bottles in the window, and a grocer's, and crossed the street. There was a small row of houses opposite a milliner and glove-maker. On the near side was a wine merchant. Would Orlando ask there? A bottle was an excellent weapon.

All Orlando had really needed to know was if Cathcart had

any resident household staff. Laundry could be done easily enough by a woman who went in every day. Cooking was another matter.

Pitt had an advantage. He knew the answers already. There was only Mrs Geddes. Orlando might have wasted much time before he had learned that. Also Pitt did not have to be discreet.

He tried the laundry, the dairy, the greengrocer and the butcher. No one remembered anybody answering Orlando's description. He might have been there, he might not. They could not say.

He was at the Crown and Anchor before one, and had a glass of cider waiting for Tellman when he arrived.

'Nothing missing,' Tellman said with a nod of thanks. He drank thirstily, looking towards the open door to the kitchen from where drifted the smell of steak and kidney pudding. He was very partial to a good suet crust, as was Pitt himself. 'Going to get some?' There was no need to specify what he meant.

In the early afternoon they started to consider where Orlando would have found or purchased a suitable weapon.

'Well, it won't have been something you'd think of as meant for harm,' Tellman said, shaking his head. He looked profoundly unhappy, in spite of his excellent meal. 'Who'd have thought people that clever would end up murdering someone?' he said miserably. 'They've got a kind of . . . magic . . . in their minds. It really had me . . .' He stumbled for words to express the wonder he had felt, the excitement and awe at the world it had allowed him to glimpse, and wooed him to enter. He had been more than willing to go. He would certainly not admit it to anyone at the Bow Street station, but he might one day go and watch a whole Shakespeare play, right from beginning to end. There was something about it. In spite of the fact that they were kings and queens and princes, the feelings in them were as real as the people he knew from day to day, it was just that they knew how to put it into those wonderful words.

Pitt knew no answer was necessary. He understood Tellman's feelings. He shared them.

They went first to the ironmonger's. It seemed the obvious place to start. The entire shop was crammed with every conceivable piece of equipment for the house, from watering cans to jelly moulds, carriage foot-warmers to chop covers and game ovens. There were gas lanterns, jelly-bag stands, corkscrews and table gongs, toast racks, cake baskets, sardine boxes, butter coolers. There were also spades, forks, scythes, baby perambulators and a newly invented torpedo washer, which claimed to launder linens better than ever before. There were tin baths, carpenter's tools and an array of knives for every purpose imaginable. They saw trussing needles, larding pins, turnip scoops, egg whisks, meat saws, and a heavy, ceramic rolling pin.

The words were out before Pitt had time to reconsider.

'That's a nice piece. Have you sold any of those lately?' He picked the rolling pin up and felt the solidity of it. It was a perfect weapon, round, hard, heavy, and easily handled.

'That's the last one I got, till more come in,' the ironmonger replied. 'You're right, sir, it's a good one. That'll be ninepence to you, sir.'

Pitt was quite sure it would be ninepence to anybody, but he did not say so.

'Did you sell one about two weeks ago?' he persisted.

'Probably. We sell a lot of those. They're very good quality.' The man was determined to do business.

'I dare say,' Pitt replied with a sudden wave of anger and

unhappiness. 'But I'm a police officer investigating the murder of Mr Cathcart, about a mile away from here, and I need an answer to my question. Did you sell one of those exactly two weeks ago, to a tall, young man, probably with fair hair.'

The ironmonger paled visibly. 'I – I didn't know there was anything wrong! He seemed . . . very quiet, very nicely spoken. But, no, not fair hair, as I recall, rather more . . . sort of—'

'His hair doesn't matter!' Pitt said impatiently. 'Was he tall, slender, young – about twenty-five?' Although Orlando could have disguised that too, if he had thought of it.

'I . . . I can't remember. I sold one that day though. I know that, because I keep very close watch on my stock. Never run out of any household ironmongery if I can help it. If it can be bought, it can be bought here at Foster & Sons.'

'Thank you. You may be required to testify to that, so please keep your records safe.'

'I will! I will!'

Outside on the footpath Tellman stopped and stared at Pitt, his face sombre.

'There isn't much more to do, is there.' It was a statement, almost a surrender. 'He could have spent the time till dark in any one of the pubs around here. If you want I'll go to all of them and ask, but I reckon we don't need to know, now that we've got the rolling pin.'

'No . . . not really,' Pitt agreed. He smiled and straightened his shoulders a little. 'We'd better go and see if we can find it, although it's probably in the river. It would be proof. We'll go through the crime, see what must have happened.'

Tellman pulled his coat collar up and they set out back to the house on the river, walking silently. They must do it before dark, and there were only a couple of hours left.

Mrs Geddes was at the house waiting, her face full of mistrust as she watched them enter the hallway and solemnly begin the re-enactment of the murder, Pitt taking the part of Orlando, Tellman of Cathcart.

Of course they had no idea of what conversation there might have been between the two men, or what reason Orlando had given for his visit. They began from a point which was incontestable.

'He must have stood here,' Tellman said, thin-lipped, placing himself near the pedestal where the vase had been smashed, and the alternative set in its stead.

'I wonder why,' Pitt said thoughtfully. 'He had his back to Orlando when he was struck, which makes me wonder how Orlando disguised the pin. No one goes to visit carrying a rolling pin, even wrapped in brown paper.'

'He'd say he'd just bought it . . . on his way?' Tellman suggested, frowning with dislike of the thought even as he said it.

'A young actor?' Pitt raised his eyebrows. 'Don't see him as a pastry cook, do you?'

'A gift?'

'For whom? A young lady? His mother? Do you see Cecily Antrim rolling pastry?'

Tellman gave him a sour look. 'Then he must have had it disguised somehow. Maybe rolled in papers, like a sheaf of pictures, or something?'

'That sounds more probable. So if Cathcart were standing where you are, and Orlando here,' Pitt gestured, 'then Cathcart unquestionably had his attention on something else, or he would have noticed Orlando unwrap his pictures and take out a rolling pin, and he would have been alarmed. It's an act without reasonable explanation.'

'Then he didn't see!' Tellman said decisively. 'He was going somewhere, leading the way. Orlando was following. He hit Cathcart from behind. We know that anyway.'

Pitt went through the motion of raising his arm as if to strike Tellman. Tellman crumpled to his knees, rather carefully to avoid banging himself on the now bare wooden floor. He lay down, more or less as he might have fallen.

'Now what?' he asked.

Pitt had been considering that. They had little idea how long Orlando had been here, but knowing what he had done, he had had no time to hesitate for more than a few minutes.

'If you think you're going to put me in any dress—' Tellman began.

'Be quiet!' Pitt snapped.

'I—' Tellman started to get up.

'Lie down!' Pitt ordered. 'Privilege of rank,' he added ironically. 'Would you rather change places?'

Tellman lay down again.

'Where were the green dress and the chains kept?' Pitt said thoughtfully. 'Certainly not down here!'

'Up in the studio, most likely,' Tellman replied, his face to the floor. 'With all the other stuff he used in his pictures. What I want to know is, how did Orlando know that the punt was here, and not somewhere else? It could have been anywhere, on any lake or river. Could have been miles away, in another country, for that matter.'

Pitt did not answer. His mind was beginning to reach for a new, extraordinary thought.

'Do you suppose he went upstairs first?' Tellman went on. 'Maybe saw the chains and the dress in the studio?' He did not say it as if he believed that himself.

'And then came down, and Cathcart was going up again, ahead of him, and Orlando killed him?' Pitt said almost absent-mindedly.

Tellman rolled over and sat up, scowling. 'Then what do you think?'

'I think he certainly didn't wander down the garden, in the dark, to see if there was a boat moored in the river,' Pitt replied. 'I think he had been here before, often enough to know that these things existed, and exactly where to find them.'

'But he hadn't!' Tellman said decisively. 'He had to ask where it was . . . from the pub landlord. We know that!'

'Or there was someone else here as well,' Pitt answered. 'Someone who did know . . . someone who finished the job that Orlando only started.'

'But he came alone!' Tellman climbed to his feet. 'You think there was someone else there the same night, also bent on murdering Cathcart?' His tone of voice conveyed what he thought of that possibility.

'I don't know what I think,' Pitt confessed. 'But I don't think Orlando Antrim murdered Cathcart in a passion of fury over the way Cathcart used Cecily, then set about searching the house to see if he could find the clothes and the chains, and the boat, to make it a mockery of the photograph. For one thing, there was no sign of a struggle when Mrs Geddes came in in the morning, which means that if he searched, he put everything back where he found it . . . exactly. Does that sound like a man in a murderous rage to you?'

'No. But Cathcart's dead,' Tellman said reasonably. 'And someone put him in that dress and chained him in the punt, then scattered all the flowers . . . and I'd swear anything you like it was someone who hated him – and hated him because of Cecily Antrim.'

Pitt said nothing. He had no argument.

'And we know Orlando was here, and he bought the pin,' Tellman went on.

'We'd better go and look for it,' Pitt said miserably. 'Before it gets dark. We've only got just over an hour.'

Together they trudged down the path towards the river, watched from the side door by Mrs Geddes.

They were sodden wet, covered in mud and it was beginning to grow dusk when Tellman slipped on it at the edge of the bank, swore, and pulled it out, washing it in river water and holding it up in angry triumph. 'So he didn't throw it after all,' he said with surprise. 'Maybe he meant to and dropped it.'

They were obliged to get the ironmonger from his dinner to identify it. He came to the door with his napkin tucked into the V of his waistcoat and a considerable reluctance in his manner. He eyed the rolling pin with disgust.

'Yes, that's one o' mine. Put my mark on 'em, in blue, I do. See?' He pointed to a tiny blue device on the end of the pin near the handle. 'Is that the one what . . . ?' He would not say it.

'Yes, it is. You sold it to a tall, young man on the afternoon of Cathcart's death?'

'Yes.'

'Are you certain?'

'Course I am. Wouldn't say so if I weren't. My books'll show it.'

'Thank you. Sorry to have disturbed your supper.'

'Now what?' Tellman asked when they were outside in the dark again. 'Is it enough to arrest him?' He sounded tired and doubtful.

Pitt was doubtful himself. He had no uncertainty that Orlando Antrim had seen the photograph of his mother and reacted with extreme distress. He had searched for the photographs and gone to the house and found Cathcart. He had purchased the rolling pin. But the dressing of the corpse in green velvet, and chaining him on the punt, with the flowers strewn around, did not follow so easily.

Could there have been two people here other than Cathcart? If so, who? He knew coincidences happened, but he did not like them. Most things had a cause, a line of circumstances connected to each other in a way which could be understood, if you knew them all and considered them long enough.

'Can we arrest him?' Tellman pressed.

'I don't know.' Pitt shook himself a little.

'But it had to be him,' Tellman said pointedly. 'He was here, we know that. He had plenty of reason to kill Cathcart. He bought the weapon and we've got it. What else is there – apart from working out how he knew where to find the dress, and the chains?'

'And the boat,' Pitt added.

'Well, somebody did!' Tellman was exasperated. 'You can't argue with that! If it wasn't him, who could it have been? And why? Why would anybody else do all that with the boat and the flowers? Wouldn't they want to get away as quickly as possible? Just leave him where he was? Why dress up a dead man – that somebody else killed – and risk getting caught?'

'Not a lot of risk,' Pitt argued. 'Bottom of a garden by the river, in the middle of a foggy night. Still, he must have cared passionately about something to have bothered.'

They crossed the road, still walking slowly, heading back towards the bridge.

'Maybe it was someone he blackmailed, after all?' Tellman suggested. 'Or more like, someone who hated that kind of picture and the way it makes people think!'

Pitt thought of Rafe Marchand. It was believable, very easily, but another idea was also forming in his mind, uncertain, perhaps foolish, but becoming clearer with each step.

As soon as he saw a hansom he hailed it, and to a sharp stare of astonishment from his sergeant, gave not the address of the theatre, but of the medical examiner.

'What do you want with him?' Tellman said incredulously. 'We know how he died!'

Pitt did not answer.

When they arrived, he told the cab to wait and ran up the steps of the building and in through the door. To his intense relief he found the surgeon still there. He knew the one question he wanted to ask.

'Was there any water in Cathcart's lungs?' he demanded.

The surgeon looked startled. 'Yes, there was a bit. I was going to tell you next time you were by.' His eyes narrowed. 'Doesn't make any difference to your case.'

'But did he actually die of the blow to his head, or of drowning?' Pitt insisted, fidgeting with impatience.

Tellman watched with what might have been a dawning comprehension. His eyes were steady and he stood motionless in the cold room, his nostrils slightly flared with distaste at the pervasive odour, real or imagined.

The surgeon stared at Pitt, shifting his weight.

'Clinically, I suppose the drowning got to him before the wound, but it's academic, Pitt. He would have died of the blow anyway . . . or exposure, in his injured state, sodden wet and left out in the river like that. It's murder any way you look at it at all! What's your point?'

'I'm not sure,' Pitt said honestly. 'Thank you. Come on, Tellman.' He turned on his heel.

'Theatre now?' Tellman asked, racing to catch up with him as he strode down the steps and swung back up into the hansom.

They rattled through the dark, gaslit streets without speaking again, Pitt leaning forward as if by effort of will he could make the horse go faster.

He was out of the door almost before they came to a stop, leaving Tellman to pay the driver and follow behind him. He raced up the steps and into the foyer, brandishing his card and calling out who he was, pushing past the usher and swinging the door wide into the back of the auditorium.

He saw with a flood of relief that the stage was still lit, although it was the very end of the final act. Gertrude and the king were both already dead, and Laertes, Polonius and Ophelia were long since gone, he by accident, she the suicide of drowning. Hamlet, Fortinbras, Horatio and Osric were left amid a sea of corpses.

There was a sound of a shot.

'"What warlike noise is this?"' Hamlet asked, swinging to face it. He seemed as taut as a wire, his nerves stretched to breaking.

Osric answered him.

Hamlet turned back toward the audience, his eyes wide with agony, staring straight ahead to where Pitt stood in the centre of the aisle.

'"O, I die, Horatio.
The potent poison quite o'er-crows my spirit.
I cannot live to hear the news from England;
But I do prophesy th'election lights
On Fortinbras. He has my dying voice.
So tell him, with th'occurents more and less
Which have solicited – "'

His voice was hoarse, cutting to the soul: '"The rest is silence."'
He crumpled and slid forward.

There was such utter stillness the audience might not have
existed, except for the tension in the air like a storm.

'"Now cracks a noble heart."' Horatio said through a throat
thick with tears. '"Good night, sweet prince. And flights of
angels sing thee to thy rest."'

Fortinbras and the English ambassadors entered and the last,
tragic words were spoken. Finally the soldiers carried off the
bodies to the sombre familiarity of the Dead March. The curtain
descended.

A complete silence filled the auditorium, thick, crackling
with emotion, then the applause erupted like a sea breaking.
As if impelled by a single force the entire audience rose to its
feet. Above the thunder of clapping voices could be heard
shouting 'Bravo!' again and again.

The curtain rose and the full cast lined up to take the call,
Orlando in the centre, Cecily radiant at his side, and Bellmaine
looking ashen, as if Polonius had risen from the grave to
acknowledge his praise.

Pitt walked down the aisle and along in front of the orchestra,
through the side door towards the back of the stage. Tellman
joined him, but still they had to wait. The applause went on

and on, drowning out every other sound. It was impossible to speak above it for almost a quarter of an hour.

Finally the curtain fell for the last time and the players turned to leave.

Pitt stepped on to the stage. He could afford to wait no longer. Tellman was on his heels.

Orlando faced him. He looked haggard and utterly exhausted. He took a step forward, but he was shaking.

'You've come for me.' His voice was clear and soft. 'Thank you for letting me finish.'

'I'm a policeman, not a barbarian,' Pitt replied just as softly.

Orlando walked towards him, his hands held as if ready for manacles. He did not once look at his mother.

'What is going on?' Cecily demanded, one way then the other. 'Superintendent, what do you want here? This is surely an inappropriate time. Orlando has just performed perhaps the greatest Hamlet there has ever been. If you still think there is anything to ask us, come tomorrow . . . about midday.'

'You don't understand, Mother,' Orlando said, still without turning to her. 'You never did.'

She started to say something, but he cut across her.

'Mr Pitt has come to arrest me for murdering Cathcart. Although I didn't put him in the river. I don't know how that happened, I swear.'

'Don't be ridiculous!' Cecily moved forward at last. This time she addressed Pitt, not her son. 'He's exhausted. I don't know why he should say such a thing. It's absurd. Why should he murder Cathcart? He didn't even know him!'

Orlando turned slowly towards her. His face was bloodless, his eyes dark-ringed as if he had come to the end of a terrible journey.

'I killed him because I hated him for what he had made you into. You are my mother! And when you debase yourself, you debase me also . . .'

'I don't know what you're talking about!' she protested. And to judge from her wide, frank eyes, Pitt believed she still did not perceive what she had done.

It was Bellmaine who told her. He moved past Orlando, close to Pitt, but turned to her. 'You made your crusade without thinking what it would do to those who loved you, Cecily,' he said in a low, painful voice. 'You had pictures taken of yourself that would shock people into thinking what you wanted them to. You woke new and powerful emotions, hurling them out of their safety of heart into the ways you wished them to be, because you thought it was good for them. You didn't stop to think, or to care, that in doing it you were destroying what they might have held too dear to lose without tearing them apart, breaking them inside.' There were tears in his throat, and a terrible grief. 'You broke your son, Cecily. The mind might tell him pornography is all right, if it breaks down old prejudices, but the heart can't accept.' His voice cracked. 'The heart only says, "That's my mother! The source of who I am!"'

At last the horror reached her. Understanding spread through her with unspeakable pain. As if she had been crippled inside, she turned her eyes to Orlando.

He did not answer. His face was eloquent enough. All the anger, and the loss and the pain were there in his haggard features. He swivelled away from her and held out his wrists to Pitt.

'No.' Bellmaine touched him with intense gentleness. 'You struck him, but you did not kill him. I did that.'

'You?' Cecily demanded. 'Why?' But there was already the

393

beginning of a terrible realisation in her.

'Because I hated him for blackmailing me,' Bellmaine said wearily. 'Over a photograph I posed for years ago . . . when I needed the money. Shown now it would have ruined me. An actor counts on image. But mostly to protect my son . . .'

'Your son . . .' Pitt began to ask, then he looked at Cecily, at Bellmaine, and at Orlando, and saw it in their faces. Orlando had his mother's hair and eyes, but there was a resemblance to Bellmaine also. And acknowledgement was in Cecily's silence.

Orlando had not known. That also was only too apparent.

'How did you know Orlando had gone there?' Pitt asked.

Bellmaine shrugged. 'Does it matter now? I knew he was greatly distressed the evening before. I did not know why. Then the day of his death Cathcart sent me a message to tell me not to go to his house to pay my usual monthly dues to him, because he had a new client coming, who had made the appointment that day. A young man called Richard Larch.'

'Who is Richard Larch?' Cecily demanded, but there was no anger in her, no spirit. The fire inside her was quenched.

'The first role Orlando ever played,' Bellmaine answered. 'Don't you even remember? I knew then – at least I feared. I've seen the Ophelia picture as well. That's why I dressed him . . .' He swallowed and seemed to stagger a little. He regained his balance with difficulty. '. . . That's why I dressed him that way, and sat him in the boat. He was still alive, but I knew he wouldn't last in the cold and the water. There was . . .' he gasped, 'there was a kind of symmetry in it. I was a good Hamlet myself, thirty years ago. Not as good as Orlando. Cecily was my Ophelia then.'

Pitt saw the sweat break out in Bellmaine's grey face and

understood what he had done. He was glad he had had no time to prevent it.

Bellmaine fell forward on to his knees.

"'O, I die, Horatio,'" he said hoarsely. "'The potent poison quite o'er-crows my spirit . . . The rest is . . . is . . .'" He did not finish.

Cecily closed her eyes and the tears ran down her white cheeks.

Orlando did not go to her. He looked at Pitt for a moment, then bent over the motionless body of his father.

"'Goodnight, sweet prince,'" he whispered. "'May flights . . .'" But he too could not complete his line. This cut the heart too deep.

Silently Pitt turned and left, Tellman behind him, his face wet with tears.

Headline hopes you have enjoyed *Half Moon Street* and invites you to sample the beginning of *Slaves and Obsession*, Anne Perry's latest compelling novel in her series featuring William and Hester Monk.

Chapter One

❧

'We are invited to dine with Mr and Mrs Alberton,' Hester said in reply to Monk's questioning gaze across the breakfast table. 'They are friends of Callandra's. She was to go as well, but has been called to Scotland unexpectedly.'

'I suppose you would like to accept anyway,' he deduced, watching her face.

He usually read her emotions quickly, sometimes with startling accuracy, at others misunderstanding entirely. On this occasion he was correct.

'Yes, I would. Callandra said they are charming and interesting and have a very beautiful home. Mrs Alberton is half Italian, and both have travelled quite a lot.'

'Then I suppose we had better go. Short notice, isn't it?' he said less than graciously.

It was short notice indeed, but Hester was not disposed to find unnecessary fault with something which promised to be interesting, and possibly even the beginning of a new friendship. She did not have many. The nature of her work as a nurse had meant they were frequently of a fleeting nature. She had not been involved with any gripping cause for quite some little time. Even Monk's cases, while financially rewarding, had over the last four months of spring and early summer been most uninteresting, and he had not sought her assistance, or in most of them her opinion. She did not mind that; robberies were tedious, largely motivated by greed, and she did not know the people concerned.

'Good,' she said with a smile, folding up the letter. 'I shall write back immediately saying that we shall be delighted.'

His answering look was wry, only very slightly sarcastic.

They arrived at the Alberton house in Tavistock Square just before half-past seven. It was, as Callandra had said, handsome, although Hester would not have thought it worth remarking on. However she changed her mind as soon as they were in the hallway which was dominated by a curving staircase, at the half-turn of which was an enormous stained-glass window with the evening sun behind it. It was truly beautiful, and Hester found herself staring at it when she should have been paying attention to the butler who had admitted them, and watching where she was going.

The withdrawing room also was unusual. There was less furniture in it than was customary, and the colours were paler and warmer, giving an illusion of light even though in fact the long windows which overlooked the garden faced towards the eastern sky. The shadows were already lengthening, although it would not be dark yet until after ten o'clock at this time so shortly after midsummer.

Hester's first impression of Judith Alberton was that she was an extraordinarily beautiful woman. She was taller than average, but with a slender neck and shoulders which made more apparent the lush curves of her figure, and lent it a delicacy it might otherwise not have possessed. Her face, when looked at more closely, was totally wrong for conventional fashion. Her nose was straight and quite prominent, her cheekbones very high, her mouth too large and her chin definitely short. Her eyes were slanted and of a golden autumn shade. The whole impression was both generous and passionate. The longer one looked at her the lovelier she seemed. Hester liked her immediately.

'How do you do?' Judith said warmly. 'I am so pleased you have come. It was kind of you on so hasty an invitation. But Lady Callandra spoke of you with such affection I did not wish to wait.' She smiled at Monk. Her eyes lit with a flare of interest as she regarded his dark face with its lean bones and broad-bridged nose, but it was Hester to whom she addressed her attention. 'May I introduce my husband?'

The man who came forward was pleasing rather than handsome, far more ordinary than she was, but his features were regular and there was both strength and charm in them.

'How do you do, Mrs Monk?' he said with a smile, but when courtesy was met he turned immediately to Monk behind her, searching his countenance steadily for a moment before holding out his hand in welcome, and then turning aside so the rest of the company could be introduced.

There were three other people in the room. One was a man in his mid-forties, his dark hair thinning a little. Hester noticed first his wide smile and spontaneous handshake. He had a natural confidence, as if he were sure enough of himself and his beliefs he had no need to thrust them upon anyone else. He was happy to listen to others. It was a quality she could not help but like. His name was Robert Casbolt, and he was introduced not only as Alberton's business partner and friend since youth, but also Judith's cousin.

The other man present was American. As one could hardly help being aware, that country had in the last few months slipped tragically into a state of civil conflict. There had not as yet been anything more serious than a few ugly skirmishes, but open violence seemed increasingly probable with every fresh bulletin that arrived across the Atlantic. All-out war seemed more and more likely.

'Mr Breeland is from the Union,' Alberton said courteously, but there was no warmth in his voice.

Hester looked at Breeland as she acknowledged the introduction. He appeared to be in his early thirties, tall and very straight, with square shoulders and the upright stance of a soldier. His features were regular, his expression polite but severely controlled, as if he felt he must be constantly on guard against any slip or relaxation of awareness.

The last person was the Albertons' daughter, Merrit. She was about sixteen, with all the charm, the passion and vulnerability of her years. She was fairer than her mother, and had not the beauty, but she had a similar strength of will in her face, and less ability to hide her emotions. She allowed herself to be introduced politely enough, but she did not make any attempt to pretend more than courtesy.

The preliminary conversation was on matters as simple as the weather, the increase in traffic on the streets and the crowds drawn by a nearby exhibition.

Hester wondered why Callandra had thought she and Monk might find these people congenial, but perhaps she was merely fond of them, and had discovered in them a kindness.

Breeland and Merrit moved a little apart, talking earnestly. Monk, Casbolt and Judith Alberton discussed the latest play, and Hester fell into conversation with Daniel Alberton.

'Lady Callandra told me you spent nearly two years out in the Crimea,' he said with great interest. He smiled apologetically. 'I am not going to ask you the usual questions about Miss Nightingale. You must find that tedious by now.'

'She was a very remarkable person,' Hester said diplomatically. 'I could not criticise anyone for seeking to know more about her.'

His smile widened. 'You must have said that so many times! You were prepared for it!'

She found herself relaxing. He was unexpectedly pleasant to converse with; frankness was always so much easier than continued courtesy. 'Yes, I admit I was. It is—'

'Unoriginal,' he finished for her.

'Yes.'

'Perhaps what I wanted to say was unoriginal also, but I shall say it anyway, because I do want to know.' He frowned very slightly, drawing his brows together. His eyes were clear blue. 'You must have exercised a great deal of courage out there, both physical and moral, especially when you were actually close to the battlefield. You must have made decisions which altered other people's lives, perhaps saved them, or lost them.'

That was true. She remembered with a jolt just how desperate it had been. It was as remote from this quiet summer evening in an elegant London withdrawing room, where the shade of a gown mattered, the cut of a sleeve. War, disease, shattered bodies, the heat and flies, or the terrible cold could all have been on another planet with no connection with this world at all except a common language, and yet no words that could ever explain one to the other.

She nodded.

'Do you not find it extraordinarily difficult to adjust from

403

that life to this?' he asked, his voice soft, but edged with a surprising intensity.

How much had Callandra told Judith Alberton, or her husband? Would Hester embarrass her friend with the Albertons in future if she were to be honest? Probably not. Callandra had never been a woman to run from the truth.

'Well, I came back burning with determination to reform all our hospitals here at home,' she said ruefully. 'As you can see, I did not succeed, for several reasons. The chief among them was that no one would believe I had the faintest idea what I was talking about. Women don't understand medicine at all, and nurses in particular are for rolling bandages, sweeping and mopping floors, carrying coal and slops, and generally doing as they are told.' She allowed her bitterness to show. 'It did not take me long to be dismissed, and earn my way by caring for private patients.'

There was admiration in his eyes as well as laughter. 'Was that not very hard for you?' he asked.

'Very,' she agreed. 'But I met my husband shortly after I came home. We were . . . I was going to say friends, but that is not true. Adversaries in a common cause, would describe it far better. Did Lady Callandra tell you that he is a private agent of inquiry?'

There was no surprise on his face, certainly nothing like alarm. In high society, gentlemen owned land or were in the army or politics. They did not work, in the sense of being employed. Trade was equally unacceptable. But whatever family background Judith Alberton came from, her husband showed no dismay that his guest should be little better than a policeman, an occupation fit only for the least desirable element.

'Yes,' he admitted readily. 'She told me she found some of

his adventures quite fascinating, but she did not give me any details. I presumed they might be confidential.'

'They are,' she agreed. 'I would not discuss them either, only to say that they have prevented me from missing any sense of excitement or decision that I felt in the Crimea. And for the most part my share in them has not required the physical privation or the personal danger of nursing in wartime.'

'And the horror, or the pity?' he asked quietly.

'It has not sheltered me from those,' she admitted. 'Except for a matter of numbers. And I am not sure one feels any less for one person, if they are in desperate trouble, than one does for many.'

'Quite.' It was Robert Casbolt who spoke. He came up just behind Alberton, putting a companionable hand on his shoulder and regarding Hester with interest. 'There is just so much the emotions can take, and one gives all one has, I imagine. From what I have just overheard, you are a remarkable woman, Mrs Monk. I am delighted Daniel thought to invite you and your husband to dine. You will enliven our usual conversation greatly, and I for one am looking forward to it.' He lowered his voice conspiratorially. 'No doubt we shall hear more of it over dinner – it is totally inescapable these days – but I have had more than sufficient of the war in America and its issues.'

Alberton's face lightened. 'So have I, but I would wager you a good carriage and pair that Breeland will regale us again with the virtues of the Union before the third course has been served.'

'Second!' Casbolt amended. He grinned at Hester, a broad, shining expression. 'He is a very earnest young man, Mrs Monk, and fanatically convinced of the moral rightness of his cause. To him the Union of the United States is a divine entity, and the Confederate desire to secede the work of the devil.'

Any further comment was cut short by the necessity of removing to the dining room where dinner was ready to be served.

Seven Dials

Anne Perry

Early one morning, Thomas Pitt is summoned to the offices of Victor Narraway, head of Special Branch. An ex-army officer has been shot and the prime suspect is the Egyptian mistress of senior cabinet minister Saville Ryerson. However some things don't add up. Why did the mistress have a gun? If she needed protection, then from whom? Is her love lying to protect her, or even himself? When the Egyptian Ambassador gets involved, it seems that a major diplomatic row is brewing.

Meanwhile Charlotte Pitt is more concerned about her husband's safety. She fears there could be involvement with the secret organisation that destroyed Pitt's police career and very nearly cost him his life. Can Pitt tread the tense diplomatic tightrope between protecting justice, the security of his country, and the safety of his family?

In her own inimitable style, Anne Perry weaves a page-turning tale of politics, passion and international intrigue set in the heart of Victorian England.

Acclaim for Anne Perry's novels:

'The author has the eyes of a hawk for character nuance and her claws out for the signs of . . . criminal injustice' *New York Times Book Review*

'We don't have a Dickens today, but Anne Perry is every bit as good' *Northern Echo*

'Offering an interesting slant on the grandeur of Britain's Empire, this novel will please fans of the series, especially those who enjoy the teamwork of Mr and Mrs Pitt' *Scottish Sunday Herald*

0 7472 6898 3

headline

Come Armageddon

Anne Perry

'You took the fire of truth from heaven. You must guard it until there comes again one who is pure enough in heart to open the seal and read what is written. It may be a hundred years, it may be a thousand, but God will preserve you until that time and the end of all things. In that day I shall come again, and we shall fight the last battle of the world, you and I together.'

'Tathea, once queen of Shinabar, has waited five hundred years for Ishrafeli's word to come true. In that time she has guarded the precious, gold Book of the word of God, and has witnessed the portentous birth of Sadokhar – a child of great significance. For he, Tathea knows, is the king who will create a golden age before the great and final war.

Now a grown man, Sadokhar has at last united the Island at the Edge of the World in peace – and four of the six warriors destined to fight Armageddon have presented themselves. But where are the other two warriors? And where is Tathea's beloved Ishrafeli who promised that he would return to fight the last terrible war against the Great Enemy, Asmodeus? Time is short – and the final conflict is about to test each one of them to their very core . . .

COME ARMAGEDDON continues the exploration of the eternal battle between good and evil which began in TATHEA. Extraordinary and compelling, this apocalyptic epic fantasy is both breathtaking and profound, as those involved face a terrifying battle – of the spirit as well as the body – with conviction and courage.

0 7472 6746 4

headline

ANNE PERRY

No Graves as Yet

In Cambridge, in 1914, the golden June days seem timeless. But for the four Reavley siblings, the summer is shattered by their parents' deaths in a car accident. Their father John, a retired MP, had apparently discovered a sinister plot. Matthew Reavley's job in the secret service means that he would understand a mysterious document John possessed. But now it is nowhere to be found and the family is convinced that their house has been searched. As their suspicions grow, they visit the scene of the crash, examine the ruined car, and find subtle evidence that the deaths may not have been accidental after all.

ANNE PERRY is a *New York Times* bestselling author of historical fiction, whose novels have been richly and widely acclaimed:

'Brilliantly presented, ingeniously developed and packed with political implications that reverberate on every level of British Society' *New York Times*

'Admirably well-written' *Guardian*

0 7553 0285 0

review

madabout**books**.com

. . . the

Hodder Headline

site

for readers

and book lovers

madabout**books**.com

Now you can buy any of these other bestselling books by **Anne Perry** from your bookshop or *direct from her publisher*.

FREE P&P AND UK DELIVERY
(Overseas and Ireland £3.50 per book)

Thomas Pitt series

Seven Dials	£6.99
Southampton Row	£6.99
The Whitechapel Conspiracy	£6.99
Half Moon Street	£6.99
Bedford Square	£6.99

William Monk series

The Shifting Tide	£6.99
Death of a Stranger	£6.99
A Funeral in Blue	£6.99
Slaves and Obsession	£6.99
The Twisted Root	£6.99

Other novels

No Graves as Yet	£6.99
Come Armageddon	£6.99
Tathea	£6.99
The One Thing More	£5.99

TO ORDER SIMPLY CALL THIS NUMBER

01235 400 414

or visit our website: www.madaboutbooks.com

Prices and availability subject to change without notice.